FOXED

Lucy Caxton Brown

© Lucy Caxton Brown 2012

All rights reserved

No part of this publication may be reproduced, stored in a retrieval system, or transmitted in any form or by any means, without the prior permission in writing of the publisher, nor be otherwise circulated in any form of binding or cover other than that in which it is published and without a similar condition including this condition being imposed on the subsequent purchaser.

First published in Great Britain

All paper used in the printing of this book has been made from wood grown in managed, sustainable forests.

ISBN13: 978-1-78003-479-9

Printed and bound in the UK
Pen Press is an imprint of
Indepenpress Publishing Limited
25 Eastern Place
Brighton
BN2 1GJ

A catalogue record of this book is available from the British Library

Cover design by Jacqueline Abromeit

Dedicated to all the unknown heroes and heroines

There is no higher ideal than the search for truth

FOXED

A family's investigation into their lost heritage

The recent discovery of the Romanov remains should have convinced everyone that the Russian Imperial Family had been executed in 1918. Yet the Soviets were never able to produce the bodies even though they said they had been shot and disposed of at the Four Brothers Mine. This led to many people harbouring misgivings about the actual fate of the Imperial Family. They chose instead to believe that the family were safely escorted to secluded exile. Stories of their escape have been around for nearly a century but where did they come from? The recently found remains do little to counteract the historic and heavily researched documentary record that categorically supports the notion that the family were rescued and lived out their life in exile. Was this fiction, as some have suggested, or was it the truth? If it was fiction why would the authors of *Rescuing the Czar*, the book that first broke the story in 1919, have risked their well earned reputations? What reason could they have had for spreading rumours that the Romanovs were quite well and living abroad if there was the remotest possibility that the bodies could be discovered? It's no wonder that many historians feel confounded and some still refute claims that the Romanovs were shot. Perhaps if the bodies had been found sooner more people would have been convinced of their execution and, even though one is inclined rationally to accept that this is what happened, there remains a lingering notion that by not getting to the bottom of this mystery and by simply accepting the gruesome version of history we do any would be rescuer a huge injustice.

Who will tell the story of those brave men and women who risked their lives to rescue the Russian Royal Family and to whom homage would be due if the story is true.

Note to readers on Calendar dates in Russia 1918

Up to and during the 19th century the calendar used throughout the Russian Empire was 12 days behind that used in the West. So for example, Wednesday 24th April 1840 in Russia was Wednesday 6th May 1840 in Great Britain, Europe and North America. These differences were due to the adoption of the Gregorian calendar in these countries. The Russian and Ottoman Empires retained the earlier Julian calendar. In 1900 the two systems became further out-of-step when Wednesday 28th February was followed by Thursday 29th February in countries using the Julian calendar, but by Thursday 1st March in those following the Gregorian. This 13-day difference lasted until the Gregorian calendar was introduced in most of Russia on 14th February 1918.

Although the Bolsheviks in the Soviet Union and the Russian Federation adopted the new style calendar on February 14th 1918 it is believed that members of the Imperial Family and many White Russians continued to hold to the "Old Style" fervently. I believe the operation of two calendars in Russia, at the same time, would have been the cause of much misunderstanding between certain negotiating parties, where timing was of the essence. This may have been the case when agents attempted to rescue the Imperial Family. If so this would certainly have meant the difference between success and failure, and perhaps more importantly life and death. Indeed it would have been the cause of much confusion pertaining to the removal of the Imperial Family, and to various other failed plots including the so called "Lockhart Plot."

While researching some of the published memoirs of White Russians I was astounded to discover that many wrote their stories without giving any dates whatsoever. So I have taken the works as I found them. The author wishes to make it clear that *Foxed* is a work of "faction". There are historic facts set within a fictitious framework and the reader should be aware that some of the dates under discussion could be either "new" or "old" style calendar. **Discussions that take place around the identity of real persons are fictitious and should not be considered as actually having taken place or as fact.**

CONTENTS

Part One Maria's Secret

One	The Baroness	3
Two	Two Women in a Grotto	8
Three	History in the Making	15
Four	Count Frederick	21
Five	Brandenberg	31
Six	Vagabonds	39
Seven	Rescuing the Czar	51
Eight	Life after Death	63

Part Two Enigma

Nine	Unlocking the Mystery	71
Ten	My Life	85
Eleven	An Agent called Fox	88
Twelve	A Wild Goose Chase	97
Thirteen	The Kaiser's Letter	110
Fourteen	William Rutledge McGarry	117
Fifteen	Jerusalem	137
Sixteen	A Letter from Heaven	147
Seventeen	A Shooting Party	154
Eighteen	Sculptress and Spy	165
Nineteen	Revolutionary Russia	178
Twenty	Comrade Relinsky	188
Twenty One	Assassination in Moscow	195
Twenty Two	The Lockhart Plot	202

Part Three Imperial Service

Twenty Three	Secrets of the German War Office	217
Twenty Four	The Old Gods Live Still	230
Twenty Five	Secrets of the Hohenzollerns	237
Twenty Six	Bertram von Ehrenkrug	251
Twenty Seven	Dr Armgaard Karl Graves	262
Twenty Eight	Bronze Venus	284
Twenty Nine	An Alibi	300
Thirty	Hetman Skoropadski	308
Thirty One	A Proposal	323
Thirty Two	Gold and Platinum	336

Part Four Mission Accomplished

Thirty Three	The File On The Tsar	359
Thirty Four	Fox's Rescue Mission	378
Thirty Five	The Great Cup Bearer	390
Thirty Six	Intrigue at Monte Carlo	395
Thirty Seven	A Mysterious Visitor	402
Thirty Eight	Disguise and Deception	418
Thirty Nine	Rome	427
Forty	Once a Knight always a Knight	436
Forty One	Revelations	449
Forty Two	Stolen Gold	456
Forty Three	A Rose By Any Other Name	463
Forty Four	Chicken Farming	473

Part One

Maria's Secret

Chapter One — The Baroness

London 1977.

The floor was crowded with old tea chests neatly sealed and addressed. Over the years Maria had astounded everyone with her energy and today was no exception because she had been hard at work for well over six hours. But now her back was aching. So, she was human after all! Maria straightened up slowly so that a sharp pain would not take her by surprise. It did and she felt that horrible dizzy feeling that made her hang onto the back of a green winged armchair until she felt better. There were still a few important parcels to be wrapped. She felt a pang of concern. Would they survive the trip? What if they got lost or were damaged? Maria rebuked herself. Don't be silly. Everything will go exactly to plan. Why, even during the 1930s – a very dangerous time – only one diary had gone missing. Luckily Maria had discovered the loss and written up the memoir even though HE had warned her not to. Well, times were different now. They were all dead. She breathed a sigh of relief. Thank God for that!

It was getting dark when Maria switched a black and gold fringed lamp on. It flooded the room with a welcome cosy light as she reached for a photograph of her only son Michael. There was no getting away from it. She would be relieved not to have to dodge his questions about her early life. Well who could blame him? She laughed at her stupidity. No one had forced her to tell him what a wild and exciting life she had led, despite the ravages of a war torn Europe. Of course she didn't divulge any of the detail to him. To all those who loved her most, her life had been a complete mystery and that was exactly how she had wanted it. She was still in control. But there was a time coming when she would not be and she knew that would be no laughing matter. Not for her and not for Michael either.

Ah, Michael! He felt he had the right to know about all her famous friends. Well what did she expect? Still she had always managed her son exceedingly well. Even when caught off guard by him as she often was, Maria would give him one of her long sweet smiles purposely designed to calm his expectations and make him feel that he was part of her big secret. Which in a sense of course, he was.

'Oh,' she would say laconically, 'There's just so much to tell, I really wouldn't know where to start and even if I told you the truth about my early life in Russia, you wouldn't believe me. I am quite sure of that!' Then, as though she relished his disappointment, she would give a long weary sigh before dismissing the conversation with a rather mysterious, 'And that, Michael, is exactly how it should be. Believe me. It's for your own sake!'

But Michael wasn't one to give up so easily. He would go on asking questions about his father and Maria would have to explain why she couldn't tell him what he wanted to know. At first Michael complained saying it was his right. But recently he hadn't shown any interest and Maria had been grateful for that. As a result they got on much better these days. In fact she was delighted when he invited her to stay with him.

Maria sat down and stared at the rest of the papers on the table in front of her. For over half a century these letters and diaries were all that remained of her extraordinary life. Now that the time to write her memoirs had arrived, the villa in Italy would be just right to get the peace and quiet she craved. Carefully she picked up one of the diaries. It belonged to a very dear friend. Instinctively a tear came into her eye as she opened it somewhere towards the centre. How could she resist reading his wonderful handwriting?

Afterwards we had supper. At the next table to us were the Misses Alexander Ivanitsky and the Baroness B. Since her return she certainly looks much better. At first I did not see her, then before all, she reprimanded me in her usual kind manner. She has grown a little thinner and has more jewels and is as fascinating as before. When she speaks one can see that she thinks of far distant things. "We all are busy these days," she said when I asked her whether she had come here from England just for curiosity to see us under the provisional government. Misha, who did not know B before, did not like her very much; in fact they all think she is suspicious. Aren't these youngsters peculiar? Especially Misha, who is so grouchy lately, all seems dangerous to him. I never think that a woman can be anything but pretty or hideous. There is no middle ground, and no suspicion about them. If a woman is what they perhaps would call "suspicious", then there is a man's influence behind her, so find the man (and it is easy) and she is as plain as a card on the table.

Baroness B. is pretty and if she likes to talk like a Pythia that's her way of making people interested in her. The Baroness said that Sophie had already reached London after the stay in Copenhagen and Paris.

Her mission as usual, she said, coquettishly and childishly looking around with a fear of being overheard, was a failure. In Copenhagen they would not even listen to Sophie, and she was told that the solution and the demarches must be made, if made, from London, as there people have every means to arrange with Berlin. Heaven knows what the Baroness has become since her peculiar conduct with the Vassilchikov and her permanent whisperings to Madame Vyrubov and the rest of the gang. But still, there was already a movement about Tsarskoe Selo. Baroness B's actions are strange. Is she paid? By whom? Cash? Promises?

Baroness B evidently communicating with Copenhagen through Sharp and Starleit, M General Z to be approached. Also Quart General R. In one instance a package carried to Sestroretsk by a lady in a blue tailored suit with white fox fur. Trail lady, arrest Baroness B. Watch Finland Depot. Radio to Generals Z. and R. No signature! My astonishment was very great and I said that though I have known Baroness B. quite well since I met her in Paris and Monte Carlo, we did not hear anything new of the poor Baroness. The only thing that we all know is she is in jail. Apparently my information is quite old. They released her about a day or two after the misunderstanding was cleared up.

'They did indeed,' Maria whispered, closing the diary and placing it carefully in the tea chest. 'Oh dear, I do hope Michael has room for this lot,' she thought as she lifted the lid into place and scribbled in bold black letters: **Literary Translations 1919-1938.**

'There! That should do. Perhaps I'll get Alice to wrap them in polythene just in case it rains.'

Maria tapped her pen nervously on the side of the tea chest. Then, checking the time she lifted out one of the books and leafed through it. A tattered letter, one that she had written, fell to the floor, its ink partially fading. It was dated 1919.

My Dearest K,

By the time you receive this I shall be back in London. Sorry to hear about your problem. An extended stay seems inevitable. Despite expected delay goods arrived safely. Write your plans soonest.

After placing the letter back between the pages she checked the condition of the binding. It was still firm. She poked into the spine and felt the rolled up tube of paper. Good – it was exactly where she had left it. No need to read it now, she thought as she placed the book back in the tea chest. Her mind flooded with thoughts of years gone by. It was a miracle that she had survived this long.

Maria rarely showed emotion but these memories brought a tear to her eye. Why had her life taken such a turn? If only, she had been born one hundred years earlier. No child should be born with such a misfortune! She pulled out an embroidered handkerchief. It had the familiar gold embossed initials. Fit for a princess she thought, wiping her eyes slowly. She wished her thoughts would go away. Then, reminded of something, she searched through one of the boxes. 'Where is it?' She muttered, her hands rummaging through until she felt the worn cover of her favourite diary. Quickly she leafed through the lilac pages, past the poetry and pressed flowers until she found what she was looking for. Words she had written half a century before. Avidly she read, reminding herself of that time in her life when nothing was certain. One passage didn't make any sense at all. Then she remembered she had written it in code for the sailors and tea traders. What a journey that had been!

Closing the diary, Maria picked up an English translation of a Russian novel she had worked on a few years earlier. Michael would be interested in this she thought, placing it back in the box and turning towards the window. It was a bleak day, one where you knew the rain would just keep falling. She would miss it of course! Dear old rainy London, so cosy, so romantic and so safe.

Walking slowly across the dimly lit room, Maria decided to play her favourite record. It would cheer her up. Silence only agreed with her when she was trying to sleep. 'Now let's see. What shall I listen to? It has to be something suitable for the occasion. Mozart? No, no, no! Let's have some Rachmaninov.' Placing the record on the turntable Maria picked up the needle and gently positioned it onto the record. She ignored the first minute of scratches as she imagined herself young again and made her way across to a large gold mirror hanging on the wall opposite. There she found an elegant woman standing in front of a huge chandelier that reminded her of the type that used to hang in the Winter Palace ballroom in St Petersburg.

As the record came to an end Maria shivered and picked up her shawl. Being that cold brought back memories of those awful winters in Moscow. Without the big ovens upon which they all took turns to sleep they would have frozen to death. Who could believe that rich Russia would have become so poor or that socialism would have lasted quite so long in the glorious motherland? What a terrible mistake it had all been! No one could escape it. Even Gorky, that great supporter of change, could not have foreseen the impact of a diminishing Russian intelligentsia on the country. Maria closed up another tea chest. 'So now my girl, we go on a big important journey. It won't be so bad! The Italian sun will help my arthritis and I can listen to Verdi over a glass of Chianti in the evenings.'

Chapter Two   Two Women in a Grotto

'If only we had said what really happened back then,' Maria said to her niece Tonya one afternoon.

'But surely they were all murdered weren't they?'

'Well as far as I know, they came to no harm at all.'

Tonya was astonished. 'What do you mean no harm? Everyone knows they were all shot!'

Maria shook her head. 'Well, I am one of those that believe they came to no harm and I have my reasons! Besides, if I can't tell my great niece....,' Maria gave her a quick hug to show her that she was special, 'who can I tell?'

Tonya had her own thoughts about the matter. Of course Maria was clever with her words.

That was to be expected from a writer and a translator. Maybe she had found the news too shocking or perhaps she was in some kind of denial and had adapted the truth to suit her own story. Maria didn't lie but her ability to dodge questions was to be admired and much as Maria loved to talk about OLD Russia she did not like to speak about the Imperial Family or other people she had known. Tonya found this frustrating, especially when Maria laughed at her persistent questioning.

'Tonya dear, you will just have to accept there is no more for me to say!'

On one occasion she asked her aunt about the paintings from Russia. 'I love those paintings, where did you get them from?'

Maria turned around to look at them. 'That one there is my favourite. It's called "Two Young Women in a Grotto" and was painted by a famous Baltic artist called Carl Timoleon von Neff. You know he was the court painter to Tsar Nicholas I. He was commissioned to paint the Tsar's two beautiful daughters, Maria and Olga Romanov. In fact he painted them many times. In this painting Maria is about forty and Olga, well I suppose she would be about thirty-eight. They are sitting in Neptune's Grotto at Tivoli. That's where the Roman emperor

Hadrian built his villa, just outside Rome. As you can see the year is 1859.' Maria pointed to the date at the bottom of the painting. 'That was the year of the Aurora Borealis. Incredibly, it could be seen as far south as Rome.'

'Wow that's amazing! But how do you know so much about it all?'

'My great aunt told me all about it. You see these were her paintings.'

Maria smiled and patted her on the back. 'It's a bit like you and me. You see, when I'm gone you can have... Ah that reminds me! I have something else to show you. Two more water-colours of Maria and Olga, this time painted by a brilliant French artist..... Well would you like to see them?'

Tonya nodded and followed her great aunt upstairs while Maria hardly drew breath as she spoke of all things Russian. 'Oh, and by the way, the name Romanov means "of Rome!"'

'It must be wonderful to paint like that. I wish I had such a talent!' Tonya exclaimed.

'Why don't you take lessons? How about writing to Alex? Michael tells me he paints very well. Maybe he can teach you?'

Tonya thought for a moment. 'Well, I'm not sure. I think I want to be a writer.'

Maria sighed at her indecision. 'In that case why not do both?'

Tonya laughed. 'Then I would be a jack of all trades and master of none!'

Maria didn't bother to reply. Her mind was on something else. Presently she spoke.

'You know I shall be leaving London for a while and going to stay in Italy with Michael?' Tonya nodded.

'Alice will accompany me but it would be delightful if you could find time to visit as well?''

Tonya clapped her hands in delight at the suggestion. "That sounds like a great idea! I love Rome. It's such a romantic place and what a history!"

Maria smiled at her enthusiasm. "You mean the art I suppose, since everywhere has history! And Russia has far more than any other country in the world. The art collections of the Romanovs and the Stroganovs can testify to that. Thank heavens those two great families had the sense to marry!'

Tonya made it clear that she didn't care to be married at all. She was quite happy as she was thank you very much! Maria giggled at the spontaneity of the nineteen year old. Tonya had no idea what Maria meant when she laughed like that but she was pleased to make her happy! Besides, she was fed up of explaining to everyone why she didn't have a boyfriend. Instinctively she knew that when the right person came along everything would fall into place. Just as it was supposed to! She might have seemed naïve to some and it is true she was bit of a dreamer, but on occasions she was prone to think quite deeply about things. Most of the time her feet were firmly on the ground even if her head was up in the clouds! Tonya thought of herself as a fisherman of ideas because if something caught her imagination, just like a fish on a hook she wouldn't let it go. Not until she had discovered all there was to know. During such conversations she would gaze at her great aunt and marvel at the colour of her cat-like eyes or watch her hands emphasise the meaning of her words.

A great amethyst ring mounted high in a gold setting sparkled at every opportunity and a string of milky pearls settled haphazardly across the front of her green satin jacket. The jewellery rattled whenever Maria moved but it didn't seem to bother her. Tonya supposed it had always been like that, ever since she was a young woman at the St Petersburg palaces. She could easily imagine the rustle of dazzling silver gowns and fragmented flashes of diamonds glistening under the light of a thousand candles, which must have been commonplace at the evening balls.

As Maria showed her the watercolours of the two princesses, Tonya questioned her aunt. 'But surely the sisters were born around 1900, so how could they have been painted in 1859?'

Maria laughed and then explained that these were the great aunts to the last Romanovs. They were the daughters of Tsar Nicholas I not of Tsar Nicholas II.

'Well it's all very confusing when they all have the same name!' Tonya exclaimed.

Maria agreed. 'The possibilities for confusion were endless in Russia. It was ever thus! But it had long been the custom in Russia for daughters to carry forward their father's name. It was particularly confusing in this case because both middle names were Nicholeavna since both generations of daughters had a father called Nicholas! Normally if the first names were the same then the middle name would have been different but in this case all three names of the princesses were the same! Historians and some art critics found it confusing too so Tonya was in good company!' she added.

Tonya found it spooky that two sets of sisters born one hundred years apart had exactly the same names and lived in the same palace and that the father of the first Maria and Olga was the great grandfather of the second Maria and Olga. Maria agreed, before adding, 'There are many Romanovs left in Russia as well as abroad.'

'Was Romanov a common name then?' asked Tonya rather innocently.

'COMMON!' responded Maria indignantly. 'Common is not a word to be used when speaking of a Romanov.'

It wasn't often that she got angry but this was one occasion when her impatience with the younger generation showed. She had always been meticulous about words and became vexed by lazy grammar. She simply could not abide slang. Tonya had assumed that her idiosyncrasy of constantly correcting everyone's grammar had come from her great aunt having been a translator. Maria was the original wordsmith, fluent in Russian, French, German, and English, which by the way she spoke with a first-class accent.

Tonya supposed that it had all been down to an excellent boarding school education. Certainly her great aunt had a lot to say on the subject of English.

'The English language is a beautifully indulgent language but lends itself easily to duplicity and double meaning. You can never be quite sure what someone may have meant. All the rules in grammar are easily broken especially that 'I before E' nonsense! And I don't think English can express the really deep feelings one may have and certainly not as well as French or Russian words can!'

Tonya wasn't sure that she agreed with everything that was said. But she did enjoy the stories. Maria's girly giggle usually signalled the launch of a previously untold tale from her childhood. They were full of romance, of bold knights rescuing damsels in distress and nothing like real life, as Tonya said afterwards much to Maria's amusement.

Maria was supposedly born in 1889. But people found it hard to believe because she looked at least ten years younger. Tonya couldn't explain how such a mixture of vulnerability and strength ended up in one person. Sometimes Tonya would feel quite strange. It happened when her aunt spoke of "OLD

RUSSIA". Straight away she would get those goose bumps and then a shiver would run down her spine. That "OLD RUSSIA" where the people loved the Tsar so much they called him Papa. Where everything smelt of frankincense and where the sound of the balalaika was accompanied by a lot of HEY, HEY, HEY and hand clapping, where all Maria's friends were famous writers like H.G. Wells, Gorky, and Chesterton. But hang on a moment. Her great aunt had spoken of a Count someone. Now what was his name? She said that HE was the love of her life, even though she had admitted to loving many people! Apparently her great aunt had been married a very long time ago. Not just once, but twice. Now she was the Baroness Maria Brandenberg. A name she had acquired that bore no relationship to her ancestry or her marriages! Maria never liked to speak of her family or of her first husband. She had always refused to discuss the matter, even with her son Michael, who surely had a right to know!

Maria always looked forward to her great niece's visit. She told Alice that Tonya reminded her of herself when she was young and studying in England. Tonya of course would never be the social butterfly that Maria had been but she was demure and attractive enough. Well, that was no bad thing. Maria liked that about her. She had plenty of common sense so it didn't matter that she didn't understand all the shenanigans of the Russian revolution!

As soon as Tonya was seated, Maria would clap her hands and Alice would wheel the prepared trolley into the room with great care. This was the 'Old Russian' way of having tea, Maria would say as Tonya feasted her eyes on the heavily laden plates, the variety of sandwiches on the top shelf and cakes and biscuits on the middle. The rattling came from the stacked crockery sitting precariously under neatly folded white napkins on the bottom shelf. Maria laughed excitedly as the trolley made its entrance into the room. Tonya could smell the freshly prepared cakes mingled with the aroma of hot tea.

'Ah! That's lovely. Just here will do nicely, thank you Alice,' Maria pointed at the side of her chair.

'Right you are,' responded Alice as she handed out the plates. 'The cake is freshly baked so it might be a little crumbly. Oh and by the way Peety-Pops has had his, so don't let him tell you any different!'

Maria laughed as her favourite dog nuzzled closer.

'Why do you call him that?' Tonya asked, bending down to pat the rather plump King Charles spaniel.

Maria smiled thoughtfully. 'Well, his actual name is Petrushka but I think that is a far too formal name for him now that he is getting so old, so we call him Peety-Pops instead.' Maria held out a piece of cake. 'You see, I have to put it close to his nose so that he can smell it because he's going blind.'

'Ah, he is cute!' Tonya exclaimed sympathetically, even though she suspected this was a daily ritual. Peety-Pops knew exactly what to expect when he heard the rattle of the trolley. Maria read her thoughts and gave her a knowing wink. 'This is the time of the day when he most likes to be treated like royalty,' Maria added, handing Tonya a teacup filled to the brim. 'We always had tea in Russia this way. Back in the really old days when there were far too many of us to have a cosy tea, well then we had to put on our very best dresses. Mama would get so angry if they were dirty, which they often were because we loved to be with Papa in the garden. I didn't mind though because as I said to my sisters more people for tea means more delicious cakes all baked with lots of cream! Oh dear me! It's so sad how the times have changed.' Maria leant forward and tapped Tonya to emphasise the point. 'And if I told you just how much they had changed I'd be here forever! Oh Jerum, Jerum, Jerum! Quae mutatio rerum!'

Tonya placed her teacup back down on the trolley just as her great aunt finished. 'Jerum, Jerum, quae mutatio what..?' Tonya laughed half way through repeating the sentence.

'It's one of my favourite sayings,' Maria added.

A couple of hours later there was a knock on the drawing room door. 'I'm off now. Are there any letters for me to post?' asked Alice.

Maria thought for a moment. 'No I don't think so. Oh, wait a moment. When you see Francesca, tell her of our plans. I'll be here tomorrow if she wants to pop in before we leave.'

Alice closed the door and Maria bent down to stroke Peety-Pops, who was taking an interest in the boxes she had packed. 'Does my little Peety-Pops want to come to Italy with Mama? Yes of course he does and so he shall.' Maria patted a comfortable rug by the fire. 'Come here. Now there's a good boy. Come and sit down.'

Having settled the dog, Maria made a start on the last of the boxes stored in the bottom of her wardrobe. They would need special packing. First she removed the mauve ribbons from around her diaries before laying them neatly on the table. She couldn't remember exactly what she had written in them, so she picked one up and turned to the first page and then to the next. Ah yes, that's right, she thought, putting a particular diary to one side. Next she held up a large bundle of papers and smelt the contents. I hope Michael will appreciate all that I am doing.

Chapter Three   History in the Making

I want the meaning of my words to shine like golden beams in your heart.

Maria sat quietly in the taxi heading for the airport. Alice read her mind and patted her arm. 'I know, I'll miss it too.' Maria leant forward and peered out of the window, eagerly absorbing every last view of the bustling city as it slipped inevitably out of sight. Only when they were rapidly approaching Heathrow did she respond.

'Well of course I'll miss it. You remember don't you? Back then, they all suggested I move to Paris or even Cannes. Well, I said no! It didn't suit me at all. Full of pretentious people, gambling and living the high life and shooting their way out of trouble after they had had one too many cocktails. They had no BACKBONE you see. I couldn't abide them. REALLY I couldn't!'

Just at that moment two motorbikes roared past. 'I wish you would sit back in the seat,' Alice said, concerned for her safety. 'You know what will happen if the driver has to suddenly brake!'

Maria laughed. 'You forget my dear. I've been in danger all my life.'

On the plane they settled into their seats and a nostalgic Maria waved goodbye to England and hurriedly ordered a Vodka Martini. 'Shaken but not stirred,' she demanded from an embarrassed steward. 'I'm sorry we only have wine or beer madam. What would you like?' Maria pulled a face and glanced across to Alice, who was busy reading the rules for emergency landings. Maria sighed. 'Well then, I'll have a glass of white wine, thank you!'

A silence ensued as Alice, who was trying to get comfortable in her seat, realised she was expected to order something as well. 'I'll just have a coffee,' she added before the steward hurried off.

Maria fidgeted in her chair as Alice rummaged through her handbag to find her Teach Yourself Italian book. 'Honestly! Do I look as though I am the sort of person who drinks beer?' She asked Alice.

'Of course not, but if you didn't want to have alcohol you should have ordered a coffee like me!' Alice gave her a knowing smile. She knew full well that Maria never went anywhere without a small bottle of Vodka in her handbag. Why didn't she ask for some ice instead of complaining?

'Because it's too early, that's why!' Maria added, opening a gold compact, powdering her nose and then applying fresh lipstick. Oh dear, she thought, gazing at her reflection. Looks that had once set a room alight were fading fast. Never mind! For her age she was still attractive. The years had been kind even though she'd put on weight and her voice was now rather deep. Alice said it was because she smoked those awful cigarettes. Still, everyone thought she was about seventy-nine and that pleased her. Heaven forbid they should find out how old she really was. Only once had she been questioned but she soon put a stop to further interrogation. 'Nonsense, I can assure you that I was certainly not born before 1900!' Only Michael had had the bravery to respond. 'I fear the lady doth protest too much!' Well, what did she expect from an only son? His father would have said as much.

The steward placed the wine on the tray in front of her and smiled. Maria wondered whether he was being cheeky. She was about to say something when Alice suddenly started pronouncing her Italian. Maria took her first sip slowly. It was surprisingly cold, which she didn't like but she indicated to the steward that he could leave anyway.

Then she turned to Alice. 'Please don't read the words out loud.'

Alice nodded as Maria took a longer sip. 'Oh! If only they would let me tell the whole story as it really was. Just this once! I mean what harm would it do? Everyone who was involved is dead, apart from me.' Maria took another sip of wine before Alice reminded her that inebriation while travelling was not a good idea. Maria gulped the rest of the wine down and promptly ordered another. 'Waiter!' she called, waving her glass furiously in the air. 'One more glass of wine please.'

Alice closed her book. 'Are you sure you want to?'

'Yes of course, it's delicious.'

Alice smiled. 'I don't mean the wine. I mean you telling the whole story. Remember your memory is not as good as it was.'

'My memory is fine thank you very much! I remember every detail.' Maria laughed spontaneously. 'Like the time I had to take the De Havilland up instead of that nippy little Gypsy Moth which I had to crash land on more than one occasion. Gosh, do you remember how cold it was in those planes! Honestly you were lucky if you didn't half freeze to death. Besides, the story MUST be told. I made that promise to him, and I won' break it.'

Alice wasn't surprised by Maria's outburst. 'That's fine. I know how important it is,' she added, watching Maria wave her empty glass in the air impatiently.

'Please try and stay calm now we have a long journey ahead of us,' Alice pleaded.

Maria placed her glass back on the tray. 'Well, who can blame me? It's my history after all! Besides, whenever I am in a plane it reminds me of what it was like on those special missions. I always felt nervous. You never knew quite how it was all going to turn out. Oh but the writing Alice? There is just so much to do!'

Alice patted her arm in a bid to comfort her friend. 'Don't worry. I'll help.'

Maria smiled and pushed her empty glass away. She knew she had drunk too much.

Sometime later the aircraft juddered to a halt and Maria woke up and looked at her empty glass. 'Hasn't the waiter been yet?'

Alice didn't bother to reply but as they queued she reminded Maria that she was there to help. 'I don't want you to worry one little bit. Once we have unpacked I will help you sort out the papers. I suggest we put the ones you want to work on in your bedroom and the rest can be stored somewhere else. By the way, I noticed you left some boxes behind in London. I hope they weren't important?'

Maria smiled. 'I'm so lucky to have you. You're as organised as ever.'

Although she was much younger, Alice knew exactly what Maria wanted to write about. She never spoke to Maria about IT unless Maria made it clear that it was okay to do so. Then they would talk for hours. Mind you this was usually after Maria had drunk copious amounts of vodka. But Alice didn't mind at all. She was pleased that Maria didn't talk about THAT particular episode of her life to anyone else. She could not remember quite as much as Maria because she had been very young at the time. Her family were from Moscow and were not grand people but they had always worked for the aristocracy. Alice had great respect for Maria, who was from a noble family even though it was not clear which family she hailed from! Still, she instinctively understood the mixed loyalties Maria wrestled with because of her own upbringing. In those days if one was to survive one had to be all things to all men! One minute a royalist, then a socialist, then a democrat, then a republican! The European aristocracy had always been a very complicated issue. Most people were loyal to their country. But Maria said that her loyalty had always been to people, not to countries! That was a very difficult position to be in during a world war. At first Alice had found Maria's views disconcerting but gradually she came to understand them. Maria had stayed loyal to her beliefs all her life. Throughout World War I and the Russian Revolution she had maintained absolute loyalty to all sides and to everyone! That meant she was a friend to the Germans and the Russians, the English and the Americans and everyone else in between, so long as they were all Christian!

'Political alliances change all the time,' she said one day. 'And the people you love are caught up in the most frightful of circumstances. What kind of person would I have been if I had not helped them? I would have found it very difficult to be happy. If I had not stepped up to the challenge and played the GAME as they requested I would not have been worthy of the title they bestowed upon me!' The title Maria referred to was that of the Baroness of Brandenberg. But on the issue of loyalty Alice found it difficult to agree. Surely loyalty was about choosing a side and then fighting for it? She was Russian and so Russia's enemies were hers. Anyway, she didn't like talking about the politics of war with Maria because the latter was far too eloquent in expressing her feelings. Feelings that Alice said bore no relationship to the requirements of the everyday world people lived in, where the power-mad, jealous, possessive, greedy and egotistical forced good ordinary people to fight wars in the first place.

Maria agreed. It was unbelievably horrific what one human could do to another in the name of God. But for all that, there was no right side to any war because innocent people got killed. All war was an abomination against the glorious planet we live on. Maria said that private thoughts mattered more than all the speaking in the world. But Alice replied that the power of prayer was even greater and that she would always fight for her faith. Maria sighed when her friend attempted to persuade her that some things were worth fighting for.

'You don't mean the word fight Alice. You are describing an internal struggle, not a violent physical episode with another human being!'

Alice supposed that Maria's outlook on life had started when she was very young. Meeting lots of people in different countries at an early age must have given her a lot of confidence. Maria had travelled to France and Germany often and that's how she came to speak both fluently. But her English was the very best it could be. In fact, if it was not for the photograph of the Tsar and his family on her bedside table and her now constant chattering about Russia, Alice could easily forget just how Russian she was.

Maria had explained it very well when she said, 'On the outside I am English, but on the inside my heart is Russian. My mind is often German because I love order and cannot abide chaos of any kind. My love of fashion is Italian and my desire to act as I think fit quite French I think!'

One day Maria had asked Alice why she didn't want to go back to Russia, even for a visit. Alice explained that she could not return until the holy church did. During the revolution, THEY – Alice never liked to mention their names – robbed and closed all of the beautiful churches and even murdered the holy men and women. THEY said that the church had kept the people ignorant and made them superstitious and that it was now time to free the peasants from their oppressors. THEY had gone much too far. They had never understood the people's need for spirituality and when they did away with the church and the Tsar... well, they did away with all that she loved about 'holy mother Russia.' Thankfully Alice had everything she wanted in London with the establishment of the Russian Orthodox Church so close to where they were living in Kensington. She even managed to add to her mystical knowledge by periodically meeting up with a group called the Theosophists.

But Alice didn't live in the past the way she thought Maria liked to. No, her view was quite different. There was no point in comparing the imperial glories of the past with the mundane bureaucracy of today's totalitarian state. 'Tsarsdom', as Alice liked to call it, was gone. It had its day of glory and now it was no more. 'Not even you can bring it back,' she had once said rather stupidly. Maria's response was frightening. First she gave a haughty devil-bedammed laugh but then suddenly broke into a fevered rant, the like of which Alice had never heard before or since.

'The only thing I'll ever accept from YOU about this new Russia is when change itself changes!' She shouted, her voice getting louder and louder. 'What they took away, what they stole, WHAT THEY DESTROYED they will jolly well HAVE to put back and this you can BELIEVE, I INTEND TO MAKE SURE THEY DO EXACTLY THAT!'

After the tirade, Maria stormed out of the room, slamming the door behind her. Alice watched as the ornate ceiling shook for a full thirty seconds as the ancient icons trembled on their huge brass chains. Maria didn't speak to Alice for more than a month. But when she did she told her that she would never accept what had happened to Russia as being a good thing. 'I know the Russian people better than anyone living today. I can tell you they will not WANT to live without their GODS for long.'

That had happened a long time ago and they had never argued since.

Now, as they walked through the airport in the heat of the afternoon, Maria came to a halt and smiled. Michael and Juliana had appeared from the midst of the crowd and were hurriedly walking towards them. As Maria waved to them she turned to Alice. 'It is quite wonderful to be in Italy again.'

## Chapter Four					Count Frederick

June 1978
'I can't believe it,' Giovanni said, wiping his forehead with a dirty handkerchief.

'We try so hard to keep it safe and then it all went up. Just like that, POOOOF! I couldn't get close. Not even with a hose. I shout for help but no one around and the Baroness she was out for the day visiting friends. She so happy to receive invite and I...,' Giovanni paused with tears welling up his eyes, 'I promised! Now all is such a mess!' Distraught, he turned and pointed at the burnt out remains of the caravan before sitting down on the bench with his face in his hands. A moment later he looked up at the burnt wreck again. 'When the Baroness came back and see caravan all burnt out. All papers lost. Mama Mia the look on her face! Then she fell down and no move again. Not at all! Then I shout and we get the doctor.' Giovanni shook his head with concern. 'She's up there now,' he said, pointing at the geranium covered balcony. 'She non parla.'

Alice didn't know what to say. She was in shock as she listened to Giovanni and looked up at Maria's bedroom window. Putting her cases down on the terrace she stood motionless, trying to comprehend what had happened. After taking only a few seconds to catch her breath she rushed up to the room where her friend lay motionless. She walked over to the bed and taking Maria's hand in hers held it for a few moments before speaking. 'Maria, Can you hear me? It's Alice.'

Maria slowly opened her eyes and managed a short smile. Alice waited for her to say something. But to her disappointment Maria only closed her eyes again. Alice sat for a while until her anxiousness got the better of her. It was no good. She must find out more about what had happened; and where was Michael? As she arrived back on the terrace, Giovanni was pacing up and down and smoking furiously. Alice immediately waved him over.

'Do you have any cold lemonade? I'm so thirsty.'

'Si, of course I get right away.' Giovanni hurriedly stubbed his cigarette out and rushed into the kitchen.

At least Maria was awake. If only I hadn't gone to Florence, Alice was in the middle of chiding herself when Giovanni placed a large jug of cold lemonade on the table. She watched him pour the lemonade out over the ice cubes and smiled when they cracked as he handed her the glass.

'Thank you,' she said, gulping the cold juice down. Giovanni poured some more lemonade into her empty glass. 'No more ice for me.'

'So are you feeling okay now?'

Alice nodded. 'I'm cooling down nicely but I am so worried. What will Maria say when she recovers and realises that most, if not all, of her life's work has gone up in flames? I should never have left her.' Alice took out her lace handkerchief and wiped her eyes.

'Si,si. But it was not my fault. The Baroness was away, I was working in the garden, busy pruning the roses she loves so much. Then I smell smoke! No understand what it was or that it was coming from the caravan. I don't know how it started and I say that to police.'

Alice listened carefully, then feeling suddenly alarmed, she whispered in French, 'I trust our little secret is safe?'

Giovanni raised his eyebrows and placed his hand on his heart. 'Mon Dieu! Oui. Certainement Madame!'

Alice smiled before asking, this time in English, 'so you didn't see anyone around the house before the fire started?'

'No no! But she has too many papers in caravan. I say no good idea. She says we wait for you. Then make good.'

Alice nodded. 'Well yes, that's right. But I didn't agree for so many of the books and papers to be kept in there. I know Maria can be pretty obstinate at times! She said to me not to worry, that they would be perfectly safe because we were in Italy and now I wish she had not said that!'

Giovanni stirred the remainder of the lemonade. 'You would like more?'

Alice shook her head. 'The trouble is, there is not enough room in the villa and so many boxes, more than even Michael had expected, and now with everyone coming to stay....' She stopped short, realising that what she was about to say next was not important, and gazed up at Maria's window.

'You see something?'

'Not sure. I thought I saw Maria,' Alice said, pointing up at her bedroom window, 'but it must have been my imagination.'

Giovanni shaded his eyes from the sun and took a step back. 'Okay! She is fine and boss, he knows more. You ask when he come back and you tell him it's not my fault, si?'

Alice patted him on the back. 'Don't worry. No one is going to blame you. Anyway, who do you think it was that first suggested storing papers in the caravan? How do you think that makes me feel?'

Giovanni shrugged, lit a cigarette and flicked the match away. 'Si, I know Alice. I not happy either. I say to her, please Baroness you no go in when you are smoking.' Giovanni held up his cigarette to make the point. 'But she likes to puff on her...'

Alice had heard enough and besides, it was getting late. Slowly she rose from the chair. 'Thank you for the lemonade, but now I really must unpack this case.' Giovanni took the hint and helped carry it up the grand staircase. Alice was pleased that her room was opposite Maria's because it meant she could keep an eye on her without being too obvious about it.

Deep in thought, Giovanni walked slowly down the stairs. It would be too awful for words if the Baroness should not pull through. He had known her for more years than he could remember. How he would miss her! She considered him a loyal and trusted friend and had treated him and his son Paul as her own little Italian family. Giovanni smiled as he thought back to when Paul and Tonya were children. Paul was only a couple of years older than Tonya and at one time Giovanni had harboured hopes of a union between them. Now Paul was a priest that was right out of the question, even though Paul found Tonya's lively mind and bouncy manner rather appealing. In fact he was forever asking when the Baroness and her niece would next visit and he had made no secret of his feelings over the years. Giovanni sighed. 'Ah well, it's no matter now.'

That evening Michael arrived back home before dinner. As a renowned historian and lecturer he often worked from home unless he was called to a meeting, in which case he stayed in town.

As he entered the open courtyard he dropped his briefcase, admired the moonlit statues and listened to the water tinkling in the fountains. Raising his gaze to the stars, he took a deep breath and caught the heady aroma of roses. Michael took another deep breath and put his hands on his hips. Ah, it was so good to be home! No wonder everyone who visited delighted in the thought of staying! The ornate gardens and rose terraces were superb at this time of year, overflowing in abundance with colour and fragrance; and the villa, although grand in architecture, was relaxed in its furnishings. Light and breezy in the summer and, once all the fires were lit, warm and cosy in the winter.

Michael turned to greet Alice warmly. 'And how was Florence, as picturesque as ever I presume?' He laughed at his own joke and Alice smiled.

'I enjoyed it very much but it was rather tiring. I was glad to get back to the hotel and put my feet up.' 'I suppose you've heard the dreadful news?' Michael could see by Alice's countenance that she had. 'Come on, let's go in. I think we could all do with a stiff drink.' Just as Michael was pouring out a glass of whisky Giovanni approached. 'And how is my mother today?' Michael asked, without looking up. 'Any better?'

'Si.' Giovanni smiled and glanced in Alice's direction as he answered.

'And has she eaten or said anything to you?' Michael sounded unnecessarily impatient and Alice could see that Giovanni was struggling to keep calm, so she decided to answer.

'Well Michael, I have been up to see Maria and thankfully she opened her eyes. Later Giovanni took her soup but she hasn't touched it. Perhaps we should go up and see her now?'

While Alice and Michael were speaking Giovanni paced up and down. Finally he stopped and leant over the large marble mantelpiece, staring into the log fire before turning and pacing up and down again. Michael watched him as Alice spoke. Eventually he'd had enough and grabbed Giovanni by the arm. 'Look here my old chap, pull yourself together. Anyone would think that you were to blame for this terrible accident.'

Alice was shocked at his intervention and watched helplessly as Giovanni stared with his mouth open before completely breaking down. Michael glanced across to Alice and raised his eyebrows before adding: 'Look man! No one blames you! Do you understand? Now stop all of this right now!' He sighed in exasperation before knocking back his whisky and slamming the glass on the mantelpiece. Giovanni composed himself and sat down. 'It was all safe. The Baroness she checks them every day, every night and then....' He broke down again in tears. 'I not forget. She fell to the ground... collapse, her face not move. I hold her hand until doctor come.'

Alice felt sorry for Giovanni and watched Michael with admiration as he handed over his handkerchief. He was always so masterful but things would only get worse if he carried on his questioning. 'Perhaps Maria would like some of that hot soup you made earlier?' she suggested, helping Giovanni back up to his feet. 'Now that's a splendid idea and while you do that I'll go and check on her now.' Michael patted Giovanni on the back as he left. Opening Maria's bedroom door, Michael was surprised to see his mother out of bed. As he entered she turned from the window and beckoned him over. 'Look at those wonderful roses Michael. They are God's treasure! Oh yes indeed. God's treasure alright.'

Michael gave his mother a long gentle hug. 'You look better now. Would you like something to eat?'

Maria shrugged. 'Well, actually I'm quite thirsty. Is there something to drink?'

'Yes of course.' Michael handed her a glass of water. 'Now come and sit over here on the bed and tell me how you are.' Maria did as she was told. Even though Michael was as controlling as ever, she was very proud of him and his interest in Russian history. It meant they could have long conversations about the past. When she had first met up with him, it had been after a twenty-five year break and she was able to tell him some stories of his early childhood and why she had not been there for him. He said he understood perfectly; that extraordinary times demanded extraordinary measures and Maria had been relieved. Thank God that he was a chip off the old block and knew how to keep secrets! Now she watched as her son walked slowly over to the window. Silhouetted against the Italian afternoon sky he looked much taller than she remembered and quite a bit thinner too. 'Darling, what am I to do? My whole life has just gone up in smoke. All my memoirs, the ones that I wanted to write up, just as I promised. They are all gone!' Michael turned into the room and walked over to his mother as she was speaking. 'I see you've lost weight again. I suppose you've been skimping on food. Now you know that won't do. You have to feed the brain if you want it to work efficiently!' she added, wagging her finger at him.

Michael sighed. 'Honestly, with all that has happened to you, you still worry about me! Now I want you to drink the hot soup that will be brought up in a moment and then I want you to rest for a while. Okay?' He didn't wait for an answer before adding, 'Now I have to go and pick Juliana and Alex up from the station, so we'll talk later.' As he made a move to depart, Maria reached out. 'I'm not hungry, how could I be after this has happened? I came to Italy to keep the papers safe! They are IRREPLACEABLE,' she shouted as he left the room. 'I think she is feeling better,' Michael said to Alice as she passed by carrying the lunch tray. He hovered to make sure all was in order and then smiled when he heard his mother ask for a vodka martini. Well, she must be feeling better! He thought as he hurried through the gardens and headed straight for the car. A surprised Giovanni watched as he drove off at high speed. Michael did not always drive himself but this route to the station was one of his favourite. With the roof down and the music playing he felt twenty years younger. As he listened to a familiar tune it brought back memories of one particular birthday in 1945.

Quite out of the blue an elderly gentleman had called and introduced himself as Count Frederick. He then proceeded to tell Michael that he had been appointed by Michael's recently deceased father. It was the count's solemn duty to inform Michael of his inheritance. Count Frederick was a tall elegant gentleman who spoke excellent Italian. Indeed he spoke a number of languages in addition to his mother tongue, which he said was Austrian. Anyway the count had proceeded to invest Michael with all sorts of goods and chattels from his late father.

Much of the silverware included ornate hairbrushes, goblets and cigarette boxes. He also gave Michael a few silk cravats and handkerchiefs, gold and silver cufflinks and a heavily embroidered waistcoat. The count also brought details of several numbered bank accounts that had been transferred over to Michael, unknown to him, at the request of his father. Having taken some light refreshment the count gave him a pink envelope. Inside it was a deposit box receipt and a key. Michael, who knew nothing of his father, was stunned by the appearance of the count bearing gifts and was eager to find out more about his father's life from him. But the count had been unable to answer his questions. He was, he explained, sworn by an oath not to divulge the true identity of his father. Michael then asked whether the count had a photograph he could show him of his father. The count said he had not. But before leaving he hugged Michael and made a request. 'Send my very best regards to the Baroness and please be sure to tell her that the Count has fulfilled his promise and his duty.' He then departed forthwith and Michael never saw him again.

When Michael told his mother the story she had been very pleased. 'Now you will not have to work quite so hard. You are extremely wealthy and you should not take too long in visiting the bank and opening the deposit box.'

Then had followed a mildly amusing conversation about what might be inside the deposit box before his mother asked about the count's appearance. Michael did his best to describe him but clearly not to her satisfaction. She kept asking questions. In the end Michael asked why, if he was such a good friend, they hadn't stayed in touch.

His mother shrugged. 'Well, it was all such a long time ago, I suppose we all just lost touch!' Of course Michael had been disappointed but he knew he would get nowhere by asking more questions and that had been the end of their conversation.

* * *

'OH NO!' Michael quickly hit the break as the car swerved and narrowly missed another car. Everything he did went into slow motion as he struggled to maintain control. *Don't tell me this is going to be the end!*

A few dangerous seconds later Michael managed to get control of the car. *Phew! How on earth did that happen?* Michael was still shaking and feeling disorientated when he remembered what had caused his near mishap. It was the recollection that he had lost the deposit box receipt and the key. *Bloody hell! It must have been at least thirty-two years ago the count gave me that key and I haven't given it a second thought until now. What on earth have I done with it? It must be somewhere in the house or in the library.*

The key, the key! I must find that wretched KEY and the receipt. Perhaps it has fallen to the back of a desk drawer? Yes that must be it. I'll look as soon as

I get back. Then Michael's next thought made him feel sick. His desk had been replaced a few years earlier. Hell! Mother will never forgive me!

The following morning Michael was still worrying about the loss when he and Juliana went up to see Maria. She was standing by the window overlooking the remains of the caravan. 'I've cried so many tears Michael dear. You can't believe how sad I am.' Maria covered her eyes as she relived the moment when she saw the smoking embers of the burnt out caravan.

'I know mother, it must have been a dreadful shock for you. But try and look on the bright side, you're feeling much better today.'

Michael sat her down on the bed. 'Now please try not to get yourself upset.'

Maria agreed reluctantly, managing a forced smile. 'But I can't remember it all without my papers. Not unless …?' She hesitated, '… UNLESS….' Maria didn't finish her sentence. Instead she pointed an arthritic finger at the tea chests in her room. Michael glanced at Juliana and raised an eyebrow. She knew exactly what her husband meant.

'Don't worry Maria. I'll stay a while with you.' Juliana sat down beside her mother-in-law.

Happy to leave them to it, Michael sighed and went downstairs. 'Ah! Giovanni, there you are, could you take my mother up some hot sweet tea when you have a moment?' Giovanni wiped his muddy hands down his apron. 'Si boss, the Baroness she is better?' Michael looked up from the letter he was opening. 'Well I should think with a day or two's rest and some good food inside her she will be fine. Now if you don't mind!' Giovanni understood and hurried back into the kitchen.

An hour or so later, over a hastily prepared meal, Juliana asked whether Michael had seen their son Alex. Michael shrugged before answering. 'He said he had an important meeting whatever that means!' He wasn't remotely interested in where Alex was. He had far more pressing things on his mind. Throwing his napkin on the table he gulped down the last of his wine.

'I'll be in the library dear if you need me. I've some papers that I really must sort out and I presume you are busy for the rest of the day?'

Juliana wasn't surprised at the question. She understood this was his way of saying that he didn't wish to be disturbed. 'Oh I suppose I shall spend a few hours sculpting after I've seen how your mother is. I hear from Giovanni that she is feeling much better but she must be so upset about the loss of all those important papers of hers.' Michael rubbed his chin and walked slowly back into the room. Resting his hands firmly on the chair he had been sitting on he gave his wife a long appreciative look. 'Yes, yes, of course. That's why I must see what I have. Maybe something can be retrieved and when she is well enough perhaps I can work with her. I really want her to be able to tell that story. Now,' he smiled, 'don't worry about our guests. I have arranged for Giovanni and his son to pick up supplies for the next few days. It's marvellous that we can all pull together this way in a crisis. Don't you think?'

Juliana agreed. When he smiled at her like that she knew why she had married him. It was such a shame they had so little in common. Juliana rose from the table slowly. 'Well then, I shall go and see Maria I think.' As she passed him, Michael caught the faint smell of Lilly of the Valley. It was her favourite perfume and it brought back happy memories for him. There was no answer when Juliana knocked on Maria's bedroom door. On entering she at once noticed Alice standing by the window and Maria lying quite still on the bed. Immediately concerned, she rushed over. Maria did not move. A strange feeling crept over her as her mind worked hard to understand what she was looking at.

When Juliana screamed Alice turned from the window. Juliana's eyes welled up with tears. 'Oh no, it can't be possible.' She sobbed hysterically as Alice put her arm around her.

'Now now my dear,' Alice whispered. 'These things happen. It is the Lord's will. Look at her face. She is in a beautiful place and at peace.' Juliana looked at Maria. Alice was right. Maria was at peace. She kissed Maria on her forehead for the last time and then became upset again. Alice did her best to comfort her, even though she was getting upset herself. 'I know, I know!' she was saying as Michael, hearing some commotion, rushed into the room. Nothing prepared him for what he saw next. The sight of his mother lying dead and his wife sobbing at her bedside was too much.

'Why? WHY NOW MOTHER?' he shouted, dropping to his knees beside the bed, his voice drowned out by the two women. Suddenly he stood up and, pursing his lips together, pulled out a silk handkerchief and blew his nose rather loudly. He stood staring at his mother, half waiting for her to say something, to smile or talk. But however much he wished it she did not move. He thought she looked thirty years younger. Then, holding onto the headboard, he said a long prayer. Afterwards he turned to his wife. 'We must tell the others as soon as possible.'

In the hall Alice met an ashen-faced Giovanni. His first concern was for his master, who he could hear wailing from the garden. Climbing the stairs two at a time he barely glanced at her. Throwing himself into the hot stifling room he hurriedly crossed himself and knelt down at the bedside and started praying. A few moments later he winced at the sight of Michael's white knuckles. They bore the testimony of how long he had been clinging to the headboard. 'Come boss. Come now. Sit over here. Gino will get some water.'

Giovanni sat him down as Juliana continued to pace up and down. 'It's such a shock, I was sure she was getting better.'

'Please, come and sit down,' Giovanni added, coaxing her over to a chair opposite Michael's. Afterwards he stood watching his beautiful princess covered in pearls and gold. She was only asleep on top of the bed clothes. Her shiny golden hair braided up around her head and that's how he would always remember her, dressed in her favourite emerald green silk gown. How he would miss her! A few moments later a cold breeze swept through the room. Michael looked up at the calendar clock on the mantelpiece. 'Remember she passed away on the 24th June.'

Chapter Five   Brandenberg

London

Sitting on a bench after the funeral, Tonya wished she could stop crying. Wherever she looked she saw an image of her great aunt lying, as if in state, in the hugely ornate Russian Orthodox Cathedral of South Kensington. She could still smell the remnants of frankincense and hear the Gregorian chanting. Oh yes! The ceremony had certainly been moving and full of deep spiritual meaning. Tonya should not have been surprised at the amount of people attending but she was astonished when all her very old Russian friends knelt down and kissed the floor just below the coffin. She was even more shocked when they kissed her great aunt on the forehead and then repeated the ritual all over again. The importance of the occasion was not lost on Tonya, who recognised what true worship was when she saw it. She was so deep in thought that she barely noticed when Michael sat down next to her. 'How are you my dear?' he asked gently. 'I suppose it must have come as a great shock to you?'

Tonya sniffled, 'I'm fine.'

'Are you sure?' Michael looked concerned.

'Well as fine as one can be on such a day!'

'I know. I hate these formal occasions, but her friends absolutely insisted. It was taken right out of my hands. The family hardly had a look in!'

Tonya didn't know what to say so she kept quiet.

Michael shuffled uneasily in his seat; 'You saw her for tea I believe?'

Tonya smiled at the thought, 'Yes, quite often. I shall miss her stories. What will happen to Peety-Pops? Surely he will need a home and what of Alice? Do we know of her plans?' Michael gazed across the city landscape before replying. 'I understand that Francesca will look after the dog for a while. As for Alice, well I know nothing of her plans, but she is welcome to come to Italy if that is what she wants. She is practically part of the family now.' Michael's tone was monotonous and he spoke with a distant look in his eyes.

Tonya had seen that look before. The Baroness used to do exactly the same thing. Stare as though she was thinking of far off things or communicating with another being.

Both Tonya and Michael continued to sit in a comfortable silence until Juliana plonked herself down on the bench. 'Gosh it's warm for London. I feel exhausted,' she said, fanning herself with a funeral card.

'Me too,' replied Tonya.

'Michael, you must be baking in that jacket. Why don't you take it off?'

Tonya thought the sculptress looked beautiful and Juliana smiled graciously as if reading her thoughts. Then she leant across Michael to speak to her. 'Why don't you come back to Italy with us for a vacation? It would cheer you up. Besides, Alex would love to see you and I can show you the piece I'm working on for the garden. It's nearly finished.'

Tonya shaded her eyes from the sun. 'What a great idea! I would love to. Thanks.'

'Good! That's settled then,' Juliana sounded excited. 'We shall all miss the Baroness so much.' She linked her arm in Michael's as she spoke.

'But was she...' Tonya hesitated for a second, not sure whether she should ask. Was Maria really a baroness? I mean are you a baron uncle, if I may call you that?'

Michael smiled. 'I believe my full title is to be Baron Michael Alexander Nicholas Brandenberg.'

'Oh I say, that is a grand name! But of what country are you a baron?'

Michael frowned. 'Russia of course, or wait a moment now, is it Germany? No, no! Silly me, it was originally called Prussia. Anyway the country does not exist any longer but the title does.'

Tonya was confused. 'Well, who made her a baroness, was it the Tsar or the Kaiser?'

Michael laughed out of embarrassment.

'I suppose you have lands and a big old castle then?'

'Why do you want to know Tonya?' Juliana was mildly amused at the conversation.

'Well, I'm just interested in great aunt's life. There were so many important people in the church. She must have been very famous. To be honest I felt a bit stupid. They all seemed to know more about her than us!'

Michael cleared his throat before speaking. 'Titles, what do titles really mean these days? You know we adopted the name Brandenberg a very long time ago and that is all you need to know and don't worry about those people in the church. They come from another time!'

'So Maria inherited the title then?' Tonya persisted.

Michael rolled his eyes, realising he had more explaining to do. 'Well I wasn't planning to give a history lesson quite at this moment but if you insist! You know, a long time ago nobility was only hereditary. If someone in your family had done a great service to the state, the monarch of the country would bestow a title on you. Your family would then benefit forever. You would have grace and favour and lands as far as the eye could see as well as serfs to work the land and produce goods for you. You would have had riches beyond your wildest imagination. So it was in our country. Many years ago, titled families lived in sumptuous palaces wearing clothes of pure gold, adorned with real crystal gems. They were knights who fought, feasted and ruled. Now, as a result of the revolution and the Bolsheviks…'

'Michael!' Juliana interrupted him. 'Please! I don't think Tonya expects a lecture! Besides, now is certainly not the time to talk of the Bolsheviks, not with all these White Russians and monarchist guests here…'

'Au contraire my dear, we are not afraid of them!'

Juliana hurriedly changed the subject. 'So will you come back to Italy and stay? We leave in two days' time. What do you say? I could do with the company!'

Tonya laughed at Juliana's exuberance but her mind was fully focused on what Michael had said. He had certainly intrigued her by his outburst and she was sure to find out more about the family history if she went.

'Yes, all right. I will come back with you but what about Alice? Can she come too?'

Juliana smiled. 'Of course she can.'

As they were walking down the path they saw Alice standing by the car. She was deep in thought. Life would never be the same again now that her dear friend had passed away. It was true the Baroness had wanted to write up her story. But the challenge now was how to do that and maintain the 'state secret'. Alice returned Juliana's wave as they approached. Perhaps if she worked with Michael they might go some way towards telling the Baroness's story. But she was perplexed. If Maria had wanted her story to be told why had she kept most of the important papers in one place? Surely she would have understood that it was careless to adopt such a relaxed approach. The more she thought about the fire in the caravan the more unlikely the whole event seemed.

'Ah Michael,' she said, speaking softly as he gave her a big hug. She was quite fond of him, not because he was Maria's son or because he was good looking and generous or because he shared an interest with her in the occult. What Alice most appreciated about Michael was his no nonsense approach. But there was one concern she did have and it was a big one. He worked far too hard and never relaxed with his family and Alice was sure that one day he would suffer a dreadful fate because of it. When such thoughts came into her mind she quickly disposed of them by forcing herself to think of something nice. But today it was hard to find anything nice to think of.

'You must be so exhausted?' Juliana commented 'And quite ready for a cup of tea I suppose?'

Once they were all seated in the car Alice peered out of the window and said goodbye to her best friend. When Michael smiled at her warmly she knew that if Maria's story was ever to be told it was the two of them that would have to piece it all together.

The next day Michael hesitantly let himself into the house. Naturally it felt empty but he had expected that, even though Alice still kept a room there. He walked slowly across to the window and looked down onto the busy London street, something his mother must have done often. He was comforted by the thought. But he had come here for a purpose and the sooner he got on with it the better. So pulling himself together he turned back into the room. Absurdly, a wave of guilt crept over him. Somehow it felt wrong for him to be here so soon after the funeral because he had come to search her belongings, but he had no choice. He was looking for something in particular and he must have it before leaving for Italy. Now where would she have put it? For a moment he tried to think as his mother would have thought. But that didn't work. Then he had an idea. Walking over to the fireplace he dropped to his knees and peered up into the chimney. Before he had a chance to fully check it out someone put a key in the front door. He rushed to stand and in doing so knocked his head. 'Damn!'

'Michael.' A cheery voice greeted him.

'What a surprise! I wasn't expecting to see you here today.' Michael smiled but he didn't feel that he had to justify his actions to anyone, let alone Alice.

'Would you like a cup of tea?' she asked, taking her hat off. 'I can go and get some milk.'

Michael grabbed the opportunity. 'Well now, that does seem like a good idea. Thank you.' After Alice had left the room, Michael got back on his knees in front of the chimneybreast. Manoeuvring carefully, he reached up and touched a metal box. It was as he thought. His mother had left something for him even if it was in a rather obvious hiding place!

A few moments later Alice was back and the kettle was boiling.

'I suppose you're just making sure that nothing important is left behind?' Alice asked knowingly as she brought in the tea on a silver tray. Michael immediately recognised the pink, green and gold tea set. 'Oh,' he exclaimed with tears in his eyes. 'That's so thoughtful of you.'

Alice smiled and handed him a slice of cake. The atmosphere was noticeably warmer between them when Alice spoke again. 'As you know Michael I was very close to your mother but I do want to say now, that if there is anything I can do to help, you need only ask.'

Michael shifted uneasily in his chair, something he was prone to do when he was embarrassed. 'Well thank you Alice, I'll remember that,' he said, clearing his throat. 'I suppose you'll want to keep this place on for a while then?'

Alice laughed out of embarrassment. 'Yes, if it's possible?'

Michael nodded 'You know Alice you're always welcome to come and stay with us in Italy. In fact I was going to ask whether you could do me a favour.'

'Oh?'

'Would you be able to pack up the rest of mother's clothes and personal items and ship them over? I'll take care of the financial arrangements of course and if you come over we can then sort everything out together.'

Alice jumped at the opportunity. 'Yes of course. But tell me, did your mother leave a will?'

'Not that I know.' Michael wasn't intending to say more but then he remembered Alice's psychic abilities and thought better of it. 'Well, just now when you came in, I was in the middle of looking for it. You know what is so strange?'

Alice shook her head. Michael continued, 'It is probably the first time in her life that she didn't forward plan. I mean, she seems to have been remarkably unprepared for what would happen if you know what ....?' He waved his hand haphazardly to express the words he didn't want to say.

'Frankly I can only draw one conclusion from this whole sorry business.' He sipped his tea and pondered over his own words.

'Now Michael, you are bound to be in shock, we all are. It was all so sudden and that's why there probably isn't a will!'

Michael didn't respond, choosing to dab up the cake crumbs on the plate. Alice gave a long sigh before continuing. 'When Maria, I'm sorry, I mean your mother, when she first told me of her plans to write up her memoirs I was quite excited if not a little concerned. That's because she said she wanted to write the truth about what happened in Russia and that it was important for it all to be set down properly. I suppose what I'm trying to say is, if you are thinking about pulling her story together, I can help. I know it's what she would have wanted.'

Michael finished his tea and placed the cup sharply down on the saucer. 'Well, thank you. I haven't quite made up my mind what I'm going to do. I won't be in a position to know until I sort through some of these papers left behind. Frankly I'm not sure her story is worth telling anyway.'

'Of course it is!' Alice blurted out. 'How can you possibly think it isn't?'

Michael looked at his shoes while he considered the question. The atmosphere had cooled and Alice watched as he stretched his legs and flexed his feet. He seemed to enjoy the squeaking sound the leather made.

'Look,' he finally replied. 'I know enough to understand that life is a very precious commodity.' He stood up and walked over to the fireplace before turning to face Alice. 'I have to tell you Alice that I believe my mother may have been murdered AND I believe the fire in the caravan was no accident!'

'No accident! What are you saying?'

Michael realised the consequence of his words as soon as Alice started to shake but there was no going back now. 'Exactly what I have just said; and for that reason, Alice, I cannot entertain the notion of writing up her memoirs while her murderers are still at large. I have a family to think of. Safety is paramount. Do you understand?'

'Yes of course,' Alice replied, 'but what does it all mean?' She asked leaning forward and clasping his arm. 'Why would someone want to kill your mother?'

Michael pulled away from her and stood up again. He didn't want to answer immediately.

Eventually he turned towards her, his face racked with anxiety.

'It's all because of that damn SECRET that she was always talking of. Did you know anything about it?'

Alice shook her head vehemently. 'No nothing.' Suddenly she felt hot and pulled herself out of the chair. 'This secret of Maria's, you think it means danger for us all then?'

Michael shrugged. 'I hope not. But who can tell?'

Alice raised her eyebrows in response. It was a silly little give-away that Michael picked up on straight away. 'I see! So you do know SOMETHING! Very well Alice, I shall not press you on whatever this secret of mother's is but the time will come when you will want to tell me. Do you hear?' He listened to himself shouting. Why was he doing that? Alice was such a warm, dear person. SHE IS NOT THE ENEMY, a voice inside his head shouted. This brought a proportion of reasonableness back to him, making him sigh. 'Look, I'm sorry Alice, that didn't come out quite as I meant ... We've all had a shock and of course you know things about my mother and ... well ...,' his words trailed off as he searched for something meaningful to say to her. Then he smiled. 'Look, come to Italy and help sort out her belongings. I don't think I can do it without you.' As he spoke, his steely blue eyes sparkled like cut diamonds. How could she possibly refuse him?

'Of course I will,' she replied and then looked down at her watch. 'Goodness. Is that the time already? I should have been at Francesca's half an hour ago.'

Michael helped her on with her coat and then gave her a hug. 'I'm sorry for shouting. It was quite unnecessary of me.'

Alice squeezed his hand. 'Just promise me that you will be careful, Michael'

'I will and I'll see you in Italy. Until then, let's not say a word to anyone.'

After Alice had left Michael rolled up his shirt sleeves and knelt down on the floor by the fireplace. Stretching his arm as far as he could, he reached up into the chimneybreast and slowly pulled out the large metal box. As he did so he heard the contents rattle. Then, washing his hands, he took a knife from the kitchen sink, went over to his mother's favourite armchair and turned it upside down. Slitting open the bottom, he extracted a bundle of papers and put them in his briefcase. As he turned the chair back up he noticed that a large key had also fallen out onto the carpet. What's this? he wondered as he picked it up. Must be for the box I suppose.

Michael placed the key into the lock but it didn't turn. Frustrated, he grabbed the knife and tried forcing the lock on the box. To his delight it sprang open. It was crammed full of precious stones. But what was the key for then? He examined it closely and found a beautiful silver fox embossed on it. Well that was nothing unusual. His mother loved foxes. Knowing how she must have valued it, he clasped the key momentarily to his chest before putting it in his pocket. Next he placed the glistening gems, which consisted of large uncut diamonds, rubies, pearls and sapphires, on a long silk scarf and wrapped them up carefully before putting them in his briefcase.

Finally he filled the box with little lumps of coal and replaced it in the chimneybreast where he had found it. As he walked out of the front door a voice in his head asked him what he intended to achieve by putting coal in the box and placing it back in the chimneybreast. Realizing his stupidity, he went back to the fireplace and emptied the box, before placing it in his briefcase. Then, after saying an emotional farewell to the house, he left.

Chapter Six   Vagabonds

Italy

Michael sat in his library, a favourite place that harboured much of what he valued in life. He was justly proud of it, not because it occupied a large part of the villa downstairs, but because it had an international reputation. His library was recognised by those in the know as one of the most important collection of books on Russia in private hands. There were many first editions, all catalogued meticulously. Scores of book-filled shelves lined the walls, each as important as the next in recording human history. Some dated back to the earliest years of European printing. Indeed it would be no exaggeration to say that Michael had many original manuscripts, which if known about on the open market, would fetch millions and millions of dollars. Michael had been lucky because his mother had helped him start the collection. Indeed, without her help it would have taken several lifetimes to collect all the published material he now had ready to hand. Knowledge is power and Michael was meticulous in the way he catalogued his library.

Near the French windows overlooking the terrace was his desk. It was a huge oak table with an angle-poise lamp on it. He had two olive green cushions on his chair, which Juliana said resembled a throne. The desk was clear of papers and had a large blotter and an ebony inkwell that had an engraved star on its lid. Michael no longer wrote with a fountain pen but was sentimentally attached to the three hundred year old inkwell because his mother had given it to him. Guarding his desk and sitting to the right of the inkwell was an old bronze lion from Kiev in the Ukraine.

Michael opened the French windows and walked out onto the terrace. It was a beautiful day and he felt the warmth of the sunlight on his face. Juliana was in the garden talking with Giovanni and waved excitedly when she saw him. 'How are you this morning darling?' she shouted. Michael waved back, despite feeling embarrassed; 'I'm fine today. Not so tired, but I have a lot of work to do!' He sipped his coffee, watching his wife as she gave Giovanni some last minute instructions.

A moment later she opened the door and Michael glanced up. 'Is everything all set for our visitors? What time are we expecting them?' he asked.

Juliana pulled out a chair and sat down. 'Well I believe they'll arrive around four o'clock,' Juliana sighed, 'but I do hope they can entertain themselves during the day since you're so busy and I really must finish that sculpture off, otherwise I will lose compete interest in it'.

Michael completely understood. 'Yes, indeed. I must have the days to sort out mother's belongings and I'm under pressure to meet the university's deadline of course! I suggest we keep the evenings for socialising. I'm sure they won't mind!'

Juliana laughed. 'We'll be lucky to get away with the evenings but we can try. Anyway how are you doing? You haven't started yet. So curiosity hasn't got the better of you?'

Michael smiled. 'Well you know mother! She was so secretive but I'm quite sure we will find some interesting objects. Hopefully a photograph album or two, maybe even a lost diary!' He laughed to show he was joking, but Juliana took him at his word.

'How exciting, I'd love to sort through some of these boxes with you.'

Michael looked across the room. 'Well I don't think that they can tell us anything we don't already know. Still, I promised her...' he paused before adding, 'Well we don't need to go into that now. Suffice to say it will take up a great deal of my time! Thankfully Alice will be here to help.'

'Aren't you going to look at any of them today? You might find some of her old diaries.' Michael sighed. 'I know I should and if I had the time... but I doubt ....' He paused, thinking of the silver fox key and the beautiful diamonds, pearls and sapphires he had found. They were all locked up safely now and he didn't want to tell Juliana about them because he was planning a surprise.

'Oh I shouldn't think we'll find any secrets written down. You know what they say......' He paused absentmindedly or so Juliana thought. She watched him walk over to the bookshelves. 'Just look at all this history on Russia, much of it written by famous Russians after the revolution. Whatever my mother's secret was I don't think there's a need for us to rewrite history!'

Juliana didn't reply right away and Michael guessed she had something on her mind. Finally she spoke. 'It's a wonderful archive, but as an artist I have to say there are always new ways of seeing things and if Maria thought her story was worth telling then I am sure it is. That secret she had always enthralled me. What was it do you think?'

Michael thought for a moment. 'Something to do with father I expect. I've never been able to get to the bottom of it!'

Juliana made a move to leave. 'Well don't give up. Just because it's been written once doesn't mean it shouldn't be corrected if it's wrong,' she added, pointing at his collection of Russian books.

Michael laughed. 'Honestly, sometimes I don't understand you. History is called history because it HAS been accepted as fact. Academics are not like artists! They can't go around rewriting history as if they were rubbing out a drawing!'

'I think that's ridiculous Michael. History has always been written by the winners and they write their own version of events. Don't deny it! By distorting history in that way, well! It can have a profound effect on future generations and it's not fair. Not fair at all to my way of thinking!'

Michael sighed wearily. 'Oh dear, I can see we are going to have one of our protracted discussions. Allow me, madam, to suggest that you are wrong. Look, here we have it...,' he said, pointing to a row of old hard-cover books. 'These are the memoirs of the exiled Russians such as Kerensky and Captain Paul Bulygin. Look, here is *The Murder of the Romanovs.* And now I'm going to prove you quite wrong, my dear, because they didn't win and defeat the Bolsheviks and yet here they are explaining exactly how the Romanovs were murdered in July 1918.'

Juliana screwed her nose up, something she was prone to do when she felt uncomfortable. 'Well, were they there at the time?'

Michael sighed loudly before replying, 'No of course not!'

Juliana thought for a moment. There was no point in arguing with him. After all, this was his specialist subject. 'Okay, in this instance you may be right but some of the memoirs that I have read, I can't think of their names now, but anyway they are just full of senseless gossip. Who said what to who and why, or who wore this piece of stunning jewellery and where! I wouldn't call that history it's just twaddle!'

Michael shook his head; 'I stand by the point I was making. Kerensky was certainly not a winner yet his book helped write history.'

'Well I don't think you have won the argument Michael. Because without knowing the full facts we cannot know whether Kerensky has given a false account or not! So of course we believe him. I mean we have no reason to question him!'

Michael smiled at her persistence. She certainly had the makings of an academic and that delighted him. So he was happy to concede the point. 'Well, I happen to know there were several versions of the book and that important initial statements made in the first edition were taken out of the following edition. I presume because they disagreed with what someone else had said. Personally, I have long since suspected that Kerensky, who was still alive long after many of his colleagues had been murdered, was in fact more involved in events that he ever let on.'

Juliana smiled. 'There, so you agree with me.'

'So you prefer to take Henry Ford's position on this?'

Juliana was confused. 'Henry Ford? What's he to do with the Russian revolution?'

'AH! HA! I've caught you out.' Michael clapped his hands, which made her jump.

She supposed that he behaved like this with all his students. Well, she didn't have time for his antics. 'I'm sorry I didn't catch what you were saying.'

Michael sat behind his desk. 'You asked what Henry Ford had to do with the Russian Revolution and my answer is A GREAT DEAL! But more to the point he agrees with you. In his mind all history was bunk!'

Juliana felt vindicated. 'Oh, how do you know that?'

Michael laughed. 'Henry Ford said it many times. Look, it's all in here.' He picked up a book that was lying open on his desk. You should read this sometime. It's quite entertaining, especially his peace ship mission.'

Juliana glanced at the book. 'Thanks, I'm sure I shall enjoy it. He sounds like a man after my own heart. Hang on a moment. He wasn't a mason was he?'

Michael rolled his eyes. 'Why are you so surprised? Most successful men are these days.'

Juliana wasn't sure whether her husband was being serious or joking. 'Well I must go. Let me have the book when you've finished with it. I would like to make a careful study of a mason who hates war and thinks all history is bugged!' Juliana laughed as she stood in the doorway.

'I didn't say he was a mason and it's bunk not bug.'

'Honestly, it's impossible to come into your library without being given some work to do.' Michael smiled. 'True, and don't you love me for it?'

Juliana allowed him the last word and closed the door gently.

After she had gone, Michael attempted to gather his thoughts together. He was slightly disturbed by Juliana's negative comments about masons; contrary to what most people believed, he was not a mason or even a master mason; although he knew a good deal about them. No, Michael's interest lay with a much older and sacred fraternity. Ever since his mother had given him his grandfather's old robes and he had seen that eight-pointed cross, his imagination had been fired up and he had spent many years researching the history of the order. This is how he combined the interests of his mother with that of his own. His mother was a great supporter of the order too. She often raised her glass of wine in memory of the 'honourable knights' who protected the innocent and distressed.

He smiled, thinking of what Juliana had said about all history being written by the winners and therefore not being a true picture. Well, if that was the case, there were some very good reasons for it. Michael hadn't got where he was today by upsetting the apple cart! But his dream, oddly enough, had been to do just that! Ever since his childhood he had hankered after international recognition. Perhaps his ambition came from his mother. After all, she had been a famous literary figure; or maybe it stemmed from him not having a father.

Of course Michael understood history was open to interpretation and had probably been adapted from time to time for the common good! Then for some reason he got to thinking about a young female student of his. Now what was her name? Oh yes, Lucinda. That was it. Lucinda wanted to find a historic event that had not been scrutinised particularly well. She wanted to uncover any lost truth! Michael had suggested *The Mines of King Solomon* but Lucinda had argued that the event she was really interested in was the origins of the Turin Shroud. He told her that it was doomed to fail and that she should consider another episode in history to research. As he later explained, 'You see the very reason why you want to investigate this story is exactly the reason why you shouldn't!' What he meant by that was that it was important for humanity to have its myths, even more so if they were related to religious symbols. She thought he was speaking in riddles. Riddles! Nothing activates the mind so quickly as a little riddle here and a little riddle there! He laughed out loud as he recalled some of the difficulties his students got into. But that was the whole point. He wanted to see into their young enquiring minds. Who had real genius up their sleeve? Who stood out among the crowd and who was the gibbering idiot?

Why sir? Why? Michael recalled their questions with much amusement.

But there was one particular episode that stood out in his mind, when the class had discussed the mystery surrounding the disappearance of the Romanovs in 1918. It was one of the proudest moments of his teaching career. His answer to his students was indelibly printed on his mind because it had become his own private mantra: 'Because even though the Romanov bones have never been discovered, the published evidence on how they died is so well documented that to write a book suggesting that they all escaped would be suicide for any budding historian.' Even now he could recall the clamour of voices protesting, just as he had suspected they would. All except Lucinda, She made sure he heard her response.

'IT WILL ONLY BE A MATTER OF TIME BEFORE THEIR BODIES ARE FOUND.' So Lucinda had spoken! Michael smiled as he picked up Henry Ford's book *My Life* and he thought about his beautiful wife Juliana. She was just like Lucinda and it would be most interesting to know what she made of a man like Henry Ford.

Then Michael got to thinking about the fire in the caravan. It made him feel so uneasy. Perhaps Juliana was right. He should put aside his career, just for a few weeks, and sort out these boxes and if there was a story to tell, well perhaps it should be told anyway! Tonya and Alice seemed more than keen to get involved. Michael gave a long sigh. Oh dear, I'll have to answer all their wretched questions! By the time the clock struck five thirty he had finished making his notes in the catalogue. It was time for a drink! He was about to leave when there was a knock on the library door and before he could say enter, the door creaked open. It was Tonya. Speak of the devil, he thought to himself as he greeted her.

'Uncle, I hope I am not disturbing you, but I just wanted to say hello and show you this interesting book that your mother left me.'

Michael was always pleased to see books, especially ones his mother had given away!

'Ah Tonya, come in and close the door. Did you have a good journey?'

'Yes, thank you. But look. This is what I came to show you, uncle. I've been reading it and it's so exciting. I had no idea they all escaped!' she added handing him a black cloth- covered book. The sort of book he loved.

'Ah, I too have a copy of this.' He read the title out loud.

'*Rescuing the Czar* by J.P. Smythe, published in 1919. A first edition and it looks in reasonable condition too. You're a very lucky girl! Did you know there's a newspaper cutting tightly folded and stuck down on the last but one page?'

Tonya hadn't seen it but for some unknown reason pretended she knew all about it.

'Oh yes, but I haven't had a chance to look at it. Why is this book valuable then? Is it worth thousands of pounds like some of those rare books you keep over there?'

Michael scrutinised Tonya from the corner of his eye as she walked over to his bookshelf and started looking through his collection. 'Have you had tea?' he asked politely. Tonya ignored the question in her excitement. 'Wow, Alex was right. You really do have some very old books. But where's the Russian section? Gosh! I bet that's exciting, *The Memoirs of a British Agent* by R.H. Bruce Lockhart.

Michael sighed, getting tired of her intrusion. 'Exciting, why would you think that?'

Tonya smiled. Here was an opportunity to impress him. 'Well! They were written at a time of historic importance. They are one-offs, A bit like this book, *Rescuing the Czar*. Have you read it uncle? Where the agent called "Fox" disguises himself as a captain of the Red Guard and arranges a pretend shooting party but really he rescues...'

'Stop right there Tonya. The book is a work of fiction. Nothing more and I wouldn't waste your time on it; not if you are serious about Russian history.' As he spoke Michael flicked through the book randomly. Tonya listened dutifully but felt disappointed at his reaction. Surely he of all people should keep an open mind but who was she to argue with such an eminent professor of Russian history!

Suddenly Michael stopped talking. He had noticed a message inside the book. 'What's this?
>*In fond remembrance of our Siberian adventure! June 1918.*
>*K.A.G.'*

Michael gave a nervous cough and shut the book promptly.

'Well Tonya, I'm sure you'll enjoy reading it! Now I must get on. I'll see you at dinner but if you have any further questions do come and talk to me,' he added, patting Tonya on the shoulders and showing her the door. 'Now remember, don't pay too much attention to what you read. It was all a very long time ago indeed.'

For her part, Tonya was far from being put off. On the contrary, she would love to be able to prove the great historian wrong and she was determined to check out his statements regarding the history of the book. When she thought of how he paced up and down with the book in his hand, it made her laugh. At one point she was sure that he was about to put the book on his shelf, and instead of listening to him, she had been working out how she was going to ask for it back if he did. But in the end Michael had smiled, realising that he had been unnecessarily harsh in his manner and that was good enough for Tonya.

After she left, Michael leant against the door and listened for her footsteps to die away. Then, rubbing his forehead, he walked back to his desk and sat down. Opening the central drawer of his desk he carefully withdrew his own copy of *Rescuing the Czar*. His book was published in 1920 and had no inscription. So, he thought, Tonya's copy must have been the original but who was K.A.G? Michael tapped a pencil on the desk as he pondered. The whole day was quite bizarre. Only a few hours earlier he had disagreed with Juliana when she suggested that all history was bunk because it had been written by the winners. Then Tonya had turned up with THAT book, believing it to be a true written account of events and then bizarrely he had been forced to say that it was a work of fiction, not real history at all; but then wasn't that the point Juliana was trying to make?

You can't trust what you read to be true and conversely, just because something appears to be fiction, doesn't mean it's not true. Oh dear! Michael rubbed his forehead again in an attempt to boost circulation and coax a nagging headache away. Juliana had made him feel ashamed. She was right; he had become narrow minded and inward looking.

'It won't do, Michael. It just won't do!' His mother's words rang in his ears and he decided that from now on it was time to make some changes to his life.

* * *

'Boxes, boxes, boxes,' Alice chuckled. 'I fly all the way from England and I still can't seem to get away from them.'

Juliana smiled. 'Well, yes I know what you mean, although I hardly notice them anymore. I've got used to all manner of things arriving from London! But it is very good of you to come out and help us sort through all of Maria's chattels. By the weight of some of these tea chests I suspect they're filled with crockery and silver.'

Alice thought Juliana looked enchanting as usual whooshing around in her linen trousers and silk scarf but it was hardly suitable attire for someone sculpting in a studio.

'You don't mind if I continue working while we chat do you?'

'No. Not at all, you're lucky to have such a wonderful light to work with'. Alice pointed to the sunshine streaming in through the French windows. 'Ah! And here is your latest piece, goodness it's so full of life! Sculpting must be very hard on the hands. Still I suppose you don't mind getting them messed up when you're creating such a statue?'

Juliana looked at her dusty hands. 'Well it's all part of getting a feel for what you're working with. It's very satisfying if not a little trying at times. But you're right perhaps I should take more care of them. 'Anyway, how was your trip?'

'Good. But I had forgotten how full of chat Tonya is. I was quite worn out by the time we arrived. Still, I do find it agreeable to have her around. I miss regular conversation now that Maria has passed over to the other side.'

Juliana looked up. 'The other side... Oh I see! Well obviously you miss her dreadfully. We all do of course!'

Alice sat in a large comfortable armchair and admired a painting on the opposite wall. 'You know, I still wake every morning expecting to see her and then it hits home. I know I shouldn't be so upset but, well, it is so difficult to accept isn't it?'

Juliana didn't like to dwell on it that much. Life was for the living and Maria would not have wanted anyone to be sad. Alice agreed and then changed the subject. 'What made you want to be a sculptor anyway?'

Juliana stuck her thumb out to measure something on the sculpted image. 'Well if I am honest I was inspired by another woman. Kathleen Scott. You may have heard of her? Like me she was a sculptress and worked on some marvellous bronzes of famous people, including one of her wonderful explorer husband Robert Falcon Scott, who so tragically died early in their marriage.' Juliana put her chisel down and poured herself some sparkling water as she spoke. 'Do you know Alice, some people are very lucky. They fall in love and stay that way for the rest of their lives. Others never find their true love and still others, in fact the vast majority of us, fall in and out of love at the drop of a hat. Can you understand it? I can't.

Alice laughed, 'We all have our own journey I suppose.'

'Ah! That sounds like you believe in destiny Alice?'

Alice shrugged. 'Please carry on with your story.'

Juliana handed her a worn out magazine. 'Here, wasn't she lovely? Just look at her long black wavy hair. I'd like to sculpt her one day! You know what I like best about her, apart from the fact she liked to chip away?'

Alice shook her head again. 'No, but I'm listening. Gosh this magazine is very old, 1912!' 'Well the other thing I like about her,' continued Juliana, 'was that she loved to go vagabonding.'

'Vagabonding? What a strange expression. Is it something to do with sculpting?'

Juliana laughed 'No. It's a form of escapism I suppose. You take yourself off into a foreign landscape and sleep out in the open. You know, in barns or out in the fields. Sleeping rough! And when you're hungry you call at farmhouses along the way and beg for food. Sometimes you do a bit of work in return but the point is you don't have any money whatsoever on you and no one can contact you because no one knows where you are or indeed who you are.'

Alice smiled. She knew exactly what Juliana was describing and they didn't call it vagabonding in her day! 'So Kathleen was living on her wits the whole time. Exactly how many years did she spend doing this so called vagabonding?'

Juliana hesitated before replying. 'I don't know. Quite a few I suppose. Anyway, I think she found it character building, she was always taking herself off vagabonding in between commissions for her work.'

'Wasn't that a dangerous thing to do? Imagine a woman going off all on her own into some strange and wild country with no money and no one to defend her honour!'

'Oh Kathleen wasn't alone. When she went to Greece and Turkey she had Isadora with her. Can you imagine what a wild time they must have had of it?' Juliana clapped her hands in delight.

'Well who was Isadora?' Alice asked.

'Isadora Duncan of course, surely you must have heard of her? The famous dancer! I believe Maria knew her too.' Alice watched in amusement as Juliana twirled around the room like a whirling dervish.

'Her forte was half naked nymphs but she danced them divinely. Eventually she married a Russian, which was daring, but then Isadora was adorably daring!' Juliana bowed low in anticipation of Alice's applause but Alice was in no mood for gaiety. The heat of the afternoon had made her weary.

'It's a strange world when sculptors become vagabonds!' She exclaimed.

'Are you feeling all right? Perhaps you're tired and need to rest.' Juliana sounded concerned. 'It must have been a long day?'

'I can't take the heat as well as I used to. I think I'll take a nap before dinner, I'm sure I'll be as right as rain after that!'

When she had gone Juliana walked over to the dresser where there was a canteen of hot coffee and poured herself a mug. She was fond of Alice but why did she always have such an air of mystery about her? This wasn't the first time that Juliana had picked up on it. In fact she used to get the same feeling around Maria as well. Oh dear, poor Alice!! I do hope she is going to be alright. Perhaps it was something to do with getting old. Why, even Michael was acting a little strange these days! Gazing out of the French windows she sipped her coffee as Alice walked across the garden towards Giovanni. Of course he was thrilled to see her. Juliana could just make out their words.

'It's so good you are here now.'

Alice smiled at him. Trust Giovanni to make her feel wanted. 'Thank you for cheering me up but it can't have been easy for you either.'

'You are right; too much change is never a good thing. You know the boss, he work all day!'

Alice patted him on the shoulder. 'Well it looks as though your hard work is paying off. I must say you really have done a splendid job with these roses!'

Giovanni grinned. 'Si of course for Maria...when shall we...?'

Alice raised her hand stopping him mid sentence, 'Please! Don't speak of it here!' Giovanni pulled away out of embarrassment, 'Si, I know. But...'

Alice quickly leant forward, cupping her hand so she could whisper in his ear, 'Look, we both made a promise to keep a secret. Let's keep to it shall we?'

Giovanni laughed nervously. 'Si, they get nothing from me. I want to live!'

Chapter Seven   Rescuing the Czar

Someday I pray that you will come to know happiness as I have known it!

Juliana looked out from the studio window and wondered what Alice and Giovanni were talking about. Giovanni was the strong silent type who hardly spoke if he could help it and recently, rather annoyingly, she had detected a lack of engagement from him. Perhaps that was because Michael was working at home. Of course Giovanni had no idea how she really felt about him. No one did. In fact she was astonished at her ability to love two men who were so different in character. Perhaps, she mused, she only had a crush on Giovanni. But she knew she didn't! If the truth be known she had been in love with him from the moment their eyes had met. Yes. She had fallen in love with him the old fashioned way, even though he was a good deal older than she. Juliana couldn't say why it had happened, it just had. His dark curly hair and romantic brown eyes hadn't helped!

Juliana smiled to herself. For an Italian male he was exceptionally handsome, as was his only son, Paul. Right from her school days Juliana had always been a sucker for the artistic look that Giovanni carried off so well. But she had met him too late and now she was married to Michael. A marvellously clever man, who loved her very much but didn't know how to show it. A tear crept into her eye and then another as Juliana thought about what might have been. Afterwards she felt stronger. Her love could not ride out in broad daylight, not like other loves, because it had nowhere to go. Besides, Giovanni was close to Michael, both as an employee and a friend. Imagine how dreadful everything would be if Michael ever found out about her feeling for the gardener! Giovanni would be a broken man and lose his job. She shivered at the thought. Oh, it would be too awful for words! He only knew how to tend the garden and cook and what about Michael? He would never recover from the shock and she would probably lose Alex as well. No, it was unthinkable and the sooner she put her feelings to one side the better. There, she had made a decision. From now on she would only think of him as a friend. She watched him prune the roses for a moment longer. He must have felt her gaze because he looked up, smiled, and gave a wave. She waved back. Now she could get on with her sculpting. What a conundrum! Married to Michael, who didn't make her happy, and worse, she didn't think she made him happy either. Still, he needed her in a way that Giovanni didn't.

Giovanni was easy-going. He enjoyed taking one day at a time and wasn't on a mission. Not like Michael, surrounded by his books and locked up in the library all day. No, Giovanni was out there enjoying the sunshine.

Oh Michael, she thought, why do you have to be the way you are? So serious and so cold! Thank heavens Alex wasn't academic like his father. Thankfully Alex took after her and had an artistic streak, even though it wasn't particularly appreciated by Michael. If only Michael would be nicer to him and give him a chance!

The sound of voices drew her attention to the garden again. Paul was talking with his father. He was serious young man and quite unlike Giovanni, but then he was a priest. Juliana thought that Michael would much have preferred to be Paul's father rather than Alex's. She smiled to herself as she pondered the notion and then, bizarrely, wondered what Giovanni's son would have looked like had she given birth to him. Realizing she was stepping into dangerous waters she quickly changed her thought process. Not an easy thing for her. Indeed, it had taken years of meditation to calm her scatty brain down. But now she was at least able to recognise when the inner self was leading the outer self up the proverbial garden path! How strange life can be when we are never happy with what we have. Oh, why couldn't life be simpler? If only Michael could be like Giovanni. Then everything would be perfect.

* * *

Having received a hostile reaction from Michael, Tonya scampered up to her bedroom. In her haste, she accidentally let the door slam and cringed as the whole room shuddered in response to her clumsiness. Oh dear, I hope I didn't disturb everyone, she thought as book in hand, she made herself comfortable. Now, how had she missed that article that Michael had spotted so easily? It must be important. Why else would Maria have stuck it so securely in the back of the book? Tonya leafed through quickly, coming upon the required page. She was amazed to find that the old tape still managed to hold the article to the book, even after all this time. Slowly she peeled the tape off the page and un-folded the article. It was larger than she expected, taking up nearly two pages, and she at once recognised that it was not from an English newspaper. It must be wonderful to write and be paid for it she thought as she skimmed the article for the name of the author. Maria had said to her that if she couldn't paint then she should consider writing for a living. Well, she had never given it much thought. Until now that is. The book in her hand had certainly inspired her and the idea was not a silly one if only she could find something half decent to write about she mused, gazing out of the window. Then she saw him – Paul! Gosh, he is nearly as tall as his father but much nicer looking.

Shame he has to wear that priestly garb all the time. He must be baking in this hot weather and he's always so serious. Just like his father. I don't think I have ever seen him smile let alone laugh. I wonder why he's miserable. Come to think of it, Alice is miserable too but then she has reason having just lost her closest friend. Tonya felt embarrassed when she thought about the flight over and what she had said to Alice about the book.

'Maria gave it to me and I don't want to let it go until I've finished reading it.'

'But I just wanted to have a quick look at it now,' a rather shocked Alice had responded.

Looking back she should have been kinder, but Alice had made her even more determined to read the book because she had said exactly the same as Michael. She had warned Tonya not to believe everything she read.

'People in those days would do or say anything for money.'

'Well that's all right,' Tonya had replied. Alice must have thought her callous but she had just wanted to end the conversation. For the rest of the journey Alice had been partial to speaking of the spirit world. Conscious of Maria's recent departure Tonya was keen not to dwell on the matter while they were so high in the sky. But it was great to be here in Italy with her and they seemed to be getting on fine now. Tonya unfolded the article very carefully. It was dated 1920 and was written by Herman Bernstein of the New York Times. This is what she read.

When I was in Siberia in the winter of 1918, I made a special investigation of the end of the czar and the imperial family. Among others, I interviewed Supreme Court Judge Sergeyev of Ekaterinburg, the man who was entrusted with the legal investigation of the Romonoff case. He familiarised me with most of the documents in his possession and the testimony of witnesses. When I asked him whether he was really convinced that the Czar was dead he said; 'I am ninety percent sure that he is dead'. In Siberia, wherever I travelled, I heard conflicting stories about the Czars end. Some versions were apparently circulated for political purposes, to create sentiment for monarchist elements. The legend kept growing and the ground was being prepared for pretenders to the Russian throne. Among the various versions I heard in Siberia, on my way from Vladivostok to the Ural Mountains, were the following; That Nicholas Romanoff was burned to death in the forest near Ekaterinburg; That he was killed by a bomb in a mine on the outskirts of the city;

That he was shot in the Ipatiev house where he was kept imprisoned by the Bolsheviki; That Nicholas was murdered in a secret passage leading from the Ipatiev house to one of the churches;

That while trying to escape by this secret passage he was caught and shot, and that his daughters, who were with him, were violated by the Red Guards; That Nicholas was spirited away by Russian officers and intimate friends to Germany, and that a large sum of money was paid to the Red Guards for permitting the Czar to escape. That the Czar and his family, disguised as poor refugees, were removed from Ekaterinburg and are living in seclusion under assumed names somewhere in the Ural Mountains.

Rescuing the Czar is the story of what purports to be two authenticated diaries arranged and translated by James P. Smythe (A.M. Ph.D), in which the story of the Czar's escape is related in great detail. There is a foreword by W.E. Aughinbaugh(M.D., LLB, LLM), who according to 'Who's Who in America', has been Professor of Foreign Trade at New York University since September 1914. Professor Aughinbaugh says in part as follows, 'Is the former Czar and his Imperial Family still alive? There are millions of people in Europe and America who are asking this question. European governments have considered the question of sufficient interest to justify the investigation by official bodies of the alleged extinction of this ancient royal line. Millions have been expended for that purpose. Commissions have pretended to investigate the subject after the event. Volumes have been returned of a speculative nature to authenticate a mysterious disappearance that has never been explained. In certain royal quarters the anxiety to disseminate the ' reports' of their commissions is too apparent to authorise a judicial mind to accept their speculative guesswork as convincing evidence of a legal 'corpus delicti' when no identified bodies have been produced. If Rescuing the Czar does no more than set at rest the fable of the Romanoff executions, it will have done its work by characterizing the source and methods and objects of its inspiration.

If it raises the presumption of generosity in quarters generally subject to suspicion, it will be equally praiseworthy for expelling the darkness that has always hovered around imperial thrones. If it performs no other service than to place upon the pale face of tragic possibility, the red-pink blush of romantic probabilities, it will have justified its presence in the society of the learned by the sincerity of its purpose and the candour of its appeal to the conscience of the world.

The first of the 'authentic' diaries by James P. Smythe, was secured in the following manner; An American named Fox who had a brother in Turkestan when the Russian Revolution took place had word from his brother that ' Nicholas R – and all the family are quite well and not a million miles distant from him'. Another American who received this letter read in the newspapers that a young commissioned officer who had returned from Siberia and who was in a hospital suffering from a wound caused by the Bolsheviki, so he went to see the wounded officer at the hospital.

'I'm as certain as I'm living' the wounded soldier said, 'that a Bolshevik is as nutty as a rabbit. The fellow I had by the neck before my lights went out was putting up a holler in German, and claiming to be a personal friend of some personal friend of the missing Czar. Before he finally passed in his chips he gave me a bundle of paper diaries he had stolen down in China and he asked me to return them to their rightful owner so that he might die without a sin upon his conscience'.

The nurse brought in an old leather bag from which the captain extracted two begrimed and blood smeared rolls written in a very small but vigorous hand.

'This diary seems to be written in very good English, Did he say who wrote this?'

'No; he cashed in as I told you; but you'll see the name Fox here and there through the diary that's written in the small hand'.

'May I take these with me?'

'Sure thing, I'll make you a present of them'.

'While the temptation is great to revise the manuscript, so as to make it read more smoothly, it has been decided not to alter a line', remarks the translator and arranger of the 'authentic' diaries. Truth will be better served by publishing what is prudent, under the complicated political circumstances of our times, word for word as it is written by its daring author. The author of the diary, under the caption; What happened at Berlin described a meeting with a Colonel Z---- S----, and how he was entrusted with a mission of Rescuing the Czar as follows; Without any preliminaries he said, 'Come with me!' We entered a cab, and a few minutes later I entered the Wilhelmstrasse and was in the presence of that tall iron-grey wiry gentleman, with eyes like a searchlight and the manners of a Chesterton.

'Thank you, Colonel'' he said. The Colonel sprang to attention, bowed, saluted and backed away. We were alone.

'In ten minutes,' he said 'You will be conducted to another room. When you arrive, advance to the middle, make a right wheel and stand at attention facing the portières. Maintain perfect silence; answer all questions- make no inquiries- understand?'

I was taken downstairs along a wide corridor to a solid oak door guarded by two sentries and an attendant in the royal livery. The door was opened by an officer of the Erste Garde. I entered a large room, advanced to the centre and faced the divided portières of an adjoining chamber. There sat the man whose nod shook the earth! Behind a heavy old-fashioned desk in dim light, apparently absorbed in writing sat a deeply tanned, lean faced, blue-grey eyed counterpart of Frederick the Great- the very embodiment of majesty!

Eyes that blazed in their defiant depths with a steady and consuming fire! The kind of eyes that seem to defy the world! I stood there fully five minutes before I heard the sharp, high pitched voice pierce through the portière saying; ' Adell, I will see the C-----'.

I was conducted to within six feet of the man at the desk, and in the same shrill voice asked me how familiar I was with Russia, with Turkestan, India, and the Far East. My answers seemed to convince my questioner. Handing me a note, he said,

'No one besides our-selves is to know that you are to undertake the mission outlined in that note.'

Then he sat forward abruptly his elbows resting on the desk, his head between his hands his eyes fixed on space. I began to study the note... I was dumbfounded. I had thought along that this man was the mortal enemy of the persons this note commanded me to rescue from danger... It was incomprehensible...And I could not ask a solitary question! In the same shrill voice the man said; 'Have you memorized it?'

I had! It was burned into my very soul. I could not forget a syllable of it. Without another word he took the note, struck a match and watched it curl into shapeless ashes. Then, making a quick gesture, he plunged into the documents before him. I backed away.

This is the account given by the author of the 'authentic' diary of how the Kaiser instructed him to rescue the Czar and his family. The author tells of a series of escapades and exciting experiences in reaching Russia, in getting into the house where the Russian royal family were imprisoned by the Bolsheviki and how he succeeded in rescuing them through a secret tunnel.

After killing a Red guard and firing several shots into the wall the author of the diary led the Czar and his family out into the night 'forgetting a jewel or two in our leisurely departure.

Out in the open we descended into an abandoned tunnel that formerly led from the Ipatiev's to the medical office of a foreign consulate a thousand feet away. The following entry was made in the tunnel;

'We are between the devil and the deep blue sea which gives me time to write. The beastly tunnel has caved in mid way in our passage. It seems from the roar overhead that we are sometimes beneath the rail road tracks.'

From this secret tunnel the author of the 'authentic' diary and the royal family could hear the commissary demanding of the Red Guards; 'What have you cut-throats done with our prisoners?'

There was a silence that could be felt. None offered an explanation that could hear. Then the report of a revolver! Then a scuffling and 'stand back another move and I'll blow you all to hell! Line up there! Now I order you to explain the whereabouts of the prisoners.'

We could hear a voice boasting.

'Did you see that blood yonder? Well?'

'That is our answer. We were suspicious of that Lieutenant of yours, so we took the matter into our own hands.'

'Who did the killing?'

'The Sergeant'

'And what did he do with the bodies?'

'Threw them into the well?!'

'The devil, you'll have to fish them out again!'

Then there was a long silence. Finally we heard; 'Here Sergeant! When will my Lieutenant report?'

'The Captain said to present his compliments and say that he is temporarily detained.' My 'prisoner' (Nicholas) poked me in the ribs impulsively and smiled.

'Where are the bodies?'

'Burned!' said the Sergeant.

'What burned up? Who burned them?'

'I did sir'.

'Didn't throw them in the well?'

'No sir.'

'Fall in! I'll court-martial every one of you'.

'Well,' ejaculated my amused prisoner (Czar Nicolas) 'It'll be exceedingly interesting to read the future accounts of my double execution! I am sure my family will read it with greater interest than they've manifested in any of London's or Gorky's fanciful novels.'

All this happened in the caved in secret tunnel in Ekaterinburg. But this is not all. There is a vivid description how the Romanov family battled for life in that secret tunnel;

'We are all about played out. The boy is exhausted and lying over in a little excavation upon his sisters wraps, His fingers bleeding and one eye blinded with the sand. The passageway behind us is almost closed up. In front of us a solid wall. The exhausted mother in binding her boys hands with a portion of her petticoat. As she kneels there she resembles Botticelli's magnificent Madonna in the Uffizi Gallery at Florence. The picture is completed by the dark background and the solicitous attitude of the girls as they cluster around the sufferer. My 'prisoner' (Czar Nicholas)' is not a bit discouraged, however. He is using his jack knife against the concrete wall with great patience and whistling softly and slowly an air from the 'Blessing of the Waters'. I know these girls are choking for a drink, as I am myself. Still not one of them has murmured at our grief, and Anastasia has become quite chummy in pretending to cheer me up. Aristocracy or royalty, even with democracy in a tunnel, makes us all one size!'

Then follows this entry;

'Water has burst through the hole my prisoner has been making in that wall. There was a flood of water in which they were almost drowned. But they managed to survive as by a miracle. They were without food in that cistern for days.' Nevertheless a long speech by the Emperor under those circumstances is recorded, He spoke of Rasputin, spooks and Jews. 'It became dark and spooky when our lights gave out and while we sat huddled together the subject of ghosts came up. 'Ghosts!' my prisoner almost snarled; 'That reminds me of the Jewish propaganda against my Government. There was hardly a Yiddish banker in the world who did not accuse me personally of inspiring Scheglovitov to have the Jews executed for ritualistic murder and I am sure their influence will be very strong with certain statesman and opportunities to have my empire dismembered when the time comes to settle the terms of peace as poor Nilus predicted.' Then follows a long tirade against the Jews and against Rasputin. The Emperor winds up by saying that there are Rasputins in all the Chancelleries of Europe and in North and South America.

According to this 'authentic' diary, the Romanovs finally succeeded in freeing themselves from the cistern and escaped to Tibet. Further details are hardly required to show the absurdity of the 'authentic' documents that are submitted in this expensively printed volume which is intended to set future historians and scholars right on what happened to the Romanovs in Ekaterinburg.

In this connection it will be interesting to reproduce some of the statements which were made to me in Ekaterinburg by the man who had access to all the material and to all the evidence of the Romanov case. Judge Sergeyev took from his desk a large blue folder which bore the inscription, The case of Nicholas Romanov and said,

'Here I have all the evidence in connection with the Nicholas Romanov case. Here are all the documents I have found, an official description of the Ipatiev house as I have found it, and the testimony of all the witnesses. No one investigated the case before I was in-trusted with this task. On July 20, 1918 the Soviet Commissary Goleschokin announced at a meeting of the Red Guards that Nicholas was shot'. He declared that he was executed for the crimes he had committed and that the Romanov family were removed. Posters to that effect were placed in certain sections of the city. The Czechoslovaks occupied Ekaterinburg on July 25th 1918. The investigation was started on July 31st. First the Czechoslovaks investigated. Then on August 15th I was appointed chief of the investigating committee. I examined the lower story of the building where the royal family lived and where the crime was supposed to have been committed. I do not believe that all the twelve people, the czar, his family and those with them were shot there. It is my belief that the Empress, the czarevitch and the Grand Duchesses were not shot in that house. I believe however, that the czar, Professor Botkin the family physician, two lackeys and the maid Demidoff, were shot in the Ipatiev house. The murder of Serguis, of Elizabeth the sister of the former Emperor, the children of the Grand Duke Konstantin Konstantinovitch, and Prince Paley took place in the coal mines of Alapayevsk on July 17th. I found the bodies and examined them, and I am convinced that the Grand Dukes were thrown into the shafts alive. I have examined two groups of witnesses.' The Judge went on. 'One group shows that all-Nicholas, the former Empress, Czarevitch and the daughters were shot by workmen and Red Guards. The other group of witnesses testifies that some of the members of the royal family were removed from the Ipatiev house alive. They talked of a mysterious German mission. This testimony is of a half mythical character and is the weaker of the two'.

'We know that auto-mobiles surrounded by Red Guards, came out of the village of Kaptiki, a summer resort about twenty versts away from Ekaterinburg. Not far away there are mines. Some of the shafts are so deep that the ice never melts there. The peasants of that village, moved by curiosity, started an investigation of their own. They found heaps of ashes near the mines and drew *attention to these. We investigated and found in one of the heaps of ashes, stripes of silk of expensive dresses, handbags, buckles of ladies slippers and buttons of ladies dresses. We also found a diamond weighing twelve carats, one of the finest in the world, which is identified as one from the Empress's necklace. She had hidden this diamond in one of her gowns. I also found a crucifix which was always worn by one of the Grand Duchesses. But we found no traces of their bodies. I had the mines examined. We found pieces of a bomb in one of them. We also found a finger of a human hand, and from certain marks I am convinced it was the finger of Professor Botkin. I have no doubt he was murdered there. The wife of one of the Red Guards who participated in the murder testifies that Nicholas and the members of his family were all shot.'*

Judge Sergeyev took out a sheet of paper and pointing to it said; 'This document I found at the headquarters of the Soviet of the Red Guards in Ekaterinburg. The pencil marks indicate it was prepared for telegraphic communication to The Central Soviet in Moscow. The document reads as follows;

'In view of the counter-revolutionary bands approaching the Red capital of the Urals, Ekaterinburg, and in view of the fact that the crowned hangman may succeed in escaping the people's judgement (a plot has been discovered among the White Guards, whose purpose it was to spirit away the former Czar and family), the Executive Committee of the Ural District Soviet of Workmen's, Peasants and Red Army Deputies performing the will of the revolution, decided to shoot the former Czar Nicholas Romanoff, guilty of innumerable bloody acts of violence over the Russian people. On the night of July 16th toward the morning of the 17th, this verdict was carried out. The family of the Romanoffs kept together with him under guard is evacuated from the City of Ekaterinburg in the interests of safeguarding public order.

 Signed; Executive District Soviet of the Workmen, Peasants and Red Army Deputies of the Urals.

 The sheet of paper containing this text bears a seal on the side reading; Russian Federal Republic of the Soviets, Ural District Soviet of Workmen, Peasants and Red Army Deputies. On the left side is a printed line reading address Ekaterinburg, Oblasoviet.'

 On the walls of the bedroom of the late Czar I found the following inscription in German: 'The Czar was killed by his slaves in the night.' Another inscription, supposed to be in his own hand, reads as follows: 'I would rather die in Russia than be saved by Germany.' While there was a slight element of doubt in Judge Sergeyev's mind as to how Nicholas Romanoff met his end, he said: 'Though we have not found the bodies of Nicholas and his family we have evidence that they have been murdered. The fact that the Grand Dukes, whose bodies we found in Alapayevsk, were murdered by the Red Guards, leads me to the conviction that Nicholas and his family met their death at the hands of the same people.'

The legend of the rescue of the Czar apparently circulated for political purposes, will hardly produce any impression in Russia, for whether the Czar was rescued or not there is no doubt that Czarism is dead in Russia.'
    Herman Bernstein,
    New York Times
    September 5th 1920

Tonya put the article aside. What a tragic story. Those poor children! How tawdry and disgusting and how repulsive it was to read. Even fifty years later! What was it Alice had said? Ah yes! In those days people did anything for money and Michael said that the book was pure fiction and written for propaganda purposes. Well, now she had read this article she was inclined to agree with them. Her tummy rumbled reminding her it was time for dinner. Up until now she had been enjoying reading the book but this newspaper article had put the dampers on it. Hang on a minute! Tonya had another thought. Maria must have put that article in the book purposely, but why? Perhaps Maria had been involved in the rescue attempt and had purposely left clues for her to find!

Chapter Eight　　　　　　　　Life after Death

Michael held the crystal in his hand and shut his eyes the way Alice had taught him. 'Who am I, what is my real name?' he whispered as he fell into a meditative state. 'Who am I? What is my real name?' He chanted as the beta rhythms began to kick in.

Now what could he see…? Nothing, Keep trying! Still nothing!!

Michael took a deep breath and held for a count of forty. He was determined to activate his third eye. Long ago Alice had explained how the third eye worked when he had first shown an interest in mysticism as a young man. Everyone knew that women had intuition, but few had linked the mysterious power of foresight to the legendary 'all-seeing-eye' that every human being possessed; so why wasn't his activating? Taking several deep breaths he slowly exhaled and held the palm of his hands upwards. Ah, at last! Something was beginning to happen.

Michael visualized the tiny bright spots dancing in front of his eyes until they merged to form a picture. He took another deep breath and relaxed, allowing the picture to form and then he asked his question again. 'Who am I? What is my real name?' Finally a jumble of lights merged into a moving picture. Michael saw an arm waving a heavy sword. The man, whose face he could not see clearly, carried a shield that was perfectly round and had a black open winged eagle embossed on its face. 'Who am I?' He asked again as the picture started to fade from his view. 'What is my TRUE name?' he shouted as a severed arm came hurtling towards him. Michael held firm as something gleamed in the sunlight. He could hear men groaning so he peered further into his vision trying to make out their faces. Too late, the vision had gone. Disappointedly he opened his eyes, endeavouring to make sense of it. A shield, an arm and a black eagle! Well an eagle was a common emblem of power and there must be hundreds of families who shared the black eagle as part of their coat of arms or insignia. Oh dear it had all been a complete flop! They were playing with him! Well, he was not surprised, given that his mind seemed to be everywhere these days. Ever since mother had died he had lost his direction. Perhaps it was something to do with working from home. After all anyone would find it difficult with the constant interruptions. If this continues I'll be forced to go back to the campus. He thought placing the crystal in an inner compartment of the lower drawer of his desk and locking it. Testing that it was secure he leant back in the chair and in doing so knocked Henry Ford's *My Life* off his desk.

'Blast! Why is nothing going right today?' Upset that some of the pages may have been damaged Michael checked them carefully. As he did so a passage in the book appeared to jump off the page at him. He had not seen it before. Ah! Perhaps this is a message from the brotherhood, he thought as he started to read what Henry Ford had to say about life after death.

'I adopted the theory of reincarnation when I was twenty-six. Religion offered nothing to the point. Even work could not give me complete satisfaction. Work is futile if we cannot utilise the experience we collect in one life for use in the next. When I discovered reincarnation it was as if I had found a universal plan. I realised there was a chance to work out my ideas. Time was no longer limited. I was no longer a slave to the hands of the clock. Genius is experience. Some seem to think that it is a gift or a talent, but it is the fruit of long experience in many lives. Some are older souls than others, and so they know more. The discovery of reincarnation put my mind at ease. If you preserve a record of this conversation, write it so that it puts men's minds at ease. I would like to communicate to others the calmness that the long view of life gives us.

Henry Ford.

Michael felt marvellously restored. Was this the answer he had been seeking all along? No of course not. He still wanted to know what his real name was. But he had learnt long ago that you don't always get what you ask for straight away from the cosmic. I suppose the brotherhood have decided that today I should receive a lesson on life after death! How fitting that by ignoring my question they highlight my vanity! He felt annoyed then a voice, sounding remarkably like his mother's, spoke: 'Michael, stop being so angry. You have nothing to prove!'

Ah, that reminded him! He must read her letter at once. Michael opened the desk drawer and pulled out the sealed envelope. The postmark showed that Maria had addressed it to herself in 1974. He had been dreading the moment for fear of the emotions it might raise. It was getting dark but for further privacy he closed the curtains and turned on the green lamp on his desk. Then, sitting in his comfortable armchair, he poured himself a large glass of wine and opened the envelope.

Brandenberg House
Kensington,
London W.8

My dear son,

If you are reading this now, it is because I am no longer with you. I'm sorry I cannot tell you who your father is but I am quite sure that if you continue in your quest to find out you will succeed. The reason I cannot tell you is that I am sworn to secrecy. It's a secret that I must keep against my better judgement and against my will. I hope you can find it in your heart to forgive me. My work was as sacred as it was secret. Remember the motto? 'To know, to dare, to do, And...... to be silent!'

If ever you do manage to find the truth, I pray that it will take away the years of hurt that you must have felt. Your father was a very brave man. Whatever you may hear in the future please remember that he sacrificed his whole life for the good of humanity and he suffered much because of it. Che Sarā Sarā! Such is the world we live in.

Now my son, the TRUTH of what happened is very important and could be told but it is not so important that you should start another war! War is a terrible crime that must be eliminated for all time. This is what your father wanted and it was what I wanted. That's why we lived the way we did. GOD willing, you will succeed in all that you STRIVE for. I have one last bit of advice for you. Learn to go with the feelings of your heart and try to subjugate the intellectual within, at least for some of the time!

Someday I PRAY that you will come to know happiness as I have known it!

So, until we meet again remember I am always with you.

Your loving mother,

Maria Brandenberg (Baroness)

Michael read the letter twice more casually noting the use of capitals, whatever they may mean. Then he read it for a third time, recognising his own form of prayer had been answered. He sat with tears in his eyes. He had much to contemplate and for once it was not to do with work. Ever since he was young his mother had been a remote and towering figure who reappeared on various occasions between the au pairs coming and going. She was forever returning from those mysterious trips of hers. Later, when he was older, he wanted to know why she was away so often. She said it was a secret and that his father would tell him one day. When he asked her where his father was she said that was a secret too! So as he grew older he gave up asking the questions. The Baroness would tell him in her own sweet time. One day she casually announced that his father was dead and it was then that Count Frederick had visited him. He had subsequently found himself in the exalted position of not knowing the true identity of either his mother or his father!

Sitting in the semi-darkness he easily recalled the day when his mother had tried to explain. She said that she was a product of her times and that most of her ilk, by which she meant the nobility in Russia, were forced to adopt as many names as necessary to ensure their survival. Michael sighed. A genealogical nightmare! He had asked her on several occasions but she would never tell. Finally she deigned to reply: 'I am so sorry Michael! When the time is right for you to know, you will surely know but I am not at liberty to say anything to you at the moment.' No wonder he felt cheated out of his family history. Michael Brandenberg indeed! Yes, even he had been forced to carry on the charade with his son Alex Brandenberg and so the lie would continue unless he could stop it by finding out his parent's true identity.

He checked his watch. There was time for another glass before dinner. Rather naively he had expected his mother's last letter to have revealed more of the family's history, especially as she knew how much it meant to him. Michael shook his head in disappointment. Then, as the clock struck seven, he raised himself out of the chair. Remember all is vanity! Michael thought he heard her voice again as he folded the letter and placed it safely in his waistcoat pocket. Taking a last sip of wine he decided to show the letter to Juliana after dinner. Then he thought better of it. She had always found his mother's life complicated and the contents of this letter would just bamboozle her further.

PART TWO

ENIGMA

Chapter Nine   Unlocking the Mystery

As always, when Giovanni finished the cooking he sang an Italian folk song. After wiping his hands on the kitchen towel he handed Juliana the cutlery while Michael busied himself choosing a wine. Alex and Paul were chatting idly with Alice, who had ensconced herself in a favourite armchair. Despite the smell of rosemary and garlic wafting through the villa, Tonya had not yet made an appearance. The sound of chairs scraping across the tiles should do the trick, Michael thought as he poured the wine. He was right, because a moment later Tonya made a hasty appearance in the doorway.

'Hey! Look at you. Have you just won a million pounds?' Alex asked, greeting her in his usual over the top manner.

'I wish!' Tonya replied, watching Paul as he lit the candles.

Once grace had been said the steaming hot pasta was served. Only the sound of cutlery could be heard until Tonya, who could never stay quiet for long, spoke. Glancing across at Juliana and then at Michael, she picked up her glass.

'Thank you for inviting me to stay with you; the meal is delicious,' she proclaimed, raising her glass in the air. 'Salute!'

Michael smiled. 'Salute! Only the best will do for such an occasion.'

'By the way uncle, I read that article we found in the back of the book.'

'Oh? What article was that?' Alice enquired.

'*A review of Rescuing the Czar* by a Herman Bernstein, I was hoping uncle would look at it and tell me what he thinks of it.'

Michael carried on eating without answering, so Juliana felt obliged to reply for him.

'Of course he will.'

Tonya blushed when she realised Paul was staring at her.

'*Rescuing the Czar*?' he enquired. 'You're not speaking of the last emperor of Russia, Nicholas II?'

'Yes, that's right. It's an intriguing read.'

'Well that does sound intriguing,' Paul smiled.

'I'm sure we would all like to see it sometime!' replied Alice before adding, 'By the way Michael, don't forget I'm coming in to help you go through some of those boxes tomorrow.'

'Don't worry, I hadn't. I'm as keen as you to get them sorted out.'

Michael sighed as he poured another glass of wine before offering the decanter to his wife. Then, sensing a growing interest, he added, 'I suppose I should explain what this is all about otherwise some of you will be left in the dark!'

Alice and Juliana laughed in appreciation as Michael cleared his throat. 'The book Tonya is speaking of is a very old story about the Tsar and his family being rescued. My mother gave me a copy of it many years ago and like you, Tonya, I believed every word. Of course mother said it was all true, every word, but I didn't see any evidence. I think it was just wishful thinking on her part.'

'Well uncle, you might change your mind when you read that article of Bernstein's. Besides, I'm of a mind to do more research on the Romanov's! They were so powerful and rich surely they could have arranged their own escape? And if they were murdered why has no one found their bodies yet? You have to agree, it's a bit of a mystery. Besides, if your mother believed they had been rescued then that's good enough for me. But I would like to know more, much more...' Tonya leant back in her chair before adding, 'Will you help me uncle?'

Michael sighed again. Somehow he knew she was going to be troublesome. 'Of course, but I warn you, you are in for a gruelling ride if you want to learn what really happened in Russia during 1918. Now then, what's for desert, Giovanni?'

'Well I may have some books that would help you Tonya,' Paul suggested in earshot of Alex, who burst out laughing.

'I know what your game is you naughty boy! You want to find the missing Romanov treasure and you think that this story will help you find it. Well let me know when you discover it. I'll get my detector out, ha ha ha! X marks the spot.'

Michael thumped the table with his fist. 'That's quite enough Alex!' he shouted out as Alex continued laughing.

'That's all right uncle. I can stick up for myself,' Tonya replied.

'Only you Alex would think of the money,' Paul added, grabbing the opportunity to defend Tonya. 'Most of us around this table would just like the story of the rescue to be true and if Tonya is able to prove the story correct then that would certainly be worth its weight in gold. Just to know that the innocent children had escaped would be a blessing from heaven.'

'Hallelujah to that,' Alice responded.

'Yes,' Juliana replied, turning to Michael. 'Whether we think the story is fiction or not I think it is admirable of Tonya to care enough to check it all out. I think she should be given as much help as possible and preferably from you.'

'Hear, hear,' Alice clapped. 'And while we are on the subject, Maria always said the truth would come out one day. I can't think of a better way for it to happen than for one of her family to find out what it was and then to write it all down in a book!'

'And if you find the missing millions, well that'll be the icing on the cake,' Alex added, still smiling. Michael was noticeably quiet. He was thinking about the letter from his mother. *What had she said? Something about the truth needing to be told? Well, well, well! I suppose I should be pleased they are showing an interest in it. This is a great opportunity for us to work together, even though Alex's main motivation seems rather mercenary. Still, he may have his uses.*

After dessert and coffee Michael yawned profusely. He was ready for bed and wanted them all to stop talking. 'Right,' he said, standing up to get everyone's attention.

Alex looked very pale and Paul supposed he'd had too much to drink so he nudged him under the table. 'Are you feeling okay?'

'Yes of course... I just wonder...' He broke off mid sentence because Michael was tapping the glass with the edge of a spoon rather loudly.

'I thought I ought to say something on this occasion as it's our first family get together since mother's death, which I know came as a great shock to you all even though she was a very decent age....' Michael's voice trailed away on the last few words until he cleared his throat again. 'Anyway, whatever your thoughts are about her life, what she did or did not do, I for one have not been happy about what happened a few days prior to her death. Now it strikes me that we as a family have one of two options. We can ignore all she stood for and all she said and remember her as, well, just an ordinary woman living in an extraordinary time or...,' Michael raised his glass and a tear fell, 'or...,' he continued, 'we can believe that she stood for something special and that her story should, no MUST be told. After all, it is what she wanted. It is why she came here in the first place and it is incumbent upon us, as her immediate family, to fulfil her wish; so no more of this Romanov nonsense tonight please.'

'Hear, hear,' Tonya responded as Michael sat down, evidently pleased with himself.

Juliana raised her glass. 'Well said my dear.'

Michael acknowledged her praise and topped his glass up.

While Juliana was still congratulating him Giovanni leant over and whispered in Alice's ear, 'So is it now we do that special something?'

Alice wagged her finger. 'No, no, no! We must wait and do as we have been instructed!'

Michael glanced at his watch. 'Alice, what time would you like to start tomorrow, about ten thirty?'

Before Alice could reply Tonya interrupted. 'You know, uncle, you were going to suggest something and then you didn't. Then you said no more Romanov nonsense! But what if this book holds the clue to your mother's secret past?'

Wretched girl, Michael thought even though he managed to smile at her. 'Well now, I was about to suggest that we approach the problem of Maria,' he laughed at his own joke and started again. 'I was about to suggest that maybe we should work on this together then. But I fear some are not as able as others!' As he finished speaking Michael glanced sideways at his son.

'Of course you can count me in,' Alex replied, 'especially as the mystery involves one of the richest families in the world!'

Michael rubbed his hands together, not out of satisfaction but because he was getting ready for bed. 'Very good and I have something that will help you. It's a book written by a man called William Clarke, *The Lost Fortune of the Tsars.*

'Great. I'll pick it up from you tomorrow then.'

Michael didn't hold out much hope of Alex turning up because his son hated reading. Still, the idea of a lost fortune was probably likely to motivate him! 'Now it would be a good idea,' he continued, 'if we all start off from the same starting point. So if you agree,' Michael glanced briefly round the room as he spoke, *Rescuing the Czar* will be the story we start with. From there we can begin to research specific areas. Paul, I know you have an interest in the Red Cross, YMCA and the Vatican library. Is there any other area you have a speciality in?'

Paul thought for a moment. 'I don't think so but surely you're not suggesting that the Vatican had a hand in rescuing the Tsar?'

'Certainly not,' Michael added defensively. 'But there may be some documents placed in that library for safekeeping. Don't forget the Romanov's were a very religious family. Russian Orthodox, practically Catholic. If any of them survived, say Olga or Tatiana, and then went on to have children themselves, well I imagine the church would want to know about it!'

Realizing Michael was deadly serious Paul wondered where it was all going to lead. Besides, he didn't want to be delving into church archives if he could help it. 'Well I do have an interest in spies. I'm reading about Sidney Reilly and his role during the summer of 1918 in Russia. Perhaps that would be more appropriate?'

Michael didn't reply; instead he stared straight ahead. Paul glanced across to Tonya, wondering what he should say next but Michael was trying to remember how many copies of *Rescuing the Czar* he had available for circulation. He didn't want to part with the copy his mother had given him, nor did he want Tonya's copy doing the rounds until he'd had a chance to study it for himself.

It was getting late and Alice yawned loudly. Juliana took the hint and rose to make more coffee while Michael sat back in his chair with both hands behind his head and smiled at Tonya. 'I wonder whether you'd let me borrow your copy of *Rescuing the Czar*?'

Before Tonya could answer, he explained the reason for wanting to look at her copy. 'It's just that yours is an original version and may contain information that is not in my copy, which of course I'm happy to lend you in return.'

Tonya hesitated. 'Of course you can have it back, just as soon as I have finished with it!' Well she could hardly refuse.

* * *

The following morning Alice knocked promptly on the library door.

'Ah! Good morning Alice,' Michael greeted her wearing a blue velvet lounge jacket and silk cravat. He looked very handsome she thought as he tidied up his desk.

'So where shall we start?' she asked.

Michael pointed to the boxes. 'You'll see that I haven't opened them yet. I suppose we will have to make room for all the contents over here. Once we have it all on the table we can invite the others to come in and take their pick. What do you think?'

'That sounds like a good idea,' Alice replied as they started to unpack the first tea chest, which contained household items wrapped up in newspaper. Towards the bottom they came across an envelope with a few photographs in it. Michael eagerly opened it as Alice looked at each in turn. 'Ah, now that's Saint Petersburg. You recognise it of course?' she added, pointing to the famous landmark. Michael nodded as she peered down at another snap shot. 'I wonder why she bothered to take a photograph of Moscow's railway station?'

Michael studied it closely. 'Well it would help if we could see who it was sitting on the cases!'

Alice laughed and picked up another photograph. 'Oh look, this is the family residence,' she said, pointing to a rather grand building. Michael took the brown sepia photograph and drew a sharp breath. 'But surely that's the Winter Palace?'

Alice laughed at his apparent surprise. 'Yes that's right. All the noble families lived in close proximity to the Romanov's. Oh look at this one. Here's your mother on horseback in Port Arthur, did you know she was a very good horsewoman?'

'Hmm, but who's that man next to her?'

'A close friend by the look of things; anyway Michael I imagine you'll want to keep these all safe?'

Michael nodded. 'Yes, Juliana can sort through this lot and put them in an album. That way they will be protected. 'Ah look, I remember this old silver candlestick. When I was young it stood on the dining room table.'

Alice picked it up. 'Gosh, it weighs a ton. The dolphin heads are sweet but those flying dragons are rather frightening. It's beautiful and ugly at the same time, good and bad all in one, very strange.'

'Just like us humans I suppose! But look at the workmanship. Juliana will want me to put it on the dining room table I shouldn't wonder.'

'That's a great suggestion,' Alice responded beaming with delight, 'and we could have it placed in the middle. That way Maria will be with us.'

'Ah you have reminded me! Remember when we were in London you said you would be happy to work with me on sorting out these wretched papers of mother's?'

Alice nodded. 'Yes but that was after the funeral and, well, I felt for your misery and when you said that you thought she had been........'

Michael suddenly raised his hand. 'Oh that! I wasn't thinking straight Alice. I was wrong. Of course she wasn't murdered. You know that. I hope you haven't told anyone?'

'No I haven't. I meant what I said to you. I'm here to help in whatever direction you want to take this. Maria confided in me from time to time but I don't think I ever got the complete picture. When she left Russia for the last time she was very sad. But she always said that she was Russian with a German heart. It never made any sense to me how she could feel like that. Oh yes, half Russian and half German, and she had the temerity to admit to it!'

'Well that makes me Russian and German too and maybe something more? I wish you could tell me where my father came from, you must have known him?'

Alice sighed. 'If there is one thing you need to understand Michael it's this. Your mother has always been a woman of mystery. It's never been my nature to pry into other's affairs. Besides, in such times of horror one just accepted what one was told. You didn't have time to question what was said. And things rarely turned out to be what you first thought they were. We were just so pleased to be alive and would do anything not to starve. Everyone was like that. In those days you kept your eyes and ears open and your mouth shut.'

'So there's no chance of finding my father either?'

'Well I wouldn't go as far as that. Who knows what we will discover in these old tea chests.'

Michael sat down and buried his head in his hands; Alice immediately felt sorry for him. 'Look, if Tonya's right about that book, *Rescuing the Czar*, well then....' Alice stopped short, not sure how to say what she was thinking without upsetting him further. 'Besides, we have other ways of finding out about your father, don't we?'

Michael glanced up at her. 'You mean crystal gazing I suppose! Ah.... now you have reminded me of something I wanted to show you. What do you think of this?' Michael handed her the heavy key with the silver fox on the front. She studied it with interest, apparently paying particular attention to the number written on the back.

'Well any ideas?' he asked.

'Sssh, I'm thinking.....A fox and the number 88... Hmm, at first I wondered if it was Russian but now it feels German. Sorry! I mean Prussian. Anyway what does it open?'

'I don't know, that's why I'm asking you. Can't you use that special intuition of yours?'

Alice smiled. 'Well have you tried?'

'Yes.'

'And...?'

'I didn't get anywhere! At first I thought it might open an old metal box of mother's that I found lying around but it didn't. So I wanted to see what you made of it. I can't tell you how annoying it is having a key hanging around and not knowing what it's for!'

'I can imagine, and such a grand looking key too. Let me sit down over here and see what powers I can muster with it. Yes, that's a good idea Michael. Shut the curtains and light a candle. I tell you what, why don't you go and make a cup of tea or something while I'm at this? I prefer to work on my own.'

Michael did as he was told. He was bound to feel down, he told himself; what with going through his mother's things and those photographs, well it was all very unsettling.

Giovanni and Juliana were talking quietly in the kitchen when Michael entered. 'I've been ordered to make the cha,' he remarked jokingly.

Juliana smiled. 'She has you well trained I see!' In a rare moment of public affection, Michael gave her a quick hug. 'It's very quiet down here, where is everyone?' he asked.

'Well you set them a big task yesterday. I expect they are hard at it. Look there's Paul and Alex reading in the garden. Even I've started reading,' Juliana remarked with a certain amount of amusement in her voice. 'Come to the studio and I'll show you the sculpture I've nearly finished. I think you will be pleased.' Michael pulled one of his faces as he arranged the teacups on a tray.

By the time he got back to the library he was full of anticipation. Alice had drawn back the curtains and was leaning rather pensively against the edge of his desk.

'So… any luck?'

Alice smiled and shook the key in her hand. 'Well I managed to pick up on a blue train with many soldiers and horses beside it. A whistle was blown loudly and the train pulled out of the station. Then something, I don't know what, made me shudder until I was forced to open my eyes. Only now do I know what it was.' Michael gave her an enquiring look.

'The train crashed, spilling the contents of its crates all over the railway tracks. Then someone waved an eagle embossed shield in my face.'

'What, the Romanov emblem?'

'No. It was not double headed. It was spread eagled! Prussian I would say. We must keep an open mind if we're to find out more Michael. By the way, what's in that cedar box over there?'

'Sssh! I think there's someone at the door.' Then, rather ridiculously, Michael motioned to her to rattle the cups and saucers so that he could creep over to the door. For all his cleverness he was still a child at heart. She watched with amusement as he stood very still for a second before suddenly opening it.

'Aaahhh!' Juliana screamed, nearly dropping a tray of home-made biscuits. Michael quickly grabbed her arm to steady her.

'God, what's wrong with you? Why do you have to open the door like that?'

'I'm SORRY. I….' Michael apologised as he took the tray. 'Mm. Thank you. These do look tasty.'

By way of reply Juliana pointed down the hallway to where Giovanni was standing. He waved back. 'Si, I make them this afternoon. Enjoy boss.'

Michael smiled. 'Thanks again and I'll see you later. Heavens that was close. They wouldn't understand all this business.' he said, placing the biscuits on the table. 'If they knew what you and I got up to they would be quite spooked!'

Alice laughed. 'SPOOKED indeed, speaking of which, you were going to show me that box.'

'Was I?' Michael questioned.

'Yes, come along now,' Alice snapped her fingers. 'Quickly, I want to see if this key fits it.'

'Don't you think I would have tried it already?' Michael sounded exasperated.

'You may have but I haven't. I know a trick or two!'

Michael heard her mumble a few words in what seemed to be a foreign language.

'Now...,' she added, holding the key jubilantly in the air. 'Let's see if it fits.' Alice gave him a knowing smile as she slotted the key into the lock. 'Well it fits but will it turn? That's the question.' She smiled as she used as much force as possible to turn the lock. Michael watched with growing concern as the key bent.

Alice felt a searing pain shoot through her hand before dropping the key and collapsing.

Horrified Michael sniffed the foul air and reached for his handkerchief. Hurriedly he rushed over to the French windows and flung them open. Alice was still lying motionless on the floor. Quickly he placed a cushion under her head and grabbed the teapot, pouring its contents into the box. His eyes streamed as a sulphurous smell made the room almost unbearable to breathe in but a moment later, a gurgling noise brought the fumes to an end.

Michael lifted Alice up and sat her in a chair carefully. Then she opened her eyes and coughed. 'Thank God. Here.... drink this. I've opened the windows so we should be safe!' Alice took the milk jug offered and drank the contents then smiled; 'If that's not the devil's work, then I don't know what is. I'm sorry Michael, I should have known better,' she added, coughing again. 'That box, whatever's in there... it's protected by a gas-filled phial located behind the lock. Now where's that key Michael? For heaven's sake don't lose it.' she urged breathlessly.

Michael did as he was told and picked up the key placing it in the inkwell on his desk. He laughed, 'Oh dear, the contents will be completely ruined now I've just poured tea over it!'

'Better the contents ruined than us dead!'

Michael glanced across in concern. 'Let me help you to your room. You must get some rest.'

Alice smiled weakly. 'That would be a very good idea the way I am feeling.'

A few moments later Michael was back in his library, staring at the cedar box soaked in tea. What a mess! Gingerly he placed it in the centre of a towel and was about to dab it dry when he thought better of it. Well that was a close call. What was that old saying? Oh yes, curiosity killed the cat. Well it very nearly did tonight! Still, if Alice was better in the morning they could try to open it again.

Just as he finished clearing up there was a knock on the door. It was Tonya. She held out her copy of *Rescuing the Czar* for him. 'Here you are uncle, as promised.'

'Thank you. You'll have it back just as soon as I'm done with it!'

As he spoke Tonya squeezed passed him into the library. He sensed she was in no hurry to leave. 'I'm sorry about the smell. Alice and I were in the middle of unpacking those boxes when....'

Tonya held her nose. 'Phew! It smells like rotten eggs in here!'

'Well I never leave the windows open when I am not in the library you see and I... '

Tonya screwed her nose up again, which annoyed Michael even more. 'But you are in the library! Anyway, look what else I have here for you. Remember that article by Herman Bernstein?'

'Ah yes of course, well done for remembering.'

Michael grinned as she handed him the old newspaper cutting. He studied it carefully. 'Of course I have seen this article before; it was written shortly after *Rescuing the Czar* was published. Bernstein interviewed Ivan Sergeyev who was the judge appointed by the Whites during the winter months of 1918 to find out what happened to the Tsar and his family.'

Tonya nodded. 'Yes! I have read the article,' she replied slightly amused that Michael was about to begin a lecture. She watched him place the article down on his desk. His shoes, as always, were perfectly shined. She listened to his footsteps as he made his way over to a large green velvet-padded oak chair. Despite the foul smell Tonya took this as an invite to take a seat as she watched him rub his chin slowly, apparently deep in thought.

Eventually he spoke. 'There are some interesting pieces of information in the original evidence uncovered by this man, such as the writing on the wall in Nicholas's own hand, saying that he would rather die in Russia than be saved by Germany; and this bit here that describes bits of clothing and jewellery, freshly cut girls' hair, the Tsar's beard having been shaved off in the bathroom, all pointing to a change in their appearance! He even mentions that controversial telegram.'

'The one written by the local soviet at Ekaterinburg, stating they had shot Nicholas. Unfortunately they could not produce the body when asked. Many White Russians and friends of the Imperial Family believed it was planted as a cover up for what really happened to the family.'

'Gosh, I'm sorry uncle but I really am going to have to open those windows!'

Tonya pushed them open and took a deep breath. 'So what do you think really happened to them?'

Michael shook his head. It was more than his life was worth to make a pronouncement without having considered all of the known facts. Even then, as he explained, a good professor asks more questions than he answers. But Tonya was having none of it.

'Please just tell me what you think.'

Michael sighed. This young niece certainly liked to nail down her target. 'Well how can I say some fifty years later what happened or whether the telegram is a fake or not? How can I say, as others have, that the wording on the telegram suggests that it was a coded message confirming the successful evacuation of the family?'

Tonya smiled. 'Of course uncle, I understand. So you think Herman wrote the article that way, to convince the general public that an execution had taken place even though they could not produce the dead bodies at the time?'

Michael winced at the way she spoke. She was not fragile like his other women students. She was rather hard, not minding at all about the talk of dead bodies. Michael glanced at his watch. 'I'm afraid I really can't give you any more time. I'm far too busy,' he added, steering her towards the library door.

'I think the Romanovs did escape and to ensure their safety they travelled to a secret hideaway in Russia and on to their final destination much later.

Perhaps all that evidence reported in Bernstein's article was purposely left lying around as a decoy to prove that they had been executed, so that the Bolsheviks wouldn't go looking for them!'

'Well Tonya I suppose if you believe in THAT rescue story you would see it that way. Personally I do not. The evidence that was produced in this inquiry and the later Sokolov investigation is absolutely watertight. TRUST ME! But look, if you don't, and you want to make a serious detailed study of it...,' Michael started to shout, 'If you want to get into the nuts and bolts of the tragedy that was Russia back then...Well I warn you, Tonya it's pretty gruesome. It is horrific, dreadfully morbid and I have no doubt it will keep you awake at nights!'

'Okay, well just answer me this. Why did the Ural Soviet want to hide the bodies when they had already owned up to shooting the Tsar? Why cover up evidence of an act they had already admitted to in their telegram to Moscow? What was so special about this execution that the bodies had to be hidden or destroyed? You see, I just don't get it.'

Michael had to admit that it was a very good question and one he couldn't answer. The girl had plenty of curiosity and there was only one way to satisfy that. He walked over to his bookshelf, quickly finding what he was looking for. 'Well, now. It's believed that the bodies were destroyed because there was a fear that the remains would be worshipped as relics. Don't forget the Romanovs were a royal Imperial Family. That translates as HOLY to the likes of you and me!'

'So they may have been,' responded Tonya, 'but I can't buy into your theory. Surely the proof is in the pudding? The Bolsheviks' inability to produce the bodies would only serve to fuel the common belief at that time that they had all escaped.'

Michael grabbed hold of a couple of books while he spoke. 'Listen, you are fully entitled to believe what you want. But I suggest you read up on all previous investigations into the disappearance of the Romanovs. It's not wise to stick to one book or one point of view. You'll find these helpful. *The File on the Tsar* by Anthony Summers and Tom Mangold and *The Hunt for the Czar* by Guy Richards.' Michael patted her on the shoulders and steered her back towards the door. 'That should keep you busy for a while. Now my dear, I really must get on.'

'Thank you. There must be so many people who remain intrigued by the mystery of what happened to the Romanov family.'

'Yes Tonya and you are clearly one of them! Remember, desperate times call for desperate measures. So when you're reading those books DO try and keep an open mind.'

Tonya smiled to herself as she left. That was so like Michael to have the last word.

Chapter Ten   My Life

The studio door was half open when Michael knocked the following morning.

'Come in darling,' Juliana called out. 'Look. What do you think of her?' she asked pointing out her latest piece of work.

'Mother!'

'You recognise her favourite pose then. I must say I'm very pleased with her.' Michael studied the statue. 'It is just as I expected, very good! But where are you thinking of putting her?'

'Well what about on the terrace or in the garden by the pond?'

'By the pond I think, just as long as she stands near the trees. I always think statues look best with a shaded light and a green background.' Michael turned the radio down as he spoke. 'By the way, I've bought you a copy of *Rescuing the Czar* to read.'

Juliana sighed as she placed it on a shelf at the back of her studio.

An ensuing silence obliged Michael to apologise. 'Look I'm sorry, I shouldn't have interrupted you but you did agree to help me discover my roots, and we should all start from the same place.'

Juliana glanced at the radio. 'I don't remember that but I seem to have little choice in the matter! Oh well, I suppose if everyone else is I might as well do my bit too!' She smiled and Michael relaxed. 'Believe it or not even Alex has started reading,' he added, hoping to encourage her.

'Really, I'm astounded! He dislikes reading as much as I do!'

As she spoke Michael ran his hands along the carefully crafted statue. He wanted to tell her that it was beautiful but instead he spoke of why Alex should find the book exciting. 'Well it's a boyish adventure and an enjoyable read. It should only take a few hours! I'm looking forward to listening to everyone's views. Ah ha... I see you have nearly finished this. Are you enjoying it?' he asked picking up Henry Ford's *My Life* and flicking haphazardly through it.

'Well to be honest, I find it a bit dry. But I'm very pleased he was a pacifist!'

'Well I told you he was!'

'Yes but that 'Peace' ship business of his. I'll give him his due he certainly stuck to his guns.' Juliana laughed at her own joke. 'Anyway, I was impressed with his commitment to the cause,' she added, wiping her hands on her apron. 'Give me the book a moment. Ah, here we are. I thought it was interesting that they used to go vagabonding, you'll remember Kathleen Scott did a lot of that too?'

Michael frowned. 'What point are you making? The term "vagabonding" was in common use in many memoirs of the time!'

Juliana sighed loudly. 'I just thought it was interesting to note, that's all. Besides I liked his opinion on the stupidity of the war. Listen to this.'

"Today I am more opposed to war than ever I was, and I think the people of the world know even if the politicians do not, that war never settles anything. It was war that made the orderly and profitable processes of the world what they are to-day, a loose, disjointed mass. Of course, some men get rich out of war, others get poor. War is an orgy of money, just as it is an orgy of blood. And we should not be so easily led into war if we considered what it is that makes a nation really great. I have never been able to discover any honourable reasons for the beginning of the World War. I believed, on the information that was given to me in 1916, that some of the nations were anxious for peace and would welcome a demonstration for peace. It was in the hope that this was true that I financed the expedition to Stockholm in what has since been called the Peace Ship. I do not regret the attempt. The mere fact that it failed is not, to me, conclusive proof that it was not worth trying. We learn more from our failures than from our successes. What I learned on that trip was worth the time and the money expended. I do not now know whether the information as conveyed to me was true or false. I do not care. But I think everyone will agree that if it had been possible to end the war in 1916 the world would be better off than it is today. But the fighting never settles the question. It only gets the participants around to a frame of mind where they will agree to discuss what they were fighting about."

'There I've finished, what do you think?'

'What do I think? I think the ship chartered was the Oscar II.'

'Michael! You know that's not what I meant! Do you think he was right to have those opinions?'

'I suppose everyone's entitled to an opinion but war makes history. Without war I'd be out of a job, along with many other millions of people I suspect!'

'Really Michael, that's absurd. I don't think we can keep going to war just to make history! Besides, I think all history is bunk and Henry said it himself, so I'm in good company!'

Michael sat on the stool and smiled. 'So you're a fan of Ford after all?'

'Partly, but I don't agree with all his ideas.'

'Oh, what don't you agree with?'

'Right,' Juliana clapped her hands, 'that's quite enough discussion Michael. Please take this back with you now because I really must get on and finish this today.'

She slapped the book into his hands and pushed him out of the studio.

As he shut the door he heard her turn the radio up.

Chapter Eleven   An Agent called Fox

Juliana was watching Giovanni tend the roses.

'Oh don't you just love this time of year?' she remarked, stretching out her arms.

'Si,' Giovanni replied, admiring her pose momentarily until he heard Tonya bound down the steps.

'Mind if I join you?' she asked.

Juliana smiled, 'Not at all. Come and tell me what you've got planned for the day.'

'Well Paul has offered to take me around the Vatican City.'

'Perhaps we can go too?' Giovanni enquired of Juliana.

She patted his arm. 'I'd love to, but really, I must finish the statue today if I'm to help Michael research his roots. He insists on giving me a history lesson even when we ...well let's just say he's given me even more reading to do!' Giovanni laughed but she could see he was disappointed. 'Why don't you go with them anyway?' she suggested.

*　*　*

Back in the library Michael and Alice had made a start on unpacking a second tea chest. Newspapers were everywhere as parcels were carefully unwrapped and placed on an old table.

'Are you sure you're feeling up to helping me today?'

'Funny you should ask. When I woke up this morning I felt as though I had a very nasty hangover but I'm fine now. By the way, what did you do with that cedar box?'

'I wrapped it up in a couple of towels and put it out of the way!'

'Good, but weren't you at all a little curious to see what was inside it?'

'Do you know Alice? After what happened to you it completely slipped my mind! Anyway, I would rather get these unpacked if you don't mind?'

Much to Michael's annoyance the first few boxes contained several more copies of *Rescuing the Czar*.

'Maria had so many of these,' Alice remarked, pulling out another two copies. 'Honestly, you'd think that she had written the book herself!'

Michael laughed. 'Well, she was an excellent writer as you know, and quite brilliant at translation.'

'Oh yes, she loved high adventure stories and the greater the mystery the more it pleased her, especially if the tale ended well.'

'Well that's more like popular fiction.'

Alice pulled a face. 'I suppose so. You could hardly have a story starting off well and ending badly. That's why the story of the Romanovs being rescued was so popular I suppose.'

While she was talking, Michael picked up a silver photograph frame with gold cherubs exquisitely carved around it. 'Just look at the work involved in this! I must show Juliana. She will adore it.' He added passing it over. 'Careful now, it's delicate.'

'So I see, and by the look of it very old indeed. It has a green velvet backing with a pink and gold inlay. I wonder what photograph was kept in there.'

'Can't you guess?'

Alice didn't reply. She was too busy unwrapping yet more silver and gold. 'Oh Michael look, a very old icon encrusted with rubies, emeralds, amethyst, turquoise and pearls. It must be fourteenth century at least!'

'I believe it's called "the Mother of Kazan" and it is sixteenth century. Mother hung it in the drawing room in the corner close to the ceiling so that it overlooked everyone seated in the room.'

Alice smiled as she recalled the house in London. 'That's the traditional place to have them, to one side of the chimneybreast. That's where the evil spirits dwelt! Remember she also had that chunk of amethyst crystal placed in the fireplace as well?'

Michael shivered at the thought. 'I don't know why she was so superstitious.'

Alice looked up. 'It's not superstition. It was her religion! Maria was no different from any other Russian of her class. In fact we all………' Alice broke off mid-sentence. 'Michael, we must hang the icon up there. Ah! And here's that amethyst you were talking about.' It was so heavy she needed both hands to hold it. 'It will require a good clean if it's to work properly!'

'Clean it! Are you sure that's wise?'

Alice sighed. 'Well how can it work with all this grime and dust on it. It must have been in that fireplace for at least fifty years. Look, don't worry, I'll soak it first and then put it out under the full moon for the evening. That way it'll be fully charged for us! And if it collects the morning dew so much the better.'

Michael had no idea what she was speaking about but was happy to defer to her in mystical matters. She was, after all, quite familiar with the occult he mused as she hurried out to get a bucket. By the time she got back Michael had hung the icon to the north side of the fireplace close to the ceiling.

'Well done, that's exactly the right position. But make sure it's tilting at an angle. The icon must face down into the room so that it can protect us.'

Michael gave it a small adjustment. 'Like that?'

Alice stepped back. 'Yes, that'll do.'

'Gosh. Feel the difference it has made already! Is that frankincense that I can smell?'

Alice smiled, 'Just you wait and see what happens once we have the amethyst fully charged!'

Michael's eyes widened in anticipation, 'So, if we hold the meetings in here, there should be no problem in us receiving divine help!'

Alice patted his arm. 'There is no reason why we shouldn't be able to make contact with the dearly departed now!'

Michael was getting on so well with Alice that he decided to read her the letter from his mother. After he had finished she expressed no surprise at the contents, saying that it all made perfect sense to her.

'Maria will be very pleased with what we have done here today,' she announced proudly.

Michael gave her one of his rare smiles. 'Now let's gather up all this newspaper and put it in that box over there.'

'Perhaps we can use it to start the fire once the evenings get a bit colder,' Alice suggested. Michael shook his head. 'I'm afraid someone has already made a claim on them! I've promised Juliana she can have them for the studio.'

* * *

In Rome, Giovanni Paul and Tonya were quite exhausted by their visit to St Peters. Tonya had insisted on going into the catacombs and looking over all the buried Popes. Giovanni had got stuck behind a never ending line of nuns and then, finding it oppressively hot, he had made his way up the winding stone staircase into the dome. There he found Paul admiring the layout of the Vatican gardens. In the meantime Tonya had toured a large metal cage that housed an electronically secure glass box. There were no signs to tell her what was inside.

Ever curious, she decided to ask a nun who was dressed in blue and white and had paused to pray at the shrine. Tonya didn't want to encroach on her privacy and waited for the moment she could ask her question. The nun told her that inside the shrine was a part of Saint Peter himself! 'Good Heavens!' Tonya exclaimed, crossing herself several times. Having thanked the nun, she felt dreadfully squeamish and made her way slowly up the stairs, where she found Paul and Giovanni busy in conversation. As she approached she heard Giovanni speaking. 'Si, the past, well it can come back to haunt you and always when you least expect it!'

Nothing more was said, but over lunch Tonya told Giovanni what she had experienced in the crypt of St Peter's. Paul was able to verify the story and Tonya was astonished that a relic of St Peter still existed. Paul then told her more stories and the importance of holy relics to Roman Catholics and to Russian Orthodox Christians. She was enthralled.

'Do you believe in reincarnation?' she asked, resting her chin on her hands.

'Depends, If by reincarnation you mean going to a higher dimension, then I suppose I would say yes.'

Tonya laughed. 'You mean up to the spirit in the sky?'

'Si,' said Giovanni. 'The body is, how you say, just a shell. The spirit lives inside. So the soul never dies.'

'So why can't we remember our past lives then?'

'We just can't!' Giovanni smiled at her trying to end the conversation.

'But some can.'

'Yes,' replied Paul. 'So they say.' 'Well how can they?' Tonya questioned.

'I don't know they just can. 'I suppose because they are meant to!'

'Will we be able to?'

'Yes, if we are meant to!'

'What does that mean?'

'Well only if there is an important enough reason to.'

'Who decides then?'

'Our heavenly Father, Jesus Christ, the only begotten son, and all the Holy Saints,' Paul whispered crossing himself.

Later that afternoon and despite Giovanni feeling tired Paul showed Tonya around the Vatican. She was mesmerised by the painted ceilings and highly coloured frescos.

'Oh Alex would love it here. He is such a fan of classical work and Michelangelo.'

'Actually, he has visited several times,' Paul replied. 'Sometimes he asks me but usually I'm too busy with my studies.'

'Si, the holy Father keeps him very busy!' Giovanni interjected.

'Otherwise the devil makes work for idle hands, eh?' Tonya replied rather flippantly.

'Not if I do my work well!'

'I'm sorry, that was a stupid remark. I don't know what came over me.'

Quite unexpectedly, Paul laughed. 'Don't worry Tonya. I don't take myself THAT seriously!'

* * *

Back at the villa, Juliana was in her studio, deciding where to store the box of old newspapers Michael had just brought up. If she could make them a bit flatter she could squeeze them into a lower drawer. As she started to flatten them out she noticed that some of them dated back to 1920. Gosh that is early she thought, separating them out of the pile of newer editions. She felt happier than she had for a long time. Ever since his mother had passed away Michael had been behaving more warmly towards her. He was less serious, almost fun! Well perhaps that was a bit of an exaggeration! Just as she was mulling over her thoughts something caught her eye. It was a headline from one the papers.

BOLSHEVIST OFFICIAL DENIES EX CZAR IS DEAD.

AMSTERDAM. June 29th 1918.
The rumours that the former Emperor Nicholas has been murdered are described as lies designed to incite the public by the President of the Executive Committee at Ekaterinburg. This message is dated June 24th and was telegraphed from Moscow by way of Berlin.

So! There were rumours of the Tsar's execution as early as 29th June 1918. *Well I never!* Juliana quickly went through the rest of the cuttings. It wasn't long before she realised that nearly every sheet contained news about Russia. The Baroness must have saved these articles but why?

Fancy Michael and Alice missing them when they were unpacking! Well I haven't got time to read it all now she thought, searching for a safe place to put them in. Michael will be pleased when he sees their contents and that I haven't remodelled them! In the midst of these thoughts another headline suddenly grabbed her attention:

EX SPY'S FORECAST FULFILLED. DR GRAVES PREDICTED FALL OF ANTWERP ONE DAY BEFORE NEWS GOT HERE. SOME OTHER PROPHECIES, ENGLAND TO BE HARRIED BY AIR ATTACKS AND TO QUIT FIGHTING IN FOUR WEEKS

The news of the fall of Antwerp in yesterday's newspapers added interest to some of the predictions recently made concerning the European conflict by Dr Armgaard Karl Graves, the former international spy, who professed to have been in the employ of the Secret Service of the German and English governments at various times.

It was dated Sunday October 11th 1914 and annoyingly the newspaper had been torn off at the beginning of the article but Juliana soon found plenty more to read about Dr Graves when she picked up another cutting dated November 1914.

SPY Dr Graves now tells of the coming invasion of England by Germany, both by air and sea. 36 Zeppelins and 375,000 men to cross the channel AND LONDON IS TO BE DESTROYED

With her interest aroused she spent an unplanned afternoon reading what she could and then putting them into neat piles to show Michael. When she had finished she was astonished to see that the pile reporting on the master-spy Dr Graves was much higher than the rest. Next Juliana picked up the Bernstein article that Tonya had found and read it with renewed interest.

* * *

Back from Rome, Tonya hurried up to her room. She couldn't wait to get back to her books! *The File on the Tsar*, *The Hunt for the Tsar* and Michael's copy of *Rescuing the Czar,* all of which lay on her bedside table. After getting comfortable she quickly flipped through the pages, searching for excerpts on the Baroness B. She soon found what she was looking for in the second diary written by Alex Syvorotka.

Quite unexpectedly the Baroness B. came today to the office. At first I did not want to see her, but then thought that it would be better not to make these dangerous people angry, as heaven knows what they are liable to do if irritated, and besides she is so fascinating. So she was shown in. She was veiled as much as only she could be, for mystery, and to conceal the slight and ingenious coat of rouge, I guess. The usual feathers, rings and perfumes; and I had thought that I would see an ascetic face tired out by seclusion! She said that she had nothing serious to tell me, but had just run in to say goodbye and calm me. She was not going to call on Maroossia. 'Too busy,' she said and 'other reasons'.

   'I appreciate your other reasons,' I said. 'You have already shown what a friend you are. Why did you drag Maroossia into your business? You probably are well protected against any disagreeable event, but we are not. So next time please use your other reasons.'

   'There was no dragging your wife into my business. The package of laces she took to Madame van der Huechts is not a crime. Besides, everything is over, so, as if nothing had happened.'

   'Yes it probably is nothing. Misha would be of a different opinion, I am sure.'
   'No, he would not.'

   There was a silence for a while, and then she said, sighing..... (here the line was illegible).

'For instance, we wanted to give you the whole outline inviting you to do something for your country and you refused to help.'

'Baroness,' I said, 'honestly and truly I don't understand these speculations. Just as honestly and just as truly I don't care for them, no matter what they are for. I hate this manner of operation. The manner! I hate plots. I hate underground work; the only thing I care for is my own comfort and my own affairs.'

'You don't know what you are talking about,' she said, 'or the atmosphere has made you so clever that I don't know whether you are trying to get something out of me or not. Very well, I am conspiring. I am now with these people with whom I would not have thought of being only three months ago. As soon as I succeed I shall leave all and become free and independent....'

Then she corrected herself. 'I don't mean to say, of course, I am not independent now but.... What time is it?'

I told her.

'Thank you. So you see.... What were we talking about? Ah, yes indeed, how silly of me! Well, so I am in a big game. It may seem that I am in the wrong. But think of the time when there will be a moment, when just a few persons, maybe only one person, will be able to appear again on the stage and become the nucleus of regeneration. And if I am wrong, and such a moment will never come, it is so easy to get rid of those whom many persons are trying to preserve.'

'Yes,' I said, smiling at her enthusiasm and innocent cynicism.

'Please omit your insinuations and sarcasm, you bad thing. I only see you are not patriotic, or you have something personal against me.'

'You can judge better than others on this last point. It looks to me as though you were wrong about the rest, however....' (a page torn out)

'... I saw Tatiana (don't ask me questions, if you please!) and the girl said that there are only two acceptable ways: to be released by the will of the people, or taken against their will, a kidnapping staged. Other methods will meet with a refusal. That is why the Emperor refused a formal foreign intervention, for it would place them in a position of parasites with the "ex" title. After everything is through, all of your Kerenskys are a parasite and could not be popular and desirable.'

'Well', she got up, 'Goodbye! Kiss Maroossia for me. And here is a friendly warning: don't talk. It is dangerous. Don't trust. It is silly. Write to Sophie's house in Paris, it will reach me. So sorry we cannot be together!'

Tonya put the book down, stretched out and considered what she had read. She assumed this part of the book had been written in October 1917, when the Imperial Family were still being held at Tobolsk and Kerensky still held power in Russia. She certainly had her work cut out for her getting through this pile of books from Michael and all before the next meeting! If only she could find out exactly who the Baroness 'B' was. A woman whose name no one dared speak?

Chapter Twelve   A Wild Goose Chase

When Michael entered the dining room he was amazed to see everyone getting on so well. Alice was in her usual chair by the fire talking with Juliana. Throughout the evening meal the excited chatting continued until Michael stood up and made a toast to the memory of his mother. Afterwards he announced that he and Alice had sorted out most of Maria's belongings and that if they wished they could all go into the library and choose something for themselves from the items lying on the large oak table behind the door.

'So you've already unpacked all the boxes then?' Juliana enquired.

'No not all,' Alice replied. 'There are still a few left. Mainly letters, translations, and that sort of thing.'

'That's right,' Michael interrupted. 'I expect they will take a little more time to sort out, but I'm not in a rush my dear!'

Juliana smiled. 'By the way, thank you for the newspapers. They will come in very useful.' 'You're very welcome my dear! 'Now Madam Tonya, what can you tell us? Have you something exciting to report on the books I gave you last week?' Michael smiled in anticipation.

'Well do you want me to give a short appraisal of what I have learnt so far?'

Michael nodded. 'Certainly, you should never put off until tomorrow what you can do today!'

Tonya shuffled her notes nervously. '*Rescuing the Czar* is made up of two diaries. One appears to be from a British intelligence operative and the other a Russian nobleman posing as a Bolshevik. The diaries describe the intricate rescue plan and finally the route taken by the Tsar and his family as they flee Russia in 1918. The hero of the story is a man called Fox who succeeds in rescuing the family.'

Michael interrupted her. 'I must say when I first read this book I found it remarkable and quite unlike any other story published about the goings on at Ekaterinburg. It was certainly a one off!'

'Anyway,' Tonya continued, 'Fox infiltrates the Ipatiev house dressed as a Bolshevik guard apparently in charge of a shooting party. Fox claims he extricated the family by shooting the guard and then taking the family through an underground tunnel, helped by the British, to a medical centre from where they were secretly removed. They hid in Russia for a couple of weeks before travelling a treacherous route through Turkistan.

Then, due to much trouble in India, which had been their intended destination, they travelled through Tibet, where with the aid of the Buddhist monks and at the request of the Dalai Lama, they were guided into China. They are supposed to have ended their flight in Chungking. Fox states that upon his arrival in Chungking he turned the Imperial Family over to the commander of a British gunboat, where they embarked on a trip down river to ….' Tonya paused. 'Oh dear, I can't remember the name of the place. Now would you mind waiting while I go and get the book?'

'Of course…' Juliana exclaimed. 'I think you have done amazingly well to have got this far.'

A minute or so later Tonya was back. 'It was Woosung, which is twelve miles from Shanghai. Fox describes a ship dressed with holiday flags. Perhaps it was Christmas or another religious holiday.'

'Or,' responded Michael, 'more likely they were celebrating the end of the war, in which case it would have been November 1918!'

Tonya took a sharp intake of breath. 'Do you know, I never even thought of that, anyway Fox ends his story with the following line: *"With his code word still ringing in my ears to be repeated to one man at Berlin, to another man in England, another in Japan, and to a dignitary in Italy, the mission I have undertaken shall have been successfully discharged, so far as history and public policy is concerned."*'

As she finished Alex responded, 'It's a clever ending but is any of it true? That's the question we need to ask!' 'One moment,' ordered Michael, 'my understanding is that the Imperial Family's destination was Ceylon, where they landed on an unnamed man-of-war accompanied by a wealthy tea merchant?'

Tonya didn't know what to say and stared blankly at her uncle.

Michael smiled. He had caught her out. 'Well, never mind that for now. What about the other diary in the book Tonya?'

'Well the second diary follows an unknown nobleman's activities. He was once a member of the Tsar's inner circle and curiously he also knows a Baroness B. who is requesting his wife to carry secret messages and convince him to join the Whites in their fight against the Bolsheviks. The Baroness B. plays a major part in both diaries. Anyway he is forced to leave his home with very little money or assurances for his future well-being.'

'After sending his wife away to what he thought would be safety, he learns that she had been shot by the Bolsheviks for being a spy. In his despair he is persuaded to join a group of agents to rescue the Imperial Family. So, assuming the identity of a Bolshevik, and taking a new identity as Alexei Syvorotka, he makes his way to Tobolsk where he lives in close proximity to the Romanovs. There he helps "The Baroness" organise supplies.'

'Who is this Baroness? Do we have a name for her apart from B?' Paul enquired.

'The trouble is she's in disguise but in this diary she goes under the name of Lucie de Clive. That's all I can tell you... Oh yes, except Alexei would have you believe there is something of a love story between him and 'his' Lucie de Clive.'

Tonya glanced at Paul who looked away mildly embarrassed.

She reverted to her notes. 'We then learn about the activities of the guards who were in charge of the family and become acquainted with numerous people who are secretly laying plans to save the Imperial Family. Syvorotka's diary then portrays his life dressed as a Bolshevik and reveals that he and the Baroness, alias Lucie de Clive, are co-operating with an English intelligence team to rescue the family. In the final pages of his diary Syvorotka is wounded and it is unclear whether he survives.'

'Thank you Tonya,' Michael remarked hesitantly. 'Now, I have always believed the story to be fiction but I must say that there are a few bewildering passages in the diaries, not least the description of the Baroness B.'

'Perhaps,' added Paul, 'it's a product of disinformation.'

Tonya didn't agree. 'What could be gained by such a publication?' she challenged. 'Surely no one would be so heartless as to lie about them escaping, knowing they had not!'

Michael interrupted. 'Well if you care to read Judge Sokolov's report there is no doubt that they were murdered. He believed their remains were buried on the outskirts of Ekaterinburg.'

'But the book doesn't try to propagandise anything uncle, except to say that the Tsar and his family were not shot at the Ipatiev House. Even Guy Richards in his book, *Hunt for the Tsar*, says that at its most dubious *Rescuing the Czar* could be a hoax, but at its least dubious, it may turn out to be a Rosetta stone of the Revolution!! A carefully prepared decoding device placed in a time capsule, ready to unscramble all the hieroglyphs the moment the right signal is given!'

Michael smiled at her tenacity. 'That may well end up being the case but what's fascinating to me is if it was simply propaganda why was it placed in the repositories most respected by scholars and historians, libraries and universities? Besides, you would expect plenty of publicity if it was propaganda. But there was no fanfare over its début. *Rescuing the Czar* is a mystery that has yet to be unravelled. As a scholar of Russian history it certainly deserves my... our attention. If we take a look at the aspects related to the publishing of this book we find the introduction was written by a highly respected person, Mr. W.E. Aughinbaugh. He was an instructor in Foreign Trade at New York University and at Columbia University, as well as being a member of the Bar of the Supreme Court of the United States and a respected author of several books on Latin America. Would such a man have risked his reputation by writing an introduction to a book which he knew was full of baloney? No of course not! So he must have believed every word in those diaries. So Tonya....,' Michael pointed his finger at her as he spoke, 'you must do more research if you are to find the truth.'

'Shall I start on the author Mr. James P. Smythe?' Tonya asked feeling confused.

'Well you'll find that very complicated because that was a fictitious name probably dreamt up between two highly respected characters of the period. One was an American businessman called Mr. William Rutledge McGarry and the other was the Russian Consul to San Francisco, a Mr George Sergius Romanovsky. As you are probably already reading Tonya in those books I gave you, they were involved with the publication of *Rescuing the Czar*, which means Mr Aughinbaugh must have discussed the contents of the book with them.'

'So what you're saying is they knew James P. Smythe was a pseudonym!' Tonya confirmed.

'Correct.'

Paul scratched his head. 'Wait a moment, a member of the Bar of the Supreme Court of the United States risking his reputation by writing an introduction to a book when he knew the authors were writing under a pseudonym? Surely he would have known they did not want to reveal their identity because they feared being ridiculed if the story turned out not to be true.'

'Quite, which means bizarrely the story may be true!'

'But I don't understand. If the story was true,' Tonya interrupted, 'why didn't they publish under their own names?'

'Probably they were frightened. People were getting knocked off left right and centre in those days!'

'Okay, so do we just accept that the name James P. Smythe was made up and leave it at that?'

Michael smiled. 'Alright, I'll tell you what I know. When I did my original doctorate I researched this part of history and got caught up with the mystery surrounding that name. Coincidentally, around this time there was a brave Canadian called Joe Boyle. He had already successfully negotiated a treaty with the Bolsheviks over Romania and had managed to rescue the Romanian Queen, her jewels, archives and millions in paper money. If my memory serves me correctly, he worked alongside an American Military Attaché called Captain William Smythe. In fact there were many famous Smythes around at this time, including a Captain Smythe of the *Moldavia*!'

'There was also a Lt. William Smythe on Robert Scott's *Discovery* expedition to the Antarctic in 1901,' Juliana added.

'And how do you know that?' Michael asked, surprised at her outburst. Juliana shrugged. 'I know most things about Kathleen Scott's life. She was someone I looked up to after all!'

Michael shook his head. 'Don't let's deviate! Now, while some believed the story told in *Rescuing the Czar* was true, others believed it to be a get rich quick scheme in the wake of the disappearance of the Russian Imperial Family. The point here is this. There was no proof whatsoever that they were either alive or dead so that is why these stories flourished. But one thing is for sure. They were most certainly either alive or dead!'

'Well I say they were definitely alive,' Tonya ventured, 'because Fox said that all governments planned to issue statements showing that their investigations would conclude that Nicholas was dead. Surely uncle, what he was saying is that somewhere there was a cover up as to exactly what happened.'

'How reliable is this Fox fellow of yours?' Alex asked.

Tonya shuffled her papers, looking for a specific page. 'Well the Baroness states that "Fox" is not his real name, although he is known by that name in the United States. In his diary he states the following:

Maria asked me today if I were any relation to Charles James Fox, whose oratory she claims to greatly admire. When I informed her that I had never met this gentleman her eyes grew very big...

"What ARE you?" she enquired. "Are you an Englishman or a Russian, you CANNOT BE A GERMAN, or ARE YOU AN AMERICAN? Oh I just hope you ARE an American!"

When I informed her that my ancestors had fought besides Kosciusko and Pulaski and that their names might be found on the muster rolls of the First Line Regiments of New York Colony and State along with the names of Goose Van Schaick and Jeremiah Van Rensselaer, she burst her sides with laughter.

"What a family you must have been!" she rippled. 'When a Fox and a Goose may dwell in peace and amity together there is nothing that is not possible for their race!"'

Alex laughed. 'Not that old chestnut! Just as we want to know more about Fox he throws in the word goose! Well we are all on a wild goose chase now.' Alex roared with laughter. Tonya hadn't seen him quite so animated before.

'Maybe he really is a Mr Fox. Besides, I wouldn't believe everything the Baroness 'B' has to say about him. One contender, so Guy Richards informs us, is a certain Charles James Fox, who was the owner of a newspaper called the North China Star, an American broadsheet produced in Tientsin, China. It reported on political and economic issues and supported Sino-American trade. Interestingly, Guy was able to interview the son of Charles James Fox, who provides an insight into the type of man his father was and it would appear that he had all the qualifications needed to get the job done. He was athletic. He spoke several languages and had a great interest in military affairs. He served as a Major in the National Guard of the District of Columbia and had many friends, some in the U.S. Secret Service. His son recalled that his father came into a windfall of money and was able to purchase the newspaper at the end of the summer in 1918 and ...'

'STOP right there!' Michael raised his hand. 'Listen Tonya, it may well be that your Mr Fox is a candidate. But the name is quite common and there could be many other contenders for this position. Besides, why are you searching for a Charles James Fox?'

Tonya looked confused. 'Well, I want to know who he really is!'

Michael banged the table in frustration, which made Alex jump.

'For goodness sake, how many times do you have to be told? IT'S A FALSE NAME! What you should be looking for is the person behind the alias of Fox and that, my dear, will be like looking for a needle in a haystack! If you hadn't suggested that my mother could somehow be involved in all this we wouldn't even be discussing it here. So stop worrying about who Fox is for the moment and concentrate on the Baroness 'B'. I want to know who she really is. Now where's that coffee Giovanni?'

'Michael is right Tonya. If you can find out who "the Baroness" is, then you will stand a much better chance of finding out the real identity of Fox and knowing whether the story told of their escape is true,' Alice added. Tonya sat back, considering what she had said.

'You know,' Alex added, pouring out a brandy for himself and Michael, 'I have always been fascinated by what happened during the Russian revolution. I could never understand how a handful of Bolsheviks managed to take over the largest and richest country in the world?'

'Perhaps I can help,' Paul offered. 'It was a very complicated affair, both politically and economically, and it involved a certain class of problem.'

'Are you sure?' Alex asked. 'I thought THAT happened during the Second World War!' 'Look,' Michael raised his hands in frustration, 'can we please try and stick to one war at a time? Now Alex, I really am too tired to explain it to you. But if you come to my library I'll give you some books to read on how it all transpired.'

Alex sighed. That was always his father's reply. Michael knew his son disliked reading. Well he wasn't going to get away with it this time! It was high time

Alex started developing his intelligence and working things out for himself instead of relying on whatever he was told and believing it to be gospel.

During coffee Tonya spoke of what she had read on the mysterious George Sergius Romanovsky. He was William McGarry's publishing partner, who claimed to be a Duke of Leuchtenburg and a distant cousin to Tsar Nicholas II. Tonya suspected that he was most likely the translator of the second diary. 'Interestingly, he was Consul General for San Francisco between 1917 and 1923. The San Francisco Russian Consulate had jurisdiction over Russian subjects residing in the western states of Arizona, California, Colorado, Idaho, Montana, Nevada, New Mexico, Oregon, Utah, Washington, and Wyoming and all the territories of Hawaii and Alaska.'

'Well that is a convenient position to hold,' Paul added quickly. 'He would naturally have had first hand information as to what transactions were taking place within the Russian community residing in the United States and that puts a very different light on the affair!'

'Does it?' Tonya asked

'Well, can't you see the point you're making? Mr Romanovsky, Duke of Leuchtenburg and self-confessed cousin to the Tsar, would not have risked his reputation by publishing a lie. So the rescue of the Russian Imperial Family must have taken place.'

'Quite!' replied Tonya jubilantly. 'That is exactly my point. This book has to be true and I believe it was published after the family had already escaped and were in safe hiding.'

'Well,' said Alice, 'I hate to pour damp water over your ideas. But that's quite a leap of faith and…'

'I agree with Tonya,' interrupted Alex. 'Mr. Romanovsky could have been instrumental in helping members of the Imperial Family make it across to the U.S. and sending them into hiding before giving them all new identities.'

'Now, Now! Don't let's jump the gun,' interjected Michael. 'We have absolutely no evidence other than this book, that the Tsar and his family survived, let alone made their way to the United States.'

Just as he finished speaking Juliana leaned across and whispered, 'You have to admit it's an intriguing point they've made.'

Michael smiled. 'Maybe, but I'm ready for bed, how about you?'

Juliana agreed 'Yes, I think it's time to wrap this one up.'

'Uncle, what does Leuchtenburg mean in English?' asked Tonya suddenly.

'Light mountain.'

'Are you sure?' Alice queried.

'Of course I am. Mother spoke of it many times.'

'Well, did the Russian consulate have access to personal records and could they have known the whereabouts of the Russian Imperial Family while they were in hiding?' Juliana asked.

Michael glanced at his watch before replying. 'Romanovsky's job would have entailed dealing with all the Russian immigrant problems. This would naturally have necessitated correspondence with Russian consulates, access to photographs, visas and passport files, documents concerning the Russians' savings bank, and various reports and correspondence that related to the changing political situation in Russia. He would have seen legal documents of individuals and papers relating to trade and commerce. Also correspondence relating to the Russian Volunteer Fleet 1914 to 1922 and documents on inheritance matters, as well as material from the Russian Orthodox Church. We know there were thousands of White Russians fleeing Russia via Vladivostok and seeking refuge in the U.S. Many of them ended up in the port of San Francisco. Obviously they were fleeing the Bolsheviks and seeking a new life and would have taken as much personal wealth as possible.'

'But most of their wealth and the income derived from it lay in the Russian motherland. This had all been confiscated by the Bolsheviks. The only way to secure their inherited lands again was to overthrow the new Bolshevik regime and reinstate the Tsar. So while they were in the U.S. the immigrant White Russians were busy, naturally enough, using the opportunity to raise funds for Kolchak, the White Russian general fighting the Bolsheviks, and crucially at this time, winning the war. So there you have it. Now are there any questions before Tonya finishes?'

'Well, contrary to what you might think father, I've been doing my own bit of research. Long before 1917, millions of dollars of Russian gold, as well as much of the personal effects of the Imperial Family, went missing. Secreted out of the country I shouldn't wonder!' Alex sounded pleased with himself.

Michael placed his cup on the saucer slowly. 'And how do you know that?'

'I read your notes of course!'

Michael sat back and folded his arms. He was intrigued by his son's sudden interest.

'Well you may well be right, but Tonya, I'm surprised you haven't mentioned a certain rumour that Mr Romanovsky may have sought a court order granting him a right of administration over the late Tsar's assets.'

'I didn't mention it because I wasn't sure whether he was acting on instructions from the Tsar.'

Alex slapped his knee. 'Ah ha, I was right!' He was delighted that his father was on his side for once. 'But we don't know what actually happened to the Tsar's gold or the beautiful gems and crystals, the state jewels belonging to his wife and daughters gone forever. All we have to go on is that much of the state gold was given to Kolchak for safekeeping. Until it mysteriously disappeared! THEY say it fell into the hands of the Bolsheviks, although they didn't get it all. Someone along the line got very rich indeed! But most went missing. So it must be out there somewhere, just waiting for us to find it!'

Tonya admired Alex's exuberance. 'I suppose you're the one who's going to find it then?'

'Yes of course! I'm not doing all this reading for nothing!' Alex glanced at his father.

'Well Michael?' asked Juliana 'Is what Alex says true? Did the gold go missing and if so where do you think it is?'

Michael took ages to answer, or so it appeared to Tonya. Even Alex yawned as he watched his father pour out another brandy. Paul, who was sensitive, picked up on the long consideration Michael gave to the question. It was as though he was weighing up the souls of dead men. Obviously he was finding it hard to reply.

Michael gave out a weary sigh. 'There was a member of General Wrangel's government who made an inquiry into the whereabouts of a million dollars worth of gold. Later it was reported to have been deposited in a bank in San Francisco. As I understand it the gentleman in question was later killed!'

'Ooh! That's scary,' Tonya hissed.

'Well I'm afraid that's not the whole story. The Grand Duke Alexander added his own twist when he said, "Until this day the participants in the Siberian epic, the Bolsheviks as well as their adversaries, are trying to ascertain the identity of the persons who helped themselves to a portion of the 600 million gold roubles of Kolchak! The Bolsheviks also claimed to have been cheated out of 90 million roubles! Winston Churchill believed that a mysterious deposit was made in one of the San Francisco banks during the summer of 1920 by individuals who spoke English with a foreign accent. But this was not the only mysterious deposit of Russian gold made in foreign banks! French experts also had similar doubts as to the origin of the Russian gold that appeared in Prague, the capital of Czechoslovakia." I'm afraid there are many such claims, all of which are very difficult to prove.'

'I find it a coincidence that this story includes individuals speaking English with a foreign accent. I'm sure I've read that statement somewhere else. I just can't think where?' Juliana responded.

Michael laughed. 'Don't be so surprised that there are people speaking English with a foreign accent in San Francisco. There were hundreds of White Russians, all well educated and most of them spoke English, French and German fluently and you know what? They weren't all spies either!'

Juliana shrugged her shoulders. She hadn't said they were! Whatever was the matter with him? Michael had a habit of dismissing her remarks as though they didn't matter and she wondered why she bothered to say anything at all.

Paul leant across to her and whispered. 'I disagree.... most of them were spies!'

Juliana bit her bottom lip. 'Is there more on the missing Tsarist millions?' She asked tentatively.

Alex rested his elbows on the table. 'Well it was reported after the Bolsheviks had replaced the Provisional Government at the end of 1917. Which means it must have been the Provisional Government that arranged the transfer of...'

'And you're surprised at that are you?' Michael interrupted his son.

Alex knew better than to push the point, even though he didn't share his father's imperialist views.

'To unravel the mysteries around the missing imperial Russian gold one has to study the complex financial arrangements that were put in place at that time. I doubt you are qualified to comment, unless of course you would like to tell us what you have read on the subject so far?' Michael challenged.

Alex gave a nervous laugh before replying. 'We know that American, British and Japanese bankers were all prominent in finding money to finance Kolchak's efforts in Siberia. Vladivostok was the physical hub of the gold for ammunition trade and San Francisco was the magnet for allied support for the White Russian effort. It makes sense therefore that Kolchak's gold would have been shipped in from Vladivostok to San Francisco to be deposited on behalf of London and New York banks as the rifles and machine guns were channelled through the port by the Remmington Arms company.'

'Remmington, that's a coincidence!' responded Paul. 'Sidney Reilly was involved with that company.'

'Reilly...?' Alice repeated.

'Yes, surely you remember him, the master spy?'

Michael suddenly clapped his hands. 'Right, that's quite enough for one evening. Paul can tell us all about Reilly another time. Now Tonya, do you mind wrapping up, I want to call it a night!' Tonya looked down at her notes. She had quite forgotten where she was until Paul kindly pointed to the paragraph. 'Okay so....it looks as though Alex is right because from what I have read, Romanovsky was at the centre of activity with regard to financing the White Russian cause and it was through his contacts, the Russian Ambassador and the Russia Financial Attaché, that he managed a complex web of financial deals involving enormous amounts of gold from the Tsarist regime. So I'll end on this question. Is it just a coincidence that one of the men responsible for publishing the book was also at the heart of plans to reinstate the monarchy to Russia?'

'Very good Tonya, and there we must leave it! But just before we do, I want to remind you all not to forget the other important Russians on the scene at the time. For example Boris Brasol who was a great friend of Henry Ford. I'm currently writing up a paper on him with regard to *The Protocols of Zion*. Interestingly he was also a friend of the Grand Duke Kyrril. He it was who planned to take the Russian throne after the Tsar had been removed in 1917. So Romanovsky may well have been at the centre of a plan to reinstate a Romanov on the throne of Russia. But first the Tsar and his family had to be rescued. Yet I am sure this does not tell the whole story!'

Michael tapped the book as he spoke. 'As to why Romanovsky would wish to publish a story about the Tsar and his family if they had not been rescued is beyond me since his reputation would have been ruined if their bodies had been discovered.'

'Well it looks as though there is only one conclusion you can come to then!'

They all thought for a moment before Paul asked what that conclusion was.

Juliana smiled at the simplicity of her reply. 'THEY KNEW THE BODIES WOULD NOT BE FOUND!'

Michael pushed the brandy glass away from him, suddenly feeling dizzy. 'Do you realise what you are saying my dear?' he asked, squinting at the light.

Juliana twiddled her pencil before answering. 'Yes, the implication is that they KNEW the Tsar and his family were ALIVE because they had ALREADY rescued them and hidden them somewhere in San Francisco.'

'GOOD HEAVENS! Is that really the way you see it?' enquired Paul, 'but what about those eyewitness accounts and statements confirming the execution?'

Alex stretched out his long legs under the table before responding. 'Well from what I have seen they all contradict each other. If a deal was done we are going to have to find a way of proving it. Coming up with yet another theory just won't do. We have got to find the lost gold!'

Chapter Thirteen   The Kaisers letter

The following morning Michael rose, nursing a very nasty hangover.

'Tut! Tut! This won't do,' Juliana remarked. 'Now eat a raw egg and drink some black coffee,' she had instructed, but Michael chose to have an English breakfast instead, fried eggs and bacon. Later when Juliana joined him she had a pile of newspaper cuttings in her hand. 'Here, I saved these for you. I think you will find them interesting.'

Michael glanced up. 'Thank you,' he replied and carried on eating. That was most unlike him Juliana thought as she went back to her studio. But Michael had other things on his mind. Today he was going to open that cedar box, the one that had caused Alice so much trouble. Then he was going to sort out the rest of his mother's books and papers. Considering he was nursing the hangover from hell he felt surprisingly motivated. You can't beat an English breakfast for getting rid of a hangover! That's what the British Empire was built on after all. Michael felt very pleased with himself. He had got the whole family working on 'the problem of Maria' as Alice had called it and very soon he expected results.

Hurriedly he finished his breakfast and made his way to the library, where he bumped into Alice. 'Ah there you are. That was good timing!' she responded as they both walked into the library and shut the door. 'Right, I'll make a start on this box over here then.' Carefully opening it, she pulled out a few books. 'Now where shall I put these?'

Michael looked up. 'Over there,' he pointed, 'just lay them on the table in the corner. We'll look at them later.'

Alice watched as Michael carefully placed the cedar box on top of his desk. 'For goodness sake,' she warned, walking over to the desk. 'Do be careful! We don't want any accidents. Let's open the windows first.' Michael smiled. 'I suppose you had better.'

He added carefully opening the box and removing a zinc phial. He peered at it for a moment, and pulled a face. 'Now what shall I do?'

'See if the ends twist off.'

Michael twisted the end very slowly. 'Ugh! It's not moving.'

'Try the other end then.'

'No, it won't budge.'

'Okay, give it to me.' Alice took the phial in her hand and closed her eyes for a moment. 'Oh dear, it really doesn't want to be opened.'

Michael shook his head. 'Doesn't look like it.

'I know! I must hold it with both hands.'

'Oh, you mean the warmth, clever you!'

Alice smiled. 'Not to mention the magic words'

'What magic words?'

Alice winked, 'As if you don't know indeed!'

A moment later Michael heard her whisper something. Suddenly there was a snap and the zinc phial split open.

'Quick, let me see what's in it.' Michael demanded.

Alice handed him the phial and at once he saw it was empty. 'There's nothing in here!'

'Look again Michael, A little more carefully this time.'

He peered into the recess of the file. 'There's nothing here at all, just a bit of white powder or something? I don't know what it is.'

'Don't get angry Michael. There's really no point,' Alice chided. 'Give me the phial. I'll take it back to my room and have a look at it later. Now let's get on with these boxes.'

Michael started to pull out the books. He barely gave them a second look, until he came across a couple of his mother's diaries. These he put to one side, intending to look at them later. Then he picked up an old scrapbook, opened it and decided to look at that later too. Towards the bottom he came across a carefully wrapped pile of old letters. They were tied with a green and lilac ribbon, which Michael recognised as two of his mother's favourite colours. He carefully untied the bow and looked at one of the letters. It was dated 1928 and addressed to the Baroness Brandenberg.

My Dear Maria,

I would be grateful if you could cast your eyes over W's letter. He requested that I write to you first for any comments you may have with regard to the facts or the arguments he states here. Of course at some stage we will need to consider how we ensure that this information remains available for those who will require it in the future.......History may have to be rewritten....

Michael sighed. It was impossible to read further because it had been torn in half. What's more, he didn't recognise the handwriting. 'Look at these,' he said, waving them in his hands. 'A right mess! I wonder she bothered to keep them after so many crossings out and tearing up.'

Alice took the first letter and studied the sheet of paper. 'Give me all of them for a moment.'

Intrigued, Michael handed her the whole pile, including the untied ribbon.

Alice smiled and held it up to the light, just as she had seen Maria do on many occasions. 'You see Michael, this ribbon has entwined silver and gold thread running thought it.' 'So?'

'That tells me everything I need to know! Now let's see what we have here.' Alice started to sift through the letters. She came across a blank piece of paper and then another and another.

Michael burst out laughing. 'See what I mean. What a mad world this is!'

Alice looked up. 'Patience is a virtue Michael. You should have realised...' She paused and held the paper up to the light again. 'Just as I thought, this has been written with magic ink. I think I may just be able to make out the signature.' She added spitting on her finger.

Michael followed her to the French windows, where they stood together peering up at the sunlight through the paper.

'Ah, here we are! It's signed by "K".'

Michael shrugged his shoulders. 'Well can you read it out to me?'

Alice cleared her throat. 'Yes. 'I believe that every statesman will admit that IF it were KNOWN generally among the old RUSSIAN people that there was an HEIR to the Throne ALIVE, and capable of being brought to Moscow, the present regime would be overthrown by a popular uprising. So there you are. That's proof isn't it?'

'Proof of what exactly?'

'The powers that be actually want us to know the truth.'

Michael sneered. 'Do they? We didn't find anything in the zinc phial except powder.'

Alice smiled. 'Ah yes, talcum powder.'

Michael was aghast, 'Talcum powder?'

'No! I have no idea what the powder is or what it was used for but we will find out.'

Alice raised the paper up to the light. 'Gracious! God does move in mysterious ways. I can barely believe what I am reading. Just listen to this.'

'No. I've heard quite enough.' Michael walked back to the middle of the room. 'I don't want to disappoint you Alice but there is nothing new in what you are reading. It's all been said before, ever since the bodies went missing in 1918.'

Alice followed him in and watched in amusement as he started to clear another tea chest. One minute he was acting like a little boy opening his Christmas presents, the next he was really grumpy.

'Blank paper indeed, I wonder why she bothered to put these letters in so haphazardly. They could have so easily been lost.'

Alice gave a wry smile. 'Or just not found!'

'What do you mean?'

'Well, by being locked in here they've been kept safe and not burnt like the other papers.'

Michael looked up. 'You're not suggesting she put them here for....,' he trailed off.

Alice shook her finger at him. 'Remember, your mother was a professional!'

'But that suggests she knew the caravan was going to burn up.'

'Maybe maybe not, I like to think she was just being her usual cautious self and covering her tracks.'

Michael grunted disapprovingly as he poked around in the tea chest.

'At last something of value, a first edition of *The Old Russian Fairy Tales*.'

Alice sat down and then noticed that a neatly folded paper had dropped out. She quickly picked it up. 'GOOD HEAVENS! It's waxy!'

'Be careful Alice!'

Alice frowned. 'I can't read it anyway,' she added, getting to her feet with some difficulty and still clutching the paper.

'I suppose you're going to tell me it's full of that hidden writing again.'

Alice shook her head.

'It might help if you bring it over here. Michael suggested as she followed him towards the French windows for a second time. Alice held the letter up so the light shone through it. 'So much of it has been corrected. It's a real mess but I can just make out a K, A, something. Anyway let me read what I can.'

'When I met Nicholas and his wife at Marseilles in 1923 we naturally did not discuss so painful a subject as the "fiction" of the Czar's murder, since our meeting was quite accidental and brief. As my wife and I plodded slowly up the steep incline to the Basilique de Notre Dame de la Garde, after alighting from the escalier, far down below us a tall, soldierly man with a grey pointed beard strode slowly down, with a lady gowned in black clinging tightly to his arm.'

Alice suddenly stopped.

'Is that all?' Michael asked.

'No, there is much more but it's impossible for me to read'

'Nicholas, the Tsar?' Michael queried 'But he wasn't THAT tall.'

'No he certainly was not. Perhaps they're speaking of the Grand Duke Nicholas? He was tall and had a pointed beard.'

Michael pondered over the letter. 'K. A. G? Mother hasn't made things very easy for me!'

'K.A.G??'

'Yes, I keep finding notes to mother from him, they were even in a book she gave Tonya but I don't know his bloody name. It's so frustrating!'

Alice smiled. 'No point in getting angry. It won't help.'

Michael stood up in frustration. 'Come on, it must be time for a coffee.'

'Yes alright, we are nearly done here, just a moment.' Alice replied lifting the last book out. Underneath she found one of Maria's translations and as usual there were all sorts of corrections and underlining to the manuscript. She studied it for a moment before handing it to Michael. 'Here, look at this, you'll recognise the text since it was later published in Guy Richard's book *The Hunt for the Czar.*

'Good Heavens!' Michael exclaimed, taking the manuscript. 'Mother has written a note beside it. Always helpful if only I could read it!'

'Do you want me to read it? I'm quite familiar with her writing.'

Michael squinted. 'No, I can manage thanks.

Gd....idea otse... sme my tk itz a frgry! The foregoing 'C.J.F.' has been inked over the original pencilled note to make certain of its preservation.

Michael angrily handed the letter back to her. 'C.J.F. More blasted initials!'

'Well this one is easy Michael! C.J.F. must stand for Charles James Fox surely?'

Michael rubbed his forehead. 'Except that was not his real name!'

'It's frustrating I know but I'm sure we'll get to the bottom of it sooner or later. Give it here. I might be able to shed some light on it. Don't forget I worked with your mother on much of this stuff over the years.'

Michael was grateful as he waited for Alice to finish. A moment later she looked up.

'That was quick. Have you read it all?'

'Yes. The upshot of all this is that someone – who, I don't know – is trying to authenticate some letters written to FOX by both the Kaiser and the Tsar. They seem convinced that the signatures are right. There is some discussion about FOX's wellbeing, but that's clearly in Maria's hand. She wants confirmation that he is being looked after. Anyway, this is what the letter from the Kaiser says:

My dear Fox,

I am profoundly pleased to learn that G--- has so good an opinion of my efforts in that matter. It strikes me with such eminent support you cannot fail to fulfil your arduous task with the very best of results.

Pense a bien

Wilhelm.'

'So, Fox not only has mother's blessing but the Kaiser's too. I must tell Tonya and Juliana, they will be pleased.'

'There's something I haven't told you,' Alice admitted, tapping the paper.

Michael smiled, 'Out with it then.'

'I recognise it as part of a letter from Mr William Rutledge McGarry, dated 22nd November 1920. It speaks of England having Nicholas in India, H.G. Wells in Moscow and the Bolsheviki bottled in a treaty. It asks what she, meaning England, intends to do with the prisoners of Tobolsk. I have not heard whether they escaped via Los Angeles or are still marooned in the Monnadnock.'

'Was H.G. Wells in Moscow at that time?'

'Yes, I believe he was.'

'So, if he is right about Wells, why shouldn't he be right about the Tsar hiding in India?'

Chapter Fourteen　　　　William Rutledge McGarry

Just before lunch Juliana found the old newspaper clippings lying haphazardly on the table. Well they can't stay here she thought, gathering them up carefully. Poor Michael, he really was missing his mother. Juliana wished she could help; he had never wanted to talk much about his feelings or about his mother but Alice had let one or two things slip recently. As she gathered up the cuttings she wondered why so many articles were about Dr Armgaard Karl Graves. Surely he must have been important to her Maria, even part of her secret? Maria must have suspected that someone would come looking for these cuttings and this was her way of keeping them safe. Ah! So that's why the caravan had been set alight. It was a decoy! But what was to fear from Maria writing her memoirs? As she glanced across to where the caravan had been, her emotions got the better of her and they were made worse when she thought of Maria's reaction to the burnt out caravan. Honestly it was just too dreadful to contemplate.

Juliana poured herself a cup of black coffee and sat down. Then she glimpsed a reflection in the window and took a second look. Who was that? Someone was sitting opposite her! Her cup rattled loudly on its saucer as she jumped up out of shock. After a bone chilling moment she dared stare at the space next to the chair from where she had risen. Of course there was no one there! Or was there? Juliana daren't move her head so she looked out of the corner of her eyes. Yes! There was definitely a woman seated, an older, plump woman. 'MARIA?' she asked hesitantly.

　'Juliana,' the voice called out in a low, softly melodic tone. Juliana sat down, her mouth dry with fear. A gust of wind directed the long white muslin curtains briefly across her face. As Juliana peeled it back she heard the words she would later repeat to her sceptical husband: 'I am who you think I am dear.. dear.. Juliana! I kept my papers safe for the sake of history AND for the sake of Michael's inheritance.' Juliana wiped her sweaty hands on her dungarees. She was sure she could still see Maria in the reflection but when the room started to warm up, she knew she had gone. A sudden knock on the door made her jump. Who on earth could that be she wondered opening the door so abruptly that Alice practically fell into her arms!

'Good heavens, you look as though you have seen a ...' Juliana grabbed her. 'Quick, come in and shut the door.'

'Why, whatever is the matter with you?'

'Maria was here a moment ago. She was sitting in that chair. I saw her reflection.'

'Well I'm not at all surprised! Maria said she would visit if it were at all possible! You are lucky to have seen her. Did she say anything interesting?'

Juliana laughed hysterically. 'Not really. She said something about being who she is and that she had kept her papers safe!'

'Whatever do you mean dear and what's that in your hand? Is that what has upset you so?'

Juliana looked down at what she was holding, screamed, and dropped it. 'I don't know where that came from. I've never seen it before!'

Alice picked it up. 'Well let's have a look shall we? Ah! It's an advert for a book, *The Secrets of the German War Office* by Armgaard Karl Graves, late spy to the German government. But where did it come from?'

'I've never seen this before. I'm sure I have no idea where....'

Alice smiled. 'Well then, it's as clear as the clay on your face! Maria must have left it with you and....' Alice trailed off, noticing that Juliana looked pale. 'Do you want me to stay until you feel better?'

'No, thank you. I'm feeling fine.'

Alice gave her a concerned look.

'No, really I am. Anyway what was it you called in for?'

'Dear me now, it's quite slipped my mind, must be my age!'

Juliana smiled. 'Why don't I put some fresh coffee on? It might help you remember!'

Alice shook her head. 'Thank you but I think I'll have some rest.'

After she had left Juliana decided to go into town and order a copy of *The Secrets of the German War Office*.

> Crown 8vo.   Cloth **2/6** net & Picture wrapper **1/-** net.
>
> # THE SECRETS OF THE GERMAN WAR OFFICE
>
> ### By ARMGAARD KARL GRAVES
>
> *Late Spy to the German Government.*
>
> ---
>
> **Unprecedented and astounding revelations of the inner workings of the German Secret Service Department. Dr. Graves, who recently was imprisoned by us for Spying at Rosyth, tells his tale without concealment or hesitation from the day when he entered the "spy school" at Berlin to the day when he finally left the service in disgust. From the first page—a scene at question-time in the English Parliament—to the end of the story the interest and excitement never flags, the most extravagant inventions of fiction are put to shame by some of the actual events of which the author writes. At any time it would have attracted universal attention; now its interest is immense. The disclosures of the hidden forces of German politics and secret diplomacy reveal the sleepless eye of their war machine and show the subterranean information by which Wilhelmstrasse endeavoured to remake the political map of Europe.**

* * *

Back in her room, Alice took a look at the cedar box and the mysterious zinc phial. At the very least she had expected to find diamonds. But whatever had been in there had succumbed to the ravages of time. All that was left was a sticky, sweet smelling white powder. As evening drew in Alice lit a couple of candles and placed them on her dressing table. She said a prayer and picked up the phial. Its contents might have disappeared but there was still a remote possibility that she could find out what had been in there. After saying a prayer she held the phial close to her and watched the candles flicker.

Good! She had evidence that the vibrations were changing in the room. She could now tune into the divine power. Psychic music was what she needed to hear. She listened carefully. At first it played quietly. So quietly she could hardly hear it at all. Gradually it grew louder until she could discern the tune. It was Hungarian. Yes, she was quite sure of that. A Hungarian Rhapsody, just right for the occasion! Now Alice must wait for the other sign that told her she was fully tuned in. Then she would be able to ask who the cedar box and zinc phial had belonged to and what their meaning was. Alice was just getting into her stride when the gong for dinner annoyingly interrupted her. Before leaving she said a prayer and extinguished the candles. Then she carefully lifted the zinc phial and placed it back in the box before putting it under her bed.

At dinner Michael made an announcement. 'I've a suggestion to make. From now on we should meet in my library rather than having long discussions over the dinner table.' Juliana watched him yawn before asking why they couldn't talk about it over dinner. He replied that dinner was a social occasion and that it wasn't right for them to be drinking and eating while they were in serious discussion about his mother's life. Juliana understood. He didn't want the alcohol disturbing his thought process and quite right too!

Alice smiled to herself. She knew exactly why Michael had suggested the library. It was to do with the power of the icon and the crystal that they had placed there together.

From now on, Michael added, they would meet on Tuesdays or Thursdays at two in the afternoon. As the meal drew to a close Michael spoke about the mysterious letters from the Tsar and the Kaiser that appeared to congratulate Fox for the completion of his mission. He also explained about the letter they had found from K.A.G. to his mother.

'If only we knew Fox's true identity life would be so much easier,' Michael added.

Juliana laughed. 'A mission can't stay secret if people admit to being part of it, can it?'

Michael didn't bother replying. Instead he poured himself a large brandy.

Giovanni said that secrets were made to be broken and that surely someone would have wanted to tell the story. At that, they all laughed because that someone of course was the Baroness herself. Maria!

Juliana reminded him that it was not secrets but promises that were made to be broken! But if this was an evening of honest speaking Juliana was careful not to mention her vision of Maria or the newspaper cuttings she had found on Dr Armgaard Karl Graves. Nor did Alice or Michael divulge the mysterious contents of the cedar box. Instead Paul became surprisingly vocal about Sidney Reilly and the Lockhart plot. He was sure that there was more to the story than met the eye. It may have even been connected to a plan to rescue the Tsar since it took place about the same time. He said no one had ever linked the two stories together. Michael agreed that Paul had raised an interesting point and it reminded him that he wanted to ask Tonya something.

'Have you read anything interesting about Mr McGarry and his involvement with *Rescuing the Czar*?'

'Yes. Those who believed the Tsar and his family had not been rescued believe the book was written to achieve a number of objectives.'

'Which were?' Michael asked.

'Firstly to arouse hopes that the Tsar was alive in order to give his supporters a figure to rally behind. Secondly to push for a freeze on Tsarist funds in the U.S. so they were not seized by the new Bolshevik regime and thirdly to lay the groundwork for imperial pretenders! However, many who knew McGarry and Romanovsky had no doubt that the story was true. The Tsar and his family had been rescued but were obliged, for reasons of honour and security, to stay submerged until the right time.'

'And of course that right time never came,' Michael interrupted. 'So he could never disclose his whereabouts or that of his wife and children. It was a state secret to be locked in the archives forever. And that's why McGarry came to the conclusion that the

"Rescinded" publication of *Rescuing the Czar,* including the authentic diary of Fox, was the only way to tell the story without invoking the fury of, if not prosecution by, one or more sovereign states. He was a clever man because he knew the book would remain in the archives and in libraries around the world and that it would be rediscovered when the time was right by future generations interested in history.'

'A "sovereign state" doesn't have to be a country, it can be a religious organisation or a charitable society,' added Paul.

Alex smiled. 'Are you saying the Vatican was involved in saving the Romanovs then?'

'No I'm not, but if they were it would have been the most unpublicised ecumenical act by the Holy See on behalf of the Russian Orthodox Church.'

Michael sighed. 'Hmm, it's interesting to hear all your points of view. Clearly there's more to McGarry and Romanovsky than first meets the eye. Romanovsky's motivation for promoting the book is easily understood; after all, he was a Russian who was related to the Tsar and would have hated the revolution and all it stood for. But what was McGarry's motivation Tonya, Any ideas?'

'Well we know he was a narrator of British war films and apparently he worked for British war propaganda efforts in America under the direction of Sir William Wiseman, head of British Intelligence in the U.S. He was also a confidant of Colonel House, President Woodrow Wilson's Secretary of State and wrote a book called *Berlin to Baghdad*, the story of the Kaiser's railroad in 1914. He was wealthy, with homes in New York and San Francisco, and he was intimately involved with the publication of....'

'Ah now,' Alex interrupted. 'You've reminded me of a point I wanted to make the other night. *Rescuing the Czar* was published in 1919 under the name of *The Prisoners of Tobolsk*. Well that's very early if you think that the rescue would have occurred sometime in July 1918 and the journey to India must have taken at least six months. I mean that doesn't leave much time for McGarry to get the book published.'

Michael agreed. 'That's a good point. It can take years to get a book to market.'

Alex laughed.

'What's so funny?'

'Well you said we shouldn't discuss this over dinner and here we are doing just that. Anyway,' Alex added, 'I can't believe McGarry became so rich or popular from writing about a train journey from Berlin to Baghdad just as his country was about to go to war with Germany!'

'Actually the U.S didn't enter the war till much later. Now, if you're going to partake in this conversation, please make an effort to get your facts right.'

'Well surely his closeness to the German Kaiser is relevant if you believe the Kaiser helped the Imperial Family to escape?' Tonya offered. 'Anyway,' she added, 'I've got something you might find interesting uncle.'

'What is it?'

'The full account of how the Fox letters were discovered. If you like I can read it out now?'

'I suppose you might as well then.'

'Not so long ago, Guy Richards, the man who wrote *Hunt For The Czar,* interviewed a New York private investigator with an army background. He asked that Guy withhold his name, although he said he would be glad to identify himself and be available for any official investigation. Guy calls him Joseph Stapleton but of course that's not his real name!'

'Michael sighed loudly, 'Another bloody alias!'

Tonya opened the book containing the notes she had made. 'He relates a story told to him by Joseph and it goes like this. One day in 1954 a retired colonel from Army Engineers called at Joseph's house in New York saying he hadn't long to live and would like to pass over some important documents for safekeeping. After the colonel had passed away a short time later Joseph sorted through the documents. Amazingly he found two letters, apparently from two emperors, Tsar Nicholas II and Kaiser Wilhelm II. He called them the "My Dear Fox" letters. They were on blueprints and attached were copies of two letters addressed to a certain Mr Boris Brasol who.....'

'Stop right there!' Michael interrupted. 'I know all about Boris Brasol. He was the former prosecuting attorney for Nicholas II and the Russian representative on the Inter-allied Conference. He died around 1963 aged seventy three. During his busy career he ran The Russian National Society in America, which favoured the restoration of the Russian monarchy under the Tsar's cousin the Grand Duke Kirrill Vladimirovich. I believe he also had links with the Russian Legitimist Monarchist Union. As it so happens, I'm writing a paper about him and his friendship with Henry Ford and a publication called *The Protocols of Zion*. Tonya smiled. 'May I continue uncle?' Michael nodded as he scribbled himself a reminder. 'Anyway, Joseph Stapleton decided it was good manners to contact Mr Brasol about the file. Joseph says he was impressed with what he called one of the most delightful and cultivated persons he had ever met! However when Mr Brasol saw what Joseph had, he asked to have the material back but when they came to the Fox letters Joseph hung onto them. He then asked Mr Brasol if he thought they were really from the Kaiser and the Tsar. Mr Brasol said that one day they would prove to be "of great historical importance". Then Joseph asked who the other letters were from. Mr Brasol said he could not say because it was a matter of honour. He said he had lost touch with the man who sent him the "Fox" blue prints. Later it was discovered that it was William McGarry who had sent the letters. He had left his initials WRM at the bottom of the letter to Mr Brasol, dated March 16th. The letter is fascinating. I'll read it to you now.

What would you say if I told you there was a document in existence dated 6th January 1919 signed NICOLAS, thanking someone for "CONSUMMATING MY ESCAPE?" As a student of literature you might say it could be Nicholas Nickleby, but it isn't. I am enclosing you a blueprint in strictest confidence as an off-set to this Sokolov invention. The inference is permissible that Fox was known to both; and the G-' above referred to could easily be George V or Galitzin and the arduous task Fox had in hand, the result of which Wilhelm advised him to think for the best in executing, could certainly NOT HAVE BEEN TO ALLOW THE BOLSHEVIKI TO ASSASSINATE the Kaiser's blood kin and thus prepare the way for a general collapse of MONARCHY. And if Lenin and Trotsky were the Kaiser's agents, the CZAR'S SAFETY must have been CERTAIN, when the treaty of Brest-Litovsk was signed or both Trotsky and Lenin would have been shot by the victorious Germans, who regarded the Empress with the liveliest feelings of affection. Let me have your criticism of this phase of the question; for some day I may imitate Victor Hugo's Man in the Iron Mask and startle my countrymen.'
   Sincerely Yours,'

Tonya looked up ' Of course Victor Hugo did not write *The Man in the Iron Mask*, Alexander Dumas did, but some have attributed this work to him, you know the way some say that Shakespeare didn't write his plays and attribute his work to Sir Francis Bacon.'

'Let me take a look at that,' Michael demanded. Tonya handed across the book and he studied the photograph of the letter. 'What a coincidence this is, Tonya, because as I mentioned earlier, Alice and I found the same letter in mother's belongings.'

'So you think these letters are authentic?'

Michael studied the letter a moment longer before handing it over to Alice.

'I simply can't say. Clearly Mr Brasol was a highly respected man who appears to have known Fox. These letters undoubtedly support the story of Fox and his mission to save the Imperial Family but more to the point they confirm that my mother was somehow involved.'

'But what does he mean by *"Let me have your criticism of this phase of the question, for some day I may imitate Victor Hugo's Man in the Iron Mask and startle my countrymen?"*

'Do you know Alice,' Juliana replied, 'I was just thinking the same. Iron Mask? Perhaps the Tsar and his family were disguised in masks when they escaped!'

Michael smiled broadly.

'What's so funny?' Juliana asked. 'Didn't you know that masks were being made for the casualties of war?'

'Actually, I hadn't given it much thought but I'm surprised you have!' Michael continued, smiling.

'Well you shouldn't be. I AM A SCULPTRESS and one of the pioneers of mask making was a sculptress too and before you ask, yes, it *is* Kathleen Scott. She worked with that great man, Sir Harold Gillies, at the London General Hospital. She called it the tin noses shop and thought men without noses were very beautiful. Just like antique marbles!'

Michael sighed again. 'Well you may have a point. The Tsar and his family could have been disguised and if their faces were hidden under masks, say aboard a hospital ship, well that would be a very safe disguise indeed. I mean who would be brave enough to raise a mask when there was a possibility of revealing the blown up face of a war veteran?'

Juliana grimaced. 'Please don't be quite so graphic.'

'Well now, you have surprised me. You haven't mentioned your favourite *iron* word. Perhaps they had iron crutches!' he added sarcastically.

'Iron...?' Alex enquired, 'Why are we talking about iron?'

'Because if you had been listening at all, you would have realised that certain words have other meanings, especially between secret agents.'

'Oh I see! That is why you laughed at my mask theory then?' Juliana taunted.

'Certainly not, anyway I didn't laugh, I just think it is ludicrous to suggest the Imperial Family of Russia were walking around with masks on for the rest of their lives. Clearly you haven't thought your theory through.'

'Well! I didn't say for the rest of their lives!!' Juliana responded angrily.

Michael pulled a face. 'Look, all I'm doing is agreeing with what you said days ago. *Iron* may have been another of those favoured words used between agents at the time. Remember even mother described herself as having an iron will, and proud that her nature was made of iron!'

'Yes, like the word vagabonding...' Juliana responded quickly.

'Oh yes...' agreed Paul. 'All the best spies used that word. They say it in all of their memoirs. Of course they weren't really vagabonding they were off on secret missions. They just told their nearest and dearest that's what they were doing!'

'How very interesting,' Michael responded sarcastically. 'But I'm quite sure that when Henry Ford and Thomas Edison said they were going vagabonding they meant it and went vagabonding. Unless of course you're suggesting they were SPIES as well!!'

This time it was Juliana's turn to laugh. 'Who would ever suggest such a thing about the great peace loving Henry Ford? But then I suppose if you were a successful agent no one would ever know would they? I mean Kathleen Scott and Isadora Duncan definitely went vagabonding together. Kathleen enjoyed vagabonding so much that all through her life she would just take off at the drop of hat! In fact some people in society where quite shocked that she should behave in such a manner but then she was no ordinary woman!'

'People were so adventurous in those days,' Paul agreed. 'Take Sidney Reilly and Robert Bruce Lockhart, for example. They went vagabonding as well. In fact I wouldn't be at all surprised to find out that Mr McGarry, Mr. Romanovsky, Charles James Fox, and Boris Brasol all went vagabonding together!' Tonya nudged him gently. 'Perhaps we should take ourselves off vagabonding too?' she suggested.

'ENOUGH of this RIDICULOUS VAGABONDING...!' Michael shouted. 'I want to continue with what I was saying about the IRON word. It might be that it was a recognition symbol, a key for people who knew and worked with each other. So when in 1921 Gorky called his secretary an "iron woman", who was he communicating with and why?'

'This is absurd Michael,' Juliana added. 'Why are we talking about Gorky? He was a socialist. Surely he would not have been interested in saving the Imperial Family?'

'No one is saying that he did, mother!' Alex protested.

Michael slammed his fist on the table. 'LOOK! Can we stick to the subject, otherwise I'm calling an end to it.''

'So, I'll continue if I may?' responded Tonya, 'but first can I ask you a question? Is Mr McGarry making some kind of link between *The Man in the Iron Mask* and the tale of the Romanov rescue?'

Michael rubbed his chin, making a grizzly scratching noise. 'I don't know.'

Silence ensued as a loud ticking clock chimed the hour. If Michael didn't know, who did? Juliana wondered.

Michael cleared his throat loudly. 'Well now. *The Man in the Iron Mask* by Alexander Dumas has always been a bit of a mystery. Some say it was a true story. At the very heart of the drama lies the unknown identity of the man hidden beneath an iron mask that was permanently welded to his face. He was taken to the fortress at Pignerol in 1679 and locked up at the Château d'If. Finally he was transferred to the Bastille, where he died in 1703. Some say the prisoner taken to the Chateau was the King of France, others say it was his unknown twin brother.'

'Well what about Gorky's iron woman? What has she to do with the Romanov rescue?' Alex enquired.

Michael appeared indignant. 'I don't believe I have ever suggested that SHE was involved in a plan to rescue the Russian Imperial Family.'

'Ah yes, but you just said there could be a link between Gorky's secretary and the *Man in the Iron Mask*. Perhaps SHE, whoever SHE happens to be, was the mysterious Baroness B?'

Michael thought he detected an edge of sarcasm in Alex's voice. 'Honestly, I have no idea what you are getting at son. What I will say, is the link that you speak of is rather tenuous! Now shall we get back to the facts?'

Juliana smiled 'Those letters are mysterious and so is the man who sent them, Mr McGarry. Perhaps he is our secret agent Fox? He's a very agile individual and from what Tonya says he had plenty of contact with the Germans and the Kaiser!'

Alex shook his head. 'No you are wrong. If Mr McGarry was Fox he wouldn't need to ask Mr Brasol for his opinion on letters written by the Tsar and Kaiser to himself, now would he?'

'Or,' Michael added, 'It's a clever ploy by McGarry to shift the focus away from him!'

'But even if McGarry wasn't Fox he could still have been a member of the rescue team.' Juliana added as Tonya continued from where she had left off.

'Now I want to get to another letter that McGarry wrote in May 1928. Astonishingly, it describes a meeting between him and Nicholas in Marseilles in 1923, five years after the disappearance of the Imperial Family in 1918. This is what he wrote.'

'When I met Nicholas and his wife at Marseilles in 1923, we naturally did not discuss so painful a subject (the "fiction" of the Czar's murder mentioned earlier in the letter), as our meeting was quite accidental and brief. As my wife and I plodded slowly up the steep incline to the Basilique de Notre Dame de la Garde, after alighting from the escalier far down below us, a tall, soldierly man with a grey pointed beard strode slowly down with a lady gowned in black clinging tightly to his arm. At a distance of about twenty feet from me, they stopped abruptly and gazed at me momentarily. As I drew closer, he spoke to me in French. His voice sounded like the voice one sometimes hears in dreams when, like a flash, the past flits by and clothes the vision with the pageantry of years.

"Ah! Mon vieux!" (My dear chap), he exclaimed, extending his hand. "Comment vas-tu? Je suis enchanté de te voir.". (How are you? I'm delighted to see you.)

We clasped hands. ' Merci, mon cher, c'est un bonheur de te revoir. Comme tu es pale! Qu'est-ce qu'il y a?'(Thank you, my dear friend, it's good to see you again. You look pale. What's the trouble?) I replied.

"Je ne me sens pas bien" (I don't feel very well), he rejoined as his eyes wandered off in the direction of the Château D'If.'

'STOP PLEASE!' Michael shouted. 'I've heard enough.'

'Well it's important uncle. He mentions the Château D'If and it just can't be a coincidence. Because that's the place where the Man in the Iron Mask was imprisoned and ......'

'Yes, yes, yes!' Michael responded adamantly. 'How many more times do we have to hear this? I tell you it doesn't MEAN anything. It's a red herring. Now just let it go. PLEASE!'

Tonya placed the book loudly on the table and slumped back into the chair.

Sensing her discomfort Paul interjected. 'Come on, let's hear it for Tonya. She's done a brilliant job!'

'Yes indeed.' Juliana agreed, while Alice clapped. Tonya bowed her head graciously. 'So...Tonya, thank you,' Paul added sincerely. 'Now don't get angry if I add something else... towards the end of the letter that you read out. McGarry uses the word Xenophon.' Paul paused, waiting for a reaction, but none came. Instead a long sigh from Michael prompted him to continue.

'Now strangely enough there was an American agent called Kalamatiano Xenophon. He was involved with Sidney Reilly in an audacious mission that had a disastrous outcome. It was called the *Lockhart Plot.* I don't know exactly what Kalamatiano Xenophon was doing on July 17th 1918 but I can tell you that during that year he was caught and jailed for three years. During that time he was reportedly shot dead but it wasn't true. He emerged via a food for prisoners deal negotiated between the U.S.A and the Bolsheviks. Why am I telling you all this? Well, I think McGarry is hinting at something by including this unusual name, Xenophon. May I suggest that he is telling us that the secret agent Kalamatiano was part of the mission to rescue the Imperial Family? These letters are a puzzle because everything he says is contrived to outwit and confuse and yet there is a silver thread of thought that runs through his words. He wants to tell us the truth but he is sworn to secrecy and can't. He desperately feels that future generations should know the truth about their history and towards the end of his life he starts to search for that one person who can reveal the truth. Unfortunately for us, he thought it was Mr Brasol but Mr Brasol had also taken the oath of allegiance and was not prepared to break it. Hence these important letters written to the agent called Fox thanking him for his help in rescuing the Imperial Family have been lying dormant; until, that is, Guy Richards makes his discoveries and publishes them.'

Michael yawned loudly. 'Please can we try Paul, for just one moment, to stick to the facts? God knows there is enough to absorb without you going off and pontificating over a wild goose chase!'

Tonya stifled a laugh. 'Well uncle I think we are all on a wild goose chase.'

'I see that McGarry also refers to a Father Edmund A. Walsh of Georgetown University,' Paul cautiously looked around the table as he spoke. 'And I know all about him. He wrote a book called *Fall of the Russian Empire*.'

'So?' Michael asked.

Paul raised his eyebrows. 'Well it was mentioned in the first paragraph of the letter!'

'So?'

'Well, he tells of a rumour that the Romanov ashes and bone relics, along with some jewellery, had been carried off in a box to Harbin. He said that his source was extremely reliable! Some say it was the Ipatiev House investigator, Sokolov, who had been stranded in Harbin with his unpublished report and a box of relics discovered during his investigations.'

'Oh dear me, that's an awful story,' Alice responded, putting her hand over her ears. 'I don't want to hear any more of it.'

Paul sighed. 'Well my point is that McGarry doesn't believe a word of it either.'

Michael listened intently with both elbows on the table. 'I didn't realise you were so informed about Russian history, Paul.'

Paul beamed. 'Oh yes. I've done a lot of research and I'm very happy to share my knowledge.'

'Another time perhaps,' Michael replied, looking at his watch. 'I think we've had quite enough on our plate with this McGarry fellow. Tonya is there much more you want to say?'

'No, I just want to finish this letter from Mr McGarry and read you what Guy Richards has to say about it.

I believe that every statesman will admit that IF it were KNOWN generally among the old RUSSIAN people that there were an HEIR to the throne ALIVE, and capable of being brought to Moscow, the present regime would be overthrown by a popular uprising. And I happen to know, personally, from the lips of both John Reed and Trotsky, that this belief was fully shared by them.

So it is not an unreasonable supposition to assume that Lenin, Kamenef, and Bukharin held similar beliefs. Indeed, it is certain they did; and knowing the Russian PEOPLE as they did, they conspired to remove OFFICIALLY this obstacle to the perpetuity of their power. Hence the "official" execution, which supplies the place of a physical execution, in creating the lingering ILLUSION, of the Royal Family's murder in thirty-six different ways.'

'Very Good Tonya,' Michael commented, 'but many would debate Mr McGarry's view that a resurrected Tzarevich would create a popular uprising that could overthrow the Bolshevik regime. However his specific reference to the OLD Russian people is accurate. He has put his finger on a real phobia of the Reds in 1928. Please continue.'

'Lastly in his letter McGarry says: *With the whole Family in their power, they could have been shot openly could they not? Then why this elaborate preparation to kill them in so many different and opposite ways, Why this "proof" of such a necessary killing by introducing evidence that six CORSET STAYS became the mute accusers of murderers who gloried in the ferocity of their immortal deed? Anastasia and Maria never wore a corset in their lives. So this disposes of the "proof du linge de dessous" and though it was necessary to convince the Russians that the whole family WAS dead, the "proof"' is that the executioners took pains to blot out the evidence of such proof. This is proving too much! The evidence offered.... would not be admitted before a coroner's jury, or in any civilian tribunal, as a basis for accusing a bandit of murder.'*

    Here, as in so much of what Mr McGarry wrote about the doings at Ekaterinburg, he seems to be leading from strength; to know more than he can tell; but to be annoyed with others for not seeing for themselves the simple verities to which he has led them by the nose. But returning to that meeting at Marseilles, how about the tall soldierly man with a grey pointed beard? Nicholas's height was between five seven and five eight. The Empress Alexandra was just a little more than an inch taller. To a man of McGarry's size, five foot two inches, the ex Tsar may have seemed tall but the word would hardly be applied to Nicholas by a trained reporter unless in comparison with someone else. Furthermore, the Romanovs were 'up' the incline, the McGarrys down. So the former could have loomed larger than they in fact were. How about the tu? Could Nicholas have known McGarrry that well? And recognised *him that quickly from a modest distance? It is by no means impossible. From the trove of McGarry documents in Saint Petersburg, Florida, it is clear that he was in and out of Moscow and Saint Petersburg before and during World War I.'*

Tonya paused from reading her notes and looked up.

'Do you know? I find that really bizarre,' Juliana responded.

'What?' Alice enquired.

'That the name of the American city where Mr McGarry's documents are stored is called Saint Petersburg even though it's in Florida! It's like, well, I don't know what it's like ...a duplication of a geographic position! Why link this man and his work with St Petersburg in such an obvious way?'

'I agree!' Tonya responded. 'But surely McGarry would have met the Tsar and Tsarina many times, since his trade trips to Russia were at the highest level. He could have been in contact with Nicholas in 1917 and 1918 at Tsarskoe Selo, Tobolsk, and Ekaterinburg! In fact McGarry may have been a field supervisor for the Romanov's escape, in which Germans, Britons and Japanese were involved. McGarry may even have met Nicholas in Vladivostok, Manila, or San Francisco during the 1918-20 period and from what I have read there is a suggestion that the ex Tsar also visited one or all of these cities under an assumed name, actually meeting with McGarry and Romonovsky and discussing various texts in the story of *Rescuing the Czar*!'

'You're not suggesting that Tsar Nicholas himself wrote part of *Rescuing the Czar*?' enquired Juliana.

Tonya shrugged. 'Who knows?'

'AH! That would coincide with the big infusion of Russian gold into Californian banks then?' Alex added.

'Wait a moment,' Michael interrupted, 'I hope you're not saying that William McGarry and Sergei Romanovsky were involved in moving shipments of Tsarist gold into U.S. banks?'

Alex smiled. 'Why not, People don't usually do a job without some form of payment!'

'Well now! Perhaps you're right son. A deal was done! Yes, a secret codicil to the Brest Litovsk Agreement. I can see that would work. The Germans were certainly in a position to demand the safe passage of the Imperial Family out of Russia in return for a reduction in the Bolshevik debt to them. Very good Alex, I am impressed.' Michael smiled at his son.

'Or,' Juliana interrupted, 'they were very short of food. Wasn't there a famine? Perhaps it was food the Germans gave them instead?'

Everyone laughed.

'What?' Juliana asked. 'Food is funny?' No, they were laughing at Michael because he had said to stick to the facts and here he was making all sorts of suppositions himself. 'Well at least I know enough about history in order to do so!' he replied curtly.

Tonya then explained that there was something intriguing about what she had read which showed up in the correspondence of McGarry and Romanovsky. 'Apparently they openly talked about publishing *Rescuing the Czar* in order to embarrass Lloyd George during his "trying times with the Irish."'

'Well that sounds like blackmail to me,' Alex replied.

'Quite.' Tonya added. ''Romanovsky wrote to a friend and said "When our day comes I will go to Ireland and kiss her revered ground". It's as if somehow Ireland had a role to play in driving out the Bolsheviks from Russia.'

'Hey, perhaps the Tsar and his family were hiding in Ireland!' Alex added.

Tonya shook her head. 'No I don't think so. The connection with Ireland may have been because McGarry was of Irish stock.'

'More to the point the Germans had been encouraging riots in both India and Ireland as part of their strategy to weaken the British Empire,' Michael elaborated. 'And don't forget the United States was a reluctant player in the First World War. Many of her important citizens, up to thirty percent, were of German extraction and many were from Irish stock too. So it's not surprising that there was so little support in the U.S. for the Imperial British in Ireland or the Imperial Russians in Russia for that matter! We know many Irish were actively seeking independence for Ireland. On top of that, the President had a real problem with this notion of imperialism. He supported democratically elected republics. The Americans did not want war but they did want Europe to change the way it was being governed and most of all they wanted to trade. Plenty of business is what they wanted. So a person like McGarry would have been highly regarded. You should remember that Russia was the wealthiest country in the world. There was a lot at stake and much to play for. McGarry and his friend Romanovsky would have seen this as a once in a lifetime opportunity. The Russian nobility were running for their lives and fleeing to the United States and whilst they may not have shared the same politics, the United States would not have ignored the plight of the Imperial Family even thought they wanted Europe to be governed by democratic leaders. Well there isn't a king of the United States is there…!'

They all laughed at his joke except Alice.
　She was too distressed at the recollection of what her fellow Russians had suffered.

'Even though I was very young,' she added, 'I can still remember how everyone suffered. You can't imagine what it was like! How we lost absolutely everything. You can't imagine what that does to your soul and what it does to the soul of a beautiful country such as Russia. I saw the evil in people and what they could do to each other. EVIL IT WAS! Not a word we like to use these days but it is the only word for what happened back then.'
　Juliana patted her on the shoulder. 'It must have been dreadful.'
　'It was. There was such a shortage of food we were all starving to death. But everyday life had to go on, through the driving rain, the pitch dark and the freezing snow, the filthy dangerous God forsaken streets where murderers and anarchists ran riot and where the horses and the dogs were shot for their meat. You never knew who was your friend or who was watching you and why. You never knew any one's real name and if you made a friend, you would never know if you would see them again. You never could believe a single thing you were told.' Alice placed her head in her hands thinking of her beloved mother Russia and Giovanni comforted her. Then Juliana leant across and gave her a long hug. 'I really do think that we have spoken on the subject long enough. Let's call it a night.'
　Giovanni agreed. 'Si, Time for rest, no think of anything now please,' he added, escorting Alice out of the room.

* * *

'Oh dear me,' Alex spoke in hushed tones, 'she's so upset. I never thought for a moment….'

'No,' replied Tonya. 'None of us did. We have been selfish. In the future we should always think about what we say and how it might affect her.'

'Anyway,' Alex continued excitedly, 'now they've gone I can tell you what I was really thinking. G-O-L-D! They must have BURIED some of the treasure in Ireland.'

Tonya smiled. 'Sounds like you want me to continue?'

Alex and Paul both nodded.

'Well,' said Tonya, opening up Guy Richards *Hunt For The Czar* again. 'Mr McGarry wrote to Romanovsky on 22nd November 1920. What he wrote appears rather cryptic now but no doubt Mr Romanovsky knew what it meant when he wrote the following:

Now that England has Nicholas in India and Wells in Moscow and the Bolsheviki bottled in a treaty, what is she going to do with the prisoners of Tobolsk? I have not heard whether they escaped via Los Angeles or are still marooned in the Monnadnock.'

'I presume that is H.G.Wells, the famous writer?' Alex enquired.

Tonya looked up. 'Yes and here we have the confirmation that England had the Tsar safe in India just like Fox's diary said. The Bolshevik Treaty that McGarry refers to is obviously the Brest Litovsk Treaty and "The Prisoners of Tobolsk" must be a code for the Tsarina and her children.'

'I don't know about that.' Alex sounded doubtful. 'What do you think Paul?'

'Anything is possible. All I can say to you both is when I was reading about Sidney Reilly I kept thinking about William Rutledge McGarry. You see, they were both clever men. But I do wonder whether this isn't just some kind of propaganda.'

'Well it can't have been propaganda supporting the Bolshevik cause because McGarry was friendly with the White Russians.' added Tonya.

Alex sighed, 'Why not make it easy and accept the British had Nicholas in India just as Fox said?'

Tonya thought for a moment. 'Going back to Paul's point about the propaganda... I suppose it is possible that the book was linked to certain officials in the British government. After all, McGarry did work for the British Film Industry and when he mentions "Bull" he may have been alluding to Sir William Bull, the Unionist Member of Parliament, who coincidentally also introduced Reilly to Churchill. But that suggests a link with Ireland and I don't know what that could be.'

'Or it could be some other "bull," responded Alex. 'Anyway, the negotiations to free the Imperial Family could have been going on between the Bolsheviks and the Allies ever since Kerensky's provisional government grabbed power and that was long before the Americans entered the war.'

'Quite ...' added Tonya. 'AND if their escape journey as told in *Rescuing the Czar* is even partly true it does show the problems encountered in planning such a dangerous mission. I bet there were plenty of failed rescue attempts going back to when the Imperial Family was imprisoned at Tobolsk. They wouldn't want the world knowing that they had agreed to release the Tsar and the Imperial Family over to the allies as part of a deal to reduce the payment of gold owed by the Bolsheviks to the Germans. It would have suited the Bolsheviks to say the family had been assassinated. After all, it was what the revolutionaries wanted.'

Alex agreed. 'It would certainly dampen expectations of the Tsar and his family ever being able to return to rule Russia.'

'But what about the British,' Paul queried. 'What was their reason for going along with the plan and announcing they were all dead?'

Tonya thought for a moment. 'Well I suppose that was the very least they could do. Keep them safe while they were hiding in exile.'

'How's that exactly?'

Tonya laughed. 'Because no one would go looking for them if they thought they were dead, Alex. As you know, the White Russians employed Sergeyev and then Sokolov to hold enquiries into the Romanovs' disappearance and get lots of witness statements to say that shooting was heard or they saw the bodies being loaded onto trucks.'

'Yes, sounds like it's a cover up to me! Paul agreed.

'Look you two, I want to believe as much as anyone that they all escaped unharmed but you have to admit the witness statements look pretty water tight.'

'No Alex they don't.' Tonya explained that the so-called witnesses were contradictory and so inaccurate as to render them worthless as far as any real evidence was concerned. 'Okay,' she added, 'so they interviewed some people who said they were involved with the disappearance of the Romanovs. But why couldn't they say where the bodies were? Surely they knew where they had been buried!'

Chapter Fifteen   Jerusalem

Despite the late night, Giovanni and Paul managed to slip away early the next morning. It was Paul's birthday and his father was going to spend the whole day with him.

'Today son I am taking you for a special surprise. Si, you must usually wear these priestly garments... I know... but I will pay for new suit for the birthday. How you like the idea? A tie eh?' Paul was delighted to spend time with his father and oddly enough didn't feel like sitting around in religious attire on his birthday either. Today they agreed but that wasn't always the case. Only the other day he had shocked his father by saying that if he hadn't been a priest he would have been a secret agent.

'Why?' a bewildered Giovanni asked.

'Well I think secret agents work for a high purpose too.'

Giovanni wasn't convinced. 'Si, I know what that is, money!'

'No papa. It's easy for people to think like that and for agents to be accused of working for the highest bidder but if you study what some have actually done, you will see that they were motivated by the highest ideals and believed they could change the world for the better. Take Sidney Reilly for example. Everyone said he did what he did for big business and money but in the end he gave up his life for those ideals. In a way he was a martyr.'

'Santa Maria!' Giovanni exclaimed.

'Well you can read it for yourself. Shall I lend you the book?'

'No,' Giovanni replied, raising both hands in the air as though he were being held up at gunpoint. 'My English isn't what it should be.'

* * *

Back at the villa Juliana was sitting at her dressing table when Michael came in.

'Good Morning,' he said, kissing her on the cheek.

'Good morning and what a beautiful day it is too!' Juliana stretched to make the point. 'Yes it is. Sorry about last night, it did go on a bit. Still at least we've agreed to hold these discussions during the day rather than over dinner. They will be much easier to control if we hold them in the library. By the way have you seen Alice this morning?' He asked putting his watch on and fiddling with his cuff links.

'Not yet!'

Michael watched as she dabbed perfume behind her ears and on her wrist. He screwed his nose up, about to sneeze, then recovered. 'Right then, I'll be downstairs if you need me.' As he left Juliana shouted after him, 'By the way I can see Alice, She is in the garden now.'

Alice waved as Michael marched over towards her. 'Alice! How are you this morning? I'm sorry about last night. It all went on far too long....' Alice tapped his arm. 'Tush! It was nothing. I had a good sleep. At my age that makes all the difference.'

'Well they should have been more thoughtful.'

'Look, I'm bound to get upset remembering those awful days in Russia. Let's forget it now.'

Michael bent down to tie his shoelace and Alice watched as he checked the other shoe.

'No loose ends?' she enquired as Michael shook his leg so that his turn-ups fell neatly back onto his shoe. He smiled, acknowledging her comment.

'I thought we'd have a day off from unpacking those tea chests. I'll see if Juliana wants to come too. We can go into town for a bit of shopping if you like?'

Alice smiled. How sweet he was to think of her feelings! 'I thought we had a lot to do?'

'Yes....but after yesterday's conversation I thought we should have a break..... But if you would rather leave it, we can go another day?'

'Yes, let's finish what we started and, contrary to what you may think, I am amazed how everyone's so involved. You have done a good job there.'

Michael sighed, 'Except Giovanni!'

'Yes, but remember he's a religious man and was very close to Maria, as we all were of course but still, he finds her loss difficult and all this delving into her life when she tried to keep it all so secret.'

'Well we're religious too and she was my mother and your best friend. If anyone should be upset about the delving, it should be one of us, not the gardener.'

'That's true.' Alice said bending down to smell a yellow rose. 'Anyway, I suppose you want to get on then?'

Michael scratched his forehead. 'Well you know what they say – the devil makes play for idle hands! By the way, I don't suppose you've managed to find anything in that cedar box or the zinc phial that was in it?'

'I've not exactly had much time. I think I'll take a turn around the garden now. Giovanni's planting arrangements are quite wonderful.'

'Alright,' Michael added patting her on the shoulder. 'Why not bring the box to the library. Say about two o'clock? I have an idea.'

* * *

An hour later, Michael was reading Tonya's copy of *Rescuing the Czar*. The following paragraphs seemed particularly significant to him and he added paper clips to mark the pages.

Under the agitated surface of this tidal wave of fanaticism that threatened to engulf the royal prisoners there were a few men in Europe and America, as well as in India and Tibet, who were slowly converging in the direction of the victims with a phrase upon their lips that none but Royalty and themselves were privileged to use. It was that ancient secret code transmitted by tradition to the followers of a sturdy Tyrian king. It was made use of by Lycurgus, as well as by Solomon and Justinian; and it was again employed by the partisans of Louis XVIII to save the House of Bourbon. It is that mystic code which binds Royalty together and is given only to those whom Royalty may trust. That ancient code meant freedom if it reached the prisoners in time! It rested with these silent men to pass the scrutiny of a million eyes to liberate the victims from the fury of the mob.

Such a rescue, as time swept by, became nothing but a slender hope with any of the women. They began to realize that their blood would not very greatly shock the nerves of statesmen who had become accustomed to the daily cataract that poured down upon the soil of Europe. They felt abandoned by the diplomats. Their only friends were busy in the red work of war. One chance alone remained. Soldiers might be deceived by men disguised as comrades. The Secret Service might overlook the hysterical entertainers who fluttered under the mask of charitable workers and skipped across forbidden lines protected by a cross. This was the only possibility, this, the phantom hope that stood trembling on the brink of the prisoners' abysmal fear.

Thus the sight of a Red Cross driver or an English uniform in the midst of their disaster became a welcome incident in the lives of these affronted women. The appearance of either seemed to carry to the prisoners a spirit of encouragement and reflect a ray of mercy into the dark corners of their hearts. They indulged the hope that some of those foreign uniforms might conceal trustworthy friends.

And they recognized a basis for such a hope in the mystifying movements of one of those uniforms that met their notice day by day. It was near them at the palace when they were thrown upon a maddened world. They saw it following onward as they passed through pathless wilds.

They could see it hovering near them on that last historic night. They learned about its manoeuvres in the morning as it moved among the silent rooms of the pretty mansard cottage that had witnessed their withdrawal from the vision of historical events, how it had paused to scan without emotion the small blood stain on the floor, how an agitated censor informed the credulous that the prisoners had been murdered in cold blood! Thus they learned that the world had heard with scepticism that, so far as history and international politicians were affected, their seven lives had been technically blotted out!'

Michael turned the page and found where Fox explains how he had been picked out for the "imperial rescue" mission.

Without any preliminaries he said: 'Come with me!' We entered a cab and a few minutes later I entered the Wilhelmstrasse and was in the presence of that tall, iron-grey, wiry gentleman with eyes like a searchlight and the manners of a Chesterfield. 'Thank you, Colonel,' he said. The Colonel sprang to attention, bowed, saluted and backed away. We were ALONE! 'In ten minutes,' he said, 'you will be conducted to another room. When you arrive, advance to the middle, make a right wheel and stand at attention facing the portiere, maintain perfect silence, answer all questions, Make NO inquiries, understand?'

I was taken downstairs, along a wide corridor to a solid-oak door guarded by two sentries and an attendant in the royal livery. The door was opened by an officer of the Erste Garde; I entered a large room, advanced to the centre and faced the divided portières of an adjoining chamber. There sat the man whose nod shook the earth! Behind a heavy, old-fashioned desk, in a dim light, apparently absorbed in writing, sat a deeply tanned, lean-faced, blue-grey eyed counterpart of Frederick the Great, the very embodiment of Majesty! Eyes that blazed in their defiant depths with a steady and consuming fire, the kind of eyes that seem to defy the world.

I stood there fully five minutes before I heard the sharp, high-pitched voice pierce through the portière saying: 'Adell, I will see the C----'. I was conducted to within six feet of the man at the desk and in the same shrill voice asked how familiar I was with Russia, with Turkestan, India, and the Far East.... My answers seemed to convince my questioner.... Handing me a note he said: 'No one besides ourselves is to know that you are to undertake the mission outlined in that note.'

Then he sat forward abruptly, his elbows resting on the desk, his head between his hands, his eyes fixed on space.... I began to study the note.... I was dumbfounded! I had thought all along that this man was the mortal enemy of the persons this note commanded me to rescue from danger. I could not understand HOW there could be the slightest co-operation between this man and the other great ones of the earth that note commanded me to call upon for assistance in case I should need it. It was utterly incomprehensible! Yet THERE were the directions in plain black and white. And I could not ask a solitary question! In the same shrill voice the man asked: 'Have you memorized it?'

    I had! It was burned into my very soul. I could not forget a syllable of it! Without another word he took the note, struck a match and watched it curl into shapeless ashes. Then, making a quick gesture, he plunged into the documents before him. I backed away until the door closed and shut out the sight of the lonely figure enveloped in a green light, his face illuminated against the shadowy background of an underground chamber of the Foreign Office. On the way to Friedrichstrasse depot I met that girl of the Metropole again!'

Michael laid the book down. So Kaiser Wilhelm is behind the mission and has hired agent Fox and the Metropole performer, who goes under the name of Lucie de Clive, but is really the Baroness B. he concluded to himself. She is involved in leading a team to rescue the Tzar and his family! He decided that there were certain elements of the story that would need further research. If he could discover Fox's real identity he felt sure he would be more than halfway to discovering whether or not the Imperial Family had survived, as McGarry had suggested in his letters to Boris Brasol.

* * *

At two o'clock sharp Alice knocked on the door, carrying that all important cedar box.
    As she entered Michael closed the door quietly behind her.

'Ah good, you have it with you,' he said, taking the box from her. Without a word passing between them Alice closed the curtains and he lit the candles.
    'Now before we start,' he broke the silence first, 'I want to read you something.'
    After he had finished, Alice told him that it had all been planned by those sworn to allegiance and that was what always felt holy to her about it all!
    Michael said he didn't understand.
    'Don't forget,' Alice reminded him. 'Whoever was involved in the rescue mission would have been risking their lives. No amount of money could compensate for losing that! The rescuers were motivated by a spiritual force, hence the mystic code!'
    'Okay Alice tell me about the mystic code.'
    'Well I can't. It's not a verbal thing.'
    Michael laughed. 'You think it was a hand shake?'
    'It's MYSTIC. Alice replied. That means it is on a higher plane, a different dimension if you like!'

'THEY said it was a phrase upon their lips that none but Royalty might use! So it must be a set of words'

Alice laughed. 'Like "Abracadabra" or "Open Sesame" or Man in the Iron Mask!'

She was in a playful mood but Michael was not amused.

'So you're not going to tell me. Very well, perhaps you can inform me about what was in that zinc phial then.'

Alice glanced down at the cedar box now in her hands. 'Unfortunately I can't tell you what that awful gas was protecting, but I have found something else of interest.' She added pointing at the side of box. 'It's a form of Sanskrit if I am not very much mistaken.'

'Sanskrit?'

'Yes, here. Look, you should just be able to make it out.' Michael took the box and held it at an angle. 'Ah yes. I can see it now.....Gosh look at that.'

असतोमा सद्गमय। तमसोमा ज्योतिर् गमया।
मृत्योर्मामृतं गमय॥

'I wonder what it says. How can we find out? Perhaps I'll take it up to campus.'

'Why don't I take a rubbing of it and ask Paul if he can help get it translated. He knows some very clever people at the Vatican.'

'What a good idea! Then at least one mystery will be solved!'

Alice smiled happy to have pleased him.

'Now,' said Michael, 'I have been thinking about who this Fox fellow could be. I am fairly sure that he is not Mr McGarry.'

Alice looked up. 'Well whoever said he was?'

Michael ignored her question. 'I'm sure when we find out Fox's true identity we will discover who the Baroness B. is.' He gave Alice a knowing smile. 'That said, if the Baroness turns out to be my mother then it should not be too difficult to find out which of her friends was Fox, if you get my drift or scent?' Michael burst into laughter. 'I know it sounds terribly confusing. I must sound quite mad!' He added watching Alice light a candle.

'I can assure you that the Baroness in *Rescuing the Czar* was CERTAINLY not your mother.'

'How can you be so sure? She had a secret and it would appear that this could be it! Anyway, contrary to what you might think Alice, I happen to believe that we can gain a lot more knowledge by having a mystical approach to our work; there, I have said it! I know I haven't always been so supportive of that sort of thing but I know you and mother were great believers in THE powers that be! Now that I have a holy Russian icon and this beautiful amethyst crystal in the library, well, I feel those powers, where ever they are and whoever they are, can be summoned to help us with the search for the truth. So any ideas as to how we should proceed?'

Alice had to hand it to him. He was certainly tenacious.

'Well for this to work Michael, it's imperative that you relax. Perhaps I should tell you a little story before we start?'

Michael laughed nervously. 'What... to get me in the mood?'

'Quite so.' Alice responded. Now there are higher beings that have entered the cosmic service of freedom and have been given dispensation by the Lords of Karma to function in the world of form as Ascended Beings. That means they can take on the appearance of any physical body at will!'

Michael looked startled. 'What are you saying? That they die and then come back to life again?'

'Yes. Not all in our world is what it seems, Michael! There are many mysteries. Not all can be revealed but some can if we open our mystic eyes and ears.'

'Being a mystic you would say that, but I've yet to be convinced.' Michael yawned. 'Anyway, why are you telling me this now? Are we going to summon one to help us now?'

'Of course not, I am just preparing your mind for any eventuality that might occur. But the most important thing is to have faith. Remember, miracles only happen to those who believe in them!'

Michael suddenly felt dizzy. 'So what happens next?' he asked, sitting down in his favourite armchair.

Alice checked to make sure the curtains were closed. 'The first thing we need to do when we have a meeting is to bless the space we are in. That makes sure there are no negative energies in the room. No demons or gremlins to ruin things for us. So we will pray for the Lord's help. After that, if all goes well, we can petition a certain person to come forth and speak.'

'What, such as FOX or K.A.G?'

'Yes or their guardian angels.'

'Hmm! And you think it is that easy, that simple!' Michael rubbed his chin before adding. 'I don't think Paul or Giovanni will warm to it. Come to think of it, neither will Juliana.'

'Tonya might, but not the others.' Alice agreed.

'Well old girl, it looks as though it's just you and me then?'

'So it would appear but Michael, I must warn you of one thing. If we do this now the very least that is demanded of you is complete sincerity of faith. Do you understand? I cannot be held responsible for anything untoward happening!'

As she spoke a candle flickered, emphasising the gravity of her words.

'Now,' she whispered, 'Let us make a start?'

Michael nodded nervously.

'I must warn you that some restless souls may enter the room and they can take on the appearance of a loved one. So remember, I am the experienced medium. You are not. Therefore listen very carefully to what I say and then do exactly what I ask. Do I make myself clear?'

Michael nodded again. Alice could see he was apprehensive.

'Just as long as you know when it is ME that is speaking.'

Michael smiled and took a deep breath.

'Look! Think of it this way Michael. You have never seen humans before so I take you to a park and show you a few at a distance. By the time you meet them you will be used to them. There is no harm done! So that is all I am going to do now. You will become comfortable with the spirit world and you will know what it feels like to be in their presence. Now! Are you ready?'

'Yes, as much as I ever will be.'

Michael took another deep breath as Alice started to chant. He wanted to shut his eyes and go to sleep but she made it clear that he was to join in the chanting. He did, but when the candles started to flicker, making wild shapes dance around the walls, he stood up, abruptly knocking a side table over. Alice broke off her chanting.

'Whatever is the matter?' she asked, watching him hurriedly draw the curtains. 'I'm not ready for this. Besides, if our research goes according to plan, we won't have to resort to this mystical intervention.'

Alice understood. 'Of course, I'm quite sure just having the icon and crystal in here will help! Anyway I'll go and see if Paul can translate the Sanskrit on the box.'

'Good idea.' Michael responded as he held the library door open for her to leave.

* * *

Back in her bedroom, Alice placed the cedar box carefully on her dressing table. It was then that she noticed a small eight-pointed star etched on the top right hand corner. It was beautifully carved and as she ran her finger along it she felt a mystical tingle. Turning over the box she found the same mark on the reverse. She had seen this sign many times before. Now the box was no longer a mystery. 'Thank you,' she whispered as she took a look inside. The box had a number of empty compartments. One had contained the poisonous phial. But what had the others contained? Looking at the size of the box she thought it too small for parchments, even if they were rolled up. Her intuition told her that the box could have held something the size of a small bottle or a piece of jewellery. After taking a sip of water Alice lifted up the box and smelt it, a dangerous thing to do, considering it had housed the poisonous powder. But all she could smell was the unmistakable scent of sandalwood. Alice closed the box and placed it back on the side table next to her bed. Then she lay down and closed her eyes and even though it was mid afternoon, a quiet melodic chant inside her head made her drift off to sleep. JE RU SA LEM............... JE RU SA LEM....... JE RU SA LEM!

Later when she awoke, her mind flooded with different images. By using a special breathing technique that had been taught her by Buddhist monks she saw past the confusion as a glowing object floated towards her, finally forming itself into the familiar object that she had always worshiped.

There was no better time than now to ask her question and Alice didn't hesitate. Who did the box belong to? What was its purpose? Why did it contain a zinc phial full of poison? Silently, she requested the information from the spinning goblet. When the goblet faded Alice heard the words she had been waiting for. Her questions had all been answered but now she wondered how Maria had come by the relic in the first place.

Chapter Sixteen   A Letter from Heaven

Paul and Giovanni relaxed in the Italian sunshine, watching the tourists mingle in the Piazza Navona and finishing off an excellent bottle of Frascati. While they waited for dessert, Giovanni picked up the book Paul had with him.

'You enjoy this story?' he enquired.

Paul smiled. 'I find it exciting because it's a world away from my work. You should read it.'

Giovanni sighed and placed the book back on the table.

'Well, can I have your opinion on something?'

Giovanni shook his head. 'From out of here? No!'

Paul gave in gracefully. Then Giovanni felt guilty. 'Why you like this book?'

Paul sipped the last of his wine. 'Mm, this is good but not as good as our church wine. I must see if I can bring some home for our meetings!'

'You no answer me? Why you like this book?'

'Because it fires my imagination and I have a theory that I need to test with someone who has read the book.'

Giovanni fiddled with his serviette

'Well, do you want to hear more?

'No! Replied Giovanni grumpily.

'You're not interested in any of this are you?'

'No.'

'Well, you must find it hard listening to us talk about it all the time then?'

'Si.'

'So you don't want to know what Maria's secret was and whether the Russian Imperial Family were rescued or not?'

'No! I miss her. I miss the baroness.'

Back at the villa Tonya was chatting with Juliana in her studio.

'So what made you start sculpting then?'

'Well I have always enjoyed making things. You know, being creative. I have never been one for reading books.'

'And yet you married a man of learning! I suppose opposites attract?'

'They did in our case. Besides, can you imagine what it would be like if there were two minds in the house like Michael's!'

Tonya laughed. Just then she noticed a pile of old newspapers on the floor and some on the workbench.

'If you're going to make something from these I'd love to help.'

Juliana smiled at her enthusiasm. 'That's very kind of you but I haven't finished with them yet. They are quite interesting.....'

'Ah ha, I see what you mean! 'Dr Graves, hmm... I'm not sure I would want him as my doctor!'

'Well quite.' Juliana added, showing Tonya the clipping that advertised *The Secrets of the German War Office*. I'm going to pick up a copy of it tomorrow from the bookseller in town. He told me that Dr Graves also wrote another book called *The Secrets of the Hohenzollerns*, which was published in 1915 or was it 1916? Anyway, it's all about secret agents working for the German Kaiser. You should read it after me.'

Tonya put the newspaper down. 'Paul would like to read it. He's really into that secret agent malarkey! So if you can't be bothered to read them, why not give them to him?'

'Look, I may not be a bookworm but I'm very interested in Dr Graves. So if you don't mind, I will look at them first!'

As Juliana spoke, Tonya sifted through the clippings. 'Hey, what's this? Look, he's been arrested for blackmailing the German Ambassador in Washington in 1916!'

Juliana gave a long sigh.

'Look here. He's making predictions about where the Germans are going to bomb next! Good heavens Juliana, these clippings are so important! You can't possibly....'

Juliana looked over and replied frostily, 'Are they?' .

'But you know that of course. You've sorted them into date order already!'

Juliana just wished Tonya would leave. Then she could get on with her sculpting.

'CRIKEY!' Tonya shouted. 'This can't be right. He's been accused of burning a woman alive! He's dangerous! Why do you want to read his books?'

Juliana gave a long sigh. 'Well you can't believe everything you read. Besides, I feel like giving the man a chance.'

'How did you get them?'

Juliana stared at her. She was becoming really tiresome and she didn't see why she should have to answer her constant stream of questions but to do so would be impolite! 'Michael gave them to me, knowing that I can always use old newspapers for my work. Anyway, more to the point,' Juliana decided to change the subject, 'how are you getting on? Any more on that secret agent Fox yet?'

'Ah! You must wait until tomorrow; then I shall reveal all!'

When Alice met Paul in the dining room it was just before dinner.

'Happy Birthday Paul, did you have a nice day out?'

'Wonderful, thank you, and how lovely the table looks for my party!'

'It certainly looks festive and I bet I know who's gone to so much trouble.'

Paul laughed at her remark as Giovanni stepped in with a full tray of drinks.

'Refreshments,' he merrily shouted, placing the tray on the sideboard.

'Ah!' Alice cried, 'Look at Giovanni's crystallized roses gracing the centre of the table.'

Paul smiled. 'I see you have something for me too?'

'Yes, it's not a present I'm afraid! We found it earlier and I was wondering whether you knew anyone who could translate it for us?'

'We?' enquired Paul.

'Yes Michael and me. We think it might be important. It belonged to Maria you see.'

Alice handed over the box to Paul and he studied it carefully. 'There are different types of Sanskrit but I'm no expert. Leave it with me and I'll see what I can do.'

The next afternoon, as a great storm struck, everyone huddled together indoors. The only person who was happy was Giovanni, whose only concern was that the hailstones didn't destroy his beautiful flowerbeds. Paul thought the weather most unusual for the time of year and so it was. But it was a great day for reading and keeping cosy near the fire. He was content, unlike Tonya, who marched up and down. She was impatient for the clock to strike two, because only then would she be able to knock on the library door.

What new revelations had Tonya to divulge? Paul wondered as he twiddled his thumbs.

'I know!' he said, grabbing everyone's attention.

Tonya paused. 'Yes?' she asked expectantly.

'While we are waiting I'll tell a story to help pass the time. Come and sit down Tonya.' He added patting the chair next to him and waited for everyone's attention.

'Have you ever heard about the "Letter from Heaven?"'

Tonya glanced at the clock before replying, 'No, I haven't and I don't think we have time to hear it Paul.'

'If it's a joke, we do!' Alex suggested.

'I think I may have heard the story before,' Alice replied. 'Does it involve a miracle?'

'Yes, and a Rabbi or two!'

Alex laughed again. 'Oh you ARE going to tell us a joke then. Great!'

'Well,' Juliana responded. 'I do hope this is not going to be in bad taste, Paul. Can't you tell us a nice story?'

'Now what can I say my son?' Alex shouted out. 'Miracles are miracles!'

'Please Paul, if you're going to tell it, you'd better hurry up. It's nearly time for our meeting.' Tonya added nervously. As he spoke Paul leant forward clasping his hands together. 'Once upon a time there was a famous Rabbi called Yisroel Odesser. He was a teacher of Breslov Hasidim, one of the first in Israel. In 1921 at the age of thirty-three, Yisroel Odesser was overcome by hunger when he was fasting. Temptation got the better of him and he ate. Immediately he regretted his action and prayed for five days continuously. Then a powerful thought came to him. So he obeyed the voice inside his head and went into his room. He randomly selected a book, which he opened. In the book he found an important piece of paper. He later called it the "Letter from Heaven". On it was written a greeting and a text that referred to the Fast of Tammuz, and the *Na Nach Nachma* mantra.'

'That's a song isn't it? Na na na na, Na na na na, hey hey hey, Na na na. Krishna Krishna, Krishna Krishna.'

'Don't be silly Tonya.' Alex chided.

Paul smiled. 'Tonya is right in a way. It is a religious mantra. But the *Na Nach Nachma Nachman Meuman* is a Hebrew mantra used by Breslover Hasidut, known as the Na Nachs. Their leader was called Nachman of Breslov and he came from the Ukraine in Russia but had died many years before and Rabbi Odesser was a follower. In his lifetime Rabbi Nachman predicted that a Song of Redemption would be revealed before the coming of the Jewish Messiah and the song would be in a single, double, triple, quadruple form!'

'Does that mean we all have to sing it?' asked Alex.

Paul sighed. 'Please allow me to continue. Now the letter from heaven said this:

It was very hard for me to descend to you my precious student to tell you that I benefited greatly from your service. And to you, I say my fire will burn until the coming of the Messiah. Be strong and courageous in your service Na Nach Nachma Nachman Me'Uman, and with this I shall tell you a secret. Full and heaped up from line to line and with strong devotional service you will understand it, and the sign? This will say you are not fasting on the seventeenth of Tammuz.'

'What does that mean?' asked Tonya.

'Never mind that for now. It's not important for us to know. For our purposes it shows how thin the veil between heaven and earth really is for those who believe.'

Paul glanced across to Alice, who nodded in agreement. 'Anyway,' he continued, 'Odesser believed the letter to be a message of consolation directly from Rabbi Nachman's spirit to himself here on earth. Odesser adopted the mantra as his personal meditation and became so totally identified with it that he later said, "I am Na Nach Nachma Nachman Me'Uman". He believed the Letter from Heaven to be a genuine miracle, pointing out that the bookcase where the note had first appeared was locked at the time and he was the only one with a key. His followers believed in the miracle and continue to this day to chant the mantra as a song of redemption for the coming of the Jewish Messiah!'

As he finished telling his story, Alex, who had been alternating between yawning and laughing throughout, was the first to respond. 'I don't believe there is such a thing as a miracle.'

'Oh there is but they only happen if you believe.' Alice whispered.

'I don't suppose there was any chance of it not being a miracle?' Juliana asked, rather amused by Alex's reaction.

'Good point. Some people believe it was a well-intentioned forgery, written by one of Odesser's students to cheer him up after he got depressed over breaking his fast. Another person later confessed to having performed the cruel prank but he was not believed.'

'The trouble is,' Alex interrupted, 'religious people would rather believe in miracles than real life!'

'Most people,' continued Paul, 'believe the letter was a note written to someone by Rabbi Nachman when he visited Tiberias during his pilgrimage to Israel in the early nineteenth century. Somehow it was placed in the old book. But crucially, Odesser finding it was a coincidence of timing, as was the reference to someone eating on the Fast of Tammuz!'

'Yes, but why are you telling us this story now?' Tonya asked.

'It was something my father said yesterday. We were talking about what happened to the Romanovs. Even though their bodies have not been discovered he is absolutely sure they were murdered and buried nearby. Now imagine this. That we have the bodies and that they are without a doubt the Romanovs. Is it still possible that they escaped?'

They all thought for a moment.

'You're right,' Juliana replied. 'How could they? It would be absurd to write of their escape if you had evidence they had been murdered.'

'Well,' Paul continued, 'what if *Rescuing the Czar* was true and they did all escape? What would you say then?'

'I would say that they can't have escaped because the bodies have been found!' Alex replied stifling a laugh at the absurdity of the discussion.

'Ah, but after how long? Over fifty years after they have disappeared? Does that mean that they did not escape? I think not.'

'This is a ridiculous conversation.'' Alex was adamant. No bodies have been found and that is precisely why we think this story of the rescue could have something to it. Besides, it isn't just about the Romanovs it's also about what happened to their gold. Christ… Paul… they were the richest family on earth, don't you think that was reason enough to want to save them?'

'My point,' replied Paul gently, 'is if you believe in miracles anything is possible. I can promise you that even if the bodies were found tomorrow there would still be millions of Christians the world over who believe they are living today.'

Alex laughed. 'Yes, but it's like people who read the Bible. They believe that it was written by God; but that doesn't mean they are right or that what they are reading is true!'

Tonya clapped her hands and stood up. 'Look! Can't you see what's just happened?'

'What?' asked Juliana obviously amused.

'We are not supposed to be talking about this until we go in and here we are doing exactly that. Anyway, it's time, let's go.'

Chapter Seventeen   A Shooting Party

'Come in everyone,' instructed Michael as he removed his glasses and started to polish them. 'Now,' he added, recovering from the noise of scraping chairs. 'I think you'll find this a very much better arrangement.'

'Why is Alice lighting the candles so early in the afternoon?' Alex asked.

'I suppose I should explain! We, that is Alice and I, we feel that our meetings will benefit from being blessed.' A cry of dismay was audible as Michael continued. 'We must remember that we are called here today on a sacred mission. If we wish to get the most out of these meetings we should approach the task in hand with due reverence! So a ritual is called for at the start of each meeting. Now let me explain what that will be. Over here we have a holy Russian icon. Can you all see? Look just up there.' Michael pointed out the heavily framed and bejewelled mosaic of the Mother of Kazan. 'This will help guide our work, and down here we have a fabulously large amethyst crystal to help channel angelic energies. You can see I have put it in the fireplace. Very important that!'

Michael sat down, noting with pleasure the solemn faces now staring at him. Very good, he thought, at last they have got the message.

'Why has Alice lit only three candles?'

'Don't concern yourself Alex. The number is of no consequence.'

The flickering candles unnerved Juliana. 'Michael, I don't think it is a good idea to have candles burning when there is so much paper in the room!' Michael gave no response.

'What's an icon for anyway, Paul?' Alex enquired.

'It's a way of connecting to God using the medium of a saint.'

Juliana sighed. 'And all this is supposed to make us feel more comfortable, is it Michael?'

'Yes, of course! Now if you wouldn't mind, Paul?'

'Almighty God, we are gathered here in your name to know the truth. If it be thy will, bless our work with success and guide us along the path so that we are not tempted into false and evil ways but come to know the divine light that is born out of every truth. Amen.'

Paul opened his eyes and was pleased to see that everyone had joined in. Alex looked pale and Alice asked him if he was feeling ill. He said he didn't like religious ceremonies.

Michael tapped him on the shoulder 'Now look son, I perfectly understand. It's not everyone's cup of tea. So if you feel uncomfortable just shut your ears and don't interrupt the proceedings! Right,' Michael added, turning to Tonya. 'You can begin.'

'Well you'll be pleased to know that I found out some more details about Fox.'

Tonya pulled out several pieces of paper from her pocket. 'I had an idea to read up on the memoirs of those who actually served in the war. Down at the library they have a whole section on it. Anyway, the first memoir is from the personal experiences of a Lieutenant-Colonel C.A. Court-Repington C.M.G, Commander of the order of Leopold and officer of the Legion of Honour. He mentions a Captain Charles Fox of the Scots Guards who dined at Maryons in 1917. Captain Charles Fox had just escaped from Germany and related his experiences of a one hundred and sixty mile journey from near Hanover to Holland. He travelled by night using a compass and lay up during the day in young plantations where children played and the Boche were not likely to come. He was nearly captured several times. Once he had to bury himself as they were about to find him. Fortunately a load of sheep ran over his "grave" and put them off his scent. He lay hidden there a whole day and then in the evening he swam across the River Ems and lost his boots! He wasn't sure exactly where the frontier was so he had to ask the first man he saw, who was dressed in a field grey uniform. Fox was ready to throw him in the river if he turned out to be the enemy but as it happens he was from Holland. He said there were very few men in Germany and he had hardly met any on his long cross-country journey. He walked about twenty miles each night from 11pm until 5am and came across some new Zeppelin sheds on the way. I found out that Fox also worked in the Indian regiment, which ties in nicely with his diary in *Rescuing the Czar*.'

'Very good.' interrupted Michael. 'Not many people know that soldiers were often moved between regiments, depending on the requirements of the day Carry on Tonya.'

'So you see, Charles Fox is thought very highly of. He is brave, clever, full of stamina, and not frightened to kill a man if he gets in the way. No wonder the Foreign Office were interested in him.'

'You've certainly done your homework. Is there anything else on Fox that you have found out?' Juliana asked.

'Not really.'

'"I have,' Paul interrupted eagerly 'I came across a rather vague reference to an operative called Captain C.M. James, who was also known as Charles Fox. He worked for British Intelligence and was Head of some British Intelligence station in New York, something to do with immigration in the 1920s. He was involved with the Lusk Committee under Raymond Finch, but then there could have been more than one Fox or maybe it's a name that many operatives used!'

Michael sighed loudly. 'I thought we all agreed that Fox was not his real name! But thank you Tonya. It helps to know that there was a Charles Fox working for the British Foreign Office and that British Intelligence Services did actually exist back then.'

'Well don't you think it's a coincidence that the agent rescuing the family is also called Charles James Fox?'

'I'm sorry, I'm not with you?'

'Well, Captain C.M. James and Charles Fox? They are Charles James Fox!'

Michael sighed again. Clearly the message hadn't got through. 'Well how about the Baroness B. What have you managed to find out about her Tonya?'

'It's not been easy. I'm wondering where to start.'

Alex nudged her affectionately. 'At the beginning might help!'

'Let's have some tea. We could do with a break!' Michael suggested.

A moment later Paul and Juliana walked into the Kitchen and disturbed Giovanni's moment of peace. 'I'll put the kettle on, you get the cups out,' Juliana instructed, making her way over to the kettle.

'Hello father, what are you doing here? Why aren't you in with us?'

Giovanni smiled as Paul drew near. 'That's not a gardening book?' Giovanni raised his eyebrows. He couldn't be bothered to reply, not over the noise of the kettle.

'I suppose,' Paul added, 'we should have lit some incense at the beginning of the meeting.'

Giovanni looked up. 'Incense, why?'

'Come on Paul, give me a hand please,' Juliana interrupted. 'Would you like a cup Giovanni?'

'Si, Grazie.'

Juliana smiled and patted him on the shoulder. 'Now please will you come and join us?' Giovanni shook his head. 'No, my work is in here.'

Back in the library Tonya was in the middle of telling Michael what she had learnt about the Baroness B. 'The Baroness 'B' plays an active role supporting those involved in arranging the Imperial Family's escape from the Ipatiev House in Ekaterinburg. Baroness 'B' is referred to in both diaries and appears to be part of a worldwide organisation's plan to rescue the Tsar and all his family. I suggest I read out a few passages from *Rescuing the Czar* that will give a good description of the Baroness.'

'That sounds like a good idea.' Michael agreed as Paul placed a plate of biscuits on the table and Juliana handed out cups of tea. Alex smiled as the cups rattled in their saucers. He much preferred to use a mug.

'Right,' Michael shouted to get their attention. 'Tonya is going to give us a description of the Baroness 'B'.' 'Yes I've taken excerpts from Fox's diary because he gives us a description of "the Baroness" and explains his relationship with her.' Tonya turned to the pages she had earmarked. 'Here we go then.'

Go to Birdcage and walk slowly back to Queen Victoria Memorial. As you pass Buckingham, observe the heavily veiled lady wearing white lace wristlets who will follow on behind. Let her overtake you. If she utters the correct phrase, go with her at once to Admiralty Arch and follow the Life Guard to the War Office. Meet number ----- there; receive a small orange coloured packet, wear the shirt he gives you, and cross the Channel at once.

'I was constantly thinking of that girl at the Metropole with her long eyelashes and dimpling smile; resembles the veiled lady at Buckingham and I was trying to make out why she managed to occupy a seat at the next table to mine at the Admiral's Palace an hour or two later. She seems to know some of the performers who mingled in the audience, especially the energetic dark-eyed Circe with the Greek nose, and said to be some sort of a Baroness, who so often approached my table. I wonder what the connection is between these two. There is certainly some sympathetic tie between those girls! This I know, for

when I had breakfast at the Cafe Bauer, U.d.L., they were BOTH there, slightly disguised, and occupying the same table! Who is Syvorotka, her lover? I wonder what the game is? Come to think about it, the titled performer of the Metropole looks like a twin sister of Marie Amelia, Countess of (Cszecheny) Chechany, a perfect composite of Juno and Venus and Hebe all rolled into one.'

'One moment Tonya,' Juliana interrupted as Paul searched his pockets for a paper and pen. 'The Buckingham connection is interesting but it's the line about the performer being an energetic dark-eyed Circe with a Greek nose. I presume by "performer" Fox means dancer. If so could it be Isadora Duncan?'

'Well anything is possible,' Michael replied impatiently, 'but can we keep our questions to the end? Now let Tonya continue. Please!'

The veiled Metropole nemesis was to see the sentry today. She seemed to be quite happy about something and looked up in the direction of my window a number of times. She was eating some of those champagne coloured rose leaves that are crystallized by the firm of Demitrof at Moscow and sold as confections to the ladies of the Court! What does it mean? Furthermore that sentry is the same man who acted as valet to Prince Galitzyn at Monte Carlo when Delcasse, Grey and Galitzyn (otherwise "Count Techlow") were gliding about the Grand Hotel de Londres. That Metropole woman was the companion to Countess C. at the Nouvel Hotel Louvre the day I met her at Monte Carlo!... and this man was the same fellow she was supping her cafe Turc and smoking her Medijeh cigarettes with out on the terrace gardens of the Hotel de Londres the night I was waiting for an American millionaire to break away from the Hungarian noblewoman at the table decorated with La France roses and the same kind of roses pinned to her corsage. The American, if he ever sees this in print, will remember the lady with the wonderful jewels flashing from her wrists and neck and whom the man with the Boulanger moustache at the adjoining table was trying hard to flirt with.

Tonya heard the scratching of pencils and noticed that Juliana and Paul were taking notes. 'Don't forget these are extracts from the story. So it's no good trying to make sense of them by joining them all together! Anyway I'll continue.'

The same dark-eyed Juno that same American met in the Salle des Etrangers at the Casino, the following day about noon. Well! That is the connection! But I did not observe that that wonderful lady wore any large SAPPHIRE that night. Nor when she changed her quarters from the Nouvel to the London did she need any such jewellery to have all the spendthrifts of Europe at her feet. If she was a "Princess" then I was completely fooled. I never saw a real princess, except Eulalia, who knew how to be democratic enough to select an American for a quiet exchange of ideas. The rest, no matter how desperately they may want to be free from Court restraint and bodyguards, remind me of the poor little caged girls at the Convent of the Sacred Heart at Seville!

'Now this is where it gets interesting.' added Tonya enthusiastically.

Well, so my captors have some connection with the Countess C---- (Cszecheny or Chechany), with the Tolna Festetics of Hungary and this is strange, for I had surmised that SHE, at least, would be friendly to MY mission if she knows anything at all about its origin. She should aid me to reach Odessa instead of having me sandbagged and cooped up here in this Soviet cage. I'm certain this Metropole lady is a TRAITOR to the Countess now and will have me murdered if I don''t produce that sapphire of the Princess's.

There is an Army Corps approaching from the southwest.... The air is surcharged with electricity and puts one's nerves on edge.... There is an ominous roar overhead that grows more nerve-racking every second.... Zip, zip, zip, bl-r-r-r-r-oo-ow! A flock of Foelkers heading east like wild ducks toward a few faint specks zigzagging in the firmament away to the north east.... Now there are a number of specks from the south speedily joining these and ALL seem to be flitting higher and higher out of sight.... Now the Foelkers are circling rapidly upward. The tramp and rattle of an Army can be heard coming up the road behind my villa....Ah! Here comes a daring plane like a streak of lightning over the Alex Nevsky Church directly toward this prison! I'm between the Devil and the Deep Sea! Whoever gets me, that flyer, or those noisy and unseen dogs of war, back yonder means nothing but plain HELL to ME!

Well, I'm not DEAD yet! A trip through the clouds is NOT the most delightful of experiences for one in summer togs. Especially when one is gagged and blind folded and roped down like a rebellious steer. So here I am cooped up again in a log cabin in the centre of an undulating plain where there might have been unending wheat fields once upon a time.... Not a solitary animal is in sight. The road out yonder looks much the worse for wear. It seems ground into a pumice stone by the hoofs of horses and the swift movement of heavy wheels.

Every gust of wind sends a cloud of fine dust pyramiding its way across the fields and through the crevices of this suffocating den furnished with a few wooden chairs, a hand-carved bedstead, a small picture of the "Virgin of the Partridges" and a brass crucifix above the bed. I greatly SUSPECT my present whereabouts. I am as much mystified as ever why that veiled Metropole Circe continues to dog my FLIGHTS.... It was she who was the daring flyer and she beat the whole army getting to my retreat in that neglected villa and spiriting me away. I am certain now that this veiled lady from Buckingham is in league with this gang of Bolsheviki, and I am also certain that I owe my life to the boast I made of being a murderer myself! A man who has escaped death is not to be trusted on a point of discretion.'He doesn't know how to select his friends.

He is like a spirit emerging from nowhere in the eternal void and grabs at the first apparition that promises companionship in his embarrassing and momentary isolation. Well, I was so glad to see that Buckingham Clorinda that I was willing to take her into my confidence at once. She seemed so sympathetic!

Tonya paused. 'Now the Baroness will speak and you tell me, if she doesn't sound the very model of Britishness!

"I commend your bravery," she said prettily, offering me her hand. It was small and beautifully moulded, yet firm and steady, and sent an electric thrill through me like a flash.... Her eyes would disarm the most suspicious diplomatic freelance in the world. Struck with admiration, hypnotized by her voice, I could only blurt, "I thank you."

"We are looking for a man of approved courage," she continued earnestly. "We are more than satisfied that YOU are the man."

Again I muttered my thanks.

"How long have you been a member?" she then asked carelessly. THIS was not so easily answered. I thought quickly.

"Long enough to KNOW my lesson." I answered.

"You still remember your instructions?"

"What instructions?"

She answered my question by asking, "Were they not BURNED?"

Who is this encyclopaedic lady? I asked myself. What manner of TRAP is she setting for me now? "Why did you SANDBAG me?' was MY answer."

"You are NOT to ask questions," she returned. "Are you not satisfied with results?'

"I am still alive."

"Well," she smiled, "A live Bolshevik, of OUR kind is much better than a dead diplomat!"

I was taken into an improvised kitchen and indulged in a splendid meal. I took no wine. My meal being finished she offered me an excellent cigarette. Glancing up through a ring of smoke my eyes fell upon a rough black-and-white sketch of a tall smooth-faced, keen-eyed man with rather large ears, firm and thin-cut lips, high forehead and steadfast gaze, dressed in the uniform of a General Officer, with a single decoration on his left breast. She observed me closely as I gazed. I KNEW this man and was about to exclaim: "The saviour of this country!" but something restrained my enthusiasm.

"You recognize him, I see!" she insinuated.

"WHO is he?" I dodged.

She merely smiled. She evidently realizes the wonderful power of that disarming smile and the fascination of good teeth in a shapely head.

"You'll do!" she said with apparent reservation as she tapped a tiny bell. A short, thickset man appeared. He is not positively ugly, but he has a way of staring at one that is rather ill-bred. There is a gold band around his left wrist and a scar upon his right cheek. I am sure he is the SAME man I met at one of Sadakichi-Hartmann's readings from Ibsen's Ghosts.

He may recall the time. It was in an abandoned palace on Russian Hill, somewhere in America; the lady at his left was discussing the difficulties of getting her motor car into Ragiz; the younger one on his right was known as Alma and gave her address as East 61st Street, New York and ALL THREE were quite convinced that the Central Powers will defeat the Allies. He is an international character and will remember this incident.

"This gentleman will join your party for Ekaterinburg tonight. YOU understand if there are any mistakes I shall not answer for results!"

There were NO introductions. The man bowed and began to back away.

"YOU may accompany him," she said, rising and flitting from the room.

I believe I understand what this party means! There is to be a SHOOTING party at Ekaterinburg under the auspices of the Bolshevists in a day or two and I may be ONE of the "mistakes" for which that mystifying lady disclaims responsibility. My companion certainly looks like a bandit and manifests the strength of a wild bull. He seems much interested in that patch on my shirt sleeve.

'The Metropole performer is a baroness sure enough. She knows a Syvorotka but declines to give his rank or whereabouts. She tells me that this place was founded by Count Tatischshev in 1721. Diagonally across the way there has been a Red Cross nurse eternally peeking through her window in this direction. If we go out into the courtyard she can see us plainly behind the other buildings, for there is nothing to obstruct her vision, and she seems mighty anxious to keep tabs on all proceedings in the yard. I have tried to figure out a resemblance between this nurse and the capricious Metropole Baroness, but the nurse seems much older. Perhaps she is disguised. If she ever reveals her identity she will remember me as the man who tipped my cap to her after posting the two sentries in front of the palisade between the telephone poles and the British Consulate.

I have lately laughed at those Italian poets who bewail the isolation of their Lauras, yet recalling my Lady Buckingham's repeated rescues, I begin to recognize a reason for the existence of that poetic fervour, which agitates the artistic heart when either its safety or its vanity is at stake.'

Tonya glanced up. 'This entry comes at the end of Fox's diary. It's after Fox has successfully rescued them and they have boarded a British gunboat which is ready to set sail.

Finally he (the captain) asked, "Would you not like to meet my SISTER who has been so much interested in you?" His sister! I had never heard of her!

"Of course," I answered, amiably enough for one completely stumped. He called a petty officer and said a few words in an undertone. In a minute a radiant young woman with springing steps glided gracefully down the deck. She was not, in her present attire, much different from Maria but as she drew near I noted the difference at a glance.

She came forward quickly and held out her hand.

"Congratulations, Mr Fox!" she said smiling.

"The Metropole!" I gasped. "What brings YOU here?"

"Still asking questions!" she coquetted prettily. "I merely called of course, to inform you that the sapphire is in America!"

I thought hard for more than a minute. Then it occurred to me that I had seen her in a dozen disguises shadowing me from Buckingham to the room upstairs on Downing Street, to charm me later at The Hague, to disappear like a will-o'-the-wisp, then to fascinate me at the Metropole.

'So, there you have it.' Tonya said putting the book down. 'The Baroness 'B' as portrayed in *Rescuing the Czar*. What do you think?'

Juliana spoke first. 'It's all very fascinating! I've got some notes written down and….' Alex interrupted before she could finish. 'It's not exactly believable. I mean what woman could fly in 1918?'

'Mmm!' Michael replied, 'She certainly has many attributes. Good looking, powerful, dark eyed, articulate, in control, and to top it all she pilots her own plane! But I must say Alex, I agree with you. This is a most dramatic story and one the film studios would certainly have been interested in.'

'I like the way Fox writes about the Baroness. My Lady of Buckingham, Juno, Venus and Hebe all rolled into one! And well, I know it seems ridiculous but I can't help thinking of Kathleen Scott!'

Michael sighed loudly. 'Why does everything have to revolve around that blessed woman?'

'Well I know you're going to think I'm stupid but Kathleen Scott, was a Lady Scott and she lived in Buckingham Palace Road. Besides, some Americans are naive about European etiquette, for example they often call a Lady a Baroness. I happen to know that Kathleen had a dynamic personality with both manly and womanly attributes. In fact her house in Buckingham Palace Road became a social centre for networking and propaganda planning amongst British and

American politicians. By the way, did you know she was a close friend of Colonel House's? He was a personal aide to President Wilson and she knew all of the powerful people of her day and was good friends with Lloyd George and Asquith, for whom she ran regular errands to Paris, Rome and Florence. If she is not the very image of the Baroness 'B' I'll eat my hat.'

Michael burst out laughing.

'Look, I've read her diary!' Juliana continued getting ever more serious. 'And I can tell you one thing for sure. She would have sworn allegiance to the Official Secrets Act. Remember it is treason to breathe a word.'

'So,' Michael responded, 'you imagine that because she lived in Buckingham Palace Road she must be "My Lady Buckingham" as mentioned by Fox.'

Before Michael could say another word, Juliana had left the room. She was obviously upset.

After an awkward silence Tonya spoke up and said what was on all of their minds. 'Well, I for one would like to hear more about Lady Scott. I think everyone should be able to have their say and what Juliana thinks is intriguing.'

Chapter Eighteen   Sculptress and Spy

When the door slowly opened, Tonya was pleased to see Juliana back again. Michael looked contrite and said nothing as she entered the library, confidentially clutching a couple of books on Lady Scott.

'I see you're intent on telling us more about this *Mata Hari* of yours!' Michael observed sardonically.

Juliana opened one of the books. 'I'm going to prove to you that she is a real contender for the role of the Baroness 'B' if you'll let me?'

'Be my guest.'

'Okay, so at the age of twenty-four Kathleen left her uncle, who she had been staying with in Ireland, and moved to Paris. Her diaries show her to have been as carefree as George Du Maurier's famous Tilby but far too independent to need a Svengali! Kathleen Scott sculpted Bernard Shaw while she was wearing unfeminine overalls. Just like me!' Juliana paused and looked down at her dirty dungarees, making Tonya laugh.

'Come on dear, do get on with it!'

Juliana smiled before continuing. 'George Bernard Shaw later said that no woman ever born had a narrower escape from being a man and he said his affection for her was the nearest he had ever come to homosexuality!'

Alex gave his mother a wide smile as she turned a page.

'Now, here is the interesting bit. Kathleen also believed in putting her own life at risk for others. She called it "the greater glory" and it manifests itself early on in her life when she wrote to her husband Robert Falcon Scott. "*If there's anything you think worth doing at the cost of your life, Do it. We shall only be glad. Do you understand me?*"' Juliana dramatized the statement before looking up to see what impact it had made. She was glad to see that everyone was still listening, except Paul, who was scribbling away again. Peering down she saw he had written the words *Juno, Hebe* and *Venus* all rolled into one and then *VEJUHENOBEUS*.

'So Paul, you think it's an anagram?' she asked inquisitively.

'Yes maybe! But please get back to your story. Just tell me. Could Kathleen Scott fly and did she have dark eyes?'

Juliana laughed. 'Everyone has dark eyes if they haven't had any sleep! But yes, she most certainly could fly, although she didn't want anybody to know she could. She was a regular at air shows with her friend Arty Paget. She spent many afternoons at the airfields chatting with flyers, learning about engines and occasionally going up herself. She admitted that she had probably been the second woman in Britain to fly and that she had flown with Mr Sopwith on dual controls. Her picture appeared in *Aeroplane* magazine without her name, much to her relief. She took the editor to lunch and asked that he stop printing stories about her as if she were a celebrity! Kathleen had a golden rule of not getting talked about, even though she was so well connected. She knew anyone who was anyone, all the important people of her day, regardless whether they were writers, diplomats, dancers, politicians, or simply adventurers. She spoke French fluently and enjoyed the opera and ballet. She dined regularly with H.G. Wells and his wife Rebecca. She loved walking across the country and sleeping rough without money. She liked to live on her wits. Kathleen was a brave, energetic, adventurous and a very attractive woman.'

Michael suddenly yawned loudly and interrupted her. 'Oh yes those infamous vagabonding trips!' Juliana ignored his comment as Tonya borrowed Paul's pencil and wrote a few notes.

'So Kathleen knew H.G. Wells. Now that is interesting. She certainly sounds like our kind of woman. But remember we are looking for a Baroness 'B' and I think the "Buckingham" connection is tenuous, even if she could be connected to the Buckingham Clorinda in *Rescuing the Czar*. Remember that the Baroness 'B' has strong ties to Berlin and goes to St Petersburg regularly. So unless you can prove that Kathleen Scott had connections further afield, I'm afraid we may have to rule her out.'

Juliana's face lit up. 'Well now! You're probably not going to believe this! Kathleen Scott's maiden name was Bruce. So her undercover name may have been the Baroness Bruce or B!'

Alex laughed. 'Well, mother, it's not a very undercover thing to use your real name now is it?'

'Oh, all right. I give up on that one. But she did have connections to Berlin and St Petersburg.'

'Oh!' responded a surprised Michael. 'That sounds promising.'

'Yes, her older brother was a Royal Navy Reserve Captain and he was on Robert Falcon Scott's ship too. Captain Wilfrid Bruce was a former cadet from the *Worcester* who was thirty-six years old and had travelled all the way from Vladivostok with Cecil Meares. They had just selected twenty Siberian-bred ponies and thirty-four sledge-dogs for Scott's expedition.'

'Wait a moment!' Tonya shouted. 'That's an important connection. In Fox's diary the Baroness is involved with a person who is organising sledges and supplies in 1917 in Tobolsk and there is a reference to old foul smelling Navy Cut tobacco that all those guys smoke! Juliana is right … they must have been the brother and sister team! You know, the bit I read out to you earlier when Fox puts the Imperial Family aboard the British Gunboat and the captain asks "Would you like to meet my sister?" and then the Baroness 'B' says "Congratulations Mr Fox" etc.'

'How clever of you Tonya, To put two and two together and come up with ten!' Michael checked the time as he gave a sarcastic reply, before adding 'Now look I want us to have this wrapped up before dinner. It all hinges on what you can tell us about Kathleen and the Berlin or Russian connection, Juliana dear?'

'Well, it just so happens that her cousin was Henry James Bruce. He was known as "Benji" to his friends. Kathleen had grown up with him before she left to study art in Paris. Now, crucially for our purposes, Benji was head of Chancery at the British Embassy in St Petersburg and worked for the Ambassador Sir George Buchanan.' Michael interrupted her. 'That's right my dear.' He encouraged. 'He was also an attaché at the British Embassy in Berlin during 1911.'

Juliana ignored the interruption. 'In Berlin, Kathleen stayed with Benji and some other American friends. She had a great time, skating, flying and attended lots of concerts. One story tells of her meeting a lady who had inherited a huge fortune and was forced to spend every penny each year.

She lived in a palace with marble floors and wore a white velvet frock covered with pearls, even during the day.'

'I wish!' responded Alex playfully.

'Yes, yes,' Michael interrupted, waving his hand around impatiently. 'Now let your mother finish please.'

'Benji took up his appointment in St Petersburg just before the outbreak of war in 1914. His story is well known. He fell in love with the city of St Petersburg and then he fell in love with its top ballerina. So it was no surprise then that in 1915 he married Tamara Karasavina, daughter of Platon Karasavin. But in 1918, St Petersburg, or Petrograd, as it had become then, was a very dangerous place for those working at the British Embassy.'

'That's correct,' Michael added. 'A decision was made to relocate to Vologda, where the Soviet Government had made provision for them all to live on a train, until they could be transferred to Archangel, where British cruisers would pick them up. Now I had no idea that Benji Bruce was related to your Kathleen Scott! It appears I owe you an apology. Now if you allow me one moment, I have a valuable contribution to make.'

Juliana folded her arms in protest. 'Honestly! I haven't finished yet.'

Tonya laughed. 'You can't complain. He's taking you seriously now.'

'Here, I've got it!' Michael shouted, rushing over with a book in his hand. 'Something was bugging me and I couldn't think what it was. Now I have found it. Did you know that Benji knew Lockhart well?'

'No!' Juliana replied.

'Well I'm surprised. You seem to know everything else!'

'I think that's a bit unfair father.' Alex responded in defence of his mother.

'Ssshh! Listen to this.' Michael opened his notebook.

'Britain was not alone. Other embassies had also been vacating the city at that time. In fact, the third Secretary of the French embassy, Louis de Robien, described the farewell scene between the young allied diplomats and their Russian friends. On the platform alongside the sleeping cars everyone was in tears. Princess Urusova stood with Gentil, (Tamara) Karsavina with Benji Bruce, Countess (Moura) Benckendorff with Cunard, and Countess Nostitz with (Jacques de) Lalaingue.'

'Well, now. The question we need to ask is this. Is Kathleen Scott a likely candidate for the Baroness 'B' or is there someone who is a rather more obvious candidate. Eh?'

Juliana shrugged. 'I don't know!'

'The point I am trying to make should be obvious to anyone with an inkling of intelligence.'

Michael sighed. 'Do I have to spell it out for you? THEY ALL KNEW EACH OTHER!'

'Who did?' Alice asked.

'Lockhart, Bruce, and Benckendorff.' Michael shouted.

'So?'

'Well clearly your Kathleen Scott must have known them too!'

'She is not *my* Kathleen Scott, just someone I admire.' Juliana couldn't help but show her anger.

Michael impatiently looked at his watch. 'Anyway, enough of this, it's almost time for a pre-dinner cocktail. But before we end, let me just say one thing. I happen to know on very good authority that Benji Bruce was so in love with his ballerina that he risked his life in 1919 to return to Petrograd and rescue her. Lockhart wrote in his memoirs that *"...his pulse quickened as he looked on with delight and admiration as Benji Bruce returned to Russia just for one day to collect his bride and take her back to England".* It was a real love story.'

'Fancy being so in love that you would risk your life like that! I can't imagine what that must feel like,' Tonya said, glancing at Paul as she finished speaking.

'We shouldn't leave out who else he took back with him,' Michael added.

Juliana had no idea what he was talking about and said so.

Michael laughed. He loved the opportunity for showing off. 'He also took Zhenya Shelepina, who was Trotsky's secretary. She married Arthur Ransome, the writer. Zhenya was the niece of ex-mayor Chelnov. He also took Lyuba Malinina, who was hastily married to Captain Hicks before his expulsion from Russia in 1918. By this time Moura and Bruce Lockhart had fallen deeply in love but unfortunately they had to stay behind in Russia!'

As Juliana watched her husband speaking, Alice couldn't help compare her soft gaze with his hard blue scrutinizing eyes.

'Now,' Michael added, looking at his wife directly. 'Exactly where your Kathleen was during this time I have no idea. Perhaps she was off vagabonding! Anyway you've given us all something to think about. Lady Scott's cousin Benji was a highly honoured and decorated man. He was invested as a Companion Order of St Michael and St George. Later he became First Secretary of the Diplomatic Service and British Delegate to the Inter-Allied Commission on Bulgaria in 1925. Finally he was advisor to the National Bank of Hungary between 1931 and 1939. He also wrote two books, *Silken Dalliances* and *Thirty Dozen Moons,* both of which I have in my collection should you wish to look at them sometime.' Michael smiled and then promptly left the room.

After he'd gone, Juliana stretched out. 'Ooh, I could definitely do with a really long soak in the bath to relax me.'

'I know exactly what you mean!' Tonya giggled. 'But tell me about Benji Bruce and his lovely Tamara. I hope they were happy in London afterwards?'

'Yes, I think so. Kathleen often joined her cousin Benji and his wife on frequent theatre trips and to the ballet, which Kathleen adored because she was friends with Tamara. Kathleen had always been interested in dance ever since her friendship with Isadora Duncan. But the point I was trying to make to Michael, even though he didn't take me seriously, was that there was a very strong Russian influence in her life, although she never liked to talk about it.'

'Yes, I did take you seriously.' Michael replied, suddenly walking back into the room.

'Did she mention her Russian connections in her diary?' Tonya asked.

'Not really. She was quite mysterious you know. I believe she once confided that if she wanted to keep a secret no one on earth would ever find out about it!'

'Just like Maria. They were two of a kind,' responded Alice. 'They would not have written about the disappearance of the Imperial Family in their diaries.'

'Well isn't that strange, given her interest in politics and her family connections to imperial Russia?' queried Tonya.

'Well it does seem strange to us, given her love of intrigue and need to see fair play. Oh that reminds me, I didn't tell you Michael.'

Michael glanced up. 'What?'

'You will recall that in *Rescuing the Czar* the Baroness travels between England, Stockholm and St Petersburg on various secret missions towards the end of 1917.' While she was speaking Juliana turned to a page she had earmarked. 'In her memoirs Lady Scott, who has now become Lady Kennet, makes an interesting post-note to the year 1917. This is what she wrote:'

"Throughout this whole year I was working as Sir Matthew Nathan's private secretary."

'She then goes on to describe a beautiful office overlooking the Thames and to say that she has some sympathy with those who work for the Government. But,' Juliana added, 'what I found really interesting was that she added this note at a much later date.

It's as if she needed to confirm her whereabouts during this time. Remember she had been spending a lot of time speaking with Colonel House, Asquith, the Chamberlains and Lloyd George! So you see, she could well have been the ...'

'Any diary can be used to fool people,' Alex interrupted. 'You just write in false entries. I know honest people think diaries are documentary proof of what happened but it can also be far from the truth! In my opinion they are only a record of what someone wants you to believe.'

'Well yes, but in Kathleen's case a lot can be understood about her life from the people she knew. For example she was good friends with Admiral Sir Reginald Hall and...'

'BLINKER as he was affectionately known,' Michael shouted excitedly. 'Head of Naval Intelligence and Master of Room Forty, Ever heard of that Paul?'

'No. I haven't.'

'Now that does surprise me! You're supposed to know all about secret agents and you have never heard of Room Forty! Well let me enlighten you. It was where counter intelligence officers worked trying to decipher codes, and at this time Blinker was quite concerned about Russia and for good reason. The British Naval Attaché in Petrograd was a certain Captain Francis Cromie, who wrote to Admiral Hall in 1918 warning him that whoever fed the Russian people would be master of the land. There was political capital to be gained because the Russians were so desperate for food. Blinker Hall was part of a team in London working to resolve the Russian problem.'

'Exactly the right time to negotiate for release of the Tsar and his family!' responded Tonya. 'And the political capital argued for could have been the reinstatement of the old regime.'

'Well I don't want to go into that now,' Michael replied. 'The question we should be asking ourselves is to do with Juliana's friend Kathleen. Bearing in mind that her cousin worked at the Embassy in Petrograd and her brother was a sea captain. That question is whether Admiral Hall was behind a plan to rescue the Tsar?'

'I suppose that is a possibility,' Juliana conceded, 'but we could never prove it.'

'Well not that it's likely, but does Kathleen mention knowing any secret agents such as Robert Bruce Lockhart or Sidney Reilly in her diary?' Alex asked.

Juliana laughed. 'Don't be silly.'

'Yet she must have known of them.'

'No. I don't recall her saying so,' Juliana was growing irritable with his line of questioning when Paul interrupted.

'It's a well known fact, by those in the know, that diaries often contain false information such as appointments never kept and journeys not taken. Time after time, when researching known operative diaries, I have found that the dates between late June and early August 1918 are either blank or have much less information than one would expect! It is all the more noticeable because all the other days they record their appointments and meetings and even their feelings. The fact that none of them make any reference to the tragic events unfolding at Ekaterinburg is quite astonishing. Nor do you find any later comments when the news of the supposed execution is out. This is all the more astounding given the fact that many of these people would have known the Imperial Family personally.'

'So Kathleen can be excused,' Added Juliana, 'because she was involved with the negotiations and attended the Paris Peace Conference. Even though Colonel House was a good friend of hers she didn't try to hide it. In fact she speaks of it quite often.'

'Is that all?' Michael asked.

'Yes, it's enough isn't it?'

'So you've answered your own question. There is no proof she helped the Imperial Family to escape.' He seemed to be enjoying his line of questioning but Alex was having none of it. 'Father, none of us can prove anything but that is not the point surely?'

'I disagree. There is no point in putting forward a case if it is not relevant and, more to the point, if it cannot be proved!'

Juliana sighed. 'Look, I wasn't trying to prove anything.'

'But surely,' added Alex, 'that is the point of a hypothesis. A statement is made that becomes the basis of discussion and research, which eventually does or does not prove the hypo....'

Michael waved his hand in the air. 'This is going nowhere fast. Are there any other contenders for the role of the Baroness 'B'?'

'Yes, how about Baroness Beckendorff?' Tonya responded.

Alice appeared shocked. 'What... Moura?

'No Alice, I'm not talking about Moura. I'm talking about Gertrude!'

'GERTRUDE!' they all shouted.

'Yes.' Tonya smiled. 'She was a beautiful actress who came from Kentucky. She left home before she was eighteen, looking for adventure, and ended up acting on Broadway. She played alongside stars on the New York stage and mixed with famous tycoons. Eventually she married the Russian Baron Beckendorff, who was a very good friend of the Tsar.'

'Ah, this is more like it,' Michael said, rubbing his hands with glee.

Tonya smiled in response. 'Gertrude was a brilliant poker player and loved horse racing. She played big money games with William Vanderbilt and John Jacob Astor. Apparently she was a good friend of Cecil B. DeMille, the film director, and confidante to Rudolph Valentino. But it was a 'rags to riches' story, from a Kentucky farm to a castle in England. In the early 1900s she had intrigued kings, presidents, nobles, diplomats and crooks. Apparently there was a sensational newspaper series written about her in 1922. Gambling, royal titles and jewels, it was all written about, as well as her stint undercover with the government when Theodore Roosevelt was President.'

'Which Beckendorff did you say she married?' asked Paul.

'It was Baron Andre de Beckendorff, a legendary figure who lived "several lives" before dying in a shroud of mystery, apparently for the second time!'

'So you're suggesting she is the person behind the Baroness 'B' in Fox's diary?' Michael enquired.

'Yes, I think it's a possibility.'

'But could she fly a plane?'

'Probably I would imagine.....'

'Not good enough. She must be able to FLY!'

Alice muffled a laugh in her handkerchief. Michael was giving his usual performance. Tonya sat back and picked at her nails.

'Tut tut, stop that.' Alice said waving her finger at her.

'SHE MUST BE ABLE TO FLY!' Michael shouted again.

'I KNOW.' Tonya quickly leafed through her notes. 'LOOK, here we are, I've got just the right person now. The first woman to win her fixed wing pilot's licence was the self-styled Baroness de la Roche. She is described in contemporary reports as a young and a pretty comedienne. At the age of twenty-four she participated in aviation meetings at Heliopolis, Budapest, Rouen, and interestingly, at Saint Petersburg, where the Tsar praised her for her bravery and audacity.'

Alex sniggered. 'Isn't it amazing how every single person is intimately involved with the Tsar!'

Paul nudged him sharply. 'Don't be so rude,' he said under his breath.

Tonya ignored them both. 'Let me finish, it's a sad story! Even though the Baroness was an accomplished flyer and had broken nearly every bone in her body she always got back into the plane after a crash.'

Alex laughed again. 'She must have been as mad as a hatter then!'

'Anyway, as I said, she performed in front of the Tsar at St Petersburg in 1911 and he congratulated her on her flying skills.'

'At last a RESULT!' shouted Michael.

'At last we have a baroness who can actually fly. Well done Tonya!'

'Except for one thing,' Tonya added cautiously. 'She wasn't a baroness, I'm afraid. She gave herself the title! Her real name was Elise Raymonde Deroche.'

Michael rolled his eyes in despair. 'Well for goodness sake.....'

'Anyway,' Tonya continued, determined to finish her story, 'it all ended tragically, because on July 18th 1919 she was killed when her aircraft crashed on a test flight. She was not the pilot though. Apparently she was learning the rudiments of becoming a test pilot when the plane lost power and some say she actually fell out of the plane!'

Juliana placed her hand over her mouth in disbelief. 'That's awful. Was it an accident?'

'I expect not!' Paul exclaimed. 'It reminds me of Isadora Duncan's death; she was apparently strangled by her scarf.' He pulled a face as he spoke. 'As you know, I have been reading about Sidney Reilly. He was a real James Bond character. Anyway I came across someone who might be of interest to our discussion here today.'

'It's relevant I hope?' Michael queried.

'Oh yes. During World War I there was a German master spy called "H" in the United States. "H" was a mysterious female who had her headquarters in one of the leading cities, probably San Francisco. From there she directed her operations to foment revolt against British rule in India and Ireland. She was so good that by the end of 1917 officials in the West conceived the idea that she was the head of all German operations in the United States. Apparently she was a German BARONESS. Now at this time, a man was arrested in San Francisco, charged with acting suspiciously in the neighbourhood of United States' arsenals in that part of the country. Papers found on him indicated that he had been under orders to destroy bridges and public buildings in Canada and to target shipping and warehouses in Pacific ports.'

'Remember the U.S.A. had not yet entered the war but was supporting the Allies with food and munitions. Unfortunately the enemy had great support from Americans who had German roots. They were trying to stop the U.S. from supporting the allies and this included them carrying out terrorist activities against the U.S. In fact many German diplomats, including Bernstorff, the German Ambassador, Franz von Papen, and Wolfe…'

'Yes, yes, I know!' Michael spat his words out. 'Just stick to the story it's the Baroness 'B' we are interested in!'

Paul raised an eyebrow, 'Well I just thought it was important to have some context, that's all! Anyway, the first clue to the woman was obtained through a letter found in the possession of this man. It was postmarked "Cleveland", and instructed him to meet her. Investigations later showed that "H" had been an agent of Wolfe von Ingel, who was at one time Secretary to Franz von Papen, Military Attaché to the German Embassy at Washington, and the reputed head of the German espionage system in the United States. When Tonya gave us a description of the Baroness in *Rescuing the Czar* I straightaway recognised "H". She was brunette, about thirty-five and of striking appearance. She had bright dark eyes, was discreet and quick in her movements, and had an altogether agreeable nature. She was well educated and spoke English, French and German with equal ease.'

'So what happened to her?' asked Tonya.

'Nothing, aside from the letter that was discovered in her effects, there was little found to make a conviction on. Anyway, she was eventually traced to a fashionable apartment in San Francisco and, at what they considered a favourable time – dawn – secret service men raided her apartment and prepared to take her into custody for questioning. But when they got there she had left. Her identity has never been established although it is believed that she was a baroness by marriage only.'

'Well could she fly?' Tonya asked.

'No not that I know of.'

'Well we ARE looking for an ENGLISH baroness who is able to fly, speaks fluent French and German, and understands a little Russian and I believe I have found her!' Tonya added adamantly.

'RIGHT NOW,' Michael intervened, 'we've had several stories of baronesses, actresses, and performers who were operating as undercover agents from time to time. Whilst the last story was of interest to budding aviators I think we can rule out Mme. de la Roche, the French "do it yourself" baroness, along with Gertrude Beckendorff and the mysterious "H"! But..,.' Michael paused and put his head to one side.

'Do you know what fascinates me most about all of this?'

They all shook their heads and said no.

''Well consider this,' he continued. 'If I was intending to write a made up story about the Tsar and his family having been rescued and I wanted to spice it up with a flying baroness or two I would have plenty of material to draw on. The American and English newspapers were positively full of such tales!'

Everyone laughed. 'That was true.'

'You know?' responded Tonya, 'I think it's brilliant how involved everyone is but I do wonder whether we will ever find out who the Baroness 'B' really is.'

Juliana patted her on the back. 'I'm sure we will it's just a matter of time!'

'You're still thinking of your Lady Buckingham aren't you?'

Juliana gave her a knowing smile. 'Maybe, but identifying the Baroness is not as important as finding out who Fox is. If we can identify him then our Baroness will surely come to light.'

* * *

The following morning Paul was in the garden speaking with his father. As Alice approached she overheard part of their conversation.

'Just forget it. It is stupid,' Giovanni concluded. Paul stared into the large hole that his father was digging as he considered the advice.

Suddenly Alice was standing next to him. 'I hope you're not looking for buried treasure?' Giovanni stopped digging and looked up.

Alice smiled at him. 'Actually, I wanted a word with Paul.'

'I have it right here Alice,' he replied, pulling out a note from his pocket.

Asato mā sad gamaya
Tamaso mā jyotir gamaya,
Mṛtyormā amṛtam gamaya,
Aum śanti śanti śantiḥ.
From ignorance lead me to truth.
From darkness lead me to light.
From death lead me to immortality.
Aum. Peace. Peace. Peace.'

Alice was delighted. 'Ah! That is so uplifting.... Michael will be pleased.'

Chapter Nineteen   Revolutionary Russia

With these dark words I begin my tale. Wordsworth.

Paul lay on his bed, taking stock of his young life so far. Ambition, success, money, and relationships had never been important to him. Instead he had a penchant for the sublime and holy. Right from a small boy he had been interested in what could not be seen, the spiritual ritual of religion. Over the last few years he had served the flock well. It had been easy because he had never been tempted to sin, unlike some of his fellow priests who had faltered and confessed accordingly. He knew some considered him arrogant but the truth was that he was bored by the drudgery and monotony of priesthood. Surely this was not how God wanted him to lead his life? He hadn't realised how depressed he was until he had seen Tonya. Unwittingly, and unfortunately for him, she had awoken all sorts of hitherto unwanted desires. Prayer would help, of course, and so would the books. He would try not to see her every day. Oh dear, there he was again, thinking of her!

All the esoteric wisdom he had absorbed through his years of study had only confirmed what everyone already appeared to know. Namely, the world was a very strange place indeed and all the more so, if you were in search of that elusive concept called truth. It was like a slippery eel. No sooner did you think you had hold of it, than it would morph into a half-truth and then into an outright lie. A prime example of the truth masquerading as a lie was that book called *Rescuing the Czar*. Paul was quite sure it was telling the truth, albeit in a most confusing manner. They say the devils in the detail but what was worrying Paul was that his old enemy was not lurking in the words of the story but rather in the shape of greed. Greed that was taking hold of young impressionable minds as they discussed the whereabouts of the Romanov treasure! Of course, he wasn't including Tonya. She was far too nice to be greedy. It wasn't her mind he was worried about at all. Ah Tonya, just at the moment when everything should have been going so well SHE had to come along and put a spanner in the works! Paul sighed. Life's a journey of discovery. I shouldn't question it too much he thought, picking up a tattered copy of *Reilly, Ace of Spies* by Robin Bruce Lockhart (the master spy's son). If the truth was anywhere it must be in here, narrated by a straight talking, no nonsense British diplomat of the highest calibre. Paul opened the book and started to read.

The road was long and unlovely. The car was long and by 1917 standards sleek. In the half-light of the Bavarian dusk, an observer, had there been one, would have but dimly discerned that both occupants of the car wore uniform. When the car slowed down and stopped by a small dense cluster of pine trees immediately to the right of the deserted road, he might have noted that the be-medalled passenger in the rear wore a colonel's uniform while his driver was dressed as a corporal. The corporal turned, spoke briefly to his passenger, then opened the door and got out. He walked back to the boot, which he opened, and took out some tools. Returning to the front of the car he opened the bonnet and started tinkering with the engine. For three minutes perhaps there was quiet except for the occasional sound of metal tapping against metal. Then the driver lifted his head. 'Herr Oberst!' His voice rang out across the silent evening.

'The Herr Oberst would be most obliging if he would assist for just one small moment. There is a loose connection in the electrical circuit. If the Herr Oberst would be so very kind as to get out of the car; and just hold a small nut in place while I deal with the other end of the cable, the car will be running again in no time at all.'

The colonel, whose uniform looked both smart and commanding even in the twilight, got out of the car, drew off his leather gloves, which he placed carefully on the running board, and bent down to peer inside the engine. He stared at the spot to which the driver was pointing with a greasy finger. If the colonel felt the heavy spanner, which cracked his skull as he peered at the magneto, it could have only been for a fraction of a second. The driver wiped his hands, carefully stripped the colonel of all his clothing, which he laid neatly in the boot of the car. To make quite sure the colonel was dead, he placed his thumbs on either side of the officer's windpipe and squeezed. When he was satisfied, he relaxed the pressure and, hoisting the naked body over his shoulders, he disappeared into the trees. The light was poor but the officer was obviously familiar with his surroundings. He made his way to a small clearing in the centre of the copse and here he dropped the Colonel's body. He pulled aside a large branch, thick with pine needles, which lay on the ground, to uncover a freshly dug grave. A small spade lay at the bottom of the pit. It took less than five minutes for the corporal to strip off his own clothing, place it on the officer's corpse, toll the body into the grave and fill it in with the spade. He then re-covered the spot with the pine tree branch.'

The naked driver trotted quietly back to the roadside. From the edge of the trees, he listened carefully for a minute or two, then stepped out onto the road and returned to the car. From the boot, he extracted the colonel's clothing and retired once more to the edge of the trees and proceeded to dress. The boots pinched a little but everything else seemed to fit perfectly. From under the driver's seat the corporal-turned-colonel pulled out what looked like a large tobacco pouch. With the aid of its contents and the use of the driving mirror, he made some simple but effective alterations to his facial appearance. The light was almost gone, but he had practised his disguise so thoroughly that he could have made the changes equally well in total darkness.

At the headquarters of the German High Command the sun shone brightly as the clock struck ten. At the great rectangular table in the large conference room were assembled, together with their principal aides, the galaxy of field-marshals, generals and admirals who controlled Germany's armed forces: von Hindenburg, Ludendorff, von Scheer, Hipper, all were there, as well as a man with a pointed beard and a withered arm, his Imperial Majesty Kaiser Wilhelm II. The chairs round the table were all occupied save one. The meeting had been in progress nearly half an hour but the representative of Prince Rupprecht of Bavaria's staff had not yet arrived and von Hindenburg was scowling; it was inexcusable for so junior an officer not to be on time. The clock had barely finished the last stroke of ten when the door of the conference room was thrown open. A click of heels, a smart salute and the absentee officer strode into the room. With a hangdog look on his face, the "colonel" apologized profusely for being late. On the journey up from Bavaria, his driver had been taken ill; he had to drop him off in hospital and drive the rest of the way himself. With a nod of greeting to one or two of his colleagues, the *"colonel" sat down in the vacant chair. Sidney Reilly had joined the council of the German High Command.*

RA-TA- TA- TAT. Four sharp knocks on the door made Paul jump. Who could that be? He opened the door to see Michael leaning against the door frame, holding a book in his hand and grinning.

'I just remembered! I wanted to give you this. I'm sure you'll find it helpful in your research on Mr Sidney Reilly.'

'Thank you! Have you read it yourself?'

'Yes, many years ago. It was one of mother's, actually. She said that it was the best telling of the Russian revolution she had heard.'

Paul read the title out: '*The Great Conspiracy, the Secret War against Soviet Russia* by Michael Sayers and Albert E. Kahn, published in 1947'.

Michael smiled again. 'This will help you get the "I"s dotted and the "T"s crossed. I know the book looks unprofessional but none of the incidents have been invented by the authors.'

Paul thought he understood what Michael was trying to tell him. 'So this is not like all the other memoirs that we seem to be getting embroiled in then? You think this is more of an academic work?'

'Quite! Unlike another book I could mention!' Michael sniggered.

'So I can read a more truthful telling of events in this then?'

'Truthful? I can't swear on the gospel that everything written here is the truth but I'm sure that when you've read it you'll be in a position to decide.'

'Well,' said Paul, 'you're the historian. It would help me to have your take on the situation. That is, if you have a few moments? It would save me a lot of work and I do want to give the family a good presentation without making any obvious mistakes!'

'You ask so politely. How I can refuse?'

'What was it like in Russia when Sidney Reilly and Bruce Lockhart worked there?'

Michael looked at his watch and sat down next to Paul.

'You're right to want to know. The study of history is the search for uncovered truths and historic context is always important if you want to get to the heart of the matter. Let's start with March 1917. At that time the Tsar had been forced to abdicate. Rioting had broken out in Petrograd and had quickly spread to Moscow. A new democratic government had been formed, headed by Prince Lvoff. It was made up mainly of Liberals, Constitutional Monarchists and Social Revolutionaries. Remember the Russians had been fighting on the side of the Allies against Germany. But Bolshevik newspapers began to appear on the streets. The future masters of Russia, Lenin and Trotsky, who had been living in exile abroad, now made plans to return and take power for themselves. Revolutionary and anti-war sentiment was increasing throughout Russia but the Social Revolutionaries had gained the upper hand and eventually it was Kerensky who took the reins of government from the Tsar. But Kerensky would not last long. The war had reduced food supplies and the people realised that life was no better under him than it had been under Nicholas II. The soldiers were starving, without equipment and completely exhausted.'

'As thousands died, many rebelled or refused to fight. By September 1917 the horses were dropping dead from starvation in the streets of Petrograd. It was then that Lenin travelled from Switzerland through to the Russian capital. Some say that the Kaiser gave him safe passage on his private train through Germany.'

'Does that mean the Kaiser helped Lenin get to power in Russia?'

'That is what some believe and that is why the western allies always believed that Lenin and Trotsky were on the German payroll. Of course Lenin and Trotsky denied it. Anyway, by the end of October 1917 the Bolsheviks had decided to act. Soldiers had been deserting the front, often murdering their officers as they went. Any officer fortunate enough to escape murder was deprived of their rank and expelled from the army by committees of privates. The latter were controlled by the Military Revolutionary Committee of the Soviets. Now, as you would expect, Kerensky had outlawed the Military Revolutionary Committee, but when he did this Lenin took his opportunity to seize power. Kerensky quickly went into hiding, fearing for his life. Many thought he had escaped Russia but there is evidence that he hung around for many months hoping to galvanise enough support to overthrow Lenin and retrieve power. This is what you have to remember, Paul, about Russia. Everything was in constant upheaval. The only thing you could be sure of was CHANGE!'

'It must have been awful! Without any law or order and no help from the government because you didn't know from one day to the next what or who the government was!' 'Quite! You are beginning to get the measure of what ANARCHY is all about.'

'Hell on earth, I don't doubt,' Paul sombrely replied.

'Now as soon as Lenin came to power he wanted to make peace with Germany and to end Russia's role in the war. He turned the old orders wherever he found them on their heads. As a result all was in turmoil and there was tremendous chaos in Russia. Overnight, privates became generals, railway porters found themselves commissars and anarchists roamed about town and country pillaging and murdering.'

'What about the soldiers loyal to the Tsar? Did they join Lenin?'

'Only if they were starving and couldn't get food. Of course, the really committed monarchists would have starved rather than join Lenin. But others had no loyalties and swapped side as the fancy took them. You must also remember that many Tsarist generals had to fight on two fronts, not only against the Bolshevik forces but against the Germans.'

'To complicate matters even further, the other political party in Russia was the Social Revolutionaries. They were fighting the Tsarist forces, the Whites, and Lenin's new army, now called the Reds or Bolsheviks.'

'So,' interrupted Paul, 'Lenin made peace with Germany and that's why he was called the Kaiser's puppet, I suppose?'

'Yes, and much to the horror of the allied forces, German troops increased on the Western Front against the Allies, since they were not having to fight the Russians! To make matters worse for us, the agreement meant that the Germans had access to the agricultural land of the Ukraine. Their soldiers became fit and strong and the outlook was disastrous for us and by March 1918 there was a distinct possibility that Germany would win the war.'

'But they didn't. So how did their position change so dramatically because, by November 1918, only seven months later, Germany had surrendered to the allied forces!'

'Well now,' Michael continued, 'we must not get embroiled in the goings on of the Great War if we are to stay focused on the events taking place during the Russian Revolution. It is a mistake of many of my students to do just that and yet a certain amount of knowledge is important; because quite clearly, these two cataclysmic events that brought so much destruction upon the human race are connected. Indeed it is probably right to say that the future

World War was born out of the seeds of the peace drawn up in November 1918.'

'But I thought the U.S. President said that the First World War was "the war to end all wars"?' Paul enquired.

'Sadly, we know it wasn't. The Kaiser was right when he said some years later that it was "a peace to end all peace".

Anyway, as time went on a rift between the future leaders manifested itself. While Lenin was determined on peace, Trotsky had other ideas. He was a flamboyant character with a great mass of black wavy hair and horn-rimmed glasses. You have probably seen pictures of him. Anyway, Trotsky fancied himself as a military commander and was committed to continuing the war against Germany. In fact he fell out with Lenin and refused to sign the treaty with Germany. But Lenin humiliated him and sent him back to Brest Litovsk for a second time, where he was forced to sign it. Now some people have said that Trotsky may have been planning to overthrow Lenin all through that year of 1918. Anyway, after signing the treaty the Germans took control of large parts of Russia.'

'They were served well in the Ukraine by the Hetman of the Cossacks, General Skoropadski. He was an imperialist who was not only fiercely loyal to the Tsar and his family in Russia but, bizarrely, to Kaiser Wilhelm II of Germany, who was now his taskmaster. This was despite the fact that these two men were mortal enemies.'

'But surely, no man can serve two masters?'

'In the normal course of events you would be right but there was more than one type of war going on. Yes, World War I was about physical boundaries but there was also a heady mix of ideologies. Imperialists stuck together, no matter what country they came from, and never more so than against the Bolsheviks, who were turning traditional values on their head and don't forget Paul, they banned religion. The Bolsheviks said they wanted to make the peasants lords of all they surveyed and so they encouraged them to set up local *soviets* to take power from the old Tsarist landlords and nobility that had ruled the land in Russia for generations. They used one of the oldest tricks in the book to get control and promised a new life of freedom, away from the suffocating regime of imperial rule. From now on the people would be in control.'

'But it didn't work!'

'No of course not, we know today that ultimate power corrupts! But look, we are running ahead of ourselves. At this time nobody really knew what the outcome would be. The allies were convinced that the Bolshevik regime could not last and that the old order would be restored. In London many did not understand the difference between a Marxist and a Bolshevik anyway, but one thing they were clear on: the danger it spelt for their systems of government if it was allowed to be successful. Some were quite sure that Lenin and Trotsky were intent on conquering the world and turning it Bolshevik. But you asked a moment ago how Germany could have been defeated so quickly having been so successful seven months earlier. All I can say is the allies must have had God on their side.' Michael smiled at his attempted joke.

'I can see I need to get this all into perspective.'

Michael waved his hand in the air. 'Yes, you do. It is complicated. But you just have to remember that people who want to be in control will use any means available to get that power, including making promises they know they can't keep. They always believe that they are right and will usually find a way of convincing the population to go to war.'

'About the Brest Litovsk Treaty, What do you think really happened between Lenin and Trotsky?'

Michael gave a long sigh. 'Well scholars say Lenin and Trotsky fell out over it and then made up. Some say that Trotsky still harboured ambitions to overthrow Lenin and take power for himself but I'm not sure about that. What you can be sure of is that both the allied powers and the Germans would have been working to ensure that whatever the outcome was it benefited their individual cause.' You see, you have to bear in mind that there were politicians, leaders of the army, navy, and fledgling air forces who were all scrambling for power in the various countries, but it was the spies that helped keep the channels of communication open. Today we tend to think of them as traitors to their country, nasty and disloyal, but we should remember that all sides employed them and that many were double and triple agents. They had their own altruistic reasons for spying and did whatever was necessary to get the war finished. Some, like Sidney Reilly, moved between the great power bases of their time, negotiating with the leaders, carrying news as well as promises, from one side to another so that peace could finally be agreed.

They gave up their lives and were vilified for their actions, but if you ask me, without them, the war would have gone on for a lot longer.'

Paul smiled. He was pleased with all that he was being told.

'That is why,' Michael continued, 'in January 1918, over the heads of the Foreign Secretary and the Foreign Office Chiefs, Lloyd George sent Bruce Lockhart, former Consul-General in Moscow, as head of a special mission to establish relations with the Bolsheviks. His brief from Lloyd George was to keep Russia in the war and stop the Bolsheviks from signing a peace treaty with Germany.'

'What was he like?' asked Paul.

'He was a brilliant diplomat, although some thought not! He knew Russia and all sections of the Russian people well and naturally spoke fluent Russian. He quickly established friendly relations with the Bolshevik leaders and in particular Trotsky, who as we know was all for maintaining the war with Germany. Lockhart was convinced that the only way of preventing a separate peace and of stopping the Germans from exploiting the position was for the Allies to co-operate with the new Bolshevik regime.'

'That seems to make sense,' Paul admitted. 'I suppose Lockhart must have befriended Trotsky to ensure he remained convinced that the Brest-Litovsk treaty was not worth signing?'

'Yes, but Trotsky didn't need any convincing. He already thought the treaty was an unworthy document because it gave so much power to Germany and took it away from the Bolshevik power base of Russia. But Lenin wanted to sue for peace with Germany and what Lenin wanted Lenin usually got. He was at the zenith of his power despite the military and economic situation in Russia being so desperate. You see, German troops were already advancing towards Petrograd. Lenin knew he could control the Kaiser and those German troops, as well as Trotsky, and he was right. Because by March, a humiliated and furious Trotsky was forced to agree to the German peace terms imposed at Brest Litovsk. The British and French Governments were convinced that the Bolshevik leaders were traitors to the allied cause and in the pay of the Germans. But in reality the Bolsheviks had little alternative but to make peace with Germany since they were in dire straits themselves. So there we have it. I hope I've helped, but please do read that book; it will help fill in any missing pieces of the jigsaw.'

Paul smiled. 'I think I have the gist of what was happening. I just need to understand Reilly's role in the Lockhart Plot. You have heard of that I presume?'

'Yes of course! Now don't forget you'll find all you need to know in that book.' Michael added, tapping the book Paul was holding.

'One moment sir, what would you say to if I told you that I thought Sidney Reilly was the man Fox in *Rescuing the Czar*?'

Michael smiled. 'I'd advise you to explore and test your hypothesis for saying so, THOROUGHLY!'

Chapter Twenty   Comrade Relinsky

After Michael had left, Paul noticed something on the floor. It was his paper full of scribbling around the words *Venus*, *Juno* and *Hebe*. He had been trying to unravel a possible anagram but the idea that Michael had seen it made him flush with embarrassment. Perhaps Michael thought him childish. Oh well, never mind he thought, staring down at the small comic book he was holding. Michael was right. It was difficult to think of it as academic literature. Well you can't judge a book by its cover! Paul sat down on the bed and randomly flicked through its pages. Then something he saw made him settle on page twenty-three. It was a description of that awful year 1918.

Revolutionary Petrograd, besieged by foreign enemies without and menaced within by counter revolutionary plots, was a terrible city in 1918. There was little food, no heat, no transport and ragged men and women shivered in endless breadlines on the bleak, un-swept streets. The long grey nights were punctuated with the sounds of gunfire. Gangster bands, defying the Soviet regime, roamed the city, robbing and terrorizing the population. Detachments of armed workers marched from building to building, searching for the hidden stores of the food speculators, rounding up looters and terrorists.

A certain Mr. Massino had shown up in Petrograd that spring. He described himself as "a Turkish and Oriental merchant". He was a pale, long-faced, sombre-looking man in his early forties with a high, sloping forehead, restless dark eyes and sensual lips. He walked with an erect, almost military carriage, and with a rapid, curiously silent step. He seemed to be wealthy. Women found him attractive. Amid the uneasy atmosphere of the temporary Soviet capital, Mr Massino went about his business with a peculiar aplomb. At evenings, Mr Massino was a frequent visitor to the small, smoky Balkov Cafe, a favourite haunt of anti-Soviet elements in Petrograd. The proprietor, Serge Balkov, greeted him deferentially. In a private room at the back of the cafe, Mr Massino met mysterious men and women who spoke to him in low tones. Some of them addressed him in Russian, others in French or English. Mr Massino was familiar with many languages. The young Soviet Government was struggling to bring order out of chaos. Its colossal organizational tasks were still further complicated by the ever-present, deadly menace of the counter-revolution.

"The bourgeoisie, the landlords and all the wealthy classes are making desperate efforts to undermine the revolution" wrote Lenin. A special Soviet counter-sabotage and counter- espionage organization was set up, at Lenin's recommendation, to deal with domestic and foreign enemies. It was called the Extraordinary Commission to Combat Counter Revolution and Sabotage. Its Russian initials spelled the word: CHEKA. In the summer of 1918, when the Soviet Government, fearing German attack, moved to Moscow, Mr Massino followed it. But in Moscow the appearance of the suave, wealthy Levantine merchant oddly changed. He wore a leather jacket and the peaked cap of a worker. He visited the Kremlin, stopped at the gates by one of the young Communist Lettish Guards, who formed the elite corps guarding the Soviet Government. Here the erstwhile Mr Massino produced an official Soviet document. *It identified him as Sidney Georgevitch Relinsky, an agent of the Criminal Division of the Petrograd Cheka.*

"Pass Comrade Relinsky!" said the Lettish guard.

In another part of Moscow, in the luxurious apartment of the popular ballet dancer Dagmara K, Mr Massino, alias Comrade Relinsky of the Cheka, was known as Monsieur Constantine, an agent of the British Secret Service. At the British Embassy, Bruce Lockhart knew his real identity: Sidney Reilly, the mystery man of the British Secret Service and known as the master spy of Britain. Of all the adventurers who emerged from the political underworld of Czarist Russia during the First World War to lead the great crusade against Bolshevism none was more colourful and extraordinary than Captain Sidney George Reilly of the British Secret Service.

"A man cast in the Napoleonic mould!" exclaimed Bruce Lockhart, whom Reilly was to involve in one of the most dangerous and fantastic undertakings in European history. Just how Reilly first came to the British Secret Service remains one of the many mysteries surrounding that very mysterious and powerful espionage apparatus. Sidney Reilly was born in Czarist Russia. The son of an Irish sea captain and a Russian woman, he grew up in the Black Sea port of Odessa. Prior to the First World War, he was employed by the great Czarist naval armaments concern of Mandrochovitch and Count Tchubersky in St Petersburg. Even then, his work was of a highly confidential character. He served as liaison between the Russian firm and certain German industrial and financial interests, including the famous Hamburg shipyards of Bluhm and Voss.

Just before the outbreak of the First World War, valuable information concerning the German submarine and shipbuilding program began regularly reaching the British Admiralty in London. The source of this information was Sidney Reilly.

In 1914, Reilly showed up in Japan as the "confidential representative" of the Banque Russo-Asiatique. From Japan he travelled to the United States, where he conferred with American bankers and munitions manufacturers. Already, in the files of the British Secret Service, Sidney Reilly was listed under the code name S.T.1 and was known as a secret agent of great daring and resourcefulness. A fluent linguist, with a command of seven languages, Reilly was soon summoned from the United States for important work in Europe. In 1916, he crossed the Swiss frontier into Germany. Posing as a German naval officer, he penetrated the German Admiralty. He secured and delivered back to London a copy of the official German Naval Intelligence Code. It was probably the greatest secret service coup of the First World War.

Early in 1918, Captain Reilly was transferred to Russia as Director of British Secret Intelligence operations in that country. His many personal friends, wide business connections and intimate knowledge of the inner circles of the Russian counter-revolution, made him an ideal man for the job. But the Russian assignment also had a deep personal significance for Reilly. He was consumed by a bitter hatred for the Bolsheviks and, indeed, for the entire Russian Revolution. He frankly stated his counter-revolutionary aims: "The Germans are human beings. We can afford to be beaten by them. Here in Moscow there is growing to maturity the arch -enemy of the human race. If civilization does not move first and crush the monster, while yet there is time, the monster will finally overwhelm civilization."

In his reports to the British Secret Service headquarters in London, Reilly repeatedly advocated an immediate peace with Germany and an alliance with the Kaiser against the Bolshevik menace. "At any price," he declared, "this foul obscenity which has been born in Russia must be crushed out of existence. Peace with Germany: yes, peace with Germany, peace with anybody! There is only one enemy. Mankind must unite in a holy alliance against this midnight terror!"

On his arrival in Russia, Reilly immediately plunged into anti-Soviet conspiracy. His avowed aim was to overthrow the Soviet Government.

Money and Murder

The numerically strongest anti-Bolshevik political party in Russia in 1918 was the Social Revolutionary Party, which advocated a form of agrarian socialism. Led by Boris Savinkov, Kerensky's one-time war minister who had taken part in the abortive Kornilov Putsch, the militant Social Revolutionaries had become the pivot of anti-Bolshevik sentiment. Their extremist methods and propaganda had attracted considerable support for them among the many anarchistic elements which generations of Czarist oppression had bred in Russia. The Social Revolutionaries had long practised terrorism as a weapon against the Czar. Now they prepared to turn the same weapon against the Bolsheviks.

The Social Revolutionaries were receiving financial aid from the French Intelligence Service. With funds personally handed to him by the French Ambassador Noulens, Boris Savinkov had re-established the old Social Revolutionary terrorist centre in Moscow under the title of League for the Regeneration of Russia. Its aim was to plan the assassination of Lenin and other Soviet leaders. On Sidney Reilly's recommendation, the British Secret Service also began supplying Savinkov with money for the training and arming of his terrorists. But Reilly, an ardent pro-Czarist, did not trust the Social Revolutionaries when it came to forming a new Russian Government to replace the Soviet regime. Apart from Savinkov, whom he regarded as completely reliable, Reilly felt that the leftist Social Revolutionaries represented a dangerously radical force. Some of them were known to be linked with the opposition Bolsheviks who followed Trotsky. Reilly was prepared to use these people for his own purposes, but he was determined to stamp out radicalism in Russia. He wanted a military dictatorship as the first step to the restoration of Czarism. So while he continued to finance and encouraged the Social Revolutionary terrorists and other radical anti-Soviet groups, the British spy was at the same time carefully building a conspiratorial apparatus of his own.

Reilly himself later revealed in his memoirs how it functioned: "It was essential that my Russian organization should not know too much and that no part of it should be in a position to betray another. The scheme was accordingly arranged on the 'Fives' system and each participant knew another four persons only. I myself, who was at the summit of the pyramid, knew them all, not personally, but by name and address only, and very useful was I to find the knowledge afterwards. Thus, if anything were betrayed, everybody would not be discovered, and the discovery would be localized."

Linking up with the Union of Czarist Officers, with remnants of the old Czarist secret police, the sinister Ochrana, with Savinkov's terrorists, and with similar counter revolutionary elements, Reilly's apparatus soon mushroomed throughout Moscow and Petrograd. A number of Reilly's former friends and acquaintances from Czarist days joined him and proved of great value. These friends included Count Tchubersky, the naval armaments magnate who had once employed Reilly as a liaison with the German shipyards; The Czarist General Yudenitch; the Petrograd cafe proprietor, Serge Balkov; the ballet dancer, Dagmara, at whose apartment Reilly set up his Moscow headquarters; Grammatikov, a wealthy lawyer and former undercover agent of the Ochrana, who now became Reilly's chief contact with the Social Revolutionary Party; and Veneslav Orlovsky, another former Ochrana agent, who had contrived to become a Cheka official in Petrograd, and from whom Reilly obtained the forged Cheka passport under the name of Sidney Georgevitch Relinsky, which enabled him to travel freely anywhere in Soviet Russia.

These and other agents, who even penetrated into the Kremlin and Red Army General Staff, kept Reilly fully informed of every measure of the Soviet Government. The British spy was able to boast that sealed Red Army orders "were being read in London before they were opened in Moscow." Large sums of money to finance Reilly's operations, amounting to several millions of roubles, were hidden in the Moscow apartment of the ballet dancer, Dagmara. In raising these funds, Reilly drew on the resources of the British Embassy. The money was collected by Bruce Lockhart and conveyed to Reilly by Captain Hicks of the British Secret Service. Lockhart, whom Reilly involved in this business, subsequently revealed in his book 'Memoirs of a British Agent' how the money was collected.

"There were numerous Russians with hidden stores of roubles. They were only too glad to hand them over in exchange for a promissory note on London. To avoid all suspicion, we collected the roubles through an English firm in Moscow. They dealt with the Russians, fixed the rate of exchange and gave the promissory note. In each transaction we furnished the English firm with an official guarantee that it was good for the amount in London. The roubles were brought to the American Consulate-General, and were handed over to Hicks, who conveyed them to their destined quarters." Finally, overlooking no detail, the British spy even drew up a detailed plan for the government that was to take power as soon as the Soviet Government was overthrown."

"Reilly's personal friends were to play an important part in the new regime. All arrangements had been made for a provisional government. My great friend and ally Grammatikov was to become Minister of the Interior, having under his direction all affairs of police and finance. Tchubersky, an old friend and business associate of mine, who had become head of one of the greatest mercantile houses in Russia, was to become Minister of Communications. Yudenitch, Tchubersky and Grammatikov would constitute a provisional government to suppress the anarchy which would almost inevitably follow from such a revolution."

Paul placed the book on his bedside table and looked out of the window. As usual, his father was hard at work tending the rose bushes. Well, it was too nice a day to be stuck in doors. Paul smelt coffee on the stove as he walked into the kitchen. His head was full of Sidney Reilly and his various revolutionary plans. Surely the plans to rescue the Tsar and family must have been linked to Sidney Reilly's plans to overthrow the Bolsheviks and reinstate a Monarchist regime? But why had no one suggested that? Paul remembered that the assassination attempt on Lenin and other events at around this time had always been referred to as the "Lockhart plot". But Lockhart had always denied any involvement. So why did the history books continue with the myth? He found it difficult to understand all the complexities. The years of prayer and ritual had taken their toll on his brain. It just wasn't flexible enough to think of so many possibilities all at once. And yet he couldn't let the question go. Why call it "The Lockhart Plot" when everyone knew that it was really Reilly's plot?

Chapter Twenty One　　　Assassination in Moscow

After finishing his coffee Paul went out into the bright warm sunshine. Seating himself on his favourite bench he watched with admiration as the rays of sunlight darted among the trees. Just as he closed his eyes he felt a thump on the bench next to him. It was Tonya.

'Paul, so you ARE here!'

Paul shaded his eyes. 'Yes, just sitting quietly enjoying the fruits of heaven.'

Tonya thought he sounded rather melancholic. 'I know! It's such a lovely day! Let's go for a picnic?'

Paul smiled as he spotted a figure walking towards them. 'Sounds like a good idea but look, here comes Alex.'

'Phew, it's hot. I could murder a cold drink. Anyone fancy a beer?'

Tonya shook her head. 'Actually Paul and I were just wondering whether we should go for a picnic?'

'That's a good idea. I'll join you. Unless of course you're thinking of taking communion together! How about Tivoli? You said you wanted to go there. I'll drive.'

Tonya jumped up. 'What a good idea! All those hidden grottos come on.' Before he knew it, she was dragging Paul along the path.

Alex shouted as he ran to catch up with them, 'Never mind making sandwiches, we'll get something on the way. Let's just go.'

Paul hung back. 'I'm not sure. I have some reading to do.'

'Oh come on Paul, don't be such a spoil sport. Please! What's more important – reading a book or going out with us?'

'Well, I'm not feeling up to it today. So I'll see you later. Have a nice time.'

A disappointed Tonya watched as Paul made his way back to his room.

'Never mind him,' Alex said, poking her in the ribs. 'You should realise he's a very busy priest. He hasn't got time to explore romantic grottos with you and me.'

'Thank you Alex, you don't need to remind me'

Paul climbed the stairs to his room, repeating as he went, 'Reilly could be Fox, Fox could be Reilly the oh so Reilly Fox!' Once in his room he grabbed a pen and paper but then, for no reason, he recalled the look of disappointment on Tonya's face. Well, there would be plenty of other times, he thought. Then, ignoring the excited hullabaloo downstairs, he sat down calmly at his desk overlooking the garden and started to write:

POINT ONE. Sidney Reilly's plans to overthrow Lenin would have started with a military dictatorship and after a few weeks of peace in the streets and the return of normality to civilian life, he would establish a new Democratic Government, which would include the reinstatement of Nicholas as the Tsar but under a new liberal constitution.

*POINT TWO. A newly reformed, less autocratic monarchy would have subdued the calls for a revolution and allowed the people to return to their religion. Therefore....*he paused for a moment. It was taking time to piece together his thoughts. *Therefore....*

POINT THREE. Part of Reilly's strategy included well formulated plans to rescue the Tsar and his family from Ekaterinburg.

Suddenly Paul had a light bulb moment. It was called the "Lockhart Plot" because it was a way of distancing Sidney Reilly and his plans for the reinstatement of the Monarchy. But why worry about that if the Imperial Family had been murdered? Unless of course, Lockhart and Reilly KNEW THEY HADN'T!

POINT FOUR. The Lockhart Plot was indeed part of a much larger plan to rescue the Tsar and his family and reinstate a constitutional monarchy in Russia.

POINT FIVE. The character of FOX as portrayed in the book 'Rescuing the Czar', was in reality Britain's so called master spy, Sidney Reilly.

'There, it's done!' Paul sat back and stared at his notes. He visualized Sidney Reilly dressed up as a German soldier and saw him accompanying the Imperial Family to a safe haven somewhere in the vast expanses of northern Russia.

How proud the brave Sidney Reilly would have been to welcome the Tsar and his family back to the Winter Palace! Siberia! Then Paul had a revelation. But that's where the white Siberian fox comes from. Ah ha! Now I know why he called himself Fox!

Downstairs, Alice knocked gingerly on the library door.

'Come in,' Michael called out confidently.

'I have the Sanskrit for you. It's all been translated, just as I promised.'

Michael took the paper and read it out loud: *'From ignorance lead me to the truth. From darkness lead me to the light. From death lead me to immortality. AUM. AUM. AUM. Peace! Peace! Peace!'*

'I see. A transcendental mantra! I particularly like the third line. But why write on the box Alice?'

'I don't know. Let me have a look at it. I'll see if I can detect a vibration.'

'We can do that later if you don't mind!'

'How about using the mantra as a blessing for our meetings then?'

Michael thought for a moment. 'That sounds like a good idea, so long as it doesn't offend anyone?'

Alice thought for a moment. 'Well, how would we know if someone was offended? People don't always say. I suppose you are right Giovanni and Paul will not like the *AUM* word; after all, they are staunch Catholics!'

Michael sighed. 'Well so are we Alice but we don't mind! Besides, I never did understand why religions have to be so precious about their words. Holy words are all the same surely?'

Alice knew exactly what he meant. 'Indeed! There is never any harm in mixing things up a little!' She replied.

* * *

Later that afternoon, Paul awoke, stretched, and felt totally refreshed. Only three hours before dinner. Hmm! That's long enough he thought, picking up his book. He wanted to check up on the events leading to the attempted assignation of Lenin. All the ends must tie up if Michael was to be convinced that Reilly was the Fox in *'Rescuing the Czar'*.

Paul turned to the book again and started reading.

The first blows of the anti-Soviet campaign were struck by Savinkov's terrorists. On June 21st 1918 as he was leaving a workers' meeting at the Obuchov factory in Petrograd, the Soviet Commissar for Press Affairs, Volodarsky, was assassinated by a Social Revolutionary terrorist. This was followed within two weeks by the assassination of the German Ambassador Mirbach in Moscow on July 6th. The aim of the Social Revolutionaries was to strike terror in the Bolshevik ranks and simultaneously to precipitate a German attack, which they believed would spell the doom for Bolshevism.

On the day on which the German Ambassador was murdered the Fifth All-Russian Congress of Soviets was in session in the Opera House in Moscow. Allied observers sat in the gilded boxes listening to the speeches of the Soviet delegates.

There was an air of tension about the proceedings. Bruce Lockhart, sitting in a box with a number of other Allied agents and diplomats, knew that something eventful had occurred when Sidney Reilly entered. The British spy looked pale and agitated. In hurried whispers he told Lockhart what had happened.

The shot that killed Mirbach was to have been a signal for a general Social Revolutionary rising, backed by dissident Bolshevik elements, throughout the country. Social Revolutionary gunmen were to have raided the Opera House and arrested the Soviet delegates. But something had gone wrong. The Opera House was now surrounded by Red Army soldiers. There was firing in the streets, but it was clear that the Soviet Government had the situation in hand.

As Reilly spoke, he was examining his pockets for compromising documents. He found one, tore it into shreds and swallowed the pieces. A French secret agent, sitting beside Lockhart, proceeded to do the same thing.

A few hours later, a speaker rose on the stage of the Opera House and announced that an anti-Soviet Putsch, designed to overthrow the Soviet Government by force of arms, had been swiftly put down by the Red Army and the Cheka. There had been no public support for the Putschists whatsoever. Scores of Social Revolutionary terrorists, armed with bombs, rifles and machine guns, had been rounded up and arrested. Many of them had been killed. Their leaders were either dead, in hiding or in flight.

Paul recalled that Mirbach had been assassinated by a Social Revolutionary terrorist named Blumkin. He had gained admission to the German Embassy by posing as an officer of the Cheka who had come to warn Mirbach of a plot against his life. The German Ambassador then asked Blumkin how the assassins were planning to act. 'Like this!' cried Blumkin, as he whipped out his pistol and shot the Ambassador. Blumkin had apparently escaped by leaping through the window and was taken away in a waiting car. He later became the personal bodyguard of Leon Trotsky.

I wonder, thought Paul, whether it is conceivable that Reilly had a deal with Trotsky and that Trotsky knew about Reilly's plans? Trotsky did not agree initially with the Brest Litovsk Treaty because he didn't want to give up so much land and power to the Germans; especially as he was Minister of War. And what about the reports that said Trotsky's hairbrush had been found at the Ipatiev House after the family had escaped? Perhaps Reilly had promised Trotsky the leadership of the new Provisional Government. Paul wrote up a few more notes and then started reading again.

The Allied representatives in the Opera House were told they could now safely return to their respective embassies. The streets were safe. Later, the news came that an uprising at Yaroslav, timed to coincide with the Moscow Putsch, had also been put down by the Red Army. The Social Revolutionary leader, Boris Savinkov, who had personally led the Yaroslav uprising, had narrowly escaped capture by the Soviet troops. Reilly was bitterly angry and disappointed. The Social Revolutionaries had acted with characteristic impatience and stupidity! Nevertheless, he declared, there was nothing wrong with their basic idea of starting a coup at a moment when most of the Soviet leaders were assembled in one place attending some congress or convention. The thought of seizing all the chief Bolsheviks at one swoop appealed to Reilly's Napoleonic imagination. He began seriously to plan to accomplish this.

During the climactic month of August 1918, the secret plans for allied intervention in Russia flared into the open. On August 2nd British troops disembarked at Archangel with the proclaimed purpose of preventing war supplies from falling into the hands of the Germans.

Paul recalled that the Americans and the Czechs had been in Vladivostok since July 1918 and that large sections of Siberia were already in the hands of the Germans and White Russians. But in reporting these events the authors had avoided discussing another critical part of Russian history, namely the disappearance of the Romanov family from Ekaterinburg. Paul wanted to know what was going on in the two weeks leading up to July 17th 1918 and the two weeks after, virtually the whole of July! The only date that had got close to being discussed was the July 6th assassination of the German ambassador Mirbach.

Now the German ambassador had insisted that the Tsar and his family be allowed to go free and shortly before his untimely death he had assured concerned monarchists that they had nothing to worry about because the matter was well in hand! Everything was going according to plan. The Tzarist General Krasnov, supported by the Germans, was waging a bloody anti-Soviet campaign across Russia. In Kiev a pro German Hetman called General Skoropadski had control of the Ukraine as well as its fertile wheat fields, which were the main source of food for both the Russians and the Germans. So it must have come as a great shock when the German ambassador was murdered. Who now was going to negotiate for the release of the Imperial Family? Well clearly there were no negotiations to be had. It must have been obvious that the only way forward now was to rescue the family and not wait for further negotiations. That's why General Skoropadski was called into action. If there was a German plan to rescue the family this man would have been very useful with his Cossack army made up of many German soldiers! In the early days of July 1918 the timing was absolutely right. There couldn't have been a better time for a rescue attempt because from the north, south, east and west, the enemies of Bolshevik Russia were preparing to converge on Moscow. But how was Reilly involved? Paul knew that any plot to rescue the Tsar and his family had to be put in context with what else was happening in Russia. So, picking up Bruce Lockhart's *'Memoirs of a British Agent'*, he turned to page 313 and made the following notes for his presentation:

It was an extraordinary situation. There had been no declaration of war yet fighting was proceeding on a front stretching from the Dvina to the Caucasus. Lockhart had several discussions with Reilly, who had decided to remain on in

Moscow after the diplomat's departure. On August 15th 1918 Bruce Lockhart received an important visitor. He was lunching in his apartment, near the British Embassy, when the bell rang and his servant announced that two Lettish gentlemen wished to see him. One was a short, sallow-faced youth called Snridhen. The other, a tall, powerfully built man with clear-cut features and hard, steely eyes, introduced himself as Colonel Berzin, the commander of the Lettish Kremlin Guard. The visitors brought Lockhart a letter from Captain Cromie, the British Naval Attaché in Petrograd, who was extremely active in anti-Soviet conspiracy. "Always on my guard against agents-provocateurs," records Lockhart, "I scrutinized the letter carefully. It was unmistakably from Cromie." Lockhart asked his visitors what they wanted.

Colonel Berzin, who had introduced himself as the commander of the Kremlin Guard, informed Lockhart that, while the Letts had supported the Bolshevik Revolution, they had no intention of fighting the British forces under General Poole which had recently landed at Archangel. They were prepared to talk terms with the British agent. Before giving an answer, Lockhart talked the matter over with the French Consul General, M. Grenard, who as Lockhart records, advised him to negotiate with Colonel Berzin but to avoid compromising our own position in any way. The next day, Lockhart again saw Colonel Berzin and gave him a paper saying, "Please admit bearer, who has an important communication for General Poole, through the English lines." Lockhart then put Colonel Berzin in touch with Sidney Reilly. Two days later, according to Lockhart, Reilly reported that his negotiations were proceeding smoothly but the Letts had no intention of being involved in the collapse of the Bolsheviks.

"He put forward a suggestion that after our departure he might be able, with Lettish help, to stage a counter-revolution in Moscow. This suggestion was categorically turned down by General Lavergne, Grenard, and myself. Reilly was warned specifically to have nothing to do with so dangerous and doubtful a move. Reilly then went underground. That is, into hiding."

Yes! Paul was elated. Now he had exactly what he was looking for: the evidence of a conspiracy to overthrow the Bolsheviks; and he was completely satisfied that his presentation was going to be the most revealing yet.

Chapter Twenty Two   The Lockhart Plot

It was two o'clock prompt and everyone except Giovanni was seated around the table in Michael's library. Alice had decided to delay the introduction of the mantra until the following week. She said she had a particular reason but Michael hadn't bothered to ask what it was.

After sorting through his notes, Paul stood up and then sat down again nervously. Moving his books to one side he leant forward, trying to get comfortable in his chair, but he couldn't and decided to stand after all. 'I'll start my presentation with an important statement, which we should keep in mind when researching any plot to rescue the Tsar.'

Paul paused to make sure he had everyone's attention. Michael smiled at the professional start. Even Alex was surprised. This was not the Paul he knew. The son of a gardener turned sombre priest and now a budding lecturer no less!

'What I'm about to tell you I have read in these books.' Paul patted the pile of books by him. 'Any plan to rescue the Imperial Family must fit into the historic context of the time. That is why I have been doing my own research into known operatives of the day. It has long been clear to us that both Fox and the Baroness 'B' are fictitiously named characters that hide the real identity of those who took part. Tonight I shall be asking an important question. Could the famous spy Sidney Reilly be Fox? But first let me tell you what was happening two weeks before the Russian Imperial Family disappeared from Ekaterinburg in the summer of 1918.'

Paul then proceeded to tell them about the murder on July 6th 1918 of the German ambassador Count Mirbach, who had been demanding the release of the Imperial Family. He explained how Sidney Reilly had purchased the support of the Letts, who were a mixture of Hungarians, Poles and Slav soldiers. 'The scene,' he explained, 'was set with all the pieces in place. The Allies were in control of Russia's major transport routes, whilst the Germans had control of the Ukraine and parts of Siberia. Remember the Allies were in Russia to fight the Germans, not the Bolsheviks! Anyway, let's move away from the war manoeuvres and concentrate on the potential of this moment in history for rescuing the Russian Imperial Family. We know the Americans and Japanese were in control of Vladivostok.

'Cossack forces helped to make up the Russian White army. These forces, loyal to the Tsar, were controlling parts of the Crimea and the Black Sea as well as the Ural Mountains. Kolchak, the great White Russian general, was on the offensive, the numbers in his army swelling as he passed the villages. But most crucially the Czechs had revolted against the Bolsheviks and were on the side of the Allies. They were now in full control of the Trans-Siberian railway and were heading directly for Ekaterinburg, where they expected to arrive no later than July 18th 1918.' Paul paused.

'Gosh, they were brave, but what did they hope to achieve in Ekaterinburg?' Tonya asked.

'Honestly,' laughed Alex, 'what on earth do you think they were going there for, to make bread?' Michael banged the table hard. 'Alex, will you keep your comments to yourself until after HE has finished!' Paul smiled. 'Well here's something strange for you to consider. Remember the Germans who the Allies were fighting? Well they now demanded the release of the family and, as I told you, they were in control of the Ukraine under the Cossack General Skoropadski. The local Reds who had been holding the Tsar and his family prisoners were not in any position to argue because they knew that Kaiser Wilhelm had been in negotiation with the Bolsheviks over food supplies, land distribution and the release of the Imperial Family into Germany's hands. However there is a possibility, at least from what I have been reading, that once the Germans had got hold of the Imperial Family they would then overthrow the Bolshevik regime and reinstate a puppet monarchy as part of a larger Prussian state. Kaiser Wilhelm II wanted to save the Russian Imperial Family; in particular the Empress and her daughters, since they were German Princesses of Hesse. So the question I am asking is this. Did the Czech army heading for Ekaterinburg beat the Germans to the rescue?'

'That's a very good question,' Michael observed, 'especially as the railroad was the most comfortable and safest form of transport in Russia. But Paul, don't forget there was another form of transport that would have been quicker, albeit far more dangerous.'

Paul frowned, but Tonya knew exactly what Michael was thinking.

'I'm speaking of the aeroplane of course, which by the way, could fly up to fourteen hundred miles without even stopping to refuel! Anyway, carry on Paul, have you finished?' Michael asked.

'No. I'd like to tell you what a certain Sidney Reilly was up to in Moscow.'

'Could I just ask a question?' Tonya interrupted. 'You seem to favour Sidney Reilly as our man Fox but surely there were many other agents who could have been Fox? Besides, Reilly was just a man interested in making money.'

Paul kept his calm. 'Reilly was not a man to sell his soul. On the contrary, he was extremely brave and committed to the monarchist cause and he appreciated the esoteric side of life. For example, he was a great expert and collector of paintings and sculpture. In fact he was famous for his Napoleonic collection.'

Tonya nudged Alex and whispered, 'Who would have thought a master spy would have been interested in paintings rather than money!'

Alex laughed. 'Yes, well it takes all sorts dear, maybe one day they'll be worth something!'

'Actually,' Michael interrupted, glancing briefly at Juliana as he was speaking. 'There have been lots of spies with an interest in the arts. Some were art critics, or painters, others sculptors, writers or journalists and woe betide anyone caught with a camera!'

Juliana thought Michael looked even more serious than usual as he spoke. But she didn't know that at that very moment his imagination had caught wind of an idea that photographic evidence of the family's escape might exist.

'I suppose during those times, anyone who had reason to travel could be used as a spy. But that doesn't mean they were full time agents!' she responded.

'Well, if an artistic temperament leads to an exploratory nature then I would be a very good spy indeed!' Alex laughed at his own suggestion.

'Wait a moment,' Tonya said. 'You're intriguing me. If I recall correctly, there is a passage in *'Rescuing the Czar'* where the rescuer of the Imperial Family gives expert opinion on a whole lot of beautiful paintings stored in a hidden chamber of a villa. Oh look, I have the passage right here I think.' She quickly pulled out the book that practically lived in her pocket. 'Here it actually informs us that this passage will identify Fox. Let me read it to you now.

I am certain that the former occupant of this villa was some Russian of taste and means. Today, while leaning against a wall that was panelled after the fashion of the walls in the Hermitage, one of the panels gave way and I found myself toppling backward into a very large room resembling a gallery There were a number of wall hangings of silk from which the pictures had been removed. The candelabra was of malachite, There were clumps of violet, jasper, porphyry, lapis-lazuli, aventurine and syenite scattered around as though the place had been divested of its furnishings in a hurry.

I have seen the same things in the HERMITAGE when for architectural elegance, richness of ornamentation and lavishness of decoration it was unequalled by any art museum in the world.'

    'While poking around among the piles of tables and vases that were moved over to one corner I came across a box of paintings that must have been STOLEN from St Petersburg.

    Here is the "Madonna del Latte of Corregio", or a mighty good imitation, that everyone remembers from the Hermitage. Here is Rembrandt's "Girl with the Broom," the "Portrait of Sobieski", and the "Farmyard" of Paul Potter. Here is the "Expulsion of Hagar" by Rubens, in which Sarah wears a white handkerchief and yellow veil around her head, with one of her hands resting on her hip and the other encased in a blue sleeve raised in a threatening gesture toward Hagar, and here is "Celestine and her Daughter in Prison", that one NEVER forgets because of the controversy between the partisans of Murillo and Velasquez over which of these two painters did the work. And here is Lossenke's "Sunrise on the Black Sea," Ugrimov's "Capture of Kazan" and "Election of Michael Romanov", in which the artist reaches the heights of Oriental splendour in colour, composition and design.... There is a FORTUNE going to the devil in this room!'

'So what do you think?' She asked closing the book again. 'I think...' Paul replied cautiously, 'that you have confirmed what I already believe. Namely that Sidney Reilly the man who adored and dealt in art was our man Fox. Now may I continue with the events leading up to the disappearance of the Tsar and his family?

    'Go right ahead,' Michael responded as Paul picked up his notes.

'Okay. So towards the end of August 1918, a small group of Allied representatives gathered for a confidential conference in a room at the American Consulate General in Moscow. The gathering at the American Consulate General was presided over by the French Consul, Grenard. The British were represented by Reilly and by Captain George Hill, a British Intelligence officer who had been delegated to work with Reilly. A number of other allied diplomats and secret service agents were present, including the French newspaperman René Marchand, who was the Moscow correspondent of the Paris Figaro. Reilly had called the meeting, according to his own account in his memoirs, to report on the progress of his anti-Soviet operations. He informed the Allied representatives that he had "bought" Colonel Berzin, the commander of the Kremlin Guard. The Colonel's price had been two million roubles. An advance of 500,000 roubles in Russian currency had been paid to Colonel Berzin by Reilly. The remainder of the sum was to be paid in English pounds when Colonel Berzin had rendered certain services and had escaped to the British lines in Archangel.'

'"Our organization is now immensely strong," declared Reilly. "The Letts are on our side, and the people will be with us the moment the first blow is struck!" Reilly then announced that a special meeting of the Bolshevik Central Committee was to be held at the Moscow Grand Theatre on August 28th. It would bring together in the same building all the key leaders of the Soviet state. Reilly's plot was bold but simple.'

'I'm sorry Paul, I have to interrupt you.' Alex demanded. 'You say August 28th 1918 but isn't that a bit late for our enquiry?'

'No, I don't think so. There is no reason why the Tsar should not have been rescued before the final act of counter-revolution was put in place.'

'Oh! So you think the Tsar and his family had already been rescued and were hiding somewhere in Russia during this time?'

'If certain reports are to be believed, the Dowager Empress Marie certainly believed her son to be safe.'

Alex rubbed his hands together. 'Well you certainly sound like you know your stuff. You'd better carry on Paul!'

'Now the Bolsheviks held their meetings in public and had planned to hold one in August. Reilly decided that in the course of their regular duty the Lettish guards could be stationed at all the entrances and exits of the theatre during the Bolshevik meeting. Colonel Berzin would choose only men absolutely faithful and devoted to the Monarchist cause. At a given signal Berzin's guards would close the doors and cover all the people in the theatre with their rifles. Then at that very moment a special detachment consisting of Reilly and his inner circle of conspirators would leap on to the stage and arrest all the members of the Central Committee of the Bolshevik Party!'

'Wow! That's adventurous if not a little reckless,' Tonya muttered as Paul stared at his notes, looking for where he had left off.

'One moment please. Ah yes, here we are. So the plan was to shoot Lenin. But before their execution the Bolsheviks would be publicly paraded through the streets of Moscow so that everyone should be aware that the tyrants of Russia were now prisoners! I won't go into the type of humiliation planned for them. But let's just say it was well below the belt!'

Alex smiled and tapped the side of his nose. He knew exactly what he meant.

'Now,' Paul continued, 'it was assumed that with Lenin and his associates out of the way, the Bolshevik regime would collapse like a house of cards. There were sixty thousand officers in Moscow, said Reilly, who were ready to mobilize immediately the signal was given. They would form an army to strike within the city while the Allied forces attacked from without.' Paul paused over something in his notes and Juliana took the opportunity to pass him a glass of water. 'Thanks... but ...er... what is that you are writing? You don't need to take notes. I can let you borrow these.'

'I'm not taking notes, just trying to work something out from the paragraph that Tonya read out. Fox's identity must be hidden in the title of the paintings. 'Look this is what I have so far,' she added, showing him the letters.

G M F D E R C N S A C N E V.

Michael glanced over and when he saw what she had written down he laughed. 'Well if you can get a name out of that you're cleverer than me. Carry on Paul.'

'Right, well the man to head up the secret anti-Soviet army was the well-known Tzarist officer, General Yudenitch. A second army under General Savinkov would assemble in the north of Russia and what remained of the Bolsheviks would be crushed between the two in a pincer movement. The British were in close touch with General Yudenitch and were preparing to supply him with arms and equipment and the French were backing Savinkov. Allied representatives who gathered at the American Consulate were apparently told what they could do to help with the conspiracy. As the day of the armed coup drew near, Reilly was meeting regularly with Colonel Berzin, carefully working out every last detail of the plot and making preparations for all possible contingencies. They were drawing up the final plans when they learned that the meeting of the Bolshevik Central Committee had been postponed from August 28th until September 6th! This came as a dreadful shock to Reilly but he kept a brave face. "I don't mind that," he told Berzin. "It gives me more time to make the final arrangements." So Reilly went off to Petrograd to make a last-minute check on the plans in that city.'

Paul put his notes down and picked up the comic looking book given to him by Michael. *The Great Conspiracy* by Michael Sayers and Albert Kahn tells us what happens next,' he said, turning to page thirty.

'In Petrograd Reilly went straight to the British Embassy to report to Captain Cromie, the British Naval Attaché. Reilly quickly outlined the situation in Moscow, and explained the plan for the uprising. "Moscow is in our hands!" he said. Cromie was delighted and Reilly promised to write out a full report for secret dispatch to London. The following morning Reilly began getting in touch with the leaders of his Petrograd apparatus. At noon he telephoned the former Ochrana agent, Grammatikov. Grammatikov's voice sounded hoarse and unnatural. "Who is it?" he asked.
   "It is I, Relinsky," said Reilly.
   "Who?" asked Grammatikov.
   Reilly repeated his pseudonym.
   "I have somebody with me who has brought bad news." Grammatikov said abruptly.
   "The doctors have operated too early. The patient's condition is serious. Come at once if you wish to see me."'

Tonya took a sharp intake of breath. 'PAUL! Those are the very same words used in *Rescuing the Czar*, remember in the second diary?' Paul smiled.

'Exactly, now you see why I wanted to tell you about Sidney Reilly. Anyway, let me continue with the story.

'Reilly hurried to Grammatikov's house and found him feverishly burning papers in the fire grate. "The fools have struck too early," Grammatikov said as soon as Reilly entered the room. "Uritsky is dead, assassinated in his office this morning at eleven o'clock!" As he spoke Grammatikov went on tearing up papers and burning the pieces. "It is a terrible risk, our staying here. I am of course already under suspicion." Reilly then called Captain Cromie at the British Embassy, and learned he knew about the assassination. Uritsky, the head of the Petrograd Cheka, had been shot by a Social Revolutionary terrorist. Everything, however, was still in order at Cromie's end. Guardedly, Reilly suggested they meet at the usual rendezvous, the Balkov Cafe. Reilly spent the intervening time destroying various incriminating and unnecessary documents and carefully hiding his codes and other papers. But Captain Cromie did not show up at the cafe. Reilly decided to risk a visit to the British Embassy.

As he left he whispered a warning to Balkov that something may have gone wrong. "Be prepared to leave Petrograd and slip across the frontier into Finland."'

'In the Vlademirovsky Prospect, Reilly saw men and women running. They dived into doorways and side streets. There was the roar of powerful engines. A car shot by, crammed with Red Army men, then another, and another. Reilly quickened his pace. He was almost running when he rounded the corner onto the street where the British Embassy was situated. He stopped abruptly. There in front of the Embassy lay several dead bodies. They were Soviet police officials. Four cars were drawn up opposite the Embassy, and across the street was a double cordon of Red Army men. The Embassy door had been battered off its hinges.

"Well, Comrade Relinsky, have you come to see our carnival?" Reilly spun around to see a young grinning Red Army soldier, whom he had met several times in his guise of Comrade Relinsky of the Cheka.

"Tell me, comrade, what has happened?" Reilly asked hastily.

'The CHEKA were looking for someone called Sidney Reilly', replied the soldier.

Later Reilly learned what had happened. Following the murder of Uritsky, the Soviet authorities in Petrograd had sent CHEKA agents to close up the British Embassy. Upstairs the members of the Embassy staff, under the direction of Captain Cromie, were burning incriminating papers. Captain Cromie dashed downstairs and bolted the door in the faces of the Soviet secret police. They broke down the door and the desperate British agent met them on the stairs with a Browning automatic in each hand. Cromie shot and killed a commissar and several other officials. The CHEKA agents returned his fire. Captain Cromie had fallen with a bullet through his head. Reilly spent the rest of that night at the home of a Social Revolutionary terrorist named Serge Dornoski.

In the morning he sent Dornoski out to reconnoitre and learn all he could. Dornoski returned with a copy of the official Communist newspaper Pravda. "The streets will run with blood," he said. "Somebody has had a shot at Lenin in Moscow, missed him unfortunately!" He handed Reilly the paper. A flaring headline told of the attempt on Lenin's life. On the previous evening, as Lenin was leaving the Michelson factory, where he had been speaking at a meeting, a Social Revolutionary terrorist named Fanya Kaplan had fired two shots point-blank at the Soviet leader. The bullets had been notched and poisoned. One of them had penetrated Lenin's lung above the heart. The other had entered his neck close to the main artery. But Lenin had not been killed.'

'His life hung in the balance. The gun which Fanya Kaplan had used on Lenin had been given to her by Reilly's accomplice, Boris Savinkov. Savinkov admitted this fact in his book, Memoirs of a Terrorist. Now with a small automatic pistol strapped under his arm for use in an emergency, Reilly left immediately by train for Moscow. En route the next day he bought a newspaper at the junction of Klin. The news was the worst possible.

There was a detailed account of Reilly's whole conspiracy, including the plan to shoot Lenin and the other Soviet leaders, to seize Moscow and Petrograd, and to set up a military dictatorship under Savinkov and Yudenitch. Reilly read on with growing dismay. René Marchand, the French journalist who had been present at the meeting at the American Consulate General, had informed the Bolsheviks of everything that had transpired there. But the final blow was yet to come. Colonel Berzin, the commander of the Lettish Guard, had named

Captain Sidney Reilly as the British agent who had tried to bribe him with an offer of two million roubles to join in a plot to murder the Soviet leaders.

The Soviet press also published the letter, which Bruce Lockhart had given Berzin to pass him through the British lines at Archangel. Lockhart had been arrested in Moscow by the CHEKA. Other allied officials and agents were being rounded up and taken into custody. All over Moscow, Reilly's description was pasted up. His various aliases – Massino, Constantine, Relinsky – were published, together with the proclamation of his outlawry. The hunt was on. In spite of the obvious danger, Reilly proceeded to Moscow. He located the ballet dancer, Dagmara, at the house of a woman named Vera Petrovna. She was an accomplice of Lenin's would-be assassin, Fanya Kaplan. Dagmara told Reilly that her apartment had been raided several days before by the Cheka. She had managed to conceal two million roubles which she had in thousand-rouble notes, part of Reilly's conspiratorial money. The CHEKA agents had not arrested her and she did not know why. Perhaps they believed she would lead them to Sidney Reilly. Now, with Dagmara's two million roubles at his disposal, Reilly was no easy game; sometimes disguised as a Greek merchant, sometimes an ex-czarist officer, sometimes a Soviet official, or a rank-and-file communist worker, always he kept on the move, eluding the CHEKA. Then, after a series of hairbreadth escapes, he made his way by means of a forged German passport to Bergen, Norway. From there he was able to sail for England. Back in London, Captain Reilly reported to his superiors in the British Secret Service.'

'He was full of regrets for lost opportunities. "If René Marchand had not been a traitor ... if Berzin had not shown the white feather ... if the Expeditionary Force had advanced quickly on the Vologda ... if I could have combined with Savinkov." But of one thing Reilly was sure. The fact that England was still at war with Germany was a mistake. There must be an immediate cessation of hostilities on the Western Front and a coalition against Bolshevism. "Peace, peace on any terms and then a united front against the true enemies of mankind!" cried Captain Sidney George Reilly.'

Paul placed the book on the table and looked up. 'There is something else I need to tell you. One day, while he was still in Russia Reilly met his former Moscow aide, Captain George Hill of the British Secret Service, who had managed to escape the Bolshevik net. The two agents checked lists of names and addresses. To his surprise Reilly discovered that a sizeable portion of his anti-Soviet apparatus was still intact. He felt there was still hope. But unlike Reilly, Captain Hill thought the game was up. He had heard that an exchange of prisoners was being arranged between the Soviet and British Governments.

The Russians were to free Lockhart and others in exchange for the safe passage home of various Soviet representatives, including Maxim Litvinov, whom the British authorities had arrested in England. Captain Hill said he was going to give himself up. He advised Reilly to do likewise. But Reilly would not admit defeat. "I'll get back without the permission of the Redskins," he told Captain Hill and he wagered his accomplice that they would meet in London in the Savoy Hotel two months later. After that Reilly remained in Russia for several weeks longer, apparently gathering espionage material and advising and encouraging anti-Soviet elements.

So that's the story of the famous "Lockhart Plot", which I think should really be called "The failed Reilly Plot!" But I suppose the whole point in telling you all this is to reinforce my theory that if the plot were to be successful in eventually reinstating a monarchist regime in Russia, Reilly would have required a Tsar! Therefore I believe the rescue plan must have been connected in some way to this plot. It gives added weight to the story because there was more than just a humane reason for rescuing the family. There was a political and economic reason as well.'

'That's really worrying Paul, because when the plot failed the Tsar and his family must have been in real trouble!' Tonya responded.

'Not necessarily,' replied Alex. 'If Paul is right they had already been successfully rescued and were hiding somewhere in northern Russia.'

'Well don't forget, at this time,' Michael interrupted, 'very few people knew that the Tsar and his family had disappeared from Ekaterinburg. Sure, as early as June 1918 there had been rumours of shootings but they had always been denied.'

'So did Reilly rescue the family then?' Tonya asked.

'Yes, surely he must have!' Juliana responded. 'He of all people would have had a back-up plan.'

'Well I have my views on the matter,' Paul continued. 'I believe they were rescued by Reilly, possibly with the help of Skoropadski's Cossacks OR by the eight hundred German soldiers stationed in Ekaterinburg at the time. Lenin was at death's door and the Whites were beating the Reds. Reilly may have failed but there were plenty of others willing to give their lives to see the Russian Imperial Family back on the throne of Russia.'

'The only worry Reilly might have had was whether two and two would be put together by the Soviets. That is why it was never referred to as the Reilly Plot but the Lockhart or Lettish Plot.'

'Yes, rather ironic when you consider that Lockhart was never actually involved with plans to rescue the Tsar or to overthrow the Bolsheviks! But it happened on his watch. That's why historians refer to it as the Lockhart Plot,' Michael added.

'Anyway,' responded Tonya, 'if we are to believe Fox, the Imperial Family escaped Russia dressed as Buddhist monks travelling on a camel train, apparently on their way to the Low White Monastery of Little Tibet and not as Paul would have us believe, on the Trans-Siberian railroad being served tea by the Czechs and cake by the Germans!'

Paul smiled. She was looking exceptionally pretty today. 'Surely you don't actually believe they escaped through India?'

'Of course I do!' replied Tonya adamantly.

PART THREE

IMPERIAL SERVICE

Chapter Twenty Three   Secrets of the German War Office

Juliana was in her studio when Tonya knocked on the door. 'Come in and have a seat if you can find one! I'm just clearing this mess up. Fancy giving me a hand?' Juliana laughed at her own cheeky question.

'If you insist, what would you like me to do first?'

'Don't be silly, I'm only joking. Anyway, how was your day with Alex? Did you enjoy your picnic?'

'Yes, that's what I came to tell you about. It was wonderful, such a romantic place. We could have stayed all week! And as for the Grotto of Neptune, I could easily imagine being there with Maria and Olga Romanov!'

Juliana was confused 'Maria and Olga Romanov?'

'Yes, the painting that Maria gave me, you know, the one painted in 1859.'

Juliana nodded. 'Ah! You mean the one the Baroness kept in her bedroom along with the other Romanov portraits?'

'Yes. I asked her once why she liked to wear her hair in the same style as the beautiful Maria Romanov, who was sitting by the river with her sister Olga. She gave me a smile and said because it was appropriately fashionable.' Tonya started giggling.

'What's so funny?'

'When she said that, I had a really silly thought.'

'Oh?' What was that?'

Tonya giggled again. 'Well I am rather ashamed to say.'

Juliana patted her on the arm. 'Come on, you can tell me.'

'Alright then, I asked her outright you know, if she was related to the Romanovs. She laughed and asked me which one! Well, then I knew she was playing me. Anyway when Alex and I were at the grotto it was so spooky. I could literally feel the princesses sitting there waiting for Neff to turn up with his brushes and palette! When Alex and I sat in the same place, just by the rushing river, I came over all goose-bumpy. Alex laughed and told me not to be so girly. What an insult! We even saw two butterflies, just like in the Neff painting. Alex told me lots of paintings went missing during the revolution.

I think it's his ambition to find a lost masterpiece or something!' She laughed at the thought. 'You must be so proud of him?'

'Yes, and I'm very glad you had a lovely day out but promise me you'll look after that painting.'

'Oh I certainly will. Speaking of which, where's your latest sculpture, or have you turned into a bookworm instead?' Tonya asked tapping the pile of neatly stacked books in front of her.

'It's funny you should say that because I'm finding it harder and harder to pick up the chisel. Do you know, I was so impressed with Paul's presentation that I felt quite moved to do another one myself.'

'Oh, so you have something important to say?'

Was she being sarcastic? Juliana wondered as she walked around the table to where Tonya was standing and picked up one of the books. 'I know it's hard to believe Tonya, but when you read this.... well, I'm hooked! Besides, I can't get a creative spark from my heart when my head is so full of this. Between you and me I'd love to believe they all escaped and yet...there is an air of tragedy I can't quite put my finger on.'

'Oh, I know exactly what you mean. I think about it all the time. Hey, I was surprised at how involved Paul is with this Sidney Reilly fellow. He's taken over Paul's life. I'm really surprised at that! Do you know, he didn't come for a picnic even though I practically begged him! He's certainly been acting strange. Not like his normal self.'

Juliana thought for a moment before replying. 'I suppose he is more communicative these days but he has always been a serious young man.'

Tonya picked up a scalpel and started tapping her palm with it. 'Do you know? The other day I found him un-wrapping a magnificent fountain pen and I swear it was solid gold. Apparently his father had asked him whether he wanted his initials engraved but all he wanted was "God is Gracious" written on it!'

'Well,' Juliana gently removed the scalpel from Tonya's hand. 'That's no surprise to me. He's a priest after all and his father, well he has always been a kind- hearted man.'

'Yes, but Giovanni must have saved for a long time to buy such an expensive present.'

Juliana dropped the scalpel into the basin for washing before wandering over to the window that overlooked the garden.

'He's a marvellous, giving kind of man who rarely thinks of his own needs, unlike someone else.... I.....' Juliana broke off, realizing what she was about to say. She smiled at Tonya before resuming again. 'You know, I often watch him in the garden. How he loves those roses of his! They are his pride and joy.'

'So they are. I bet you didn't know that he has asked Alex to paint them?'

'Paint the rose bushes, whatever next?'

Tonya giggled. 'I mean do a painting of them of course!'

'Really, well did Alex agree?'

'Yes, he said it was easy.'

Juliana laughed. 'That's Alex all over. Nothing is too difficult for him if he puts his mind to it. But he will need a very large canvas if he's going to get all the roses in. I wonder where Giovanni wants to hang it.'

'In the kitchen so he can look at the roses while he is cooking!'

Juliana laughed. 'Steaming roses, a kitchen is not exactly the best place for a painting! Still, I do worry. Giovanni is so melancholic these days. I think he misses the Baroness dreadfully. Oops! I shouldn't say that. I mean Maria.'

Tonya sighed as she listened to Juliana before picking up a scrap of paper that Juliana had scribbled on. 'Have you worked out what these letters mean yet?' she asked, waving the paper in the air.

'No I haven't. It's not easy. There are hardly any vowels you see.'

Tonya pulled a face as she read them out. G M F D E R C N S A C N E V. The problem is we have the F but there is no O or X!'

'Ah! But that's not his real name, remember?' Juliana mimicked Michael as she spoke.

Tonya laughed. 'Well there is no Sidney Reilly hidden in here either. Paul will be disappointed.' Saying this, she took her leave

Afterwards Juliana poured herself a cup of strong black coffee and sat down. She was tempted to light a cigarette but thought better of it. Instead she picked up a pen and tried to makes sense of the letters. After a moment she scribbled SAC, NEV, FRED, FED ER, MAC, CAM, DEF VAN, NAV, NERD, DEN, REN, NER, D R E A M,... Oh dear, it was quite useless! What a day this was turning out to be. She glanced across at the cigarettes again. 'No, no, I mustn't weaken!' she said aloud in an attempt to make herself stronger. Quickly she picked up the book she had been looking forward to reading all day. *The Secrets of the German War Office* written by Dr Armgaard Karl Graves in 1914. But, as she opened the front cover she noticed that it was written in collaboration with an Edward Lyell Fox! Now then, that is a coincidence! I must show Michael she thought, curling up on her favourite sofa and turning to the first chapter.

How I became a Secret Agent

Half past three was heard booming from some clock tower on the twelfth day of June, 1913, when Mr King, the Liberal representative from Somerset, was given the floor in the House of Commons. Mr King proceeded to make a sensation. He demanded that McKinnon Wood, the House Secretary for Scotland, reveal to the House the secrets of the strange case of Armgaard Karl Graves, German spy.

A brief word of explanation may be necessary. Supposed to be serving a political sentence in a Scotch prison, I had amazed the English press and people by publicly announcing my presence in New York City. Mr King asked if I was still undergoing imprisonment for espionage; if not, when and why I was released and whether I had been or would be deported at the end of my term of imprisonment as an undesirable alien.

Permit me to quote verbatim from the Edinburgh Scotsman of June 12 1913: "The Secretary for Scotland replied Graves was released in December last. It would not be in accordance with precedent to state reasons for the exercise of the prerogative. I have no official knowledge of his nationality. The sentence did not include any recommendation in favour of deportation."
 Mr. King: "Was he released because of the state of his health?"
 The Secretary for Scotland: "I believe he was in bad health, but I cannot give any other answer."
 Mr King: "Were any conditions imposed at the time of his release?"
 The Secretary for Scotland: "I think I have dealt with that in my answer." (Cries of "no")
 Mr. King: "Can the Rt. Hon. Gentleman be a little more explicit?" (Laughter) "We are anxious to have the truth. Unless the Rt. Hon. Gentleman can give me

an explicit answer as to whether any conditions were imposed I will put down the question again." (Laughter)

The Speaker intervened at this stage, and the subject dropped. Heckling began at this point; word was quickly sent to the Speaker, and he intervened, ruling the subject closed.

Now consider the Secretary for Scotland's statement: "It would not be in accordance with precedent to state reasons for the exercise of prerogative." In other words, high officials in England had found it advisable secretly to release me from Barlinney Prison by using the royal prerogative. Why? Later you will know. Also, consider the Secretary for Scotland's statement that he had no official knowledge as to my nationality, significant that, as you will realize.

There are three things which do not concern the reader: my origin, nationality and morals. There are three persons alive who know who I am. One of the three is the greatest ruler in the world. None of the three, for reasons of their own, is likely to reveal my identity. I detest sensationalism and wish it clearly understood that this is no studied attempt to create mystery. There is a certain deadline which no one can cross with impunity and none but a fool would attempt to. Powerful governments have found it advisable to keep silence regarding my antecedents. A case in point occurred when McKinnon Wood, Secretary for Scotland, refused in the House of Commons to give any information whatsoever about me, this after pressure had been brought to bear on him by three members of Parliament. Either the Home Secretary knew nothing about my antecedents, or his trained discretion counselled silence.

I was brought up in the traditions of a house actively engaged in the affairs of its country, for hundreds of years. As an only son, I was promptly and efficiently spoiled for anything else but the station in life which should have been mine, but never has been and, now, never can be. I used to have high aspirations, but promises never kept shattered most of my ideals. The hard knocks of life have made me a fatalist, so now I shrug my shoulders. Che sarā, sarā! I have had to lead my own life and, all considered, I have enjoyed it. I have crowded into thirty-nine years more sensations than fall to the lot of the average half a dozen men.

Following the custom of our house, I was trained as a military cadet. This military apprenticeship was followed by three years at a famous gymnasium, *which fitted me for one of the old classic universities of Europe. And after spending six semesters there, I took my degrees in philosophy and medicine. Not a bad achievement, I take it, for a young chap before reaching his twenty-second birthday. I have always been fond of study and had a special aptitude for sciences and the languages.*

On one occasion I acquired a fair knowledge of Singalese and Tamul in three months.
     From the university I returned home. I had always been obstinate and wilful, not to say pigheaded, and being steeped in tales of wrongs done to my house and country, and with the crass assurance of a young sprig fresh from untrammelled university life, I began to give vent to utterances that were not at all to the liking of the powers that were. Soon making myself objectionable, paying no heed to their protests, and one thing leading to another, my family found it advisable to send me into utter and complete oblivion.

To them I am dead, and all said and done, I would rather have it so. After the complete rupture of my home ties, I began some desultory globetrotting.

I knocked about in out-of-the-way corners, where I observed and absorbed all sorts of things which became very useful in my subsequent career. The natives, and by that I mean inhabitants, of non-European countries always fascinated me, and I soon learned the way of disarming their suspicion and winning their confidence, a proceeding very difficult for a European. After a time I found myself in Australia and New Zealand, where I travelled extensively, and came to like both countries thoroughly. I have never been in the western part of the United States, but from what I have heard and read I imagine that the life there more closely resembles the clean, healthy, outdoor life of the Australians than any other locality. I was just on the point of beginning extensive travels in the South Sea Islands, when the situation in South Africa became ominous. War seemed imminent, and following my usual bent of sticking my nose in where I was not wanted I made tracks for this potential seat of trouble.

I caught the first steamer for Cape Town, landing there a month before the outbreak of war. On horseback I made my way in easy stages up to the Rand. Here happened one of those incidents, which, although small in itself, alters the course of one's life. What took place when I rode into a small town on the Rand known as Doorn Kloof one chilly misty morning was written in the bowl of fate. Doorn Kloof is well named: it means "the hoof of the devil." A straggling collection of corrugated iron shanties set in the middle of a grayish sandy plain as barren of vegetation as the shores of the Dead Sea, sweltering hot an hour after sunrise, chilly cold an hour after sunset, populated by about four hundred Boers of the old narrow-minded ultra Dutch type with as much imagination as a grasshopper, that is Doorn Kloof. When I rode into the village I was in a decidedly bad temper. Hungry, wet to the skin, the dismal aspect of the place, the absence of anything resembling a hotel, the incivility of the inhabitants, all contributed to shorten my, by no means long, temper. I was ripe for a row. As I rode down the solitary street I found a big burly "Dopper" flogging brutally a half-grown native boy.

This humanitarian had the usual Boer view that the sjambok is more effective than the Bible as a civilizing medium. After convincing him of the technical error of his method, I attended to the black boy, whose back was as raw as a beefsteak. Kim completely adopted me and he is with me still. I christened him Kim, after Kipling's hero, for his Basuto name is unpronounceable. He has repaid me often for what he considers the saving of his life. Not many months later Kim was the unconscious cause of a radical change in my destiny. I have ceased to wonder at such things. By the time Kim had learned some of the duties of a body servant we had reached Port Natal. War had broken out and I volunteered with a Natal field force in a medical capacity. Field hospital work took me where the fighting was thickest.

During the battle of the Modder River, among the first of the wounded brought in was one of the many foreign officers fighting on the Boer side. It was Kim who found him. This officer's wound was fairly serious and necessitated close attention. Through chance remarks dropped here and there, the officer placed my identity correctly. It developed that he was Major Freiherr von Reitzenstein, one of the few who knew the real reasons of my exile. In one of our innumerable chats that grew out of our growing intimacy, he suggested my entering the service of Germany in a political capacity. He urged that with my training and social connections I had exceptional equipment for such work. Moreover, he suggested that my service on political missions would give me the knowledge and influence necessary to checkmate the intriguers who were keeping me from my own. This was the compelling reason that made me ultimately accept his proposal to become a Secret Agent of Germany.

No doubt, if the Count had lived, I would have gained my ends through his guidance and influence, but he was killed in a riding race, three years after our meeting in the Veldt, and I lost my best friend. By that time I was too deep in the Secret Service to pull out, although it was my intention more than once to do so. And certain promises regarding my restoration in our house were never kept. Coming to a partial understanding with Count Reitzenstein, I began to work in his interests. The Boer War taught Germany many things about the English army and a few of these I contributed. As a physician I was allowed to go most anywhere and no questions asked.

I began to collect little inside scraps of information regarding the discipline, spirit and equipment of the British troops. I observed that many colonial officers were outspoken in their criticisms. All these points I reported in full to Count Reitzenstein when I dressed his wound. One day he said: "Don't forget now. After the war, I want to see you in Berlin." In my subsequent eagerness to pump more details from the Colonial officers, I too criticised, and one day I was told Lord Kitchener wanted to see me. "Doctor," he said curtly, when I was ushered into his tent, "you have twenty-four hours in which to leave camp." Whether that mandate was a result of my joining in with the colonial officers' criticism, or because my secret activity for Count Reitzenstein had been suspected, I cannot say. But knowing the ways of the "man of Khartoum", I made haste to be out of camp within the time prescribed.

Later I learned that the Count, being convalescent and paroled, was sent down to Cape Town. After the occupation of Pretoria, I got tired of roughing it and made my way back to Europe, finally locating in Berlin for a prolonged stay. I knew Berlin, and had a fondness for it, having spent part of my youth there in the course of my education. It has always been a habit of mine not to seem anxious about anything, so I spent several weeks idling around Berlin before looking up Count Reitzenstein.

One day I called at his residence, Thiergartenstrasse 23. I found the Count on the point of leaving for the races at Hoppegarten. He was one of the crack sportsmen of Prussia and never missed a meeting. He suggested that I go to the track with him, and while we waited for the servant to bring around his turn-out, he renewed his proposals about my entering Prussian service.

"I expected you long ago," he said. "I have smoothed your way to a great extent. We are likely to meet one or two of the Service Chiefs out at the track, this afternoon. If you like, I'll introduce you to them."

"Is there any likelihood of my being recognized?" I asked. "You know, Count, it will be impossible for me to go under my true flag."

He assured me there was not the slightest chance. "Your identity," he explained, "need be known to but one person."

Later I was to know who this important personage was.

"Very well," I agreed. "We'll try it."

The Count always drove his own turn out, and invited me to climb up on the box. When his attention was not occupied with his reins and returning the salutes of passers-by, for he was one of the most popular men in Berlin, we discussed my private affairs. The Count showed a keen interest and sympathy in them and his proposal began to take favourable shape in my mind. As he predicted, we met some of the Service Chiefs at the track. Indeed, almost the first persons who saluted him in the saddle paddock were Captain Zur See von Tappken and a gentleman who was introduced to me as Herr von Riechter. The Count introduced me as Dr von Graver, which I subsequently altered, whenever the occasion arose, to the English "Graves".

After chatting a bit, Captain von Tappken made an appointment with me at his bureau in the Koenigergratzerstrasse 70, the headquarters of the Intelligence Department of the Imperial Navy in Berlin, but made no further reference to the subject that afternoon. I noticed though that Herr von Riechter put some pointed and leading questions to me, regarding my travels, linguistic attainments, and general knowledge. He must have been satisfied for I saw some significant glances pass between him and the Captain. The repeated exclamations of "Grossartig!" and "Colossal!" seemed to express his entire satisfaction. Following my usual bent, I did not call at Koenigergratzerstrasse 70 as the Captain suggested. About three days passed and then I received a *very courteously worded letter requesting me to call at my earliest convenience at his quarters as he had something of importance to tell me. So I called...*

Juliana stopped reading and stretched. Something was niggling but she couldn't put her finger on it. She was sure that she had heard the term "Koenigergratzerstrasse 70" before. Never mind, she thought, picking up from where she left off; it would come to her eventually.

Koenigergratzerstrasse 70 is a typical Prussian building of administration. Solid but unpretentious, it is the very embodiment of Prussian efficiency, and like all official buildings in Germany is well guarded. The doorkeeper and commissaire, a taciturn non-commissioned officer, takes your name and whom you wish to see. He enters these later in a book, then telephones to the person required and you are either ushered up or denied admittance.

When sent up you are invariably accompanied by an orderly; it does not matter how well you are known, he does not leave you until the door has closed behind you. When you leave, there is the same procedure and the very duration of your visit is entered and checked in the doorkeeper's book. I was admitted immediately.

After passing through three anterooms containing private secretaries not in uniform, I was shown into Captain von Tappken's private office. He wore the undress ranking uniform of the Imperial Navy. This is significant, for it is characteristic of all the branches of the Prussian Service to find officers in charge. The secretaries and men of all work, however, are civilians; this for a reason. The heads of all departments are German officers, recruited from the old feudal aristocracy, loyal to a degree to the throne. They find it incompatible, notwithstanding their loyalty, to soil their hands with some of the work connected with all government duties, especially those of the Secret Service. Though planning the work, they never execute it.

To be sure, there are ex-officers connected with the Secret Service, men like von Zenden, formerly an officer of the Zweiter Garde Dragoner, but with some few exceptions they are usually men who have gone to smash. No active or commissioned officer does Secret Service work. Von Tappken greeted me very tactfully. This is another typical asset of a Prussian Service officer, especially a naval man, and is quite contrary to the usual characteristics of English officials, whose brusqueness is too well and unpleasantly known. After offering me a chair and cigars, Captain von Tappken began chatting.

"Well, Doctor," he said, "have you made up your mind to enter our Service? For a man fond of travelling and adventure, I promise you will find it tremendously interesting. I have carefully considered your equipment and experience and find that they will be of mutual benefit." I asked him to explain what would be required of me, but he replied: "Before my entering upon that, are you averse to telling me if you have made up your mind to enter the Service?" It was a fair question, and I replied:

"Yes, provided nothing will be directly required of me that is against all ethics."

I noticed a peculiar smile crossing his features. Then, looking me straight between the eyes and using the sharp, incisive language of a German official, he declared: "We make use of the same weapons that are used against us. We cannot afford to be squeamish.

"The interests at stake are too vast to let personal ethical questions stand in the way. What would be required of you in the first instance is to gain for us information such as we seek. The means by which you gain this information will be left entirely to your own discretion. We expect results. We place our previous knowledge on the subject required, at your disposal. You will have our organization to assist you, but you must understand that we cannot and will not be able to extricate you from any trouble in which you may become involved. Be pleased to understand this clearly. This service is dangerous, and no official assistance or help could be given under any circumstances."

To my cost, I later found this to be the truth. So far so good! Captain von Tappken had neglected to mention financial inducements and I put the question to him. He replied promptly: "That depends entirely on the service performed. In the first instance you will receive a retaining fee of 4000 marks ($1000) a year. -You will be allowed 10 marks ($2.50) a day for living expenses, whether in active service or not. For each individual piece of work undertaken you will receive a bonus, the amount of which will vary with the importance of the mission. Living expenses accruing while out on work must not exceed 40 marks ($10) a day. The amount of the bonus you are to receive for a mission will in each case be determined in advance. There is one other thing. One-third of all moneys accruing to you will be kept in trust for you at the rate of 5 per cent interest."

I laughed and said: "Well, Captain, I can take care of my own money.'"

He permitted the shadow of a smile to play around his mouth. "You may be able to," he said, "but most of our agents cannot. We have this policy for two reasons. In the first place, it gives us a definite hold upon our men. Secondly, we have found that unless we save some money for our agents, they never save any for themselves. In the event of anything happening to an agent who leaves a family or other relatives, the money is handed over to them."

I later cursed that rule, for when I was captured in England there were 30,000 marks ($7,500) due me at the Wilhelmstrasse and I can whistle for it now. Captain von Tappken looked at me inquiringly, but I hesitated. It was not on account of monetary causes, but for peculiarly private reasons, the dilemma of one of our house becoming a spy. The Captain, unaware of the personal equation that was obsessing me before giving my word, evidently thought that his financial inducements were not alluring enough.

"Of course," he continued, 'this scale of pay is only the beginning. As your use to us, and the importance of your missions increase, so will your remuneration. That depends entirely on you." He raised his eyebrows inquiringly.

"Very well," I said. "I accept."

He held out his hand. "You made up your mind quickly."

"It is my way, Captain. I take a thing or leave it."

"That's what I like Doctor, a quick, decisive mind." That seemed to please him.

"Very well, to be of use to us, you will need a lot of technical coaching. Are you ready to start tomorrow?"

"Now Captain!"

"Very good," he said, "but tomorrow will do. Be here at ten am. Then give us daily as much of your time as we require." He called in one of his secretaries, gave him command briefly and in a few minutes the man was back with an order for three hundred marks. This, Doctor, is your first month's living expenses. Retaining fees are paid quarterly."

As I pocketed the check I remarked: "Captain, personally we are total strangers. How is it that you seem so satisfied with me?" Again his peculiar smile was noticeable. "'That is outside our usual business procedure," he said. "I have my instructions from above and I simply act on them."

I was young then and curious so I asked, "Who are those above and what are their instructions?" No sooner had I put that question than I learned my first lesson in the Secret Service. All traces of genial friendliness vanished from von Tappken's face. It was stern and serious.

"My boy," he said slowly, "Learn this from the start and learn it well. Do not ask questions. Do not talk. Think! You will soon learn that there are many unwritten laws attached to this Service." I never forgot that. It was my first lesson in Secret Service.

Juliana placed the book down and patted the top of it, the way she did her sculptures when she was particularly pleased with them. Now she understood why Michael got so excited about his books. But for her, well it was a new experience altogether and it was no exaggeration to say that she was enthralled by the antics of this man von Graver or Dr Graves as he was known in England. But just a moment now, he says that Graves or von Graver is not his real name! Hmm! I wonder... perhaps this Dr Graves is of European royalty. Oh how exciting it would be if he was really a prince or a duke or something! Juliana stood up and stretched. I really ought to get out of these old dungarees, she thought, especially as Michael is so moody about them; besides, there was no point in wearing them if she wasn't sculpting... Oh, but they are so comfortable, I think I'll leave them on for the rest of the day. But now it's time for a long cool glass of wine!

Chapter Twenty Four   The Old Gods Live Still!

Down in the kitchen Giovanni and Alex were mixing up some pasta and setting the table. 'Rosé?' Giovanni asked, handing the bottle to Paul to open. For once he appeared in a cheerful mood. Paul assumed it was because Alex had agreed to paint the picture of the roses for him.

'When you go Roma?' he asked.

Paul shrugged.

'De poor....Dey need your help...... Si?'

'Please father, not now.' Paul was irritated by the cross questioning. 'Look, it won't be long before I return but even priests deserve a little holiday!'

'Si, si, si... de poor.... dey go ungry... no time for stupid oliday.... Eh!'

'I am not the only one serving in the community! They will be looked after in the usual way. I can assure you!'

'Si, si, si. What about your poor cousin with six bambinos, dey all go ungry too! No job, no nothing! When you last visit, eh? When you last take a food parcel, eh?' Giovanni demanded as Juliana walked into the kitchen.

'Now, now, what's all this about?' she asked.

'Never mind, you o-l-y man, I go if you are too busy.' Giovanni stopped waving his hands in the air as Paul tried to explain why he was so upset.

'He wants me to go to back to Rome tomorrow. He doesn't like it when I am here at the villa.'

'Si, It is time you go!' Giovanni turned and as soon as he caught sight of Juliana he smiled.

For her part she thought it was a good idea to change the subject. 'Mm, something smells delicious, I'm so hungry.' She said helping herself to slices of avocado. 'Come now, Giovanni, what's there to be upset about?'

'Nothing, all is fine, all is okay now you are here!' Giovanni smiled politely.

'You see, your father can be quite the charmer when he wants to be. But I'm glad I've caught you Paul. Presumably you speak Latin?'

'Si, he does, if he has not forgotten!' Giovanni exclaimed as he left the room.

'Right then, here goes. 'O Jerum, Jerum, Jerum. Quae mutatio rerum. Tempora mutantur et mutantur tempora….. Any idea what it means?'

Paul pursed his lips together before answering. 'The times are changing or… how the times have changed!'

'Okay and the Jerum bit? Is it a shortened word for Jerusalem?'

Paul shrugged. 'I can't say. It could be. If it's a famous saying Michael will know it.' Juliana sighed. 'Well of course! Why didn't I think of that? Anyway, where is everyone? I'm starving.' Juliana poured herself a glass of wine before offering Paul the decanter. 'Come on,' she added, 'let's eat. They'll all be here any moment.'

Later that afternoon, Michael was working when Juliana knocked on his door.

'I hope I'm not disturbing you?'

He smiled. 'You, you never disturb me!' he joked, drawing up a chair for her. 'Ah! You've bought me an old book with an interesting title. May I have a look? Ah, the *Secrets of the German War Office,*' he added, noting that it was written by a Dr Armgaard Karl Graves in collaboration with a Mr Edward Lyell Fox. 'Well done! You have found our Fox!'

'Yes, it would appear so, unless you think otherwise?'

He didn't reply.

'Michael?'

He shook his head. 'I'm sorry dear, I was just looking, there's something familiar about the initials of the doctor's name. Michael repeated the letters as he walked across to his bookshelf. 'A.K.G, A.K.G. Now where have I heard that before…?'

Juliana watched him leaf through a couple of books before picking up Tonya's copy of *Rescuing the Czar*. 'Of course, here it is. The dedication to mother is signed by a K.A.G.

'I'm not with you!' A confused Juliana responded.

Michael sighed. 'It could be the same person? K.A.G is a Dr Karl Armgaard Graves and A.K.G. is Dr Armgaard Karl Graves!'

Juliana wasn't convinced. 'So you're saying your mother knew Dr Armgaard Karl Graves!'

'She must have, and if you read what's written you'll see why I am so excited.'

Juliana peered down at the book. 'They took part in a Siberian adventure together!'

'When I think of how long I've been looking for that name and now you casually walk in and....' Michael stopped mid sentence and gave her a big kiss on the cheek. 'You've no idea how desperate I've been to find out more about mother's life and the name of my real father. As soon as I saw this message a strange feeling came over me and well... I can't explain it... I just knew THAT was my father and now at last I know HIS name. Dr Armgaard Karl Graves.'

'Don't get your hopes up. It might not all be good news! If you're right and A.K.G is really K.A.G then your father was....Oh dear, I'm almost afraid to say it... He admits to having been a German spy, who later worked for the British and Americans.'

Michael covered his eyes. 'Don't say that they were both secret agents! God help me!'

Juliana laughed at his reaction. 'Well I always said there was something...' She didn't finish the sentence. 'Anyway, how are you going to prove that A.K.G. is K.A.G or that he is your father for that matter?'

Michael's mind was elsewhere. 'I wonder, this Edward Lyell Fox... did he have a brother in Turkestan?'

'You're falling into the same trap as everyone. Fox was not his real name!'

He laughed and put the book down. 'Was there anything else my dear?'

'Yes, this,' Juliana replied pointing at the Latin inscription in *The Secrets of the German War Office*. What does it mean and any ideas where it comes from?'

'Let me see if I have anything in the German section. But if my memory serves me right it is an ancient verse from the days of the Teutonic knights'

'I see I've come to the right place!' Juliana stared at his desk covered with heraldry books, royal banners and various crests. 'Are you thinking of registering a coat of arms for us?' she joked.

'Would you object?'

Juliana shrugged. I've never given it a thought!'

'We could choose any name we like with the heritage I appear to have!'

'Yes, that's true, a fox and a goose at the very least!' Juliana joked as Michael sifted through a few rare books on the top shelf. Finally he pulled out a thin black book with gold leaf, some of which had rubbed off. Expertly he flicked to the right page.

'I see my dear, as usual, that I am NOT wrong! According to this version, it's over a hundred years old. Six verses of eight lines each. Alice would say that added up to a holy number. Here, I'll read it out.

'Rückblick Eines Alten Burschen 1843 (Engl. Höfling, 1825)

O, old sounds and jubeltied,
Your memory shall remain
And yet the harsh battle of life
One rosy glow give!
Soon silenced all our dizzy joke
Our song is dumb, our glam förstämt;

O,Jerum,Jerum,Jerum, O, JERUM, JERUM, JERUM,
O, quae mutatio rerum! O, quae mutatio rerum!

Where are they, who were all,
Only not betray his honour,
Halt who were men of genuine content
And masters of the world alike?
They drew away from wine and song
To everyday life boring and coercion.
O, Jerum, Jerum, Jerum, O, JERUM, JERUM, JERUM,
O, quae mutatio rerum! O, quae mutatio rerum!

One of science and common sense
In scholars quantities,
The other sweat of their brows
In paragraphs perverteth,
One plaster soul who is shaky,
A piece hop its tattered sleeve;
O, Jerum, Jerum, Jerum, O, JERUM, JERUM, JERUM,
O, quae mutatio rerum! O, quae mutatio rerum!

A tames wild rapids cases,
Another gives us the paper,

One engineer engaged in cold,
One masters volts so brave,
One draws the house, a measure the soil,
A mixed hop mixture so strong;
O, Jerum, Jerum, erum, O, JERUM, JERUM, JERUM,
O, quae mutatio rerum! O, quae mutatio rerum!

But the heart of a true student
No time can freeze to death,
The glad jeeld which he lighted,
His whole life will shine.
The old skin has been broken,
But the kernel remained healthy,
And what he may lose
It shall never fail!
So secret, brothers, settled our circle
The joy-tank and honour!
Despite all that we secure and well satisfied
Our friendship and loyalty oath.
Lifting Bagar'n high, and the blade, friend!
The old gods live then
Among bowls and cups,
Among bowls and cups!

'Well I like the last verse. It sounds so full of chivalry don't you think?' Juliana queried.

Michael laughed. 'Some old drunk's song, I shouldn't wonder!'

'No, I don't think so. It's Grail orientated!'

Michael grew serious. 'Hmm, I can see why you say that. All cups and bowls!'

'Perhaps it's older than a hundred years,' she ventured. 'Maybe I'm right and it originates in an original song of the Knights Templar. I really like the Jerum, Jerum, Jerum, bit, it's so melodic.'

Michael laughed. 'Sometimes I wonder where you get your ideas from. Dr Graves probably learnt it at a German university or some military academy during the early 1900s. Anyway, if I'm to learn more about my father I should start reading some of the books he has written!'

Juliana agreed. 'Of course, why don't you make a start on the *Hohenzollern* book, I'll fetch it right away.'

* * *

The following morning Giovanni was in Rome for an eleven thirty appointment. Located in a dark narrow street just off the main thoroughfare was a special type of shop. Giovanni knocked three times and waited anxiously. Less than a minute later, after a protracted creaking, the door was opened and he stepped cautiously inside. He found himself standing in a semi-darkened, cool room. As his eyes became accustomed to the light he recognised the man standing opposite.

'Buon giorno, amico carissimo. Son oltremodo felice di vederla!' Giovanni smiled and slowly laid ten gold coins in a row on the counter.

'Mama Mia, Benissimo!' the dealer exclaimed before biting into one of them.

Giovanni watched as the imperial coat of arms and seal of Nicholas II was inspected carefully.

The double-headed eagle with three crowns flashed under the light and for a moment Giovanni felt guilty. The dealer studied the shield hanging over the eagle's breast on which a horseman was slaying a dragon.

'Authentico, si?' he asked, before biting into it again.

Giovanni nodded eagerly. 'Quanto vale questo? Antico!'

A moment later the dealer appeared satisfied but just to be sure he weighed them one by one. 'Che vuole?' He asked.

Giovanni thought for a moment. 'Che oro prezzo?'

The dealer shrugged. 'Uno moneta, uno mommento!'

Giovanni suddenly felt chilly and rubbed his hands together as the dealer left the counter, taking one of the coins with him.

Presently he returned smiling.

'Che vuole?' Giovanni asked again, this time more determinedly. He had no idea what they were worth but he must have at least twenty thousand lira.

The gold dealer smiled. 'Ahh! Si! Il danaro e`fratello del danaro,' he added, handing Giovanni thirty five thousand lira. Giovanni's eyes widened. Surely the dealer had paid him too much. 'Amigo, lei ha fatto uno sbaglio!'

'Ben detto..... Arrivederla signore!' the dealer added hurriedly, waving him out of the shop.

Back at the villa Juliana was congratulating her son. 'This is super, Alex, a real masterpiece.' she said, admiring the painting.

Alex looked on proudly. 'I'm glad you like it. As you can see I painted it in oils rather than watercolours. I think it was the right choice.'

Juliana agreed. 'The yellow, pink and red are picked out beautifully against the green. Oh! I see you have included my statue. But honestly, I can't believe how you were able to paint so many roses.'

Alex smiled. 'Giovanni made me promise to paint each one individually and I don't mind telling you how difficult that was!'

Chapter Twenty Five   Secrets of the Hohenzollerns

Later that evening Alex gave the painting to a delighted Giovanni.

'Grazie! Benissimo!' He said as Alex embellished on the detail of his hard work.

'It wasn't easy, especially that one there,' He added pointing to a rather complicated bush stroke.

'Si, I can see! Ah, excuse!...' Giovanni angled the canvas awkwardly as he spoke.

Alex sighed. 'The statue's in the background so that's your point of reference. Comprende?'

'Si, grazie!'

Alex shook his head. Not only did he have to paint the picture, he had to tell Giovanni how to look at it as well!

'I presume you have signed it?' Michael enquired.

Alex glanced across to where his father was standing. 'Of course, I must. Give it here, I'll sign it now.'

'Artists should also give their work a title,' Michael added impatiently.

'Oh, I haven't thought of one.'

'I know,' Tonya suggested, 'let's think of a name for the painting and write it down and then have a lucky dip, so to speak.' Before anyone could say no she started to tear up bits of paper and hand them out. 'Don't forget to put your initial in the corner so that we know who suggested the name.'

'That won't work my dear,' Responded Alice, 'because Alex and I share the same initial!' 'Well just write AX or AE then!'

A moment later they were all thinking hard. Giovanni appeared to take longer than most. Eventually he put his submission in and Tonya gave the cap to Alex. 'That's it. Give them a good mix round.'

Alex waved his hand in the bunch of papers while they all counted to ten.

'Okay, that's enough. Alex can pick the winner,' shouted Tonya, walking back to where Giovanni was seated. 'Now shut your eyes and choose one.'

Alex did as he was told. 'OOH LA LA, here we go then!' He added pulling out a folded piece of paper, which he handed to Tonya. 'It's from Alice. She thinks the painting should be called "Treasure from Heaven".'

'That's a good title. Thank you!' Responded Alex as he gave Alice a kiss. 'I would never have thought of that.'

'Well, can't we see what everyone else has suggested?' Juliana enquired, picking up the cap and emptying the contents on the table.

'Ah! Paul's put "Roses by the Terrace", very appropriate. Tonya, yours is "Flower Power", while Giovanni suggests "Maria Fiori", which is a pretty title; and now what have we here? Ah, Michael's! "Garden near Rome"! Well, that's a rather boring title for your son's first masterpiece! Finally, the last one is my suggestion, "Roses with Statue".'

Michael burst out laughing. 'And yours I suppose is by far the best, shame it wasn't chosen!'

Juliana ignored him. 'Oh that wasn't the last; there is one more. Alex, now what did you call your own painting darling?' Juliana opened the last paper slowly. '"Royal Roman Roses", how very poetic.'

Michael frowned and turned to Giovanni. 'So where do you intend to hang this newly acquired… painting?'

'He wants to hang it in the kitchen!' Tonya butted in.

'Not for parlour. Too mucho cooking! No! I hang in my room if okay with boss?'

Michael smiled.

'Of course it's okay with father!' Alex shouted.

'Since the painting has been such a success, I hope we are all at liberty to request a masterpiece from our own resident artist?' asked Juliana.

Alex smiled at the suggestion and turned to his father. 'I could do one of you in the library if you like?'

Michael grimaced. 'I'd rather you painted your mother in her studio. That would be a little more challenging than painting my plain old books!'

Alex thought he detected some sarcasm in his tone. 'Well, it might surprise you to know that I have a penchant for books at the moment. There you are! I must be a chip off the old block after all.'

'If you say so!'

As they were getting ready for bed Juliana handed Michael *The Secrets of the Hohenzollerns* by Dr Armgaard Karl Graves. 'I know you'll enjoy reading this.' She added closing the shutters. Michael eagerly leafed through its pages and

Juliana was amazed at how quickly he became absorbed by its contents. He was so wrapped up in his own world she thought as she climbed into bed next to him. He carried on reading.

'You know,' Juliana was determined to get his attention. 'I do wish you would be nicer towards Alex. He tries so hard to please you!'

Michael closed the book unnecessarily loudly and placed it on the bedside table.

'Well he shouldn't bother. I don't want a son who wants to please me. I just want him to be normal!'

'He is normal Michael. It's normal for him to be the way he is and you had better get used to it. What would you prefer? That he pretended to be something that he is not? To marry and all the time having to live a lie just to please you? Is that what you want for your son?' 'Well, why did we have a son like that anyway? I mean where did he get it from? It was certainly not from my side of the family.'

Juliana was barely able to contain her fury. 'How dare you speak of your son like that and infer that your side of the family is so dam good and mine is bad! God made gay people too! And you... you know something? I'm beginning to wish I was as well!' With that, Juliana turned her back on him put the light out and pulled the covers over her head.

Michael didn't like sitting in the dark in silence. 'I didn't mean to … he paused halfway through his sentence, not quite bringing himself to apologise. Then he got out of bed. 'For goodness sake,' He shouted, 'I said I'm sorry! Are you going to ignore me all night? Is that it?... Well?'

Juliana refused to speak so he tapped her on the shoulder. Still she did not respond.

'Fine, I've got the message.' He added picking up the book and walking out. The bedroom door slammed louder than he had intended. Perhaps she would call out? No. Well he wasn't going to lose face by going back in. Downstairs Michael quietly opened the library door. Two could play at her game! Damn! He thought, if only I could control my anger. Well there was nothing for it now. I'll have to spend the night in here!

Giovanni, who had heard the raised voices and then the slam of the bedroom door, was trying to decide where to hang his picture. At first he was going to position it over the headboard but then he wouldn't be able to sit in bed and look at it. Finally he opted for the wall opposite. After banging in a nail as quietly as he could he lifted the painting into position and was just about to hang it when there was a knock on the door. He put the painting down and looked at his watch. It was late. Perhaps it was Michael wanting to talk. Not Juliana surely? Perhaps the boss was so pleased with his work that he was going to give him a rise! He smiled at the prospect as he opened the door.

'There you are!' Alice whispered. 'I know it's late but I wanted to... Oh! Do you want some help hanging that picture?' she asked, pushing past.

Giovanni shook his head nervously. This was a rather late visit. Something must be wrong he thought as he shut the door.

'Now look, I know the last few months have been difficult but this is silly of you!' Alice held up a gold coin in front of Giovanni's shocked face.

'Che?'

'You left it on the kitchen floor in full view of everyone. Lucky for you, I was the one who found it. You're supposed to be keeping our secret safe!'

Giovanni grabbed the gold coin. 'Si, it go back tomorrow.'

'Well, what is IT doing out in the first place?'

'Non comprende...'

'Of course you do. Now you better tell me.'

Giovanni sat down on the bed with his head in his hands. Something was clearly wrong so Alice decided to be lenient. 'Look, I know it's been hard but this was a silly mistake. But on the other hand,' she added, pointing at the painting, 'that was a very good idea!'

Somewhat relieved, Giovanni smiled. 'Si, but why you call the painting, "Treasure from Heaven"?'

'Don't you worry about that, you know I always have a reason!

Giovanni scowled.

'Well for heaven's sake man, how do you think they are going to respond when we tell them?'

'Please, they no find out.'

'Dear me, wake up. You carry on being sloppy like this and we will have a lot of explaining to do.'

Giovanni thought for a moment. 'Why we no say truth now.'

'Don't be ridiculous. You know we can't.'

Giovanni sat down on the bed and rubbed his face hard. He was tired but she needed answers. 'Well?' She demanded.

Giovanni looked up. 'Me non comprende!'

Alice stood opposite with one hand on her hip. 'That's not an answer! How did this coin come to be on the kitchen floor?'

Giovanni stared at the carpet.

'Well I haven't got all night!' She watched him walk across to the window.

A silver moon hung in the sky, sending intermediate beams of light onto the rose bed. As he turned to speak Alice saw he was near to tears.

'Si Alice, you are right. You are always right. I didn't tell you about my sister?'

'No you did not.'

Giovanni blew his nose. 'Well she is poor, too many children and no money.'

'Please,' Alice raised her hand, 'don't tell me you are giving her the GOLD COINS!'

Giovanni sat down on the bed. 'No. I have no money, so I get MONEY by selling coins, just a few!'

Alice sat down. 'What on earth possessed you?'

'I told you!' Giovanni spoke louder than usual.

'You stupid man, didn't you think that questions would be asked? Selling an illegal currency, STUPID, and whoever you've sold them to, well, they probably think there is more! You dare to put all our lives at risk! How long have you been doing this for?' Giovanni lowered his head. 'Not so long,' he mumbled.

'HOW LONG, I asked?'

'About nine months.'

'Nine months?' Alice crossed herself while she was speaking. 'That's just after Maria... God bless her soul... died!'

'Si, I know. That is why I so upset. After the fire, I thought someone would come!'

Alice stood up and walked away from him. 'Well who knows? I wouldn't be at all surprised if someone isn't looking for them at this very moment! Honestly, how long have you worked for this family? And this is how you repay their kindness! I am shocked. You're prepared to put the whole family at risk by your ignorant behaviour.'

Giovanni covered his face in shame. Then he glanced up. 'So what I do now?'

'Stop selling the coins for a start. We'll have to think of a new plan, you should have come to me for help in the first place.'

'I tell my sister no more money now. I tell her to go to church for help.'

'Well that may be some relief to you, but whatever you do this family must not be put in any further danger. Do I make myself clear?'

Giovanni didn't reply. Instead he started to shake uncontrollably making Alice feel sorry for him. She sat down and put her hand in his. He looked up with a sheepish look on his face 'So sorry for trouble I cause.'

Alice nodded. 'Very well, in the future never do anything without speaking to me first. Do you understand?'

* * *

Downstairs, Michael stood in his library, admiring the brown and gold cover of the book Juliana had given him. *The Secrets of the Hohenzollerns* was published by McBride Nast and Co. in 1915. He adored rare old books, especially when they were printed on thick parchment paper and had wavy edges. As he studied the Hohenzollern coat of arms on the cover he believed that what he was about to read was from his father. After pouring himself a large malt whisky he turned to the first page.

You say this is fiction.
I say it is not.
You say that I lie.
I say I do not.
Quien Sabe?

My first book, The Secrets of the German War Office, has been the target of much criticism. Some of the criticisms I appreciated and found more or less justified. Others were too ill informed and contemptible to represent even a casual judgement of the facts. It appears that the purchase of a book entitles the buyer to criticize; be it so. Some official representatives of governments, notably the German, have seen fit to attack in their usual underhanded way. I understand their necessity for so doing. Also, I expected this, for I have been long enough in their employ to know the wherefore and the why. I have made no answers to these attacks, for I hold, with the sages of old, that too strenuous a denial is the natural act of a guilty conscience. I do not ask for sympathy or tolerance, for neither has ever been mine, besides I can do very well without them. My veracity and morals have been, and will be doubted. Well, that is my concern. One thing I never have been, and that is a coward. I have taken the Persian Satrap's advice to his son:

"My Son, if bad luck does pursue thee,
Yield not, though in courage you lack;
A fighter goes scathe less through battle,
When a coward is shot in the back!"

My son! A thrill ran through Michael at the sound of those words. He had never known what it was to have a father but now he did. Resting the book on his lap, he savoured the moment and sipped his whisky. Then he thought of Alex and his argument with Juliana, which he promptly dismissed. Eagerly he read a note from the publisher of the book.

In order to consolidate into a consecutive narrative the varied events in which the present two generations of the Hohenzollerns have taken part, the author has adopted the name of Bertram von Ehrenkrug. Under this pseudonym he is able to relate not only his own experiences but those of Secret Service agents who were working with him. The bulk of the missions, however, were undertaken solely by the author.

So for Armgaard Karl Graves, A.K.G. read Bertram von Ehrenkrug. Right, I've got that, Michael thought as he turned the first page and started to read.

Explanatory Note: Whenever a King of Prussia lies on his death bed there is handed to his successor a small, time-scarred black ebony box, nine inches long by four inches wide. This box is sent immediately after the demise of the reigning King to the hereditary Truchsess of the Kingdom, who acknowledge its receipt by returning one of the only two existing keys to the secret royal archives. In these archives, (accessible only to the King, the Truchsess and the Reichs Chancellor) are stored the innermost secrets of the Royal House and the Empire. Although officially the keeper of the King's secrets is never in evidence, unofficially and unobtrusively he wields a tremendous power, much as did in the olden days the keeper of the King's conscience.

Well that is a coincidence, Michael thought, rushing across to his desk and pulling out the cedar box before measuring it. It was exactly the same size, but not made of ebony; that didn't matter to Michael, because it was still a box measuring nine inches by four inches wide. With shaking hands he poured himself another whisky. As he did so he glanced out of the window. It was pitch black except for a full moon that shone back at him. He closed the shutters, fetched pen and paper and marched swiftly back to his chair, where he began avidly reading again.

In the heart of the Mark of Brandenburg, called "The Streusand-Biichse", of Prussia, about fifty miles from Berlin, in the midst of one of the magnificently, well-cared-for Prussian domain forests, stands the hereditary castle of the Freiherren von Ehrenkrug. This stronghold is the seat of the Koenigliche Oberfoerstereij, the officially known position of the Masters of Ehrenkrug and the only one known to ninety-nine out of every hundred of their fellow men. To the remaining few, Derer von Ehrenkrug are of vastly greater significance.

Since the days of the accession of the first Markgraf of Brandenburg, the House of Ehrenkrug has been closely identified with the aims, ambitions and successes of their Liege Lords of Hohenzollern. Even prior to this time, they were Reichsgraven and Trustees in the old German Empire. They were king-makers in the truest sense of the word.

Michael knew that the word "truchsess" (trustees) literally meant "sitting on the coffer". It was the medieval title of the most trusted official of the ancient Saxon kings and early German emperors. But at the back of his mind something was disturbing him about the name "Ehrenkrug" and he couldn't put his finger on it. Well never mind, it would come to him. He topped up his scotch and continued to read.

Grim and silent, surrounded by historic oak and fir trees, stood the ancient castle of Ehrenkrug. On the night of June 15, 1888, a drizzling rain was falling upon the battle-scarred walls. Grim and silent, swaying in the chilling blasts, stood the countless majestic trees like an outer guard, as if aware of portentous events. Grim and silent, human sentinels, clad in the dark green and silver uniform of the Prussian Royal Foresters were guarding the passage to the big oak-panelled refectory of the castle.

Around a solid wine-stained oak table were seated six men, reclining in deep leather cushioned arm chairs, their faces fitfully illuminated by a crackling log fire burning in a huge, brass-bound hearth. At the head of the table was a commanding figure, tall, six feet two in his stockings, wide *of shoulder and deep of chest, with the traditional bearing and carriage of a Prussian officer; the big massive head framed with deep gold hair and beard, slightly streaked with gray; keen steel blue, clear eyes, set wide apart, Truly a magnificent type of Teuton, this Wolfgang von Ehrenkrug, head of his house. At his right sat an equally tall but more slender man, his South Germanic origin clearly indicated in his dark hair and eyes. Clean shaven, with a thin-lipped, closely compressed mouth and high forehead, his severely intellectual, almost clerical aspect, easily stamped him for what he was, the Minister Plenipotentiary of the Bavarian court, Graf von P .....*

To the left was seated a short, stocky built, almost rubicund gentleman, whom one, even without glancing at his canonicals, or without looking at the gold cross suspended from his neck, or the big blood red, gleaming carbuncle on the third finger of his right hand, would have pronounced a dignitary of the Church and such he was, the Prince Bishop of Mayence. Seated in the other chairs were three high officials of the German Empire.

All their faces reflected deep, earnest, almost solemn thoughts. No one had uttered a word since they had been ushered into the hall by equally silent retainers, an hour before midnight. Only von Ehrenkrug, the head of the table, cast frequent glances at the big, dully-ticking wanduhr. It struck the hour of twelve. Almost simultaneously the door opened and a somber-clad, gray-haired servant walked up to his master, and saluting, said in a trembling voice, "Gnadiger, Herr, the messenger has come." Deep emotion was reflected in von Ehrenkrug's face and voice; as he arose, he placed his hand on the old servant's shoulder: 'It had to come, Herman.'

Quietly sobbing, the servant retired from the circle of men and took his place in the back of the room. Turning to the others present, the Master, in his low, deep voice, said: "Gentlemen, is it your pleasure to have the messenger sent in?" A silent nod was their answer. The watching servant, receiving the sign, almost immediately returned with the messenger, a clerk of the Royal Household. All had arisen. Walking straight up to the Freiherr, the officer saluted, and handing him a small black ebony box, said at the same time, "Der Kaiser ist todt." (The Emperor is dead).

Although everyone in the room had expected this message for hours, all were visibly affected. The Freiherr had drawn from his closely buttoned coat a thick black silk ribbon, on which were suspended two curiously wrought silver keys, one of which he handed to the messenger, who, saluting, left. The door closed, the Freiherr turned to his waiting companions, saying, "It behooves us to do our duty. Follow me." Opening a door at the farther end of the hall he led them down a flight of narrow, stone stairs into the keep of the castle. There in the flickering candlelight the six men gathered about a time-marred, brassbound cedar and sandalwood catafalque wrought with curious Sanscrit designs. Reverent and noiseless their movements, this was the catafalque in which was borne back to his home in 1040 the founder of the House of Ehrenkrug, who had perished during the Crusades in a valiant attempt to save Wolfram of Heckingen, one of the noble ancestors of the Hohenzollerns. Ever since that day this coffin has been the repository for the most important documents of House and State. Inserting a key into the ancient lock, Wolfgang von Ehrenkrug strove to throw the bolt. Years of idleness had stiffened the lock. But with oil and many manipulations the bolt was finally thrown. The lid turned back, there appeared a black hole. The old Freiherr took up the black ebony box. Carefully he touched the edges with oil and gently he placed it in the hole. It fitted perfectly.

A perceptible glance of relief passed over the faces of the group. A moment later there was handed into the room two buckets of water. Wolfgang von Ehrenkrug motioned to his companions to stand back. As they withdrew he poured the water over the box until the crevices were filled. Then, taking a heavy wooden mallet, he struck the ebony box, now in position, a sharp blow. With a clicking noise a seam in the extreme right opened and disclosed a hollow compartment. Bending over, the old Freiherr abstracted a zinc cylinder containing closely written parchments yellow with age. These parchments were sealed with the great seal of Prussia.

Michael froze. Zinc cylinder? Sanskrit! THE SILVER KEY! He shivered as he recalled Alice fainting and their disappointment at not finding anything in the zinc container. Still, never mind that. His father, or so it would appear, had been heir to a noble Prussian family! And that box he had removed from his mother's London home may have been part of that Prussian treasure chest. But why did she have a key used to open secret archives that dated from the crusades and how did she come by the box in the first place?

Michael replenished his glass with another large measure of whisky. Then, for no particular reason, he stood up and walked over to the mirror. There he stood, slightly lopsided but tall, admiring his own image. He pushed back his hair and stroked his chin before running his finger down the line in the middle towards the slight dimple at the bottom. He was a true Prussian! What breeding! As he walked away from the mirror, he knew he shouldn't feel better than everyone else, but tonight, well it was hard not to! Gulping the rest of his whisky, he grabbed the half full decanter and sat down. Then he read how the powerful deadly poison in the form of fine powder was sprinkled freely between the outer lid and the inner secret cubicle of the catafalque. The drenching eliminated the risk to those acquainted with the secret. Those unacquainted with the secret paid the price of their unwarranted trespass. On two distinct occasions, attempts were made by unauthorized persons to delve into this chest and on both occasions they had been found dead alongside it. So he and Alice had a lucky escape by the sound of it! As the clock struck one thirty, Michael considered retiring for the evening. The trouble was, he couldn't bring himself to go back to Juliana. So instead, he pulled an old tartan blanket across the chair and snuggled up underneath it. This is what he read next.

Calling his companions, he had them bear witness to the fact that the seals were intact and unbroken. Thereupon they signed a paper, which the Count placed with other similar vouchers in another compartment of the chest. Returning the documents to their tube, he carefully abstracted the ebony box, closed the lid and locked the outer covering of the catafalque. A few moments later the party was driven to the station, whence a special train conveyed them to Berlin.

Berlin was cast in gloom. The usual rather boisterous gaiety of the Berliners was very much subdued. On Unter den Linden a fine drizzling rain made the great globes of the electric arc lights gleam as through a hazy nebula. A great rain-soaked throng of humanity moved slowly up to the Palais on the Schloss-Platz, becoming denser as it neared the royal residence, where other masses of loyal citizens had stood for hours, awaiting the dread news. The idol of the German Empire, the hero of the Franco-Prussian War, the ideal of Teutonic manhood, lay dying. Anxiously every face was turned toward the flagstaff on the roof of the Palais, where the royal standard was drooping. A dim figure was seen fumbling with the halyards, and slowly the standard was lowered to half mast. The indistinct murmur of the vast crowd was instantly hushed, and with bared heads they listened to the booming of the minute guns. Frederick III, Emperor of Germany, King of Prussia, lovingly called "Unser Fritz", was dead. For the second time within one hundred and two days the Empire was cast into deep mourning.

The new ruler, in certain sections feared and hated on account of supposed intolerance and ambition, was largely an unknown, but all important factor in their destinies. No wonder anxious faces were lifted to the dim outline of the emblem of royal power.

Inside the Palais, in the anteroom leading to the royal death chamber, were assembled the principal office holders of the Empire, led by Fürst Bismarck, who stood nearest to the folding doors. He stood alone, evidently sunk in deep reflection. Curious glances and significant shoulder shrugs were directed toward him, plainly showing the rather ill-concealed thoughts of some of the courtiers present. Bismarck, the man of blood and iron, the Iron Chancellor, almost undisputed head in Prussia and Germany for nearly twenty years, awaited his new master. A Portentous meeting this, the folding doors were pushed back, and with short, jerky steps Prince Wilhelm of Prussia, who only in the last ten minutes had become King of Prussia and Emperor of Germany, stood before them.

A medium tall, slimly built, fair-haired young man, remarkable only by reason of his intensely sharp, clear, steel blue eyes and proud bearing. Almost insignificant in this group of exceptionally tall, broad-shouldered, imposing-looking, grey haired men, he was nearly dwarfed by the masterful presence of the Iron Chancellor. Hardly noticing the deep obeisance of the dignitaries, he stood gazing for fully a minute at the maker of his empire. Bismarck, drawn to his full height, looked straight at his new king. Slowly a quiet, almost paternal, smile appeared on the ruggedly lined face of the Chancellor.

A deep nervous flush overspread the young king's countenance. What were the thoughts coursing through those two minds? The one, by hereditary, inalienable and, to his mind, divine right, emperor of forty million people, placed there by an accident of birth; the other, a mastermind seen but once in a century, the instrument that made possible his elevation to imperial power. The smile and flush can easily be interpreted. Bismarck took two steps toward the King. William II held out his hand. Bismarck bent over it, stooping low to imprint the kiss of homage. Then the young monarch, his blue eyes alight with pride, showed one of his rare flashes of intuition and tact by placing his arm around the chancellor with an intimate gesture. Still keeping his left arm on Bismarck's shoulder, he turned to the others, saying, "Gentlemen, the Kaiser, my father, ist zur Ruhe gegangenf " Turning to Bismarck, he said in his sharp, rather shrill voice "Your Excellency will issue all necessary orders and send out the summons." With a wave of his hand he dismissed his audience, and, beckoning to Bismarck to follow him, he re-entered the death chamber.

Six hours after the young emperor had led Bismarck to the bed of the dead king there was held in the Royal Palais a secret conclave. The King, Bismarck, von Ehrenkrug, and three others debated long behind closed doors, which opened only when Wilhelm II and the tall Ehrenkrug descended into the royal archives. What transpired there no one (except the Emperor and von Ehrenkrug) knows, for Wolfgang von Ehrenkrug had delivered to the new emperor the black box with the secrets of his house. Secrets, that were later to soak Europe in blood.

Michael stopped reading. What secrets could that family have? Well, his certainly had secrets, all of which would be resolved if only he knew the real names of his mother and father! He yawned and stretched. It was late and he really should go to bed, well just one more page he thought, raising the book to his blurred vision. A moment later he closed his eyes and felt the weight of the book on his chest as he fell asleep.

Chapter Twenty Six   Bertram von Ehrenkrug

The next morning Juliana knocked on the library door. She had expected Michael to return to the bedroom so they could make up. But he had not. That was unusual and Juliana did not like unusual events. She knocked again, harder this time. Still there was no answer. Well, she certainly wasn't going to run after him she thought as she made her way into the kitchen. Anyway where was everyone this morning, she wondered pouring herself a coffee. By the time she had finished breakfast still no one had appeared, so she made her way back to the studio.

'Have you seen your father this morning?' she asked Alex, who she met in the hallway.

'No. Why should I have done?' He replied bounding past.

'Well if you do, ask him to pop up and see me.'

Alex thought that was strange coming from his mother. Usually it was his father who gave the orders! Perhaps he should go and look for him. A moment later he opened the library door and got a shock. Michael was sprawled out across the floor.

'HELP!' Alex shouted as he rushed over to him.

'Dad, dad, are you okay?' he implored, shaking him rather unwisely. Michael did not respond. 'Dad?' Still there was no reply. Alex laid him gently back down and ran into the hallway. 'Quick, I found him, he's collapsed.'

Juliana rushed down the stairs. 'Whatever has happened to him?'

'I don't know but he's not moving.'

'Oh my God,' Juliana rushed over. 'Call for the doctor, QUICKLY!'

Alex hurriedly made the call. By the time he got back, she had made Michael comfortable. All they could do now was to wait for the doctor to arrive. Juliana paced up and down. 'I'll never forgive myself if anything happens to him.'

Much to everyone's relief the doctor arrived soon afterwards.

'I'm sure there is no need to worry but if you wouldn't mind I'd like to examine him.'

'But I'm his wife, I should stay!'

'Yes, I'm his son. I want to be here too!'

'Very well, but will someone fetch a glass of water?'

A concerned Juliana looked on as the doctor listened to Michael's breathing. 'How long has he been unconscious for?'

'I've no idea. I think he may have been there all night!' she whispered.

'I see! And you were not concerned for his well being?'

'Well of course, if I had known he was ill, I would have been worried but I didn't know until this morning when we found him!' Juliana was irritated by the doctor's questioning and was just about to say something when the door flew open. It was Alice.

'Oh my God, what's happened?'

'That's what I am trying to determine,' the doctor replied, his impatience beginning to show. 'Now please, allow me some room.'

Alex placed the water on the table and made his way across to the window. Tonya and Paul were seated in the garden, enjoying the early morning sun. He frowned then his thoughts were interrupted by the doctor.

'I'm afraid it would appear that he is still in some type of coma. Where is the ambulance?'

'It's not here yet,' fretted Juliana.

'In that case, where is the telephone?'

'This way please doctor,' she replied as Alex followed them out.

When they had left Alice hurriedly closed the door and returned to Michael's side. Kneeling beside him she grabbed hold of his hand and said a special prayer aimed at aiding his rapid recovery. She fully expected his fingers to move and they did. But he didn't open his eyes. 'Michael?' she called out. 'Please! Still he did not stir.

'Asato Ma Sad Gamaya, Tamaso Ma Jyotir Gamaya, Mrtyorma, Amrtam, Gamaya, Aum... Santi, Santi, Santi,' she urgently whispered.

Michael opened his eyes. 'ARMGAARD, did you say Armgaard?'

Alice threw her arms in the air. 'Thank the Lord!'

'Water, I'm so thirsty,' Michael pleaded clasping his throat.

On hearing the commotion Juliana and Alex rushed back in. Alex quickly poured a glass of water. 'Here Dad, drink this slowly.'

Michael took a long gulp. 'What happened? Who are you? Oh, the doctor! What's wrong with me?'

'Darling, we were so worried! Alex couldn't wake you so we called the doctor. But I see now that all you did was fall asleep while you were reading,' Juliana added.

'He was going to send you to the hospital,' Alex pointed to the doctor as he spoke. 'He thought you were in a coma!'

Michael took another sip of water before replying. 'I was in a deep sleep. I'm fine. No need to worry. Let the doctor go.'

'You've been overdoing it.'

'Yes, he has Alice. I keep telling him to take it easy,' Juliana added.

The doctor smiled. 'Well, he appears to have made a remarkable recovery, so I am happy to leave but I want you to promise me one thing. If there are any further attacks, you'll bring him straight to the hospital. We must do some tests. We can't have this happening again to our esteemed professor!'

After seeing the doctor out Juliana went back into the library, where Michael was thanking Alex for his help and Alice was folding up the blanket. After they had left the room Juliana spoke to Michael. 'Well you certainly know how to pick your moments! You gave us all quite a fright!' she rebuked.

'I suppose I have to be sorry for that.' Michael barely looked at her.

'Don't be silly, there is no need to be sorry. I just want you to be careful! I DO CARE ABOUT YOU, YOU KNOW. Now about last night...'

'Look,' Michael interrupted, 'I was wrong to say what I said. I'll make it up to you. I'm not making excuses for my behaviour, but perhaps it's because I've never known my own father that I find it... well.... difficult to relate to a son, my son!'

Juliana frowned. 'You think you don't know how to be a loving father. Is that it?'

'Yes, but I'm going to make a big effort and change my ways''

Juliana smiled. 'I'm glad Michael. Now let's forget all about it. I love you but sometimes you aren't the easiest person to live with!'

Michael gave her a big hug. 'You wait and see. Things are going to get much better. I promise!'

Juliana pulled away. 'Well I think that calls for coffee. What about something to eat?' He shook his head. 'Coffee is fine but I'm staying put for a while. Can you stay with me?'

'Yes of course, I won't be long.'

Upon her return Michael told her that he felt cold. He asked her if she wouldn't mind reading the rest of the chapter to him. She agreed, placed a blanket over his shoulders and felt his forehead. 'I don't think you have a temperature just a hangover!' Michael flushed as she glanced at the empty decanter. Juliana smiled then turning to chapter two of *The Secrets of the Hohenzollerns*, she started to read to him.

'When Wilhelm II came up from the secret room he was a changed man. From a rather gay, somewhat dissipated, broad-minded Bohemian prince, Wilhelm II had changed mysteriously into a stern, almost puritanical king, with no thought but for his house and empire. He had read the message, the instruction that was to fashion his destiny. Some, indeed most, of those documents are in the handwriting of Frederick the Great. The exact purport is known only to those directly concerned and only given to the ascending kings.

'Oh look,' said Juliana, pausing for a moment. 'There's a note at the bottom of the page. Do you want me to read it?'

'It probably says the writer, Dr Graves, has adopted the name Bertram von Ehrenkrug.'

'No it doesn't.' Then she laughed.

'What's so funny?'

'Ehrenkrug it's a strange name.'

'Why?'

'Because ehren means "honour" and krug means "jug".'

Michael laughed. 'Oh, I see! He hails from a family of honourable mugs then! Well never mind that for now. Read me the note at the bottom of the page.'

'The author wishes it clearly understood that his knowledge of these things is derived and pieced together solely from conversations overheard in his own family circle, from personal observation and disjointed scraps of documentary evidence which have at times passed through his hands. He does not claim a personal perusal or contact with the documents mentioned in this chapter.'

Michael shrugged. 'Well at least he's honest.'

'Quite!' Juliana added picking up the book again.

'It is a notorious fact that wars and acts of aggression are never entered into by the Hohenzollerns until they have reached the age of forty. This is of remarkable significance when history has shown us that acts of conquest are made at an extremely early age and in the first years of manhood, when ideals and ideas pulse powerfully and run high. In the instances of Genghis Khan, Tamerlane, Alexander the Great, Attila and Bonaparte, their conquests were made in their early manhood, in some instances even in their teens. The history of the Hohenzollerns, with one or two exceptions, shows the distinct opposite.

'The empire and reign of these youthful conquerors has never lasted longer than the second or third generation, whereas the Hohenzollerns, with ever-increasing power, have reigned for nearly eight centuries. In natural traits and impulses they have the same tendencies of making their power and might felt, they have the same desire as is shown in the history of Frederick the Great and the attitude of the present heir apparent to give to primeval and martial instincts. Nevertheless, these desires are curbed and undergo a complete change on attaining supreme command. William II made no exception to this mysterious influence. The first act of the young Kaiser after his view of the contents of that box was to place his own mother under arrest.

Now, between Wilhelm II and his mother, no love was ever lost. The reason for this dormant ill-feeling goes back many years. When he was about two years of age, his mother, then Crown Princess Frederick, rigidly adhered to her English habits, one of these being her daily morning ride. These rides were looked upon rather askance, as it was not the custom for princesses of the Prussian court to show their equestrian abilities. Her Royal Highness also had a habit of taking her little son in front of her saddle, all remonstrance being of no avail. On one of these morning constitutionals, having to manage a rather restive animal, she dropped the infant. Somewhat alarmed, in view of the antagonistic attitude of the Court toward these morning canters, the accident was not mentioned and no medical attendance was called in at the time. After about three weeks, alarming symptoms appearing in the left arm and one side of the young prince, professional advisers were summoned. They had come too late; muscular atrophy resulting from a fracture had set in. Hence dates the Emperor's crippled left arm. Wilhelm, who was an intense admirer of all perfection, physical and otherwise, never forgave his mother. It was not likely then, that suspecting his mother of having appropriated one of the most important documents from the secret archives of the Hohenzollerns, Wilhelm II would blush at drastic measures. Wherefore there came a conference with von Ehrenkrug. The Emperor imprisoned his mother in the palace. She was under guard, of a polite guard to be sure, but utterly unyielding for two days. At the end of that time Wolfgang von Ehrenkrug was summoned. Imprisonment had affected the desired result. The document was restored.'

Juliana paused and turned a quizzical eye on Michael. 'Are you quite comfortable? Would you like some more coffee?' He nodded, and afterwards he asked her to sit closer. 'Then you won't have to shout,' he explained, as she continued.

'Freiherr Wolfgang von Ehrenkrug was seated in his study reading the daily newspapers just arrived from the capital, a frown on his forehead getting deeper and deeper. The news contained in the papers was of an alarming nature. Sweeping changes were taking place in the army and civil cabinets. The martial, and somewhat bombastic, utterances of the new Emperor had created a lot of ill feeling in France. Affairs up to now solely directed by Bismarck, in an even, if iron tenor, were becoming unsettled through his continual clashing with the new imperial will. Bismarck, long used to undisputed sway and a free hand, was becoming more or less handicapped by the Emperor's growing habit of personally conducting affairs of state, and a break, sooner or later, became daily more apparent.

Von Ehrenkrug's perusal of the papers was disturbed by a servant announcing a visitor, who proved to be the Minister of Police, a cabinet officer of high rank, Count von P-------. Von Ehrenkrug and the minister were life-long friends and comrades-in-arms. Von P-------- unburdened himself without hesitation. "Things are moving fast in the capital, Ehrenkrug. We've got a new master with a vengeance. Every report goes to him direct, instead of to the Chancellory. There's a deal of disappointment amongst his old cronies. I've had instructions to intimate to quite a few of them that a change of air, considerable air, would be very beneficial for their health.'' Bending forward, he said in a tense whisper, "He's inaugurating his own private Secret Service; messengers of his own choosing are coming and going hourly. The ambassadors to St Petersburg and the Quai d'Orsay are being recalled. Changes, Ehrenkrug."

Von Ehrenkrug had listened in silence, nodding his head now and then. Now, raising his head, and looking his old friend straight in the face, he quietly remarked, "And the object of your visit, Alter Freund, is what?" The Minister of Police fidgeted somewhat, and after a slight hesitation said, "It is about your nephew. Have you heard from him lately? Receiving a negative reply, he continued, "Well, the young fool has been at it again. He has compromised himself to such an extent that a prolonged absence would be very advisable. I have received, so far, no official orders, and it is only on account of our long friendship that I am here to advise you in this matter. Your nephew, as you may or may not be aware, has identified himself with the Revolutionary Socialistic Party, and has been indiscreet enough to advocate their radical theories, not only in speeches, but in writings; brilliant writings, I must admit but nevertheless highly dangerous, bound to come to the Emperor's notice.'

'I would advise you to use your influence to stop this foolishness, or send him out of the country." Von Ehrenkrug had listened without comment, and now simply said, "Thank you, old friend." Touching a bell, he instructed the answering servant to telegraph immediately to the young Freiherr at the University of Bonn to return home at once.

The railway station at Furstenwalde an der Spree is small and sleepy. It is not a usual stopping place for express trains, so that when the eastbound through train slowed down and came to a halt it drew quite a few curious onlookers. A young man descended, carrying overcoat and cane. The station master gave a startled look then rushed forward, giving the youth an effusive greeting, which was returned in a very debonair manner. Most of the idlers gathered also extended familiar, yet very respectful, greetings, and one of them being asked by a stranger, 'Who is this young man? He seems pretty popular," was informed with no little pride of tone and gesture, 'That is our young Freiherr, Bertram von Ehrenkrug.'

The station master, who knew young Bertram since he was knee-high, expressed his wonderment at the sudden appearance of the Freiherr, at the same time querying about luggage and means of transportation, to all of which queries he received the laughing answer, "Oh, the Governor wired for me and, Donnerwetter, I've left my grip in the train. I forgot to let them know at home that I was coming by this train. You had better telegraph to the Schloss and have them send in the dog cart. I am going over to the Black Eagle Inn."

Michael stood up while Juliana was reading, took hold of a notepad and scribbled down Furstenwalde? Revolutionary Socialistic Party? University of Bonn? 1898?

Juliana paused, watching him with interest. 'Have you finished?'

'Carry on,' he grinned back at her.

'All of which was very characteristic of Bertram Erwin, hereditary Freiherr and heir of Derer von and zu Ehrenkrug, for a more unconventional, Bohemian scion the rather staid, conventionally conservative and proud house of Ehrenkrug had never produced. This trait of character, manifested since the early childhood of Bertram, was a continual source of discord between him and the Head of the House. Bertram was soon comfortably ensconced in the beer garden fronting the inn, and quickly surrounded by a coterie of old cronies, hugely enjoying their gossip'.

'All too soon the dog cart drove up. All too soon, for Bertram had a decidedly uneasy feeling in regard to his sudden summons home. He was received by his uncle's own body servant, upon whose countenance, at no time cheerful, rested an extra funereal gloom. With a muttered, "B-rrr, the weather gauge points to storm," I'm in for it, he thought as he walked into his uncle's study.

The old Freiherr was standing in front of the fireplace. Acknowledging the salute of his nephew with a curt nod he queried, "Have you eaten, Bertram?" receiving an equally curt, "Yes, thanks, sir." There was no hint of familiarity or close relationship in their attitude. Notwithstanding, they bore a striking resemblance to each other. Bertram was as tall as his uncle but of slimmer build. The same widely set-apart blue eyes, the same high forehead and firmly moulded chin, in the case of the younger man as yet softer and unlined.

Without preamble, his uncle began: "I suppose you know why I have recalled you from your university?" Without waiting for an answer, he continued: "I have received a visit from Count von P----.who unofficially informed me that your activities have attracted the seriously displeased attention of the Government. It is only your position as my nephew and heir to the House of Ehrenkrug and the personal friendship to me of the Minister of Police that has saved you from most serious consequences. Von P--- warned me that the Emperor's attention was bound to be drawn toward you. I intended to send you abroad, but Von P-----'s warning came too late. I received, this morning, a peremptory order from the Emperor for your instant removal from the University. You are to report yourself to the Military Kadetten-Anstalt of Lichterfelde within forty-eight hours. You can count yourself fortunate, for instead of a punishment, it is more of an honour." "Not a word!" the Freiherr commanded, raising his hand in a gesture of silence. "I know what you wish to say. We have gone over all this before. I know your ideals about being a free agent and leading your own life. You are not a free agent, and you cannot lead your own life. You have to pay the penalty, if penalty it is, of being born into the House of Ehrenkrug, which for five hundred years has observed tradition and served its rulers and country with unsullied honour and fidelity. Be silent!" the Freiherr exclaimed again, as he noticed an attempt on the part of Bertram to interrupt him.

Your free thought ideals and tendencies you have without doubt derived from your mother, who, excellent woman though she was, could never control her hot, independent Polish blood, and to my intense sorrow she has bequeathed you her temperament.'

'You will from now on be subjected to an iron military discipline, which will teach you obedience, the first rule necessary in those who wish to command others. This is your last chance, for although the House of Ehrenkrug has always sufficient power and influence to advance and protect, this power would never be used for the benefit of an unruly member of the family. You will clearly understand this. That is all. Go to your quarters." Bowing to his uncle, and turning on his heel, Bertram walked out. Like the Emperor, his star was not yet in the zenith.'

Juliana glanced up. 'IRON military discipline! I think that's a good place to finish for now.'

Michael scribbled another note. After he finished he glanced up and smiled. 'That means I may have a Polish grandmother and Alex could have a .....'

'Yes,' Juliana interrupted, 'and speaking of family traits, we can see where he gets his from!'

Michael raised an eyebrow before replying. 'I know! It's quite uncanny. We must find out more about this man but tell me, you understand why I think he's my father and why I must know absolutely everything there is to know about him, especially what his relationship was to my mother. I must know what his real name was and hers of course.'

Juliana tapped the closed book on her lap. 'You mean Dr Armgaard Karl Graves?'

Michael smiled. 'Or as I like to call him, Dr Karl Armgaard Graves.'

'Hm! It shouldn't be too difficult to piece his life story together! We have much of it written down here, all be it under a different name! By the way, do you remember giving me lots of old newspapers from out of those tea chests?'

Michael frowned. 'Vaguely, why do you ask?'

'Well quite by chance I happened to read one and then another. You'll be pleased with what I discovered.'

'Spill the beans then.'

'They were nearly all on this Dr Armgaard Karl Graves, which makes me think you may be right. Why else would your mother keep them?'

'I must see them at once. Where are they?'

'Well I thought you would say that so I'm busy putting them in date order. But I must warn you they are fragile and some are badly damaged.'

Michael smiled. 'Well there is something I should show you first.' Juliana watched him rummage through a desk drawer. He wondered whether he should show her the cedar box and then thought better of it.

'Here,' he said, passing her the letter.

'You've read it to me before. Don't you remember?'

'Have I? Well I couldn't have asked for more. At least she took the trouble to explain why she could never tell me who my father was!' As he finished speaking Michael walked slowly across the room and stood silhouetted in front of the French windows with his hands clasped behind his back. Juliana had never seen IT before but now IT was very much in evidence! Though his suit was crumpled and his face grey, his forbearance was exactly like one of the Prussians described by Dr Graves. Michael turned towards her. 'You know, it's such a beautiful day, I've a mind to take a turn around our rose garden. Will you join me?'

Chapter Twenty Seven   Dr Armgaard Karl Graves

When Giovanni heard of the doctor's visit he was shocked and asked Alice what had happened. After she explained they decided to call in on Michael.

'Come in, come in! Take a seat,' Michael said, smiling.

Giovanni removed his cap. He was glad to see that Michael was looking so well and was about to congratulate him on his recovery when he spotted the icon in the corner.

'Haven't you seen that before?' Michael asked.

Giovanni shook his head.

'Well come over here and take a closer look if you like. Alice came up with the idea of placing it here. It will keep us all focused on the discussion in hand.'

Alice smiled in agreement.

'Si,' replied Giovanni nervously. He wasn't sure what else he should say.

'And look over here,' Alice pointed to the huge piece of amethyst sitting in the fireplace. 'You see how they bring safety to this place? Oh I do hope you will join us tonight? It promises to be rather exciting!'

'Well, er...,' Giovanni stumbled over his words.

'Just having you here will be good,' Alice insisted. 'The more brains we have around the table the better!'

That made Giovanni smile. No one had spoken about his brains before. 'Si, si, but who will make the supper?'

'Oh don't worry about that, we can prepare it beforehand. In fact...,' Alice added, patting his back. 'Let's get the lasagne and salad put together right now.'

* * *

Juliana was putting the newspaper clippings together when Michael strode into her studio later that day.

'Well?' he demanded. 'I can't wait to see what you've got for me.'

Michael picked up a musty green and gold book. 'So this is *The Secrets of the German War Office!*' He flicked through the first few pages. You're a secretive one too. I wonder what else is my little squirrel is hiding?' Michael laughed to show he was joking. Then he saw the table where Juliana had neatly laid out the newspaper clippings all in date order.

'Doctor Armgaard Karl Graves,' Michael pronounced the name slowly. 'I must say this one is in excellent condition considering it dates back to 1916. Mother was clever to keep hold of them for so long.'

Juliana glanced at the newspaper clipping in Michael's hand. 'That one isn't bad but some are barely legible and there are others where bits are actually missing. Take this one here,' she added, holding up a delicate newspaper. 'You have to be careful. Some of the print is barely readable. Anyway, I've done my best with them!'

Michael picked the clippings up one after another until he had a pile in his hand. Juliana sighed. 'Please try and keep them in order.'

'I assume by the time I've finished reading this lot I'm going to know all about my father the good doctor!' Juliana remained silent as she watched her husband browse somewhat haphazardly through the clippings.

'Ah! Ha! November 4th 1914. Listen to this.

'**MORE PREDICTIONS BY EX-GERMAN SPY:** *Dr Graves now tells of Coming Invasion of England by Germany both by Air and Sea*, *Thirty Zeppelins and three hundred and seventy five thousand men to cross the Channel.* **LONDON IS TO BE DESTROYED. EX SPY'S FORECAST IN WAR FULFILLED;** *Dr Graves predicted fall of Antwerp one day before news got here.*'

ENGLAND TO BE HARRIED BY AIR ATTACKS AND TO QUITE FIGHTING IN FOUR WEEKS

The news of the fall of Antwerp in yesterday's papers added interest to some of the predictions recently made concerning the European conflict by **Dr Armgaard Karl Graves,** *the former international spy, who professed to have been in the employ of* the German and English Governments *at various times.*

'Well, he's certainly making the headlines!' Michael noted, picking up another cutting.

Juliana smiled. 'As you can see, some are...'

'Good Heavens June 27th 1915!' He interrupted. 'This one's about the book I'm reading.

GERMAN SPY TELLS HOHENZOLLERN SECRETS. *Another book by* **Dr Armgaard Karl Graves** *professes to make new disclosures regarding the Kaiser and his Court.*

UNPRECEDENTED AND ASTOUNDING REVELATIONS OF THE INNER WORKINGS OF THE GERMAN SECRET DEPARTMENT

'Dr Graves, who recently was imprisoned by us for spying at Rosyth, tells his tale without concealment or hesitation from the day when he entered the "spy school" at Berlin to the day when he finally left the service in disgust. From the first page, a scene at question time in the English parliament, to the end of the story, the interest and the excitement never flags. The most extravagant inventions of fiction are put to shame by some of the actual events of which the author writes. At any time it would have attracted universal attention; now its interest is immense. The disclosures of the hidden forces of German politics and secret diplomacy reveal the sleepless eye of their war machine and show the subterranean information by which Wilhelmstrasse endeavoured to remake the political map of Europe.'

Michael lay the crumpled cuttings down. 'I can't believe that no one has ever heard of this man before. He was as famous as that Sidney Reilly that Paul's always going on about!'

Juliana laughed. 'Now you can see why I had to order those books of his. But look here Michael, not all the publicity was good, I'm afraid.' She pointed to a clipping that she had purposely left to one side. 'Listen to this.

The publisher assures us that Dr Armgaard Karl Graves's Secrets of the German War Office has reached over one hundred thousand American readers and was translated into six languages. This may be so, but it only proves how easily we are enthralled, for a greater collection of arrant nonsense we never heard!'

'Who wrote that?'

'I have no idea. Only the article has been cut out of the paper. But it must be from an American newspaper, perhaps the New York Times or the Washington Post. I think we can assume that Dr Graves was in the newspapers on a regular basis. Look! Here is another eye catching story.'

Michael laughed. 'Don't you mean spy catching!'

'Apparently in November 1916 he was accused of blackmailing the German Ambassador in Washington, a certain Count Bernstorff and his wife.' Juliana added.

Michael sat down. 'Ah yes. Germany still had an embassy in the United States because the U.S. did not enter the war until much later.'

'Ssshhhh! Listen!' Juliana demanded.

'Dr Graves admitted that his name was not Graves and that his alias was Meinke. When arrested he said that he would like to escape spending the night in a cell. So bail was set at $2000 and was paid by a professional bondsman. According to Department of Justice officials, Graves came to Washington from New York last Monday and called on Prince von Hatzfeldt-Trachenberg, Counsellor at the German Embassy.

At the latter's residence, he told the Prince, officials said, that he had some letters, the publication of which might be embarrassing to Countess von Bernstorff. He did not know who had written the letters, Graves was represented as saying. He had nothing to do with the matter other than to serve a friend, Graves said, according to the account given after his arrest. All he wanted was to serve Germany, but his friend desired compensation for delivering the letters and it is alleged that the sum of $3000 was suggested. As evidence that he had letters addressed to the Countess, Graves exhibited an envelope addressed to the Countess, which he said had contained one of the letters that he thought might be embarrassing to the Ambassadress if they were published. A second conversation took place on Monday between Prince Hatzfeldt and Graves at the German Embassy. It was arranged that Graves should call on Prince Hatzfeldt on Friday. Graves is supposed to have returned to New York. He didn't call on Prince Hatzfeldt yesterday but returned to Washington from New York this morning and went to Prince Hatzfeldt's residence, where he was arrested.

Meanwhile Prince Hatzfeldt had told Graves's story to Count von Bernstorff. The latter notified the State Department and asked that Graves be arrested. Washington police had a detective stationed at the Prince's house to wait for Graves. Graves arrived at 10 o'clock. The conversation between the Prince and Graves was overheard by the Inspector, who arrested Graves as he was leaving. According to the story told by Department of Justice officials, Graves asked for $3000 for the return of the letters.'

Juliana looked up to see Michael shaking his head. 'Well I'm in shock,' he responded. 'Blackmailing the German Ambassador, Perhaps he is not my father after all!'

'Don't be so quick to judge, Wait until I have finished you might be pleasantly surprised.

A curious weapon, a combination of a pistol and jack-knife was found on Graves. He said it had been given to him by a New York police captain. In giving the details of the case federal officials said that upon entering the office of Prince Hatzfeldt, Graves made it known that he had in his possession the papers which brought about his arrest. One letter, which he exhibited, was to the Countess von Bernstorff from her son, an officer in the German army. Graves said, according to statements made by Federal officials tonight, that he had other letters that would prove embarrassing should they be published.

Officials of the German Embassy allege that Graves had in his possession what apparently were confidential coded dispatches from the German Government to Count von Bernstorff. The prisoner said that he had obtained all the documents from persons who smuggled them past the British censors on the steamship Oscar II.'

Juliana paused for a moment while she thought. 'Oscar II? Wasn't that the ship Henry Ford chartered as his Peace Ship in 1914?' she asked.

Michael shrugged. 'I can't remember the date off hand but yes, that was the name of the ship. Anyway, carry on!'

'Well isn't that another piece of the puzzle found?' Juliana asked.

Michael shrugged. 'Possibly, Carry on!'

'The official dispatches were said to be useless to him, because he could not decipher them. The letters showed no postmark and officials at the embassy were convinced that they had been obtained in some manner from a confidential messenger whose identity still is undisclosed.

Then we have this but I'm not sure whether it is part of the same article.

Much interest is being shown in Washington tonight in Mr Graves's statement that the correspondence which he held reached this country by a messenger on the Oscar II. This was regarded as revealing how persons and officials apparently avoided the British censorship in communicating with the Germans.'

'Graves first appearance in public after his arrest was at the office of United States Commissioner Taylor, where, surrounded by Federal Agents and police detectives, he was brought for arraignment. He was faultlessly attired, swung a light walking stick and viewed the proceedings with a faint smile until the question of bail was brought up. He requested that, should he be unable to secure a bondsman, he be permitted, to spend the night in a hotel, under guard of detectives, whose expenses he offered to pay. "I should like," he said, "to escape spending the night in a cell." In reply to questions, Graves provided the following reply:

'"I have nothing so important to say. I may never make a complete statement. I am an American in every sense of the word. I have American ideas. I have declared my intention of becoming a citizen of this country and have taken out my first papers. I am now a writer, a lecturer, and lately have been writing scenarios about my experiences as an international spy. I have been in this country two years and nine months. Yes, it is true that I was once connected with the British Foreign Office but I am no more. I came to Washington for the sole purpose of disposing of the papers. I had no intention of blackmailing Countess von Bernstorff. I object to the charge of blackmail. I do not like the word. I made no attempt to communicate with the Countess. I do not deal with women. I did deal with Prince Hatzfeldt. I will not at this time discuss the contents of the papers I had. I will say, however, that I was just employing the same methods which the German Embassy has used in this country for the last two years and four months. In my business transactions with Prince Hatzfeldt, I considered that I was rendering the Embassy a great service, letting the original letters go into the hands of the Embassy for $3000. The parties who conveyed the letters from Germany to the United States incurred $2480 in expense.'"

Michael stood up and walked around the room. He was genuinely upset.

'To think that we are listening to the words of a man who died so long ago and he was a lecturer just like me.' Michael turned to Juliana. 'You know what? I LIKE him. He's as honest as the day is long! Is there more?'

'Yes there is.'

'Well come on, I haven't got all day!'

'Well before I start Michael, I want you to sit down and relax. You know what the doctor said. Now please!' Michael did as he was told while Juliana read Dr Graves's defence statement.

'"Not one cent of the $3000 would have been mine. The benefit to me in handing these letters over to the German Embassy was in what good service the Embassy would be to me in Germany. Those documents were official and would have helped men in certain quarters in Germany to get what has been long overdue to me in the way of money owed me there. At no time in my interviews and conversations with Prince Hatzfeldt was Countess Bernstorff mentioned. In fact, Countess Bernstorff has nothing at all to do with it. It is true the letters were addressed to her, but that was just a cover. Those letters were entirely official documents. I have not said they were brought on the Oscar II. That's surmise.'"

'Why is he so worried about that?' Michael shouted. 'Unless of course he knows that the Oscar II is a courier ship of some kind?'

Juliana ignored the comment and carried on reading.

'According to the Frankfurt Gazette, Dr Armgaard Karl Graves, who describes himself as an international spy of worldwide fame, at one time in the confidence of the highest officials of Germany including the Kaiser himself, is in reality Max Meincke, at one time connected with a more or less private detective agency in Brussels.'

'Max Meincke!' Michael interrupted again. 'What a name!'

'A recent issue of the paper reviewing his career asserts that Graves or Meincke has never been connected with the German Secret Service. According to the story as told by the Gazette, Graves has served terms in prison in both Germany and in Great Britain. John J. Halligan, his lawyer, of 303 Broadway, admitted yesterday that Graves had been sentenced to eighteen months in Scotland several years ago and also that his client had been sentenced to four months in jail in Bulgaria prior to his conviction in Scotland. On both occasions, he added, the offence was one of espionage undertaken on behalf of and at the instigations of the German Government. Mr Halligan said yesterday that Graves had told him that he had used the name Meincke as an alias while working as a spy in Belgium before the present war started.'

'Oh no,' Michael said, rubbing his forehead.

Juliana looked up. 'Do you want me to stop?'

'No, of course I don't. I'm just trying to digest it all. Why does he keep changing his name all the time! It makes life so damn difficult!'

Juliana laughed. 'Well, he is a spy. That's what they are supposed to do, be under cover!'

'I'm only interested in this baloney if he is definitely my father.'

Juliana thought for a moment. 'Unless we come across a birth certificate or some other documentation we won't know whether he is your father, but surely your mother wouldn't have collected all this information about him if he wasn't important in some way.'

Michael watched Juliana pour out a coffee. 'Surely there must be a clue to his real identity somewhere in these cuttings?'

'Yes, we just have to be a patient.'

'Of course I know that. I'm not stupid!'

Juliana slammed the coffee cup down. 'Don't get irritable with me.' She added picking up a large tattered cutting. Carefully she opened it and turned it to the light in order to see the print more easily.

Michael looked on inquisitively, until he could contain himself no longer.

'Well what does it say?'

Juliana took a purposely slow sip of coffee before replying. 'It's a cutting from the Frankfurt Gazette and says:

'Dr Armgaard Karl Graves, who has been lecturing and writing books against Germany in the United States, is Max Meincke who was born in Berlin May 7th 1882. He studied dentistry for a time and was later in the employ of a merchant. In 1898 he left Germany for the first time. In 1911 he appeared in Wiesbaden as Mr A.K. Graves, M.D. and on May 27th of the same year was sentenced in a German court to six months imprisonment but before the sentence was imposed he fled to Stettin. Meincke first asserted when examined in court that he had earned the title of doctor of medicine at the University of Adelaide in Australia and that his right to the name Graves was due to the fact that he had been adopted by a Major Graves in Tavistock, West Australia. Investigations by the proper authorities disclosed that no such person as Major Graves mentioned by Meincke existed, and furthermore that there was no town in West Australia called Tavistock....'

'Ah!' Michael interrupted. 'I'm sure there's a Tavistock somewhere in Australia and that Major Graves, I wonder if that isn't.....'

'MICHAEL! Can you STOP interrupting me unless you have something really important to say, now look what you've done! I've lost where I was up to.'

Michael leant over. 'There!' he said, pointing to the paragraph.

'When confronted with these facts Meincke admitted that he had been exaggerating. While still living in Wiesbaden Meincke endeavoured to attract attention to himself by veiled allusions to acts involving espionage which he said he had accomplished. Subsequently he left Germany and went to Scotland and in 1912 was arrested at Glasgow, tried and sentenced to serve eighteen months in prison for having in his possession ciphers, which he refused to decipher.'

'Oh! No!' Michael rubbed his head and sat down. Juliana felt sorry for him. It must be awful, she thought, not knowing your parents names and especially for a man of his elevated reputation. 'Don't forget, what I've just read WAS from a German newspaper. Not everything printed is necessarily the truth Michael. Besides, his lawyer denies every word. Listen to this.

'"All of these statements against my client," said Mr Halligan, 'are inspired by the German Government. He may have been known as Meincke in Brussels and probably was! Dr Graves tells me that he has so many aliases that he has *forgotten some of them and that the name Meincke may be among those which have slipped his memory. Any statement that he has served terms in German prisons is false and nobody knows that better than do the German authorities.*

When he was in Belgium before the war, he was not there in the employ of any private detective agency, but as the agent of the German Government sent there to get military maps of the country. He was sent to England for the same purpose and would have succeeded but for the fact that he was betrayed by an enemy at the German court who wanted him out of the way. That enemy was very close to Crown Prince Frederick William. He did not serve the sentence imposed in Scotland, but was released for "Reasons of State" by the British Government. A copy of the article which appeared in the Gazette has been placed in the hands of the United States naturalization authorities in New York and it was said yesterday that in the event Graves applied for full citizenship, he would be asked to explain certain statements made in the article. Up to the present he has only asserted that it is his intention to apply for citizenship. Dr Graves issued the following statement last night in regard to the article in the Frankfurt Gazette:

"The whole article is malicious and unfair and I do not wish at present to make a detailed statement in regard to it. I will however call attention to certain points, which I want to make clear. First, concerning the assertion that I was ever connected with a detective agency in Brussels: I was there as the head of an institution, a college of philosophy, the funds of which were supplied by the German Government and the faculty of which were my subordinates in the Imperial Secret Service. Second, as to my serving terms in English prisons: I was caught, tried, and convicted in 1912 in England as a German spy. And after fighting the British Government to a standstill when I was convicted, I admitted that I had a fair and square trial.

The British Government is not in the habit of convicting any man without an exhaustive trial, and if the British Government found me guilty of being a German spy you may rest assured that a German spy I was. Third, I was never convicted in Bulgaria. I was arrested there and released after forty-eight hours. Fourth, as regards the statement about my veiled allusions to espionage in Weisbaden, this must seem a joke to anyone acquainted with German officialdom, for no one with even the slightest suspicion of espionage attached to him would be able to travel 100 meters in Germany, especially in Prussia.'"

'Damn it! It wasn't Bulgaria!' Michael shouted. 'It was Belgrade. He said so in his book!' Juliana put the clippings down on the table. Michael was getting far too irritated and it worried her. 'Perhaps it's a printing error! Anyway, what do you think of all of this?' she asked, trying to calm him down.

Michael rubbed his forehead from side to side and then rubbed his eyes rather hard. His face was very red.

'I hope you haven't got high blood pressure!'

Michael sighed. 'Oh I don't know, woman. What's more, I don't care!'

'Well you should care. I want you to see the doctor next time you're in town and get it checked out!'

'Yes alright. Please don't fuss. Now look, I'm thinking! This Count Bernstorff, well he was no angel. I read that he was accused of being involved with many treacherous acts against the United States, Canada and Britain and being German and living in the U.S. he was able to obstruct the arms shipments to the allies.'

'Isn't that what you would expect from a German whose country is at war?' Juliana responded.

Michael laughed sarcastically. 'Well, not from a diplomat who is a guest of the United States! Anyway some of the plans, or so I believe, included destroying the Welland Canal, which circumvents Niagara Falls. This was attempted in September 1914 but failed. In 1914 the German diplomatic mission began supporting the expatriate Indian Movement who wanted independence from British rule. You see, the Kaiser had long wished for a German Empire that would include Britain's "jewel in the crown", India. A certain Captain Franz von Papen, who later became Chancellor of Germany and Captain Karl Boyed, a naval attaché were also involved or so it was reported at the time.'

'Oh, now you've just reminded me,' Juliana responded, 'I meant to tell you that not all the articles that Maria collected relate to Dr Graves. Look at this one; it's just what you were saying.

VON PAPEN ARRESTED. MAN CALLED WOLF VON IGEL SEIZED BY FEDERAL AGENTS AFTER A STRUGGLE. MASS OF PAPERS TAKEN, SAID TO INVOLVE EMBASSY AND WELLAND CANAL FIGURES IN DOCUMENTATION.

Michael read the headlines and handed the article back to Juliana. 'I know about this. Are there any more on Dr Graves?'

'Yes, here are a few more.' Juliana handed them over, one by one.

A FEARSOME WARNING BY DR GRAVES A SPY, DEADLY BACTERIA BOMBS, BLINDING VAPOUR RAYS AT GERMANS' CALL. HE SAYS GOING TO SUE BERNSTORFF.

Will ask a modest $200,000 out of millions in gold he says envoy has cashed in banks.

DR GRAVES GUARDED BY A GRIM SENTINEL, *a solemn man with acrobatic eyes on duty at portal of a German spy's home.*

DOCTOR TO FACE THE MUSIC, *the charge of attempting to blackmail is to be pressed.*

Juliana looked up. 'Do you want to hear more?'

Michael nodded.

'Dr Armgaard Karl Graves, self styled "'international spy", who was arrested in Washington on Saturday charged with attempting to blackmail the Countess von Bernstorff, wife of the German Ambassador to the United States, announced from his sixty-ninth street headquarters yesterday afternoon that he would return to Washington this afternoon "to face the music". He declared that he had no fear of the outcome and added that tomorrow, when the time came for him to be arraigned before a United States Commissioner to answer the charges against him, "he would be there with bells on". Dr Graves, minus collar, and grave in appearance as well as in name, talked at length when seen at 65 West Sixty Ninth St yesterday.

'And here's another article.

'GRAVES AS CITIZEN WILL DEFY GERMAN KAISER'S ALLEGED FORMER CONFIDENTIAL AGENT, TAKES OUT FIRST PAPERS HERE, FEARS FOR HIS LIBERTY.

Refuses to reveal his birthplace other than to say it is in Central Europe. On Monday Graves appeared in the Supreme Court of New York County and announced his intention of becoming an American citizen. In his application he gave the name under which he is known in this country, said that he was born in Central Europe, was a subject of the late Franz Josef (Austria/Hungary) and that he was born May 7th 1878.'

Michael interrupted. 'That makes him about thirty seven years old.'

'Dr Graves fears that an attempt will be made by the German Government to get possession of his person. As a citizen he could demand the protection of this Government if any attack was made upon his liberty by a foreign power. That explains his application for his papers at this time. Dr Graves answered all the questions of the clerk until he was asked where he was born. He declined to reply and it was not until a telephone message was sent to the Federal Bureau and an answer received that specific information on this point could be dispensed with, that his papers could be made out.'

'So he thinks the Germans will kill him, poor man,' Michael elaborated.
　'I know, but at least the Federal Bureau backed his application for American Citizenship. They must have believed in him,' Juliana replied.
　'More importantly, imagine if they actually knew his true identity but for some important reason could not reveal it!' Michael's eyes widened as he considered the implication of what he was saying. 'He must have been a very important person, a count? A PRINCE even! This is so intriguing I just wish we could get to the bottom of it all.''
　Juliana agreed. ''And according to this, everything he predicts comes true. Listen:

'GRAVES CASE TO GO TO KAISER. IMPERIAL PERMISSION NECESSARY FOR EMBASSY ATTACHÉ TO TESTIFY:
Formal request that Prince Hatzfeldt, Counsellor of the German Embassy, appear as a witness against Karl Armgaard Graves, self styled international

spy, has been made by the State Department in a note to Count von Bernstorff, the German Ambassador. The request has been forwarded to the German Foreign Office in Berlin. Ultimately it will come before Emperor William, who must give his personal approval before the Prince can appear.'

Michael glared at Juliana.

"What? You're not surprised that the Kaiser will have his say on a German citizen!'

'No, but this is the first time that I have seen him referred to as Karl Armgaard Graves. So now I am certain that he really IS mother's friend, K.A.G!' Michael flicked through the cuttings quickly. 'If only we knew what papers these articles all came from we could get copies. There is probably much of the real story missing.'

'Well let's assume they are from the major papers of the day. Besides, even if we could get hold of them it would be a huge job trawling through them all.'

As she spoke Michael's eyes settled on one of the articles.

San Francisco. November 20th, 1916. *Graves furnished a dramatic conclusion to negotiations which had been in progress for a week between Prince Hatzfeldt and Graves. The latter said he had paid for the papers and asked the Prince for $3000 for the documents. As Hatzfeldt could not get the papers without payment he had Graves arrested. Graves considers he has evidence sufficient to cause Bernstorff and Hatzfeldt to be expelled from America as "persona -non grata" officials. "The master spy", as Graves styles himself, intended publishing the contents of the German documents, failing their sale to Hatzfeldt and says it was purely a business proposition.*

'Well at least we have San Francisco and a date, but it doesn't give the name of the paper. Damn it! What date was that other article you read to me, the one about Bernstorff?'

Juliana started searching. 'I think it was 1916 but I can't say for sure!'

'Oh well, it doesn't matter. I just want to know whether he was telling the truth. Would you like another coffee? I'm desperate for one.' Michael carried on talking as he put the kettle on. 'I seem to recall a story that Bernstorff also helped organize what became known as the "Great Phenol Plot!"'

'That sounds explosive,' Juliana joked.

'Yes, it was an attempt to divert phenol from the production of high explosives in the United States, presumably because it would end up being sold to the British. The most famous in 1916 was called the Black Tom explosion and was the most spectacular of the sabotage operations.'

'But do you really think the German ambassador was involved?'

'I wouldn't have thought so. But you see, Bernstorff, along with all the other German diplomats, had to leave the United States in 1917 when Woodrow Wilson severed diplomatic relations with Germany. When Colonel House heard the news he wrote to him saying "The day will come when people in Germany will see how much you have done for your country in America."'

'So what happened to Bernstorff? Was that the end of his career?'

'I believe he retired to Berlin'.

'What I find intriguing,' Juliana added, 'is that Karl Graves predicted that Prince Hatzfeldt would never give evidence against him in court and he was right! But how did he know that?'

'I don't know. Prince Hatzfeldt came from an eminent family in Germany, as did Bernstorff of course.'

'But if Karl Armgaard Graves was able to get a Hatzfeldt and Bernstorff on the run and I can only imagine they knew Graves's real identity, then he must have been, as he always claimed, superior to them!'

Michael smiled before replying.' I think they were afraid of him and what he could tell! That's why the Kaiser got involved and put an end to it all.'

'Good Heavens Michael, you think Karl was a prince!' Michael winked and smiled again.

'Surely you're not suggesting he was a member of the Hohenzollern family?'

Michael's grin grew wider. 'No just a spying prince!'

'But if that was the case surely the U.S. would want to lock him up and throw away the key?'

'Not according to this,' Michael replied, picking up another cutting.

'Although initial charges were made against Graves they were dropped as he predicted when the German Reich rejected the testimony of the embassy staff and he was then discharged.'

'Ah yes but it wasn't for very long I'm afraid, according to this.' interrupted Juliana.

'*August 1917. Germany asks the U.S. to intern Karl Armgaard Graves. Master Spy worries German officials.*''

Michael took a deep breath. 'Well I'm not surprised they wanted him locked up. He was giving all their secrets away. Aha! Look here at last, retribution!' He shouted in excitement.

'*GRAVES LIKELY TO GO FREE, DEPARTURE OF GERMAN EMBASSY MAY SAVE HIM FROM PROSECUTION* '

'What a day this has been my dear.'
   'Well, it's not over yet, I'm afraid I have some bad news for you.'

At first Michael thought she was joking, then he realised her tone was deadly serious. He watched her take up a cutting from the table and prepared himself for the worst. Juliana looked at her husband. Good, he appeared quite calm. 'It's dated August 18th 1917 somewhere in Kansas City. Are you ready for this?'

'*Kaiser's Spy Arrested.*
Karl Graves asserted he was working for the State Department.'

'Oh no.' Michael shouted, putting his head in his hands.

'Dr Karl Armgaard Graves, self styled international spy, who came into some prominence in 1914 after the publication of a volume of his experiences as the personal spy of the Kaiser, was arrested by federal agents last night at the Union Station for being in a zone closed to enemy aliens without permits. Dr Graves told the authorities that he was working for the Department of State. He also gave out statements that he was on his way to Denver in an effort to obtain papers that would prove the illegitimacy of the Hohenzollern family.'

'Among his possessions were found documents relating to the establishment of a Saxon union in this country. The self-styled spy was almost without funds when arrested and poorly dressed.'

Juliana paused, sensing his disappointment.

'There's more isn't there?' he asked reluctantly.

'I'm afraid so. This is from Washington and is dated August 17th 1917.

'*Dr Graves's statement that he was working for the State Department was the direct cause of his arrest in Kansas City. Graves, the Federal Authorities say, has been passing in several Western cities as representing the State Department, and in view of his status the authorities thought it wise to take him into custody.*'

Michael gave a loud sigh. 'Oh, well. That's it I suppose. It sounds to me as though he has had a complete breakdown and no wonder! With all that he has gone through!'

'Yes,' agreed Juliana. 'It sounds as though he was arrested for his own protection, but what do they mean by his status, are they suggesting he was royalty?'

Michael shrugged. 'Anyway, I thought he was protected. Didn't he have American citizenship or something? It is so confusing and it doesn't help not having all the newspaper articles. It's most unlike mother to be so haphazard. Are you sure there aren't any more cuttings?'

'I think this is the last one.'

'Well, I haven't got my glasses but even I can see there are two cuttings stapled together here! Do try and be careful dear. Now tell me quickly, what does it say?'

Juliana read out the cuttings in a louder than normal voice:

'*The internment of Dr Karl Armgaard Graves, said to be the Kaiser's personal spy, was ordered today in a telegram to Federal..... I'm afraid the print is so faded I can't make the words out. Ah this bit I can. Attorney General Gregory, who says he was taken to the federal prison at Fort Leavenworth in Kansas, where he was confined for the duration of the war.*'

Juliana glanced across before turning to the other cutting.

'This one is dated September 27th 1917. It's in much better condition,'

'Karl Armgaard Graves, the international spy, who was identified by a photograph by Charles Levine as Louis Clement, was sent to Leavenworth Prison as a dangerous alien on September 23rd 1917.'

Michael rubbed his eyes. 'I feel exhausted. It's far too much to take in all in one go. Shall we leave it?''

'Well I suppose he was locked up, by that I mean in jail, until the end of November 1918?' 'Michael sighed. 'So it would appear.'

'But who is this Louis Clement?'

'Search me!'

'So there we are. At least we know a little more about the mysterious Dr Graves. I hope it has answered some of your questions darling?' Juliana gathered up the papers.

Michael stood up and stretched. 'Yes some but not all, by any means! For a start I would like to know more about this Edward Lyell Fox, Karl's collaborator in writing *The Secrets of the German War Office*.'

'Surely you don't think he was....?' Michael didn't let her finish.

'I've never been so sure in my life! After all, here we are looking for a man called Fox and we find him working in collaboration with Dr Karl Armgaard Graves, who was quite possibly the greatest spy that ever lived.'

'I see, you think that Karl Graves used the name Fox as an alias and then went on to rescue the Imperial Family whilst pretending to be locked up in jail?'

Michael smiled. 'Well what other conclusion can I draw?'

Juliana opened the studio door for him. 'Knowing him as we do, don't you think he would have told us later that he had saved the Russian Imperial Family?'

'He did, but not under his real name. Fox admits in his diary to working for the British, the German Kaiser and the Americans. He was the perfect person to manoeuvre his way through enemy lines, a man to be trusted above all others, a man to be trusted with the lives of royalty.'

'Do you think he was a mason then?'

'I didn't say that, but since you insist on harping on about this, let me explain that you don't have to be a mason to keep an oath or break a promise! Whether he was a mason or a member of the secret squirrels' club should be of no consequence to us.'

Juliana clasped his arm affectionately in an attempt to calm him down. 'You're right of course. I don't wish to make a window into his soul. But Fox did speak of the freemasonry of royalty and I wondered what he meant by mentioning it at all. I mean, it must be a club for the very privileged and I wonder if it...' Juliana paused as Michael stepped back into the room.

'Wait a moment now,' he interrupted, 'Armgaard! It's such an unusual name. Have you ever come across it by any chance?'

Juliana thought for a moment. 'Armgard is a girl's name in Holland. I presume when it's spelt with a double "A" that it must be the male version.'

'Ah, I've an idea. I'll research all the ancient family lines of Europe and see which one carries the name Armgaard."

Juliana laughed. 'Well I suppose it's no good researching the name Karl. There'll be hundreds if not thousands of noble families carrying that name.'

'Yes indeed... Karl... Charles! There is absolutely no reason to research that name!'

As he was speaking Michael subconsciously pulled out the letter from his mother and unfolded it. Juliana instinctively understood why her husband felt the need to read it yet again. Afterwards he smiled. 'You do see, dear, why this man Armgaard could be my father don't you?'

'Yes, of course I do.'

After Michael left the studio, Juliana meandered over to the table. She had not shown him everything on Dr Graves. Now she found herself frantically searching for THAT article because for one awful moment, while they had been talking, she had worried that Michael had scooped it up along with the rest of the cuttings. It's not that she wanted to keep secrets from him, and she positively hated to lie, but his health was important. She wanted to protect him from his fate for as long as possible.

Then she found it. Thank God, she said to herself as she opened a purple folder and slipped the precious cuttings into it. We've had enough shocks for one day. She thought as she placed the folder back in a drawer under a pile of sculpting utensils.

Back in his library Michael called Alice in. 'This is all very mysterious,' she exclaimed, delighted to be called in.

'Sorry, it's not meant to be. What can you tell me about the origins of the name Armgaard?'

'Armgaard?'

'Remember K.A.G?'

Alice nodded. 'Of course I do. Karl, Maria's friend, a wonderfully brave man!'

'Well it might surprise you to know that I know who he really was now.'

'Indeed!'

'Oh yes, you're going to be very proud of me. Would it surprise you to know that K.A.G stands for Karl Armgaard Graves, an international spy of some renown?' He asked watching for any sign of recognition on Alice's face. There was none. 'Oh Yes,' he continued 'it appears that K.A.G. – the writer of the fanciful letter to my mother, I quote, "In Remembrance of our Siberian Adventure" – is no lesser a person than the famous Dr Armgaard Karl Graves, a secret agent who wrote several best sellers. In fact I have one here. Look!' Michael held up The Secrets of the Hohenzollerns as he spoke.

'I also believe, and Juliana is totally with me on this, that Dr Graves, alias K.A.G., is not only my father but also THE AGENT CALLED FOX who rescued the Tsar and his family!'

'My! You have been busy.'

'We have a problem though! Graves was not his real name!'

Alice laughed as she sat down. 'Oh I know that's what it says in *Rescuing the Czar*!''

'No! I'm not talking about FOX.'

'Oh, I thought you just said he was Fox.'

Michael put his head in his hands and gave a long sigh as Alice strolled across to the window. 'I do love this view of the terrace and garden,' she added almost melancholy.

Michael grunted. 'I'm talking about Dr Armgaard Karl Graves! We know that Graves is not his real name, but I think the other two, or at least one of his other names, may be. By the way, I am quite sure he is a prince.'

'The name Armgaard sounds Danish or Dutch to me.' Alice replied fixing her gaze on the garden below. Michael joined her by the window. 'Giovanni works so hard on the garden. He does you credit, Michael.'

He patted her shoulder. 'Yes, yes! Now Alice, I've got a favour to ask you.'

'Go on!'

'Is there any chance that you can find out from some of your old friends whether they knew of a noble family that carried the name Armgaard or Armgard in their ancestral tree?'

Alice walked slowly back to her chair and sat down. 'Well most are... WAIT A MOMENT! I've just had a thought. Do you remember when we opened the cedar box and you asked me to....'

'Yes?' Replied Michael expectantly.

'Well, remember what I saw?'

Michael scratched his head. 'Oh yes, you said you saw a battle scene, a shield and arm with a sword in it. I can't remember what you said.'

'That's EXACTLY what I saw. YES!'

He shook his head. 'You've lost me Alice!'

'Try to say it backwards!' Michael turned around with his back towards her.

Alice laughed. 'Don't be STUPID!'

'Oh, you mean the words... sword, arm, shield, spear....'

'Put the two middle words together.'

Michael thought for a second. 'Arm shield?'

Alice raised both her arms in the air. 'Arm! guard! That's what the cosmic was trying to tell me. I am quite sure of it now. So! We need to find out from the powers that be on the other side, who exactly this Armgaard fellow is, then we can ask about...'

'Why not just contact mother?'

'Honestly Michael! Your mother has only relatively recently passed over. It would be quite disrespectful to make demands so early on in her.....' Alice stared straight ahead, not bothering to finish her sentence. Something seemed to be bothering her.

Michael frowned aware the room was suddenly getting colder.

'What about if I gave you another name, do you think you could ask about it?'

Alice sighed. 'Well I can try. But obviously not at the same time! It would have to be on another occasion. Anyway what's the name?'

'Edward Lyell Fox, he was a very good friend of Armgaard's and ...' Michael stopped short as Alice's face became blurred. He heard his words sound as though they were being absorbed into some kind of electrically charged atmosphere that Alice was creating.

'What's happening?' he asked nervously.

Alice didn't reply. Instead she turned and walked across to the corner of the room where the icon hung.

'Well?' he enquired again gently, noticing the strong smell of incense suddenly wafting towards him. Alice didn't reply. Instead, her face had hardened and her lips were set firm. Gone were the familiar rosy cheeks and sparkling eyes. In their place was a pallid, stony cement-coloured mask that made him shiver. Suddenly she clapped her hands and Michael fell completely under her spell. Words floated in white ink all around him. He tried to make sense of them as several "Edward Lyell Fox" signatures, all in different handwriting, appeared before him.

He shook his head, trying to free himself of the images and all the while half conscious, he was aware of Alice standing right by him. After what appeared to be eternity to him, Michael heard her clap her hands again.

'If you want to know the answer to your questions it's time you left.'

Michael tried to move his legs but just now they felt like iron. He even tried to speak but no words came forth, then the room warmed up and Alice looked quite normal again.

'Did you do THAT?' he asked.

Alice gave a knowing smile and helped him to his feet.

'You really must teach me how to freeze time like that,' he added nervously as Alice stood by the fireplace, staring at the amethyst crystal.

'Michael, you've asked me to find something out for you and for that reason I will need some space.' Alice spoke in a rich vibrant tone that reminded Michael of his mother.

'Yes, of course, is there anything else you require?'

'Only that you light the candles before you leave.'

Chapter Twenty Eight   Bronze Venus

Tonya and Paul were speaking in hushed tones when Alex walked into the dining room.

'Looking forward to the meeting?' he asked as he helped himself to an orange.

'Yes we certainly are.'

'And have you done your homework?' he joked.

'Of course,' said Paul. 'We've been working very hard on the project.'

'What project?'

Tonya laughed.

'Don't you want to tell me?'

'All will be revealed soon!' Paul replied patting him on the back as he left.

'That sounds mysterious.' Alex responded.

Tonya smiled. 'It's not for me to say. Paul's put in a lot of work, which should pay dividends, because I don't think that we've got to the heart of the matter yet.'

Alex pushed his hair from his eyes. 'I know what you mean, but I don't think you can rush an investigation like ours. It will have its own momentum, if you know what I'm saying?'

Tonya eagerly agreed, even though she wasn't sure what he was talking about. All she cared about was spending the afternoon with Paul and for that reason she was very pleased.

Alex read her thoughts. 'I say you and Paul? Well, you seem to be spending a lot of time together now. Anything I should know?'

Tonya blushed. 'No.'

'Oh come on. I wasn't born yesterday! If I didn't know for a fact that Paul was committed to his work as a priest and with all that being a priest entails, well, I would have thought you two were attached at the..' Alex paused when he saw her blush. She was clearly uncomfortable with his interrogation but why? Then he felt bad. 'Oh look!' he said, reaching out. 'I'm sorry, Tonya.'

She pulled away then managed a short smile. 'Well, what about you Alex? Is there a man in your life too?'

'No one that's particularly special.'

Tonya didn't believe him but was satisfied that she had made her point. There was no need to press him further.

'Actually,' added Alex, 'I've been concentrating on my part of the project and I have decided to make an effort and get on better with father. You heard about his collapse I suppose?'

'Yes. Alice told me. But he's made a rapid recovery. Thank God!'

'So far, but none of us know what really happened to him. All I can say is that it gave me an awful fright. Besides, since then he has behaved much nicer towards me. And for my part, I have found a new hobby!'

Tonya smiled. 'Well, everyone should make an effort to get on with their parents!' 'Surprise! Surprise! I love reading old books, especially when they speak of missing treasure. Guess what I've found?'

Tonya suppressed a smile. 'What?'

'Romanov treasure being smuggled out of Russia during the Revolution. It makes me want to track it all down and trace where it has ended up. Honestly, I can't stop thinking about it.'

Tonya laughed. 'You have the gold bug that's for sure!'

'It's not about the money. I just want the satisfaction of finding something that has been lost for years! By the way, did you like the painting I did for Giovanni?'

'Yes, and what's more so did Giovanni. He was over the moon!'

Alex grinned and then glanced at his watch. 'Come on, it's time. I'm really looking forward to Paul's talk.'

Once they were all seated Michael welcomed Giovanni to the meeting.

'Now before we start, Alice and I have decided that we shall open with a mantra to guide our work. Are you all ready?'

Tonya and Paul looked at the icon hanging in the corner.

'I presume it will be a prayer?' Paul asked.

'No. We have chosen a mantra that is specifically tailored to our needs,' he replied as Alice handed out a sheet of typed verse. 'Now repeat after me, one, two, three, From ignorance lead me to truth. From darkness lead me to the light. From death lead me to immortality. Aum, Aum, Aum! Peace, Peace, Peace!'

A long silence ensued.

'Can we make a start?' Juliana asked.

Michael looked up. 'Right Paul, I believe you are going to give your latest ideas on the mysterious Baroness. Alex, I am sure you wanted to speak but I can't remember what it was about?'

'The White Russians and the missing gold but if we haven't got time we can leave it for another day.'

'No, no! We will try and make time so long as you think it is relevant to our story? Now Giovanni, welcome to our gathering,' Michael paused and glanced at Juliana. He wasn't sure whether he should mention the newspaper clippings that they had been looking at earlier. Reading his mind she gave him a look that said "no". Giovanni put his hand to his mouth and coughed several times, probably from nerves, or so Juliana thought as she poured out a glass of water.

'Is there something you would like to say?' Michael asked.

'Si,' Giovanni cleared his throat before adding, 'I no involved but I have a question. If all Maria's papers burn, how you know what you know?'

'Let me explain.' Michael replied. The ones in the caravan were all burnt, of course. But in her belongings we found her scrapbooks. Remember mother came to Italy to write her memoirs and Tonya suggested that we should do it for her now that she is no longer able, so we have these meetings to share information.' Giovanni took a sip of water before he replied. 'I come only to hear my son speak. I don't like you search for Tsar and try and involve Baroness Brandenberg.'

Michael sighed. 'Let's get one thing sorted out straight away. You shouldn't refer to my mother as "the Baroness". If anything, she was probably a princess. Anyway, it is better you call her Maria for now. Do you understand?'

Giovanni pulled a face then shrugged. 'Si but *she* say I must only call her Baroness, not I!'

'I know,' said Michael. But times have changed. Besides, it will become very confusing if you do, because today we will be discussing the role of another Baroness. I don't want any silly confusion over the two. So please do as I ask and call her Maria.'

'That's a very interesting point you've just made, uncle!' Tonya leant forward and rested both arms on the table. Paul looked up. He had been busy scribbling some last minute adjustments to his presentation but something in Tonya's voice caught his attention.

Afterwards a certain type of silence fell upon the room, a silence that accentuates the ticking of a clock and makes you aware of your own mortality. Tonya took a deep breath and Paul noticed she had goose bumps on her arms. He shot her a look of concern and she smiled briefly. Then he held her hand. When she saw Alex had noticed, she pulled it away. Juliana sat pensively staring at the amethyst crystal until Alice sighed loudly, prompting Michael to speak.

'Well Paul, you have something to say or not?'

Paul gathered his papers and stood up.

'You don't have to stand. Please sit. I want these meetings to be as informal as possible. Michael responded.

Alex sniggered at the absurdity of the comment, given the earlier mantra chanting. 'Actually, I prefer to stand,' Paul replied. 'That way everyone can hear me.'

'Very well, as you please!'

Paul cleared his throat. 'Well now, at our last meeting mention was made of the Countess Benckendorff and you will recall that she was at the station with Lockhart and Benji Bruce. Do you all remember?'

Everyone nodded except Giovanni, who concentrated on picking the dirt from his fingers.

'Alex, you have a question?' Paul asked.

'Not a question, rather an observation. I think she would be the Countess 'B' not the Baroness 'B'!'

'Well, my understanding is that she was often referred to as the Baroness Benckendorff in British and American newspapers of the time. Her maiden name was Baroness Maria Ignatievna Zakrevskaya. First she married a Count Benckendorff and then a Baron Budberg. But if the book *Rescuing the Czar* is telling us the truth then being able to identify the Baroness 'B' is crucial to authenticating the rescue story. In *Rescuing the Czar* the Baroness 'B' plays an active role supporting those who are involved in arranging the Imperial Family's escape from the Ipatiev House in Ekaterinburg. Baroness B. is referred to in both diaries and appears to be part of a worldwide organisation's plan to rescue the Tsar and his family. Fact or fiction, the story is intriguing and deserves further investigation.' Paul quickly glanced at his father, half expecting him to be asleep. Instead he found he had his full attention. Giovanni smiled. He was pleased that his son was using the gold pen he had bought him for his birthday.

'So,' Paul added, 'in order to discover the identity of Baroness 'B' we have researched some real life baronesses of the time. In my humble opinion only one stands out. Only one has all the credentials necessary to get the job done. Only one baroness was in the right place at the right time and knew all the appropriate people and because of her charming personality only one baroness could get away with what others dared not do, and that was to bridge the divide between two ruthlessly opposing forces, the Reds and the Whites, and to bring about a more humane situation than otherwise could have been the case during 1918. Because her role was part of a secret operation, these momentous events that she took part in could never fully be appreciated for what they were. That is until now, if we are to believe what we read!

We know that Moura Benckendorff was a favourite of the Empress and acquainted with Rasputin! Against all the odds she had weathered the Russian revolution and remained a life-long friend of Kerensky. She was a true European but as a Russian aristocrat she lived in the lap of luxury until the Bolshevik uprisings forced her to live by her wits. Though history doesn't record it, she may well have been more involved in the so-called Lockhart Affair that almost brought down the fledgling Soviet state. She was his mistress, after all. Later she would work for Maxim Gorky and become the mistress of H.G Wells. She was famous for her energy, intelligence and charm.'

'A mistress of H.G. Wells you say?' Michael interrupted. 'That reminds me of the poem that McGarry sent to Brasol. Remember now that England has Nicholas in India and Wells in Moscow etc. etc?' Michael sat back and twiddled his thumbs, expecting a response. There was none. 'REMEMBER ANYONE?' he shouted out.

Of course they did. They just weren't sure what point Michael was trying to make. Michael caught their drift. 'Well, I'm just saying about Wells. I believe we discussed earlier whether H.G Wells could have been part of the plan to rescue the Tsar? Now, coincidentally, we hear that Moura and H.G. Wells were lovers.' Suddenly aware of how loud his voice was, Michael looked up. A sea of blank faces met his gaze.

'It's a good point,' Paul agreed, coming to the rescue. 'I'll continue. Now I told you that Moura was called Countess Zakrevskaya. It was said that she was a descendant of Agrafena Fyodorovna Zakrevskaya, the wife of a Moscow governor, who was a great beauty to whom Pushkin had written poems. Modern day poets believe that Moura was a descendant of Pushkin's *Bronze Venus*.'

'Ah! Ha! Stop right there!' Michael said getting out of his chair and picking up a copy of *Rescuing the Czar*. 'Listen to this. I just need to read you something from Fox's diary. It is the description of the Baroness B.... Now where is it dam it? Ah yes, here we are. A perfect composition of Juno, Venus and Hebe all rolled into one! Well, well, well! What do you think of that? Yet another coincidence or what?'

Paul considered the point for a moment. 'It would appear so! I stupidly thought that was an anagram of some sort when I first read it but I see now what you mean. You think it was his way of confirming the identity of the Baroness because she was known as a descendant of the recipient of Pushkin's Bronze Venus!'

Juliana gasped. 'Well I never! Michael is right. That is too much of a coincidence!'

Michael smiled broadly. 'Quite so Paul, please continue with what you were saying.'

'Well I shan't go into details about her early life except to say that she was very well connected. She was born in 1892 and was the youngest of four children. Her father was Ignaty Platonovitch Zakrevsky, whose great grandfather was Andrei Osipovitch from Kiev in the Ukraine. But more to the point, and relevant to our enquiry, Moura's step-brother, Platon Ignatievitch, was working at the Russian Embassy in London and later as an attaché in Berlin. So Moura was educated at boarding school. She was clever and tough and right from the beginning she relied on her health, energy and considerable charm as a woman to get by in those exceptionally cruel times.'

'That's right,' Michael interrupted, wagging his finger. 'Remember that it was her generation, the same as mother's, born between 1890 and 1900, who were almost completely destroyed by war, revolution, emigration, the camps, and the terror of the '1930s.....'

'NOW,' Paul interrupted. 'Here comes a crucial bit of information. Fox tells us that the 'Baroness B.' is English. So how can Moura, who we know is Russian, be the English Baroness 'B'?'

'Go on,' encouraged Michael.

'How can a Russian be English? Well, that would depend on how well she could speak English. Moura also had strong German connections, even though part of her family came from the Ukraine. After boarding school she came to Britain to perfect her English, a language she had spoken since childhood. Luckily her step- brother Platon was stationed in London and the Russian ambassador Count Benckendorff was his patron. Moura often visited the Count and met many of his guests, including diplomats from the Foreign Office. One in particular became a close friend. He was called Maurice Baring and he was on the best of terms with everyone!'

'Ah!' Alex interjected. 'Remind me to tell you a neat little story about Barings and Russian gold later.'

'Now then,' Paul continued reading from his notes. 'Maurice got on very well with the Benckendorff family. Not only Count Alexander Konstantinovitch, Steward of the Imperial Household and Knight of the White Eagle, but also Count Pavel Konstantinovich, Grand Marshal of the Russian Imperial Court and Minister of the Crown Domains. Through the Benckendorffs Maurice Baring met other aristocratic Russian families, including the Shuvalovs and the Volkonskys. But his closest friends were the young men at the Russian Embassy, including Moura's brother Platon. Like Baring they were embarking on diplomatic careers as attachés. It was at Maurice's house that Moura met her future husband, as well as many other people from London society, including Robert Hamilton Bruce Lockhart and H.G. Wells.

In 1911, aged only nineteen, she married Ivan Benckendorff, who a year later was appointed secretary at the embassy in Berlin. There in Berlin Moura was introduced to the Kaiser at a court ball. She even said that Wilhelm had a sense of humour when at the Potsdam Palace she danced with him two or three times on one night. So here we have a strong German connection and it appears she quite liked the Kaiser! In 1914 when war broke out they left Berlin. Moura returned with her husband to Russia and rented lodgings in St Petersburg. In 1913 she gave birth to a son, Pavel, and a little girl called Tania in 1915.

During the next three years, while caring for her children, Moura worked in a military hospital as a nurse. So here we have the nursing experience.'

'You will recall that in *Rescuing the Czar*, the Baroness works as a Red Cross nurse! Anyway, by November 1917 she was in St Petersburg, now called Petrograd. While there she witnessed dreadful conditions. One evening just before Christmas, she received some dreadful news. Peasants from a neighbouring village had clubbed her husband to death in their home in Estonia. Thankfully the governess, Missy, had managed to escape with the children and was in hiding. Shortly afterwards Moura was evicted from her apartment in Petrograd and was forced to roam the streets penniless. Travel to Estonia had become impossible since the train service had stopped in October. After the October Revolution and the murder of her husband, Moura found herself in a completely different world. Her class was now doomed to destruction.'

Paul paused noticing that Alice had gone dreadfully pale. But Michael was oblivious. He took the opportunity to push his chair back and stretch his legs.

'*O Jerum, Jerum, Jerum, Quae Mutatio Rerum!* How the times change and...I suppose changing times demand changing practices! Now take a break while I explain what was going on in Russia at this time.'

Paul smiled and obediently put his paper down.

'Mother said that when the revolution first started the aristocracy were in great shock. They were completely paralysed and unable to react in any constructive way to their demise. It took less than a year for the whole of the aristocracy to fall. Such was their elimination! It is a lesson to us all! They succumbed because they were unable to understand the difference between a hunger strike and calls for a revolution. What is the peasant complaining about, slavery? But serfdom has been abolished by law and the peasant ought to be grateful! Let no man lay a hand on the Tsar. He is God's deputy and rules by divine right!'

'Ah,' Alice interrupted tearfully. 'I remember small bits. Such a wide difference between the people in Russia and it was dangerous to be in the streets for too long. Everyone was armed. It was mob rule, except no one knew who the ruling mob was! People were so hungry that they changed sides just for a slice of bread! They ate the starving horses and even started to eat the dead corpses in the street. Oh God it was...,' Alice stumbled over her words before pulling out her handkerchief and everyone fell silent.

Juliana comforted her. Then Alice, dreadfully distressed, pushed her away. 'Please! You have to excuse me. I don't feel well. I'm sorry, it's brought it all back to me now.' she added, leaving the room in a hurry.

Michael sat down and twiddled his thumbs, considering whether he should send his wife out after her. But Juliana was angry. 'You see the effect it has on someone to witness such atrocities?' she shouted. 'This is why I hate war!' She added shaking her finger at him.

Michael laughed nervously and put his hands up. 'Don't shoot the messenger!'

'It's not funny. I don't know why you are laughing.'

Michael sighed. 'Heavens, if I didn't laugh I'd probably burst our crying!'

Juliana wasn't sure how to take his last comment. 'Well perhaps you can explain to us how the situation got out of hand so quickly. Why were the people starving and why was Russia so dreadfully poor?'

'Now that Alice has left the room I can tell you,' Michael replied in a more serious tone. 'You see, many wars had taken their toll on Russia. Ever since the time of Peter the Great, Russia had been fighting her neighbours. But when she entered into the First World War in 1914 she was already feeling the effects in her treasury and arsenals. Remember, Russia is an enormous country. It has to feed millions of soldiers as they trek across vast swathes of harsh, often cold, if not mosquito-ridden land just to shoot a few bullets or fire their cannons. The truth is the Russians were tired of fighting long before they entered the war. So it was down to the frail and elderly to keep the home fires burning and get the crops to market.' God, how I hate war, it never pays. It should be banned immediately!' Juliana responded emotionally.

Michael grimaced. 'Well that's easier said than done my dear! Anyway that's enough from me. Paul, will you continue please?'

Paul stood up and shuffled his papers. 'As I said, during this time Moura had no money and desperately needed help, so she went to the British Embassy where the Ambassador, Sir George Buchanan, was packing up to leave.'

'Moura was welcomed by his daughter Merrill and Captain George Hill on the morning of January 7th 1918, as embassy staff got ready to leave by train. This ties in, with Sir Alfred Knox's report, when he said that on that morning most of the British colony, and a few others from the diplomatic corps, accompanied the British Embassy staff to the station.

Remember he recalled that only one Russian came, a Madam B. You won't be surprised to find out that I think that this Madam B. is none other than Moura herself. If I am right it means that she could have been known as Madam B. by the British. The French may have called her Countess B, which of course at this time she was, and the Germans and the Americans Baroness B!'

Tonya laughed at his extended explanation. Then, realising she was the only one, fell silent.

'Anyway,' Paul continued, 'I am sure you can see how this story is repeated in Fox's telling of events leading up to the Tsar's rescue. Now pay attention, because I've something very special for you all. Paul glanced up and winked at Tonya, before adding, 'In his book, *Memoirs of a British Agent*, Lockhart describes what it was like to meet Moura. I'd like to read it to you and see whether it rings any bells?'

'Do,' Michael replied, mildly amused. 'I'm sure it will be full of romance.'

Paul held the heavy old book with a reverence normally accorded to the New Testament, or so Tonya thought as she listened to him read.

'It was at this time that I first met Moura who was an old friend of Hicks and Garstin and a frequent visitor to our flat.'

'Wait a moment. I thought you said Lockhart met her many years before when she was in London during 1911?' interrupted Alex.

'Yes, that's right!'

'Well why does Lockhart say that he has just met her then?'

Paul sighed. 'I don't know, perhaps he's speaking figuratively or he has forgotten.'

Alex laughed. 'No, no! Something's not right. Are you sure you've done your homework properly?'

'Please let me continue without further interruption.' He demanded, picking up the book again.

'She was then twenty-six, a Russian of the Russians. She had a lofty disregard for all the pettiness of life and a courage which was proof against all cowardice. Her vitality, due perhaps to an iron constitution, was immense and invigorated everyone with whom she came in contact. Where she loved, there was her world, and her philosophy of life had made her mistress of all the consequences. She was an aristocrat. She could have been a Communist. She could never have been a bourgeoisie. During those first days of our meeting in St. Petersburg I was too busy, too preoccupied with my own importance, to give her more than a passing thought. I found her a woman of great attraction, whose conversation brightened my daily life.'

'Can I just flag up the word IRON, it's appearing again. You know as in the book *The Man in the Iron Mask*?' Juliana interrupted. 'That "iron constitution" of hers! Can't you see what I mean? It's such a coincidence, I'm sure it's a code of some kind.'

Michael frowned. 'I'm not on the same wave length as you, obviously!'

'Well, it's the same as when you mentioned H.G. Wells. You know, when McGarry spoke of the Iron Mask and that he might write his own story and so now we have Moura or Madame B. being described as "iron". She must have been part of the team who tried to rescue the Tsar!'

Alex nodded enthusiastically, supporting her hypothesis. 'Quite!'

'Please let Paul finish without your constant interruptions and diatribe.'

Paul sensed he was running out of time.

'Why can't you all just concentrate on what I am reading, it's so important.' He continued.

'Besides William Hicks and Dennis Garstin, there was a naval attaché at the embassy, a Captain Francis Cromie, another of Moura's old friends from London. On Francis Cromie's birthday Moura hosted a luncheon for all of them. She could not invite them to her place so she arranged the party at their apartment. They had a great time and it was their last carefree party together.'

Just as Paul came to the end they were interrupted by the library door slowly opening. It was Alice. She said she was feeling much better. Juliana pulled a chair out and she sat down.

'Hope I haven't missed too much?'

Michael raised a finger to his lips. 'Ssshh! Paul is reading from his notes.'

'By March 1918 the embassy in Petrograd was down to skeleton staff. Francis Lindley, Charge d' Affairs, and Buchanan's unofficial replacement, was the last embassy official to depart for Vologda, leaving Lockhart in charge. Lockhart was now the senior man in charge, with Captain Hicks acting as military attaché. They took an apartment on Neva embankment with tall windows that looked out onto the Peter and Paul Fortress across the other side of the river. Before long, relations between Moura and Lockhart had intensified and they fell deeply in love. Lockhart had already made new friends with Trotsky and Lev Karakhan, who he met regularly. He was also speaking with Lenin, Radek, Yakov Peters, Felix Dzerhinsky and Grigory Zinoviev. With George Buchanan gone, Trotsky now treated Lockhart as the only true representative of His Majesty's Government.'

'Very good Paul, THIS IS SO IMPORTANT,' Michael interrupted. 'Because if a deal was done to free the Russian Imperial Family we now have all the key players in place and they are ready to act!'

Giovanni nodded enthusiastically. 'Si,' he shouted as Paul continued.

'Lockhart later wrote this:

'In varying degrees of intimacy I got to know nearly all the leaders from Lenin and Trotsky to Dzerhinsky and Peters. I had a special pass into Smolny, the Bolshevik headquarters in Petrograd. More than once I attended a meeting of the Central Executive Committee in the main restaurant of the Metropole Hotel in Moscow where in Tsarist days I had taken part in entertainments of a very different kind, and....'

'THE METROPOLE HOTEL' Tonya shouted out exuberantly. 'Did you hear that? Remember in *Rescuing the Czar,* when Fox said he was constantly thinking of that girl at the Metropole with her long eyelashes and dimpling smile resembling the veiled lady at Buckingham?'

Paul smiled. 'Yes, the Metropole! So now you see why I was so looking forward to telling you all this. This is what Lockhart said next.

'On my journey from Petrograd to Moscow I travelled in Trotsky's troop train and dined with him. My daily work was with Trotsky, Chicherin, Karakhan, and Radek, who after Trotsky's appointment as Commissar for War formed the Triumvirate of the Soviet Commissariat for Foreign Affairs. When the peace deal at Brest-Litovsk was signed he understood that his real place was now in Moscow.'

'I'm sorry to interrupt you,' Michael broke in. 'but I must add this important point. The Bolsheviks had moved their headquarters from Petrograd, the new name for Saint Petersburg, to Moscow out of fear that the Germans would soon occupy Petrograd. In fact mother told me that there were already hundreds of German soldiers walking the streets in Petrograd. Often they went completely unnoticed by the people, as many were disguised as Russian soldiers!'

Juliana burst out laughing. 'Well if they were dressed as Russians how did she know they were German?'

'Because if you were near them you could hear them speaking German.' Alice replied quietly. 'You see, nearly all the Germans could speak Russian. But the Red Russians, uneducated as they were, could not speak German. Only the Russian nobility had the privilege of learning foreign languages.'

'Remember too,' added Paul, 'that although Lockhart thought the allies should support the new Bolshevik regime, he knew that London did not agree with him. By April he understood that London had only one goal and that was for the allies to defeat the Germans and win the war. Now recall the so-called Lockhart Plot, where Reilly tried to overthrow Lenin and oust the Bolshevik regime in August 1918? Well we agreed some time ago that any plan to rescue the Tsar must have been tied into that plot.....'

'Yes, we all remember, except your father, who wasn't here! Now get on with your point.' Alex interrupted again.

'Si, Maria said the Tsar will rule Russia one day!' Giovanni added for good measure.

'Look Paul, the events that we are really interested in knowing about have to be around 17th July 1918,' Alex admonished. 'That's the date when the Tsar and his family disappeared from the Ipatiev House in Ekaterinbug. Okay, you've told us some interesting information about Moura Benckendorff and her involvement with the Lockhart Plot and we know she helped Lockhart get out of jail but what else is new? Can you tell us what she was doing around 17th July 1918? Eh? I bet Mr Lockhart hasn't anything to say about that in his diary!' Alex jeered.

'Well if you'd just let me finish....'

'Ekaterinburg?' Alice whispered.

Juliana poured her a glass of water. 'Are you sure you want to stay?'

Alice nodded. 'I just feel cold. I'm probably coming down with something!'

'Can we continue please Paul?' Michael asked impatiently, tapping the table while Alice blew her nose.

'Not only should we be interested in the dates around mid July but some others as well and I'll tell you why! As you know, there were two calendars in operation in Russia during this period! That means that there was thirteen days difference between the calendars.'

'Really,' Alex exclaimed, 'how convenient!'

Michael stepped in. 'Let me explain it to you, so that you are clear. The new style Gregorian calendar was already in use on the continent and in Great Britain but it didn't replace the old style Julian one in Russia until 1918. That's when the new style dates moved thirteen days ahead of the old style dates. So, for example, once the new style calendar was introduced the old style 1st of February became new style 14th February.'

Tonya scratched her head. 'Well, when exactly was the new style calendar introduced to Russia anyway?'

Michael sighed. 'In 1918, I have just said!'

Tonya smiled. 'I'm sorry, what month in 1918?'

'That's a very difficult question to answer. Perhaps Alice can throw some light on when the new style calendar was exactly introduced?'

'Well, I was very young as you know, but I remember it causing much confusion for a long time. During most of 1918 many people, especially the aristocrats, the White Russians, well they refused to budge from the old calendar. Long into 1918 people were still using the old calendar dates. That is because they did not want to change the days of when the religious festivals were being held.'

'It was very upsetting when we lost thirteen days! Most of the nobility, and of course all the Imperial Family, refused to change. They only EVER used the old style calendar. Later people said the new regime had brought it in on purpose to disorientate the church and its teachings. So Russia was split into two different time zones. Some thought it was 1st February and others the 14th February! It played havoc with forward planning because those working for the Bolsheviks thought it was one day and all those working against them quite another! So, for example, when they said "we'll meet you on the 14th June in Kazan" they often had to wait a further thirteen days before anyone arrived; either that or THEY were thirteen days too late!'

'Oh Jerum, Jerum, Jerum! How the times change.' Michael added unaware of the significance of his statement.

Now the revelation that there were two different calendars being used at the same time in Russia during 1918, intrigued Tonya and she considered the full implications. Could this have affected those who were planning to rescue the Imperial Family she wondered? Paul too, was considering the impact this might have had on carefully laid plans.

'How do you know the Imperial Family used the old calendar?' he asked.

Alice was about to answer when Giovanni interrupted. 'Maria, she tell me, after Tsar and family leave friends, found a calendar on the wall. You see, every day the Tsarina would write in an entry. But her last entry was on the 23rd of June 1918. So why did she not write any more?'

'He's right,' Alice added, 'the Empress religiously made notes in her diary and on the wall calendar. So if she was at the Ipatiev house until the 17th July as they say she was, then all the dates between 24th of June and 17th of July should have had something written on them but they didn't! That's why some believe they escaped much earlier.'

'That's St John's Day, the same day Maria....' Paul whispered, but Michael was too busy making notes to reply. Tonya watched with interest as her uncle circled the 23rd of June in pencil several times. That gave her an idea and she started to count on her fingers as she worked out the number of days between the 24th of June and the 17th of July. Then, seeing the absurdity, she burst out laughing. 'Honestly, as if there wasn't enough to consider, what with everyone changing sides, hiding their identities, and now to top it all changing the dates as well!'

'I suppose we can be sure that the rescuers and the Imperial Family were using the same calendar, since they were all aristocracy,' added Alex, concerned that carefully laid plans would go haywire. 'But wait a moment, there may be some advantage to having two calendars at work; but then if what Giovanni says is right, we must be extra careful when researching the memoirs and diaries of the nobility because they often do not say which calendar they are using. For instance, I'm reading some very old diaries written by White Russians who are reporting on the various events around the time of the Tsar's disappearance. Are they writing in the old or new style calendar when they refer back to 1918?'

'Well they should say what calendar they are using.'

Alex laughed. 'Yes Dad, but they don't.'

Michael shrugged. 'I don't know what else to say. You'll have to use your common sense for a change! Okay I'll spell it out for you if I must! if you take the 17th of July 1918, depending on what diary was used and by whom, you could have thirteen days either side to play around with.'

Alex scratched his head. 'What, from the 4th to the 30th of July?'

'But that's practically the whole of July!' Tonya added.

Michael sighed. 'A serious researcher must consider all possibilities.'

'So uncle, maybe the family disappeared thirteen days before the 17th July, which would be.....'

Alex laughed. 'You've struck gold, Tonya. What better day for the Americans to rescue the Tsar and his family than on Independence Day!'

Chapter Twenty Nine   An Alibi

A heavy silence hung over the room as they recognised the magnitude of what had been discussed. Juliana stared at the amethyst, Giovanni at the icon, and Paul at his notes, trying desperately to fathom the full impact of a changing date.

Alex was the first to speak. 'Wait a moment. I've had an idea...forget Independence Day, if that calendar is right and the 23rd of June was the last entry made by the Empress, they must have escaped on June 24th?'

'Do you know?' Michael stood up as he spoke. 'I feel so overwhelmed with the way this is all coming together I feel we must give thanks and chant our mantra.'

'From Ignorance, lead me to Truth,
From darkness, lead me to the light,
From death lead me to immortality.
Aum. Aum. Aum.
Peace. Peace. Peace!'

Michael looked up. 'While we were chanting I asked a question and Alice you will be amazed! I have already received a reply from our guide.'

'Oh!' Juliana responded, raising an eyebrow.

'Yes, I have been told we are to take the dates as the record account suggests!' Alex and Tonya were surprised but Paul seemed pleased. 'I'm glad because I have prepared my prognosis on the basis of the Imperial Family disappearing around 17th of July 1918. But if they had disappeared earlier, say either the 4th of July or even as far back as the 24th of June, then what I am about to tell you may be even more relevant.'

'How is that?' Michael enquired.

'Because as the Imperial Family were being held hostage, Savinkov, Reilly's friend, had escaped from prison and as we know, the White Russians were strategically placed to inflict a great victory for the Tsar. They planned to trap the Bolshevik forces in a pincer movement and put an end to their rule.'

'Serious trouble was brewing for the Bolsheviks, not from the Germans, but from the White Russians and the situation was about to be exacerbated. You see, General Poole and the Allied Expeditionary Forces began to move south from Archangel. At the same time the Czechs were moving west to secure the all-important Siberian Railway. The Cossacks had already secured the Ukraine under the pro-German *Hetman* Skoropadski. Alarmed at the way events were turning out, Trotsky hurriedly mobilized the Red Army.'

'I'm sorry Paul, but I thought you were going to inform us about the Baroness B's role in all of this,' Interrupted Tonya 'That's what we want to hear, not all this revolutionary mischief!'

'Don't worry, I haven't forgotten. This is what I wanted to tell you. At this time Moura had moved into the apartment with Lockhart. Apparently she didn't have many friends and so Lockhart's friends became hers. As the summer progressed her behaviour became quite strange. Perhaps I should add that through most of her life there was a sense of mystery about her and during this crucial time, according to Lockhart's diary, he knew nothing of her whereabouts.'

'It's uncanny but it sounds so much like mother,' Michael whispered to Alice.

'One day,' Paul continued, 'Moura announced that she would leave. She said she wanted to visit her children in Revel, Estonia. Naturally she was worried about them since she had not seen them since September 1917. So on July 12th 1918 she departed Petrograd. At such a dangerous time this was an act of sheer madness and Lockhart cursed himself for letting her go. In his memoirs he records how he spent ten days beside himself with worry. He couldn't eat or sleep. On the brink of utter despair, he had fainting fits and found himself unable to speak. Finally the telephone rang. She was back, calling from Petrograd and he collected her from the station in Moscow the next day. She had been away at least eighteen days. That means she arrived back in Moscow at the end of July 1918.' Paul placed his notes on the table and continued. 'Now remember, in Fox's diary, the Baroness B. is keeping an eye on activities at the house where the family are imprisoned. She is stationed in a nearby building and disguised as a Red Cross nurse and ...'

'Wait a moment, Paul you're saying that she COULD have been the Baroness B. as reported of in *Rescuing the Czar* because she would have had enough time to get to Ekaterinburg, do what she had to do and get back again. Yes?'

'Please Tonya! Will you stop and allow Paul to continue with his story.'

'Well hold on a moment Michael,' Juliana demanded. 'If Tonya is right we know why Lockhart was so sick with worry now.'

'Yes,' Paul added. 'He said it was because he was unsure of whether she had the right documentation to travel. Moura said she was travelling by train to Estonia. But Lockhart must have known that all travel to Estonia was impossible because there weren't any trains going in that direction!'

'So he can't have been anxious about whether her documents would pass inspection on the train when there were no trains. So how did he think she was going to get to Estonia then? Why did he let her go if it was so dangerous?' Juliana asked, clearly concerned for Moura's welfare.

Paul smiled, encouraged by the reaction he was getting.

'I suppose she could have travelled by truck or car or plane to Estonia,' Alice suggested, 'although that would have been very dangerous.'

'Quite,' added Paul, 'and answer this. If Moura did leave for Estonia why did she choose such a dangerous time to go?'

'Because it was all part of THE PLAN, that's why,' Alex added confidently.

'More to the point, if what you say is right Paul, and I have no reason to doubt you,' added Michael, 'Why risk returning to Moscow eighteen days later? Paul's right, it must have been part of a much bigger plan, a plan that had agreement. Clearly she is not so vulnerable when she can move this safely around a war torn country.'

'Anyway,' Paul added. 'We know for sure that train services to Estonia had been terminated the year before! So I really don't know where she went.'

Alex laughed. 'That's the way it is with secret agents. They are really clever at covering their tracks!'

Michael smiled. 'Never a truer word was said. I suppose there are a number of other possibilities that we could consider. She could have travelled to Petrograd instead, possibly at Lockhart's request, on a mission for British Intelligence! So his anxiety for her was not that she had gone to Estonia but that he knew she was in great danger. On the other hand he may have sent her on a secret errand to Vologda. Or she may have had some private business in Petrograd that she didn't want to discuss with Lockhart. Or she could have stayed in Petrograd in complete seclusion on business unrelated to British intelligence or she might have gone somewhere else entirely unknown to us! The list is endless.'

Juliana laughed. 'Not endless, because you haven't mentioned Ekaterinburg.' 'Would she have had enough time to get to Ekaterinburg, free the Tsar, and get back by train?' Tonya asked Alice.

'Oh yes, plenty of time. The line between Petrograd, Moscow and Ekaterinburg was a very punctual route and in full use. She wasn't glued to Lockhart you know! Why should she answer to him just because they were.....' Michael coughed. 'Less of this title tattle, I want to know exactly what she was doing on those dates, because they are close to one of the most important dates in Russia's history, namely the disappearance of the Imperial Family from Ekaterinburg.'

Juliana sighed loudly. 'Don't be silly Michael, how can we get to know the truth after all this time?'

'Can I finish please?' Paul asked politely. 'When Lockhart found out that Moura was coming home he was elated. Nothing mattered more than seeing her again and he felt he could face any crisis, any unpleasantness that the future might have in store for him. So now I'm coming to the end. Without going into details it was lucky for Lockhart that Moura did return to Russia because not so long afterwards he was arrested and placed in jail and after some serious negotiations, it was Moura who was able to secure his release. She was clearly a woman of great influence.'

'She fits the description of the 'Baroness 'B' in *Rescuing the Czar* but I cannot confirm whether she flew a plane. Oh and ...' Paul raised his finger in the air as he spoke, 'there is one last important point I want to make; even though it happened in 1932, it has a bearing on this episode in Russian history. Lockhart was writing up his memoirs and, quite naturally, he asked for her approval on what he had written. But the reaction he got was not expected. In fact he was so shocked that he recorded how he felt in his diary on June 18th 1932.'

'This morning I had a shock, a letter from Moura in which she requests me to alter the part in my book referring to her. She wants it made more formal. She wants to be called Mme Benckendorff all through. She is as conventional as a Victorian spinster and why? Because I said that fourteen years ago (1918) she had waving hair, whereas it is as flat as a Ukrainian's! Therefore my description is shallow, false etc and this is obviously all that the episode meant to me; therefore either the full love story or nothing.'

'This will be very difficult. The book, however, will have to be altered. She is the only person who has the right to demand an alteration.'

'Perhaps Moura had other reasons for wanting the words taken out?' Tonya suggested. Maybe she didn't want to be referred to as a baroness or be linked to the Ukraine because she didn't want to be identified as the Baroness 'B' in Fox's diary. 'Or,' added Alex confidently, 'she didn't want her name linked to the Ukrainian Hetman Skoropadski because he supported the German Kaiser.'

Michael stood up and reached for some water. 'You may have a point son.' He added pouring himself a glass. 'It is common knowledge that both Hetman Skoropadski and Gorky helped some Romanovs to escape.'

'Oh!' Juliana sounded surprised. 'I thought Gorky was a socialist writer, Why would he want to save members of the ruling Imperial Family?'

'Not all socialist writers agreed with Bolshevik ideas,' Michael hastily replied. 'Gorky was a great humanitarian; of course he would want to save innocent members of the Imperial Family.'

Alex looked up from his doodling, 'Not to mention the rewards! I'm sure saving the Imperial Family would have had paid handsomely. A million at least I shouldn't wonder!'

'You shouldn't jump to such a conclusion,' Alice objected. 'Everyone knows that the imperial gold, estates and works of art were all confiscated by the Bolsheviks when they came to power. The Imperial Family were as poor as church mice.'

Alex shook his head. 'Not according to my research. Gold was sloshing about all over the place. I've always said if you want to find the people you have to follow the money trail and...'

'Well now, that's all been done before and no one ever found anything.' Michael suddenly felt irritated by his son's mercenary attitude.

'Si, boss is right,' Giovanni agreed.

'Right then,' Alex replied. 'I guess I'll have to prove it to you all.' He rose as if to leave the room but then thought better of it and sat down.

Michael sighed. 'Is there any more you wish to say Paul?'

'Only to add that Lockhart made the changes that Moura requested. But my question to you is this. Why did he bother recording that she had asked him to make the changes?'

'Oh, I see!' Tonya exclaimed. 'I'm getting your drift. You suspect he left this as a clue for us to pick up on much later. A bit like McGarry's correspondence and the "Dear Fox" letters from the two Emperors.'

'Yes. I'm quite sure Lockhart put it in his diary so that it could be read later by whoever was investigating the disappearance or whereabouts of the Romanovs. He probably expected the truth would come out one day. But Moura would have wanted it hidden because she was afraid. Don't forget she was still living in Russia at that time.'

'That's right,' Michael added. 'The 1930s was a very dangerous time and there were plenty of unexplained deaths, not just in Russia, but right across Europe!'

'She had every reason to be worried, mixing with the likes of Reilly and the other agents who visited Lockhart from Petrograd. I mean, being his interpreter she must have accompanied him to the theatre and restaurants and met all his political acquaintances.'

'But,' added Paul, 'Lockhart did not take her with him on his official business and it is unlikely that she knew of the private addresses he had in Moscow for meeting with disguised Tsarist generals before they journeyed south to join forces with the White volunteer army.'

'I shouldn't think Moura was with him when he met with the ex-leader of the Provisional Party, Mr Kerensky, who had been hiding in Russia and now wanted to get out. Lockhart found him a passport in the name of a Serbian officer and an introductory letter to General Poole which enabled him to escape.'

'Ah, that reminds me. Did you manage to find out why Kerensky used to call Lockhart "Roman Romanovitch"?' Michael asked.

'What does that mean?' Tonya asked.

'Literally it means "Roman, son of Romanov",' Michael replied.

'Why would Kerensky call Lockhart a son of Romanov? Does Kerensky think that Lockhart helped the Tsar escape or something?'

'Certainly not, there is absolutely no historic evidence to suggest that Mr Lockhart was involved in a plan to rescue the Tsar and his family,' Michael replied curtly.

'However, there is evidence to show that another man of the Revolution that Moura was involved with was helping to save the Romanovs. The information comes from Lili Dehn's memoirs. She was a great friend of the Tsarina. Gorky apparently sheltered at least one of the Romanovs and that man successfully crossed the Finnish border to his freedom sometime after 1921. Remember, by now Moura was living with Gorky. He called her his iron woman! Later she herself claimed that if you looked at her very closely you could see in her an undeniable resemblance to Peter the Great!'

'Good heavens!' exclaimed Juliana. 'So she actually left Lockhart to live with Gorky! I suppose she was called "iron" because of her will but I wouldn't want to be called that, not ever!' Juliana leant across to Alice. 'You know, the more I hear from Paul the more I believe I was wrong. Kathleen Scott was definitely not the Baroness.'

'So,' Paul added, 'to close my presentation here are two verses written by the Russian poet Pushkin that I would like to read to you. I do so in memory and in homage to a very brave Moura Benckendorff And a very brave Baroness, whoever she might be!

The first lines are taken from Pushkin's *Portrait*, written in 1828.

'With fire blazing in her soul,
Her heart a storm of passion:
She makes the partial universe whole,
Among our northern women of fashion;
And heedless of society's rules,
She races on till breath is scarce:
The way a lawless comet hurls,
Across the stationary stars

'And secondly, perhaps more aptly,' Paul added, 'here are a few lines from The Confidant, written in the same year by Pushkin. I have chosen this because I feel this aptly describes Mr Lockhart's feelings for Moura at this time.

'I strain to capture every cry,
Of hard confession, tender pain;
Your language makes me wild again,
With passions storm and mutiny;
But hide your stress, hide the now,
And hide your dreams from my inspection;
I fear the feverish sweet infection,
I fear the knowledge of what you know!'

Chapter Thirty   Hetman Skoropadski

'Goodness Alex, you are a dark horse. I had no idea you had quite so many books up here!' Tonya exclaimed.

'Well it's not a secret! Actually, most belong to father. Take this one for example.'

'*Researches in Sinai* by W.M. Flinders Petrie; I don't suppose there can be too many of these about!'

Alex laughed. 'You're right, of course, but the reason I picked this out was because I wanted to have a go at drawing the ruins as they were seen fifty odd years ago.'

Tonya sat down on the bed. 'Gosh! I didn't realise Egypt interested you so much!'

Alex rummaged around with his other books before replying. 'Most artists like Greece or Italy but I'm intrigued by the Egyptian mysteries. You know the *Book of the Dead*, and all those enchanting spells that you have to memorise in order get to the Field of Reeds.'

Tonya sighed. 'I'm afraid I know nothing about the Field of Reeds Alex, but I imagine they will be easy to paint!'

Alex laughed and sat down next to her. 'The Field of Reeds is where you go when you die. If you know how to get there you can live forever. It's fascinating stuff when you get into it.'

Tonya stood up to leave. 'Well as I said, I've never heard of the *Book of the Dead* but by the look of some of these titles I can see you have an interest in discovering hidden treasure.'

Alex laughed again. 'I know. It's a bit juvenile I suppose. But there must be so much buried out there, just waiting to be found.'

'If only you could find it, I know! So come on Alex, where's the metal detector hidden?'

'Honestly! What do you take me for? I'm not such a greedy treasure hunter!'

'Actually I thought you were a painter, but now I see you have become a bookworm instead!'

'No I haven't. I still love to paint. I'm really only doing this to please father and to show him that I've got an interest in this rescuing the Tsar malarkey. Besides, don't forget I'm researching how the Tsarist gold was lost. Father gave me these brilliant books and to be honest there hasn't been much research to do. All I do is chose various passages that are relevant to our story and put them together.' As he was speaking he handed Tonya a book to leaf through. Afterwards he showed her the notes he was making.

'Wow! another old book. This one is published in 1922, *Russian Gold Reserves* by V.J. Novitsky. But Alex, you surprise me! I had no idea you could speak French!' Before Alex could reply she picked up another book. 'Oh and look, Maurice Collis's *Wayfoong* and here, a first edition of *The Fate of Admiral Kolchak* by Peter Fleming. Goodness me, you do have a lot to read!' She placed the books back on the table and smiled. 'I've got you sussed Alex! You aspire to some of that gold for yourself.'

Alex sighed. 'Every country kept a war chest and during the war much went missing. It would be naive to assume that it reappeared after the war. In fact my grandmother told me a story. I don't know where she got it from or whether it was true. But she said that Germany's war chest of gold was kept at Spandau and that out of the five milliards of Francs paid as a war indemnity to Germany from France in 1871, over 200,000,000 marks in gold coins, mostly French, had been saved as a nucleus for a ready war chest by the Kaiser's ministers. You know, I can still see my grandmother winking at me when she told me the story! Just before she came to the end she rubbed her hands together as if she was cold. But she wasn't, she was just excited. Then she bent low and whispered in my ear. She said that some of it was still hidden in a mediaeval looking watchtower called the Julius Thurn. Imagine that Tonya! All those gold coins just waiting to be found!'

Tonya's eyes widened at the thought. 'When do we leave?'

Alex laughed. 'Seriously though, Paul's presentation was interesting but mine will really get the juices flowing. I intend to reveal absolutely everything. He'll be so jealous.'

'I don't think there is much chance of that. Everything he does is perfect. I've quite given up trying to make an impression on him!'

'Oh I don't know. Responded Alex, 'You seem to be working your magic to great effect on him. I mean only the other day...'

'Oh that! It was silly, but yes I suppose we kind of get on, I just wish he wasn't a priest because …….. Ssshhhh! I think there's someone at the door!'

Alex raised his eyebrows. 'Come in. Come in whoever you are.' he sang out loud.

It was Giovanni. 'Ah! Buono giorna signor! La disturbo forse?'

'What could you possibly be disturbing, my old tutti frutti?' Alex replied before turning to Tonya. 'Comprende l'Italiano?'

Tonya shook her head.

Giovanni stood patiently in the doorway, waiting for them to finish.

'Lo capisco un poco, pero non tanto! Che peccato!'

'Please come in, I'm just leaving.' Tonya replied politely.

'No, not on my account signora?' he replied, handing Alex a tray of homemade sweets.

'Ooh la la! Mio favouratio! Chocalatio! Grazie amigio!'

Tonya smiled. Alex was so light on his feet he really should have been a ballet dancer! 'You spoil him Giovanni. I suppose these are for the picture he painted you?'

'Si, excusee Tonya, fafa fouri, I humbly ask you a favour. The File on the Tsar, may I borrow it?'

'Certainly but you'll find it difficult to follow. It's quite academic.'

'Si…. Il leggere libri utili giova a tutti'

Tonya turned to Alex. 'I wish he wouldn't suddenly break into his own language like that, what's he saying now?'

Alex laughed. 'He says reading useful books helps everyone.'

Tonya smiled. 'So! You speak Italian as well as French! My, you are a dark horse,' she added, picking up a paint brush and spraying out the bristles. 'Oh yes indeed. You are obviously a man of hidden talents!' Alex giggled in delight as she turned to reply to Giovanni. 'About that book, I'm afraid I'm still reading it but as soon as I have finished I'll let you have it!'

Giovanni bowed low again, 'Mucho grazie!'

'Good, that's settled then.' Tonya added dawdling over towards one of Alex's easels.

'If only I could paint like you Alex. Imagine being able to paint Maria and Olga in the "Grotto of Neptune at Tivoli."' Alex looked up and frowned. 'You remember, the one painted in 1859 by Carl Timoleon Neff,' Tonya reminded him.

'Ah! You mean the one grandmother gave you? You're brave, wanting to copy a masterpiece! Still, as mother would say, there's no harm in trying.'

Tonya waved the paintbrush in the air. 'Perhaps I can borrow one of these from you?'

'Absolutely not, it is completely out of the question! We artists never share our tools, only our models!' He giggled infectiously.

'Hey, I've just had a thought.' Tonya raised both eyebrows as she spoke. 'Do you think there is any treasure buried up in that grotto?'

Alex suddenly grew serious. 'What on earth makes you say such a thing?'

Tonya started laughing. 'I just wanted to see how quickly you stopped giggling. Now I know what really motivates you and it is not your painting.'

Alex stared at Tonya, trying to make out whether she was serious or not. 'So you've found my metal detector then!'

'Che? What buried treasure?' Giovanni enquired.

'Oh ignore him. Alex is working on his presentation and looking for the missing gold.'

'But how you say he find, you say metal tector?'

'Ah! Ha!' Alex sprang out and made him jump. 'You, my little Italian friend, will have to be patient. Now if you don't mind, out the pair of you.' He corralled them towards the door. 'I really must get ready. Cinderella can't afford to be late for the ball.'

Just as he was about to leave Giovanni noticed a newspaper article lying on the bed.

'So many paintings, they go missing in revolution,' he added walking over to read it. 'Mona Lisa,' Petrograd and the art which may have been looted. Mama Mia! Loss of so many masterpieces! Ah non! Raphael, Murillo and Rembrandt, all these taken from the Hermitagio, huh! Allora vedra! Who know how much they must be worth now? Si allora, but you know what is so sad?' Giovanni asked, turning to speak to Alex, who was merrily whistling. 'How bad war is. So much hurt many great masterpieces and they go forever. Poof, just like that!'

Alex laughed. 'Now poof yourself, my little amigo with a bee in your bonnet, it's time for you to leave.'

Giovanni smiled and Tonia followed him out. As she turned to close the door she saw Alex take a cream shirt from the wardrobe before matching it with a boisterous blue silk cravat.

'Going somewhere exciting then?' she enquired.

Alex stopped whistling and waved. 'Bye bye!'

* * *

The following morning Alice was enjoying sitting in the garden when Giovanni hurriedly caught up with her, 'Momento, Mucho problemo!'

Alice stopped and turned around.

'Si, Yesterday Alex, he say about the buried treasure!'

'What treasure?'

'Is what I say! The BURIED TREASURE! He has a metal tector!'

'Ssh!' Alice put her finger to her lips. 'Someone may hear you. Now relax, I'm sure there is nothing to worry about.' She patted him on the back. 'Try not to worry so much.'

Giovanni shrugged. 'Si, but I do. I must see father. Confession will be good.'

Alice made her way towards a garden bench and sat down. 'A confession is not good!'

Giovanni sat down next to her and covered his face. 'I should never have done it. If they find out … Mama Mia! No home. No job.'

'Don't fret so much. You'll make yourself ill. Tomorrow will take care of itself. I promise you.'

Giovanni glanced up, hope written all across his face. 'Si, our lady will make it so?'

Alice smiled and patted his arm. 'Anyway, how is the painting?'

'Percho me lo domanda?'

Alice sighed. 'Dove l'oro parla ognilingua tace!' she replied in her best Italian. 'Where gold speaks every tongue is silent.'

Giovanni slapped his head. 'I wish it were so!'

Alice smiled. 'Well you know what you must do! So do it quickly. *DOVETE!* God forbid something should happen!'

'Si, si. But how we do it?'

Alice thought for a moment before whispering something to him.

'Si, si!' he enthusiastically agreed.

'And then we…' Alice whispered again to him. First he smiled then he jumped up like a new born lamb. 'Ah! Ha! Perfettamente! Benissimo angelica! Grazie!'

***

Sometime later Michael was leaving the library when Alice bumped into him.

'I'm just going to join Juliana for some coffee on the terrace, How about you?'

'I'd love to. By the way, I thought that mantra worked very well.'

He agreed. 'Yes, just as we anticipated.'

'That pink shirt really suits you!'

Michael smiled. 'Yes. Mother gave it to me many years ago. I've never been brave enough to wear it. I have always preferred white shirts but this morning, well I was feeling so rejuvenated, that I decided to put it on. I'm glad you like it. I hope Juliana doesn't get too much of a shock. She always said I was such a boring dresser. By the way, I wanted to ask you if... oh never mind. Let's go and see if Juliana is ready for that coffee.'

Three slow knocks warned Juliana that her husband was at the door.

'Come in Michael,' she replied, surprised that Alice was with him.

'Ah, music while you work. I do so love listening to Mozart.' Alice added following Michael into the studio.

'Yes, providing I can keep up with it. Actually I was going to work outside this morning but it was so overcast I thought it might rain. Whatever is the matter with the weather these days?' She added walking over to the window. 'I suppose that's why Giovanni isn't tending the roses this morning! Oh but look, it seems to be brightening up.' Michael put his arm around her. 'Well then, perhaps we should have coffee on the terrace if you're ready for a break?'

As Michael carried a tray with coffee and home baked biscuits out to them, Juliana remarked how well she thought the meeting had gone.

'Considering he's a priest Paul's summing up was very comprehensive, especially when he said that Fox may be Sidney Reilly and the Baroness 'B' may have been Moura Ben...'

Michael interrupted his wife. 'Well I don't agree. Having read some of Reilly's writings I can say there is no comparison in the writing styles.'

Juliana sighed. It was just like Michael to argue over the detail. 'Anyway,' she added, 'how are you getting on with *The Secrets of the Hohenzollerns*?'

He leant back in the chair. 'Oh, it's a marvellous read. I can't put it down. Alice, you should take a look. The doctor is a splendid writer. Speaking of which, that reminds me, I was thinking about Gramatikov's comment to Reilly. Remember, when he said "*the doctors have operated too early and the patient's condition is serious*"? That must have been a coded way of saying that the rescuers had messed up the dates. You know, because of the use of both the new and old calendars. One can just imagine the problems that would have caused. I can't understand how no one saw the danger of confusion, with one team working to the old calendar date while the other worked to the new?'

'If that had happened, it would certainly have upset the apple cart,' Alice observed. 'One party would have had to act without the other's knowledge. One can only imagine the confusion and panic that would have caused!'

Juliana stirred her coffee slowly thinking about the implications for the Imperial Family.

'By the way, have you seen Tonya this morning?' Michael asked, interrupting her thoughts.

'Yes, she's gone shopping for a new dress.'

'A new dress!' exclaimed Alice 'That's unusual for her. I always expect to see her in trousers like you. What's the occasion I wonder?'

Juliana burst out laughing. 'Oh dear, I'm so bad at keeping secrets! Paul has invited her out for dinner. He's taking her to Rome, possibly a meal at the Piazza Navona. Remember darling? That delightful restaurant we went to last year.'

Michael grunted. 'That'll cost a pretty penny. I wasn't aware that priests enjoyed such luxuries!'

She sighed. 'We should be pleased for Tonya. I'm glad she's settling in so well.

Alice nodded. 'Yes, she's a very sociable girl.'

Michael poured himself another cup of coffee. 'Well I hope she hasn't got her hopes up too high. I always thought she and Alex might...' He trailed off, recalling a previous conversation he'd had with his wife. 'Ah well! What's the use? I hope they have a good time and it doesn't all end in tears.'

Juliana patted him on the arm. 'Let's hope not. By the way,' she said, reaching inside her dungarees, 'I've got a surprise for you!'

Michael's face lit up as she took out two photographs and handed them to him.

'I found them amongst the old German newspaper clippings of your mother's. Here's one of the articles from the *Berliner Tageblatt*, written by a German journalist called Leo Lederer. Apparently he visited General Skoropadski in Kiev on May 10th 1918. Here what do you think of this one?'

Michael studied the photograph. 'How clever of you, so we are finally face to face with General Skoropadski the famous Hetman of the Ukraine and isn't he the very image of a Cossack leader. Well, well, well! But who is that in the middle?'

Alice leant across. 'It looks like a member of the Russian Orthodox Church because he has a long dark beard. My! Just look at the diplomat in the white suit. He must be an American if I am not very much mistaken!'

'Let me see,' Juliana interrupted. 'Oh yes, he is dressed like an American.'

'Has he got glasses on?' Alice enquired. 'I can't see too well.'

'No I don't think so.' Juliana replied unfolding the article.

'Well come on,' Michael demanded, 'what does it say?'

"'The General lives in one of many houses that he himself owns in Kiev. A simple one story building with a large balcony, the light carpeted veranda swarms with men. Soldiers with fixed bayonets keep guard at all the doors. In the anteroom there is a ceaseless coming and going. Young officers of the newly established bodyguard of the Hetman, who have again put on the varnished boots and the gold shoulder brades (epaulets) of the Russian Guard, stand near, Government officials grown old in service and young students hurry through the rooms.

At the green table the new commander of the palace Pressolovsky is holding an informal conference with General Alexandrovitch and other high officers. In the corner stands an assistant to the Ministry of Foreign Affairs with two young persons. Wild looking and collarless the representatives of the Great Russian Government, who have just come from Kirsk to Kiev for a short conversation with regard to peace negotiations. The physician of the Hetman appears. The "Baroness" comes, a young vivacious lady with rich dark brown hair. Deputations have themselves announced and pass with light step through the white rooms.'"

'AT LAST WE HAVE THE BARONESS!' Michael shouted.

Juliana smiled. 'I knew you'd be happy when I told you.' He gave her a hug. 'To tell you the truth, I'm aghast at the regularity of her appearance. She seems to be popping up all over the place, just like a bad penny.'

Alice smiled wryly. 'So you think this is the same Baroness as spoken of in *Rescuing the Czar* then?'

'Oh yes. Here,' Michael pointed to the article, 'look at that. They have put quotation marks around the word "Baroness". That tells me everyone at the time would have known who she was. There was no need to say her name you see!'

Alice laughed. 'But unfortunately Michael, we still don't know who SHE was.'

'Is there a picture of her?' Juliana asked, noting Alice's comment.

'No.' Michael replied.

'Well perhaps the Baroness is General Skoropadski's wife then.' Alice ventured.

'No, no, no! Otherwise she would be known as the "Baroness S". As usual, you've both got it wrong! It is quite clear who she is. Recall the other night when we said our mantra? We all came to the agreement that the Baroness must be Moura Benckendorff because she has brown wavy hair and now we see she has arrived in the Ukraine. But for what reason, I wonder? Perhaps she is a member of the peace negotiating team?'

Juliana thought for a moment. 'The Ukraine, isn't that what she said to Lockhart? Going to see her children?'

Alice sighed. 'No, no! She went to Estonia.'

'Anyway, before we discuss it further let me read the rest of it. There may be more secrets to be revealed about this enigmatic Baroness.

'"*Despite the many guards, I succeed without being held up further in reaching the room of the Hetman. A man in a bearskin cap and a red Cossack coat admits me. Pojtavetz-Ostranizki, Chancellor of the General, his white mantle thrown over the scarlet cloth of the Ukrainian Ataman, introduces me to the Hetman. With friendly words the new chief of the Ukrainian Government greets me as the first flying journalist to visit him. This tall slender figure is clothed in the black Cossack coat such as his predecessors in the Hetman's office have worn. His blond head with closely cropped hair and his blue eyes and the well- modelled nose may have belonged to a German aristocrat. His movements allow one to recognize the former cavalry officer.*"'

Michael put the article down. 'Shame there is not more about him here.'

'I must say he sounds most distinguished and very German, even though he is a Russian.'

'That's what makes him a true Prussian, Alice.'

'Surprise, Surprise!' Juliana shouted, startling both of them. 'Let's see what you make of this photograph.'

'Good Heavens! That's the Kaiser, Wilhelm II, having words with General Skoropadski,' Michael gasped, 'if I didn't know better I would say they look like brothers. When was this taken, do you know?'

'I'm not sure. I presume about the same time as the other one. It's part of an old newspaper cutting that I found folded inside of ...' Juliana wasn't able to finish because Alice was reading the headline out loud.

'"**HETMAN SKOROPADSKI VISITS THE KAISER IN BERLIN. 8th September 1918**. Gracious me, this is taken only six weeks after the Tsar and his family disappeared!"'

'Yes, and a full two months before Germany would sign the Armistice with the Allies,' Michael added.

'Okay, so why did General Skoropadski visit the Kaiser?' Juliana asked.

Michael looked up. 'I haven't a clue!'

'Well perhaps this article can shed some light. It's just a shame we haven't got all of it,' Juliana added as she unfolded a cutting that she had been holding onto.

'"*The German Emperor recently entertained at luncheon General Skoropadski, Hetman of the Ukraine, and both generously expressed the admiration for one another. The Emperor, according to a Berlin dispatch, said he had offered a helping hand to afflicted Ukraine, which had suffered by the war "brought upon the world by the machinations of the Entente and continued by them with criminal madness, in spite of the recognized unattainable nature of their aims of domination". Germany had furnished Ukraine with a basis for existence as a State, he said and added, "Henceforth a citizen can follow his vocation undisturbed and a peasant can cultivate the soil in safety and enjoy the fruits of his labour. There still remains much to do, but under the direction of your Highness, Ukraine has already made considerable progress in international consolidation and has thereby assured to itself a basis for future development." He proposed a toast. "To his highness, the Hetman of the Ukraine, Hurrah! Hurrah! Hurrah!" General Skoropadski said, "The very gracious reception which your Imperial Majesty has granted me will be regarded by the entire Ukrainian people as a sign of your Majesty's good will towards young Ukraine and it will lend strength to carry through the heavy* tasks which are still awaiting." He offered a toast. 'To His Majesty, the German Kaiser, Hoch! Hoch! Hoch!"'

'Ah, that's sweet. Now what's this I see written in italics at the bottom of the page?' Alice enquired, leaning across. 'Oh dear, I can't make it out without my glasses. Can you see it any better Michael?'

Juliana passed the cutting across to Michael for his inspection. 'Mother's hand, quite likely, and it's written in turquoise ink and says, *Our raison d'etre our work will prove!*'

Michael laid the article down. 'Is it cryptic enough for you?' he asked Alice as Juliana took a closer look at the writing.

'But that's not your mother's handwriting!'

Michael took a second look. 'No on second thoughts I don't believe it is. But I do recognise the hand and the ink. There is something strangely familiar about it. I know! It's the same as the handwriting in the front of Tonya's copy of *Rescuing the Czar*. The one mother gave her. Remember the message from K.A.G?'

Juliana nodded. 'Of course, I'm not likely to forget it, am I?'

'I wouldn't put too much store by that notion of yours!' Alice added. 'In those days they all had similar writing. We called it an educated hand.'

Michael laughed. 'I suppose they all used the same kind of ink too? Oh never mind, let me take it back to the library and compare it with the inscription in *Rescuing the Czar*.' He coughed before adding, 'Don't worry, we'll soon get to the bottom of this.'

'Just a moment Michael, the photographs and newspaper clippings must have a meant something to your mother. Please Michael, look after them they are precious.'

'Oh I will, don't you worry. I get the distinct feeling that these photographs are a record of something very important, especially with that mysterious Baroness hovering in the background.'

'Gracious,' Alice responded. 'You sounded just like Fox then! Before you go Michael, mark the date. Some of the Romanov family would still have been trapped inside Russia. Might they not have headed for Kiev or Odessa in the hope of escaping and if so, General Skoropadski could have been the man to help them.'

'What about the British? Didn't they help rescue the Tsar?' Juliana queried.

'To my mind there now seems little doubt that a plan to rescue the Tsar was being mobilized from the Ukraine. But more to the point,' added Michael, 'this photograph is evidence that the Kaiser was serious about rescuing his cousin Nicholas II. Certainly the Kaiser and General Skoropadski were close friends!'

Alice agreed. 'Yes, and if it were known that the Kaiser was thanking the General for rescuing his cousin the Tsar, this picture would be worth its weight in gold!'

'Gosh! To think at the very time this photograph was taken, Skoropadski could have been providing a safe haven within Russia for the Imperial Family and at the same time mobilizing troops with a view to mounting a monarchist uprising against the Bolsheviks. Or do you think the Kaiser is thanking him for delivering the Imperial Family to Germany?' Juliana questioned. Michael appeared irritated. But Juliana carried on. 'And the Baroness B. Lockhart says she went away for quite a few …,' Juliana paused. 'NO! That can't be right. Estonia is not near the Ukraine? But hang on! I know EXACTLY what happened now. THINK Michael! How did General Skoropadski travel to Berlin?'

Michael shrugged. 'By horse I imagine.'

Juliana sighed. 'No, he would have gone by train probably travelling with his Cossack bodyguards. I can see them all dressed up as German soldiers. Remember the Ukraine was flooded with them anyway.'

'Well he may have flown, and without any military support whatsoever! That would take only a few hours.'

'Not if he was escorting the Imperial Family or part of it, to safety in Berlin.'

Alice burst out laughing. 'What an imagination you have! If only it was true.'

'I don't know why you find it so funny Alice! I don't think it is beyond the realms of possibility,' Juliana replied indignantly.

'Well, my dear wife! You can't have it both ways.' Michael added kissing her on the forehead. 'Fox tells us they all escaped through Tibet to India or Ceylon, not that they travelled to Berlin via the Kaiser's railroad!'

'Well darling, I don't suppose he would give away the exact route if it was meant to be a secret! Anyway, even if they did travel to Germany or were saved by the Kaiser, no one would admit it because of all the anti-German feeling in England at that time! We were at war after all!'

Alice agreed. 'Imagine how the King of England would have reacted had he known that the Russian Imperial Family were being held in a secret *Schloss* at the request of the Kaiser!'

'For someone who doesn't really care about history or books, you seem to be showing a remarkable interest in this story, my dear.'

'Juliana has a point. I am surprised that you are not congratulating her for her logic. If it was Paul, you would have done so!' Alice patted Juliana on the back as she spoke.

'Look,' Juliana added, 'If it's fine to assume that Fox was really Sidney Reilly and the Baroness 'B' was Moura Benckendorff then why is it beyond the realms of possibility to think India might mean Berlin! Come on! You don't actually believe Fox when he says they trekked out on camels through some of the most dangerous and desolate parts of Asia, where murders were taking place every minute!'

Michael smiled and finished his coffee. 'There I was, thinking that we could enjoy a peaceful half an hour sitting on the terrace in the warm sunshine. I should have known better! You, my dear, are quite the Sherlock! I take my hat off to you! But now I must leave you. I want to check whether this handwriting in green ink is the same handwriting in Tonya's copy of *Rescuing the Czar*.'

Juliana watched him stride off in the direction of the house. Then she burst out laughing. 'Oh what fun Alice! I love surprising him like that. He hates to admit that he is impressed but I know he is! Now, if you have a moment Alice, I have something else to show you.'

Chapter Thirty One A Proposal

When Tonya and Paul arrived at the restaurant, the waiter asked them where they would like to sit. 'Somewhere with a nice view' Paul suggested, so the waiter took them to a table by the window. 'This is the best we have!' he told Tonya as she sat down and admired the flowers on the table.

'It was such a surprise when you suggested going for a meal,' she whispered, leaning over to pat Paul's hand. 'I hope you didn't mind me agreeing to lunch rather than dinner!'

Paul smiled. 'It's all the same to me.' He replied handing her the menu.

Tonya barely glanced at it. 'Is there anything you recommend? Have you eaten here before?'

'Yes, once or twice. I recommend the insalata to start and perhaps a pasta dish or maybe you prefer fish? If so, the lemon sole is my favourite. I usually have it with asparagus and fried potatoes.'

Tonya smiled at his enthusiasm. 'It sounds delicious; I'll go along with that. Let's order a bottle of white wine to go with it.'

As Paul called the waiter over, Tonya took the opportunity to glance around the restaurant. She liked the music and the vibrant chatty atmosphere.

'I think Italian waiters are so charming,' she confided as the waiter left.

'Not as charming as you.'

Tonya blushed. 'Do you like the dress I am wearing? I bought it especially!'

Paul cast an admiring glance over it. 'Yes, it suits you perfectly. I much prefer to see you in a dress rather than trousers all the time.'

Tonya scowled. 'Do you? Why is that then?'

'Well, it's more, how do you say?' Paul laughed nervously, 'It's good for a woman to look like a woman!'

'I'm not sure I get your drift. Can't a woman still look like a woman in trousers then?'

Paul laughed again. 'Of course, I was just saying!'

Tonya unfolded her serviette and placed it firmly on her lap while Paul watched silently as the waiter poured out the wine.

'You priests wear long frocks and no one says you look like women!'

Paul gave a nervous cough. 'Well, that's very different. Everyone knows we are priests and that is what we priests must wear!'

Tonya sipped the wine, wondering whether to continue with the conversation. She decided not, and as a result the atmosphere during the meal was awkward. To make things worse Paul made no effort to speak.

'Shall we have a dessert?' she asked finally.

'You go right ahead. I'm no longer hungry.' He added without looking at her.

She hoped she hadn't offended him and hurriedly thought of something to say.

'Well, I'll just have a coffee unless you're having a liqueur, perhaps a Sambuca?' She asked giving him the sweetest smile she could. Paul looked away.

'Okay, I'm sorry for…..' She paused, not sure what to apologise for.

'It's fine Tonya. I'll join you in the coffee and liqueur if you wish. We got off to a bad start. Come and sit over here next to me now.' Paul patted the empty chair beside him.

Tonya felt much better when he put his arm round her and gave her a big squeeze.

'You know, I am so happy that you agreed to come and have a meal with me because I have something I want to ask you later.'

Paul explained what it was like to grow up in Rome and told her a funny story about his childhood. She laughed, even though looking sideways made her neck ache. 'If you don't mind Paul, I'll go and sit opposite. Ah, here is our liqueur. Let's light them?'

'Si' Paul replied, 'it's the Italian way! But don't leave it alight too long, not if you value the alcohol!'

Tonya blew hers out, watching the dark coffee beans bleed into the drink.

'And careful you don't burn your fingers when you pick the glass up,' Paul warned.

'So what's it like being a priest then?' Tonya asked, slightly irritated by his constant concern. Paul placed his coffee cup gently on its saucer. 'Well I've always had a calling. It came naturally to me.'

'Oh! So you didn't have any other ambition?'

'No. As I said, it just happened and I have always accepted that, until now that is!'

'Oh?'

Tonya was surprised and leant forward, her eyes magnetically drawn to his. His were so utterly absorbing she could stare into them forever. A moment or two later Paul was still talking when she realised she hadn't taken in a word he'd said.

'I'm so sorry Paul, why are you having second thoughts about being a priest?'

Paul smiled before replying. 'After I gave the presentation I enjoyed it so much and doing the research into the past, well I did find it more rewarding than some of my priest work. Then I got a terrible feeling of guilt and asked myself can this be right, you know, when you are enjoying yourself. Then I decided I didn't want to be a priest anymore.' Paul reached out for her hand and clasped it tightly as he spoke. 'Imagine how exciting it would be to make some new discoveries and then write about them! I'll tell you something. I won't write a book unless I can reveal the mystery to the reader. I'm not one for leading them up the garden path.'

'I'm in shock, whatever will your father say?'

Paul shrugged. 'Of course he won't be happy, but it is my life!'

Tonya pulled her hand away gently. 'You should get together with Alex, he is intrigued by the Egyptians and some dead book as well!'

Paul laughed. 'I think you mean the Dead Sea Scrolls.'

'He said it was Egyptian!'

'Yes Tonya, but I wish for more truths to be unearthed. That is for sure!'

'You sound as if you really mean to give it all up then?'

'I have been called to make this change'

'But you can't just stop being a priest, surely?'

'No, no. I must speak to them first. They will make sure that I am doing the right thing. You know, they will ask me lots of questions.'

She leant back and folded her arms. 'I can see it's not going to be easy. What if they say that it is perfectly possible for you to remain a priest and do your research? Then what will you say?'

Paul gave her a wide smile. 'I tell them the real reason! I tell them I want to marry and have children.'

His reply made her blush and she realised there was more to come when he stood up and ceremoniously pulled another chair out and sat next to her.

'I think you know what has changed my mind!'

Tonya didn't know what to say. It was all happening so fast.

'Si, I know!' Paul hugged her really tight. 'Plenty of bambinos for us but now we celebrate eh?' Paul stood up and snapped his fingers at the waiter. It was then that he noticed Tonya was shaking. 'Mama Mia, you are so cold. Have another Sambuca and coffee that will warm you up.'

'Thank you. You know, listening to you just then, well it reminded me of something. When Maria died I was sure I wanted to write her story. I still do. But look where all the research has taken us, and to think that you and I ... well we may not have....'

Paul squeezed her hand as she spoke. 'You haven't said anything about my proposal?'

Tonya smiled. 'It's too early to say anything. The church may not let you go.'

'Paul reached for his coffee and sat back. 'Did you understand my presentation?'

Tonya sighed. 'Yes, of course. But I was sure that Maria had left us the clues because SHE was going to turn out to be the Baroness 'B', not who you are suggesting or Juliana's Kathleen Scott.'

'Well I could be wrong!'

Tonya smiled. 'I worry over Alex chasing hidden Russian gold. I feel his motivation is too materialistic.'

'The fact he is looking for treasure?'

'Yes. I know he calls it the "Tsar's missing millions" but the whole emphasis on why we got involved has changed. I thought it would be easy to write the story of Maria's life but I'm beginning to see how complicated it is. I'm never going to be able to do it.'

'Please Tonya, don't be despondent. Try and enjoy the journey for what it is! You never know where it might take you. Besides, it is good to discover the truth even though it seems complicated now. Think of it as exponential growth!'

'Exponential?'

Paul laughed. 'It means the more you see, the more you are able to see. Or the more you learn, the more you can learn. As our Lord said, nothing is hidden that will not be known and there is no secret that will not come to light!'

'I thought you didn't want to be a priest!' Tonya laughed.

'Once a priest, always a priest, isn't that what they say?'

'Well I don't mind, you can stay a priest for as long as you like, just so long as you marry me eventually!'

Paul laughed. 'Si, of course, but one thing I wanted to ask you since you made a study of the book too. Do you think Fox is telling the truth when he says the Tsar and his family escaped to Ceylon as guests of that British tea magnate?'

'Yes, the book says so and I believe Mr McGarry thought so too when he wrote *Now that England has Nicholas in India and Wells in Moscow*. But I admit to giving it plenty of thought. I even did some research into various tea companies such as Twinings, Brook Bond, and Liptons. They all had estates in India and Ceylon but there was only one man that stuck out in my mind because he had a large bungalow in Ceylon and was always inviting people over for a stay and he was a famous sailor.'

'Oh! Who was that?'

'Sir Thomas Lipton. He was a best friend of King George V and was well known for using his ship to rescue royalty. In fact he employed Red Cross nurses to treat the ill and wounded. His first boat was called *Erin* and was used as a Red Cross ship that helped rescue the Serbian Royal Family. Unfortunately that sank before 1918 but was replaced by the steam yacht *Victoria* in 1920. Sir Thomas was a gifted sailor and often raced against the Kaiser and the King in the America Cup, which he eventually won. He was a marvellous philanthropist and a handsome bachelor all his life.'

Paul smiled. 'You have done well. But how can you be sure that the tea magnate mentioned in *Rescuing the Czar* is really Sir Thomas Lipton?'

'I can't, but I think the book wants us to believe that.'

Paul looked at his watch. 'You speak like a diplomat and I see a pattern developing throughout this investigation.'

'What do you mean?'

'The story is too plausible.'

'Hmm, well don't worry about that. I am sure Alex will come up with something to get us all going again! He's very confident. He says the gold is buried out there and he thinks he can find it!'

Paul laughed. 'Tell me something I don't know!'

* * *

Back at the villa Alice was in Juliana's studio. 'What a peaceful atmosphere! So inspiring and the light is very good for you to work in I think.'

'That's true but there is a downside! It gets very hot in the afternoon and I have to walk around the house to keep cool. Sometimes I pop into the library to see Michael. I don't know why, but it seems much cooler down there.'

'He closes the shutters around two and even when he has the French windows open he draws the curtains to get a bit of a breeze. Anyway dear, I mustn't stop too long, what have you got to show me?'

Juliana smiled knowingly as she pulled out two old photographs. 'Here, take a look at Maria when she was young. Wasn't she beautiful? And check out her gorgeous clothes!'

As Alice held the photos up to the light Juliana noticed her hand was shaking.

'Now let me see.., no.... I don't think this is Maria.'

'Well have a look what's written on the back.'

Alice did as she was told. 'Oh! Baroness 'B' in Berlin! I was going to ask whether they are of the same person. But clearly they are!' Alice peered closer at the photos.

'Well you knew Maria back then. Don't you recognise the clothes she's wearing?'

Alice shook her head. 'No. This one might be her but I'm really not sure about the other. Anyway where did you get them?'

Juliana smiled triumphantly. 'They were tucked away in the back of this old photograph frame, which also had this picture of Maria in it.' Juliana held up a picture of Maria in her seventies.

'Oh I remember this frame, quite delightful, all those little gold cherubs and angels on it.' Alice ran her fingers lovingly along the carved outline as she spoke.

'It's polished up really well even though I say it myself! I thought Michael would like it on his desk. The photographs fell out when I was cleaning it.'

'Well dear, I really can't say one way or another. It may be Maria, it may not!'

Juliana pointed at the photograph again. 'You see here Alice. If this is Maria then she is definitely sloe-eyed and has that lovely brown wavy hair. Look at the clothes. A fox or an ermine stole. That's exactly how Fox described her in his diary and what a coincidence, me finding it in here! But I wonder who the gentleman is, her brother perhaps?'

Alice laughed. 'Who can say?'

'Well I will have to ask Michael then, but I thought out of everyone you would remember!'

Alice sighed. 'I'm sorry dear. I don't think it is Maria. It looks more like Baroness Benckendorff to me. Trouble is, they all dressed the same in those days. They all wore their jewels to show off. Come to think of it.... this second photograph, the one taken in Berlin around 1916. That looks as though it's taken at the races at Hoppegarten.'

'Or is it an airport?' Juliana asked

Alice quickly polished her glasses. 'Could be, could be! She is standing with her husband or brother I suppose.' Alice laid the photographs down and smiled.

'So you can't tell me whether it is Maria or Moura?'

Alice didn't reply.

Juliana sighed 'Well okay, suppose I go along with your view, that this isn't Michael's mother Maria. Explain to me why she would have had these photographs tucked away in this frame then?'

Alice shrugged. 'Perhaps you're letting your imagination get the better of you. I mean, thinking that Maria is the Baroness 'B' in Fox's diary. Anyway, Michael will be very interested in seeing them. Well done for finding them.'

'Great! You have just given me an idea. All I have to do is get hold of a photo of Moura and one of Maria taken at the same age and compare them. That way we will definitely know who is who.'

'Well, you would have to get a photo of her when she was very young. That will not be easy although Michael might have one somewhere I suppose.'

'Thank you, Alice. I had quite forgotten that Michael hadn't opened all the boxes yet. But before you go, I wanted to show you another of Maria's friends. I say "friend" because she took such an interest in him; you may know him, Dr Armgaard Karl Graves?' Juliana handed Alice a few newspaper cuttings. 'You'll note they go back to 1937.'

Alice quickly flipped through them before placing them on the table.

'Goodness, you have been busy.'

'Don't you want to read them?' Juliana asked, watching her head for the door. 'There were some awful things written about him. I am sure they can't all be true.'

Alice paused and turned back. 'I can tell you now. Maria always spoke very highly of him. I wouldn't believe everything you read. Anyway I suggest you hear what Michael has to say on the matter. Ah! That reminds me. He wanted a quick word. I'll pop down to see him now.'

Alice made her way slowly down the stairs pondering over what Juliana had shown her. Maria had done a good job of leaving clues about the place but Alice worried that everyone was getting the wrong end of the stick. When she opened the library door, Michael was sitting at his desk, the outline of his absurdly large chair framed by the light entering from the French windows. As she entered Michael looked up.

'You wanted a word?' she asked, still unable to see his face properly.

'Alice, come in.' He said pulling a chair up for her. 'Take a seat. Now, I've been thinking. I really do want to contact Dr Graves and the sooner we do it the better.'

Alice smiled. 'I see! But he has been dead for thirty-two years and ....'

Michael raised his hand. 'Before you say anything, let me tell you why. I've been reading about his early life and researching his name and that of his friend Edward Lyell Fox. My wife has shown me some cuttings that mother kept. He may be my father, although we have yet to discover his real name. Did you know he was famous? He made predictions about the outcome of the war. Many of them came true. In fact, much of the work he did during his life has gone unrecognised.' Michael clasped his hands together before adding 'Now I want to try and put all of that right. So is it possible to contact the dead?'

Alice rose from the chair and walked slowly round the room. She was deep in thought.

'Well?' He asked 'Can it be done?'

Alice pursed her lips together, deep in thought as she sat back down. 'Give me a moment while I think. He's been gone long enough. But we must ensure that we contact his spirit without interfering with his karma! It won't be easy. But aren't you afraid Michael?'

'Afraid!'

Alice half smiled. 'I haven't done a proper séance for a long time. In fact the last one was with Maria in….'

'Mother, really? Who on earth did she want to contact?'

Alice laughed. 'It wasn't anyone on earth, Michael!'

Michael sighed.

'Never mind me,' she added hastily. 'We usually had about five or six people around the table and …..'

'NO. I don't want anyone else in the room.'

'Well I'm not sure it can be done with any less than five. Too much energy required, you see.'

Michael sighed again. 'Surely there must be a way. If we say a holy mantra and burn some incense. Perhaps meditate for a few minutes before. Surely it's possible with just the two of us?'

Alice shook her head. 'I have never done it like that and besides, if we are to be successful in lifting the veil, the angels must be with us right from the start. Frankly I don't think they will be impressed with just you and me! '

Michael stood up and looked out through the French windows. Down below Giovanni was attending the roses. He watched his gardener at work, admiring the way he handled the secateurs. Presently he turned to Alice. 'How do we manage it then?'

Alice thought for a moment.

It was longer than Michael was prepared to wait. 'Well?'

'Don't rush me. Let me think…We'll need a cosmic alignment.'

'COSMIC ALIGNMENT' Michael blurted out, 'what has a cosmic alignment got to do with contacting the dead?'

'Alice laughed at his reaction. 'Don't be so surprised. Haven't you heard of "windows of opportunity" and "feedback loops?"'

Alice mimicked exclamation marks with her fingers in the air as she spoke. 'There are certain times of the year when the spirits of dead people are more easily contactable than at others! We must have the right window and all the angelic powers we can muster with us on the night. Now what month was the doctor born?'

Michael opened his notebook. 'May or June, 1878 or 1882, I'm really not sure what year.'

'Oh dear, that's no good. I'll have to ask for special dispensation. I know it all sounds mysterious to you Michael but knowing the terrestrial date is absolutely critical. The only other way is to know what date he died, then if I do my arithmetic correctly.... I should be able to work out what window he went back through!'

'Dam it Alice, I don't know the exact date he died. Surely there must be another way?' 'There is, but I need to hold something he owned.'

'Would this do?' Michael suggested, waving a stick in the air. 'Or what about cuff links, silk ties? I still have them in this cupboard somewhere.'

'A walking stick is fine and if you have a watch even better.'

Michael groaned. 'Oh dear, I thought I had one. Does it matter?'

Alice sat back down. 'No. I don't suppose it does.'

'I know, How about a piece of paper with his handwriting on it? Surely that would help?'

Alice smiled. 'Good man. That means we can hold the séance on a night when the veil is at its thinnest. Late October should do nicely.'

'HALLOWEEN, I'm not sure I can wait that long!'

Alice laughed at his impatience. 'I don't see why not! It's only five weeks away. By the way, from now until then you mustn't eat any meat or fish. Only fruit, vegetables and nuts are allowed. No alcohol either or cigars!'

Michael stood up abruptly. 'A séance may not be an appropriate step after all! Is there another way we can contact him?'

'I suppose you could pray and ask a question. The answer could come in the form of a dream!'

Michael laughed at the suggestion.

'Why are you laughing?'

'Come to me in a dream, honestly Alice, my name's not Joseph!'

'You asked me a question and I give you an answer and then you laugh! To find out in a dream Michael, is the best way because you are inviting Karl to come to you when he is ready. It is much better than forcing his attendance at a séance!'

Sensing the conversation was over Michael sat back in his chair. Alice rose to leave and Michael leant forward and rested his face on his hands, staring blankly at the green leather desk top. Alice felt sorry for him. He was disappointed but she wasn't going to change her advice. As she made her way to the door he looked up.

'I suppose you're right. I'll give it a go then.'

As she turned to leave, Alice bumped into Juliana. 'Is he in?' she asked, 'I'm just going to show him the photo of the Baroness in Berlin. See what he makes of it!'

Alice smiled. 'Oh yes, I'm sure he will be very intrigued and I hope you have given up on that idea of yours, that somehow Kathleen Scott was the mysterious Baroness 'B' 'Indeed I have. It was quite foolish of me! If she is listening I crave her forgiveness. I don't know why I persisted along that path for so long!'

Alice laughed. 'Well it's not easy to get rid of a bee in the bonnet!' She muttered closing the door behind her.

'Look, photos of the Baroness in Berlin,' Juliana said, waving them in front of Michael.

'That's mother. I'm sure of it,' he said enthusiastically. 'I've often seen photographs of her in similar outfits.'

Juliana sat down. 'Well I'm sorry to disappoint you but Alice says it is not! It just looks like her. She is sure this is Moura Benckendorff at Hoppegarten in Berlin, you know the famous race course.'

'Well I never! Where did you find these?'

'It was hidden in the back of a picture frame that I was cleaning up for you, along with this much more recent one of your mother. You see Michael, all these photos in Berlin have got me wondering about the Kaiser and what his role might have been in helping to rescue the Tsar.'

'Well come over here. As you know, my collection is extensive!'

Juliana giggled and followed her husband to the bookshelf. 'Here I have a large German section to my library. The Kaiser's role is well recorded throughout the First World War and the Russian Revolution. She peered at the books on the shelf. 'These look ancient!'

Michael laughed. 'They're not so ancient but they are delicate. Please be careful if you handle them! But you are most welcome to have a look. Let me draw your attention to these three shelves in particular. This is where I keep my most valuable works of literature. Here you will find everything on the Kaiser and his life. You may be surprised to know that after the war he wrote a series of articles for American newspapers. He was popular even after he was exiled to Holland. Paul has been looking at them too, so if you can't find what you're looking for, he may still have it!'

'Thank you, anyway, how are you getting on with your search for the name Armgaard?'

'I'm not doing well! I'm currently going through the Austro-Hungarian aristocracy, having finished with the Bulgarian dynasties. I haven't found one man with that name.'

'Well don't give up hope. If anyone can find it, you can!'

'I'm glad you have such faith in me my dear. But guess what? I did find something out about Edward Lyell Fox. Apparently he wrote a book in 1917 called, *Willhelm Hohenzollern and Company*. It is full of his memoirs as a war correspondent in Germany. In fact I wouldn't be at all surprised to discover that Dr Graves didn't lift some of the material for his book, *The Secrets of the German War Office*, from it!'

'Well you can't accuse him of stealing words, because it states quite clearly in the front that it was written in collaboration with Edward Lyell Fox. They must have very been good friends.'

'Yes, I suppose so and it is sad that he died so early in 1920. Dr Graves must have missed him a lot.'

'1920! He must have been quite young then?'

'Yes, in his thirties or so I believe.'

'How did he die? Was he shot?'

'No. He died off duty. Apparently there had been a lot of influenza that year. Young and old caught it alike.'

'Well that's a great shame! Thank goodness he wasn't murdered.' Juliana paused for a moment. 'I've just had a thought. If Dr Graves knew that Edward Lyell Fox rescued the Tsar, then him getting the flu and apparently dying would be a very convenient way to disappear don't you think?'

Michael was shocked. 'Where have I heard that before? But I'm surprised at you my dear! You sound... well almost cold hearted. Let me remind you that Edward had a family and a loving wife whom he left behind. I feel I must assure you that he is most definitely *not* the Fox we are looking for in *Rescuing the Czar*.'

'By the way, I've found a few more clippings that you might like to look at. They are mainly of the Tsar and contain speculation as to whether he managed to escape. Your mother seems to have collected everything printed on the subject.'

'Come on, let's get something to eat,' Michael suggested putting his arm around his wife. 'We must remember that Mother had a vivid and wild imagination. Like many writers she was prone to illusions about just how good her work was. It's not that she purposely misled or told lies. I am sure she really believed what she said.' Michael gave his wife a squeeze to emphasise the point. 'She would have witnessed shocking events and the end of a great dynasty that had ruled Russia for hundreds of years. How could she live with herself if she had not had some role in helping to save the family? I am sure she was not alone in her machinations. Along with other members of the Russian nobility she must have found the whole episode very upsetting indeed. It must have felt like the end of the world for everyone. It's no surprise to me that she hung on to these mementos. It's all she had to remember those awful times by.'

'Yes, poor Maria!' Juliana agreed. 'What an awful thing to have gone through!'

Chapter Thirty Two   Gold and Platinum

The following afternoon Alex stood in the library. 'I have something to show you all,' he announced flamboyantly, taking a coin from his pocket and flipping it in the air. 'Here everyone, take a look at the imperial currency of Russia. I want you to know exactly what I am talking about today.'

Tonya sighed. He was such a prima donna. Still, he had caught their attention. There was Giovanni staring wide-eyed at the coin, totally mesmerised by it. She noted the beads of sweat breaking out on his forehead.

Alice held her hand out. 'May I see it? Ah! A gold rouble dated 1914. Where did you get it from?' She waited for a reply but none was forthcoming. Alice passed the coin to Tonya, who pulled a squeamish face before handing it quickly to Paul.

'How do you know this is authentic?' Paul enquired.

Alex laughed. 'I am as certain as I'm alive that it is very real indeed!'

'So how did you come by it?' Juliana repeated Alice's question, but Alex still refused to answer.

As Giovanni pulled out his handkerchief and wiped his brow, Alice leant across. 'Do try and relax PLEASE!' she whispered as Michael now held the coin high in the air.

'Come on son, spill the beans. Where did you get it from?'

Alex gave a broad smile. 'Okay, okay! It's a kind of a loan shall we say but really I just wanted everyone to get a feeling of what we are talking about this afternoon.'

Tonya laughed. 'Honestly Alex! I do think we all know what a gold coin looks like!'

'Look here. What I've got to say is important. I've prepared some notes but to be frank it's all too academic. I prefer to have an interactive session because lecturing, well, it's not really my style!'

Michael raised an eyebrow as he examined the coin further. Such was the continuing interest in the coin that Alex wondered whether anyone was listening.

'Okay! Can I have it back now?' He asked stretching his hand out.

'Not so fast son! You have not answered my question. Where did you get this from?'

'All will be revealed in good time.' He added watching Giovanni hurriedly leave the room.

'Is he unwell?' Juliana asked.

'No, he's fine. He must have forgotten something in the kitchen. Don't worry I'm sure he'll be back shortly.' Alice assured her.

Michael tapped the table loudly. 'Well can we get on? I haven't got all day!'

Alex cleared his throat. 'If Fox's diary is to be believed, Nicholas and his family would have needed plenty of money to cover living expenses while they were in hiding and also to buy the silence of the rescuers. Earlier we spoke of a possible secret codicil to the peace treaty signed at Brest-Litovsk, where the Bolsheviks agree to release Nicholas II and his family in return for a huge reduction in their debt to the Germans.'

'I don't remember us speaking about that!' Paul exclaimed.

'Well, we sort of mentioned it,' Tonya reminded him.

'Anyway,' Alex continued, 'another fact is that the Imperial Family and their rescuers would have required bucket loads of money if they were to survive in secret. So in my opinion if we want to find where the family ended up, all we have to do is follow the trail of loot! But it would be silly to think that Nicholas and Alexandra walked out of Russia with boxes of gold coins clonking about them.' He laughed at his own joke. 'So they must have had help in transporting the gold or is it possible that they were able through some kind of prior agreement to convert existing foreign deposits of Tsarist gold coins or bullion into the currency required for their new existence wherever that was?'

'I believe what you're trying to say,' interrupted Michael, 'is that any negotiation must have taken place long before they actually escaped and some form of agreement was probably reached on exactly how much gold would be needed to support the Imperial Family whilst they were in hiding. Maybe the money was even sent in advance to the rescuers?'

'Do give him a chance,' Juliana requested.

'We know,' Alex continued, 'that the Tsarist gold reserves amounted to roughly half of the available gold supplies in Siberia during 1918.'

'How do you know?' asked Paul. Alex ignored the question and turned a page of his notes.

'I'm sorry. Did you not hear my question? How do you know that?' Paul repeated his question.

Alex sighed loudly. 'Let me say here and now. I will provide you with a list of my sources at the end of this presentation and then you can ask questions. All the questions you want. So please don't interrupt me now.'

'I thought you said this was going to be an interactive session!' Tonya jested.

'No, Alex is quite right,' Michael added. 'He can say what he likes so long as he tells us the source of his misinformation!'

Alex sighed as Giovanni walked melancholically back into the room and sat down next to Alice. 'Excusee!' He added apologising for his absence.

'That's all right! You haven't missed much,' Alice patted him reassuringly.

'NOW,' Alex shouted. 'Bearing in mind my previous statement, you may be surprised to know that in 1914 Russia held the largest stock of gold in the world. It was estimated around 1,700 million roubles. However, seven traumatic years later there was nothing left. NOTHING! So the question is where did it all disappear to?'

Michael started laughing.

'What's so funny?' Juliana asked.

'Nothing, I'm just being silly,' he whispered. 'Ignore me.'

'Now there have been all sorts of stories,' Alex continued. 'Some true and some false!' Michael couldn't contain himself any longer. 'Well I hope what you're going to tell us is the truth because we haven't got time to listen to lies!'

Alex twiddled the gold coin in his hand as he spoke. He obviously had no intention of being waylaid by his father's sarcastic comments. 'I will TRY and tell you where the money went between 1917 and 1920. So, at the start of the war there was plenty of financial cooperation between Russia and the Allies, Just as you would expect really.'

Alice squinted. 'Would you mind not fiddling with that coin Alex, it's blinding me!'

'Oh I'm sorry. Let's shut the sun out.' Alex put the rouble in his pocket while Tonya closed the shutters.

'Now I want to move on to an important story.'

Juliana coughed and then apologised.

'PLEASE! Why won't any of you let me make a start?' He heard himself demand as he waited for silence in the room. 'THANK YOU. Now towards the end of 1917, Red guards stormed the Imperial Bank in Moscow. The new Bolshevik government was facing difficulties and there had been many strikes. Banks had gone out of business and as inflation was rising there was an urgent need to circulate millions of roubles. Desperate times demand desperate measures, so on November 7th1917 the Commissar of Finance turned up at the State Bank accompanied by armed sailors and a military band! Significant that, if you think about it! Anyway, he demanded the immediate handing over of ten million roubles! But the state bank refused to pay up. It took a further two visits and the presentation of an ultimatum. Eventually, late at night, armed guards forced an entry and the bank officers were forced to open the vaults. On that night five million roubles in notes were taken.'

'This was the beginning of the handing over of Russian core state wealth. Some called it Tsarist funds but to the Bolsheviks it was theirs to do with as they wished. Now as worrying as the raiding of bank paper notes and securities was, it was nothing in comparison to the devastation that would be caused to the Imperial Bank building where the country's gold reserves and imperial jewels were being held. All of it would go and much of it would disappear forever! But before I tell you how, I must first say that it is unfair of me to put all the blame at the Bolsheviks' door. They were not the only ones trying to get their hands on Russia's gold. The White Russians fighting against the Bolsheviks were after it as well.'

'And,' Michael intervened, 'The Whites weren't stupid! They knew the revolutionaries would not survive if they had no money, but what of the Czechs Alex? You have not mentioned them. They are so important in this story!'

'Well I was just coming to that! Now the Czechs had been fighting on the side of Russia and the Allies against Germany. But after the Brest-Litovsk agreement, when Russia made peace with Germany, they found themselves without a war to fight and they were to all intents and purposes disbanded. The Czechs were, however, about to become involved in the civil war in Russia because the White Russians asked them to fight on their side against the Bolsheviks. The Czechs were tired of fighting and wanted to go home if only they could find a speedy and safe route out of Russia and they looked to the Allies to provide them with a route. Is that about right?'

'Yes,' agreed Michael, 'but you have forgotten to mention Trotsky.'

Alex shrugged. 'I just want to tell them about the gold. Trotsky's not relevant; besides I don't have any information on him here!'

'Very well,' Michael responded getting to his feet. 'I'll say something. By the summer of 1918 several counter-revolutionary forces were settled in Russia. They held areas close to Vladivostok, as well as the Manchurian border and the Urals. Bear in mind this is only a matter of weeks before the Imperial Family were to disappear. Trotsky was nervous about allowing the armed Czechs, who were hostile to the Bolshevik regime, into Moscow to move through Russia. So Trotsky bombastically insisted that the Czechs lay down their arms and proceed to Vladivostok unarmed. Of course they refused to do that and instead established themselves in groups across the route to Vladivostok. This included the strategic Trans-Siberian Railway. In Moscow the Bolsheviks feared that the Czechs planned to team up with the White forces around Samara, head for Ekaterinburg and free the Tsar and his family.'

'No surprises there then,' Alex interrupted his father, trying to get a word in.

Michael took the hint. 'Well alright if you want to carry... Carry on then!'

'Thanks, now where was I? Oh yes! The gold reserves that the Bolsheviks inherited from Kerensky's provisional government were likely to be severely depleted by the terms of the Brest-Litovsk Treaty. The Bolsheviks had already shipped one hundred and sixty million dollars worth of gold from Moscow to Berlin.'

'Why Berlin,' Juliana asked. 'Surely it should have gone to London or New York?'

Michael sighed. 'Obviously it was part of the DEAL!'

'What, THE RESCUE?' Juliana was frantically trying to keep up.

'No!' Michael shouted. 'Part of the peace treaty at Brest-Litovsk!! Do pay attention dear!'

Juliana looked confused. 'Well why are we talking about gold if it is not to do with rescuing the Tsar and his family?'

'Si,' Giovanni agreed. 'No understand this gold business!'

'Well in that case let me explain,' Michael offered. 'The gold in Berlin was eventually shipped to London but that was much later, after the war. With the advance of the combined White and Czech forces towards Samara, Trotsky became nervous about where the Russian gold reserves were being held. So just before the Czechs and the White Russian Army arrived, Trotsky moved the gold stored at Samara in scores of barges down to Kazan. But his plan was stupid and I'll tell you why. Kazan already had a large Russian gold stock. Now with this additional eastern gold added to it, the reserve increased to thirty two million pounds worth of gold. It was a staggering amount of gold to be stored in one place and in such an unstable environment. Trotsky had made a big mistake. The Whites and the Czechs took hold of Kazan and acquired all of the gold. This was one of the biggest treasure hauls of the war and very few people knew about it. But what happened next is an enduring mystery and may be linked to what really happened to the Romanovs. Alex, I'm sure can tell us more.'

Alex smiled as Tonya poured him a glass of water. 'Now, here comes the interesting bit. During the next eighteen months, one hundred and twenty million dollars worth of gold went missing, over five hundred million dollars in today's terms. Spent, lent, lost or stolen! No one knows what happened to it.'

'I can't imagine what one hundred and twenty million dollars worth of gold coins must look like!' interrupted Tonya. 'How on earth did they transport it, surely not by barge?'

'Many a true word…said in jest… rumour has it that some of the gold did physically sail away. That's if your books are anything to go by father?'

Michael raised an eyebrow. 'That's news to me.'

'In November 1917,' Alex continued, 'a former Commander-in-Chief of the Russian Black Sea Fleet Admiral Alexander Kolchak, dropped by the British Embassy in Tokyo. He offered to work for the British Government and was immediately accepted. After working in Mesopotamia, Kolchak was persuaded to help in Manchuria, which he did. But by 1918 he was the man fully in command of the White Russian forces in Siberia.'

'Oh, I know which story you're about to tell!' Michael shouted excitedly. 'You've got it from one of my old books that Mother translated. *The Russian Gold Reserves*, written in French by that Russian finance minister, V.J. Novitsky. He wrote all the incredible details after he had escaped from Russia and was living in Paris.'

'That's right, but what I have to say happened a few months after the disappearance of the Russian Imperial Family from Ekaterinburg. In October 1918 Admiral Kolchak took charge of the army and navy in Omsk and was offered the title "Supreme Ruler of the Siberian Government". He managed a coalition of warring factions against the Bolsheviks, coordinating his military actions with those of the allied governments.'

'All this war talk is so depressing and long after the Imperial Family disappeared. I wonder why you bother telling us all this.' Alice rubbed her forehead irritably but Alex ignored her.

'Now the Siberian Government had gold reserves amounting to three hundred and thirty two million dollars in Omsk. Kolchak had access to the gold and spent some of it on munitions and military equipment, which he brought in through the port of Vladivostok. But someone had very sticky fingers or so rumour has it!'

'Sticky fingers, what mean sticky fingers?' Giovanni enquired.

Alex laughed. 'Whoever was handling the shipments was thieving the gold.'

'Oh, I don't know about that son. I think that's hearsay. Kolchak spent more than one hundred and twenty two million dollars financing the White Russian armies alone.'

'And what a shame that was,' replied Alex. 'Anyway a year later, towards the end of 1919, the Bolsheviks advanced on Kolchak. Suddenly his life was in danger. He was forced to leave Omsk and move his headquarters further east to Irkusk. Of course that meant taking the remaining gold reserves with him along the Trans-Siberian railroad.'

'Not an easy task. It took more than ten days to load the two hundred and ten million dollars of gold bullion into forty special reinforced cars. But this is where it gets interesting. Kolchak left Omsk on the night of November 12th 1919, at least two days before the Bolsheviks were due to arrive.

He travelled in a convoy of trains which he named A,B,C,D, and E, and they were accompanied by an armoured train. Kolchak travelled in train B. His staff the Chancery and the guards were in trains A, B, C, and E and the gold was placed in train D! So far so good, but their luck was not to last. Not long after their departure from Omsk, two of the trains were moving through the station of Tatarskaia, roughly eight miles east of Omsk, when Train B ploughed violently into the back of the gold train D. The catastrophic crash started a huge fire in the station and eight railway cars were destroyed. More than eighty guards were killed or wounded in the explosion and all the boxes of gold were scattered over the railway line.' Alex's eyes widened as he described the scene. 'Just imagine all the ingots and gold coins spread over the railway line, just ready for the picking!'

'How much gold was there?' Paul asked.

'I don't think the amount lost in the chaos is actually known.' Alex looked across to Michael for a reply.

'Well the reason we don't know how much was lost is because events moved very fast. As Alex said, by the end of November 1919 the Bolsheviks were firmly back in control of the country. They were closing in on the remnants of the White armies and some of the Czechs who were still trying to escape Russia. Of course, after this dreadful accident Kolchak lost his authority. Remember he was in train B, so he would have been badly injured.'

'Who picked up all the gold that was spread across the railway lines?' Juliana enquired. 'Surely someone must have?'

'Otherwise,' interrupted Alex, 'Mother will be taking a first class ticket to Omsk I guess!'

'You may well joke about such things but this is a very sad story indeed. If I recall correctly,' Michael continued, 'the Czechs were still in control of the Trans-Siberian railway and through a series of negotiations were able to arrange their escape route and control movements along that transport corridor and out of Russia. But the congestion along the line had severely reduced freight movements to only two trains a day. Kolchak was told by the Czechs that his train, which now contained the remnants of the gold, could continue only as far as Nijnneudinsk.'

'Of course,' Michael continued, 'there were delays and as the political tension rose, General Janin, a French commander of the Allied forces, suggested that Kolchak for his own safety should leave the gold train and travel under his protection to Vladivostok. Tragically, Kolchak never reached the coast. What happened next has been clouded in mystery but some believe the Czechs handed him over to a newly established revolutionary socialist regime in Irkusk. Ah yes, Kolchak! What a magnificent leader,' Michael added. 'Many, including Mother as well as your family Alice, would have pinned their dreams of freedom upon his success. But unfortunately their hopes were dashed when two months later he was brutally executed by his enemies. It was a very sad day for the Whites.'

'Well If I had my way I would ban war forever,' Juliana interrupted. 'It's a crime against humanity.'

'I agree,' said Paul. 'Blessed are the peacemakers for they shall be called the children of God.'

Alex shuffled his papers, frustrated he wasn't holding their attention.

'I haven't finished the story of missing Russian gold! Look right from the start, I said that if my theory was right, the gold should follow the Tsar into exile.'

Michael chuckled to himself. 'Well you've done your best son. It's a complicated subject and you can't be expected to know everything. Luckily I was here to fill in the gaps.'

'I THOUGHT IF I COULD FIND A LARGE AMOUNT OF GOLD BEING SHIPPED OUT OF RUSSIA THEN THAT WOULD CONFIRM THE TSAR AND HIS FAMILY HAD SUCCESSFULLY ESCAPED.'

Alex repeated his theory then realised he was shouting and lowered his voice. 'But it wasn't that easy because much of Russia's gold had been leaving the country long before 1918 and of course there were significant amounts shipped out when it became obvious that the White Russians would not be able to reinstate a monarchy in Russia. Most of the gold that officially left Russia before 1918 was in payment for weapons and traded items. There were also the normal financial arrangements, such as interest bearing certificates that needed to be settled, all of which you would expect to find between trading partners. But I did find a blip!'

'Oh!' Michael reacted. 'What kind of a blip?'

'In 1919, when it became clear that the Bolsheviks would remain in control of Russia and the Tsar would never return, well it's then that we start to see the transportation of huge amounts of gold around the country. The Czechs, who have much of the gold, promise to hand it all back to the Bolsheviks in return for a safe route out of Russia.'

Michael interrupted. 'Whether the full amount of gold was ever returned is open to debate.'

'You're absolutely right, of course!' Alex agreed. 'However there were rumours of large quantities of gold coins being sold in Harbin shortly afterwards. So much in fact that the sales taking place, depressed the market price!'

'This led some scholars to believe that the Czechs or someone else lucky enough to gain from the earlier train crash was unloading their recently acquired booty.'

'I remember,' Added Alice, 'years later that many White Russians in exile were convinced that the Czech Legions had taken up to thirty-two million dollars worth of gold from Admiral Kolchak.'

'Well,' responded Alex, 'of course the Czech Consul denied the charges against the Czech Legion and explained how the missing gold was lost. They said that the gold had been guarded by three hundred men as it left Kazan on its long journey through Siberia under the combined eyes of Kolchak and General Janin. After General Janin entrusted the gold to the Czech Legion for safe keeping it was immediately put in the care of three Czech officers and three Russian officials. The boxes all had original seals on the cases of gold, to which were added further Czech seals.

But on January 12th 1920, the Czechs discovered that the seals on one case that had been guarded by the Russians at the station of Tiuret had been broken and thirteen cases were missing! The rest of the gold consignment was guarded by the 7th Company of the Irkusk Soviet Regiment from February 28th and formally handed back to the Bolsheviks by the Czechs on March 1st 1920. So this was the detailed response to the charges of the alleged looting of thirty-two million dollars worth of gold by the Czechs and it had a ring of truth about it. At least it did until more of the truth was discovered in Hong Kong. The Czechs had supposedly sold the gold on the international market through Vladivostok and perhaps they did lose a part of it in the way they officially described but it takes two to tango! It was later discovered that the bank where they had off loaded some of the gold still held the details of the transaction in its vaults! Now I may not have all the facts but I have made some notes from your old books, father. They are written in French so my translation may contain a few errors. Apparently the Hong Kong and Shanghai Banking Corporation had opened a branch in Vladivostok in 1918 at the request of the British government. One day it was approached by the Czechs. At the time the local manager was a Mr. B.C. Lambert. He recorded that the

Czechs sold part of the bullion they had with them to the Hong Kong Bank. But in *Wayfoong* Maurice Collis tells us that these gold bars were offered to the Bank of England, which refused them. Lambert then made an offer for them through a Mr. A.G. Stephen, the manager of the Shanghai branch. They were shipped by yacht under Commander Baring to Shanghai and then sent to India where gold was badly needed.'

'So between 1917 and early 1920 the Bolshevik gold stock more than halved. From six hundred and thirteen million dollars to three hundred million dollars worth and guess what? A year later it was down to one hundred and seventy million dollars. Not very soon after that it was completely gone. Now listen to what the Tsar's own brother-in-law, Grand Duke Alexander, had to say on the matter in his book *Once a Grand Duke*:

"Until this day, the participants in the Siberian epic, the Bolsheviks as well as their adversaries, are trying to ascertain the identity of the persons who helped themselves to a portion of the six hundred and fifty million gold roubles of Kolchak. The Soviet rulers claim to have been cheated out of some ninety millions. Winston Churchill believes that a mysterious deposit was made in one of the San Francisco banks during the summer of 1920 by a group of individuals who spoke English with a strong foreign accent.'"

Michael clapped his hands just as Alex finished. 'Very good, you have told us how millions of dollars worth of gold left Russia in only three years but you haven't said how this was linked to the Tsar and his family's escape.'

Alex thought for a moment. 'Well there are many stories that I haven't told you. I have only tried to pick up on the points that may have had a bearing on the disappearance of the Tsar and his family.'

'Yes I realise that. But what's the connection between the disappearing millions and the disappearing Tsar?'

Alex shuffled his notes as he thought of an answer to impress his father.

Juliana felt sorry for him and stepped in. 'Well, I found it interesting but I've got a couple of questions which may be relevant, dear.'

Michael checked his watch. 'Yes alright I suppose we have time. What are they?'

'Well now If I've got this right, some gold went to Berlin and then to England or the United States. Some gold went to India, where it was badly needed, and some gold, according to the Tsar's brother-in law, ended up in a Californian bank! So, perhaps that's where the Tsar went! CALIFORNIA! It all makes sense from what we know about McGarry and his partner Romanovsky.'

'Secondly, regarding this Brest-Litovsk agreement, obviously the Germans did a deal with the Bolsheviks and told them they wouldn't have to pay so much if they released the Tsar and his family.'

Alex sighed loudly. 'But that would add to the Russian gold reserves, mother, not detract from them!'

A slow smile crept across Michael's face. 'Yes but wait a moment, your mother is right. The Bolsheviks should have paid the Germans at least three hundred million. Instead we know they only paid half the amount requested in the original treaty, that is to say only one hundred and sixty million.'

'Shall I repeat what I said before?' Alex enquired.

'No, you don't have to,' Juliana replied. 'Some of the gold must have ended up in India as Fox said, along with the Tsar and his family.'

'If only life was so simple,' Michael responded. 'I'm afraid it's not possible to put two and two together and come up with six! Not in this case. The chaotic circumstances rule out any proof as to where the missing millions ended up.'

Michael picked up the book, *Wayfoong*, and started to leaf through its pages; then, sensing a change in atmosphere, he looked up. Alex was flushed with anger because he was fed-up with his father continually checking up on his facts. Michael chose to ignore his son's discomfort and turned to page one hundred and seventy seven and started to read to himself. Presently he closed the book. 'Though I say it myself son, I think you have done a good job at relaying the facts. But I'm afraid there is one important point that you have missed.'

'Oh!' Alex exclaimed.

'Yes, when you spoke of the missing gold millions you should have stated that the bullion also included platinum. Now excuse me a moment. There is something I must check.'

Alex put the gold coin in his pocket and watched as his father picked out another book from his collection.

'PLATINUM,' repeated Juliana. 'Didn't Fox speak about confirming the status of the gold and the platinum?'

'Yes, I'm sure he did,' replied Tonya, 'but perhaps it was a code for asking about the arrival of the Tsar and his son in the U.S?'

Juliana laughed. 'That's way too clever for me but if Alex is right and the gold was to follow the Imperial Family out of Russia, then the words should mean exactly what they say!'

Alex took the gold coin out of his pocket again and threw it up in the air. 'Yes, everything points to the Tsar and his family being financed in exile by the missing Kolchak gold and platinum and it all ties in with Mr Romanovsky receiving the gold in San Francisco.'

'I hope you're not all jumping to conclusions,' Michael admonished, returning to the table with two more books.

'Definitely not,' Tonya replied. 'Alex must be right and the Czechs have to be at the heart of the deal. Also, we know McGarry and Romonovsky supported Thomas Masaryk for the presidency of a new country called Czechoslovakia and Mr Romanovsky married Goldie Biakini, who was allegedly Thomas Masaryk's niece!'

'Stop right there, before you all jump to the stupidest of conclusions! Now son, you didn't do your research properly! You have missed vital information about a gold shipment in 1918 and it's lucky I am here to correct you. Otherwise, heaven knows what a wild goose chase you would be on.' Michael laughed quietly to himself as Alex shifted uneasily. 'I have here a book published in 1966 called *The End of the Romanovs* by Victor Alexandrov.' Michael held the book up before turning to page seventy-two. 'This has a direct bearing on our discussions and I'll be interested to see what you think. So here we go! In his report to Lenin and Trotsky, A.A. Joffe, the Soviet Ambassador in Berlin and a member of the central committee of the party added that the Tsarina's brother, the Prince of Hesse-Darmstadt, had called on him on two separate occasions. This aristocrat had courteously offered his services to the Soviet representative as a mediator between Moscow and Berlin so as to save Soviet Russia from the burden of total occupation by the Germans.' Michael paused. 'Before I go on, let me explain something to you. In 1918 the Germans had control of large parts of Russia. They occupied Kiev and the Ukraine and, as we know, there were at least nine hundred Germans in Ekaterinburg disguised at Red Army soldiers. This is what Joffe said in his report to Lenin and Trotsky on the matter of the Tsar's release:'

"The Prince has offered to negotiate a suspension of the Soviet war debt amounting to three hundred million gold roubles as fixed by the treaty of Brest-Litovsk, or at least to reduce it. Naturally the release of the Tsarina Alexandra and her family would be the ultimate proof of the Kremlin's goodwill."

'Behind this move there appeared the very clear intention of getting the ex-Tsar Nicholas, once free of his jailers, to accept and endorse the peace of Brest-Litovsk. The Prince of Hesse-Darmstadt had let Joffe understand that this offer was unofficial and was to be kept secret. So Alex, why do you insist on suggesting the Czechs were in a deal to free the Tsar and his family?'

Alex was about to reply when Michael unexpectedly interrupted. 'I suspect you're not able to answer but I can reveal why some historians believe it to be the case. Michael turned the page and started to read.

'There was a Central Committee meeting held on May 23rd 1918. Suddenly, up jumped a little man with a face framed in a frill beard. He was wearing a well-cut suit and had been sitting on Lenin's left like an old companion in arms. He had travelled across Germany with Lenin in the famous sealed coach. His horn-rimmed spectacles jumped on his bony nose as he leapt to Vladimir Ilytch's defence. Karl Bernodovitch Radek easily reduced the barrackers to silence. The news he had brought from Stockholm seemed important and contributed a new element to the general discussion. This is what he said:

'"My Swedish informers have learned quite recently that close interest in the butcher Nicholas is being shown on the other side of the Atlantic. If the City of London is mainly concerned with hundreds of gold pieces buried in the cellars of Kazan, Wall Street is showing a philanthropic interest in a thoroughly devalued personality, the head of the Romanovs. The National City Bank is financing the operation. The broker is Thomas Masaryk, a professor who is preparing to install himself as liberator in the Hradshin in Prague. He is the man who has remote control over the Czech legions in Siberia and he it is who has promised his associates to free the ex-Tsar. All the deliveries made on credit to the Whites by Remington Arms and the Metallic Cartridge Union depended on the speed with which the Czechs approach Ekaterinburg and the prisoners in the Ipatiev House. Three million gold dollars, machine guns and rifles, in exchange for the puppet Nichlachka is how Masaryk sees the business proposed to him by the American bankers." Careful to produce the desired effect Radek paused for breath before continuing in a low voice. "The American cargo ship Thomas, which is expected at Vladivostok in mid July, is due to land 14,000 rifles as well as doubtless embarking the Romanov family."'

Michael moved the bookmark back to page seventy-four. 'You have done well, Alex, in explaining how plans to rescue the Romanovs were being linked to the financial arrangements that were agreed at Brest-Litovsk. But whatever the Germans want they usually get. The Russians weren't in a position to negotiate. Many historians believe there was definitely a secret codicil to the Brest-Litovsk treaty. The Germans had control of most of the food and Russia was starving. Without Germany's help the Bolshevik revolution would have floundered.'

'Wait a moment. If the Russians should have paid three hundred million dollars to the Germans and instead only paid one hundred and sixty million, surely that confirms the Prince of Hesse-Darmstadt was successful and got the Royal Family safely out of Russia, otherwise Germany would have invaded the whole country.'

Michael shrugged his shoulders. 'It's a good point Tonya but it's one I can't answer.

'What is the *Hradshin*?' Juliana asked.

'It's a castle in Prague,' Alice replied before adding, 'Of course the Tsar and his wife must have had bank accounts all over the world. I presume the Empress had a bank account in Berlin, since she was a princess of the House of Hesse?'

'Well apparently they had many accounts,' Michael confirmed, picking up another book.

Alice smiled. 'I know there were deposits in his daughters' names at the Mendelssohn Bank.'

Michael tapped the book in his hand. 'Now listen to me! Quite by chance I have a wonderful surprise for you all. Gather round quickly! In this book are the most amazing photographs. I wanted to show you a particular....'

'STOP,' shouted Tonya, 'ISN'T THAT'S THE TSAR'S HANDWRITING?'

'Yes it is. But it's very faint and you'll need a magnifying glass to see it.'

'But don't you see? I can match his handwriting with that of the Fox letter. Remember, the one supposedly written by the Tsar, thanking Fox for his help. Just wait a moment while I go and get it.'

While she was gone Michael got up to fetch a magnifying glass and Juliana and Alice flipped through the pages of photographs.

'Gosh, look at this! A picture of the investigator Sokolov as he arrives in Russia and here, Olga all dressed up in a traditional mediaeval dress.' Giovanni leant over to take a closer look, paying special attention to Maria Romanov.

'Ooh la la! Bella!' he said, pointing at her photograph.

'Oh yes! The girls were beautiful,' Alice responded, 'and so charming. Oh I adore this one of Maria and Tatiana and here, and little Alexei playing with the spaniel.' Alice sat back in the chair and wiped her eyes dry.

Noticing she was upset Juliana leant over to comfort her. 'You met them I suppose?' she asked. Alice mumbled something but Juliana wasn't sure what. 'It must have been a great shock to you when they disappeared?'

Alice looked up and smiled. 'Not really. Everyone was disappearing and then reappearing again. It was a symptom of the times. Besides, we were quite sure they were safe. We knew people who said they had all escaped. Well, Maria did. But then, as time passed, we heard so many different stories. Some said they had been executed, found like so many other members of their family who had died inside Russia, in suspicious circumstances. In the end we did not know what to think. Many believe they escaped and most of the time I did too. But every now and again I get a horrible feeling that they might not have made it.'

Alice dabbed another tear from her eye as she spoke. 'It's so confusing. We met people who had seen them alive. They said they could not tell us where they lived for fear they would be discovered by the Reds. They were disguised, you see, and wanted their faithful followers to know that they had all escaped and were safe. Maria always said they would return to rule Russia when the people wanted them to. Well, we all thought that until the mess up occurred.'

'Mess up?' Juliana asked.

'Yes, the Bolsheviks managed to cling to power. After Kolchak's murder all plans for a revival of the White Army's fortune went astray. There was no one to lead them, you see, and as you have heard all the money, the gold, well it was all spent. Maria used to say all hope was lost after 1925 following that "'Trust" fiasco and the capture of ...' Alice's story was interrupted by the sound of running feet.

'I'VE GOT IT. Quick, let's check the handwriting.' An out of breath Tonya burst into the room with several books in her hand.

Paul laughed at her exuberance and Michael reached for the magnifying glass, examining the two signatures carefully. 'What do you think?' he asked, passing it over to Alice. She took the magnifying glass and peered at the signature. 'Well, the writing is similar but it is very difficult to tell if it belongs to the same hand. Good heavens! I have just noticed something. Look here, in the *Dear Fox* letter, he has signed himself as *Nicolas* not *Nicholas*!' Alice added pointing to the *h* that was missing.

'Now that *is* peculiar,' Michael agreed, stroking his chin. 'It can't be a spelling mistake surely? Do you know whether the Tsar signed his name in that way Alice?'

Alice shrugged. 'Perhaps it's the Russian way?'

'Well now, finding that little detail could give us a clue as to who may have written these letters in the first place.'

'Don't you mean "forged"?' Alice enquired.

Tonya laughed. 'Well, clearly the person can't spell, but does that make it a forgery?'

Alice threw her hands up in despair while Juliana continued to stare at the handwriting. 'Well I can't tell whether it is or it isn't. I suppose you have to consider the context in which it was found.'

Michael sighed. 'Never mind, it was worth having a look at. Now are there any other photographs of his handwriting in these books Tonya?'

'I don't know.'

'GOOD GRACIOUS!' Michael shouted, picking up the magnifying glass again and studying a photograph carefully. 'There's no mistaking those fine features. Juliana, remember that old photograph you showed me, the one with the diplomat dressed in the white suit, the one we thought was an American standing with the Cossack General Skoropadski in the Ukraine? Can you go and get it for me? Quickly! The GERMAN connection is about to be confirmed!' He shouted exuberantly, slapping Alex on the back.

A few moments later the door burst open as Juliana returned with the photograph.

Michael compared the two images. 'AH! HA! It's just as I expected. They are the same. This is Count Alvensleben, the famous German diplomat, with the *Hetman* of the Ukraine, General Skoropadski. This is the significant other that I have been searching for.' His eyes lit up as he spoke. 'Come and have a look. I give you the connection between Wilhelm II and Skoropadski: the German Kaiser's messenger, Count Alvensleben. So despite the bitter war raging across the land, Russia and Germany were negotiating in the Ukraine. But what for I wonder?'

Michael handed the book to Alice, who stared at the photograph.

Then, rather uncharacteristically, Giovanni showed some interest. 'You really think this is the same?' he asked, pointing to the two pictures of Count Alvensleben.

'Yes, clearly it is the same man. There can be absolutely no doubt it in my mind.'

Giovanni smiled. 'Si, no doubt as you say boss.'

'Well then, there is only one conclusion we can come to!' Alice exclaimed. 'The Kaiser must have helped the Tsar and his family to escape!'

'Of course, why are you so surprised?' Tonya asked. 'Isn't that what Fox said in his diary all along! And don't forget we have even heard about the Remington Arms company! Which reminds me, there can be no doubt that Sidney Reilly must have been involved with some plan to rescue the Romanovs because, as we know, he had very close business connections with this company too!'

Michael clapped his hands. 'Very good, I see you are all putting two and two together and coming up with four AT LAST!'

Alex flipped the gold rouble onto the table and watched it fall in front of Giovanni. 'Heads or tails?' he asked, grinning.

'I dunno?'

Alex picked up the coin. 'Come on Gio playa da game!'

Sensing his discomfort, Juliana stepped in. 'He wants you to get it wrong but you're too clever for that.'

'I no play stupendo, mio non stupendo!'

Alice sensed an awkward situation arising. 'Now come on you two, it must be time for tea.'

Giovanni smiled at the suggestion, all the while watching Alex continue to toss the coin in the air.

'Now you see it, now you don't!' He shouted childishly, throwing the coin ever higher into the air.

Then, as it fell, Giovanni lunged forward and grabbed it. 'WHERE IS IT FROM, EH?' He demanded, incandescent with rage.

Alex bubbled up with laughter again. 'Hey! What business is it of yours my little Gio amico eh?'

Giovanni threw the coin in a temper. 'Stupidaggine sospettare sorella..... sosp...!' He added, foaming at the mouth.

Alice tugged his arm. 'Tea, NOW PLEASE!'

Afterwards, Alex continued to giggle like a schoolboy. So wrapped up was he in his joke that he hadn't noticed his father staring at him in disbelief. Michael couldn't abide that type of arrogance from anyone. Let alone his son.

'You find it funny do you, mimicking his accent like that?'

Alex turned on his heels to see his father standing close by. 'No, I wasn't laughing at that!'

'Well what was so funny then?'

Alex shrugged and made a move towards the table.

'Perhaps you can tell me where you got the coin from?'

Alex started to gather his papers together. 'A friend gave it to me after I told him that I was researching our family history.'

'Gave it to you? Well he must have been a very good friend! Do you have any idea how much that is worth?'

'Well by the fuss you're all making I should think it must be worth at least a million!' Alex drew out the coin and bit it before placing it back in his pocket. 'Now, may I leave the room?'

Michael impatiently waved his son out. 'I don't know where he gets his ideas from!'

Juliana laughed out loud. 'You enjoy talking to yourself do you?' she asked as he admired her silhouette in the open doorway.

'Ah just the woman, this German connection of yours needs investigating further. What do you say to you doing a bit more research in that direction?'

As he spoke Juliana picked up the photos of Count Alvensleben and

General Skoropadski. 'You know, I really feel these two gentlemen are the key to us finding out the truth.' Michael walked over and gave her a big squeeze. 'In which case my dear, I'm sure any future discovery will be particularly revealing!'

PART FOUR

Mission Accomplished

Chapter Thirty Three   The File On The Tsar

'Do thou thy duty as thy forebears have done before thee'

After the incident with Alex, Michael took Giovanni under his wing, allocating him a special place in the library. Giovanni didn't want to give a presentation because his English wasn't good enough.

'Don't worry about that. Just get on with reading what you're interested in. The nearer you can get to the event, the nearer the truth you will find yourself,' Michael advised.

So, after finishing his chores he would go into the library and search Michael's extensive collection of early works on revolutionary Russia. Besides, it was peaceful in there and he could avoid Alex, who was behaving rather strangely towards him. Giovanni had no idea why. Perhaps it was something to do with the painting that he had given him; although he knew hiding away in the library was not the answer and that he would have to face him sooner or later.

That opportunity came when Alex caught him tending the roses the following morning.

'Ah there you are my old fruit. I haven't seen you for a while. How are you? Better I hope?'

'Si.' replied Giovanni avoiding his gaze and continuing with the gardening.

Alex noted his frosty reception. 'Look, about the other day. I am sorry. I was only playing. I had no idea that you would take it so seriously.'

Giovanni felt obliged to look up then. 'No problemo.' He added attempting a smile.

Alex patted him on the shoulders. 'So we are friends, yes?'

'Si, amico.'

'Good.' Alex replied admiring a droplet of water sitting on a rose petal. 'You wanted to know where the gold coin came from I believe.'

Giovanni shrugged. 'It means nothing to me.'

'In that case I shall definitely tell you!' Alex laughed. 'I was given it by a friend. You see, his father is a coin dealer in Rome. He knew I was researching the missing Russian gold and he lent it to me.'

'Benissimo!' Giovanni replied, carefully dead-heading another rose.

Alex frowned. 'You don't seem to be yourself these days. What's wrong?'

Giovanni didn't reply.

'Would you like me to do another painting for you?'

'No grazie!'

Alex kicked the soil twice while he thought of what else to say. 'I think it's going to be very hot today.'

Giovanni dropped the scissors so that he could tie up a drooping vine. 'Si maybe.' He spoke nonchalantly.

Alex got bored and patted him on the back. 'Well at least we are friends again,' he said, taking his leave.

'Amico?'

Alex turned around. 'Yes?'

'My Paulo and Tonya, How you say?... Amor?'

Alex smiled. 'Ding dong! Ding dong! Ding dong!! Ding dong!!' He sang, cheekily patting Giovanni on the back again.

'Why he no tell his father?'

Alex suddenly felt awkward and picked up the scissors, choosing to cut a red rose for his buttonhole. 'Don't worry. He's still a priest at heart. Anyone can see that.'

After lunch Alice and Juliana met Michael in the library to make a start on emptying the last of Maria's boxes. 'Remind me why we didn't empty this one before now?' Juliana asked, pulling out a silver candlestick and admiring the engraving on it.

'Probably because I didn't ask you to, No I'm only joking!' Michael added hastily. 'Now then Alice, don't forget to keep any newspapers you find, just in case.' Michael laughed at his own pun as he watched Alice hold up a huge iron sculpture of two Cossacks on horseback.

'Shall I put this over here for now? Then we can use this part of the table for emptying the boxes.'

'Good idea, but mind those books. I told Giovanni he should put them back on the shelf if he's not using them.'

While they chatted Juliana studied the candlestick. A small gull had been engraved on the side and she wondered whether it was part of a family coat of arms. She showed it to Michael but he didn't seem that interested, so she put it to one side and delved into the box. Towards the bottom she came across a large gold-coloured scrapbook.

'Look at this!' she called out. 'Some more family photos, I shouldn't wonder. Hey, perhaps we'll come across a young Maria.'

Michael glanced up. 'Oh, never mind that now. Put it down here, we can look at it later. Now! Is there anything else of value in that old tea chest?'

'Santa Maria!' Alice let out a blood-curdling scream.

'What is it?' asked Juliana.

'Look what I've found!' She added holding up a long ornate cream silk dress. It was beautifully embroidered with gold silken thread and hundreds of seed pearls. 'And look here, a head dress to match!'

'Gracious!' Michael exclaimed. 'Do you think it was Mother's wedding dress?'

'Maybe,' Alice replied.

Juliana held it up against her, even though her arms were aching with the weight. 'Oh I wish I'd got married in this. Hang on a moment. What's this?' Juliana picked at a hard lump sewn into the seam and then finding herself unable to release the object she laid the garment carefully on the table and pulled a grip from her hair, which she poked into the seam of the dress. 'Look, there's a stone in here.'

'Well I never! Look at the size of that!' An astonished Michael held the diamond between his index finger and thumb. A peculiar smile crept across his face. 'We should have opened this much earlier!'

'What's that?' Alice asked pointing at the dress. 'Is that another one?'

'Oh yes, look, there are so many.' Replied Juliana extracting a second and then a third diamond from a closed seam. A moment later all three sat back, completely flabbergasted. In front of them lay eight large diamonds of perfect proportion.

'Maybe we shouldn't have removed them?' Alice whispered.

'I don't see why not,' Michael replied, picking one up to examine it.

Alice gave an unhappy sigh, stood up and walked between the boxes. 'Because they've been in the dress a long time, it's bad luck.'

'Well, I'm not going to put them back if that's what you think!' Michael responded sharply as he wrapped them up carefully in his white handkerchief and deposited them in his safe. Juliana picked up the dress. 'It feels so dusty and it smells of ...sweet...no stale Lily of the Valley. We'd better send it to the cleaners.'

'Send it to the cleaners!' Alice repeated apparently in shock. 'I can hardly believe my ears. You certainly cannot. There are far too many exquisite pearls sewn onto it. It has never been cleaned nor must it be.'

'You're right of course,' agreed Juliana. 'Let's put it back in the box.'

'Now what do you think of these? Put them up for auction perhaps?' Michael suggested, placing two small icons on the table. 'Mother must have had so many. I wonder she could be bothered to keep them all. Now what else do we have here? Ah, three brass incense burners. Hmm! I like them very much. I think I'll hang this one over here in the corner under that large icon. What do you think Alice?'

Juliana laughed. 'If you're not careful Michael you'll turn this room into a Russian Orthodox Church!'

'Actually, I think that is rather the point!' Alice replied watching Michael pick up an amber broach. 'This is quite nice, but it's not your style, Juliana. Perhaps you would like it Alice?' Alice smiled. 'Why thank you, you know I shall always treasure it,' she added, fastening it to her dress.

'It's my pleasure! Now what else do we have here? Ah a silver cigarette case. Here you are my dear. I know how much you enjoy a cigarette. Would you like it?'

Juliana took the case. 'I most certainly would. It is so elegant and look, it even has an emerald clasp. I wonder how old it is.' She asked turning the case over to look for a hallmark.

'Don't worry, it is silver. I can assure you of that.'

Juliana opened the case and to her amazement found three musty old cigarettes. She smelt one and pulled a face, which made Alice laugh.

'I wouldn't smoke those if I were you. They are far too strong. Medijeh, I shouldn't wonder. Maria loved them.'

Juliana closed the case. 'So this was Maria's! Well, I shall treasure it. By the way, did you notice the intertwined initials in the lower corner? Perhaps you can make them out?' Juliana passed the cigarette case to Michael.

'I think that's just a pattern, nothing of consequence. Now, what else do we have in here? Ah! Look Alice, just what we need!' Michael held up a box of crimson red cubes and then unwrapped one. He took a deep sniff and closed his eyes. Alice raised an eyebrow as he handed her one to smell. 'Frankincense if I am not very much mistaken, and we know exactly what that will come in handy for.' Michael gave her a knowing smile and she returned his look.

'Well I'm sure this is very valuable too,' Juliana held up a large beaded necklace against herself. 'Amber the size of walnuts, imagine the weight if you had to wear that all night!'

Alice smiled and then noticed Michael was hovering over them. He looked very pleased with what he was holding. It was a glittering white enamel and gold cross.

'Now this is exactly what I expected to find! A Knight of St John's cross. The most important find of the afternoon.'

Juliana glanced up. 'Well that's far too large to wear on a chain, even for you!'

Michael laughed. 'You are right it would have to be worn on my lapel.'

'Actually, you should wear it on the left breast,' Alice replied 'Anyway, why did you say you were expecting to find it?'

Michael ignored her question in his eagerness to wear it. Juliana watched as he fumbled with the clasp, managing eventually to secure it. 'There!' he said. 'I think this calls for a celebratory drink, don't you?' He asked patting the cross.

A few moments later the glasses were set out on the table and Michael was pouring out the wine. 'Salute, it feels like Christmas!'

'Nastravia!' Alice replied in her best accent.

'I know, let's open the scrapbook,' Juliana suggested as she finished off her glass of wine.

'Yes, I don't see why not,' Michael agreed, before topping up their glasses.

Juliana drew the scrapbook towards her and opened it up carefully. Alice thought she recognised the writing on the inside cover, which was in a familiar Russian hand.

'Michael?' she asked. 'Can you put another light on?'

'I certainly will and while I'm about it, I'll light a few candles too. That will make it nice and cosy!'

'Are you able to tell us what it says?' Juliana asked, leaning over Alice's shoulder.

Alice muttered something before putting the book down on the table.

'I know! It's very heavy isn't it?'

'No. It's not that,' Alice replied, her face as white as a sheet.

Sensing a change in atmosphere, Michael sat down next to his wife while Alice took off her glasses and cleaned them before repositioning them. 'What is it Alice?' he asked impatiently.

'This reads *Statements of Denial on the Romanov Murders* and there is something else written here in large block letters. Just here, look.' Alice pointed out a word and then glanced up at Michael, who was clearly in shock. 'Now hold on a moment while I work out what this says.' Alice's finger trembled as she pointed to the words. '*He lies like an eye witness.*'

Michael gave a nervous cough as Alice stumbled over the words. 'That's a strange thing to write,' he responded uneasily.

'Yes.... Alice replied in a hushed tone. 'It's a very old Russian saying and it's a long time since I....' Alice stopped and took a gulp of wine then she turned the fragile pages slowly. 'Well! Well! Well! What have we here? Goodness gracious me! Maria has been busy!' Look, pages of newspaper articles and handwritten memos in English. But they are not in her hand and they run all the way from 1918 to...' Alice turned to the last page. 'Well I never!'

As she spoke Michael and Juliana peered over her shoulder.

'Ah! Ha! I recognise that writing,' he said, rubbing his hands together.

'Whose is it then?'

Michael tapped his glass with a pencil. 'If I'm not very much mistaken it belongs to Dr Karl Armgaard Graves. Now let's see what he has to say. Come on, make yourselves comfortable. I'll read it to you. Right, to start with, we have a cable sent to London dated October 5th 1918. Apparently it's from a Sir Charles Eliot and says:

'Mystery surrounds the fate of the Tsar, who is stated by the Bolsheviks to have been shot here on the night of the 16th of July and some of the highest and best informed officials cling to the belief that his imperial majesty was not *murdered but removed and placed in German custody, story of murder being invented to explain his disappearance. Officer Sergeyev, appointed by present government to investigate crime, showed me over the house where imperial family were confined and where his imperial majesty is supposed to have been shot. He dismissed as fabrications all stories respecting discovery of corpse, confessions of soldiers who had taken part in the murder, and on the other hand all narratives of persons who declared that they had seen the Emperor after 16th July...'*

Michael paused and poured out some more wine. He knew from experience how traumatic these documents could be to those old enough to remember. Even *his* hand was trembling. 'Are you quite ready for me to continue?' He asked out of concern for Alice, whose face was grey with anguish.

'Yes, I suppose you must.'

'Very well I'll begin.'

'The house was quite empty. On the wall opposite, the door and on the floor were the marks of seventeen bullets or, to be more accurate, marks showing where pieces of the wall and floor had been cut out in order to remove the bullet holes. The officials charged with the investigation having thought fit to take them away for examination elsewhere. They stated that Browning revolver bullets were found and that some of them were stained with blood. Otherwise no traces of blood were visible. The position of the bullets indicated that the victims had been shot when kneeling and that other shots had been fired into them when they had fallen on the floor. Mr Gibbs thought that for religious reasons the Tsar and Dr Botkin would be sure to kneel when facing death.

There is no real evidence as to who or how many the victims were but it is supposed that they were five, namely the Tsar, Dr Botkin, the Empress's maid and two lackeys. No corpses were discovered, nor any trace of them having been disposed of by burning or otherwise, but it was stated that a finger bearing a ring believed to have belonged to Dr Botkin was found in a well. On the 17th of July a train with the blinds down left Ekaterinburg for an unknown destination and it is believed that the surviving members of the imperial family were in it.'

When Michael paused to take a sip of wine, Juliana took the opportunity to say what was on her mind. 'It's as I said all along. They all escaped by train to Berlin!'

Michael nodded. 'Hmm! Part of the family may have escaped but it is unlikely they all did. But more to the point, I am reminded of what Fox said.'

Alice frowned. 'What was that?'

'Surely you remember?' Juliana exclaimed.

Michael smiled. 'Well you obviously do, so why not tell her?'

'You mean when the Baroness 'B' told Fox about the arranged shooting party at Ekaterinburg?'

Alice shivered. 'I must say it makes for very unpleasant listening. I feel quite ill!'

Michael put his glass down. 'Take courage, Alice. Searching for the truth is never a pleasant task. Now bear with me as I read out these numbered points to you.'

Michael adjusted his chair to get closer to the page. 'Lucky it is written in English, otherwise you'd have to do the honours of translation Alice!' Michael cleared his throat and Juliana noticed the candle flicker again.

'One, the marks in the room at Ekaterinburg prove at most, that some persons unknown were shot there and could even be explained as a result of a drunken brawl.

Two, there was an aeroplane flying low over the garden of the house several times backwards and forwards.

Three, soldiers were running everywhere with much activity.

Four, general opinion in Ekaterinburg that Empress, her son and four daughters, were dispatched on 17th July to the north or to the west.'

Michael squinted. 'I can't make out the rest of these points because the writing is so faded. I'll have to skip these.' Juliana was sure he could and that he was simply sparing Alice undue upset. She watched as he ran his finger quickly down the page. 'Ah, now this is more legible.

'At the bottom of the ashes was a diamond and as one of the grand duchesses is said to have sewn a diamond into the lining of her cloak it is supposed that the clothes of the imperial family were burnt here. Also hair, identified as

belonging to one of the grand duchesses, was found in the house. It therefore seems probable that the imperial family were disguised before their removal. At Ekaterinburg I did not hear even a rumour as to their fate but subsequent stories about the murder of various grand dukes and grand duchesses cannot but inspire apprehension.

I have the honour to be with the highest respect Sir,
Your most obedient humble servant
C. Eliot.'

Juliana stared at the cream dress lying on the floor and the candle flickered ominously again.

'Is there a draft in here?' Alice asked, pulling a shawl over her shoulders. Suddenly the candle spluttered its wax across the table and threatened to go out. Then, quite unexplainably, took on a new life. As the room grew noticeably brighter, Alice could clearly see the writing in the scrapbook.

'Have you heard of Charles Eliot before?' Juliana asked her husband.

'Yes. He was High Commissioner and Consul-General for Siberia and was asked by the British to investigate the mysterious goings on at the Ipatiev House because there were so many conflicting reports coming out about the Romanovs' whereabouts. Some said they were alive and others said the Tsar had been shot but Moscow remained quite silent on the subject. Ah that reminds me! When Sir Charles Eliot wrote of the mysterious train standing at Ekaterinburg station with its blinds down, he was probably referring to what we know as the *Varakushev Account*. Varakushev said he was at the Ipatiev House on the 17th July 1918. Now let me see if I can find exactly what he said, Michael added walking over to where Giovanni had been working.

A moment later he picked up *The File on the Tsar* and flicked through its pages. Eventually he found what he was looking for on page one hundred and thirty, which he noticed had been ear-marked by Giovanni. 'I'll read what it says here:

'*Alexander Varakushev was a former mechanic from St Petersburg and a guard at Ipatiev House. He also worked at the headquarters of the Red Army in Ekaterinburg. His friend, a conductor on the Omsk railway was a man called*

Samoilov. He testified in September 1918 and said that he was told by Alexander Varakushev that the Romanovs had been removed from Ekaterinburg alive.'

'Surely that's just hearsay? It can't be relied upon!' Juliana interrupted.

Alice agreed. 'You're right, we shouldn't rely on it.'

Michael sighed. 'Well it's as good as anything else we have and, more to the point it's an early recorded statement. So I'll read it if you don't mind? Here goes.

'I worked as a conductor on the Omsk railway. In June and July of this year I lived in Flat 2 at Vostochnaya Street, Ekaterinburg, in a wing together with a Red Army man, Alexander Semyenovich Varakushev. Varakushev served in a unit of the guard of the former Tsar Nicholas II. After the Bolshevik announcement that they had shot the former Tsar, having read about it in the newspaper, I asked Varakushev if it was true. He replied that the dog Goloshchokin was putting out these stories but in reality the former Tsar was alive. Then Varakushev told me that Nicholas and his wife were put in manacles and taken in a Red Cross motor car to Ekaterinburg station, where they were put in a railway carriage and sent off to Perm. As for the former Tsar's family, Varakushev stated that they were still in the Ipatiev House but said nothing was said about where they were going to be sent. During this conversation Varakushev suggested to me that if I wanted to see Nicholas at the station I could but on that day I did not go to the station. However a couple of days before the surrender of the city, I was at Ekaterinburg station to pick up wages and I met Varakushev there. He showed me a train of several first and second-class carriages standing on track 5 or 6, to which at the front was attached an engine with steam up. Beyond this train on the next track stood one first class carriage, the windows of which had been painted black or covered with black curtains. According to Varakushev, the former Tsar and his wife were in this carriage. The carriage was surrounded by heavily armed Red Army personnel. Varakushev told me that the carriage with the former Tsar was to go on the mining line. When and where this carriage was sent to I do not know and I did not see Varakushev anymore.

When the Czechs attacked, they (the Bolsheviks) sent us several units, first to Bogdanovitch station, then to Yegoshino, where meeting Commissar

Mrachkovsky I asked where Varakushev had gone and in general where all the former guards of Nicholas had gone. He replied that they had gone to Perm. From Yegoshino I went with other units by a roundabout route to the Alapayevsk factory, where there was talk about the former Tsar amongst my comrades. The Bolsheviks asserted that he had been killed. I asserted that he was alive, referring to Varakushev. For this I was reported to Mrachkovsky. He summoned me and ordered me to say nothing about it or I would be severely punished.'

Michael snapped the book shut. 'So there you have it, the source of Sir Charles's report to London!'

Alice had been flicking through Maria's scrapbook while he had been reading.

'I've come across a few interesting notes as well. This one is dated 16th October 1918 and it's a telegram to the Foreign Office from Consul Thomas Preston at Ekaterinburg. This is what it says:

On July sixteenth at a meeting of the Ural Provisional Government of soldiers and workman delegates it was decided to shoot the Tsar and this was communicated to him and sentence carried out same night by Lettish soldiers. No trace of the body however has ever been found. The rest of the members of the imperial family were taken away to an unknown destination.'

'Now at the bottom of the page and underlined is another entry which is dated December 1918. It reads: *I do not believe that all the people, the Tsar, his family and those with them were shot there.* It is signed by Judge Sergeyev who, you will recall, was appointed by the Whites to investigate the disappearance of the Romanovs.'

Alice turned the page. 'This is from the daily papers of 1918 and 1919. Underneath Maria has glued various newspaper cuttings to the page.' Alice fell silent for a moment as she read the first few lines. Presently she looked up. 'Well now, there can be no doubting Maria's intention here.' Alice spoke in hushed tones as Juliana and Michael leant across to get a better view.

'Warsaw December 16 1918.
The mother of former Emperor, who is living near Livadia in the Crimea, has

been receiving letters every ten days purported to come from the former ruler, according to Polish officers who have arrived here from Sebastopol.

++++++++

'Warsaw December 24 1918.
"There is no doubt that the Czar and his entire family are alive. I am positive of this." Was the declaration made to the correspondent today by Michael Chikhachev, a nephew of General Skoropadski, who has just escaped from the Ukraine after a recent trip to Petrograd, Dvinsk, Vilna and Rovna. "I cannot reveal where the Czar is because he does not wish it,'" he added.

++++++++

'London January 8th 1919. (British Wireless Service)
According to a story sent by a special correspondent of the Morning Post at Archangel which it is necessary to treat with reserve, the former Emperor of Russia is still alive. The correspondent telegraphs: "A friend of mine, Prince M-, who has just arrived here from Petrograd, informed me that he had a long talk with Grand Duke Cyril on November 18. The Grand Duke told him that he had just received a letter from Grand Duchess Tatiana, daughter of the Emperor, who wrote that the Empress and her daughters were still alive and that the Emperor had not been shot.'"

++++++++

'That's amazing!' Juliana cried. 'Fox was right all along!'

Michael laughed. 'That's a conclusion you can jump to if you want, but life is rarely as simple as that! Is there more Alice?'

Alice was so engrossed with what she was reading that she didn't hear him. Juliana prodded her gently.

'GOOD GRACIOUS!' Alice blurted out then hurriedly polished her glasses. 'Listen to this:

14 March 1919. Rome. Italy.

According to an interview with Stephania Turr, a daughter of a noted Hungarian general, printed today in the Giornale d' Italia, the belief still exists that Emperor Nicholas and his wife, as well as some of the Russian Grand Dukes, were not put to death by the Bolsheviki. The interview quotes a conversation between Miss Turr and Prince Obolensky, a former Captain of the Russian Imperial Guard, in which the Prince expressed his firm belief that the Russian royal family is still alive. He is reported to have refused to give details as to the basis for his beliefs except that the former Emperor and Empress were perhaps hidden in Northern Russia.'

++++++++

After she had finished reading she noticed the look of amazement on Michael's face.

'I can't believe that Warsaw article actually mentions Skoropadski's nephew! What a coincidence.'

Juliana agreed as she reached for the wine. 'It's quite uncanny how only the other day we were talking about Skoropadski and discussing his possible involvement with the rescue operation and here we find his nephew confirming that they were all saved! Is this the proof we've been looking for?'

'We must try not to jump to conclusions tempting as it is. You see the way this information has been put together is very one sided.'

'Maybe, but it's all we have to go on Michael!'

'That's true if we are just relying on what Mother says. But luckily I have someone else's testimony and I think you'll find this far more reliable. Forget Varakushev! If you really want to know what happened,' Michael added, picking up *The File on the Tsar*, 'listen to this account of one of the few men who actually guarded the Imperial Family. His name is Medvedev and this is what he is reported as saying.....'

'Well why should we believe this Medvedev chap any more than anyone else?' Juliana interrupted.

'Because,' Michael responded, 'he was the ONLY eyewitness who said he saw the bodies being carried out of the house.'

Alice winced and put her hands over her ears. 'I really DON'T want to hear this.'

Michael ignored her and started to read:

'On sixteenth of July 1918 towards seven o'clock in the evening, the commandant Yurovsky ordered, him Medvedev to collect the revolvers from all the guards who were on duty around the house. There were twelve revolvers in all, all of them of the Nagant type. Having collected the revolvers he delivered them to the commandant Yurovsky at the office in the house and put them on the table. Earlier that day, in the morning, Yurovsky had given instructions for the boy who was the waiter's nephew to be taken from the house to the guards' quarters next door, the Popov house. Yurovsky did not give him any reason for all this, but shortly after he had delivered the revolvers to Yurovsky, the latter said to him: "Today Medvedev, we are going to shoot the whole household" and ordered him to warn the guards on duty that if they heard shots they were not to be alarmed.'

When Michael paused to draw breath, Alice took the chance to stretch her legs. She walked slowly across the room towards the window. Michael watched her with concern and was about to ask if she wanted to leave when Juliana spoke. 'This sounds exactly like Fox's report! In fact, if I didn't know better I'd think you were reading straight from the account in *Rescuing the Czar*!' Michael agreed. 'I know it's uncanny. But this is what he says next:

He suggested that he should warn the sentries about this at about ten o'clock in the evening. At the appointed time, he Medvedev, warned the guards about this and then went back into the house. At about 12 midnight, Commandant Yurovsky started to wake up the imperial family. Nicholas II himself, all his family and also the doctor and servants got up, dressed, washed and about an hour later all eleven people left their rooms. They all looked calm as if they did not suspect the slightest danger.

Alice turned from the window. 'I'm sorry I just can't hear anymore,' she said. So if you don't mind I'll see you both later.' Michael pursed his lips as she hurriedly left. 'Are you sure you still want to listen to this?' he asked.

Juliana smiled. 'Of course, how many hours did I have to spend listening to your mother speak of the horrors of the Revolution? Anyway, I bet I've heard it all before! Besides, we have to remember that for Alice it's quite a different matter. She was so much closer to it than us.'

Michael smiled. 'Well, I'll continue then. Now remember, this is the ONLY eyewitness account so what he says is important.

From the upper story of the house they came down the stairs leading from the outside. Nicholas II himself carried his son Alexei in his arms. When they were downstairs they entered the room at the end of the main part of the house. Several had brought a pillow with them and the maid was carrying two pillows. The Commandant Yurovsky ordered chairs to be brought in. Three chairs were brought. By this time two members of the Cheka had arrived at the House of Special Purpose; one of them, as he found out later was Yermakov (he didn't know his first name) from Verkh-Isetsk Plant and the other was a complete stranger to him. The first of these, Yermakov, was small, dark, looked about thirty, clean shaven, with a black moustache. The other was tall, blond and looked about twenty-five or twenty-six. Commandant Yurovsky, his assistant and these two people came downstairs where the family was already.

Of the guards downstairs in the room where the imperial family was, seven were Letts; and the other three Letts were also downstairs but in a special room. The revolvers had already been distributed by Yurovsky to the seven Letts in the room, to the two Cheka members, to his assistant, and to Yurovsky himself. In all eleven revolvers were given out and Yurovsky allowed him, Medvedev, to take one revolver back. Besides this, Yurovsky had a Mauser revolver. Thus there were twenty-two people gathered together in the room downstairs, eleven who were to be shot, and eleven men with weapons, all of whom he had summoned.'

'Twenty-two people in one room? That seems an awful lot,' Juliana interrupted.

Michael shrugged and took a gulp of wine before continuing.

'Seated on the chairs in the room were the wife of Nicholas II, Nicholas II himself, and his son. The others remained standing by the wall. All were calm. A few minutes later Yurovsky came out to him, Medvedev, in the adjoining room and said to him: "Go outside Medvedev and see if there are any unauthorised

people about and listen whether the shots can be heard or not. He Medvedev, went out to the other side of the fence, immediately heard gunshots, and went back into the house to tell Yurovsky that the shots could be heard. When he entered the room where the imperial family was, they had all been shot already and were lying on the ground in various positions; beside them was a mass of blood, which was thick like liver.'

'Oh God, stop Michael it is disgusting! I can't listen to it any more either. Really, I can't!' Juliana hurried out of the room leaving Michael to read the final paragraphs on his own.

With the exception of the Tsar's son Alexei, all seemed to be already dead. Alexei was still moaning. In his Medvedev's presence, Yurovsky shot Alexei two or three more times with the Nagant and then he stopped moaning. The appearance of the victims so affected him Medvedev, that he began to feel sick and left the room. Yurovsky then ordered him to run over to the guard post and tell them not to be worried if they had heard shots.

As he went over to the post, two more shots came from the house, and he met the corporal of the guard, Ivan Starkov and Konstantin Dobrynin running across from the guard post. Meeting him in the road near the house, these two said: "You will have to be able to say that they have really shot Nicholas II and not someone else in his place. You saw him often enough." At this, he told them that he had personally seen only too well that they had been shot, that is Nicholas II and his family, and he told them to go to the guard post and calm the guards so that they would not get excited. Thus he, Medvedev, saw that the following people had been shot: the former Emperor Nicholas II, his wife Alexandra Feodorovna, his son Alexei, his daughters Tatiana, Anastasia, Olga, and Xenia (sic), Dr Botkin, and the servants, the cook, the waiter, and the maid.

So! Michael thought to himself. Medvedev confirms he saw them all shot yet he calls Maria by another name altogether, Xenia! He didn't recall his mother ever referring to the Tsar's daughter Maria, as Xenia! Perhaps it was a middle name or was Medvedev just not familiar with the names of the Imperial Family? In which case how could he be so sure they had all been shot? Michael carried on reading.

Each had several bullet wounds in various parts of their bodies. The faces of all of them were covered in blood and the clothing of all of them was also bloody. The dead persons apparently were unaware of the danger threatening them until the very last moment of the shooting. He himself, Medvedev, did not take part in the shooting. When he, Medvedev, came back to Yurovsky in the room, Yurovsky ordered him to bring several men from the guard to carry the corpses of the victims to a motorcar. He called up more than ten men from the guard, but does not recall exactly whom. Stretchers were made from the shafts of the two sledges standing in the courtyard under the shed. Sheets were tied to them with cord, and thus all the corpses were carried to the automobile. They took from all the members of the imperial family, whoever had them, rings, bracelets, along with two gold watches. These were handed over at once to Commandant Yurovsky. He does not know how many rings or bracelets were taken from the dead persons. Then all eleven corpses were taken from the courtyard to the motorcar. The vehicle in which the corpses were placed was a special truck which had been brought to the courtyard in the evening. Two members of the Cheka went off in the vehicle with the bodies, one of them being Yermakov, and the other man described earlier whom he did not know. The driver of the vehicle, it appears, was surnamed Lyukhanov, a man of average height, stocky, looked rather over 30 with a spotty face. The corpses of the victims were placed in the vehicle on a grey army cloth and were covered up with the same cloth. The cloth was taken from the place in the house where it had been kept in one piece. He, Medvedev, does not know for sure where the bodies were taken and at that time asked nobody about it. After the corpses had been taken from the house, Commandant Yurovsky ordered the guard to be summoned to wash the floor in the room where the shooting had taken place, and also to wash the blood on the wall of the house, at the main entrance in the courtyard, and where the vehicle had stood. This order was then carried out by those who made up the guard. When all this had been done, Yurovsky left the courtyard and went to the office in the house. He, Medvedev went off to the Popov House, where the guard's quarters were, and did not leave the quarters until morning.

Michael lay the book down on the table and sighed. He had read this testimony before and was quite familiar with it. He wondered why he had bothered to read it again, since neither Juliana nor Alice could bear to hear another word.

Well, he couldn't blame them. A most unpleasant affair, but this reading had revealed a possible error in the witness statement.

He remembered that Medvedev had unexpectedly died of typhus shortly after giving testimony in March 1919. Crucially, he had died before Sokolov, who was the second investigator, could interview him. But what of those who said they saw the family shot? Were their statements reliable?

As early as October 1918, Judge Sergeyev, head of the first investigation, had questioned a former guard. He was Mikhail Letemin. Michael turned to *The File on the Tsar* to check his facts. It was exactly as he thought. Letemin was not an eyewitness but explained that he had been told of the murders when he came on duty the next morning. His informant was Andrei Strekotin, who claimed he had seen the family led into the basement and shot while he was on guard between midnight and four o'clock in the morning. Letemin said he had queried the story, pointing out there ought to be a large number of bullet holes in the room, which there were not!

Strekotin replied "Why so many? The tsarina's maid hid behind a pillow and lots of the bullets went into the pillow." Letemin also suggested that there should be a great deal of blood but was told it had been cleaned up during the night.

Michael checked the time. It was just coming up to five o'clock, yet he felt really tired. It must be that red wine he thought, closing the book and placing it back on the table. Then he yawned even louder and walked across to his favourite chair. Dragging a blanket over himself, he settled into the chair and fell asleep.

A few moments later he was dreaming........ Through a hazy mist, a roaring bear rushed towards him. He heard himself say 'RUSSIA is rushing!' He was falling. Then someone shouted from out of the mist. It was that unmistakable high-pitched voice he had been reading about. A squeaky, demanding voice: 'Time is of the essence, do you HEAR me? Operation OBIV.. LION...' The words faded as Michael stood to attention along with several others.

'You have your instructions for the Moscow plan?'

They all said yes. Someone stepped forward and saluted.

'Eagle, you will take your orders from the Ukraine bear. NOTHING IS TO GO AMISS, AM I UNDERSTOOD? Secure all transport routes and food stocks without delay.'

'Fox, you have your orders. The state valuables are to be delivered to me. All of them!

Gentlemen! Baroness, the future of the civilised world rests in your hands. Good luck and goodbye!'

Chapter Thirty Four   Fox's Rescue Mission

Later that evening Juliana knocked on the library door. Getting no reply, she entered to find Michael still fast asleep in the chair. Repositioning the blanket that had fallen off him she picked up the book he'd been reading and made her way over to the table where a light was still on. She also had with her a copy of the book *Rescuing the Czar*. She wanted to compare Fox's account of the rescue with what she had heard already, so turning to the bottom of page thirty-five she began to read from it.

Alice will give up her wheel chair when the NUN gives the word ...she is worrying about my prisoner's sister, Olga, and her two companions, who insist on offering their services to the poor in the Crimea ... and well she may!... Facing the East they are likely to travel south! I must get rid of this old valet, Parafine Domino, who makes a nuisance of himself, hovering around my prisoner like a hawk. Gallipoli says he'll get rid of Alice's physician before the TENTS arrive, substituting a fake doctor from the Red Guard, who'll tell me when the prisoners are fit to travel. As "Captain" of this Soviet Guard I am as cold-blooded as Gallipoli before the spies and hangers-on. Captain! That title seems to stump the old Russian soldiers, they claim that there is no such animal. The Sergeant has suggested that I put the prisoners under a SMALL GUARD when we take them to the Ural District Soviet Court of Workmen. Nice trap to catch me.

If I agreed to this I'd be in the same category as Denikin or Dutov or Ekhart and be shot by the gang outside by mistake, so as to fulfil the prophecy of my lady of Buckingham. My answer was to order the guard on the balcony to keep their guns pointed at the prisoners whenever they appear in the garden. This will satisfy the eavesdropper in the red brick across the way and scare the wits out of old Parafine besides giving him something to talk about when we get away.... To satisfy that suspicious Sergeant that there is no Japanese money secreted by the prisoners I have ordered my men to use their bayonets against the walls and ceilings ... even the frame of the bathroom is not to escape!... Gallipoli is growling around that I'm doing my work too damned well to seem reasonable! The poor boob! His idea of being reasonable seems to consist in spreading rumours that the prisoners have been disposed of in a dozen different ways.

When Maria and Tatiana mounted the truck in the yard this confiding swaggerer started the gossip that they were being loaded up to be taken out of town and shot. Now I am told by some of the excited guard that that report is TRUE because they heard someone in the attic of the red brick yelling: "The baggage is at the station!" When I asked them what we wanted with "BAGGAGE" they went away growling that I wasn't playing fair! To my sombre-robed lady of Buckingham, who seems to have deserted me as well as the slender guard at the Huis ten Bosch, as well as those at the Wilhelmstrasse and Odessa who are part of this "BAGGAGE," my guard's agitation will assume the humorous character of unconscious prophecy. Suspicion is in the air! This undisciplined gang of cut throats under that half-baked Sergeant are demanding HOSTAGES from me for my conduct of this business; they want the Grand Duchess Olga, her two companions, and FIFTY other women!

AT LAST! The planes are buzzing in the sky. The icon of holy Nicholas is being wrapped up. The NUN has copies of the letters to Oldenburg and Gendrikov. It's time to say to my prisoner: "Come with ME to the U.D.S. of W.A.R.A.D." If he has the code from Odessa he will ask: "Are you taking me to be shot? RUN MOBS."
I'll have the guard go through his pockets to find the letters that'll turn him over to my vengeance; then for Ekhart's tunnel and OBLIVION!

Half an hour later, Michael grunted in his sleep. Oh, I do hope he doesn't start snoring Juliana thought, before noticing the blanket had slipped off again. She got up, rearranged it and after making sure he was comfortable, picked up where she had left off. Tsar Nicholas was explaining to Fox what effect his "arranged" disappearance would have on the world.

''It is understood already in certain chancelleries how my execution will be publicly accounted for. Each Ministry will appoint a Commission suggested by the Crown to investigate and publish its own report. The report published will be given out under the name of a Naval or Military Commission to impart an official sanction to the supposed inquiry and support the authenticity of the document agreed upon. Naturally these prearranged reports will vary so as to satisfy the state of mind in each particular country."

"If regicides are so easily arranged," I observed cautiously, 'perhaps the duration of this 'Revolution' is also definitely determined?"

"There'll be a period of revolution and distress," my prisoner remarked, "before our country settles down to industry and contentment. But the desire of 'self-determination' will mislead the unfortunate and cause them to embrace a tyranny of the most cruel and selfish type. This will last for a time until gluttony destroys itself as all excesses do."

Juliana paused and rested the book on her lap. Is this really Tsar Nicholas II speaking to Fox, she wondered. Well his description of the Ipatiev House sounded accurate so he must have been inside it and in any case Juliana was sure that his diary would have been published long before any photographs of the Ipatiev House had been circulated. Suddenly Michael stirred and she turned to see if he was awake. His eyes were closed. Good he should sleep!

'LIONS' Michael suddenly shouted, making her jump. Juliana put the book down. 'Michael! Wake up, you're dreaming! Michael?'

'No! No! NO! Ah Hahahaha! Madame... comment appellez-vous?'

'Come on Michael, wake up!' Juliana shook him and he opened his eyes. She waited for him to get his bearings.

'I wasn't snoring was I?'

'No, you were shouting though, something about lions.'

Michael growled, laughed and then stretched before checking the time. 'Did I say anything else?'

'Not that I heard. Were you playing rugby?'

Michael frowned, 'No, that wasn't it. Ah, now I remember! It was something to do with what we were reading. That's it. The Kaiser spoke to me in that squeaky voice of his and well, it was very strange! He was giving me orders bold as brass. Can you believe it?' He folded up the blanket neatly and laid it on top of a stool by the fire.

'Anyway, what have you been up to while I've been napping, apart from keeping an eye on me that is?'

'I've been reading! I thought I'd compare Medvedev's story with what was written by Fox in *Rescuing the Czar*.'

'And?'

'Well, as I keep saying, I think Fox is telling the truth. There are so many verifiable facts. Why, only this afternoon, I came across one in *Hunt for the Czar*.

'Go on,' Michael encouraged, signalling for Juliana to sit opposite him.

'Well as you know, a good part of Guy's book is taken up with analysing the content of *Rescuing the Czar,* so I was paying particular attention to what I was reading. As I was going through it I came across an interesting conversation which took place between a Mr Wilton and a Mr Lasies at Ekaterinburg station in 1918.'

Michael slapped his knee. 'I know all about him. He was a well respected journalist who promoted the story that the Tsar and his family had been shot at the house.'

'Promoted? You make it sound as if he was purposely spreading propaganda.'

Michael smiled. 'Do you know what I find so fascinating about Fox?'

'No.'

'All the so-called "coincidences" that bring the story to life and make it so believable and now here you are mentioning a conversation between Lasies and Wilton. A story you've casually picked up in a book by Guy Richards. I presume you are about to say that Mr Aughinbaugh also mentions Mr Lasies in his introduction to *Rescuing the Czar*? Therefore the particular story that you're about to tell me must be true! The problem is what appears to be a coincidence in your eyes could be a contrived plot!'

'Yes alright Michael. You have your opinion but whether you like it or not, I do believe Fox and this is why. Let me first read the paragraph that refers to Lasies in the introduction of *Rescuing the Czar*.

'On April 5th 1920, the Universal Service carried a cable from Paris reading, "Czar Nicholas and all the members of the Imperial family of Russia are still alive, according to Mr Lasies, a former member of the Chamber of Deputies,

who has just returned from a mission to Russia." This was several weeks after the manuscript of the following account of the Czar's escape was in my possession (Mr Aughinbaugh). Yet this confirmation of the manuscript has not sufficiently overcome the universally persistent doubt that has grown out of many previous imposing reports.'

Juliana looked up to see Michael helping himself to a glass of wine.
'Michael, you haven't been listening!'
'Of course I have. Would you like a glass?'
Juliana shook her head. 'Not now! Look Michael, Mr Aughinbaugh is confirming that due to all these other reports, presumably from the likes of Wilton, that he feels it is important to draw our attention to the fact that Lasies insists the family is alive and he hopes that this will encourage the American public to read Fox's diary.'
Michael yawned. 'Yes, yes! So what's your point?'
'Well, in *Hunt for the Czar*,' Juliana turned to page one hundred and thirty, 'Guy says this: "There is however no further reference to Lasies in Rescuing's 269 pages. The Frenchman arrives and departs in the same paragraph like a porpoise jumping through the surface of history only to plunge once more out of sight."
Michael laughed. 'Rather like someone else I know. Carry on!'
Juliana stared at her husband. He was obviously enjoying the wine!
'Right Michael, here is what Guy concludes:

'Dr Aughinbaugh would never have let Lasies disappear if he had known as much about him as we do now. This stubborn, enquiring soldier-politician from the French provinces is an important figure in the assassination controversy. Joseph Lasies was a wit, a politician, a newspaperman, a cavalry officer and gifted public speaker. He was drawn into the Romanov controversy quite by accident. He made a long study of it at the Ipatiev House and elsewhere and then he ran into another journalist, an Englishman, who had done the same. The force of their impact was felt strongly among Lasies' French readers. Lasies, aged fifty-two, was on the editorial staff of the Paris daily newspaper Le Matin. After the war he was assigned to Ekaterinburg as commander of a cavalry squadron.

Lasies made his first visit to Ipatiev on May 11th 1919. A week later this important incident occurred. The place was the platform of the Ekaterinburg railroad station. The date was May 18th 1919 and the Englishman in question was Robert Wilton, correspondent of The London Times. His stories from Ekaterinburg were to gain a large audience in English language newspapers. The dispatches of Joseph Lasies, correspondent of Le Matin, garnered a similar large French readership.

Here is what happened. Lasies and Commander Bolifraud, a member of the French Military mission at Ekaterinburg, were talking on the station platform. Wilton joined them. The Romanov mystery soon became the subject of their conversation. Lasies expressed his many mental reservations about the claimed effects of the inferno that supposedly caused so many cadavers (those of the Romanovs and their aides) to vanish into thin air.

At this point Wilton remarked, "I shall have a clear mind about it. Wait for me a few minutes and I shall return." He walked off and didn't come back for about half an hour. Returning, he was barely within earshot when he called out, "I have the explanation!" When he rejoined the other two on the platform he said, "Here is what happened. The victims were burned with eleven carboys of sulphuric acid." There followed, according to the Frenchman, a discussion of the acid and its chemical properties, with Lasies questioning Wilton about the amount, the supplier, the containers etc.

Then after a moment of reflection, Lasies remarked, "My dear Wilton, only English sulphuric acid diplomatically prepared can produce magic effects. Moreover, your magistrate instructor (at Ipatiev House) had discussed with us the matter for more than two hours and he did not speak to us at any time of sulphuric acid!"

Then Wilton lost patience. Addressing Lasies in a tone that both Frenchman stated they long remembered, he said, "Commander Lasies, even if the Czar and the Imperial Family are living, it is necessary to say that they are dead!" At the conclusion of this exchange of thoughts at Ekaterinburg, Mr Wilton's parting words were, "I am going to do articles in The Times, to affirm the death of the Czar and of his family."

"Go to it Wilton," says Lasies.

"I shall do some articles in Le Matin to say that you know nothing about it. Nor do I." Both men lived up to their promise. Each wrote articles and a book to back up his contention. Wilton's remarks on the station platform at Ekaterinburg have been used over the years by the anti-assassins to reinforce their theory that British Foreign Office policy embraced the massacre version as a cover to be followed devoutly regardless of the facts.

Almost a year later Lasies found himself unable to resist the temptation to expand the scope of his witticism about British diplomatic acid. The occasion was April 22nd 1920.

Havas: Dispatch from New York quoted reports that the Imperial Family were safe in England. Lasies concluded that British Government censors no longer had any objections to a Romanov resurrection. He was now convinced that the Whitehall brand of sulphuric acid was even more miraculous that he had given it credit for. "It not only burns like any other acid and causes bodies to vanish into thin air but it can restore them on command." The views that Lasies conveyed to Wilton were not frivolous afterthoughts to a bit of light conversation. He had done a lot of legwork on the case.'

'He had reached his conclusions slowly and carefully. It is worth noting that Mr Wilton's articles and book were instrumental in the English speaking world's readiness to believe in the Romanov assassination. When Lasies first visited the Ipatiev House the magistrate instructor gave him what was then the orthodox briefing on the last hours of the Romanovs, including the massacre in the basement, the burning of the bodies near the mine pit etc and though he had an open mind on the subject, his first reactions were: "I remained sceptical about the facts such as they were related to me."

Revision of his scepticism towards outright disbelief began in conversations with Bolifraud, who had arrived in Ekaterinburg four months before Lasies. Bolifraud's disbelief had sprung, in turn, from conversations with a Russian general who had arrived long before Bolifraud, a general who had come to Ekaterinburg with the Reds and converted to the Whites when the Reds left. In his published letter Bolifraud covered all this.

'I was especially shaken following a conversation with General Bogoskovski at the Headquarters. General Bogoskovski had been in the service of the Bolsheviks since the coup d'etat of November 1917 and had held an important post in the war school of Petrograd. He had been transferred to Ekaterinburg by order of the Bolsheviks at the time of the German advance in March 1918. General Bogoskovski thus was there at Ekaterinburg carrying on official functions, when the Romanov drama was fulfilled. Upon recapture of the city he took up service with the Czechs and became afterwards Chief of Headquarters of the Army of Siberia, which was commanded by General Gaida. I saw General Bogoskovski daily, and each time that I tried to open a conversation on the fate of the Imperial Family he obstinately resisted all attempts at confidence. But one day, returning with him from the front, in the course of lunch that we took together in the train between Glosov and Perm, my having insisted again, General Bogoskovski, after a few moments of hesitation almost whispered to me: "I am convinced that His Majesty the Czar Nicholas is alive, as well as his whole family." Since then my doubts have only increased about the drama of Ekaterinburg. General Bogoskovski, in his official position with the Bolsheviks, was probably aware of many of their secrets. Lasies endorsed his friend's scepticism, but it was from two other Russian officers, first a lieutenant, and then a colonel, that Lasies gained persuasive intelligence that all the Romonovs had escaped and were alive and well, just a few weeks prior to Lasie's arrival in Siberia.'

'On May 12th 1919, the day after his first visit to Ipatiev House, Lasies made a trip to General Pepelaev's headquarters at Berechagino. He talked with a lieutenant whom he refuses to name for security reasons. He calls him Lieutenant X. The lieutenant spoke French well and remarked, "You doubt the reported fate of the Imperial Family? Perhaps you are right, for I in particular, have serious reasons to believe in their survival." The lieutenant read Lasies two letters from a member of his family, whom, he said, was an important functionary in the imperial regime. One of these passages he translated and dictated as Lasies made notes.'

'Let me see,' Michael demanded, just as Juliana finished reading the sentence.

She handed him the book and then poured herself a glass of wine.

'Guy Richards has certainly done his homework. I'm most impressed. But I see much of his quest is taken up with looking for the Tsar's son and there lays the rub. If he really believed the Tsar had lived he would have done far more to find him!'

Juliana sighed. 'Yes, I know Michael, but that's not the point I'm trying to get to! Why don't you look at the letter on the next page?'

Michael frowned. 'What am I supposed to be looking at? OH MY GOD, I see what you mean!'

Juliana smiled. 'Please read it out while I enjoy my wine.'

Michael cleared his throat.

'**April 1919**

The Emperor is here! How to understand it? I think that you will understand it as we have understood it ourselves. If that is confirmed, the festival of Christ (Easter) will be for us all bright and infinitely joyful.

Lieutenant X showed Lasies another letter from the same source, written a few days after the first. It read:

These last days we have received confirmation on the subject of the health of those of whom we love, may God be praised!

'The lieutenant referred Lasies to a colonel in Perm who had gotten the same kind of information by mail. Passing through Perm Lasies looked him up and was told by him that he had indeed received similar advices from those who ought to know. Lasies appeals to the readers' intelligence to understand why he is concealing the identity of the two officers and why he has not included in his book a copy of the photograph of Lieutenant X that the officer had presented to him as a memento of their meeting.

Armed with a supply of tough questions to fire at the magistrate-instructor at the Ipatiev house, Lasies asked General Janin for permission to make a second visit. Janin passed on the request to General Gaida, who approved. Lasies arrived for his second inspection of the mansion on May 15th 1919. This time not only was the magistrate-instructor present but several of the persons, including the residence's wealthy merchant owner N.N. Ipatiev and his wife.

Point by point, Lasies reports he went over the official story of the Imperial Family's last day on the premises and listened to the magistrate-instructor, "who no longer believed with either his eyes or his ears". Then he wrote an entry in his diary:

Imperial Family has not been assassinated here, not as it has been told to us. At the very most, the Czar alone had been executed.

By the time Lasie's book was published, he had made it very clear that he had information that none of the Romanovs had been killed. Several documents about the Romanov case have spilled out of classified files into the National Archives. A State Department spokesman said they never had a Romanov file and therefore couldn't be hiding it. The facts are in conflict with this statement. There are two documents in the National Archives that bear heavily on the Romanov case. Both originated in the State Department. One clearly refers to "the Romanov File" and the other has blurred inked inscription that could be the same thing. Both have been initialized by a number of officials in the State. One bears the stamp and scrawl of an otherwise indecipherable "Chief Special Agent". The first set of documents are stapled under a message from **Rome, dated December 7th 1918 and addressed to the Secretary of State, Washington**

For your confidential information,

I learned that in the highest quarters here it is believed that the Czar and his family are all alive.

Paris informed.

Nelson Page.

'Attached to this telegram are a number of other messages querying other embassies about this report in the name of The Division of Near Eastern Affairs. They are all splotched, pockmarked, and griddled with signatures. On the upper right hand corner of the first sheet is a notice to the effect that the papers were declassified (and consequently sent to the National Archives) by authority of a letter of 1.8.58 from W.H. Anderson, State Department.'

Michael rested the book on his knee and looked up. 'I have to take my hat off to you. You've certainly done your homework.'

Juliana smiled. 'Yes, well I'm not finished yet. Remember Alex mentioned General Janin when we were talking about how Kolchak lost the Tsar's gold?'

Michael nodded.

'Well, Guy Richards lists all the discrepancies between the testimonies given by the guards and guess what? They hardly agree. In fact they disagree on the last words spoken before the shooting started and they disagree on the time of night it took place, varying from midnight to dawn. Two accounts say chairs were brought for members of the party, whilst another states specifically that everyone was shot standing up. Sometimes the testimony is so contradictory that one wonders whether the speakers were there at all, or whether they actually said what has been written into their statements.'

Michael laughed. 'Well I don't think we are going to solve this mystery, my dear. At the end of the day I'm only interested in one thing.'

Juliana looked up. 'Oh?'

'Yes, the real name of my mother and father.'

'But don't you see Michael, that's why we are doing the research! Look, I've nearly finished. Just listen to how different the various testimonies are. For example, there's the maid Demidova. She is described by Proskuryakov as about forty, tall thin and dark, but Yakimov describes the same woman as stout, blonde and aged thirty to thirty-five. Surely you don't need a photographic memory to remember the only maid you saw daily over a period of weeks! This primary evidence leads me to only one conclusion. They didn't really know what they were talking about and ....' Juliana paused as Michael opened the window for some fresh air. 'You do realise,' he interrupted, 'you're falling into the same trap as the investigator Sokolov?'

'What do you mean?'

'You're getting bogged down in the detail. Without the bodies, dead or alive, you'll never know what really happened to them!'

Juliana sighed. 'Well even if they find the bodies tomorrow, it's been so long it wouldn't disprove the rescue. They could have died quite naturally and then been reburied. Anyway, plenty of people said the family were transferred from Ekaterinburg to a place of safety and were not shot.'

Michael sat down as Juliana placed the books back on the table. 'You know, with all that we've discussed I don't think Giovanni needs to work on these Russian files.'

Juliana smiled. 'I agree. He is such a sensitive soul. I can't imagine how he would have coped reading all those detailed witness statements. Just look at how Alice reacted!'

As she was speaking Juliana noticed something glistening under the table. 'What's that?' She asked kneeling down to get a closer look.

Michael also bent down to have a look. 'A gold rouble, it must be Alex's; he must have dropped it, the careless lad!'

Chapter Thirty Five   The Great Cup Bearer

'Damn!' shouted Michael.

Juliana stopped what she was doing and turned around. 'What's the problem?'

'I can't find it! It's so annoying!'

Juliana smiled. 'Don't worry. It can't be far. Here, let me help. What exactly are we looking for anyway?'

Michael sighed. 'The notes I've made on a Danish family.'

'Well, let's see what you have here,' Juliana suggested, sifting through the papers on his desk before picking up a large handwritten document and laughing. 'Well I really don't think he was a member of the Kaiser's family, so we can put this one to one side. Ah, that reminds me. Alice said you wanted some candles.'

'Yes, black ones.'

'Black, that's a bit morbid.'

'No, it isn't. Besides, Alice said they would do just right for the occasion we have in mind!'

Juliana was just about to ask what occasion, when Alice appeared in the doorway.

Michael beckoned her in. 'Anyway, you can see the glow of the candle much better when they are black, isn't that right Alice?' He added smiling as she walked in.

'It certainly is!' she responded, heading for the table where Michael had carefully laid out his research.

Juliana sighed. 'Well good luck you two, and have a productive afternoon!'

Michael looked up. 'Before you go my dear take a look at this. He suggested pointing to a set of name cards.

Juliana returned to the table. 'My! You have been busy!'

'Yes, as I said, I'm only interested in finding out about whether Karl Armgaard Graves is my father and if so, what his real name was. He said he belonged to the high nobility of Prussia, so these are the ancient lines of aristocracy that Dr Graves wrote about. Remember?'

Juliana read them out slowly. 'Holstein, Wernigerode, Hohenzollern, Eulenberg, Furstenberg, Hadtzfeldt, Bernstorff, Kanitz, and finally…' Michael joined in on the last name, 'TRACHENBURG.'

'Very impressive, but what exactly are you trying to achieve?'

Michael tapped his pen on one of the cards. 'Remember what we discussed the other day? I want to see whether any of these families carry that unusual name Armgaard. If my theory is right, I should discover what noble family Dr Graves belonged to.'

Juliana ran her finger down the line of one of the family trees. 'So you've made up your mind not to look for Bertram Von Ehrenkrug then?'

Michael shook his head. 'I don't think there is any point. He said it was a fictitious name.'

Juliana sighed. 'Yes, but you have to admit "Ehrenkrug" is an intriguing name. Perhaps his real name is connected to it in some way?'

Michael burst into laughter. 'What, HONORARY MUG?'

'So, he had a good sense of humour! But I've just got a feeling about this Michael. He chose that name carefully and I'm sure it's a clue to who he really was.'

Michael smiled. 'Well, I must admit, only yesterday I was thinking along similar lines. The "honorary mug" may refer to a noble family that held the highest position at the Kaiser's court. Namely, the Master Of Ceremonies! That is why I took a very close look at the old Duke Trachenburg. His title was "The Great Cup Bearer to the All Highest". All Highest being Kaiser Wilhelm II.'

'Yes of course! Ehren krug. Honourable mug. He must be from the cup bearing family and now you've just reminded me. *Jerum! Jerum! Jerum*!'

'*Jerum, Jerum, Jerum*, what's that got to do with the Master of Ceremonies to the All Highest?'

Juliana sighed. 'Honestly Michael, for someone who is supposed to be so intelligent you can be really stupid! They were singing about "Ye old gods that live in cups". Can't you see Dr Graves was giving us a clue to his ancestral roots?'

Michael raised an eyebrow and was about to say something when Alice butted in. 'Trachenburg, that rings a bell. I'm sure they were a Silesian Catholic family.'

'You are correct,' added Michael. 'But do you remember who he was married to?'

Alice shook her head.

391

'Well, it's such a coincidence that I can hardly believe it myself. He was married to Countess Benckendorff, a niece of the Russian Ambassador in London. At first I wondered whether he was the uncle that Bertram Ehrenkrug visited in Furstenwalde. Oh I forgot! You don't know the story. Well Bertram, alias Dr Graves, said his uncle accompanied the Bishop of Mayence and Wilhelm II down into the crypt for a secret ceremony before he was crowned the Kaiser.'

Alice smiled. 'Well if Karl comes from this noble family and he is your father.. well...what can I say? I suppose even royalty has to be initiated into how to harness the secrets of divine power and as we know the power is conferred only through a secret ceremony steeped in tradition. All very mysterious and certainly something one would not wish to hold in public.'

Michael rubbed his hands together, unable to hide the delight he felt. 'Very good Alice, but I was reminded of a story Juliana told me.'

At the mention of her name Juliana sat down again. 'Oh! What was that?'

'Remember when Dr Graves was accused of blackmailing the Countess Bernstorff?' Michael glanced at his wife for confirmation. 'Well, you'll recall he took his enquiry to Prince Herman Hatzfeldt, who along with the rest of the family, threatened to sue him for blackmail; but after much ado, including the personal intervention of the Kaiser, all charges were mysteriously dropped. So I am assuming that Dr Graves may have been closely involved or even related to the Kaiser.'

Alice sighed. 'But Michael, this is all conjecture. Without knowing Dr Graves's true identity you can't prove a thing. You know, it's an impossible task, unless of course you find a secret diary written by him that explains all his different names and characters.' Alice laughed at her own joke.

Michael thumped the table in friendly frustration. 'No! Don't tell me I've got this far only to be turned back at the last hurdle!'

Alice gave him a comforting pat on the back.

'Well there has got to be a way of finding out,' Juliana added, doing her best to encourage him.

Michael sat down and rubbed his forehead. For a moment there was silence in the room.

'Wait a moment,' Juliana announced. 'I know how we can prove whether Dr Graves is telling the truth.'

'How?' asked Michael.

'Test one of his claims. Remember in *Secrets of the German War Office* he said he was exiled and had no alternative but to become a secret agent so that he could get back a title that was rightfully his. So Michael, all you have to do is find a member of the Prussian nobility who was exiled around the 1900s.'

Michael gave his wife a broad smile. 'Sometimes you really surprise me with your ideas. But finding such a person would be a miracle in itself!'

'Yes,' Alice agreed, 'there are so many families to go through. It's not easy conjuring up names of those who don't want to be found!'

'I suppose you're right,' Michael concurred. 'Look at the trouble I've had finding out about the name Armgaard.'

Alice laughed. 'It sounds like you're on a bit of a wild goose chase. I should give it up if I were you.'

'I know the name Armgard means immense or universal yet there does not appear to be a male equivalent, or at least I haven't come across it. I don't suppose you've ever heard of the name have you?'

Alice smiled. 'All you have to do, I would have thought, is find a female in one of these noble families with the name Armgard!'

'Alice, you're a genius too! I might even find her exiled son, born around 1875!' Michael rifled through his papers as he spoke. 'You see he must come from one of these two families because they are the only ones that carry the name Armgard.'

Juliana sighed. 'Well, good luck. I must get on. I'll see you both later.'

Michael ran his pen down a long list of names. Presently he stopped. 'Alice, I want you to be honest with me. Did you ever meet my father?'

'If ever I did, he was not introduced to me as such. Your mother had a lot of admirers. Some of whom she was in contact with over the years. Yes, she spoke of her friendship with Karl, but she never once spoke about your father to me.'

'You see, I still don't understand why she couldn't tell me about him. I mean, what was the big secret? Shall I tell you something?'

'Do!' Alice responded, sensing there was more to come.

'It's something I have suspected for quite a while now.' Michael stood up and gave a deep sigh. 'Look Alice, why can't you just be straight with me? Did you meet Karl?

'Oh dear Michael, it was such a long time ago, how do expect me to remember?'

Michael laughed falsely. 'Well you must have seen a photograph of him at least.'

Alice patted him on the shoulder. 'I didn't and you really shouldn't spend too much time worrying about it,' she added, leafing through the pages of *The Secrets of the Hohenzollerns*.

Michael watched suspiciously, wondering whether she was telling the truth. He was about to ask another question when Alice looked up.

'What's this?' Alice asked, handing the book over. 'There, towards the middle of page eleven.' She added pointing to the text. 'You see where I mean? One minute he is talking about Ehren KRUG and the next Ehren BURG!'

'Great! Why didn't I notice that? A Freudian slip if ever there was. So Alice, our Dr Karl Armgaard Graves may be an Ehrenburg, not an Ehrenkrug. Well, well, well, what a family to hail from. So prestigious! Mother told me all about the Lords of Ehrenburg, with their magical castles and estates and their sumptuous treasure!'

Chapter Thirty Six   Intrigue at Monte Carlo

Juliana cradled a mug of hot coffee as she watched Giovanni water the roses from her studio window. But it wasn't Giovanni who was on her mind. She had been worrying about Michael's preoccupation with his mother's life. If only she could help him find the answer to his question! At least then they could all return to some kind of a normal life. Finishing her coffee, she picked up a fine chisel and approached a nearly completed statue. She should work on it today but...

'Oh why did all this stuff have to happen now?' she yelled, throwing the chisel across the room. 'Bloody *Secrets of the German War Office*, it's completely ruined my life!' Juliana felt like crying but was not going to give in. No, she would keep a stiff upper lip; after all, a clear mind was crucial for her creativity she thought, locating the chisel and picking it up. All morning her attempts to complete a relatively simple task had proved ridiculously arduous. 'It's no good,' she whispered, listlessly allowing the chisel to slide down the face. Juliana loosened her grip, knowing that it would mark her work but somehow, just at that moment, being rebellious was more important. So she allowed the force of gravity to draw it noisily downwards over the contours of the body. Then, springing her fingers apart, she released her grip so the chisel bounced onto the bench before hitting the marble tiles. She listened to it making a sharp clinking iron sound that was only just bearable and it reminded her of the IRON WILL POWER of Michael's mother. What a mystery she was and how she missed her! Heaven knows what she would think of their antics now!

Juliana turned towards the sunlit window. Would Maria appear again she wondered, as she had before? No. She wouldn't. Instead, a faithful Giovanni was digging away. She wondered how he didn't get bored tending the flower beds every day. Well, she supposed he was devoted to his work, just as she was usually! But today she couldn't stop thinking about Dr Karl Armgaard Graves. That might have been because she had promised to give Michael the book later and she knew she should finish reading it beforehand. Besides, there were a couple of points she wanted to investigate. Firstly, what was Dr Karl Armgaard Graves's real identity and secondly, what relationship did he have to Maria?

Juliana made herself another coffee and settled herself on her favourite sofa. Then, turning to page ninety-four, she started to read.

As I hurried back to my rooms I went over what von Wedel had said: "You are to be ready to take the midnight express to Monte Carlo. You will there keep watch on and report any possible meeting between the Russian, French and English ministers, at present travelling about the Riviera. You will have the assistance, if necessary, of the Countess Chechany. If you need her, send her this card." (he had given me the card with his signature across it, a reproduction of which is presented on this page). "If meetings or conferences take place, you must obtain the tenor thereof. Here is an order for your primary expenses." He had flicked an order for 3000 marks, about $750, across his desk. "Anything you wish elucidated?"

Not having met the Countess, I had requested her description. Pushing a button, Count von Wedel had given the answering secretary an order; within three minutes I was shown the photograph of the lady and her signature, of which I took a copy. Having no further requests I had bowed myself out. My first act was to cash the order; second to decide and prepare the character I wished to assume in Monte Carlo. I decided on a South African mine owner. I know considerable about mining, and being well acquainted with South Africa, the Rand and Transvaal, I had the advantage of knowing my locality first.

A Secret Service agent is always careful to choose a character with which he is fully familiar. One is certain to meet, sooner or later, men in the same walk of life; and unless one be well primed one is bound to be "bowled out". I knew there would be South African mining men at Monte Carlo. Procuring necessary papers, such as mining journals, quotations, a couple of South African newspapers and photographs, I went home and had my man carefully select and pack my wardrobe. I caught the midnight Lloyd Express. Selecting a pleasant middle compartment, and getting my seat registered, I made myself comfortable and began to map out a campaign. This was rather a tough problem. To be in the slightest degree successful, I had to get near, and if possible in touch with, the ministers that Count von Wedel had designated. How is this to be done? I knew it was far from easy, almost impossible, to make their casual acquaintance. I began to cast the personality of the three men over in my mind. There was Prince Kassimir Galitzin, at that time high in the favour of the Czar. There were Delcasse of France and Sir Edward Grey of England. All three were gyrating about the Riviera and the Savoy; ostensibly it was for their health, possibly for other reasons. In any case the health of these gentlemen seemed a matter of some concern to the German Emperor.

Health trips of more than one statesman in or about the same locality are looked upon with much suspicion and promptly investigated; more so when there is any extra political tension. At that time, it was in 1910, the air was tense; Germany was in the dark, unable to distinguish friend or foe. Sir Edward Grey's habits were unknown to me. With Delcasses I was somewhat familiar. Prince Galitzin. Ah, yes! I knew him pretty well, "Bon vivant", extremely fond of a pretty face. Um! I began to see light. Here is where the Countess might come in. By her photograph, an extremely beautiful woman; but photographs often flatter and do not give an indication as to personality. Festina lente, I could see.

Five forty-five the next afternoon and I was installed at the Hotel Metropole in Monte Carlo. After a refreshing bath, I had supper served in my room and sent for the hotel courier. This an old globetrotter trick, hotel couriers or dragomen are walking encyclopedias. They are good linguists, observant and shrewd. They are masters of the art of finding out things they should not know, and past grand masters in keeping their mouths shut unless you know how to open them. Not with palm oil. Oh, no, nothing so crude! You would never get any truths or anything worthwhile, with bribery.

Juliana stopped reading. 'MONTE CARLO! HOTEL METROPOLE! I've heard that somewhere before! she thought, before turning the page.

I had to find out local intrigues and gossips, who was in Monte Carlo and what were they doing. Who were the leading demimondaines and gamblers? Were there any possible secret service men? Hence the courier, a Swiss from Ober Arau, a district of Switzerland I luckily knew well. When he knocked at the door, I cheerily bade him come in. I made my manner as good-natured as possible. I offered him a real Medijeh cigarette.

Juliana lay the book down. 'MEDIJEH!' she said out loud, 'Maria's favourite cigarette!' Michael will be amazed at this she thought, taking a cigarette and lighting it as she walked across to the window. Dear Giovanni, still working hard! Juliana inhaled deeply, fighting off the desire to blow circles in the air. I wonder who this Countess is and what her relationship is to Dr Graves? Juliana finished her cigarette and returned to the sofa where the book lay open and picked up where she left off.

As befitting his station, he was slipping the cigarette in his pocket. "Light it, won't you? Have a little smoke with me here. I'm a bit lonesome. I want to get my bearings. Won't you join me in a glass of wine?" That was my first oar in.

After some commonplace conversation, as to how the season was, I asked: "Anybody of interest here?" I winked knowingly. Possibly it pleased the courier to have someone to chuckle over a secret. All my oars were in. "At the Grand Hotel de Londres," he said slyly, "there is a gentleman who does not fool me."
  I offered him another cigarette, helped him to another glass of wine.
  "He is registered there as Count Techlow, but he can't fool me. He is the Prince Galitzin."
  What's he doing; gambling a lot?" (I knew he wasn't.)
  "No," replied the courier, 'he's keeping pretty quiet."
  "Is there a Countess Techlow?"
  The courier shook his head. Bueno! The coast seemed clear. I knew it was extremely awkward and often dangerous to tempt the quarry away from a demimondaine, especially at Monte Carlo. After chatting some more I bid the courier good night. I would see the Countess the first thing in the morning.'

Along toward noon I called at the Nouvel Hotel Louvre where von Wedel had told me I would find Countess Chechany. I sent in my own card bearing the name of H. Van Huit, Doorn Kloof, Transvaal (the reader will recall my experience at Doorn Kloof); also von Wedel's card with his signature. I had to wait for some time, but finally the Countess received me in her boudoir. She was in bewitching negligee. From the photograph I was prepared to find a very *handsome woman, but shades of Helen! This was Venus, Juno and Minerva, the whole Greek and any other goddesses rolled into one! Tall and willowy, superb of figure, great dark-blue eyes, masses of blue-black wavy hair, full red lips forming a perfect Cupid's bow. But why go on? I might get too enthusiastic, and mislead the reader. After my adventure I never saw the Countess again.*

VENUS, JUNO, and MINERVA.... all rolled into one! Juliana was sure she had read the very same thing in Fox's diary! She scribbled herself a quick note before returning to the book.

I knew that by birth the Countess Chechany was a high Hungarian noblewoman. By marriage she was related to the Counts of Tolna Festetics, a leading house in Hungary. Also, she was one of those marvellously beautiful women peculiar to that country.

Waving a small jewelled hand she begged me to take a chair beside her. A cigarette was daintily poised in her fingers. "Be seated, Mr. Van Huit of Transvaal," she said, gazing at me with a roguish grin. We both burst out laughing. Of course she knew what I was; von Wedel's card showed her that. But, as her next words plainly showed, she knew a great deal more. "I've got a badly sprained ankle, doctor! Can you do anything for me?"

I must have shown a pretty stupid face, for she laughed amusedly again. I certainly was surprised, for up to now I had never met her and my being a doctor was known only to one or two persons in the Service. Besides, it is strictly a rule of the Imperial Secret Service never to discuss or divulge personal matters. Her attitude by no means pleased me. I cordially hate anyone, especially women, knowing more than I do. One never knows where one is standing in a case like this. I decided not to show my curiosity, but I was determined to learn how she knew about me. Coolly I said: "Well, Countess, you have somewhat of an advantage. But if I can be of any assistance to you, pray command me."

As answer, she sprang up, and pirouetting around the room, "Now, why be peevish? If you're good and nice, I shall tell you sometime all about it."

She never did, for with all her ingenuous mannerisms, my lady was about the deepest and least fathomable bit of femininity I have ever met, besides being the possessor of a devil of a temper. After some more banter, which I instigated to become somewhat acquainted with my prospective partner, I came to business.

"Do you know Countess, the object of my mission?"

"Nothing beyond the intimation of your coming and the command to cooperate with you if necessary, so you had better enlighten me mon cher."

I did so with some reservation, it being my habit not to let anyone into a thing too much, least of all a woman. I suggested that our first object was to make Prince Galitzin's acquaintance. As his Serene Highness resided at the Hotel de Londres, we agreed to dine there. After accepting a dainty cup of chocolate I departed, purposely returning home by way of the Londres. Here, with a little diplomacy, I managed to reserve for dinner the table I wanted, one next to the Prince.

Well pleased, I later dressed, armed myself with a bouquet of La France roses and called on my partner. I had the roses sent up and waited.

The Countess sent word that she would be down shortly. I smoked three cigarettes. Still no Countess! I have yet to meet a woman who could or would be punctual. Finally I heard the soft swish and frou-frou of silk garments and looking up saw her ladyship coming down the grand stairway. She was brilliantly robed, jewels flashed at her neck and wrists. She was of that type of beauty difficult to classify, although assured of approval in any quarter of the world.

"Tired of waiting, mon ami?" she said, tapping me playfully on the arm. "See, in return for your patience, I am wearing your roses." She had them pinned on her corsage. We entered our carriage and drove to the Hotel de Londres, discussing the parts we were going to play. Would the Russian Bear be caught? I wondered.

When we arrived, I saw that the hotel was pretty well filled. Everybody who was anybody seemed to be there. I noticed a number of prominent American society ladies. Experience has taught me that there are three places where you meet sooner or later every known person in the world: Piccadilly Circus, the terrace of Shephard's Hotel, Cairo, and Monte Carlo. Remembering our diplomatic conversation of the afternoon, the maître d'hôtel came rushing forward and with profound bows directed us to our table, which was tastefully *decorated with La France roses, the Countess' favourite (charged to expenses). As we walked slowly down the passage to our table, many eyes were turned toward us. The Countess appeared unconscious of it all. Lazily, half insolently observant, yet wholly unconcerned, she was without doubt the most strikingly beautiful woman in the assembly.*

Juliana paused and scribbled another note. Prince Galitzin! Medijeh cigarettes! Monte Carlo! Countess! Baroness! But hang on a moment, when was this book written? Juliana turned to the front to check. August 1914! That's at least five years before Fox's diary was published in *Rescuing the Czar*! So the author of Fox's diary, presumably Fox himself, has told the same story as Dr Armgaard Karl Graves in *Secrets of the German War Office*! Then, as Juliana was considering the implications, she recalled a certain passage describing paintings hanging in a villa where Fox had been imprisoned on his way to rescuing the Tsar.

When she and Alex had first read the paragraph they naturally assumed that it was a spy who had a penchant for art, such as Sidney Reilly. But now Juliana suspected something quite different. Turning to page twenty-seven she found the paragraph where the paintings were listed and read the cryptic message at the top of the page: This entry may serve to identify the author. Underneath there were block capitals spelling out the words HERMITAGE, STOLEN, NEVER, and FORTUNE. Juliana messed the letters up and rewrote them out in capitals.

E. N. U. N. T. R. O. F. R. E. H. R. E. V. E. N. E. L. O. T. S. E. G. A. T. I. M.

Next she picked up her earlier workings, taken from the titles of the paintings that were listed on the same page. In her search for the hidden identity of Fox, she extrapolated certain letters. Juliana knew that if she was right the name revealed would confirm everything she suspected. Then carefully she double-checked the letters she had written down.

M.O.G. M. G. M. F. D. E. R. C. N. S. A. C. N.E. V.

Chapter Thirty Seven   A Mysterious Visitor

*He was known in the diplomatic circles of a dozen courts as the
Stormy Petrel for his appearance ever heralded coming troubles.*

A smell of garlic and pasta sauce wafted up the stairs and as usual Giovanni was shouting in the kitchen. 'E voler di Dio che vi amiate l'un l'altro come fratelli!'

'What's that he's saying?' asked Alex, frustrated that he couldn't translate.

'He said it's the will of God that we should love each other as brothers,' Paul replied.

Alex poured out a cold beer and laughed. 'Oh, but I do love you very much!' he added blowing him a kiss and then winking.

Paul shook his head. 'No absolutely not!'

Alex sat down. 'Love has no boundaries. Jesus loves me too!'

Paul smiled. 'Not in that way.'

Alex turned serious. 'Anyway, what were you talking about when I came in?'

Paul placed a carafe of water in the centre of the table.

'My nephews, they are always fighting. They cause their mother dreadful problems.'

'Iddio ci ha dato la coscienza affiche la ascoltiamo!' Giovanni shouted from the kitchen again.

'Now what's he saying?' Alex asked irritably.

'God has given us a conscience that we may listen to it.'

'Ah ha, if he's talking about ME having a bad conscience, forget it! I don't have one. But on the other hand if I was to pretend to be something I wasn't and to lie about what I am, well then, I would have mucho bado consciencanio Gio, comprende?'

Giovanni was purposely whistling loudly, making it clear he didn't want to get involved in another argument. Alex sipped his beer contentedly but Paul couldn't contain his anger. 'God has ordained that the love between a man and a woman is for procreation. To have bambinos, and before you say anything, if God wanted the human race to procreate in a different manner he would have given everyone the right equipment to start off with!'

Alex leapt from his stool. 'Well you would say that. TWIT! Life isn't just about procreation. You can't stop love EVER! As for marriages, christenings and church services, well I suppose they keep the church coffers going.'

Giovanni looked up. 'Eh! No fighting you two.'

Alex turned his back and finished off his lager as Giovanni came over and patted Paul on the back.

'You two, everything is fine now, Si? Nelle amicizie e necessarion che si aprano gli occhi!'

Alex laughed. 'He's saying something about us being friends?'

Paul smiled. 'Yes. He said when it's a question of friendship it's always necessary to open one's eyes!'

While they were talking, Alice busied herself emptying the contents of a drawer. She was sorting out the candles for Michael. Some were black and some white but she must have eight of each. 'Giovanni, have we any more black candles?'

'How many do you need?' he asked, pulling a funny face.

'As many as you have,' she replied sharply.

'Ah!' Giovanni understood. This was another of Michael and Alice's secrets. Like the icons and the crystals it was all part of the special goings on of their spiritual partnership! He remembered Maria liked these rituals, especially when it involved the use of incense. The church used it for high masses and festivals. But Maria, Michael and Alice liked to hold ceremonies at home and, most shockingly of all for Giovanni, they did so without a priest!

Alice struggled to her feet. 'Well, have we another white candle somewhere?'

Giovanni pointed at the dining room table. 'Only what you see in there.'

'Perhaps you can get some more in Rome tomorrow?' Alice suggested.

'Oh don't worry,' Juliana interrupted. 'I have a few in the studio you can borrow. Now come on everyone, let's eat. I'm starving.'

Alice placed the candles on the dresser and sat down. 'You look tired, what's wrong Juliana?'

'Nothing, I've just been reading. I am not used to it. I find it hard to absorb all the information.'

'What information?' Alex asked his mother.

'Oh, never mind that now. I'll tell you once I have had a chance to figure it all out! But more to the point, Alex, haven't you lost something?'

Alex checked his pockets. 'No, I don't think so.'

Juliana smiled. 'So what's this I am holding?' She said throwing the gold coin in the air. Alex laughed, his eyes gleefully following the sunbeams as they shot around the room.

'You shouldn't be so careless Alex,' she scoffed. 'I thought you were going to look after it?'

'But it's not mine. Look!' He added pulling a coin from his pocket.

'Well if it's not yours, whose is it?'

Alex put his hands in the air. 'Search me!'

'Well it's a mystery how gold coins keep popping up everywhere and no one admits to owning them! Anyone would think they grow on trees, and as for you Alex, what hope is there for a treasure hunter who can't spot gold when it's right under his nose?'

Alex blushed as his mother finished speaking. 'Bella Donna ...Excuse, I must...'

Alice nudged him under the table, making him stop mid sentence.

'Well,' interrupted Alice, 'perhaps the coin has fallen out of one of Maria's cases.'

Juliana placed the coin on the table. 'Really, I wasn't aware that Maria had a collection of Russian roubles stored away in her case!'

Alex sighed. 'You see how easy it is to make the wrong assumptions, especially when you're not aware of all the facts!'

Juliana smiled. 'Do you think there may be more in Maria's case then?'

Alice blushed. She hated to lie. 'I have no idea. It just came to me when Alex said he still had his coin and....'

Juliana didn't wait for her to finish. 'But how did you know that we had found it under the table when we were emptying Maria's boxes?'

Alice faltered before replying. 'I didn't.'

'But you said...' Juliana broke off mid sentence and put the coin in her pocket. 'On second thoughts, forget about it.'

'Gold, gold, gold, tra la la, tra la la, all you need is gold, de de de de.'

'Very good Alex, you should have been an entertainer!'

Tonya smiled, but as Juliana joined her son in singing, Alice whispered to Giovanni, 'Don't worry, they'll know the real truth soon enough.'

* * *

The following day Paul and Tonya were sitting in the garden.

'It's such a beautiful day!' Paul exclaimed, putting his arm around Tonya. 'And I have the day free. What would you like to do?'

Tonya thought for a moment. 'I really don't mind.'

'Shall we take a walk? Good for the body and the mind!'

Tonya rose reluctantly to her feet. 'I suppose I'm going to have to get used to you talking like this when we're married!'

For a moment Paul looked serious. Tonya laughed to show that she was joking. Then he understood.

'Well how about if I take up another profession, maybe become a writer?'

'You can do both. A priest who writes about mind, body and soul and finishes with blessings all round.'

Paul laughed. He was beginning to understand her sense of humour.

'Oh yes. I'll write about what happens to their spirit after they die.'

Tonya frowned. She wasn't quite sure what to say next. 'Well, I'm sure that will sell many books! Perhaps I can help?'

'Certainly, but I think you will be very busy, eh?' Paul replied, winking at her.

Tonya sighed. 'I can still study!'

Paul pulled a face. 'Study what?'

'Italian cooking of course, speaking of which, when are we going to announce our engagement? You know I haven't told anyone yet.'

Paul thought for a moment. 'Let's wait for this other business to finish.'

Back in the library, sun was streaming onto the books as Michael dipped the shutters and picked up *The Secrets of the German War Office*. He was eager to find out more about the man he suspected of being his father so he turned to page seventy-six, which Juliana had conveniently earmarked for him.

There is no lack of pine forests in Germany or Norway; and I had plenty of acquaintances in both countries. To any one of them I would have been welcome, but this would have entailed social obligations and I wanted to be absolutely alone. There were but two of my friends at whose places I could do exactly as I wished, where man and beast knew me. One whose place was in the Pushta, Hungary, was probably away on a hunting trip and Hungary was too remote. The other, a schoolmate of mine, lived near Furstenwalde, about fifty-eight kilometers from Berlin. Furstenwalde I decided, was an ideal spot, near Berlin, yet isolated enough and in the heart of one of the largest of the well-cared-for Prussian domain forests. So Ehrenkrug, the seat of the Koenigliche Ober Forsterei and the family seat of the Freiherren von Ehrenkrug was the place I selected.

Michael paused. Dr Graves had always referred to himself as an Ehrenkrug but was he really an Ehrenburg? Just as he was looking for his notes, Juliana knocked on the door. 'Oh good, you've got the book I left. How are you feeling, still tired?' she enquired, placing a glass of wine next to him.

Michael stood in front of the fireplace and smiled. 'Bit early isn't it?' he said, nevertheless taking the opportunity to raise his glass.

'So, have you had any luck finding a family with the name Armgard in it?'

'I fear it's beginning to get the better of me but I'm addicted of course!' Michael laughed. 'I just can't stop! I'm not getting very far, but still, this book should help. Thanks and salute!'

Juliana raised her glass in response. 'Well I'm not surprised you feel like you do. It's exhausting when everything we read is only half true!

Michael agreed. 'It's all very disconcerting.'

Juliana sipped her wine slowly. 'Guess what I have just found out?'

Michael looked excited. 'What?'

'I've discovered something intriguing about Dr Graves. Did you know he was on tour with the Crown Prince in 1909 when he visited the shipyards of Essen?'

'So, he's actually mixing with royalty. To tell the truth, I suspected as much. I'm not surprised to find that he is a good friend of Wilhelm II's eldest son. They were probably in the same class at school. Is there any more wine?'

Juliana rose to fetch the bottle. 'Yes, in the kitchen but when I get back I've something even more important to tell you. By the way, this gold rouble we found, it's not Alex's!'

'Well whose is it?'

'I don't know. I'll leave it to you to figure it out!'

Michael stared at the gold rouble in his hand. 1914? It looked authentic enough but where on earth had it come from? Then an idea came to him. Smiling to himself he put the coin back in his pocket.

A few moments later Juliana placed a fresh bottle of wine on the table. 'Well, what do you think?'

'Any peanuts?' enquired Michael.

'Yes here, but there are no olives I'm afraid. By the way, Alice is still looking for another white candle. I told her I've got a couple in the studio but surely you must have a spare one in here?'

Michael sighed. 'Yes. There are several in my desk but I wanted black candles!'

Juliana poured out the wine slowly then tasted it. 'Mm! This is delicious.'

Michael agreed and sat down.

'I know,' suggested Juliana, 'let's put some music on. It'll cheer us up a bit.' She added pulling Michael to his feet. 'Remember when we used to do this?' she asked, linking her arm through his. 'That's it! Hold your arm up. Now drink!'

Michael laughed. 'Of course I remember! It's a very romantic touch, if not a tad awkward! Anyway, Salute!'

'I think you're supposed to drink it all in one go.' Juliana replied topping up his glass. Michael promptly knocked the glass back in one gulp. 'Do you know what day it is?' he asked.

Juliana pretended to be confused until she saw his disappointed face. 'Yes, of course I do! Silly!' She replied.

'Well then, it's worth a double celebration!' Michael walked over to his desk and opened the drawer. 'I hope you like it?' He added handing her a beautifully wrapped box.

Full of anticipation, Juliana opened her gift. What she saw took her breath away. 'Oh! Michael! You shouldn't have. Opals and diamonds, you know they are my favourite. What have I done to deserve this? They are exquisite.' Juliana held the necklace up to the light and admired the stones.

'See how it sparkles!' Michael added, giving her a kiss on the cheek.

'Please help me to put it on?'

'AHA HA-HA.'

'What's so funny?'

'Nothing! HA-HA-HA! Well perhaps the dungarees and old shirt don't quite do it justice! Never mind, you can put something a little more fetching on later!'

Juliana giggled. 'I'll do better than that. I'll wear this in bed for you!'

Michael blushed at the thought and poured another glass of wine. 'Well happy anniversary anyway!' he said, sitting back down. 'Now what was it you wanted to speak to me about?'

'Oh dear, It's quite slipped my mind.' Juliana thought for a second. 'Oh yes, I know. It was about that gold coin. Alex has his.....so that means the one we found is new!'

Michael looked surprised. 'Well where did it come from I wonder?'

Juliana watched as he pulled the coin from his pocket.

'Maybe it fell out of one of the boxes we were unpacking the other day and rolled under there.'

Michael bounced to his feet and scrambled under the table. Getting his drift, Juliana burst into laughter and followed him.

'Honestly, look at us,' she said awkwardly, keeping her head down. 'We're behaving like a couple of school kids!'

'Ouch! OUCH!' Michael shouted. 'Ooohh! That really hurt!'

Juliana giggled and rubbed his head, then fell silent. 'SSSSHHH! There's someone in here.'

Michael peered out from under the table. Alice was standing in the doorway, hands on hips.

'Serves you both right!' She responded looking across at the two empty glasses on the table. 'Honestly, a couple of glasses of wine and you're on the floor. You should be ashamed of yourselves!'

'AH HA- HA –HA, you mean under the table!' Michael joked as he crawled out.

Alice bent down to see Juliana still crouched down. 'Are you intending to stay there all night?'

Juliana laughed as Michael helped her to her feet. Then she noticed a cut. 'Oh dear, Michael, you've hurt yourself. Look, there's blood everywhere, quick, sit down.' Juliana patted the chair as she spoke.

'It takes more than a little bump on the head to... em.. to er... to ..!'

Juliana glanced across to Alice with a look of concern. 'You'd better get some salt water and a cloth for me Alice, quickly!' she shouted as Michael wavered for a second before pulling out his handkerchief.

'Don't worry Alish, I've got thish... I can er...'

'Just ignore him and do as I say,' Juliana instructed, waving Alice out of the room as Michael wriggled in his chair.

'I'm fine. Come on. Let me get up!'

'Not until the bleeding has stopped.' Juliana lifted the handkerchief as Alice returned. 'Dear me, it's nasty. It will need stitches. We'd better call the doctor and, Alice, if you wouldn't mind, can you get some ice?'

Michael forced himself to stand up. 'NO!' he shouted. 'Pleesh! I'm fine now. Don't fush!'

Alice handed the ice to Juliana, who expertly wrapped it in a napkin. 'Here, hold this in place while I make that phone call. I don't want you collapsing on us again. You know how long it takes you to stop bleeding!'

Michael fumbled with the napkin.

'Oh for HEAVENS SAKE Michael, take hold of the damn thing and hold it firm. You know you're not like ordinary people.' With that, Juliana rushed out of the room.

Michael watched her leave then handed the blood-stained napkin to Alice. 'What was it you wanted me for anyway?' he asked.

'Well it can wait for now.'

'What can wait?'

'I was looking for a white candle. Juliana said there might be one in here.'

Michael sighed. 'Alice, I don't know what's going on but you know full well I have plenty. There are some in the third drawer down,' he pointed out as blood continued to drip down his neck.

'Quick, take this and hold it firm,' Alice requested, handing him a compress.

Michael did as he was told until Juliana returned.

'Oh dear, I can't get hold of the doctor at the moment so all we can do is dress the wound and hope for the best!'

Michael sighed as Juliana applied a stinging round of antiseptic cream and a gauze bandage. He cradled his head, complaining of a nasty stinging sensation.

'Oh no, it's still bleeding.' Alice watched thick drops of blood appearing on the dressing. 'This is no good. It will have to come off. Look, I'll tear this clean tea-towel in half. Now hold it as tight as you can to your head until the bleeding has stopped. Do you hear?' Michael nodded.

'And there's no need to make such a big deal of this,' Juliana added trying to convince herself that everything was okay. Then she noticed his dilated pupils.

'Have you got a headache?'

Michael shook his head and then shouted with the pain.

'Careful! You'll make it worse. Just try and keep your head still if you can.' Juliana wiped the blood off his face and hands. 'There now,' she said, getting up to leave, 'If you're okay for a bit I'll see if I can get hold of the doctor.'

'Look,' Michael interrupted, 'Give me that brown tape over there. I don't want to hold this in place all night!'

Alice suppressed an urge to laugh as she watched him bind his head in copious amounts of plastic tape.

'Anyway,' Alice asked, 'what were you both doing under that table? Did you lose something?'

Michael shakily poured himself a glass of water before sitting down in his favourite armchair. 'It was stupid really we were just wondering whether there were any more gold coins about. Anyway,' he added, changing the subject, 'more to the point, did you get hold of the BLACK candles that I was after?'

'I certainly did.' Alice replied, 'They're in the kitchen. So, are we ready for our little séance tonight?'

Michael tapped his head, which made her cringe. 'I want you to talk me through the prochess firsh. Ish my head shtill bleeding?'

'It looks to be holding for the moment but don't keep touching it! Now, about the séance, I know we shouldn't rush it but we must take full advantage of the full moon and guess what? Tonight we have one!'

Michael checked his watch. 'Good!' he replied, before shakily pouring himself a glass of wine.

'Should you be doing that?' Alice enquired.

'Probably not but it is our anniv.....' Michael broke off mid sentence and stared into his glass of wine.

Presently he looked up. 'Let's start thish now.'

'But it's not dark, we can't see the moon. Besides, you wanted me to explain the process?'

'Itchs not neshasherry. Have you got the black candlesh to hand?'

'No, but I can get them!'

'Before you go, jush explain how we make contact with the .... brotherhood.'

Alice sighed. 'I would have thought that you knew all about that.'

'Yesh of coursh, I jush need reminding of the exact proshess that's all.'

Alice looked worried. 'I'm not happy about this; you're not in a fit state for this sort of encounter. Just listen to you, your speech is slurred.'

Michael put his empty glass on the side table. 'If not now, when? Can you get me another glash of water.'

When Alice passed her in the hall, Juliana was just finishing off her phone call.

'His speech is slurred. Have you managed to get hold of the doctor yet?'

'Yes. He'll be here in an hour or so. Is Michael resting now?'

'He says he wants to have a séance! Honestly, I told him he's not thinking straight and it's not advisable tonight but....'

Juliana frowned. 'I don't want him doing anything of the sort until the doctor has given him the all clear...Ssshh! What's that?'

Alice listened and then smiled. 'Ah good, he's snoring.'

Juliana smiled. 'Come on. We'll sit with him and wait for the doctor.'

Sometime later Michael stirred. 'Water, is there any water?'

Juliana held the glass as he drank. She was pleased that his speech was no longer affected and decided he was well enough to hold the glass for himself. They both watched as he gulped until the glass was empty. But as he finished he let the glass drop to the floor and rolled his head back against the back of the chair. Alarmed by his grey appearance, Juliana leant forward and grabbed his arm. 'Michael, Are you feeling alright?'

Suddenly he leant forward. 'Listen' he demanded.

'Yes. Of course.' Juliana replied glancing across to Alice with a worried look on her face.

'Good! Now there's no time to lose! We have all been seeking answers for far too long. It is time for us, and by that I mean Alice and myself, to contact those in higher realms. Juliana, you may stay if you wish!'

Numb with shock, Juliana found herself unable to reply.

Michael picked up on her silence. 'Very well STAY. Now Alice let us begin immediately there is no time to waste.' As he finished speaking Juliana felt a tingling sensation run up her back. The hall clock mysteriously struck the hour for the first time in years and a window rattled noisily in its frame. Michael was now sitting rigidly and his face had a purple hue to it, accentuated by the dark shadows circling his eyes.

'Is anyone there?' he demanded as Juliana stared back marble eyed into the darkening room, not blinking for fear of missing something.

'Knock three times if you wish to be heard.' Michael spoke in a sharp rasping accent, his eyes now firmly shut.

A chill ran through Juliana as she watched an empty wine glass apparently come from nowhere and roll slowly but surely across the floor towards Alice.

'Good, we have our signal to proceed. Light the candles and incense. No one speak.'

Alice rose, handed something to Michael and then lit the candles. The room was slowly bathed in golden flickers of candlelight as Michael held open his mother's copy of *Rescuing the Czar*. Juliana could just make out Karl's handwriting on the page.

In Memory of our Siberian Adventure, Summer 1918 K.A.G.

'Are you there?' Michael asked again, this time in a deep voice.

'Yes,' whispered Juliana, immediately realising she should have kept quite. Alice placed her finger to her lips. Just at that moment three loud knocks reverberated around the room. Juliana covered her face, her heart pounding as the black candles shot spluttered wax, first this way then that. It had the potential of a horror scene and Juliana wanted to leave. Glancing up she saw Alice drawing in the air. What was she trying to say? Oh, she wanted a pen and paper.

Suddenly Michael lurched forward in the chair. 'So! You have heard our call. You have come!' He stated, with eyes wide open. Juliana was about to say something when she became aware of a strange noise, interspersing whistles followed by a sharp snapping sound. The sort you get when you press a button on the camera and take a photograph. Chick, chick, chick! As the room became progressively darker, Juliana realised it was the sound of doused wicks, the candles were blowing themselves out, one by one. Soon they were all out.

It felt chilly and Juliana instinctively folded her arms in an attempt to keep warm. She wondered whether Alice was feeling the cold but it was too dark for her to make eye contact. Michael had sunk back into his chair. How long they sat there for Juliana couldn't tell. But all was quiet except for Michael' rhythmic breathing. She was sure he was asleep.

It was while she was wondering whether she might leave that the room was bathed in a warm and welcoming light. But where was it coming from? Juliana checked the half melted candles. They were all out. Well then Alex must have managed to get the doctor after all. It must be the headlights of his car turning into the drive. She turned to look out of the French windows. But there was no sound of the doctor's siren. Then with amazement she looked on as a welcoming silver light grew in strength. The glow of the full moon had passed to the side of a huge poplar and was now squeezing itself demandingly through the wooden shutters. She watched it grow in brightness as it projected a larger than life silhouette of Michael onto the wall behind. It was eerie and Juliana fidgeted as the shadows started to play tricks with her mind. Well! She wouldn't be frightened. She wouldn't let IT get the better of her. She would close her eyes and IT would go away.

A few moments later she opened them. All was silent and the shadows in the room had disappeared. She could just make out the shape of his bandaged head as a rogue beam of moonlight slowly passed over his face.

Juliana peered across half expecting him not to look human. She wanted him to move, to look at her and say something. Anything that would prove he was still conscious. Alice observed how she nervously fiddling with her necklace but there was nothing she could do. Events would have to take their own course now.

Juliana would have left the room there and then but for the weakness in her legs. How long was all this going to take anyway? She asked herself. Suddenly the candle burst into flame, making Juliana grip the side of her chair as a second wave of fear swept over her. Then she caught a brief glimpse of Michael's face. Gosh, he did look different.

'Das ist Wunderbarste! Wunderbarste!' He shouted, clapping his hands, the force of which startled her. Then she smelt the recognisable scent of incense and knew from previous conversations with Alice that if everything was going according to plan, the constant flickering candle would herald the arrival of an invited guest. Now she could clearly hear the music, faint at first, but growing clearer. Bach, Wagner? It definitely wasn't Mozart.

Juliana presumed that being able to hear the music was evidence of some kind of psychic activity. It made her feel peaceful but her thoughts were interrupted by a spluttering candle. As the moment slipped by, her wish to ignore the lighting phenomena became impossible as more candles absurdly relit themselves in time to the heavy beat of Siegfried's *Funeral March*. Something dramatic was about to happen. She checked her watch, nervously trying to make up her mind whether this was a good time to leave, when quite out of the blue she heard what sounded like a choir singing. HALLELUJAH, HALLELUJAH, HALLELUJAH! She wondered if Alice could hear it. She waved to her but all Alice did was raise her eyebrow in response. Juliana felt sick so she closed her eyes to get rid of the nausea. Then she heard it. A strange rustling sound came closer, forcing her to look but she fought it. It didn't help. Even with her eyes closed a horrible image appeared before her accompanied by the sound of a dead body being dragged around the room. Just when she thought she could bare it no long and would have to let out a dreadful scream, it stopped. She opened her eyes. Michael's head had dropped to one side and his mouth was open. Before Juliana could do anything he slumped forward and fell to the floor.

'Michael! Oh no. NOT AGAIN!'

Alice rushed over. 'Dear oh dear, He's not breathing. I did warn him! I knew this was a bad idea!' She added checking his pulse. He should have listened to me. Wherever is that doctor?'

Hearing the mayhem, Paul, Alex and Tonya all rushed in and looked on as Juliana screamed, 'He's gone... He's dead! Oh why did he have to leave us like this?'

'Pray to God it's not too late and call for the doctor AND TELL HIM TO HURRY!' Alice shouted.

* * *

Michael was enjoying the music and floating high in the room. He knew he was in some sort of transition but was amazed to learn that his senses all seemed to be working perfectly normally. He heard Alice tell Tonya to get the doctor and could see Juliana rocking him backwards and forwards, his body lying limp in her arms. Poor Juliana, if only she had felt the great surge of energy that had raised his spirit, she would know that he was still with her. Now, as he floated precariously in mid air, completely detached from the emotional scene being played out below, he shouted loudly, hoping they could hear him.

'I'M FREE! I'M LIGHT! OH SO LIGHT!' Then he laughed because no matter how loud he shouted they could not hear.

'I'M ALIVE. I'M NOT DEAD! Why CANT YOU SEE I'M NOT DEAD?' Amazingly he saw Juliana look up. It was as if she could hear him but then disappointingly he watched her place a blanket over his lifeless body and a cushion under his head. Alice prayed while Tonya and Paul anxiously waited for the doctor to answer.

'PLEASE GOD BRING HIM BACK TO ME,' he heard Juliana sob as Giovanni did his best to comfort her. Perhaps he was dead? No, he mustn't give in to THAT feeling, even though he was being drawn ever higher, travelling at the speed of light through a blue green silvery mist. Then he saw THEM! They tried to join hands with him and he knew they were all heading for the same place! 'NO! NO! I'M NOT READY! NOT NOW, IT'S NOT TIME FOR ME.'

* * *

Wherever Michael was, he didn't see the blue flashing light of the ambulance arrive or his motionless body carried onto the stretcher. He didn't see Juliana administering oxygen as the vehicle careered at barely a safe speed down the mountainside. Juliana didn't want anyone with her, so the distraught family had no option but to wait at home, hoping that against all odds the doctor could save Michael's life.

A dejected Alice wandered aimlessly back into the library. What could have gone wrong? Surely that fall wasn't enough to kill him, unless... unless something else had affected him? Somewhere in the distance, she heard the clock chime eleven as she pushed open the library door.

'GOOD EVENING!'

Alice hesitated in the doorway, straining her eyes into the dark room. She could just make out the figure of a tall man.

'Good evening,' she replied, watching him rest his foot on the fire bender. The gentleman wore an exquisite waistcoat, which was heavily embroidered in green and silver thread. It had loops instead of buttonholes but annoyingly his face was still hidden from her view.

'I see you have taken well care of it.' The stranger commented, pointing at the silver candlestick on Michael's desk. His voice was deep and resonating. 'When the candles are lit, one can admire the Storm Petrel etched thereon most satisfactorily!'

'You mean the little bird, I suppose?'

The scent of Eau de Cologne wafted across and Alice recognised her visitor. Well almost.

'Come over here,' he demanded.

Alice did as she was told, hoping to get a better view. She noted the long black gloves that he wore but dared not look directly into his face. An unusual ring sat on top of the third left finger and it flashed in the light as he pointed to the engraving on the candlestick. She thought she recognised it but would need to take a closer look before being sure.

'This bird is special to you?' she asked, bravely fixing her gaze on him.

'I shall divulge my knowledge forthwith! It flies so!' He said placing his hands together in the shape of a bird and holding them against the wall so that the shadow resembled a bird flying. 'Its wings are delicate, yet it flies in a V shape fighting off all manner of forces as it hovers above the blustery oceans, such a courageous bird.'

'Why are you telling ME this?'

'Why should I answer YOU when it was Michael who called me?'

Alice was quite taken aback by his reply. 'Yes, well I'm afraid Michael has been rushed to hospital, he may even be dead as we speak unless you can ...' Unable to finish, Alice hurriedly pulled out a handkerchief and wiped her eyes.

The stranger bent down and looked her directly in the eye. 'I know.'

'Well, he wanted to contact the...... and request information about Dr Karl Graves. He wanted to know if he was his father and also what noble family he really comes from and...'

Before she could finish the stranger raised his hand.

'I am bound by an ancient motto, I cannot tell but he will know...........' Alice strained to hear every word as his image and voice started to fade.

As the room became noticeably warmer she heard the mysterious echoing words. 'To Know, To Dare, To Do.... To Know, To Dare, To Do.... To Know, To Dare, To Do....'

'Please, PLEASE don't go until you tell me that Michael will live. I KNOW YOU CAN HELP HIM PLEASE!'

Chapter Thirty Eight   Disguise and Deception

A live Bolshevik of OUR kind is much better than a dead diplomat!

Michael opened his eyes. He knew exactly where he was. The view from the window was a familiar one but how long had he been here? At the sound of voices he tried to raise himself up.

'I'm pleased to tell you Baroness Brandenberg that all the tests have come back and they are normal, so your husband is free to leave.'

'Phew! That is a relief. Thank you for all you've done, doctor.' Juliana gave Michael a smile. 'You have given us all quite a shock, now how are you feeling? Are you ready to come home darling?'

Michael smiled in response and nodded.

'Giovanni will be here in a moment, so let's get you ready.'

Michael smiled again. 'Well what a night I had! I don't know whether it was the drugs they gave me but I had the most amazing dream. I must write it down before I forget!'

Juliana laughed at his enthusiasm. Considering his ordeal, he was in remarkable spirits.

* * *

Back at the villa an ashen faced Alice greeted them. 'Michael! Thank God you're here!'

'Thank you Alice,' he replied, making his way slowly up the stairs.

'Oh Michael, there's something I have to tell you.....'

He stopped and turned. 'Yes?'

Alice smiled. 'Last night, after you were taken away in the ambulance, we had a visitor. You know the kind I mean, AND I'm certain it was HIM!'

Juliana sighed. 'What are you talking about now?' She asked feeling angry that Alice hadn't given Michael any space to relax.

'Well, I know it was HIM because he pointed out the birds engraved on the candlestick.'

Michael rubbed his head gently checking to see if it still hurt. 'Which candlestick are you talking about Alice?'

'The one on your desk, he was such a gentleman AND he wore a very smart waistcoat. It was silver and ……' Alice paused as Michael suddenly faltered on the stairs. Luckily Juliana was there to steady him.

'Why not tell us tomorrow Alice? Michael has had quite enough to deal with over the last couple of days.'

The following morning, Alex and Giovanni were talking about recent events. Both were relieved to have Michael home again. Alex took out his gold coin. 'Don't you think it is strange how there are now two of these in the house?' He asked holding the coin up in the air.

'Si,' Giovanni agreed in a bored tone.

'And strange too that both are from exactly the same year, I wonder if there are any more lying around?'

'Per dir la verita non lo so nemmen io.' Giovanni mumbled.

'What's that you say?' Alex asked as he got up and scraped his chair along the floor.

'Oo can say?' Giovanni said, cringing at the noise.

Alex laughed. 'Well now that I've got a metal detector I'm hoping I can!'

'Buono and have a nice day tectoring.' Giovanni added watching Alex leave the dining room.

Upstairs, Michael was laughing loudly. He had been told by his wife to take it easy this morning and that's exactly what he intended to do. So that he wouldn't get bored and while she was getting dressed, Juliana had left him a copy of *Rescuing the Czar*. He was reading Fox's account of how the Baroness 'B' helped to rescue the Tsar and his family. Juliana had thoughtfully earmarked pages that told of the intriguing and often romantic relationship between the Baroness and the secret agent called Fox.

A man who has escaped death is not to be trusted on a point of discretion. He doesn't know how to select his friends. He is like a spirit emerging from nowhere in the eternal void and grabs at the first apparition that promises companionship in his embarrassing and momentary isolation. Well, I was so glad to see that Buckingham Clorinda that I was willing to take her into my confidence at once. She seemed so sympathetic!

"I commend your bravery," she said prettily, offering me her hand. It was small and beautifully moulded yet firm and steady and sent an electric thrill through me like a flash. Her eyes would disarm the most suspicious diplomatic freelance in the world. Struck with admiration, hypnotized by her voice, I could only blurt, "I thank you."

"We are looking for a man of approved courage," she continued earnestly. "We are more than satisfied that YOU are the man."

Again I muttered my thanks.

"How long have you been a member?" she then asked carelessly.

This was not so easily answered. I thought quickly. " Long enough to know my lesson!" I answered oracularly.

"You still remember your instructions?"

"What instructions?"

She answered my question by asking, "Were they not BURNED?"

Who is this encyclopaedic lady? I asked myself. What manner of TRAP is she setting for me now?

"Why did you SANDBAG me?" was MY answer.

"You are NOT to ask questions," she returned. "Are you not satisfied with results?"

"I am still alive."

"Well," she smiled. "A live Bolshevik of OUR kind is much better than a dead diplomat!"

I was taken into an improvised kitchen and indulged in a splendid meal. I took no wine. My meal being finished she offered me an excellent cigarette. Glancing up through a ring of smoke my eyes fell upon a rough black-and-white sketch of a tall, smooth-faced, keen-eyed man with rather large ears, firm and thin-cut lips, high forehead and steadfast gaze, dressed in the uniform of a General Officer, with a single decoration on his left breast. She observed me closely as I gazed. I KNEW this man and was about to exclaim: The saviour of this country! But something restrained my enthusiasm.

"You recognize him I see," she insinuated. "WHO is he?"

I dodged. She merely smiled. She evidently realizes the wonderful power of that disarming smile and the fascination of good teeth in a shapely head.

"You'll do!" she said, with apparent reservation as she tapped a tiny bell.

A short, thickset man appeared, he is not positively ugly, but he has a way of staring at one that is rather ill-bred. There is a gold band around his left wrist and a scar upon his right cheek. I am sure he is the SAME man I met at one of Sadakichi-Hartmann's readings from Ibsen's Ghosts. He may recall the time. *It was in an abandoned palace on Russian Hill somewhere in America; the lady at his left was discussing the difficulties of getting her motor car into Ragiz; the younger one on his right was known as Alma and gave her address as East 61st Street, New York and ALL THREE were quite convinced that the Central Powers will defeat the Allies. He is an international character and will remember this incident as well as the following.*

"This gentleman will join your party for Ekaterinburg tonight YOU understand. If there are any mistakes I shall not answer for the results!"
   There were NO introductions. The man bowed and began to back away.
   "YOU may accompany him," she said, rising and flitting from the room.

I believe I understand what this party means! There is to be a SHOOTING party at Ekaterinburg under the auspices of the Bolshevists in a day or two and I may be ONE of the "mistakes" for which that mystifying lady disclaims responsibility. My companion certainly looks like a bandit, and manifests the strength of a wild bull. He seems much interested in that patch on my shirt sleeve.

Michael paused for a moment as he recalled that Sidney Reilly had written in his memoirs about patches sewn into the sleeves of shirts; but then he supposed all agents and diplomats knew about such intrigues. Michael turned to the last page that Juliana had earmarked. Fox was about to say goodbye to the Baroness 'B', having successfully delivered the Russian Imperial Family to the Captain on board a British gun boat.

He called a petty officer and said a few words in an undertone. In a minute a radiant young woman with springing steps glided gracefully down the deck. She was not, in her present attire, much different from Maria but as she drew near I noted the difference at a glance. She came forward quickly and held out her hand.
   "Congratulations Mr Fox!" she said, smiling.
   "The Metropole!" I gasped. "What brings YOU here?"

"Still asking questions?" she coquetted prettily. *"I merely called, of course, to inform you that the sapphire is in America!"*

I thought hard for more than a minute. Then it occurred to me that I had seen her in a dozen disguises shadowing me from Buckingham to the room upstairs on Downing Street, to charm me later at The Hague to disappear like a will-o'-the-wisp, then to fascinate me at the Metropole.

Michael closed the book. "The Sapphire is in America"! What could that mean? A coded way of saying that the Tsarevich, the young Alexei, was safe in America or that the Romanov funds had safely reached the bank! Michael slumped back on the pillow and wiped his brow with a handkerchief.

Just then a ray of sunshine hit the dressing table and reminded him that it was time to get up.

Once dressed, Michael sat watching his wife brush her hair. She wanted him to stay in bed but he had reassured her that he was feeling as fit as a fiddle.
    'Well promise me you'll take it easy.'
    'Of course I will.'
    'And that means no work in the library either.'
    Michael saluted. 'Yes Ma'am!'
    'Why not go for a gentle walk in the garden before it gets too hot and then you can join me in the kitchen for some lunch. Oh! By the way, what was that dream you had?'
    Michael sat on the end of the bed and rubbed his head.
    Juliana sighed. 'Surely you remember? When we came out of the hospital you said you had a dream.'
    'Did I? I thought that was Alice who said that. I'm sure she spoke about the candlestick with the bird on it called a Storm Petrel.'
    Juliana sighed. 'Yes, apparently someone paid a visit after our attempted séance and after we had left for the hospital!' Juliana sighed again because she realised it was no good pressing him on the matter of his dream if he had completely forgotten. Picking up *The Secrets of the Hohenzollerns* she sat down next to him. 'Have you read this bit that I earmarked for you yet?' she asked, turning to page fifty-four.

Michael shook his head.

'Well it could be about your father's early life, you know.'

Michael smiled faintly. 'Is it relevant?'

'I would say so, yes!'

'Well read it to me then.'

'Bertram von Ehrenkrug entered and remained standing at a salute, two paces inside the door, his close-fitting uniform of an officer of the Guard Uhlans setting off his tall remarkably well-knit frame. The Emperor, after sharply appraising the general appearance of the young officer, returned the salute and said, in a pleasant, non-official tone:

"Stand at ease Ehrenkrug. Come over here." Pointing to a spot within two feet of himself, he turned to the Count, who was standing at his right, and commanded, 'Begin your examination, Wedell."

"It has pleased His Majesty, Your King, to use you from now on in a private and confidential manner. Your house has served the throne faithfully and well for hundreds of years. The confidence now placed in you is partly due to your family connections, partly to the satisfactory reports received of you. You will have to relinquish your military career, but," with a smile, 'from all accounts this will not be any great sacrifice on your part. I have here a report as to your knowledge of languages and other attainments, which I wish to verify. You will answer the questions put to you in the language in which you are addressed." The Count put his next questions in French, English, and Russian, which were promptly answered in a faultless accent. The Emperor, who had taken up a document, at this point looked up and said: 'Wedell I am satisfied, I shall leave the rest in your hands."

The Emperor arose and walking over to Von Ehrenkrug, placed his arm on the young man's shoulder, saying: "Ehrenkrug, I must have men I can trust. You will learn that I have to do many things in an unofficial way and that I have to issue many unofficial orders; that is why I need men of intelligence and integrity. See to it that you do not abuse my need and the trust placed in you. You are from now on my personal messenger, accountable only to me and in my absence to Count Wedell. Go now to your home and await instructions. You are dismissed." Retiring to the door, and saluting, Bertram von Ehrenkrug, messenger of the King, went out embarking on a career, the like of which has *fallen to the lot of few men. Years after he was known in the diplomatic circles of a dozen courts as "The Stormy Petrel", for his appearance ever heralded coming troubles.'*

Juliana closed the book. 'So you see, what Alice said last night about the visitor and the engraved bird on the candlestick that belonged to your mother...'

'OF COURSE, Storm Petrels,' Michael interrupted loudly. 'The visitor was my father. The séance worked after all, even though I wasn't there to see it! He must have wondered where I had gone'.

Juliana smiled. 'Well if he was a spirit I'm sure he would have known.'

Michael scowled before replying. 'Yes, yes! But going back to what you were reading in Dr Graves's book, it sounds as though he was done out of his inheritance. That means that we have been done out of ours too.'

'It is pointless getting all het up about it or jumping to wild conclusions. You need to find out what family he came from before you can discover what it is you should have inherited!'

Michael rubbed his chin. 'That's easier said than done. Many noble families in Prussia held a hereditary title. Let me see now, there was Eduard Liebenau and er... August Eulenburg.. and ...well at least another six families!'

She understood his frustration and wanted to help. 'By the way, I was looking through your papers the other day and I see they had a girl in the family called Armgard.'

Michael smiled. 'Yes, I think the Kaunitz family did as well. Honestly, it's so damn frustrating not being able to put a name to my father!' He smiled again and stretched his legs.

'Well, if Bertram von Ehrenkrug, alias Dr Karl Armgaard Graves, is the friend of your mother's called Karl, who wrote the message in *Rescuing the Czar* about remembering the Siberian adventure, then surely he must have left some other clues in his writing ?'

Michael agreed. ' Yes you are right... if I recall correctly he used the name Dr Cannitz as an alias on one occasion and if he is the nephew of the Lord High Steward then I cannot be blamed for assuming that he could be a nephew of either August Eulenburg or Eduard Liebenau, or that princely family of Ehrenburg. But even if I can prove I'm his son, what chance do I have of retrieving what's legally mine?' Michael slumped back, 'and another thing, do you honestly think that an exiled Ehrenburg or a Eulenburg would choose such a ridiculous name as Ehrenkrug? It's nothing more than an insult to our family, honorary mug indeed!'

'Karl's a master of disguise, that's for sure. I bet he's having a good laugh at us!' Juliana attempted to lighten the conversation but it didn't work.

'Well I don't think it's very funny! Being forced to join the Secret Service and go abroad on the understanding that after a few years' service he would be allowed to return and claim the family title. Instead his cover is blown and he is reported to the authorities and then imprisoned and when that didn't work, they try and blacken his name by accusing him of blackmail and get him arrested all over again!' Michael marched across the room and threw open the windows. 'It beggars belief, IT REALLY DOES!' he shouted. 'No wonder he went to work for the British and Americans. I mean, what was the man supposed to do? All along he is warning about the coming war and trying to save millions of lives. He even tried to stop the bloody war and what appreciation does he get? Eh? *NADA!* Instead he is treated like a common criminal! It's DISGUSTING!' Michael realised he was getting too angry and stopped abruptly.

'I do hope I'm not disturbing you two?' Alex tapped gingerly on the door. 'How are you this morning father?' he added, sheepishly poking his head round the corner.

Michael smiled. 'Ah Alex, I'm much better, thank you.'

Juliana watched her son hop from one foot to another.

'Was there something on your mind?' Michael enquired, wondering whether Alex had overheard their conversation.

'I was just wondering when you were planning to hold another meeting. We seem to have forgotten all about *Rescuing the Czar*?'

'Not at all,' Juliana replied sternly. 'In case you hadn't noticed, your father has been unwell! Besides, we have all been busy and......'

'No. No! The boy's right. We ought to have one soon.' Michael suddenly felt a sharp stab in his chest but, not wanting to give the game away, he continued to gaze out of the window. When he spoke again it was in a barely audible voice and Juliana sensed something was wrong.

'What a beautiful day it is. After all that has happened I think we should have a day out together in Rome, perhaps stay overnight in a hotel so we don't have to rush back?' He looked at his watch. 'It's only 9.30 ... we've got plenty of time!'

Juliana gave him a hug. 'Sometimes you do surprise me!'

Alex laughed. 'That bump on the head seems to have done him the power of good!'

Michael grimaced. His chest was feeling tight but he was not about to let on. Turning to Juliana, he smiled. 'I could do with a break. I spend far too much time working and not enough time with you and Alex. Besides, I know the fresh air will do us all the power of good!'

Chapter Thirty Nine   Rome

'Come on Gio! Hurry up! We need to go now! Where are Paul and Tonya? What about Alice? Oh there you are! Come on you lot, let's go!'

Giovanni scratched his head. He wasn't a man for last minute plans but he was amused to see Alex so excited. 'The boss, he will take his own car?'

'Well yes! We can't all fit in this one! Come on, we'll follow him out.'

Giovanni started up the engine while Alice made herself comfortable next to him in the front. Paul, Tonya and Alex, who were all squashed in the back, were giggling like school children.

'There they go. Come on chauffeur don't let us get left behind!' Alex shouted as Michael pulled out in front of them. Giovanni had a habit of whistling when he was happy and he was never happier than when he was driving through the Italian countryside. Alice wanted him to stop because she was trying to overhear the conversation taking place in the back of the car. As far as she could make out Paul wanted to stay longer than a day because he wanted to show Tonya around.

Almost an hour later they turned onto the Via Giulia. Giovanni followed the car in front at a respectable distance because Michael as usual was driving the Maserati too fast for his liking. As they neared the city centre Michael was forced to slow down as he looked for a place to park. During the journey he had listened to Juliana singing along to Frank Sinatra but now he wanted her to stop, so he coughed loudly. A concerned Juliana leant across. 'Are you alright?' Michael smiled. 'Yes, of course I am. Now look, I have some small business I wish to attend to when we park up, so...'

'Well I should have known better,' interrupted Juliana, pretending to be annoyed. 'There I was thinking I was going to have you all to myself today. Well how long do you need for this little business of yours?'

Michael indicated loudly and turned left.

'Well?' she asked.

'Oh not long, I just want to pop into that shop on Via Dei Coronar. You know, the one where I saw the statue, I'm sure I told you.'

'Michael! Surely you're not going to buy it? It'll cost a fortune, besides I can make you one for half the price!'

'Yes, but it won't be the real thing. You know what a stickler I am for authenticity. Now where would you like to be dropped off?

'Via Condotti will be fine,' Juliana added adjusting her silk scarf and sunglasses in the mirror. 'Better wave the others down so we can make arrangements for meeting up,' she added just as Giovanni pulled up next to him, 'Where we go now boss?'

'We'll park up here and do a spot of shopping. I suggest we all meet up at Cafe Greco for coffee in an hour or so?'

Giovanni scratched his chin loudly. 'Buono! I go barbiere first.'

'In that case,' 'may I join you and Juliana?' Alice asked, smiling.

'Yes, of course. What about you three?' Michael enquired, leaning through the front window. 'And is a late lunch at the Trattoria Trastevere alright by everyone?'

'Yes, that's fine because I want to show Tonya around San Giovanni in Laterno, so we'll meet you there later,' Paul replied.

'Good and what about you Alex, any plans? Or do you want to join us for a spot of shopping?'

'No thanks. Places to go, people to see. I'll meet you at the Cafe Greco about 12.30'

Soon after the arrangements had been made Michael found the shop he was looking for but much to his frustration it was shut. Too early I suppose, he thought, admiring the stonemason artefacts in the window. Now where was it? Ah yes, I see! A glass cabinet is standing in its place. Oh dear, I hope it hasn't been sold. Just as he was about to leave a light shone out from the shop. Michael stepped back to avoid the glare, then moving slightly to the left, took a closer look. From the window several gold coins caught his eye. Curiosity got the better of him so he walked over to the doorway, shaded his eyes and peered in. Now he could see the coins clearly. One was turned over to show the head of Tsar Nicholas II and the other was dated 1914. He couldn't see a price tag but imagined they were worth more than their weight in gold. Michael sighed. How inconsiderate not to show opening times on the door or prices on the items.

A mile away Juliana paused in front of her favourite shop, 'I love that ring but I can't make up my mind whether it's made of platinum or white gold.'

Alice studied the ring. 'Oh, I know what you mean. It's so difficult to tell. It's definitely not silver!'

Juliana laughed. 'I should think not! Not at that price anyway. I suppose it would cost a lot more if it was platinum. I think it must be gold. Let's ask.' Juliana tried the door and found it locked.

'It's too early,' Alice responded.

'Of course, I forget these shops don't open until the afternoon. Never mind, we'll come back another day.' As they walked slowly towards Cafe Greco Alice told Juliana more details about her mystery visitor.

'You must have been so scared. I would have screamed!' Juliana exclaimed.

'Well, I was more in shock over Michael being taken ill again. But when the stranger appeared, well, I suppose I was in double shock, although I was as cool as a cucumber at the time! As I told you, I first saw him standing by the fireplace and noticed he was dressed in rich attire. He wore a flamboyantly embroidered waistcoat with thick intertwining loops instead of buttons and he recognised the candlestick at once and the Storm Petrels. Anyway, I was just about to ask who he was, when he started to well....take his leave... He didn't want to answer my question. It was as though he just evaporated into thin air. He must have read my mind. Spirits have special powers you know.'

'Really, so who do you think it was then?'

'Well at first I told myself that it could be any number of counts or princes that Maria knew but to be honest I knew all along it had to be HIM!'

'You mean Dr Karl Armgaard Graves, I presume?'

'How did you know?'

'Well it wasn't difficult. He wrote in his book that he was called a "Stormy Petrel", a harbinger of doom!

'Speaking of harbingers of doom, shall I tell you what else he said to me?'

'Only if you want to frighten me,' Juliana laughed. 'I still can't get used to the idea that he was in our library. It's so spooky!'

'Well, he told me a story the like of which I have never heard and I only remembered it this morning when I woke up.'

Juliana reached out to Alice. 'Would you like to sit and rest a moment?' She asked pointing to a well-positioned bench.

'Oh, that's thoughtful of you dear. Thank you.'

Alice sat down and sighed with relief. 'Now where was I? Oh yes. Karl said that on very special occasions the Kaiser always wore a talismanic ring, which had been passed down through all his Hohenzollern ancestors. But one day, things changed after his courtiers had noticed that he refused to take it off and was wearing it every single day. Apart from its apparent talismanic power they also wondered why he wanted to wear it all the time, since it was not at all valuable or particularly attractive.'

'Oh!' Replied Juliana wondering what the point of the story was. 'Is that it then?' 'Gracious no! Let me explain. The Kaiser obviously felt that this quaint old ring, set with a stone of no intrinsic value, held the magical power of protection. Legend has it that a toad hopped onto the bed of the wife of the Elector John of Brandenburg and deposited this pebble right there in front of her! The toad then mysteriously disappeared. Karl told me that the pebble has been zealously treasured by the family ever since and is still kept in the family archives. Apparently the father of Frederick the Great had it mounted in a ring and he...Karl... told me that the ring is always worn by the head of the House of Hohenzollern!'

'It's a fascinating story but I don't understand why it was considered to be a talisman?' Alice frowned. 'One can only imagine. I am presuming that John of Brandenburg's wife became pregnant with a male heir after the toad put the pebble on her bed!'

'Perhaps she kissed the toad and he turned into a prince!' Juliana giggled at her own interpretation.

'I wouldn't mock if I were you. Many a true word is said in jest!'

Juliana stifled another giggle as she checked the clasp on her handbag, which was unusually filled to the brim. 'I'm sure Michael will be enchanted by the adventures of the Brandenburg toad and his magic pebble. Now come on, we mustn't keep him waiting; but Alice, why did Karl tell you that story?'

'I've no idea. Perhaps he saw the book about the Hohenzollerns on Michael's desk and wanted to emphasise what a superstitious lot they were.'

Juliana stood up and brushed the back of her jacket. 'BRANDENBURG! But that's our name! That's why he told you.'

Alice sighed. 'Yes but it is spelt differently and I'm sure Maria only chose that name because she had to hide her true identity.'

'But if she chose such a great name to hide behind one wonders what family she really hailed from.'

'True, there's no greater name in Berlin than Brandenburg!'

'So you think Maria was German or Prussian then?'

'Maria could have been English, French, and Russian but she would never have been that!' Juliana wasn't sure what Alice meant. 'Well, did Maria wear a toad ring? Has Michael seen it?'

'Oh dear me,' Alice replied, patting her arm gently as they started to walk. 'I only told you the story because I thought you would find it amusing. You see, when Karl told me I thought of the grail legends. Not once did I think about the name Brandenburg and for that I feel quite ashamed but...' Alice raised her finger in the air as she spoke. 'Whatever that stone was, it must have been very important. Why else would the Kaiser want to wear it every single day?'

'I don't know. I'll be interested to hear Michael's reaction to the tale. These things mean so much more to him. Anyway, it's not the first time that a stone has played a role in human destiny and I don't suppose it will be the last,' Juliana philosophically mused as they walked into the Cafe Greco. 'Here we are then,' she added, holding the door open. 'There's Michael seated in the corner.'

Michael roared with laughter when Alice told him about the toad ring. 'Well if you think that was strange, listen to this.' He added sipping his cappuccino. 'I had a dream too. Remember that night I was away? Dr Graves appeared to me. It all came back when I was walking around this morning. In my dream he said I should call him by his first name.'

'What, Armgaard?'

'No, KARL! And he wanted to share a secret with me. He said it was my right to know!'

'Do tell,' Alice encouraged.

'He told me that it was him that wrote Fox's diary!'

Alice laughed out of disbelief. 'Why would he do that?'

Michael shrugged. 'I only know what he told me in the dream, Alice. Oh yes, he was being looked after in a Fort at the time.'

'Did he tell you who asked him to write it?'

Michael shook his head.

'Well I'm not at all surprised' interrupted Juliana. 'I suspected as much after I read his books.'

'He said that he wrote the story of Fox and emphasised that he was especially fond of Maria!' Michael added.

'Is that your mother or the Tsar's daughter?'

Michael shrugged his shoulders. Then he turned to Alice and said very quietly but firmly, 'All I want to know is, if he is my father, what's his real name and did he rescue the Romanovs? Tell me, with all that we have gone through, why is it proving to be AN IMPOSSIBLE TASK?'

Juliana placed her coffee cup slowly on the saucer. As Michael's voice reached a crescendo she considered whether to tell him what she had discovered about the doctor. Seeing Alice's face she thought better of it and said instead, 'Well Michael, HE MUST BE Fox because I can't see what he had to gain by publishing a fictitious story detailing a rescue mission that never took place.'

Michael appeared to calm down and nodded in agreement. 'I couldn't have put it better myself. But where do we go from here? How can we find out the real truth about Fox?'

Juliana watched him closely as he stared lethargically into his empty coffee cup. She knew the worst thing for Michael's health was to succumb to a depression.

'Look at these paintings. Aren't they wonderful? Let's have a wander round.'

Michael looked up and smiled wistfully. He was about to agree when Alice leant across and whispered in his ear. 'Was there anything else he told you?' she asked as Juliana walked over to look at the paintings hanging on the wall opposite. Michael made a move to follow her but Alice grabbed his arm. 'Come on, you can tell me and there is no need to be disappointed. Your father was honest as the day is long and very brave too. That much I do know.'

Michael smiled. 'Well, there was something in the dream. I didn't want to...'

'Come on, quickly now,' Alice encouraged.

'Well...I ...,' Michael hesitated as Juliana returned to the table.

'Please! Don't let me interrupt.' She responded apparently offended by the sudden silence.

'Oh, don't be silly! There's nothing we are not telling you.' Michael added resting both elbows on the table. 'I was just about to explain what else I saw in my dream. Now, it's very strange. Karl said he was imprisoned at Fort somewhere.... I can't recall the exact name. Anyway, I was transported back to his room somewhere in the U.S. He and I sat chatting for a while until we were interrupted by a visitor. He was tall and very elegant and Karl knew him well. Then suddenly in my dream I realised that this tall stranger looked exactly like the Count who had came to see me all those years ago. You know the one who gave me my inheritance.'

'As I said, Karl knew him well and was not at all surprised to see him. By the way, although Karl was living in a fort of some kind he was in opulent surroundings. He had two servants and his rooms were well furnished and he had all the books and writing material he could possibly want. In fact it looked like a palace but of course he was held for his own security.'

Michael paused to sip the last of his coffee.

'Well that certainly rings a bell,' Alice responded. 'I remember Maria saying that he was very well looked after. She told me that Karl had only been arrested for his own safety, since he was German and the United States was now at war with Germany. You won't remember this but I do. Enemy aliens were not to be treated as prisoners because they were not convicts. They were all to be treated with courtesy, especially a man of Karl's background.'

'You mean because he was a Brandenberg?' Juliana enquired.

Alice continued without replying. 'I remember Karl could afford all the trappings of a luxurious life. He wrote in 1920 to Maria saying that he fully expected to become an American citizen. They had promised him that much!'

'And,' Juliana added, 'From what I've read he was fully entitled to receive it, given how much information he had passed to the U.S. and British about the Kaiser's ambition to conquer the world.'

'Anyway, getting back to my story,' Michael interrupted. 'This important visitor explained to Karl that they needed him and that he was exactly the right person for the job. He half joked with Karl, saying he knew that Karl had a mission to fulfil and that if he was successful he would not only be able to write history he would be responsible for making it! Karl laughed very loudly. In fact he was laughing so loudly that I started to laugh with him. I could actually hear myself laughing in my sleep; it was very peculiar. "MAKE HISTORY" I heard him say. But here's the strangest thing. Halfway through my dream the man who was asking Karl to make history turned into a woman and what she had to tell Karl was, and always would be, A STATE SECRET. In fact, it was more than a state secret, it was a universal secret! This beautiful woman told me that the Russian Imperial Family had been successfully rescued and were being hidden safely at a secret and secure retreat where they were awaiting the outcome of certain events in Russia. Remember, it was August 1918 and she didn't go into detail as to what those events were. But here's the thing. The monarchy was to be restored in Russia towards the end of 1919. However it would not be Tsar Nicholas II on the throne.'

'You see, he didn't have the heart for ruling any more. Apparently another member of the family would rule in his place. Then, and this is spooky, Karl winked at me and he stretched out his arm towards the female visitor. It was bizarre. He was saying something but I couldn't hear what it was. Anyway, no one suspected HER of being an agent too. They must have been writing up their story together. Everyone naturally assumed that she was his fiancée as they huddled together, drafting up every step of the rescue mission into Fox's diary. I could see she had many letters and all sorts of papers. Then she turned round and this is what really got to me...'

Michael took a deep breath before continuing. 'She called out to me to bear witness. But I couldn't see her face. Try as I might, I could not make out one of her features. Then, in my dream my father asked her where the Russian royal family were living. She could not divulge the secret whereabouts of the family but said that she would bring him more notes that should be incorporated into the diary. You see, she said, when certain events had taken place everyone would want to know HOW they had ALL escaped.

"You!" she said, pointing at him, "will become very wealthy because film directors will want to make a film and you should remember that when you start writing up their journey to safety; you should make it as dramatic and colourful as possible because no expense will be spared in making the film and you will be paid handsomely for it. Unfortunately you cannot put your name to the Russian masterpiece! I know the reasons will be clear to you!"

Then I saw her hug him before taking her leave. Oh yes, and she gave him one more order. "No one is to know. The well being of the state relies on your silence. Do I make myself clear?" I heard her say as she swept from the room and there my dream ended.'

'Goodness me, that was a detailed dream. I wonder you didn't tell me earlier! Well, at least we know why he named the rescuer of the family, Fox.' Juliana stated triumphantly.

Michael scowled. 'Why is that?' he asked.

Juliana grinned. 'Well don't forget, Fox is also the name of a well-known filmmaker but there's just one thing that doesn't add up. If the family had already escaped and were safely hidden, why couldn't they just tell the real story of their escape? Why was it so important for Karl to write a made up version of the journey they took out of Russia?'

Michael sighed. 'I don't know.' He replied glancing at Alice for support.

'Oh dear me, just because you dreamt it Michael, doesn't make it true!' Alice laughed at the absurdity of the situation as Juliana continued to make suggestions.

'How about this, Dr Graves called his hero Fox because he wanted to pay tribute to his dear friend Edward Lyell Fox, who had just died. Besides, I'm quite sure Karl was not involved in the rescue personally because he would have been too old.'

'Too old,' repeated Michael. 'He was only about forty. I don't think that's too old for such a mission!'

'Ah! Now you have reminded me of something!' Alice stepped in. 'Can you remember exactly what time you had the dream?'

Michael sniggered. 'Don't be ridiculous. How am I supposed to know?'

'Think please!'

'Well, it must have been about one or two in the morning.'

'Ah! Ha! Now I know why he was in such a rush to leave me!'

Michael looked amused. What on earth was Alice talking about now?

He was about to ask when Juliana sighed and checked her watch. 'Come on you two, we should head up toward the restaurant, otherwise we'll be late.'

Chapter Forty   Once a Knight always a Knight

In the restaurant, Alex had been explaining why he had taken photographs of the Piazza de Popola.

'And now I've a great idea for painting it too!' he continued enthusiastically as Tonya reached across for a bread stick to nibble on.

'Oh good, I can't wait for you to start, I love the smell of the oil paints. Don't forget you promised to give me some lessons.' Tonya took off her jacket as she spoke. 'And there's another great place to take great photographs just across the way there. Paul showed it to me, it's called the Piazza Santa Maria and has a stunning fountain. Oh, that reminds me Alex, can you take a photo of the two of us?' Tonya asked leaning against Paul.

Alex smiled. 'Yes of course!' He replied getting up and adjusting his lens. 'Just a little closer please, smile! Ah, that's lovely! I'll do another one, just in case!' Tonya smiled as he repositioned the camera, refocused the lens and clicked the button. 'There, that should do nicely. By the way, I met my friend who gave me the gold coin this morning. It was quite by accident! Anyway, he's going to join us later. His name is Alonzo.' Alex went on. 'He's very handsome and I am pleased to say that he hardly speaks any English!' Alex winked to emphasise the point.

'Why so pleased?' Paul asked.

'Becaaaause,' Alex drew out his answer. 'It's so much moooore exciting getting to know one another without using booooring woooords. It means you have to rely on other forms of communication!'

Paul flushed as he listened, partly out of anger and partly out of embarrassment. Eventually he had to say something. 'So you think you're right to have an unfair advantage over him? You understand Italian perfectly well, what if he finds out one day?'

Alex laughed again. 'But he doesn't know that and he won't find out until I'm ready for him to!'

'Well I should be careful if I were you!' Tonya warned. 'You might hear something you don't like. Then how would you feel?'

Alex shrugged, wondering why they took everything so seriously.

'Why don't you tell him that you speak some Italian and get him to teach you more?' Paul suggested.

'That's a great idea,' Tonya added. 'Then you can teach him English in return.'

Alex burst out laughing again. 'I think we have rather more interesting things to do than give each other language lessons!'

As Michael, Juliana and Alice walked into the restaurant they bumped into Giovanni. 'Good timing' Michael ventured. 'Right let's see, where are they sitting?' He murmured peering into the semi- darkened room.

'I see them!' Alice replied pointing to a long table with a red and beige checked table cloth. 'Right now Giovanni, you come and sit next to me,' she demanded, watching Michael seat himself at the head of the table as usual.

'I'll keep this one for Alonzo if you don't mind,' Alex said, hastily grabbing hold of the chair next to him.

Michael sighed loudly. 'Would you mind?' he asked Paul, who immediately got up and gave his chair to Juliana. Michael then ordered the wine as everyone settled themselves.

Once Juliana was seated Michael tapped a wine glass with the edge of his butter knife to get their attention. 'Now, before we decide what to eat there is something I would like to say. First of all, the lunch is on me as a thank you for helping me to unravel mother's mysterious past. Thanks to all your hard work I have acquired enough evidence to prove that Fox's diary in the best seller *Rescuing the Czar* was actually written by my mother's good friend Dr Armgaard Karl Graves. The story is intriguing and it would seem that the role of the Baroness is certainly based on my mother's life.' He took a sip of wine before continuing. 'Now, we know she had a secret; but helping to rescue the Tsar and his family was not it. I suspect her real secret was that Dr Armgaard Karl Graves, and please remember this was not his real name, may also have been my father. Of course, I have no way of proving the hypothesis and it is very upsetting for me to have to..,' Michael paused and thumped his chest as he repeated the words, '...to have to admit that as a result I am not a Brandenberg and neither is my son! However, I have it on very good authority that Dr Graves hails from the Prussian aristocracy, his name being every bit as good as the name Brandenberg. I have always known that my father was a special man and his name may have been so important that my mother was unable to divulge it during her lifetime. Of course, I am yet to find out her real name as well; but Juliana and I think we could be onto something and we will be able to reveal all to you shortly. So,' Michael raised his glass in the air, 'enjoy your meal.' He shouted and they all raised their glasses in return.

Afterwards everyone was deep in thought. Eventually Michael looked up. 'Shall we order?' he suggested, lifting up the menu. Juliana leant over and gave him a big hug. 'That was well said. Now let's enjoy the meal!' she added, noticing that Alice and Giovanni were still deep in conversation.

'Come on you two take a look at the menu so that we can finish ordering.'

Alice laughed. 'Don't worry. We know exactly what we're having. It's always the same with us. Spaghetti, spaghetti, Spaghetti!' She added tunefully.

'Right, let me see exactly how many there are of us.' Michael started counting as the waiter stood by patiently. 'Seven! So that's two more bottles of red and two bottles of white and some Vichy as well, say two bottles of that should do.'

'By the way, does anyone remember what day it is?' Alice asked, quite out of the blue. 'The 22nd of June. Why?' Juliana was mildly amused.

'Oh dear,' replied Michael, suddenly remembering something he shouldn't have forgotten. 'Tomorrow is the anniversary of ......' He glanced across to Alice as he spoke. 'Of course how forgetful of me not to mention it, that's another reason why I gathered us here today. I was waiting for the wine to arrive before I said something.' Michael cleared his throat, watching impatiently as the waiter finished pouring the wine. 'So please everyone, raise your glass in remembrance of the Baroness Maria, my wonderful mother, your grandmother, your mother-in-law, your great aunt, and your very close friend, Alice, too!'

The chair legs made a loud screeching noise on the marble tiles as they all stood up. 'To Maria Brandenberg, Cheers! Santé! To the Baroness 'B', Cheers! Santé! To Lucy, Santé!'

'LUCY? Why did you say Lucy?' Alex asked Giovanni.

'Leave him alone.'

'Well, I only asked why he said Lucy. There is no need for him to get upset about that surely?'

Alice sighed as Paul grinned like a Cheshire cat and tapped the glass to get everyone's attention.

'Buono! It must be the day for announcements and I hope our news will make you all so happy.' As Tonya stood beside him, Paul clasped her hand and looked directly at his father. 'Si, with your blessing we wish to get married. So first I am asking Tonya and now I am asking you. What do you say, father?'

Giovanni wanted to turn away but knew how impolite that would be. Instead he muttered something unintelligible.

'Oh, and you're all invited to the wedding here in our wonderful AMOR ROMA!' Paul added, turning to Tonya and kissing her cheek.

'That's wonderful news!' Michael responded by clapping. 'We knew that an announcement was imminent, didn't we Juliana?'

Juliana smiled 'Yes, congratulations. We are very happy for the two of you. Have you set a date?' As she spoke she glanced across to Giovanni, who had tears welling up.

'Well, we were thinking of the autumn, perhaps November.' Giovanni leant over and gave his son a big hug. 'Molto bene.' He added raising his glass and downing the contents. 'Si, so we are now one big family.' he told Alice as Michael tapped his wine glass three times. 'Three cheers for Paul and Tonya! Hip Hip Hooray! Hip Hip Hooray! Hip Hip Hooray!' Michael replenished his glass and handed the bottle to Juliana. 'This time we'll say it properly! Hock! Hock! Hock! And since family tradition dictates it, we'll down our wine all at once... all together now!'

HOCK! HOCK! HOCK! They shouted, all except Giovanni. He cut a lonely figure as he stood fiddling with his tie and hoping his son would not be too ashamed of him. What luck he'd decided to go to the barber's earlier! So, Paul was going to leave the priesthood for good. That would be difficult for his family. To think of all those years of study all gone to pot! It was such a disappointment. But he knew better that to indulge his fondness for sadness at such a time, not when everyone else was enjoying themselves. Instead he smiled at the happy couple whenever they looked at him. He even raised his glass to Alex the tormenter, who was as unpredictable as ever. Dancing one moment and taking photographs the next. He could not remember when he had been so happy or so young and carefree. Ah well that is what life does to you. It makes you yearn for the days when you were young. By the time the food had arrived Giovanni felt a lot better. Change happens, he told himself. Well, he knew that as well as the next man but he was still harbouring *that* secret. Soon it would come out. What would they think of him then?

'This is very tasty,' Alice remarked, heartily tucking into her spaghetti.

'Si,' Giovanni agreed tucking his napkin in as Michael leant across to Alice and whispered, 'Remember when I said that I thought Mother had been murdered?'

Alice almost dropped her fork, 'Well, yes of course I do,' she whispered back, 'but why are we …..' Michael waved her concern away. 'I just wanted to say that I don't think that's the case anymore. However, I do believe that the fire in the caravan was no accident. Someone wanted those papers destroyed because THEY didn't want the TRUTH to come out.'

Michael took a sip of wine before continuing. 'I remember years ago when the Count delivered my inheritance, he told me that one day I would learn who my real family was. But despite the work we've put in we're no closer are we?' Alice shook her head in agreement with him.

'But you see Alice I have always suspected that you knew more. That you kept a secret out of some misguided loyalty to my mother. So Alice why have you refused to tell me? What's your reason?' Alice turned deadly serious. 'What else did this Count tell you?' she hissed watching Michael tap his bottom lip.

'He said that my father was sorry that he had not known me as a father should know a son and that I have siblings that one day I should meet.'

'Well, he seems to have told you quite a lot then.' Alice placed her cutlery neatly together on the plate and folded her napkin. 'But there is something else you need to know! Legend has it that there is nothing more important in life than the swearing of an oath and GOD HELP YOU, if that oath is broken!' Alice shouted the words out as she spoke. 'Because a legacy left behind of a broken oath can be handed down from generation to generation, in fact up to seven times!'

Michael laughed nervously as a candle on the table caught Alice's breath and flickered.

'Ah! Ha! Legacy you say? Well is it a good legacy or a bad legacy? Magic, like miracles, only work if you believe in them and I don't! Anyway, tell me what would happen if YOU broke THAT sacred oath and told me mother's secret?'

Alice sighed. She hated being put on the spot. 'I'm sure you don't need me to spell it out for you but I will anyway! I'd put at risk all the members of the family and call into question the validity of my life continuing! Please Michael, don't ask me to say more. Especially not today! Remember, I'm a great believer!'

'What's going on? Who are you upsetting now?' Juliana demanded.

'We're just talking about the meaning of taking an oath and what the consequence would be if you broke it.' Alice replied.

Juliana was shocked. 'Today of all days is not a day to be morbid. I'm sure Paul and Tonya will be very happy together!'

Michael raised an eyebrow. 'Actually, we were talking about bold knights of old and their secret societies and the oaths that members must take and what effect this might have on future generations of a family.'

Alice smiled. 'Yes, I was reminding Michael that the brotherhood is always there no matter what.'

Juliana burst out laughing. 'Do you know, Alice, I haven't got a clue what you're talking about.'

Michael sighed. 'Let me explain, dear,' he responded, taking her literally. 'Some orders go way back. Their members took sacred oaths in order to be accepted into the brotherhood. So for example, take the Red Cross. It is sworn to provide shelter and refuge. Well, imagine something similar for a knight of a secret order where whole generations have sworn allegiance. You'll give him shelter no matter what, and you'll protect him no matter what, because your life and the life of future generations in the family depend on it.'

'One law for the few, another for the many, is that what you're saying?' Juliana paused due to a mild intoxication of wine. Michael frowned as he thought about what might be coming next. 'And this is what I do for your so-called business of honour.' Michael watched horrified as she put her thumb under her front teeth and flicked it out at him. He wasn't sure what to say to his wife, who had given him a very Italian insult; so he poured her a glass of water instead.

'Well my dear, it's not as simple as that,' Alice replied. 'Tradition and establishment play a large part in maintaining the status quo, for which we must all be thankful. There are many orders that trace their roots back to 1099, and don't forget, most of the monarchs of Christian Europe are members. Let me give you an example of what we are talking about here. When the peace treaty was signed in 1918, Kaiser Wilhelm II was still alive. He was offered sanctuary by Count Goddard von Bentinck. The order he belonged to had three thousand knights worldwide. Michael knows about the Rechtsritter, who are the Knights of Justice, but perhaps he has not heard of the Ehrenritter, who were Knights of Honour.'

'OF COURSE ALICE, now I see what you're trying to tell me!' Michael sounded euphoric. 'My father was from a family of Ehrenritter, not Ehrenkrug or Ehrenburg. That's why he was sworn to secrecy. Oh my God! EHREN RITTER! That's why he couldn't tell the truth about his role in the rescue of the Russian Imperial Family. That's why he wrote the false account of their journey too.'

Alice leant back in the chair. 'So there you are, Michael. Now you know your father was an Ehrenritter!'

'Yes, thank you. Is there any more?'

Alice shook her head.

'Can women become Ehrenritter?' Juliana asked.

'Usually it is for the eldest son!' Alice replied glaring at Michael and half expecting him to say something about the Kaiser's talismanic ring.

'Well, that's a shame, because it would explain a lot. I mean, just imagine if your mother had been tied up by a whole host of intergenerational secrets as well! Juliana squeezed Michael's arm affectionately.

He smiled 'I'm sure you would like it to be full of secret conclaves and femme fatales but there is only one type of "night" that you should know about!'

Juliana pulled away from him flirtatiously before replying. 'And pray tell, kind sir, what do you have in mind?' Michael hesitated unsure of how to react.

Juliana leant forward again. 'Very well, since you are unable to speak perhaps this will loosen your tongue?' Juliana handed him a half full carafe as she spoke. 'Or,' she added, 'perhaps there are other ways of making you talk! How about your accomplice, Alice? She looks as though she's in cahoots with you and hiding the esoteric knowledge about these knights of old from me.'

'Well, as you have already guessed, I'm bound not to reply!'

'Come along, I'm sure you really don't want to upset me! I wish to hear everything NOW!' Juliana shouted out, slightly inebriated.

'Well,' continued Alice 'I understand there are only eight surviving hereditary knights of the eight-hundred-year-old order in Germany. You'll not be surprised to learn that the order I speak of was founded by crusading knights who protected pilgrims along the route to Jerusalem.'

'Ha! I knew it!' Juliana winked at Michael. 'Exactly what Dr Graves said in his book; so now we know his family belongs to one of those eight surviving members'.

'Well if that is the case, he would have had the protection of Kaiser Wilhelm II.'

'That's just it Alice! The Kaiser did come to his defence,' Michael interjected.

'So which Ehrenritter did Dr Graves's family belong to then?' Juliana demanded as Michael sat pensively listening.

'Well, there is a name for this ancient order, although it is not used much today and...' Alice paused again, choosing her words carefully.

Juliana sighed with impatience, sensing she was about to be fobbed off, or at the very least for Alice to say that her lips were sealed! Why was she so hesitant about saying the name out loud? Juliana wondered growing more impatient by the minute.

'Honestly, anybody would think I was asking you to divulge the whereabouts of the Holy Grail!'

A smile crept across Alice's face as she turned her wine glass to catch the glistening crimson glow of the candle light at regular intervals. To Juliana it flashed like a lighthouse, warning intrepid travellers to stay away and then when Alice spoke it was as if time itself stood still.

'Deep in the Neumark of Brandenburg, east of the Oder River, lies an ancient castle which was the headquarters of one such brotherhood. If the walls had ears then the sentries at Sonneburg Castle could tell us a mighty tale or two. Of that I'm sure! But whatever those tales may have been, there is something far more precious, far more important, about that particular order today. The order has created and supported thousands of charitable activities. It runs hospitals and ambulance services and provides first aid training and manages disaster relief across the frontiers of Europe.'

While Alice was talking Juliana picked up an olive, bit into it and discarded the stone. 'You're speaking about St John's Ambulance or the Red Cross I suppose?'

Alice shook her head. 'If you'll just let me finish before you jump to conclusions! Nowadays the Grand Master is elected and no longer nominated by the King of Prussia or Emperor of Germany, since he no longer exists. What I tell you is important in terms of the period of time we are speaking about, which is the first quarter of the twentieth century.' Alice paused for a moment and took a handkerchief out from her pocket.

Juliana hurriedly drank her wine as Alice neatly twisted a corner and dabbed the corner of her right eye. 'Are you okay?' she asked.

Alice smiled in response. 'Now where was I?' She asked patting Juliana's hand.

'You were about to tell us why the order that Dr Graves belonged to was so important.'

'Ah well, I don't know about that! But what I can tell you is that since 1693 the Grand Master of the Johanniter Orden has always been a Hohenzollern.'

'Well, they must have been very good people then,' Juliana suggested.

Alice didn't bother replying. 'There were only eight families who were original members, so if Dr Graves's family was one of them, it shouldn't be beyond the wit of man to find him.'

Michael's eyes lit up. 'Of course, why on earth didn't I think of that? Nothing is hidden that will not be made known! Do you know, I was thinking only the other day about the "My Dear Fox" letters, you remember, the ones supposedly written by Tsar Nicholas and Kaiser Wilhelm in 1919 and shown to Boris Brasol in 1931?'

'What, the ones William McGarry sent?' Juliana asked.

'Yes. Now if Karl Graves is our man Fox then Mr McGarry must have got the letters from him. That means William Mcgarry knew Dr Armgaard Karl Graves in November 1918.'

'Well, that sounds logical,' interrupted Alice. 'But what about the Baroness 'B' who was she and have you managed to discover what part she played in all of this? After all Michael, we could be talking about your mother here.'

'Let's keep the Baroness out of this for the moment. Now, if the Tsar wrote to Karl in 1919 and the Kaiser wrote to him sometime before May 1918...?' Michael paused as he counted on his fingers.

'Darling,' interrupted Juliana, 'why are you calling him Karl and not Armgaard?'

'Because my middle name is Karl and I'm one hundred percent sure he is my father. You remember that message he left. 'In Remembrance of our Siberian adventure.' and he signed himself K.A.G. So he wanted to be called Karl. Besides, Armgaard is not a name I recognise or particularly like!'

'Well I suppose that's a good enough reason, but if you could make a wish come true, what would it be?'

'For you to stop interrupting me because now I've completely forgotten what I was about to tell you, but since you ask,' Michael raised his glass, 'There are many things I would wish for.'

'Be serious Michael, we are talking about Karl here!' Alice admonished.

'I see you've put my wife up to this little game.'

'I assure you I haven't!' Alice replied indignantly.

'Come on darling let's hear your wish. Whisper it to me. You know I can make it happen!'

Michael flushed and Alice wondered whether he'd drunk too much wine.

'Ha! Ha! I don't know. I suppose I'm curious as to what Karl looked like and what happened to him after he saved the tsar and his family.'

Juliana was jubilant. 'DA-DAA! I told you I could make it happen! Look what I have here.' She added opening her bag and pulling out a pile of old newspaper cuttings. Michael couldn't believe his eyes as she laid them one by one on the table in front of him. After she had finished Juliana glanced down the table. Apart from Giovanni, everyone else was busy chatting and laughing. She immediately felt sorry for him and waved him over, patting the chair next to her for him to sit on.

'Okay darling, you wanted to know what Dr Graves looks like. Well here you are.' Juliana handed Michael a photograph as she spoke and Alice looked on in astonishment. 'It was taken around 1937 or so I believe'.

'God Almighty, I really do look like him! Mother said I was the spitting image of my father!'

'Give it to me,' Alice demanded, leaning over Giovanni. 'Where on earth did you get that from?' she asked.

'Well you're never going to believe this. It was stuck to the lining of that old tea chest in the library. I nearly missed it.'

'But how did you realise the significance of it?' Michael asked.

Juliana smiled. 'It looked like you. Then I read this. You see, everything now falls into place.' As she spoke Juliana handed him the article.

Michael listened carefully to what his wife was saying before passing the clipping to Alice. 'But you've known about this for some time. Why have you taken so long to tell me?' Michael found it hard to accept that his wife could have secrets from him. He reached for an almost empty wine bottle and poured out the remainder into his glass.

Alice stared at the photograph with tired and bleary eyes as Giovanni looked on.

'Che significa?' he asked, as Alice passed it to Tonya. She was far too wrapped up in her own world to show any interest but Alex's reaction, well that was to be expected. 'Soooo! This is what my grandfather looks like. Wow! He's mighty fine looking.' He added studying the photo. Then the smile left his face. 'Actually, he looks a bit uncomfortable don't you think?'

Juliana took a second look. 'Yes. He's clearly not happy about being photographed; remember he likes his privacy!'

Alex scowled. 'But he looks ashamed, Mother.'

'Give me that now, how dare you speak of him in that manner!' Michael shouted as Alex kept a firm grip on the photograph.

'Don't take it personally. I was only commenting from an artistic point of view. I mean, if I wanted to paint a guilty look on a face I would paint one like that!' Michael's face looked as though it was about to explode.

'Now that's quite enough Alex,' Juliana reprimanded, snatching the photograph from his hand and handing it back to Michael.

'Oh dear,' Tonya sighed, leaning across to Alex. 'It seems every time you start discussing Dr Graves you end up in a row and you're always in the middle of it!'

Hearing what Tonya had to say, Michael glanced up. 'I'm not angry with you son, I just want you to show some respect. After all, we don't know the full story and none of us are in a position to judge or criticise Dr Graves! Besides, you shouldn't speak ill of the dead.' he chastised, waving an empty wine bottle at the waiter.

Alex didn't like being reprimanded in front of everyone. He'd better not do that in front of my friend he thought, watching his father gesticulate frantically at a passing waiter. Oh that's good. That's very good! Alex watched as the waiter immediately responded to his father's demands.

A few moments later Juliana held a paper in the air. 'That's not the only surprise I have for you Michael! You wanted to know about Karl's life after 1918 and I have it ALL here.'

Michael groaned and put his head in his hands.

'What's wrong? I thought you'd be happy.'

'We are only approaching the anniversary of Mother's death, that's all!'

'Quite!' agreed Alice angrily, reminding Juliana. 'Whatever you say will be heard by both Maria and Karl in the spirit world. Look, it's a full moon, you know what that means?'

Juliana shook her head. 'No Alice, I'm afraid I don't.'

'On a night like tonight the dimension they are on and the frequency at which they communicate is closely connected to our vibrations. It means they can communicate with us as we can with them. So let me give you this bit of advice before you start, my dear. It must all be vetted and scrutinised closely by someone they trust and love.'

Alex shivered in rather an exaggerated manner, which made Tonya giggle but Alice had their full attention.

'Well, who would you suggest Alice?' Juliana demanded.

'I would have thought that was obvious! Unfortunately however, we, that is Michael and I, are unable to scrutinise the records, so we cannot verify what you're about to divulge.'

Juliana smiled. 'Well you'll just have to trust me then. Anyway, if Maria bothered to collect these then it must have meant something to her. I'm not going to make any judgements. That's for Michael to do, once he has heard what they say.'

Michael groaned, placed his head in his hands and wondered where this was all going. Presently he looked up and, judging by his demeanour, he was apparently inspired. 'After careful consideration it strikes me that even though we are in relaxing circumstances, with wine and food on the table, our interests are always best served when we are guided by the spirits. This should be a serious moment. So before we listen to what Juliana has to say let us…'

'Guided?' Giovanni butted in. 'How you mean guided boss? Not those strange words we said before?'

'HA, HA, HA, HA, I'll drink to the SPIRITS!' Joked Alex holding up his glass of wine, then he checked his watch, hoping that Alonzo would not arrive at such an embarrassing time.

Chapter Forty One   Revelations

'Right my dear!' Michael said, turning to Juliana. 'We are ready to hear what you have to say now!'

'Remember when the caravan burned? How we thought we'd lost everything, but then Maria cleverly left us these clues so that we could piece together the truth about her SECRET life. Well, what I'm about to reveal will astonish you and it is only fitting that tonight, on the evening before the anniversary of her death, that I am able to do so. Let us remember all that she was to us before history took its fateful turn.'

'Amen to that,' Michael added.

'Without a doubt, Maria was a woman of mystery with oh so many secrets....many of which we will never get to the bottom of. But thanks to her I can reveal that I have been able to unravel yet another perplexing mystery. Before I do, let's please all raise our glasses to our wonderful time with Maria, the Baroness Brandenberg, may she always be with us!' Juliana raised her glass high into the air and everyone stood up.

'Nastravie!' Alice shouted across the table. 'Nastravie!'

After the toast, Juliana held up the photograph of Dr Armgaard Karl Graves.

'You all saw this earlier. To us he is known as Karl because that's who he was to Maria but as we have found out, he also went under the name of Dr Karl Armgaard Graves, a pseudonym for a secret agent who called himself Fox and wrote Fox's diary in the best seller *Rescuing the Czar*. We know that Dr Graves copied text from his best seller *The Secrets of the German War Office* into the diary of Fox, the man who says he rescued the Russian Imperial Family in 1918. Now, even though Fox's diary is contrary to all that we know about the end of the Imperial Family, namely that they were all executed at Ekaterinburg, crucially we now have documentary evidence to suggest that part of the story Karl tells in Fox's diary may actually be true. But before I get onto that let me say this. Whatever else Karl may or may not have been, one thing is for sure. He was a highly successful author who sold hundreds of thousands of books in the U.S. during the First World War. But it would appear, from what I have here, that he was no more than a common criminal who used the art of extortion to earn a living.'

As Juliana finished speaking a gasp went up.

'Yes! I know it's shocking but bear with me while I set the scene for you. It's September 1917 and the United States has made a decision to back the Allies and enter the war. However, not everyone in America is happy. That's because a substantial part of the American population is German and quite obviously would not want to go to war with their relatives in Germany. Who could blame them for that? In addition, there were many Germans seeking citizenship in the U.S. Now when war breaks out between the two countries the U.S. Government becomes nervous about allowing German nationals, especially if they were influential, to roam freely around the country. They were to be treated as enemy aliens and in most cases they were locked up, not for what they had done but for what they might do!

It should come as no surprise to you then that Karl was one of those suspected. He was caught loitering in a forbidden zone without a permit. As a result he was sent to a detention centre called Fort Leavenworth. However, there was some debate as to whether this was the right course of action or whether he should be considered for parole. Remember, he was not a convict in the true sense of the word and so was not handcuffed. Karl becomes a guest at Fort Leavenworth towards the end of 1917 but it is by no means certain that he spent all of his time there. I say this because amongst Maria's papers I found a copy of a letter dated May 13th 1918.

It was from the Office of the Attorney General in New York and addressed to the U.S Department of Justice in Washington. The letter thanked them for their communication containing information on Dr Armgaard Karl Graves. Unfortunately I have been unable to find out what that information was but the date is an interesting one because if Karl had been on a mission to save the Tsar in Ekaterinburg then this was exactly the right time to get permission to leave the U.S. So this communication with the Department of Justice, dated May 13th 1918, could be the documentary proof we are looking for that Fox, really Dr Armgaard Karl Graves, was telling the truth when he says the Imperial Family were all rescued.'

'Wow!' Tonya interrupted. 'He really was Fox!'

'Now,' continued Juliana, 'I have thought long and hard about what other reason the Justice Office may have had for communicating over an internee and I have not been able to think of any other reason apart from registering special release papers for this secret mission.'

'Maybe he became ill and needed special drugs or had to go into hospital?' Paul suggested.

'Or how about this?' interrupted Alex. 'He'd been commissioned by the authorities to write up the story of the Romanovs' escape in the format of a lost diary and they were communicating about what privileges or payments he should receive for doing the work.'

'Yes, that's quite possible,' agreed Juliana, 'but if he wasn't freed so that he could go and rescue the Imperial Family in Russia, then we can assume that he would have been released at the end of the war in November 1918. Of course, any friendships or affiliations that he had developed during his internment would have continued afterwards. If Fox's diary was written up during his so-called internment, then William Rutledge McGarry and Mr Romanovsky may have visited him at Fort Leavenworth to provide him with the information he would have needed to write Fox's diary, unless of course there was a go between, and this is where the enigmatic Baroness 'B' could have had a role.'

Tonya reached across the table for the last slice of garlic bread. 'Well, if the authorities did ask Karl to write the story, why in 1920 did they demand that it was withdrawn from the market?'

Juliana shrugged. 'I have no idea,' she replied, looking at Michael for clarification.

'Well,' he responded, 'during the latter part of 1918 there was still every chance that the Whites would beat the Reds and gain control of Russia but when Kolchak was killed the tide turned. It became clear that the Reds would maintain their grip on the state and create a new Bolshevik regime across the country. By 1920 it was obvious that Russia would not be returning to its former imperial state anytime soon and so that's why I think it was withdrawn from sale.' Michael sneezed and pulled a handkerchief from his pocket.

'Bless you!' Alice responded watching him rub his nose hard.

'Right where was I? Oh yes, so to publish *Rescuing the Czar* would have been to put the lives of the Imperial Family at risk. It would have provided the Bolsheviks with certain knowledge that the Imperial Family was alive and well. They feared the Bolsheviks would make a concerted effort to find and annihilate them, since their exiled existence would pose a continual threat to the new Bolshevik State.'

'Indeed, as we have discussed before, the Bolsheviks may have been looking for the remnants of Russian royalty when they lured Russian monarchists back into Russia with the enticement of positions of power, culminating in the infamous "Trust" conspiracy which was sprung in 1925.'

'Ah!' Alex responded, 'I remember reading about that plot. It was designed to root out imperialist supporters from exile and trick them into going back to Russia. The organisers of "The Trust" lured them back by telling them that there was a huge underground movement ready at any moment to overthrow the Bolsheviks and reinstate the monarchy. That's how Sidney Reilly was eventually caught and executed. Right, Paul?'

'Yes, but as Michael says, the heart of the plan was to capture exiled members of the Russian Imperial Family so that they or their relatives could not ascend to the Russian throne in the future.'

'That makes me think the Bolsheviks believed members of the Imperial Family were still alive at that time then.'

Alice smiled. 'We shall never know Tonya. Luckily, any remnants of the Russian Imperial Family were far too clever for that and stayed well away from Russia.'

'So now we know why Mr McGarry withdrew *Rescuing the Czar* from sale,' Juliana went on. 'But let me get back to my story about Dr Armgaard Karl Graves! It's 1918 and he is freed from internment. Now as we know, he has been trusted with a secret, quite possibly one of the biggest secrets of all time. Either he personally rescued the Tsar and his family or he knew they had been rescued; but even though he was a Prussian noble from one of the greatest dynastic houses of Europe, he now finds his circumstances greatly reduced through no fault of his own. Without the sale of the book he is virtually a pauper. All the promises of a new life in America have evaporated into thin air. Despite this, he never once let the cat out of the bag. To his credit he never spills the beans, yet he could have so easily sold his story and made the millions he wanted to. All that hard work for no pay, it would make anyone angry.'

Alex agreed as he watched his mother open her handbag and pull out more newspapers.

'These articles, dated from 1925, do not make for pleasant reading. Dr Graves is accused of trying to extort money to fund a trip to uncover buried treasure.'

Alex's eyes opened wide. 'Ah! Ha! I was right buried treasure! I just knew we would find some.' Juliana smiled. 'Well I shall come to that in a moment. But first let's order some dessert. I like the look of the zabaglione.'

While they all chose from the menu, Juliana busied herself checking that the articles were in date order. Then Alonzo arrived and Alex introduced him to everyone. Tonya noted his distinct smell of aftershave, which she found surprisingly refreshing. After making sure his friend was settled, Alex made his way over to his father. 'I'm a bit worried about Alonzo getting bored since his English is practically non-existent and he won't understand what's being said. Do you mind if we leave?'

'You must do what you think fit but if you stay you'll hear what your mother has to say about the man who could be your grandfather. I'm sure your friend will understand when you tell that tomorrow is the anniversary....'

'You're right, Father! I'll order him a dessert and coffee. He'll be fine.'

A few minutes later Juliana tapped the wine glass with her pen. 'Right everyone, if I could have your attention for a few moments! I promised to tell you about Dr Grave's life after the war. So here we are.' She added holding up an old newspaper.

'This article is dated May 28th 1929. I'll read it to you;

The notorious international war spy Armgaard Karl Graves has been arrested in Los Angeles on bunko charges that were brought against him in San Francisco. Henry Kirchmann Jr. alleges that Graves swindled him out of $3,500 as part of a scheme involving the promise of buried treasure in Haiti. He is in jail! To search for the treasure, Clarence Saunders gave him $1,500 but saw no more of him!'

'I believe this next one comes from the Los Angeles Times.

Buried Plunder Inquiry Widens. Amazing tale spurs Investigation. Dr Graves tells of plan to get one million eight hundred thousand dollars. Former activities recounted. Authorities last night began a canvass of the United States for information on the activities of Dr Armgaard Karl Graves, self styled master spy who is held here on a charge of grand theft through a complaint filed against him.

Alex put his hand over his mouth in disbelief. Nearly two million dollars! But where did he get that amount of money from? Juliana ignored her son and carried on reading. 'This article is dated May 29th 1929 and reads as follows:

"Spy faces trip north today. Dr Graves will be taken to San Francisco. Swindle accusation must be answered there. Effort to trace treasure fails. Dr Armgaard Karl Graves, self styled promoter of an expedition to Haiti to search for three million dollars in buried gold treasure, will be taken to San Francisco to answer a swindle charge according to information received yesterday by the police.'

'THREE MILLION DOLLARS,' Michael repeated. 'That's a big payoff!' he mumbled, watching Juliana place the papers neatly in her bag. 'So you're saying my father is just a common swindler.' He groaned, 'Mad, bad and dangerous to know.'

'Dear me, Michael, don't take on so. You can't believe everything you read in the paper,' Alice added trying her best to comfort him.

'Well what else am I to believe? SHE hasn't got any good news for me!'

Juliana patted his shoulder in sympathy. 'Try and read between the lines or at the very least, see the big picture. These articles, I should say headlines, are not telling us the full story. Besides, I may yet surprise you! Now, according to your mother's scrapbook he was jailed again in 1934. Now we don't know why, but there was a note saying that he was released in 1937 and afterwards things seem to have got a lot better for him. In fact, what happens next is really quite unexpected and backs up ALL that Karl has ever said.'

'Well I think I've heard FAR too much already!' Michael shouted. 'AND I'd be grateful if you would consider the company we're in! It is hardly enjoyable for me to listen to all this news of my father's criminal record sitting here in the middle of a public restaurant!'

'Now Michael, don't take on so. Juliana was only trying to help. There are always two sides to a story,' Alice replied. 'Besides, I do want to hear more and…..'

'Look, what we really want to hear about is the treasure and where it's buried. THREE MILLION DOLLARS! COME ON MOTHER, SPILL THE BEANS!' Alex shouted, rubbing his hands together and laughing madly.

Tonya smiled. 'You're right! It could all be true. Imagine all those gold coins and sparkling gemstones, rubies, sapphires and pearls just waiting to be found underneath the sand. We should go looking for it. You never know!'

'Well, I'm not so sure,' Paul added. 'It sounds like a typical tale of extortion. Greedy people always fall for them.'

'Why do you think the treasure included rubies, sapphires and pearls when I only mentioned gold?' Juliana asked Tonya.

'That's easy to answer. If the treasure Dr Graves was referring to was part of the lost Romanov fortune, then it would more than likely include jewellery. Sapphires sprung to mind because the Baroness B told Fox that "the sapphire was safely in America"!'

Michael laughed loudly. 'Well, if that's not the most ludicrous assumption I've ever heard, I'll eat my hat!'

'You're not wearing one, father.'

'Wait now,' Paul interrupted. 'Let me get this clear. You're saying that Dr Graves may have known of the treasure when he wrote Fox's diary because he had already buried it in Haiti specifically for the use of the …'

'That's a ridiculous assumption.' Michael interrupted. 'The Imperial Family did not casually drop anchor at a beach on Haiti, on their way to California from Vladivostok. Nor did Dr Graves carry a crate of jewels and coins off the waiting cruiser and bury them in a secret hiding place!'

'Come on Dad! Play the game! X marks the spot. We're one of the few who know where it's buried and I bet you it's still there.'

'Where on Haiti do you think it is then?' asked Tonya

'It's buried on a beach between the high and low tide line of course!'

Chapter Forty Two   Stolen Gold

Alice watched Giovanni with concern. Large beads of sweat glistened and ran down his face. She handed him a paper napkin and he smiled in gratitude, dabbing his forehead dry. 'Please Alice! We must say now. It is the right time.'

Alice gave a heavy sigh and patted his arm reassuringly. 'Yes, I know.' She replied watching Juliana struggle to close her handbag. 'Here, let me help,' Alice said holding one side. 'Gracious! You really do have a lot of papers in here. Perhaps you should take some out or get yourself a larger briefcase!'

Juliana smiled. 'You're right, and I have much more to show you, but somehow I don't think a restaurant is the right place to reveal it in.'

Alice glanced across to Michael, who was leaning back, staring at the photograph of Dr Graves. Every now and again he muttered something under his breath then, sensing he was being watched, he looked up. 'You know? I really wish we had those Fox letters so I could read them again.'

Alice pulled a face. 'Well surely you can remember what they said?'

Michael shook his head.

'Well,' she replied, 'if I recall correctly, they went something like "My Dear Fox, thank you for consummating my escape. Nicholas."

'No, no, no!' Juliana butted in, 'I know it off by heart. It said "My Dear Fox, I need not tell you how I feel indebted for all that you have done towards consummating my escape. I feel that you will do all you can to maintain my state secret. Believe me, Sincerely Nicolas."

Michael smiled. 'She's right. Nicholas said CONSUMMATING my escape, not rescuing me. It's quite different. Consummating, to bring to completion and fulfil. To sum up! You see, it could mean THANK YOU FOR PERFECTING MY ESCAPE! But there is another anomaly in the letter that's worrying me. Nicholas signed his name with only a *C* in the middle not a *CH*! Do we have any evidence that is how he liked to write his name? You see, I'm not convinced, nor am I about this,' Michael held up the photograph of Dr Graves and angrily waved it in the air. 'Is this man really my father? I think not!'

As he finished speaking a sharp snap announced that Juliana had finally managed to close her handbag. She turned away from him as she prepared to leave.

'I really worry about him Alice. I fear for his state of mind, I really do. You see how he reacts! There's so little positivity in him these days. Not like the old Michael. In fact I'm seriously wondering whether I should tell him the rest. I just don't know how he'll react.'

Alice patted her on the shoulder. 'He's just tired, as we all are. Why don't we leave the youngsters and head back to the hotel? Besides, Giovanni and I have something important to tell you both.'

Juliana looked surprised. 'Don't tell me you're getting married too!'

Alice burst into laughter at the thought.

'What's so funny?' Michael asked grumpily.

'Ah, we'll tell you back at the hotel. Are you ready to leave?'

'As ready as I'll ever be!'

* * *

Back at the hotel Giovanni insisted he was tired and said he wanted to go to bed but Alice was having none of it.

'You can't go to bed yet. We must tell them everything tonight.'

Giovanni watched as she made herself comfortable on a large soft green sofa and then he sat down next to her.

'A black coffee should help you stay awake!'

Giovanni smiled politely. 'Si, buono, quando vuol farlo?'

'Because we promised, remember?'

'Si, si but will you tell them ALL of it?'

Alice glanced across to Michael, who was deciding where he would be most comfortable. 'Yes, I suppose I will have to. You don't need to speak but I want you here just in case!' She said watching Juliana return having ordered the coffee.

'So Alice, what's the big surprise?' Michael asked, sitting down opposite.

'Before she tells you can I just finish where we left off at the restaurant?' Juliana interrupted hastily.

'Not more revelations!' Michael grimaced at the thought.

'I know it was a shock to hear about Karl's arrest and subsequent imprisonment but amongst your mother's papers were some documents relating to a certain Count Hochberg. I thought you might find them interesting. Have you heard of him before?'

'Of course I have! He was my father's best friend and gave me my inheritance. In fact, I still have the key to a safety deposit box that he left me.' Michael laughed at the absurdity of his last remark.

'You have not opened it yet?' Giovanni asked.

'No. I know it sounds ridiculous and I did give it some thought a while back but what with one thing and another I completely forgot. I really should....'

'Wait a moment now. I hope you don't mind if I say something,' Alice leant forward in earnest. 'Michael, we, that is, Giovanni and I, we have something important to tell you. We should have told you before now but the right moment never presented itself. Look, I need you to promise me that you won't get annoyed with us?'

Michael smirked as he picked up his coffee cup. 'Get annoyed, whatever next!'

'PLEASE! Just do as I say. Make the promise so we can get this over and done with.'

Michael was clearly taken aback by Alice's sharp tone. 'If I didn't know better I'd think there was some sort of conspiracy going on.' He sipped his coffee and placed his cup back on the saucer noisily.

'See! You're beginning to get angry. Now please! You promised us you that you wouldn't!'

Michael started laughing. 'So! An oath is what you want! Very well, I promise not to get angry. Now for HEAVENS SAKE TELL ME.'

Alice cleared her throat before speaking. 'Well now, remember last year when your mother and I first arrived here?'

Michael nodded politely. 'Yes.'

'You will recall that she and I spent much time together in the caravan and then with Giovanni on the..,'

Michael interrupted her. 'Actually I don't recall that,' he said dismissively. 'Oh bloody hell! Will someone tell them to turn that stupid music off, it's far too loud!'

Alice laughed. 'I don't think the pianist will be very happy if we do!'

'Well tell him to play quieter then. I can't hear myself THINK.' Michael sat down abruptly. 'NOW DO GET ON WITH IT ALICE PLEASE,' he added in a louder voice.

'Michael, I Have some very good news for you. You are a very rich man indeed,'

'TELL ME SOMETHING I DON'T KNOW.'

'Ah yes ...,' whispered Alice, 'but you don't know HOW rich you are! You see, it's all been ferreted away over the years for you. The Baroness, your mother, made me – well Giovanni and me – the guardians of your inheritance. All was to be revealed on the first anniversary of her death, when we were to discharge our duty and make the fabulous wealth known to you.' As Alice finished speaking the pianist stopped playing, much to Michael's relief.

'Okay,' he responded, rubbing his hands together. 'So how much are we talking about and where is it?'

'Now here's the thing.' Alice sat back in her seat. 'I can't tell you exactly how much there is but it's safely buried.'

'What do you mean it's buried? Not in Haiti?'

Alice laughed. 'Good heavens! No, it's much closer to home than that. It's buried under the rose bushes.'

'WHAT?' Juliana screamed.

'Well, surely you must have suspected something when you found that gold coin in the library?' Alice asked incredulously.

Juliana didn't have a chance to reply; instead she watched incredulously as Michael turned on Giovanni, who had been sitting quietly and prodded him with his finger.

'So you thought to make an idiot out of me. You thought to keep my inheritance safe by burying it under those damn rose bushes of yours! HOW DARE YOU! I've got a jolly good mind to take you outside and give you the beating of your.... NO! I'll sack you here and now that's what I'll do....' Fearing the worst Alice grabbed hold of Giovanni quickly.

'But don't you see Michael?' Juliana intervened in his defence, 'That's why he cared for them so lovingly over all these months.'

'Si, and the painting from Alex, you see it was like a map boss, just in case something should happen to us. Then there was a letter telling you everything,' he added, watching a furious Michael pace up and down. Eventually he stopped in front of Alice and gave her a look that made her shiver.

'So! Russian gold roubles! I see! ILLEGAL tender! AND STILL YOU HAVE NOT TOLD ME. Exactly how much are we TALKING ABOUT?'

'Well .... It's difficult to quantify. Look, please don't shout at me.' Alice raised her hands in the air, trying to placate him. 'About three million dollars, of course we would have told you sooner,' she continued, 'but we were sworn to secrecy. Well, it was what your mother wanted and she...'

'QUIET! I'm THINKING!' Michael shouted as he sat back down again.

'Really Michael, there's no need for you to be quite so rude,' Juliana admonished, watching him twiddle his thumbs and stare at Alice.

Finally he broke the silence. 'So what are we to do with you two?' he asked threateningly, pointing at Giovanni and Alice. Alice ignored him and gingerly sipped her coffee. As usual Michael was over reacting. A family trait if ever there was one. Ignore him and he would calm down eventually, but as for Juliana, well that was quite another story. She looked genuinely unsettled by the revelation and was probably wondering how they had managed to keep it a secret for so long. Perhaps they were right to feel betrayed after all.

'Look, it's not something we wanted to do.' Alice confirmed. 'Maria asked us to do it for you. We didn't really have a choice!' As she stopped speaking she heard her words ring out into a heavy silence. There was nothing more they could say in their defence. It was up to Michael to understand their situation.

'It really isn't their fault,' Juliana insisted, adding her support. 'They only...'

'Yes, yes! I see all that now...Perhaps I was too hasty and over reacted.' Michael rubbed his hands together as though he was rubbing out the words of the last conversation. Clearly he had a change of heart. 'Well now I suppose you are right. This is a cause for celebration. Let's order some champagne.'

'If you don't mind I'll stay with the coffee for now,' Juliana replied.

'No we must celebrate. I insist.'

All remained quiet as Michael hurriedly ordered the champagne and filled their glasses.

'A toast to mother! Alice, thank you for all that you have done over the years.' Michael then peered down at Giovanni. 'I suppose I have to thank you too,' he added somewhat reluctantly. 'Si. God rest her soul. God rest the Baroness!' Giovanni raised his glass in reply. 'I'm so Appy. No more secrets now boss knows!'

Michael forced a smile. 'That's right. No more secrets and no more anger from me either. I promise!' Giovanni gave him a broad smile before finishing off his champagne.

'You see, I told you they would be fine about it. You can tell them now,' Alice suggested, patting his arm reassuringly.

Giovanni put his glass on the table and cleared his throat. 'Si boss, I must make confession. I took some gold coins for my very poor sister! I sell some but can pay you back unless you see me as a good charity which I hope ....?'

'YOU DID WHAT? I can't quite believe my ears. YOU ACTUALLY STOLE FROM ME? Please tell me it's not true Alice, my own servant!' Michael started to shout at the top of his voice. 'YOU UN-GRATEFUL... PEA-SANT,' he cried, pointing a menacing finger at Giovanni. 'YOU DARE TO STEAL FROM ME!' he yelled, incandescent with rage.

'Now, now, Michael, remember your blood pressure,' Juliana reminded him. 'You promised not to get angry and here you are... well quite frankly, making a real spectacle of yourself.'

'GET HIM OUT OF MY SIGHT before I do something I'll regret!' Michael punched the air, just missing Giovanni as he stood up to leave.

Luckily Juliana managed to grab Michaels arm and pull him towards her. 'No Michael, I won't let you sack him, he's not going anywhere. For years he has been our faithful servant. I know he's only ever had our best interests at heart. Okay, he's owned up to a ... well let's say a misjudgement, but you! Really there is no need for you to be so unforgiving with all the luck you have had in your life.... NOW CALM DOWN!'

Michael sat tensely with his hands clasped together in front of his face, staring into his champagne glass.

'Please Michael!' Alice implored him. 'Don't let the evening end like this. I know it was wrong of him to take the coins but he saw it as the lesser of two evils. He only borrowed the money. He always intended to pay it back.'

'Damn right he'll pay it back!' Michael snarled.

'Well I don't see why he should have to!' interrupted Juliana. 'He should keep it as a fee for looking after your bloody inheritance all these years! In fact, Alice should have a fee as well!'

Michael said nothing as her words sank in. Presently he stood up. 'Juliana is right,' he agreed, offering Giovanni his hand. 'It's uncharacteristically ungenerous of me. I apologise, but it's not every day I hear of a hidden fortune coming my way so I think I can be forgiven for my over-reaction. Thank you for being so honest. It can't have been easy for you!'

'Honestly Michael, you do surprise me. Really you do.' Juliana gave a sigh of relief. Michael smiled and sat down, putting his arm around her. 'Why do I surprise you my dear?'

'You didn't ask Alice where the gold came from.'

Michael sneered. 'I don't need to. Alice said it came from mother.'

'Ah! But where did *she* get it from?'

'Ssshhhh!' Alice warned. 'I don't think we should be speaking about the details of it here.'

Michael poured out another glass of champagne. 'I suppose the gold must have come from ...'

Alice put her finger to her lips, once again reminding him to speak in a lower voice. He smiled, seemingly enjoying the intrigue.

'Russia!' he whispered.

Alice shrugged but Giovanni nodded. 'Si, they are mostly 1914 but there are also some pink notes in very bad condition with blood and what looks like tiny pinholes. They are dated 1919 and not worth much.'

Juliana suddenly felt squeamish as her lively imagination got the better of her.

'Well, well, well!' Michael pulled at his bottom lip as he spoke. 'I think we all know exactly where mother GOT THE GOLD FROM NOW.'

'Actually we don't' responded Alice, growing more alarmed at Michael's loudness.

'OF COURSE WE DO!' Michael shouted.

'Right, that's quite enough. No more discussion around this table. It's too dangerous.'

'You're right of course but there's one point I must insist upon,' Michael whispered behind his hand. 'I don't want Alex, Tonya, or Paul hearing about the gold buried in the garden business. So we'll have to find an appropriate opportunity to dig it up!' Michael patted Giovanni as he spoke. 'Your rose bushes will have to get a very nasty disease and die!'

Giovanni smiled. 'Of course, it can't be helped.'

'Then all the gold will be put safely into my vault while I speak to my accountant. Heaven knows what the tax liabilities will be!'

'Well never mind all that for now,' interrupted Juliana. 'I didn't finish telling you about Count Hochberg.'

Michael gave her a mischievous look as he picked up his half empty wine glass. 'Why do I get the feeling there's something you're not telling me?'

Chapter Forty Three   A Rose by Any Other Name

Giovanni stretched out his legs and yawned. 'Excuse me,' he immediately apologised. 'Go on now. You get yourself off to bed,' Alice suggested, pushing him off the settee. 'Yes, you look exhausted,' agreed Juliana, rising to say goodnight before settling herself back down again.

After Giovanni had left Alice moved closer so she could hear what Juliana had to say about the Count.

'Well I know it's late but this won't take long and it's strangely appropriate that you hear about the Count's story along with all the other revelations of this evening.' Juliana paused as she sorted through a mix of papers from her handbag.

'Which Count are we talking about?' Michael asked, watching her pull out some handwritten notes.

Juliana didn't bother to reply since what she was about to say was all consuming. 'Now, according to Maria, this is a tragic story of a certain noble's fall from grace. You will recall that in his two books Dr Graves referred to himself as Bertram von Ehrenkrug, an exiled scion of a Prussian noble house that stretched back to the crusading knights of the eleventh century. You will remember then that I suggested if we wanted to know who Betram von Ehrenkrug moulded his character on we would have to find a Prussian noble family who had exiled an heir at about the same time as Bertram von Ehrenkrug.'

Alice placed her hand to her mouth, unable to conceal her astonishment at what Juliana was about to reveal.

'So here amongst your mother's papers I found what I was looking for. It's about Ferdinand Hochberg, a nephew of Princess Marie von Saxe-Weimar and a member of the Pless family. He was also a close friend of Crown Prince Wilhelm and his father was a distinguished diplomat, director and composer.'

'Wait a moment,' Alice interrupted, 'is he the same Count who visited Michael all those years ago?'

Juliana shrugged. 'I don't know.'

'No. Definitely not! The man who visited me was a Count Frederick who gave me a silver key with a fox on it.'

'Ah, here we are. This is the bit I was looking for. Can you confirm this is your mother's handwriting?'

Michael leant over to take a closer look. 'Yes, I see it's partly written in that green ink!'

Alice smiled. 'Ah! How Maria loved that colour. Reading between the lines she said it was able to hide a multitude of sins!'

'Right, let me read out what she has written here then,' Juliana added.

'Count Ferdinand Hochberg had a twin brother and just like Bertram von Ehrenkrug, Count Ferdinand was forced to give up his inheritance because he wanted to marry a woman below his station. She was very beautiful but worked in a glove store in Berlin.'

Michael sat bolt upright. 'I'm quite sure that my Count did not have a twin brother called Ferdinand who was exiled. This is clearly some clever diversion away from the real truth of the matter. You can't take everything mother wrote as gospel dear.'

A slow smile crept across Alice's face.

'What now?' He asked, clearly perplexed.

'Perhaps that's what William McGarry meant when he said that one day he would write his own *Man in the Iron Mask* story. If I recall correctly, in that particular story the prisoner, who was locked up in the Chateau d'If was none other than the identical twin brother of the King of France!'

'Good God, woman! You're not suggesting that my father Dr Karl Armgaard Graves, the man called Fox is the twin brother of the Crown Prince?'

Alice gave a knowing smile, 'Certainly not but may I politely suggest, that you listen carefully to what Juliana wants to read to us.

'The news of a torrid love affair between a rich aristocrat and a common shop girl caused a huge sensation in the Berlin court and was a major upset for the family. The Count was asked to stop the liaison and give up the girl for someone more appropriate to his station in life. When he refused he was

forced to resign his commission as First Lieutenant in the Royal Foot Guards and leave Germany so as not to embarrass his family. His father gave him some money to see him through his exiled period. I suppose the whole family was hoping that he would change his mind and not marry the girl. But in 1906 he did just that. The ex-count and his new wife then went to live in the United States, where they eventually established a chicken farming business.'

Juliana glanced up as she turned the page. 'But before all this, I must tell you that he was embroiled in a most unfortunate incident, one that may ring a few bells with us.'

Michael laughed loudly. 'Chicken farming and she speaks of embroiled accidents. Whatever next? Before we get too involved in this tale let's order some more coffee.'

'Oh that's a good idea.' Alice responded, beckoning the waiter over.

'Right now,' Juliana continued, returning to Maria's notes.

'When the exiled Count first arrived in the United States he met up with a certain Mr Barnes, who encouraged him to invest what little savings he had in the Cottonwood Creek Copper Company.'

'Well I can quite understand that he would want to invest in mining if he was of true Hochberg stock. Gold mining would have run through his veins. It was in his blood! For generations that family had been known for their involvement in that industry but chicken farming, well I am so surprised at that!'

'PLEASE MICHAEL!' Juliana shouted. 'Will you let me continue without these constant interruptions of yours? Now, since the Count had been ostracised by his family, Mr Barnes adopted him as his own in the United States. So the ex-Count Ferdinand von Hochberg changed his name to Mr Ferdinand Barnes and worked for his adopted father. After a period of time, Mr Barnes persuaded ex-Count Ferdinand to go back to Germany with the aim of encouraging all his wealthy friends to invest in the Cottonwood Creek Copper company.

'When Ferdinand arrived back in Berlin, he was greeted as a hero. Society welcomed him because all his ex-friends, including the Crown Prince, believed he had made millions in American mining stock and they were eager to share in his wealth and good fortune. Still conscious of the delicacy of his newfound position in Berlin society, the exiled Count led a bachelor's existence. While he socialised with his old friends in Berlin, his young wife and child were kept in the background, living far from Berlin. German society was excited at the prospect of investing in American mining shares and the Count spent most of his time collecting funds from his friends and associates for future mining projects, promising large returns on the money invested.....'

'Well I'm not surprised. He was bound to be successful,' Michael responded, 'coming from a family that had already made a fortune in mining.'

'QUIET!' Juliana replied irritably before continuing. 'Now, it was rumoured that many of the Count's investors included royalty and this drew even more interest from the nobility. But as time went on things were not what they first appeared to be. There were no fabulous returns on the money, not for the investors nor for the unlucky Count. In fact there was no copper in the mine and the company was not worth a dime. Naturally, all the German investors were furious and demanded their money back. What followed was a particularly nasty and protracted court case. One of the outcomes was that Ferdinand Hochberg, alias Ferdinand Barnes, sued his adopted father Mr Barnes because he had also invested in the venture. It's not clear from your mother's scrapbook what happened next but after a prolonged court case his real father in Germany felt sorry for him and sent him a monthly allowance to help support his now growing family. Shortly after doing this his father died. Of course Ferdinand's twin brother inherited everything in Germany. Needless to say, the allowance ceased and Ferdinand was left to fend for himself, his wife and four children.'

Juliana paused to pick up her coffee cup.

'He must have been very much in love with the girl to give up all his inheritance. What an honourable man!' Alice commented.

'More stupid than honourable, if you ask me!' Michael interjected. 'As the eldest twin he could have had it all if only he had been a bit crafty! I'll not bother you with the intricacies around having your cake and eating it but us men understand the concept very well!'

'By the way, before I continue Michael, can you remember what year Count Frederick visited you?' Juliana enquired.

'Let's see. It must have been sometime in the 1940s. He was well into his seventies anyway.'

'And what did he say to you?

Michael shrugged.

'Think hard, Michael. This could be crucial,' Alice implored.

Michael rubbed his brow. 'Well …only that he had been very happily married. Oh now wait a moment it's all coming back to me. He did mention that he had a large family who lived in a magnificent castle somewhere in Germany or was it Austria.. I can't remember now!'

'There, you see it could very well be the same person, Michael. He speaks to you of the brother who had inherited the title and lived in the castle instead of him!' Alice exclaimed enthusiastically.

'No, he didn't exactly say that…'

'Right, well before we come to any conclusions let me get back to what Maria has said here:

'Now before the Count lost his inheritance, there had been plenty of family discussion over him giving up the title. His father and mother did everything to dissuade him from marrying the poor shop girl. The ancient noble house was not going to lose its scion that easily. But in the end their attempts were to no avail. Ferdinand chose the girl over his family and his estate. In doing so he let down generations, or at least that is how his parents saw it. The family were unable to contain the fallout and the story was told and retold by members of Prussian society and in local newspapers. Everyone in Berlin knew about this unfortunate affair, much to the embarrassment of his father. So when Ferdinand returned to Germany and promised to make good, everyone believed him even though there was a matter of a court case to be resolved. Those that had lent Ferdinand the money were sure they would get their funds returned and that eventually Ferdinand would make them all very rich indeed. They all believed in him bar one person.

'Look at what Maria kept.' Juliana added holding up an old letter apparently written by Wilhelm II's son, the Crown Prince of Germany. 'As you can see much of the handwriting has worn disappeared away. But thankfully Maria has done much to preserve it.'

As she held the wafer thin paper to the light Michael gasped. It was so fragile he could practically see through it. 'Anyway,' Juliana continued, 'I'll read it out to you. But when you hear me say the word, "something", that's in place of the word I cannot read, okay?'

Michael laughed at his wife's predicament. 'All I can say is I'm glad you're not a lawyer defending me!'

'Well it's a great shame that it hasn't been better protected but I suppose we should thank God for small mercies! At least we have *some* of this precious correspondence. The letter is dated December 18th 1908, from Berlin, and reads as follows:

'Dear Mucki,
Many thanks for your last card today. I'll have to be "something", with you for once. The other day I was in Rohstock. Under the present circumstances it was naturally not a very pleasant "something". Your father still loves you very much and is quite "something" over the affair. Your mother, I hate to say it, has given you up "something, something". Your father showed me a piece of writing written by you, in which you declared on your word of honour you would give up your name the moment you married the woman of "something". Mucki, think this over. There is no going back from having given up your name. You must keep your word of honour "something" matter becomes known and it surely will become known "something" impossible here and lost for all of us "something". Take this step and "something", old friend. I have talked with your father about this matter "something". Write, and you can believe me, your parents have "something" influenced me, but you can't get around your declaration "something" written word of honour. If I had written that in the "something" I should marry the aforesaid person, I shall give up my "something", then, I would have done it by all means.

Dear Mucki, doesn't make the least difference to me personally what name you give yourself, you will remain my good "something" to whom I'll always have a helping hand but with your new friends you cannot suddenly get new ideas of "something". ..."Something" are no mental reservations for a respectable person....Of this Mr Barnes (really American and theatric)... Please write me once more exactly about this point. ...Realize that he is simply using you for advertising. Take this picture of you and the good man together, Mucki. Well as for the rest........!'

Juliana stopped reading. 'That's the end I'm afraid.'

'What, no more?' Michael enquired.

'I'm afraid not. But I did find this folded up in the cutting.' Juliana handed him a page out of an English newspaper to read. Michael opened it excitedly and read the contents out loud.

'A 1908 edition of the Almanach de Gotha carries confirmation of the story sent over here from the United States in September 1906, that Count Hans Ferdinand von Hochberg, a member of the Pless family, had renounced the title of Count and adopted the name Barnes.'

After he finished Michael handed the article back to his wife. 'I suppose he continued living in the U.S?'

'Yes, as far as we know,' Juliana replied, 'although he must have found it difficult when the country went to war with Germany. Amazingly, he would have been in exactly the same situation as that other German nobleman we know of who was living in the U.S.'

She paused, expecting Michael to pick up on who she was talking about but he didn't 'I mean of course, Dr Graves, who, by his own admission, was considered an enemy alien. Anyway, Count Hochberg seems to have kept himself very much to himself because we don't hear much about him except that Maria wrote in her scrapbook that he rented a large farmhouse for his wife and four children and set them up running a big chicken farm.'

'Well thank you for taking the trouble to explain that all to me.' Michael patted her on the knee as she passed the paper to Alice to look at.

'Aren't you going to ask me why I bothered showing you all this tonight? It's late after all!'

Michael stuck his bottom lip out, something he was prone to do when he was thoughtful.

'I suppose there must be a reason why Mother followed the Count's story so closely. But I am unaware that he meant anything specific to her. She certainly never mentioned his name to me. Oh! Wait a moment. She did visit him in the U.S. once.'

Alice coughed and Michael glanced across to her. She had just finished reading the old newspaper and was staring wide eyed at him.

'WHAT?' he asked. 'You know something more? Was he my uncle? Don't tell me I'm a Hochberg?'

Juliana sighed 'Well think, MICHAEL! What could this story possibly have to do with YOU?'

Michael shrugged. 'That's what I'm trying to find out! Perhaps one of you would be kind enough to inform me what's going on. All my life my name has been Brandenberg AND all my life I have known that Brandenberg was not my REAL NAME!'

'COME ON MICHAEL. You can do better than that surely! Why do you think your mother collected all these cuttings and carefully put them together? Your mother, THE BARONESS! MICHAEL?' DO I HAVE TO SPELL IT OUT FOR YOU?' Juliana became increasingly exasperated with her husband. 'OH FOR HEAVEN'S SAKE!'

Michael rubbed his eyes. 'Look, I am tired. I can't possibly think at this time of night. It's far too late.'

'Okay, okay...' Juliana replied. 'This is the point I want to make. Dr Karl Armgaard Graves said that he had been exiled by his family. He said the only reason that he got involved with the intelligence services in the first place was to redeem his lost position in society. Remember, he told us that he was assured that once his missions had been successfully completed, he would be reinstated as a Count and be rewarded with his lost inheritance in Berlin?'

Michael vigorously rubbed his forehead. 'Alright, I see where you're going with this but I think it is a bit rich assuming that Dr Armgaard Karl Graves was really the Count. Only a moment ago Alice was insinuating that my father was a brother to the Crown Prince of Prussia! NOW you're trying to tell me I might be a Hochberg! She's trying to tell me I am a Hohenzollern and, quite frankly, I am tired of it. I can see that both of you are jumping to all sorts of conclusions for which you have no proof whatsoever.'

Juliana burst into laughter. Her old Michael was back again. 'You're not fooling me for one moment, Michael. I know what this is all about. You're frightened and your pride is holding you back from recognising the truth when you hear it. In fact you couldn't see the truth if it stared you in the face. It's so much easier to pretend that you're related to the Romanovs or the Hohenzollerns, than to acknowledge that your real roots are slightly lower down the Royal Oak tree!'

'HA! The old nag's got some spirit in her after all!'

'Really Michael, there is no need to be so rude about your wife. It's common of you!' Alice scolded.

'It's because he's scared of what I'll say next. Isn't that right Michael?' Juliana continued with her antagonism.

'I doubt very much that you have the capability of frightening me my dear!'

'We will see about that.' Juliana smiled as she pulled out another sheet of paper from her handbag and unfolded it slowly. Michael's frown disappeared when he saw her handwriting on it. 'What's this? Yesterdays shopping list?' he asked sarcastically.

Ever the joker, Alice thought, as she followed their conversation with growing interest. She had always thought that it would be Tonya who would unravel the clues cleverly hidden by Maria; but Juliana had surprised her with her tenacity and her honesty. The sculptress was turning into a proper little Sherlock Holmes, a persistent and tenacious investigator who was summing up with an eloquent narration to boot!

'Come on, admit it Michael, you were annoyed when I suggested that Dr Armgaard Karl Graves's real name might have been Ferdinand Barnes, alias Count Hochberg. Well! I don't see why you should be so surprised. Think of all the names he used throughout his life. Let's see, how many were there? Trenton Snell, James Stafford, Dr Franz von Cannitz, Max Meinke, Bertram von Ehrenkrug, A. Graham, Karl Graven, A. Greenbaum, P. Gunther, Dr von Graver, Count Arthur Zu Wernigrode, H. Van Huit, Dr Armgaard Karl Graves, and last but not least FOX! That's fourteen names that we know about. God knows how many more there are. So whatever you say Michael, there is a chance that he also took the name of Barnes!'

'No Juliana, I'm sorry. I can't believe for one moment that Dr Graves is related to Count Hochberg, or for that matter the Prussian Crown Prince. So if you don't mind, let's have an end to this nonsense.'

'But how can you be so sure?' Alice asked.

'Because I met the Count and he looked nothing like this photograph of Dr Graves.' Michael handed Alice the photograph that he had been holding onto.

'Don't be so silly! You can't compare images in that way. People change as they get older. Anyway this photograph was taken of Dr Graves as a secret agent. He was probably disguised. Don't forget he was a consummate actor!'

Realising the discussion was leading nowhere Michael stared into his empty glass and then ordered another brandy. 'Would you two like a coffee or something?' he asked nonchalantly.

Juliana shook her head. 'Not for me. I'll never sleep. Anyway, it'll soon be time for breakfast.'

Alice laughed. 'Ah, how time flies when you're enjoying yourself,' she added philosophically.

'Come on Michael, it's time for you to face the truth.' Juliana had turned serious again. 'But can you take it I wonder?'

Michael smiled at his wife. 'Of course I can. If you're sure it IS the TRUTH.'

Juliana watched him light a cigar and puff on it several times. She considered having a cigarette herself but thought better of it. Michael picked up his brandy and looked her honestly in the eye.

'In fact, if I didn't know better, I would think you were trying to drag this out for as long as possible. You just love knowing something that you think I don't. Well I can't blame you I suppose. You rarely have the opportunity to outshine me. Besides, I know my father for the man he was. The saviour of the Romanovs and you can't take that from me.'

It all reminded Alice of a similar discussion that had taken place many years ago between herself and Maria. So now all was to be revealed.

Chapter Forty Four   Chicken Farming

Juliana watched Michael raise his brandy glass against the electric light and admire the soft amber lights glowing in the liquor. He could be quite artistic sometimes and that was so much preferable to the pompous lecturer that he almost always was. There must have been a reason why she had fallen in love with him in the first place but she couldn't remember what it was! But one thing she did know. He always had to be right. He always had to be better and out-perform everyone. He always had to be a winner. It was all so tedious. Well, he's not going to get away with it tonight. I'll teach him to insult my intelligence! Juliana swirled the remnants of her coffee around in the cup so fast that they nearly spilled over.

For his part Michael was oblivious to her thoughts and gave her one of his charming and disarming smiles. His wife was probably going to play devil's advocate; well that was fine but he would not be fooled into believing something that was not true just because it sounded plausible. 'Well now Michael, I wouldn't be so quick to worship this Dr Armgaard Karl Graves if I were you.' Juliana returned his smile before adding, 'I've tried to tell you all along that he is not the man you think he is. Count Hochberg was a genuinely decent and honest man who had dreadful things happen to him, whereas Dr Graves was a ...'

'RUBBISH!' shouted Michael indignantly. 'I won't let you say that about him.'

'Well I'm afraid he was the first to admit to it. He did some very bad things, even though he says bad things always happened to him! You can see it in the stories he tells. He says he had no choice but can we believe him? I think you just have to bite the bullet on this one Michael! You still think of this man as your father because your mother called him Karl. He was a gifted writer but let's face it he made all these stories up, including the story of his own life AND now, after I have shown you these clips of Maria's, you must be able to see where he got the material to invent his life from.'

Juliana waved a few papers in the air as she spoke. 'There were lots of tragic stories just ready for the telling and to a gifted writer such as Dr Graves this must have been heaven sent. A little tweaking here, and a little tweaking there! No wonder he had so many best sellers on his hands!' Juliana triumphantly through her head back and laughed.

Michael gulped his brandy down and placed the glass precariously on the table. He had never seen his wife act like that and where did that mad laugh come from? He turned to Alice. At least she looked like she felt sorry for him.

'Don't you see dear? It was all in the papers. Perhaps Juliana is right and we've spent all this time investigating, well what appears after all, to be a bit of a fairy tale. At the very best it would appear that somewhere through the mists of time the truth has been lost. It would be a miracle if we were to find it now.'

Michael relit his cigar. 'Well I thought you believed in miracles?'

Alice didn't respond instead she adjusted her seating to avoid his cigar smoke as he ordered another brandy.

'My dear wife,' He went on, 'You as usual, have over simplified a very complicated subject. You want to make it all fit into some explainable pattern of events. You want to make order out of chaos. Well I have news for you. You're not sculpting a statue now! Sometimes....SOMETIMES, NOT ALL the pieces fit together as you would like them to. But that doesn't mean you should believe that it is all rubbish.'

'Michael?' Alice spoke softly but firmly. 'Are you telling your wife how to think? Because it occurs to me that Juliana has done a fine job and could be right to a certain extent in this instance. Maybe Karl did read about the sad tale of Count Hochberg, who lost his title and fortune out of love for a beautiful shop girl, and perhaps he did adopt the story as his own.'

Michael shot her a look of disapproval. 'EXCEPT THAT YOU FORGET. MY FATHER TOLD THE TRUTH ABOUT HIS LIFE. HE WOUDLN'T STEAL SOMEONE ELSE'S IDENTITY, LET ALONE A DEAR FRIEND'S!' Michael only realised he was shouting when he saw the look on their faces. 'Look, I admit I was as guilty as anyone of not believing in him at first but now, well so much water has gone under the bridge. Whatever my head might argue, and yes Juliana may be right, but whatever my head may argue, my heart says something quite different.'

'But you can't ignore the evidence!' Juliana added incredulously.

'What evidence? SHOW ME IT IF YOU DARE!' Michael bellowed like a caged lion. Juliana wasn't going to stand for that. She immediately rose from the settee. 'Excuse me!'

'Honestly Michael, what on earth has come over you, speaking to your wife like that?' Michael looked contrite for a moment. 'Well, she will insist on poking her nose into my business. Where's that bloody brandy I ordered?'

Michael snapped his fingers impatiently at a passing waiter, who turned sharply on his heels. 'BRANDY, SAMBUCA! HERE NOW!' He hollered gesticulating at the table. All was silent as a few moments later the waiter served the drinks. He sipped his brandy and waited for his mood to miraculously lift. 'I wasn't too hard on her, was I Alice?' he asked contritely.

'She'll be alright. She's just not used to this sort of heated debate.' Alice could see there was no point in trying to convince him of Juliana's point of view. He would just get angrier and that would be no good for his blood pressure. Michael must have read her thoughts because a second later he pulled out his handkerchief and wiped the sweat from his brow. Then he smiled warmly. 'You're right. I do take this too seriously.' he ventured.

Alice nodded. 'I think so. Life is unfair but it is something we all have to come to terms with. We win some and we lose some and for all our hard work, as you say, we may never know the truth for what it really was.' Michael patted Alice's arm gently. 'Thank you for understanding me.' He added generously as he watched Juliana approach. As she drew close he stood up in his usual gentlemanly way and she immediately detected a more conciliatory attitude. 'I've ordered a drink for you, my dear, to celebrate the good news about the gold. Oh, I'm sorry Alice. I didn't ask you what you wanted.'

Alice looked at her empty glass. 'A glass of water will do, it's getting rather late for me.'

Michael sat down and savoured his brandy, watching Juliana sip her drink. That'll relax her he thought. 'Now where were we? Ah yes!' He remembered and turned to Juliana.

'You were saying something about my father being a bad man, weren't you? And I said to you "show me the evidence". You see, I don't think you can show me that.'

'On the contrary,' Juliana replied. 'According to these papers he was deceiving everyone. He was jailed for extorting money to fund a trip in search of three million dollars worth of gold coins on a Haiti beach! You have to admit it Michael, your judgement is clouded by your emotions! Look, it's all here in black and white.' Juliana tapped the papers as she spoke and Michael flushed red with anger again. At that point Alice decided she'd had enough. It was clear to her that Juliana had no further information to divulge and so it was time to intervene. 'You say this with such conviction Juliana; but I know exactly how Michael is feeling because despite your evidence I can vouch that Maria absolutely adored Karl. She would have done anything for him and that would not have been the case if he had been a charlatan. Anyway, she would never have kept all these papers if it was not for a very good reason. That reason was so Michael could get to know who his real father was.'

Alice had barely finished speaking when Michael jumped out of his chair and threw his jacket down. 'THANK YOU ALICE!' he shouted, loosening his tie and clumsily pulling his shirt out. Then he sat down and rubbed his face hard. Presently he looked up. 'Is no one else hot?' He asked.

Juliana gave Alice a knowing look as Michael picked up the last of his brandy and gulped it down. 'I've had enough.' Michael rubbed his forehead with his handkerchief. 'You know what? It's late! I don't think I care anymore. I've had enough! I'll get some water.'

'He's right,' Alice agreed. 'But let me say one thing before we retire. No matter who your father and mother were, there are two important things you should remember. Firstly, it is clear that your family history goes back a very long way indeed and secondly, you know they cared about you because they left you a hugely important legacy and they left you the gold to prove it!'

Michael swayed dangerously for a moment as Juliana passed him the water, which he eagerly drank. But it was Alice's words that soothed his troubled mind. They acted like a magic tonic. So much so that when he put his glass down, he looked twenty years younger. He said it was as though a huge weight had been lifted from his shoulders and for the first time in a long while he could think clearly. Everything was back in perspective and he had them both to thank for that. He didn't care whether he was a Hohenzollern, a Trachenburg, an Ehrenkrug, a Hochberg or a Brandenberg.

Michael smiled triumphantly. He had overcome his demon, a demon that had haunted him all his life. He stood up and brushed his hair back, pushing his shirt into his trousers as he spoke. '...A rose by any other name....that saying is so true! I'm so sorry about my behaviour.'

Juliana placed her hand over his. 'Michael, you don't have to apologise to me for showing your emotions. It's what makes us human and none of would be human if we were perfect!'

Michael smiled warmly at his wife. 'But some are more perfect than others and you are one of them. You know, we really must look after these cuttings. I think we should put them into a scrapbook when we get home.'

'Yes, indeed,' Alice interrupted. 'They should have pride of place in the library.'

Michael appreciated the comment. 'You know, I often wish that I had been a country fellow, by that I mean happy to follow the simple joys of life such as farming. Why did I have to be so cerebral? Heaven only knows!'

Juliana squeezed his hand. It wasn't often that Michael was self-critical, even if it was a rather half- hearted attempt.

'So,' Alice responded. 'If not a miner, then a farmer you will be! Perhaps it's in the blood after all!'

Michael looked up. 'I think not.'

'I don't see why. It's a very useful industry to have under your belt.' Alice continued, 'For instance, if I was on a dangerous mission to rescue the Romanovs and there was a possibility that I may not return, I would want to make sure that my wife and family had some kind of income to rely on. There again, as an alien agent or spy, or diplomat, call it what you will, I would have known that at any time throughout the two wars there was a huge risk of being killed or locked up in prison for years on end. If that happened, and for reasons of state security, I would not have been able to explain who I really was or prove it. Having gone under so many different names in the past and probably worked for a number of different people I would realise that my position was untenable. So...'

Michael interrupted her. 'Well his wife could have worked in a shop like she used to in Berlin!'

'Perhaps she didn't speak English very well or had a strong German accent or just needed to look after her children and the farm. Anyway more to the point, what do Foxes like?'

Michael frowned. 'What on earth are you talking about?'

Alice smiled. 'Foxes... Foxes like chickens, Hence the CHICKEN FARMING!'

'Well that SURE DOOOO sound like woman's work to me. OH YES, SIRREE!' Michael replied mustering the best southern drawl he could.

'That's my point!' Alice continued. 'If I were a man of multiple identities, an international spy that had been arrested under various false identities and imprisoned for many years, I would want my family to be in a position to look after themselves while I was locked up. As you say, chicken farming is easily managed by a woman and her four children.'

Michael gave her a quizzical look. 'Yes, but I'm not sure where this is taking us. That's all.'

'Alice smiled and leant across. 'Aren't you? Well perhaps you should take some time to think about it then?'

Michael stubbed his cigar out. 'Yes perhaps I should, but in case you haven't noticed, this whole thing has practically sent me mad!'

Juliana laughed. 'That's true, but please Alice, continue with what you were saying.'

'Well now, let's presume everything that we have read is true. If I was Fox, alias Dr Graves, I would want my family to know the truth about my life so I would keep some kind of a written record. A diary and a bestseller or two would help! A photograph album and a scrapbook could help fill in the missing pieces pointing to my true identity. Surely it can't have escaped either of you how similar Dr Graves's life was to that of the Count's? That's why he wrote *The Secrets of the Hohenzollerns* and *The Secrets of the German War Office*. As for the rest, burying the gold on a beach in Haiti and setting up a chicken farm, well that was the best thing he could do to secure your future, Michael.'

Suddenly Juliana had a thought. 'Good heavens, I've just remembered William Rutledge McGarry's claim to be able to write his own *Man in the Iron Mask*. I thought he was talking about the escaped Tsar living with a fresh identity but perhaps he was talking amount Dr Armgaard Karl Graves not being known for WHO he really WAS! Like *The Man in the Iron Mask,* possibly being a twin of the King of France and.......gracious me! Count Hochberg also had a twin so... that means....'

Alice quickly interrupted. 'Juliana, all we can say is that Dr Armgaard Karl Graves was probably once a Count of Prussia who went under the secret agent name of Fox, that he was commissioned by the Kaiser to rescue the Tsar and his family using the help of General Skoropadski and the Baroness 'B'. In addition, we can assume that if the family had been successfully rescued the public would want to know the story of how they had escaped. Since the Allies were at war with Germany they couldn't possibly tell the truth. So they commissioned Dr Armgaard Karl Graves to write the story, but with a fictitious journey added to it so that the actual whereabouts of the Tsar and his family would not be known. Having read the story people would think they were still living in India or Ceylon. While it looked as though the Bolsheviks would be defeated, the plan to publish *Rescuing the Czar* was on track but as soon as it became evident that the Imperialists or Whites weren't able to win, then the book had to be quickly withdrawn from sale. That's because it endangered the members of the Imperial Family who had already escaped. So! Yes, while you should not assume that what I tell you is necessarily the truth I would advise you for your own sanity to regard what Maria has left us in the way of evidence as a story worth telling!'

Michael detected irony in Alice's voice as she spoke. 'Interpretation, as any historian will tell you, is at the very heart of what us humans call the truth.'

Michael smiled. 'Well that certainly makes sense to me, Alice.'

'No, wait a minute you two,' Juliana responded. 'Don't you want to know what happened to Dr Graves in the end?' she added, emptying the contents of her handbag onto the table. 'Here listen to this.

'**DEPORTEE TAKEN OFF SHIP**

Dr Armgaard Karl Graves, self-styled former German spy, who was put aboard the **President Roosevelt** *of the United States Lines at 10am yesterday for deportation to Germany, obtained a last minute stay half an hour later and was sent back to Ellis Island. Byron H. Uhl, Eastern District Commissioner of Immigration and Naturalization, said he had received instruction from*

Washington yesterday morning to give Dr Graves an indefinite stay. The only explanation Mr Uhl could give was that the request for the stay had been made by another Federal Department. Dr Graves, who had insisted that death awaited him in Germany, was ordered deported after his release from Tennessee State Penitentiary, where he had been serving a term for fraud.'

'What's the date of that article?' Alice asked.

'Fifteenth of April 1937.'

Michael moaned. 'But that's a long time after the Tsar and his family were said to have been rescued! Please don't tell me he spent seventeen years behind bars? It just wouldn't be fair,' he added, watching Juliana fold up the cutting and place it back in her bag.

'I suppose we should be satisfied with small mercies,' Alice sighed. 'And at least we know that someone actually cared enough to save him from a certain death in Nazi Germany. You have to admit, there is a marvellous poignancy to our brave rescuer being rescued himself. Surely that must please you Michael?'

'Yes it does and after all that HE has done, it should be the very least you would expect! Of course, I am pleased that America thought highly enough of him to accept him as an American citizen. Mother always said she had friends in high places!'

Michael gave Juliana a hug. 'You know, I should have realised you had some secrets up your sleeve when you came out with that large handbag today!' Then, turning to Alice he added, 'I wonder if Karl ever returned to Haiti to pick up the treasure that was buried on the beach? Come to think of it! We'll have to get Alex down there with his metal detector. I wouldn't be surprised if it isn't still buried in that scenic little bay I visited when I was a little boy with Mother.'

Alice smiled knowingly. 'Do you remember what it was called, Michael?'

'The bay of Monte Cristi I believe just on the border with.....'

Juliana laughed. 'Honestly, you're so funny Michael, especially when you've had too much to drink.'

'What have I said that is so amusing?'

'You said the beach was called Monte *Cristi*, surely you meant to say MONTE CRISTO?'

'No, the beach is called Monte C…'

Michael paused, His eyes lit up and Juliana watched as a triumphant smile spread across his face. 'GOODNESS ME, YOU REALLY ARE A DIAMOND,' he added, giving her a big squeeze before turning to Alice. 'AND YOU, You knew all along but it took yet another coincidence for us all to believe. The Romanov gold really was buried on that beach just as Dr Karl Graves said.'

Alice smiled. 'Certain words have a magic all of their own!' Then she giggled, recalling Maria, who had said so on many occasions.

'Like the word "iron", part of a secret language known only to the operatives in the field?' Juliana enquired.

'Absolutely.' replied Michael, 'I shall never think of the 'The Count of Monte Cristo' and 'The Man in the Iron Mask' in quite the same light. On a more serious note, I can now reveal to you that Dumas bought the land and built the Château de Monte Cristo, which he then called Château d'If! The very same that McGarry spoke of when he met Nicholas and his wife in Marseilles. If you read the story I'm sure even more clues will come to light. The Tsar and his family may even have been living there while they were in hiding! Dr Graves was telling the truth after all, but no one believed his story, poor fellow.'

'Yes, Michael…,' Alice's voice was heavy with emotion. 'So now you know what a brave man he was and why the President felt compelled to intervene and save his life.'

Further Reading

Alexandrov. V.	The End of the Romanovs	Hutchinson and Co. Ltd	1966
Anonymous.	The Fall of the Romanoffs	Herbert Jenkins Ltd.	1918
Berberova. Nina	Moura	New York Review Books	1988
Bruce. H.J.	Silken Dalliance	Constable London.	1946
Bulygin Paul.	The Murder of the Romanovs	Hutchinson & Co	1917
Churchill. Winston.	The World Crisis 1911-18	Odhams Press Ltd	1920
Clarke. William	The Lost Fortune off the Tsars	Weidenfeld and Nicolson	1994
Collis. Maurice.	Wayfoong	Faber and Faber	1965
Dukes. Sir Paul	Come Hammer Come Sickle	Cassell &Co	1947
Fleming. Peter.	The Fate of Admiral Kolchak	Rupert Hart Davis	1963
Fox. Edward Lyell.	Wilhelm Hohenzollern & Company.	Robert M McBride and Co.	1917
Kennet. Lady K.	Self-Portrait of an Artist	John Murray. London.	1949
Kerensky. A.F.	The Road to Tragedy	Hutchinson & Co.	1917
Kiste John Van Coryne Hall	Once a Grand Duchess, Xenia , Sister of Nicholas II	Sutton Publishing	2002
Graves, DrArmgaard. Karl	The Secrets of the German War Office	McBride Nast & Co New York	1914

Further Reading

Graves. Dr Armgaard Karl.	The Secrets of the Hohenzollerns	McBride Nast & Co New York	1915
Bruce Lockhart R.H.	Memoirs of a Secret Agent	Putnam.	1932
Lockhart. Robin.	Reilly, Ace of Spies	Futura Macdonald & Co.	1967
Novitsky. V.J.	The Russian Gold Reserves; Before and During the World and Civil Wars 1883-1921 Paris		1922
Reilly. Sidney.	An Autobiography; Britain's Master Spy, The Adventures of Sidney Reilly	Carroll & Graf	1986
Richards. Guy.	The Hunt for the Czar	Peter Davis, London	1970
Sayers. Michael. Khan. Albert	The Great Conspiracy	Boni and Gaer Inc. N.Y.	1946
Stafford, David	Chuchill & Secret Service	Abacus	1995
Smythe. James. P.	Rescuing the Czar	Henry Haskins Printing Co.	1920
Smythe. James. P.	The Prisoners of Tobolsk	Henry Haskins Printing Co.	1919
Summers. Anthony. Mangold .Tom	The File on the Tsar, The Fate of the Romanovs	Book Club Associated	1976

Other books by Lucy Caxton Brown

The River Centaur　　　　　　*Available on Kindle*
978-1-78003-274-0

Half Human, Half Horse. She's got a wild story, To tell of course. So come with me, On a journey of delight, Galloping fast under silver moonlight. She promises you, her suprise won't fail, When you've read the poetry Of the River Centaur's tale.

The Small book of Poems including Golden Ray and Cupid's Child　　　*Available on Kindle*
978-1-78003-273-3

Time to transend the days woes, So kick off your shoes, And twiddle your toes, Stop all that mindbending flannel. And open up your free flowing channel, So...Here we go now! When the day becomes dusk, It's then I hear you ask, What of me and what of you? Was it love or was it lust? To each their own heart. We all play a frantic part. Then we take our leave in flight, N'er to return until summer's light!

The Key
978-1-78003-419-5

She stands alone with many faces, In wild and desolate places, She's greater than a mountain, More fluid than a fountain! It's long since she was worshipped, but all of that's to be eclipsed, Now it's time to wake humanity, And show them divine duality.

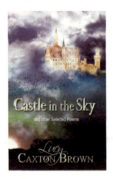

Castle in the Sky and other Selected Poems
978-1-78003-420-1

There is a centre within our hearts, That links us to all parts. We call it cosmic consciousness, And the smell of a rose, its delicateness, Can take you to that holy place, That's inside you and full of grace.